MW01231996

Anne

Constance Fenimore Woolson

ISBN: 1545241856

ISBN-13: 978-1545241851

Table of Contents

CHAPTER I.

"Heaven lies about us in our infancy!

Shades of the prison-house begin to close

Upon the growing boy;

But he beholds the light, and whence it
flows,

He sees it in his joy.

The youth who daily farther from the East

Must travel, still is Nature's priest,

And by the vision splendid

Is on his way attended;

At length the man perceives it die away,

And fade into the light of common day."

—Wordsworth.

"It is but little we can do for each other. We accompany the youth with sympathy and manifold old sayings of the wise to the gate of the arena, but it is certain that not by strength of ours, or by the old sayings, but only on strength of his own, unknown to us or to any, he must stand or fall."—Emerson.

"Does it look well, father?"

"What, child?"

"Does this look well?"

William Douglas stopped playing for a moment, and turned his head toward the speaker, who, standing on a ladder, bent herself to one side, in order that he might see the wreath of evergreen, studded with cones, which she had hung on the wall over one of the small arched windows.

"It is too compact, Anne, too heavy. There should be sprays falling from it here and there, like a real vine. The greenery, dear, should be either growing naturally upward or twining; large branches standing in the corners like trees, or climbing vines. Stars, stiff circles, and set shapes should be avoided. That wreath looks as though it had been planed by a carpenter."

"Miss Lois made it."

"Ah," said William Douglas, something which made you think of a smile, although no smile was there, passing over his face, "it looks like her work; it will last a long time. And there will be no need to remove it for Ash-Wednesday, Anne; there is nothing joyous about it."

"I did not notice that it was ugly," said the girl, trying in her bent posture to look at the wreath, and bringing one eye and a portion of anxious forehead to bear upon it.

"That is because Miss Lois made it," replied William Douglas, returning to his music.

Anne, standing straight again, surveyed the garland in silence. Then she changed its position once or twice, studying the effect. Her figure, poised on the round of the ladder, high in the air, was, although unsupported, firm. With her arms raised above her head in a position which few women could have endured for more than a moment, she appeared as unconcerned, and strong, and sure of her footing, as though she had been standing on the floor. There was vigor about her and elasticity, combined unexpectedly with the soft curves and dimples of a child. Viewed from the floor, this was a young Diana, or a Greek maiden, as we imagine Greek maidens to have been. The rounded arms, visible through the close sleeves of the dark woollen dress, the finely moulded wrists below the heavy wreath, the lithe, natural waist, all belonged to a young goddess. But when Anne Douglas came down from her height, and turned toward you, the idea vanished. Here was no goddess, no Greek; only an American girl, with a skin like a peach. Anne Douglas's eyes were violet-blue, wide open, and frank. She had not yet learned that there was any reason why she should not look at everything with the calm directness of childhood. Equally like a child was the unconsciousness of her mouth, but the full lips were exquisitely curved. Her brown hair was braided in a heavy knot at the back of her head; but little rings and roughened curly ends stood up round her forehead and on her temples, as though defying restraint. This unwritten face, with its direct gaze, so far neutralized the effect of the Diana-like form that the girl missed beauty on both sides. The usual ideal of pretty, slender, unformed maidenhood was not realized, and yet Anne Douglas's face was more like what is called a baby face than that of any other girl on the island. The adjective generally applied to her was "big." This big, soft-cheeked girl now stood irresolutely looking at the condemned wreath.

The sun was setting, and poured a flood of clear yellow light through the little west windows; the man at the organ was playing a sober, steadfast German choral, without exultation, yet full of a resolute purpose which defied even death and the grave. Out through the eastern windows stretched the frozen straits, the snow-covered islands, and below rang out the bugle. "It will be dark in a few moments," said Anne to herself; "I will do it."

She moved the ladder across to the chancel, mounted to its top again, and placed the wreath directly over the altar, connecting it deftly with the numerous long lines of delicate wreathing woven in thread-like green lace-work which hung there, waiting for their key-stone—a place of honor which the condemned wreath was to fill. It now crowned the whole. The little house of God was but an upper chamber, roughly finished and barren; its only treasure was a small organ, a gift from a father whose daughter, a stranger from the South, had died upon the island, requesting that her memorial might be music rather than a cold stone. William Douglas had superintended the unpacking and placing of this gift, and loved it almost as though it had been his own child. Indeed, it was a child, a musical child—one who comprehended his varying moods when no one else did, not even Anne.

"It makes no difference now," said Anne, aloud, carrying the ladder toward the door; "it is done and ended. Here is the ladder, Jones, and please keep up the fires all night, unless you wish to see us frozen stiff to-morrow."

A man in common soldier's uniform touched his cap and took the ladder. Anne went back. "Now for one final look, father," she said, "and then we must go home; the children will be waiting."

William Douglas played a few more soft strains, and turned round. "Well, child," he said, stroking his thin gray beard with an irresolute motion habitual with him, and looking at the small perspective of the chapel with critical gaze, "so you have put Miss Lois's wreath up there?"

"Yes; it is the only thing she had time to make, and she took so much pains with it I could not bear to have her disappointed. It will not be much noticed."

"Yes, it will."

"I am sorry, then; but it can not be moved. And to tell the truth, father, although I suppose you will laugh at me, *I* think it looks well."

"It looks better than anything else in the room, and crowns the whole," said Douglas, rising and standing by his daughter's side. "It was a stroke of genius to place it there, Anne."

"Was it?" said the girl, her face flushing with pleasure. "But I was thinking only of Miss Lois."

"I am afraid you were," said Douglas, with his shadowy smile.

The rough walls and beams of the chapel were decorated with fine spray-like lines of evergreen, all pointing toward the chancel; there was not a solid spot upon which the eye could rest, no upright branches in the corners, no massed bunches over the windows, no stars of Bethlehem, anchors, or nondescript Greek letters; the whole chapel was simply outlined in light feathery lines of green, which reached the chancel, entered it, played about its walls, and finally came together under the one massive wreath whose even circle and thick foliage held them all firmly in place, and ended their wanderings in a restful quiet strength. While the two stood gazing, the lemon-colored light faded, and almost immediately it was night; the red glow shining out under the doors of the large stoves alone illuminated the room, which grew into a shadowy place, the aromatic fragrance of the evergreens filling the warm air pungently, more perceptible, as fragrance always is, in the darkness. William Douglas turned to the organ again, and began playing the music of an old vigil.

"The bugle sounded long ago, father," said Anne. "It is quite dark now, and very cold; I know by the crackling noise the men's feet make across the parade-ground."

But the father played on. "Come here, daughter," he said; "listen to this waiting, watching, praying music. Do you not see the old monks in the cloisters telling the hours through the long night, waiting for the dawn, the dawn of Christmas? Look round you; see this dim chapel, the air filled with fragrance like incense. These far-off chords, now; might they not be the angels, singing over the parapet of heaven?"

Anne stood by her father's side, and listened. "Yes," she said, "I can imagine it. And yet I could imagine it a great deal better if I did not know where every bench was, and every darn in the chancel carpet, and every mended pane in the windows. I am sorry I am so dull, father."

"Not dull, but unawakened."

4

"And when shall I waken?" pursued the girl, accustomed to carrying on long conversations with this dreaming father, whom she loved devotedly.

"God knows! May He be with you at your wakening!"

"I would rather have you, father; that is, if it is not wicked to say so. But I am very often wicked, I think," she added, remorsefully.

William Douglas smiled, closed the organ, and, throwing his arm round his tall young daughter, walked with her down the aisle toward the door.

"But you have forgotten your cloak," said Anne, running back to get it. She clasped it carefully round his throat, drew the peaked hood over his head, and fastened it with straps of deer's hide. Her own fur cloak and cap were already on, and thus enveloped, the two descended the dark stairs, crossed the inner parade-ground, passed under the iron arch, and made their way down the long sloping path, cut in the cliff-side, which led from the little fort on the height to the village below. The thermometer outside the commandant's door showed a temperature several degrees below zero; the dry old snow that covered the ground was hardened into ice on the top, so that boys walked on its crust above the fences. Overhead the stars glittered keenly, like the sharp edges of Damascus blades, and the white expanse of the ice-fields below gave out a strange pallid light which was neither like that of sun nor of moon, of dawn nor of twilight. The little village showed but few signs of life as they turned into its main street; the piers were sheets of ice.

Nothing wintered there; the summer fleets were laid up in the rivers farther south, where the large towns stood on the lower lakes. The shutters of the few shops had been tightly closed at sunset, when all the inhabited houses were tightly closed also; inside there were curtains, sometimes a double set, woollen cloth, blankets, or skins, according to the wealth of the occupants. Thus housed, with great fires burning in their dark stoves, and one small lamp, the store-keepers waited for custom until nine o'clock, after which time hardly any one stirred abroad, unless it was some warm-blooded youth, who defied the elements with the only power which can make us forget them.

At times, early in the evening, the door of one of these shops opened, and a figure entered through a narrow crack; for no islander opened a door widely—it was giving too much advantage to the foe of his life, the weather. This figure, enveloped in furs or a blanket, came toward the stove and warmed its hands with deliberation, the merchant meanwhile remaining calmly seated; then, after some moments, it threw back its hood, and disclosed the face of perhaps an Indian, perhaps a French fisherman, perhaps an Irish soldier from the barracks. The customer now mentioned his errand, and the merchant, rising in his turn, stretched himself like a shaggy dog loath to leave the fire, took his little lamp, and prepared to go in quest of the article desired, which lay, perhaps, beyond the circle of heat, somewhere in the outer darkness of the dim interior. It was an understood rule that no one should ask for nails or any kind of ironware in the evening: it was labor enough for the merchant to find and handle his lighter goods when the cold was so intense. There was not much bargaining in the winter; people kept their breath in their mouths. The merchants could have made money if they had had more customers or more energy; as it was, however, the small population and the cold kept them lethargically honest.

Anne and her father turned northward. The southern half of the little village had two streets, one behind the other, and both were clogged and overshadowed by the irregular old buildings of the once-powerful fur company. These ancient frames, empty and desolate, rose above the low cottages of the islanders, sometimes three and four stories in height, with the old pulleys and hoisting apparatus still in place under their peaked roofs, like gallows ready for the old traders to hang themselves upon, if they came back and saw the degeneracy of the furless times. No one used these warehouses now, no one propped them up, no one pulled them down; there they stood, closed and empty, their owners being but so many discouraged bones under the sod; for the Company had dissolved to the four winds of heaven, leaving only far-off doubtful and quarrelling heirs. The little island could not have the buildings; neither could it pull them down. They were dogs in the manger, therefore, if the people had looked upon them with progressive American eyes; but they did not. They were not progressive; they were hardly American. If they had any glory, it was of that very past, the days when those buildings were full of life. There was scarcely a family on the island that did not cherish its tradition of the merry fur-trading times, when "grandfather" was a factor, a superintendent, a clerk, a hunter; even a voyageur had his importance, now that there were no more voyageurs. Those were gay days, they said; they should never look upon their like again: unless, indeed, the past should come back—a possibility which did not seem so unlikely on the island as it does elsewhere, since the people were plainly retrograding, and who knows but that they might some time even catch up with the past?

North of the piers there was only one street, which ran along the water's edge. On the land side first came the fort garden, where successive companies of soldiers had vainly fought the climate in an agricultural way, redcoats of England and blue-coats of the United States, with much the same results of partially ripened vegetables, nipped fruits, and pallid flowers; for the island summer was beautiful, but too short for lusciousness. Hardy plants grew well, but there was always a persistent preference for those that were not hardy—like delicate beauties who are loved and cherished tenderly, while the strong brown maids go by unnoticed. The officers' wives made catsup of the green tomatoes, and loved their weakling flowers for far-away home's sake; and as the Indians brought in canoe-loads of fine full-jacketed potatoes from their little farms on the mainland, the officers could afford to let the soldiers do fancy-work in the government fields if it pleased the exiled ladies. Beyond the army garden was the old Agency house. The Agency itself had long been removed farther westward, following the retreating, dwindling tribes of the red men farther toward the Rocky Mountains; but the old house remained. On its door a brass plate was still fixed, bearing the words, "United States Agency." But it was now the home of a plain, unimportant citizen, William Douglas.

Anne ran up the path toward the front door, thinking of the children and the supper. She climbed the uneven snow-covered steps, turned the latch, and entered the dark hall. There was a line of light under the left-hand door, and taking off her fur-lined overshoes, she went in. The room was large; its three windows were protected by shutters, and thick curtains of red hue, faded but cheery; a great fire of logs was burning on the hearth, lighting up every corner with its flame and glow, and making the poor furniture splendid. In its radiance the curtains were damask, the old carpet a Persian-hued luxury, and the preparations for cooking an *Arabian Nights'* display. Three little boys ran forward to meet their sister; a girl who was basking in the glow of the flame looked up languidly. They were odd children, with black eyes, coal-black hair, dark skins, and bold eagle outlines. The eldest, the girl, was small—a strange little creature, with braids of black hair hanging down behind almost to her ankles, half-closed black eyes, little hands and feet, a low soft voice, and the grace of a young panther. The boys were larger, handsome little fellows of wild aspect. In fact, all four were of mixed blood, their mother having been a beautiful French quarter-breed, and their father—William Douglas.

"Annet, Annet, can't we have fried potatoes for supper, and bacon?"

"Annet, Annet, can't we have coffee?"

"It is a biting night, isn't it?" said Tita, coming to her sister's side and stroking her cold hands gently. "I really think, Annet, that you ought to have something substantielle. You see, *I* think of you; whereas those howling piggish bears think only of themselves."

All this she delivered in a soft, even voice, while Anne removed the remainder of her wrappings.

"I have thought of something better still," said William Douglas's eldest daughter, kissing her little sister fondly, and then stepping out of the last covering, and lifting the heap from the floor—"batter cakes!"

The boys gave a shout of delight, and danced up and down on the hearth; Tita went back to her corner and sat down, clasping her little brown hands round her ankles, like the embalmed monkeys of the Nile. Her corner was made by an old secretary and the side of the great chimney; this space she had lined and carpeted with furs, and here she sat curled up with her book or her bead-work all through the long winter, refusing to leave the house unless absolutely ordered out by Anne, who filled the place of mother to these motherless little ones. Tita was well satisfied with the prospect of batter cakes; she would probably eat two if Anne browned them well, and they were light and tender. But as for those boys, those wolf-dogs, those beasts, they would probably swallow dozens. "If you come any nearer, Louis, I shall lay open the side of your head," she announced, gently, as the boys danced too near her hermitage; they, accustomed alike to her decisions and her words, danced farther away without any discussion of the subject. Tita was an excellent playmate sometimes; her little moccasined feet, and long braids streaming behind, formed the most exciting feature of their summer races; her blue cloth skirt up in the tops of the tallest trees, the provocative element in their summer climbing. She was a pallid little creature, while they were brown; small, while they were large; but she domineered over them like a king, and wreaked a whole vocabulary of roughest fisherman's terms upon them when they displeased her. One awful vengeance she reserved as a last resort: when they had been unbearably troublesome she stole into their room at night in her little white night-gown, with all her long thick black hair loose, combed over her face, and hanging down round her nearly to her feet. This was a ghostly visitation which the boys could not endure, for she left a lamp in the hall outside, so that they could dimly see her, and then she stood and swayed toward them slowly, backward and forward, without a sound, all the time coming nearer and nearer, until they shrieked aloud in terror, and Anne, hurrying to the rescue, found only three frightened little fellows cowering together in their broad bed, and the hairy ghost gone.

"How can you do such things, Tita?" she said.

"It is the only way by which I can keep the little devils in order," replied Tita.

"Do not use such words, dear."

"Mother did," said the younger sister, in her soft calm voice.

This was true, and Tita knew that Anne never impugned the memory of that mother.

6

"Who volunteers to help?" said Anne, lighting a candle in an iron candlestick, and opening a door.

"I," said Louis.

"I," said Gabriel.

"Me too," said little André.

They followed her, hopping along together, with arms interlinked, while her candle shed a light on the bare walls and floors of the rooms through which they passed, a series of little apartments, empty and desolate, at the end of which was the kitchen, inhabited in the daytime by an Irishwoman, a soldier's wife, who came in the morning before breakfast, and went home at dusk, the only servant William Douglas's fast-thinning purse could afford. Anne might have had her kitchen nearer what Miss Lois called the "keeping-room"; any one of the five in the series would have answered the purpose as well as the one she had chosen. But she had a dream of furnishing them all some day according to a plan of her own, and it would have troubled her greatly to have used her proposed china closet, pantry, store-room, preserve closet, or fruit-room for culinary purposes. How often had she gone over the whole in her mind, settling the position of every shelf, and deliberating over the pattern of the cups! The Irishwoman had left some gleams of fire on the hearth, and the boys immediately set themselves to work burying potatoes in the ashes, with the hot hearth-stone beneath. "For of course you are going to cook in the sitting-room, Annet," they said. "We made all ready for you there; and, besides, this fire is out."

"You could easily have kept it up," said the sister, smiling. "However, as it is Christmas-eve, I will let you have your way."

The boys alertly loaded themselves with the articles she gave them, and went hopping back into the sitting-room. They scorned to walk on Christmas-eve; the thing was to hop, and yet carry every dish steadily. They arranged the table, still in a sort of dancing step, and sang together in their shrill childish voices a tune of their own, without any words but "Ho! ho! ho!" Tita, in her corner, kept watch over the proceedings, and inhaled the aroma of the coffee with indolent anticipation. The tin pot stood on the hearth near her, surrounded by coals; it was a battered old coffee-pot, grimy as a camp-kettle, but dear to all the household, and their principal comforter when the weather was bitter, provisions scarce, or the boys especially troublesome. For the boys said they did not enjoy being especially troublesome; they could not help it any more than they could help having the measles or the whooping-cough. They needed coffee, therefore, for the conflict, when they felt it coming on, as much as any of the household.

Poor Anne's cooking utensils were few and old; it was hard to make batter cakes over an open fire without the proper hanging griddle. But she attempted it, nevertheless, and at length, with scarlet cheeks, placed a plateful of them, brown, light, and smoking, upon the table. "Now, Louis, run out for the potatoes; and, Tita, call father."

This one thing Tita would do; she aspired to be her father's favorite. She went out with her noiseless step, and presently returned leading in the tall, bent, gray-haired father, her small brown hand holding his tightly, her dark eyes fixed upon him with a persistent steadiness, as if determined to isolate all his attention upon herself. William Douglas was never thoroughly at ease with his youngest daughter; she had this habit of watching him silently, which made him uncomfortable. The boys he understood, and made allowances for their wildness; but this girl, with her soft still ways, perplexed and troubled him. She seemed to embody, as it were, his own mistakes, and he never looked at her little pale face and diminutive figure without a vague feeling that she was a spirit dwelling on earth in elfish form, with a half-developed contradictory nature, to remind him of his past weakness. Standing at the head of the table, tall and straight, with her nobly poised head and clear Saxon eyes, his other daughter awaited him, and met his gaze with a bright smile; he always came back to her with a sense of comfort. But Tita jealously brought his attention to herself again by pulling his hand, and leading him to his chair, taking her own place close beside him. He was a tall man, and her head did not reach his elbow, but she ruled him. The father now asked a blessing; he always hesitated on his way through it, once or twice, as though he had forgotten what to say, but took up the thread again after an instant's pause, and went on. When he came to the end, and said "Amen," he always sat down with a relieved air. If you had asked him what he had said, he could not have told you unless you started him at the beginning, when the old formula would have rolled off his lips in the same vague, mechanical way. The meal proceeded in comparative quiet; the boys no longer hummed and shuffled their feet; they were engaged with the cakes. Tita refrained from remarks save once, when Gabriel having dropped buttered crumbs upon her dress, she succinctly threatened him with dismemberment. Douglas gazed at her helplessly, and sighed.

"She will be a woman soon," he said to his elder daughter, when, an hour or two later, she joined him in his own apartment, and drew from its hiding-place her large sewing-basket, filled with Christmas presents.

"Oh no, father, she is but a child," answered Anne, cheerfully. "As she grows older these little faults will vanish."

"How old is she?" said Douglas.

"Just thirteen."

The father played a bar of Mendelssohn noiselessly on the arm of his chair with his long thin fingers; he was thinking that he had married Tita's mother when she was hardly three years older. Anne was absorbed in her presents.

"See, father, will not this be nice for André? And this for Gabriel? And I have made such a pretty doll for Tita."

"Will she care for it, dear?"

"Of course she will. Did I not play with my own dear doll until I was fourteen years old—yes, almost fifteen?" said the girl, with a little laugh and blush.

"And you are now—"

"I am over sixteen."

"A great age," said Douglas, smoothing her thick brown hair fondly, as she sat near him, bending over her sewing.

The younger children were asleep up stairs in two old bedrooms with rattling dormer windows, and the father and elder daughter were in a small room opposite the sitting-room, called the study, although nothing was ever studied there, save the dreams of his own life, by the vague, irresolute, imaginative soul that dwelt therein, in a thin body of its own, much the worse for wear. William Douglas was a New England man of the brooding type, sent by force of circumstances into the ranks of United States army surgeons. He had married Anne's mother, who had passionately loved him, against the wishes of her family, and had brought the disinherited young bride out to this far Western island, where she had died, happy to the last—one of those rare natures to whom love is all in all, and the whole world well lost for its dear and holy sake. Grief over her death brought out all at once the latent doubts, hesitations, and strange perplexities of William Douglas's peculiar mind—perplexities which might have lain dormant in a happier life. He resigned his position as army surgeon, and refused even practice in the village. Medical science was not exact, he said; there was much pretense and presumption in it; he would no longer countenance deception, or play a part. He was then made postmaster, and dealt out letters through some seasons, until at last his mistakes roused the attention of the new officers at the fort; for the villagers, good, easy-tempered people, would never have complained of such trifles as a forgotten mail-bag or two under the counter. Superseded, he then attended nominally to the highways; but as the military authorities had for years done all that was to be done on the smooth roads, three in number, including the steep fort hill, the position was a sinecure, and the superintendent took long walks across the island, studying the flora of the Northern woods, watching the birds, noticing the clouds and the winds, staying out late to experiment with the flash of the two light-houses from their different distances, and then coming home to his lonely house, where the baby Anne was tenderly cared for by Miss Lois Hinsdale, who superintended the nurse all day, watched her charge to bed, and then came over early in the morning before she woke. Miss Lois adored the baby; and she watched the lonely father from a distance, imagining all his sadness. It was the poetry of her life. Who, therefore, can picture her feelings when, at the end of three years, it was suddenly brought to her knowledge that Douglas was soon to marry again, and that his choice was Angélique Lafontaine, a French quarter-breed girl!

Angélique was amiable, and good in her way; she was also very beautiful. But Miss Lois could have borne it better if she had been homely. The New England woman wept bitter, bitter tears that night. A god had come down and showed himself flesh; an ideal was shattered. How long had she dwelt upon the beautiful love of Dr. Douglas and his young wife, taking it as a perfect example of rare, sweet happiness which she herself had missed, of which she herself was not worthy! How many times had she gone up to the little burial-ground on the height, and laid flowers from her garden on the mound, whose stone bore only the inscription, "Alida, wife of William Douglas, aged twenty-two years." Miss Lois had wished to have a text engraved under this brief line, and a date, but Dr. Douglas gently refused a text, and regarding a date he said: "Time is nothing. Those who love her will remember the date, and strangers need not know. But I should like the chance visitor to note that she was only twenty-two, and, as he stands there, think of her with kindly regret, as we all think of the early dead, though why, Miss Lois, why, I can not tell, since in going hence early surely the dead lose nothing, for God would not allow any injustice, I think—yes, I have about decided in my own mind that He does not allow it."

Miss Lois, startled, looked at him questioningly. He was then a man of thirty-four, tall, slight, still noticeable for the peculiar refined delicacy of face and manner which had first won the interest of sweet, impulsive Alida Clanssen.

"I trust, doctor, that you accept the doctrines of Holy Scripture on all such subjects," said Miss Lois. Then she felt immediately that she should have said "of the Church"; for she was a comparatively new Episcopalian, having been trained a New England Presbyterian of the severest hue.

Dr. Douglas came back to practical life again in the troubled gaze of the New England woman's eyes. "Miss Lois," he said, turning the subject, "Alida loved and trusted you; will you sometimes think of her little daughter?"

And then Miss Lois, the quick tears coming, forgot all about orthodoxy, gladly promised to watch over the baby, and kept her word. But now her life was shaken, and all her romantic beliefs disturbed and shattered, by this overwhelming intelligence. She was wildly, furiously jealous, wildly, furiously angry—jealous for Alida's sake, for the baby's, for her own. It is easy to be humble when a greater is preferred; but when an inferior is lifted high above our heads, how can we bear it? And Miss Lois was most jealous of all for Douglas himself— that such a man should so stoop. She hardly knew herself that night as she harshly pulled down the curtains, pushed a stool half across the room, slammed the door, and purposely knocked over the fire-irons. Lois Hinsdale had never since her birth given way to rage before (nor known the solace of it), and she was now forty-one years old. All her life afterward she remembered that night as something akin to a witch's revel on the Brocken, a horrible wild reign of passion which she trembled to recall, and for which she did penance many times in tears. "It shows the devil there is in us all," she said to herself, and she never passed the fire-irons for a long time afterward without an unpleasant consciousness.

The limited circle of island society suggested that Miss Lois had been hunting the loon with a hand-net—a Northern way of phrasing the wearing of the willow; but if the New England woman loved William Douglas, she was not conscious of it, but merged the feeling in her love for his child, and for the memory of Alida. True, she was seven years older than he was: women of forty-one can answer whether that makes any difference.

On a brilliant, sparkling, clear June morning William Douglas went down to the little Roman Catholic church and married the French girl. As he had resigned his position in the army some time before, and as there was a new set of officers at the fort, his marriage made little impression there save on the mind of the chaplain, who had loved him well when he was surgeon of the post, and had played many a game of chess with him. The whole French population of the island, however, came to the marriage. That was expected. But what was not expected was the presence there of Miss Lois Hinsdale, sitting severely rigid in the first pew, accompanied by the doctor's child—a healthy, blue-eyed little girl, who kissed her new mamma obediently, and thought her very sweet and pretty—a belief which remained with her always, the careless, indolent, easy-tempered, beautiful young second wife having died when her step-daughter was eleven years old, leaving four little ones, who, according to a common freak of nature, were more Indian than their mother. The Douglas family grew poorer every year; but as every one was poor there, poverty was respectable; and as all poverty is comparative, they always esteemed themselves comfortable. For they had the old Agency for a home, and it was in some respects the most dignified residence on the island; and they had the remains of the furniture which the young surgeon had brought with him from the East when his Alida was a bride, and that was better than most of the furniture in use in the village. The little stone fort on the height was, of course, the castle of the town, and its commandant by courtesy the leader of society; but the infantry officers who succeeded each other at this distant Northern post brought little with them, camping out, as it were, in their low-ceilinged quarters, knowing that another season might see them far away. The Agency, therefore, preserved an air of dignity still, although its roof leaked, its shutters rattled, although its plastering was gone here and there, and its floors were uneven and decayed. Two of its massive outside chimneys, clamped to the sides of the house, were half down, looking like broken columns, monuments of the past; but there were a number left. The Agency originally had bristled with chimneys, which gave, on a small scale, a castellated air to its rambling outline.

Dr. Douglas's study was old, crowded, and comfortable; that is, comfortable to those who have consciousness in their finger-ends, and no uncertainty as to their feet; the great army of blunderers and stumblers, the handle-everything, knock-over-everything people, who cut a broad swath through the smaller furniture of a room whenever they move, would have been troubled and troublesome there. The boys were never admitted; but Tita, who stepped like a little cat, and Anne, who had a deft direct aim in all her motions, were often present. The comfort of the place was due to Anne; she shook out and arranged the curtains, darned the old carpet, re-covered the lounge, polished the andirons, and did all without disturbing the birds' wings, the shells, the arrow-heads, the skins, dried plants, wampum, nets, bits of rock, half-finished drawings, maps, books, and papers, which were scattered about, or suspended from the walls. William Douglas, knowing something of everything, was exact in nothing: now he stuffed birds, now he read Greek, now he botanized, now he played on the flute, now he went about in all weathers chipping the rocks with ardent zeal, now he smoked in his room all day without a word or a look for anybody. He sketched well, but seldom finished a picture; he went out hunting when the larder was empty, and forgot what he went for; he had a delicate mechanical skill, and made some curious bits of intricate work, but he never mended the hinges of the shutters, or repaired a single article which was in daily use in his household.

By the careful attention of Anne he was present in the fort chapel every Sunday morning, and, once there, he played the organ with delight, and brought exquisite harmonies from its little pipes; but Anne stood there beside him all the time, found the places, and kept him down to the work, borrowing his watch beforehand in order to touch him when the voluntary was too long, or the chords between the hymn verses too beautiful and intricate. Those were the days when the old buckram-backed rhymed versions of the psalms were steadfastly given out at every service, and Anne's rich voice sang, with earnest fervor, words like these:

"His liberal favors he extends,

To some he gives, to others
lends;

Yet when his charity impairs,

He saves by prudence in
affairs,"

while her father followed them with harmony fit for angels. Douglas taught his daughter music in the best sense of the phrase; she read notes accurately, and knew nothing of inferior composers, the only change from the higher courts of melody being some of the old French chansons of the voyageurs, which still lingered on the island, echoes of the past. She could not touch the ivory keys with any skill, her hands were too much busied with other work; but she practiced her singing lessons as she went about the house—music which would have seemed to the world of New York as old-fashioned as Chaucer.

The fire of logs blazed on the hearth, the father sat looking at his daughter, who was sewing swiftly, her thoughts fixed upon her work. The clock struck eleven.

"It is late, Anne."

"Yes, father, but I must finish. I have so little time during the day."

"My good child," said Douglas, slowly and fondly.

Anne looked up; his eyes were dim with tears.

"I have done nothing for you, dear," he said, as she dropped her work and knelt by his side. "I have kept you selfishly with me here, and made you a slave to those children."

"My own brothers and my own little sister, father."

"Do you feel so, Anne? Then may God bless you for it! But I should not have kept you here."

"This is our home, papa."

"A poor one."

"Is it? It never seemed so to me."

"That is because you have known nothing better."

"But I like it, papa, just as it is. I have always been happy here."

"Really happy, Anne?"

The girl paused, and reflected a moment. "Yes," she said, looking into the depths of the fire, with a smile, "I am happy all the time. I am never anything but happy."

William Douglas looked at her. The fire-light shone on her face; she turned her clear eyes toward him.

"Then you do not mind the children? They are not a burdensome weight upon you?"

"Never, papa; how can you suppose it? I love them dearly, next to you."

"And will you stand by them, Anne? Note my words: I do not urge it, I simply ask."

"Of course I will stand by them, papa. I give a promise of my own accord. I will never forsake them as long as I can do anything for them, as long as I live. But why do you speak of it? Have I ever neglected them or been unkind to them?" said the girl, troubled, and very near tears.

"No, dear; you love them better than they or I deserve. I was thinking of the future, and of a time when,"—he had intended to say, "when I am no longer with you," but the depth of love and trust in her eyes made him hesitate, and finish his sentence differently—"a time when they may give you trouble," he said.

"They are good boys—that is, they mean no harm, papa. When they are older they will study more."

"Will they?"

"Certainly," said Anne, with confidence. "I did. And as for Tita, you yourself must see, papa, what a remarkable child she is."

Douglas shaded his face with his hand. The uneasy sense of trouble which always stirred within him when he thought of his second daughter was rising to the surface now like a veiled, formless shape. "The sins of the fathers," he thought, and sighed heavily.

Anne threw her arms round his neck, and begged him to look at her. "Papa, speak to me, please. What is it that troubles you so?"

"Stand by little Tita, child, no matter what she does. Do not expect too much of her, but remember always her—her Indian blood," said the troubled father, in a low voice.

A flush crossed Anne's face. The cross of mixed blood in the younger children was never alluded to in the family circle or among their outside friends. In truth, there had been many such mixtures on the island in the old times, although comparatively few in the modern days to which William Douglas's second marriage belonged.

"Tita is French," said Anne, speaking rapidly, almost angrily.

"She is more French than Indian. Still—one never knows." Then, after a pause: "I have been a slothful father, Anne, and feel myself cowardly also in thus shifting upon your shoulders my own responsibilities. Still, what can I do? I can not re-live my life; and even if I could, perhaps I might do the same again. I do not know—I do not know. We are as we are, and tendencies dating generations back come out in us, and confuse our actions."

He spoke dreamily. His eyes were assuming that vague look with which his children were familiar, and which betokened that his mind was far away.

"You could not do anything which was not right, father," said Anne.

She was standing by his side now, and in her young strength might have been his champion against the whole world. The fire-light shining out showed a prematurely old man, whose thin form, bent drooping shoulders, and purposeless face were but Time's emphasis upon the slender, refined, dreamy youth, who, entering the domain of doubt with honest negations and a definite desire, still wandered there, lost to the world, having forgotten his first object, and loving the soft haze now for itself alone.

Anne received no answer: her father's mind had passed away from her. After waiting a few moments in silence she saw that he was lost in one of his reveries, and sitting down again she took up her work and went on sewing with rapid stitches. Poor Anne and her poor presents! How coarse the little white shirts for Louis and André! how rough the jacket for Gabriel! How forlorn the doll! How awkwardly fashioned the small cloth slippers for Tita! The elder sister was obliged to make her Christmas gifts with her own hands; she had no money to spend for such superfluities. The poor doll had a cloth face, with features painted on a flat surface, and a painful want of profile. A little before twelve the last stitch was taken with happy content.

"Papa, it is nearly midnight; do not sit up very late," said the daughter, bending to kiss the father's bent, brooding brow. William Douglas's mind came back for an instant, and looked out through his clouded eyes upon his favorite child. He kissed her, gave her his usual blessing, "May God help the soul He has created!" and then, almost before she had closed the door, he was far away again on one of those long journeyings which he took silently, only his following guardian angel knew whither. Anne went across the hall and entered the sitting-room; the fire was low, but she stirred the embers, and by their light filled the four stockings hanging near the chimney-piece. First she put in little round cakes wrapped in papers; then home-made candies, not thoroughly successful in outline, but well-flavored and sweet; next gingerbread elephants and camels, and an attempt at a fairy; lastly the contents of her work-basket, which gave her much satisfaction as she inspected them for the last time. Throwing a great knot, which would burn slowly all night, upon the bed of dying coals, she lighted a candle and went up to her own room.

As soon as she had disappeared, a door opened softly above, and a small figure stole out into the dark hall. After listening a moment, this little figure went silently down the stairs, paused at the line of light underneath the closed study door, listened again, and then, convinced that all was safe, went into the sitting-room, took down the stockings one by one, and deliberately inspected all their contents, sitting on a low stool before the fire. First came the stockings of the boys; each parcel was unrolled, down to the last gingerbread camel, and as deftly enwrapped again by the skillful little fingers. During this examination there was not so much an expression of interest as of jealous scrutiny. But when the turn of her own stocking came, the small face showed the most profound, almost weazened, solicitude. Package after package was swiftly opened, and its contents spread upon the mat beside her. The doll was cast aside with contempt, the slippers examined and tried on with critical care, and then when the candy and cake appeared and nothing else, the eyes snapped with anger.

The little brown hand felt down to the toe of the stocking: no, there was nothing more. "It is my opinion," said Tita, in her French island *patois*, half aloud, "that Annet is one stupid beast."

She then replaced everything, hung the stockings on their nails, and stole back to her own room; here, by the light of a secreted candle-end, she manufactured the following epistle, with heavy labor of brains and hand: "Cher papa,—I hav dreemed that Sant Klos has hare-ribbans in his pak. Will you ask him for sum for your little

11

Tita?" This not seeming sufficiently expressive, she inserted "trez affecsionay" before "Tita," and then, folding the epistle, she went softly down the stairs again, and stealing round in the darkness through several unused rooms, she entered her father's bedroom, which communicated with the study, and by sense of feeling pinned the paper carefully round his large pipe, which lay in its usual place on the table. For William Douglas always began smoking as soon as he rose, in this way nullifying, as it were, the fresh, vivifying effect of the morning, which smote painfully upon his eyes and mind alike; in the afternoon and evening he did not smoke so steadily, the falling shadows supplying of themselves the atmosphere he loved. Having accomplished her little manœuvre, Tita went back up stairs to her own room like a small white ghost, and fell asleep with the satisfaction of a successful diplomatist.

In the mean time Anne was brushing her brown hair, and thoughtfully going over in her own mind the morrow's dinner. Her room was a bare and comfortless place; there was but a small fire on the hearth, and no curtains over the windows; it took so much care and wood to keep the children's rooms warm that she neglected her own, and as for the furniture, she had removed it piece by piece, exchanging it for broken-backed worn-out articles from all parts of the house. One leg of the bedstead was gone, and its place supplied by a box which the old-fashioned valance only half concealed; the looking-glass was cracked, and distorted her image; the chairs were in hospital and out of service, the young mistress respecting their injuries, and using as her own seat an old wooden stool which stood near the hearth. Upon this she was now seated, the rippling waves of her thick hair flowing over her shoulders. Having at last faithfully rehearsed the Christmas dinner in all its points, she drew a long breath of relief, rose, extinguished her light, and going over to the window, stood there for a moment looking out. The moonlight came gleaming in and touched her with silver, her pure youthful face and girlish form draped in white. "May God bless my dear father," she prayed, silently, looking up to the thick studded stars; "and my dear mother too, wherever she is to-night, in one of those far bright worlds, perhaps." It will be seen from this prayer that the boundaries of Anne Douglas's faith were wide enough to include even the unknown.

CHAPTER II.

"Heap on more wood! the wind is chill;

But let it whistle as it will,

We'll keep our Christmas merry still.

The damsel donned her kirtle sheen;

The hall was dressed with holly green;

Forth to the wood did merry-men go,

To gather in the mistletoe."—Walter
Scott.

"Can you make out what the child means?" said Douglas, as his elder daughter entered the study early on Christmas morning to renew the fire and set the apartment in order for the day. As he spoke he held Tita's epistle hopelessly before him, and scanned the zig-zag lines.

"She wants some ribbons for her hair," said Anne, making out the words over his shoulder. "Poor little thing! she is so proud of her hair, and all the other girls have bright ribbons. But I can not make ribbons," she added, regretfully, as though she found herself wanting in a needful accomplishment. "Think of her faith in Santa Klaus, old as she is, and her writing to ask him! But there is ribbon in the house, after all," she added, suddenly, her face brightening. "Miss Lois gave me some last month; I had forgotten it. That will be the very thing for Tita; she has not even seen it."

(But has she not, thou unsuspicious elder sister?)

"Do not rob yourself, child," said the father, wearily casting his eyes over the slip of paper again. "What spelling! The English is bad, but the French worse."

"That is because she has no French teacher, papa; and you know I do not allow her to speak the island *patois*, lest it should corrupt the little she knows."

"But she does speak it; she always talks *patois* when she is alone with me."

"Does she?" said Anne, in astonishment. "I had no idea of that. But *you* might correct her, papa."

12

"I can never correct her in any way," replied Douglas, gloomily; and then Anne, seeing that he was on the threshold of one of his dark moods, lighted his pipe, stirred the fire into a cheery blaze, and went out to get a cup of coffee for him. For the Irish soldier's wife was already at work in the kitchen, having been to mass in the cold gray dawn, down on her two knees on the hard floor, repentant for all her sins, and refulgently content in the absolution which wiped out the old score (and left place for a new one). After taking in the coffee, Anne ran up to her own room, brought down the ribbon, and placed it in Tita's stocking; she then made up the fire with light-wood, and set about decorating the walls with wreaths of evergreen as the patter of the little boys' feet was heard on the old stairway. The breakfast table was noisy that morning. Tita had inspected her ribbons demurely, and wondered how Santa Klaus knew her favorite colors so well. Anne glanced toward her father, and smiled; but the father's face showed doubt, and did not respond. While they were still at the table the door opened, and a tall figure entered, muffled in furs. "Miss Lois!" cried the boys. "Hurrah! See our presents, Miss Lois." They danced round her while she removed her wrappings, and kept up such a noise that no one could speak. Miss Lois, viewed without her cloak and hood, was a tall, angular woman, past middle age, with sharp features, thin brown hair tinged with gray, and pale blue eyes shielded by spectacles. She kissed Anne first with evident affection, and afterward the children with business-like promptitude; then she shook hands with William Douglas. "I wish you a happy Christmas, doctor," she said.

"Thank you, Lois," said Douglas, holding her hand in his an instant or two longer than usual.

A faint color rose in Miss Lois's cheeks. When she was young she had one of those exquisitely delicate complexions which seem to belong to some parts of New England; even now color would rise unexpectedly in her cheeks, much to her annoyance: she wondered why wrinkles did not keep it down. But New England knows her own. The creamy skins of the South, with their brown shadows under the eyes, the rich colors of the West, even the calm white complexions that are bred and long retained in cities, all fade before this faint healthy bloom on old New England's cheeks, like winter-apples.

Miss Lois inspected the boys' presents with exact attention, and added some gifts of her own, which filled the room with a more jubilant uproar than before. Tita, in the mean while, remained quietly seated at the table, eating her breakfast; she took very small mouthfuls, and never hurried herself. She said she liked to taste things, and that only snapping dogs, like the boys, for instance, gulped their food in a mass.

"I gave her the ribbons; do not say anything," whispered Anne, in Miss Lois's ear, as she saw the spectacled eyes turning toward Tita's corner. Miss Lois frowned, and put back into her pocket a small parcel she was taking out. She had forgiven Dr. Douglas the existence of the boys, but she never could forgive the existence of Tita.

Once Anne had asked about Angélique. "I was but a child when she died, Miss Lois," said she, "so my recollection of her may not be accurate; but I know that I thought her very beautiful. Does Tita look like her?"

"Angélique Lafontaine was beautiful—in her way," replied Miss Lois. "I do not say that I admire that way, mind you."

"And Tita?"

"Tita is hideous."

"Oh, Miss Lois!"

"She is, child. She is dwarfish, black, and sly."

"I do not think she is sly," replied Anne, with heat. "And although she is dark and small, still, sometimes—"

"That, for your beauty of 'sometimes!'" said Miss Lois, snapping her fingers. "Give me a girl who is pretty in the morning as well as by candle-light, one who has a nice, white, well-born, down-East face, and none of your Western-border mongrelosities!"

But this last phrase she uttered under her breath. She was ever mindful of Anne's tender love for her father, and the severity with which she herself, as a contemporary, had judged him was never revealed to the child.

At half past ten the Douglas family were all in their places in the little fort chapel. It was a bright but bitterly cold day, and the members of the small congregation came enveloped in shaggy furs like bears, shedding their skins at the door, where they lay in a pile near the stove, ready for the return homeward. The military trappings of the officers brightened the upper benches, the uniforms of the common soldiers filled the space behind; on the side benches sat the few Protestants of the village, denominational prejudices unknown or forgotten in this far-away spot in the wilderness. The chaplain, the Reverend James Gaston—a man who lived in peace with all the world, with Père Michaux, the Catholic priest, and William Douglas, the deist—gazed round upon his flock with a benignant air, which brightened into affection as Anne's voice took up the song of the angels, singing, amid the ice and snow of a new world, the strain the shepherds heard on the plains of Palestine.

"Glory to God in the highest, and on earth peace, good-will toward men," sang Anne, with all her young heart. And Miss Lois, sitting with folded hands, and head held stiffly erect, saw her wreath in the place of honor over the altar, and was touched first with pride and then with a slight feeling of awe. She did not believe that one part of the church was more sacred than another—she could not; but being a High-Church Episcopalian now, she said to herself that she ought to; she even had appalling visions of herself, sometimes, going as far as Rome. But the old spirit of Calvinism was still on the ground, ready for many a wrestling match yet; and stronger than all else were the old associations connected with the square white meeting-house of her youth, which held their place undisturbed down below all these upper currents of a new faith. William Douglas was also a New-Englander, brought up strictly in the creed of his fathers; but as Miss Lois's change of creed was owing to a change of position, as some Northern birds turn their snow-color to a darker hue when taken away from arctic regions, so his was one purely of mind, owing to nothing but the processes of thought within him. He had drifted away from all creeds, save in one article: he believed in a Creator. To this great Creator's praise, and in worship of Him, he now poured forth his harmonies, the purest homage he could offer, "unless," he thought, "Anne is a living homage as she stands here beside me. But no, she is a soul by herself; she has her own life to live, her own worship to offer; I must not call her mine. That she is my daughter is naught to me save a great blessing. I can love her with a human father's love, and thank God for her affection. But that is all."

So he played his sweetest music, and Miss Lois fervently prayed, and made no mistake in the order of her prayers. She liked to have a vocal part in the service. It was a pleasure to herself to hear her own voice lifted up, even as a miserable sinner; for at home in the old white meeting-house all expression had been denied to her, the small outlet of the Psalms being of little avail to a person who could not sing. This dumbness stifled her, and she had often said to herself that the men would never have endured it either if they had not had the prayer-meetings as a safety-valve. The three boys were penned in at Miss Lois's side, within reach of her tapping finger. They had decided to attend service on account of the evergreens and Anne's singing, although they, as well as Tita, belonged in reality to the flock of Father Michaux. Anne never interfered with this division of the family; she considered it the one tie which bound the children to the memory of their mother; but Miss Lois shook her head over it, and sighed ominously. The boys were, in fact, three little heathen; but Tita was a devout Roman Catholic, and observed all the feast and fast days of the Church, to the not infrequent disturbance of the young mistress of the household, to whom a feast-day was oftentimes an occasion bristling with difficulty. But to-day, in honor of Christmas, the usual frugal dinner had been made a banquet indeed, by the united efforts of Anne and Miss Lois; and when they took their seats at the table which stood in the sitting-room, all felt that it held an abundance fit even for the old fur-trading days, Miss Lois herself having finally succumbed to that island standard of comparison. After the dinner was over, while they were sitting round the fire sipping coffee—the ambrosia of the Northern gods, who find some difficulty in keeping themselves warm—a tap at the door was heard, and a tall youth entered, a youth who was a vivid personification of early manhood in its brightest form. The warm air was stirred by the little rush of cold that came in with him, and the dreamy and drowsy eyes round the fire awoke as they rested upon him.

"The world *is* alive, then, outside, after all," said Miss Lois, briskly straightening herself in her chair, and taking out her knitting. "How do you do, Erastus?"

But her greeting was drowned by the noise of the boys, who had been asleep together on the rug in a tangled knot, like three young bears, but now, broadly awake again, were jumping round the new-comer, displaying their gifts and demanding admiration. Disentangling himself from them with a skill which showed a long experience in their modes of twisting, the young man made his way up to Anne, and, with a smile and bow to Dr. Douglas and Miss Lois, sat down by her side.

"You were not at church this morning," said the girl, looking at him rather gravely, but giving him her hand.

"No, I was not; but a merry Christmas all the same, Annet," answered the youth, throwing back his golden head with careless grace. At this moment Tita came forward from her furry corner, where she had been lying with her head on her arm, half asleep, and seated herself in the red light of the fire, gazing into the blaze with soft indifference. Her dark woollen dress was brightened by the ribbons which circled her little waist and knotted themselves at the ends of the long braids of her hair. She had a string of yellow beads round her neck, and on her feet the little slippers which Anne had fashioned for her with so much care. Her brown hands lay crossed on her lap, and her small but bold-featured profile looked more delicate than usual, outlined in relief like a little cameo against the flame. The visitor's eyes rested upon her for a moment, and then turned back to Anne. "There is to be a dance to-night down in one of the old warehouses," he said, "and I want you to go."

"A dance!" cried the boys; "then *we* are going too. It is Christmas night, and we know how to dance. See here." And they sprang out into the centre of the room, and began a figure, not without a certain wild grace of its own, keeping time to the shrill whistling of Gabriel, who was the fifer and leader of the band.

Miss Lois put down her knitting, and disapproved, for the old training was still strong in her; then she remembered that these were things of the past, shook her head at herself, sighed, and resumed it again.

"Of course you will go," said the visitor.

14

"I do not know that I *can* go, Rast," replied Anne, turning toward her father, as if to see what he thought.

"Yes, go," said Douglas—"go, Annet." He hardly ever used this name, which the children had given to their elder sister—a name that was not the French "Annette," but, like the rest of the island *patois*, a mispronunciation—"An´net," with the accent on the first syllable. "It is Christmas night," said Douglas, with a faint interest on his faded face; "I should like it to be a pleasant recollection for you, Annet."

The young girl went to him; he kissed her, and then rose to go to his study; but Tita's eyes held him, and he paused.

"Will *you* go, Miss Lois?" said Anne.

"Oh no, child," replied the old maid, primly, adjusting her spectacles.

"But you must go, Miss Lois, and dance with me," said Rast, springing up and seizing her hands.

"Fie, Erastus! for shame! Let me go," said Miss Lois, as he tried to draw her to her feet. He still bent over her, but she tapped his cheek with her knitting-needles, and told him to sit down and behave himself.

"I won't, unless you promise to go with us," he said.

"Why should you not go, Lois?" said Douglas, still standing at the door. "The boys want to go, and some one must be with them to keep them in order."

"Why, doctor, imagine me at a dancing party!" said Miss Lois, the peach-like color rising in her thin cheeks again.

"It is different here, Lois; everybody goes."

"Yes; even old Mrs. Kendig," said Tita, softly.

Miss Lois looked sharply at her; old Mrs. Kendig was fat, toothless, and seventy, and the active, spare New England woman felt a sudden wrath at the implied comparison. Griselda was not tried upon the subject of her age, or we might have had a different legend. But Tita looked as idly calm as a summer morning, and Miss Lois turned away, as she had turned a hundred times before, uncertain between intention and simple chance.

"Very well, then, I will go," she said. "How you bother me, Erastus!"

"No, I don't," said the youth, releasing her. "You know you like me, Miss Lois; you know you do."

"Brazen-face!" said Miss Lois, pushing him away. But any one could see that she did like him.

"Of course I may go, father?" said Tita, without stirring, but looking at him steadily.

"I suppose so," he answered, slowly; "that is, if Erastus will take care of you."

"Will you take care of me, Erastus?" asked the soft voice.

"Don't be absurd, Tita; of course he will," said Miss Lois, shortly. "He will see to you as well as to the other children."

And then Douglas turned and left the room.

Erastus, or Rast, as he was called, went back to his place beside Anne. He was a remarkably handsome youth of seventeen, with bright blue eyes, golden hair, a fine spirited outline, laughing mouth, and impetuous, quick movements; tall as a young sapling, his figure was almost too slender for its height, but so light and elastic that one forgave the fault, and forgot it in one look at the mobile face, still boyish in spite of the maturity given by the hard cold life of the North.

"Why have we not heard of this dance before, Erastus?" asked Miss Lois, ever mindful and tenacious of a dignity of position which no one disputed, but which was none the less to her a subject of constant and belligerent watchfulness—one by which she gauged the bow of the shop-keeper, the nod of the passing islander, the salute of the little half-breed boys who had fish to sell, and even the guttural ejaculations of the Chippewas who came to her door offering potatoes and Indian sugar.

"Because it was suggested only a few hours ago, up at the fort. I was dining with Dr. Gaston, and Walters came across from the commandant's cottage and told me. Since then I have been hard at work with them, decorating and lighting the ball-room."

"Which one of the old shells have you taken?" asked Miss Lois. "I hope the roof will not come down on our heads."

"We have Larrabee's; that has the best floor. And as to coming down on our heads, those old warehouses are stronger than you imagine, Miss Lois. Have you never noticed their great beams?"

"I have noticed their toppling fronts and their slanting sides, their bulgings out and their leanings in," replied Miss Lois, nodding her head emphatically.

"The leaning tower of Pisa, you know, is pronounced stronger than other towers that stand erect," said Rast. "That old brown shell of Larrabee's is jointed together so strongly that I venture to predict it will outlive us all. We might be glad of such joints ourselves, Miss Lois."

"If it will only not come down on our heads to-night, that is all I ask of its joints," replied Miss Lois.

Soon after seven o'clock the ball opened: darkness had already lain over the island for nearly three hours, and the evening seemed well advanced.

"Oh, Tita!" said Anne, as the child stepped out of her long cloak and stood revealed, clad in a fantastic short skirt of black cloth barred with scarlet, and a little scarlet bodice, "that dress is too thin, and besides—"

"She looks like a circus-rider," said Miss Lois, in dismay. "Why did you allow it, Anne?"

"I knew nothing of it," replied the elder sister, with a distressed expression on her face, but, as usual, not reproving Tita. "It is the little fancy dress the fort ladies made for her last summer when they had tableaux. It is too late to go back now; she must wear it, I suppose; perhaps in the crowd it will not be noticed."

Tita, unmoved, had walked meanwhile over to the hearth, and sitting down on the floor before the fire, was taking off her snow-boots and donning her new slippers, apparently unconscious of remark.

The scene was a striking one, or would have been such to a stranger. The lower floor of the warehouse had been swept and hastily garnished with evergreens and all the flags the little fort could muster; at each end on a broad hearth a great fire of logs roared up the old chimney, and helped to light the room, a soldier standing guard beside it, and keeping up the flame by throwing on wood every now and then from the heap in the corner near by. Candles were ranged along the walls, and lanterns hung from the beams above; all that the island could do in the way of illumination had been done. The result was a picturesque mingling of light and shade as the dancers came into the ruddy gleam of the fires and passed out again, now seen for a moment in the paler ray of a candle farther down the hall, now lost in the shadows which everywhere swept across the great brown room from side to side, like broad-winged ghosts resting in mid-air and looking down upon the revels. The music came from six French fiddlers, four young, gayly dressed fellows, and two grizzled, withered old men, and they played the tunes of the century before, and played them with all their might and main. The little fort, a one-company post, was not entitled to a band; but there were, as usual, one or two German musicians among the enlisted men, and these now stood near the French fiddlers and watched them with slow curiosity, fingering now and then in imagination the great brass instruments which were to them the keys of melody, and dreaming over again the happy days when they, too, played "with the band." But the six French fiddlers cared nothing for the Germans; they held themselves far above the common soldiers of the fort, and despised alike their cropped hair, their ideas, their uniforms, and the strict rules they were obliged to obey. They fiddled away with their eyes cast up to the dark beams above, and their tunes rang out in that shrill, sustained, clinging treble which no instrument save a violin can give. The entire upper circle of society was present, and a sprinkling of the second; for the young officers cared more for dancing than for etiquette, and a pretty young French girl was in their minds of more consequence than even the five Misses Macdougall with all their blood, which must have been, however, of a thin, although, of course, precious, quality, since between the whole five there seemed scarcely enough for one. The five were there, however, in green plaided delaines with broad lace collars and large flat shell-cameo breastpins with scroll-work settings: they presented an imposing appearance to the eyes of all. The father of these ladies, long at rest from his ledgers, was in his day a prominent resident official of the Fur Company; his five maiden daughters lived on in the old house, and occupied themselves principally in remembering him. Miss Lois seated herself beside these acknowledged heads of society, and felt that she was in her proper sphere. The dance-music troubled her ears, but she endured it manfully.

"A gay scene," she observed, gazing through her spectacles.

The five Misses Macdougall bowed acquiescence, and said that it was fairly gay; indeed, rather too gay, owing to more of a mingling than they approved; but nothing, ah! nothing, to the magnificent entertainments of times past, which had often been described to them by their respected parent. (They never seemed to have had but one.)

"Of course you will dance, Anne?" said Rast Pronando.

She smiled an assent, and they were soon among the dancers. Tita, left alone, followed them with her eyes as they passed out of the fire-light and were lost in the crowd and the sweeping shadows. Then she made her way, close to the wall, down to the other end of the long room, where the commandant's wife and the fort ladies sat in state, keeping up the dignity of what might be called the military end of the apartment. Here she sought the brightest light she could find, and placed herself in it carelessly, and as though by chance, to watch the dancers.

"Look at that child," said the captain's wife. "What an odd little thing it is!"

"It is Tita Douglas, Anne's little sister," said Mrs. Bryden, the wife of the commandant. "I am surprised they allowed her to come in that tableau dress. Her mother was a French girl, I believe. Dr. Douglas, you know, came to the island originally as surgeon of the post."

"There is Anne now, and dancing with young Pronando, of course," said the wife of one of the lieutenants.

"Dr. Gaston thinks there is no one like Anne Douglas," observed Mrs. Bryden. "He has educated her almost entirely; taught her Latin and Greek, and all sorts of things. Her father is a musical genius, you know, and in one way the girl knows all about music; in another, nothing at all. Do you think she is pretty, Mrs. Cromer?"

Mrs. Cromer thought "Not at all; too large, and—unformed in every way."

"I sometimes wonder, though, why she is not pretty," said Mrs. Bryden, in a musing tone. "She ought to be."

"I never knew but one girl of that size and style who was pretty, and she had had every possible advantage of culture, society, and foreign travel; wore always the most elaborately plain costumes—works of art, in a Greek sort of way; said little; but sat or stood about in statuesque attitudes that made you feel thin and insignificant, and glad you had all your clothes on," said Mrs. Cromer.

"And was this girl pretty?"

"She was simply superb," said the captain's wife. "But do look at young Pronando. How handsome he is to-night!"

"An Apollo Belvedere," said the wife of the lieutenant, who, having rashly allowed herself to spend a summer at West Point, was now living in the consequences.

But although the military element presided like a court circle at one end of the room, and the five Misses Macdougall and Miss Lois like an element of first families at the other, the intervening space was well filled with a motley assemblage—lithe young girls with sparkling black eyes and French vivacity, matrons with a shade more of brown in their complexions, and withered old grandams who sat on benches along the walls, and looked on with a calm dignity of silence which never came from Saxon blood. Intermingled were youths of rougher aspect but of fine mercurial temperaments, who danced with all their hearts as well as bodies, and kept exact time with the music, throwing in fancy steps from pure love of it as they whirled lightly down the hall with their laughing partners. There were a few young men of Scotch descent present also, clerks in the shops, and superintendents of the fisheries which now formed the only business of the once thriving frontier village. These were considered by island parents of the better class desirable suitors for their daughters—far preferable to the young officers who succeeded each other rapidly at the little fort, with attachments delightful, but as transitory as themselves. It was noticeable, however, that the daughters thought otherwise. Near the doorway in the shadow a crowd of Indians had gathered, while almost all of the common soldiers from the fort, on one pretext or another, were in the hall, attending to the fires and lights, or acting as self-appointed police. Even Chaplain Gaston looked in for a moment, and staid an hour; and later in the evening the tall form of Père Michaux appeared, clad in a furred mantle, a black silk cap crowning his silver hair. Tita immediately left her place and went to meet him, bending her head with an air of deep reverence.

"See the child—how theatrical!" said Mrs. Cromer.

"Yes. Still, the Romanists do believe in all kinds of amusements, and even ask a blessing on it," said the lieutenant's wife.

"It was not that—it was the little air and attitude of devoutness that I meant. See the puss now!"

But the puss was triumphant at last. One of the younger officers had noted her solemn little salutation in front of the priest, and now approached to ask her to dance, curious to see what manner of child this small creature could be. In another moment she was whirling down the hall with him, her dark face flushed, her eyes radiant, her dancing exquisitely light and exact. She passed Anne and Rast with a sparkling glance, her small breast throbbing with a swell of satisfied vanity that almost stopped her breath.

"There is Tita," said the elder sister, rather anxiously. "I hope Mr. Walters will not spoil her with his flattery."

"There is no danger; she is not pretty enough," answered Rast.

A flush rose in Anne's face. "You do not like my little sister," she said.

"Oh, I do not dislike her," said Rast. "I could not dislike anything that belonged to *you*," he added, in a lower tone.

She smiled as he bent his handsome head toward her to say this. She was fond of Rast; he had been her daily companion through all her life; she scarcely remembered anything in which he was not concerned, from her first baby walk in the woods back of the fort, her first ride in a dog-sledge on the ice, to yesterday's consultation over the chapel evergreens.

The six French fiddlers played on; they knew not fatigue. In imagination they had danced every dance. Tita was taken out on the floor several times by the officers, who were amused by her little airs and her small elfish

17

face: she glowed with triumph. Anne had but few invitations, save from Rast; but as his were continuous, she danced all the evening. At midnight Miss Lois and the Misses Macdougall formally rose, and the fort ladies sent for their wrappings: the ball, as far as the first circle was concerned, was ended. But long afterward the sound of the fiddles was still heard, and it was surmised that the second circle was having its turn, possibly not without a sprinkling of the third also.

CHAPTER III.

"Wassamequin, Nashoonon, and Massaconomet did voluntarily submit themselves to the English, and promise to be willing from time to time to be instructed in the knowledge of God. Being asked not to do any unnecessary work on the Sabbath day, they answered, 'It is easy to them; they have not much to do on any day, and can well take rest on that day as any other.' So then we, causing them to understand the articles, and all the ten commandments of God, and they freely assenting to all, they were solemnly received; and the Court gave each of them a coat of two yards of cloth, and their dinner; and to them and their men, every one of them, a cup of sack at their departure. So they took leave, and went away."—*Massachusetts Colonial Records.*

Dr. Gaston sat in his library, studying a chess problem. His clerical coat was old and spotted, his table was of rough wood, the floor uncarpeted; by right, Poverty should have made herself prominent there. But she did not. Perhaps she liked the old chaplain, who showed a fine, amply built person under her reign, with florid complexion, bright blue eyes, and a curly brown wig—very different in aspect from her usual lean and dismal retinue; perhaps, also, she stopped here herself to warm her cold heart now and then in the hot, bright, crowded little room, which was hers by right, although she did not claim it, enjoying it, however, as a miserly money-lender enjoys the fine house over which he holds a mortgage, rubbing his hands exultingly, as, clad in his thin old coat, he walks by. Certainly the plastering had dropped from the walls here and there; there was no furniture save the tables and shelves made by the island carpenter, and one old leathern arm-chair, the parson's own, a miracle of comfort, age, and hanging leather tatters. But on the shelves and on the tables, on the floor and on the broad window-sills, were books; they reached the ceiling on the shelves; they wainscoted the walls to the height of several feet all round the room; small volumes were piled on the narrow mantel as far up as they could go without toppling over, and the tables were loaded also. Aisles were kept open leading to the door, to the windows, and to the hearth, where the ragged arm-chair stood, and where there was a small parade-ground of open floor; but everywhere else the printed thoughts held sway. The old fire-place was large and deep, and here burned night and day, throughout the winter, a fire which made the whole room bright; add to this the sunshine streaming through the broad, low, uncurtained windows, and you have the secret of the cheerfulness in the very face of a barren lack of everything we are accustomed to call comfort.

The Reverend James Gaston was an Englishman by birth. On coming to America he had accepted a chaplaincy in the army, with the intention of resigning it as soon as he had become sufficiently familiar with the ways of the Church in this country to feel at ease in a parish. But years had passed, and he was a chaplain still; for evidently the country parishes were not regulated according to his home ideas, the rector's authority—yes, even the tenure of his rectorship—being dependent upon the chance wills and fancies of his people. Here was no dignity, no time for pleasant classical studies, and no approval of them; on the contrary, a continuous going out to tea, and a fear of offending, it might be, a warden's wife, who very likely had been brought up a Dissenter. The Reverend James Gaston therefore preferred the government for a master.

Dr. Gaston held the office of post chaplain, having been, on application, selected by the council of administration. He had no military rank, but as there happened to be quarters to spare, a cottage was assigned to him, and as he had had the good fortune to be liked and respected by all the officers who had succeeded each other on the little island, his position, unlike that of some of his brethren, was endurable, and even comfortable. He had been a widower for many years; he had never cared to marry again, but had long ago recovered his cheerfulness, and had brought up, intellectually at least, two children whom he loved as if they had been his own—the boy Erastus Pronando, and Anne Douglas. The children returned his affection heartily, and made a great happiness in his lonely life. The girl was his good scholar, the boy his bad one; yet the teacher was severe with Anne, and indulgent to the boy. If any one had asked the reason, perhaps he would have said that girls were docile by nature, whereas boys, having more temptations, required more lenity; or perhaps that girls who, owing to the constitution of society, never advanced far in their studies, should have all the incitement of severity while those studies lasted, whereas boys, who are to go abroad in the world and learn from life, need no such severity. But the real truth lay deeper than this, and the chaplain himself was partly conscious of it; he felt that the foundations must be laid accurately and deeply in a nature like that possessed by this young girl.

"Good-morning, uncle," said Anne, entering and putting down her Latin books (as children they had adopted the fashion of calling their teacher "uncle"). "Was your coffee good this morning?"

"Ah, well, so-so, child, so-so," replied the chaplain, hardly aroused yet from his problem.

"Then I must go out and speak to—to—what is this one's name, uncle?"

"Her name is—here, I have it written down—Mrs. Evelina Crangall," said the chaplain, reading aloud from his note-book, in a slow, sober voice. Evidently it was a matter of moment to him to keep that name well in his mind.

Public opinion required that Dr. Gaston should employ a Protestant servant; no one else was obliged to conform, but the congregation felt that a stand must be made somewhere, and they made it, like a chalk line, at the parson's threshold. Now it was very well known that there were no Protestants belonging to the class of servants on the island who could cook at all, that talent being confined to the French quarter-breeds and to occasional Irish soldiers' wives, none of them Protestants. The poor parson's cooking was passed from one incompetent hand to another—lake-sailors' wives, wandering emigrants, moneyless forlorn females left by steamers, belonging to that strange floating population that goes forever travelling up and down the land, without apparent motive save a vague El-Dorado hope whose very conception would be impossible in any other country save this. Mrs. Evelina Crangall was a hollow-chested woman with faded blue eyes, one prominent front tooth, scanty light hair, and for a form a lattice-work of bones. She preserved, however, a somewhat warlike aspect in her limp calico, and maintained that she thoroughly understood the making of coffee, but that she was accustomed to the use of a French coffee-pot. Anne, answering serenely that no French coffee-pot could be obtained in that kitchen, went to work and explained the whole process from the beginning, the woman meanwhile surveying her with suspicion, which gradually gave way before the firm but pleasant manner. With a long list of kindred Evelinas, Anne had had dealings before. Sometimes her teachings effected a change for the better, sometimes they did not, but in any case the Evelinas seldom remained long. They were wanderers by nature, and had sudden desires to visit San Francisco, or to "go down the river to Newerleens." This morning, while making her explanation, Anne made coffee too. It was a delicious cupful which she carried back with her into the library, and the chaplain, far away in the chess country, came down to earth immediately in order to drink it. Then they opened the Latin books, and Anne translated her page of Livy, her page of Cicero, and recited her rules correctly. She liked Latin; its exactness suited her. Mrs. Bryden was wrong when she said that the girl studied Greek. Dr. Gaston had longed to teach her that golden tongue, but here William Douglas had interfered. "Teach her Latin if you like, but not Greek," he said. "It would injure the child—make what is called a blue-stocking of her, I suppose—and it is my duty to stand between her and injury."

"Ah! ah! you want to make a belle of her, do you?" said the cheery chaplain.

"I said it was my duty; I did not say it was my wish," replied the moody father. "If I could have my wish, Anne should never know what a lover is all her life long."

"What! you do not wish to have her marry, then? There are happy marriages. Come, Douglas, don't be morbid."

"I know what men are. And you and I are no better."

"But she may love."

"Ah! there it is; she may. And that is what I meant when I said that it was my duty to keep her from making herself positively unattractive."

"Greek need not do that," said Dr. Gaston, shortly.

"It need not, but it does. Let me ask you one question: did you ever fall in love, or come anywhere near falling in love, with a girl who understood Greek?"

"That is because only the homely ones take to it," replied the chaplain, fencing a little.

But Anne was not taught Greek. After Cicero she took up algebra, then astronomy. After that she read aloud from a ponderous Shakspeare, and the old man corrected her accentuation, and questioned her on the meanings. A number of the grand old plays the girl knew almost entirely by heart; they had been her reading-books from childhood. The down-pouring light of the vivid morning sunshine and the up-coming white glare of the ice below met and shone full upon her face and figure as she bent over the old volume laid open on the table before her, one hand supporting her brow, the other resting on the yellow page. Her hands were firm, white, and beautifully shaped—strong hands, generous hands, faithful hands; not the little, idle, characterless, faithless palms so common in America, small, dainty, delicate, and shapeless, coming from a composite origin. Her thick hair, brown as a mellowed chestnut, with a gleam of dark red where the light touched it, like the red of November oak leaves, was, as usual, in her way, the heavy braids breaking from the coil at the back of her head, one by one, as she read on through *Hamlet*. At last impatiently she drew out the comb, and they all fell down over her shoulders, and left her in momentary peace.

The lesson was nearly over when Rast Pronando appeared; he was to enter college—a Western college on one of the lower lakes—early in the spring, and that prospect made the chaplain's lessons seem dull to him. "Very likely they will not teach at all as he does; I shall do much better if I go over the text-books by myself," he said, confidentially, to Anne. "I do not want to appear old-fashioned, you know."

"Is it unpleasant to be old-fashioned? I should think the old fashions would be sure to be the good ones," said the girl. "But I do not want you to go so far beyond me, Rast; we have always been even until now. Will you think *me* old-fashioned too when you come back?"

"Oh no; you will always be Anne. I can predict you exactly at twenty, and even thirty: there is no doubt about *you*."

"But shall I be old-fashioned?"

"Well, perhaps; but we don't mind it in women. All the goddesses were old-fashioned, especially Diana. *You* are Diana."

"Diana, a huntress. She loved Endymion, who was always asleep," said Anne, quoting from her school-girl mythology.

This morning Rast had dropped in to read a little Greek with his old master, and to walk home with Anne. The girl hurried through her *Hamlet*, and then yielded the place to him. It was a three-legged stool, the only companion the arm-chair had, and it was the seat for the reciting scholar; the one who was studying sat in a niche on the window-seat at a little distance. Anne, retreating to this niche, began to rebraid her hair.

"But she, within—within—singing with enchanting tone, enchanting voice, wove with a—with a golden shuttle the sparkling web," read Rast, looking up and dreamily watching the brown strands taking their place in the long braid. Anne saw his look, and hurried her weaving. The girl had thought all her life that her hair was ugly because it was so heavy, and neither black nor gold in hue; and Rast, following her opinion, had thought so too: she had told him it was, many a time. It was characteristic of her nature that while as a child she had admired her companion's spirited, handsome face and curling golden locks, she had never feared lest he might not return her affection because she happened to be ugly; she drew no comparisons. But she had often discussed the subject of beauty with him. "I should like to be beautiful," she said; "like that girl at the fort last summer."

"Pooh! it doesn't make much difference," answered Rast, magnanimously. "I shall always like you."

"That is because you are so generous, dear."

"Perhaps it is," answered the boy.

This was two years before, when they were fourteen and fifteen years old; at sixteen and seventeen they had advanced but little in their ideas of life and of each other. Still, there was a slight change, for Anne now hurried the braiding; it hurt her a little that Rast should gaze so steadily at the rough, ugly hair.

When the Greek was finished they said good-by to the chaplain, and left the cottage together. As they crossed the inner parade-ground, taking the snow path which led toward the entrance grating, and which was kept shovelled out by the soldiers, the snow walls on each side rising to their chins, Rast suddenly exclaimed: "Oh, Annet, I have thought of something! I am going to take you down the fort hill on a sled. Now you need not object, because I shall do it in any case, although we *are* grown up, and I *am* going to college. Probably it will be the last time. I shall borrow Bert Bryden's sled. Come along."

All the boy in him was awake; he seized Anne's wrist, and dragged her through first one cross-path, then another, until at last they reached the commandant's door. From the windows their heads had been visible, turning and crossing above the heaped-up snow. "Rast, and Anne Douglas," said Mrs. Bryden, recognizing the girl's fur cap and the youth's golden hair. She tapped on the window, and signed to them to enter without ceremony. "What is it, Rast? Good-morning, Anne; what a color you have, child!"

"Rast has been making me run," said Anne, smiling, and coming toward the hearth, where the fort ladies were sitting together sewing, and rather lugubriously recalling Christmas times in their old Eastern homes.

"Throw off your cloak," said Mrs. Cromer, "else you will take cold when you go out again."

"We shall only stay a moment," answered Anne.

The cloak was of strong dark blue woollen cloth, closely fitted to the figure, with a small cape; it reached from her throat to her ankles, and was met and completed by fur boots, fur gloves, and a little fur cap. The rough plain costume was becoming to the vigorous girl. "It tones her down," thought the lieutenant's wife; "she really looks quite well."

In the mean while Rast had gone across to the dining-room to find Bert Bryden, the commandant's son, and borrow his sled.

"And you're really going to take Miss Douglas down the hill!" said the boy. "Hurrah! I'll look out of the side window and see. What fun! Such a big girl to go sliding!"

Anne was a big girl to go; but Rast was not to be withstood. She would not get on the sled at the door, as he wished, but followed him out through the sally-port, and round to the top of the long steep fort hill, whose snowy slippery road-track was hardly used at all during the winter, save by coasters, and those few in number, for the village boys, French and half-breeds, did not view the snow as an amusement, or toiling up hill as a recreation. The two little boys at the fort, and what Scotch and New England blood there was in the town, held a monopoly of the coasting.

"There they go!" cried Bert, from his perch on the deep window-seat overlooking the frozen Straits and the village below. "Mamma, you must let me take you down now; you are not so big as Miss Douglas."

Mrs. Bryden, a slender little woman, laughed. "Fancy the colonel's horror," she said, "if he should see me sliding down that hill! And yet it looks as if it might be rather stirring," she added, watching the flying sled and its load. The sled, of island manufacture, was large and sledge-like; it carried two comfortably. Anne held on by Rast's shoulders, sitting behind him, while he guided the flying craft. Down they glided, darted, faster and faster, losing all sense of everything after a while save speed. Reaching the village street at last, they flew across it, and out on the icy pier beyond, where Rast by a skillful manœuvre stopped the sled on the very verge. The fort ladies were all at the windows now, watching.

"How dangerous!" said Mrs. Bryden, forgetting her admiration of a moment before with a mother's irrelevant rapidity. "Albert, let me never see or hear of your sliding on that pier; another inch, and they would have gone over, down on the broken ice below!"

"I couldn't do it, mamma, even if I tried," replied Master Albert, regretfully; "I always tumble off the sled at the street, or else run into one of the warehouses. Only Rast Pronando can steer across slanting, and out on that pier."

"I am very glad to hear it," replied Mrs. Bryden; "but your father must also give you his positive commands on the subject. I had no idea that the pier was ever attempted."

"And it is not, mamma, except by Rast," said the boy. "Can't I try it when I am as old as he is?"

"Hear the child!" said Mrs. Cromer, going back to her seat by the fire; "one would suppose he expected to stay here all his life. Do you not know, Bert, that we are only here for a little while—a year or two? Before you are eighteen months older very likely you will find yourself out on the plains. What a life it is!"

The fort ladies all sighed. It was a habit they had. They drew the dreariest pictures of their surroundings and privations in their letters homeward, and really believed them, theoretically. In truth, there were some privations; but would any one of them have exchanged army life for civilian? To the last, thorough army ladies retain their ways; you recognize them even when retired to private and perhaps more prosperous life. Cosmopolitans, they do not sink into the ruts of small-town life; they are never provincial. They take the world easily, having a pleasant, generous taste for its pleasures, and making light of the burdens that fall to their share. All little local rules and ways are nothing to them: neither here nor anywhere are they to remain long. With this habit and manner they keep up a vast amount of general cheeriness—vast indeed, when one considers how small the incomes sometimes are. But if small, they are also sure.

"Rast Pronando is too old for such frolics, I think," said Mrs. Rankin, the lieutenant's wife, beginning another seam in the new dress for her baby.

"He goes to college in the spring; that will quiet him," said Mrs. Bryden.

"What will he do afterward? Is he to live here? At this end of the world—this jumping-off place?"

"I suppose so; he has always lived here. But he belongs, you know, to the old Philadelphia family of the same name, the Peter Pronandos."

"Does he? How strange! How did he come here?"

"He was born here: Dr. Gaston told me his history. It seems that the boy's father was a wild younger son of the second Peter, grandson, of course, of the original Peter, from whom the family derive all their greatness—*and* money. This Peter the third, only his name was not Peter, but John (the eldest sons were the Peters), wandered away from home, and came up here, where his father's name was well known among the directors of the Fur Company. John Pronando, who must have been of very different fibre from the rest of the family, liked the wild life of the border, and even went off on one or two long expeditions to the Red River of the North and the Upper Missouri after furs with the hunters of the Company. His father then offered him a position here which would carry with it authority, but he curtly refused, saying that he had no taste for a desk and pen like Peter. Peter was his brother, who had begun dutifully at an early age his life-long task of taking care of the large accumulation of land which makes the family so rich. Peter was the good boy always. Father Peter was naturally angry with John, and inclined even then to cross his name off the family list of heirs; this, however, was not really done until the prodigal crowned his long course of misdeeds by marrying the pretty daughter of a Scotchman, who held one of the smaller clerkships in the Company's warehouses here—only a grade above the hunters themselves. This was the end. Almost anything else might have been forgiven save a marriage of that kind. If John Pronando had selected the daughter of a flat-boat man on the Ohio River, or of a Pennsylvania mountain wagoner, they might have accepted her—at a distance—and made the best of her. But a person from the rank and file of their own Fur Company—it was as though a colonel should marry the daughter of a common soldier in his own regiment: yes, worse, for nothing can equal the Pronando pride. From that day John Pronando was simply forgotten—so they said. His mother was dead, so it may have been true. A small sum was settled upon him, and a will was carefully drawn up forever excluding him and the heirs he might have from any share in the estate. John did not appear to mind this, but lived on merrily enough for some years afterward, until his sweet little wife died; then he seemed to lose his strength suddenly, and soon followed her, leaving this one boy, Erastus, named after the maternal grandfather, with his usual careless disregard of what would be for his advantage. The boy has been brought up by our good chaplain, although he lives with a family down in the village; the doctor has husbanded what money there was carefully, and there is enough to send him through college, and to start him in life in some way. A good education he considered the best investment of all."

"In a fresh-water college?" said Mrs. Cromer, raising her eyebrows.

"Why not, for a fresh-water boy? He will always live in the West."

"He is so handsome," said Mrs. Rankin, "that he might go Eastward, captivate his relatives, and win his way back into the family again."

"He does not know anything about his family," said the colonel's wife.

"Then some one ought to tell him."

"Why? Simply for the money? No: let him lead his own life out here, and make his own way," said Mrs. Bryden, warmly.

"What a radical you are, Jane!"

"No, not a radical; but I have seen two or three of the younger Pronandos, of the fourth generation, I mean, and whenever I think of their dead eyes, and lifeless, weary manner, I feel like doing what I can to keep Rast away from them."

"But the boy must live his life, Jane. These very Pronandos whom you describe will probably be sober and staid at fifty: the Pronandos always are. And Rast, after all, is one of them."

"But not like them. *He* would go to ruin, he has so much more imagination than they have."

"And less stability?"

"Well, no; less epicureanism, perhaps. It is the solid good things of life that bring the Pronandos back, after they have indulged in youthful wildness: they have no taste for husks."

Then the colonel came in, and, soon after, the sewing circle broke up, Mrs. Cromer and Mrs. Rankin returning to their quarters in the other cottages through the walled snow-paths. The little fort was perched on the brow of the cliff, overlooking the village and harbor; the windows of the stone cottages which formed the officers' quarters commanded an uninterrupted view of blue water in summer, and white ice fields in winter, as far as the eye could reach. It could hardly have withstood a bombardment; its walls and block-houses, erected as a defense against the Indians, required constant propping and new foundation-work to keep them within the requirements of safety, not to speak of military dignity. But the soldiers had nothing else to do, and, on the whole, the fort looked well, especially from the water, crowning the green height with buttressed majesty. During eight months of the year the officers played chess and checkers, and the men played fox-and-geese. The remaining four months, which comprised all there was of spring, summer, and autumn, were filled full of out-door work and enjoyment; summer visitors came, and the United States uniform took its conquering place, as usual, among the dancers, at the picnics, and on the fast-sailing fishing-boats which did duty as yachts, skimming over the clear water in whose depths fish could be seen swimming forty feet below. These same fish were caught and eaten—the large lake trout, and the delicate white-fish, aristocrat of the freshwater seas; three-quarters of the population were fishermen, and the whole town drew its food from the deep. The business had broadened, too, as the Prairie States became more thickly settled, namely, the salting and packing for sale of these fresh-water fish. Barrels stood on the piers, and brisk agents, with pencils behind their ears, stirred the slow-moving villagers into activity, as the man with a pole stirs up the bears. Fur-bearing animals had had their day; it was now the turn of the creatures of the deep.

"Let us stop at the church-house a moment and see Miss Lois," said Rast, as, dragging the empty sled behind him, he walked by Anne's side through the village street toward the Agency.

"I am afraid I have not time, Rast."

"Make it, then. Come, Annet, don't be ill-natured. And, besides, you ought to see that I go there, for I have not called upon Miss Lois this year."

"As this year only began last week, you are not so very far behind," said the girl, smiling. "Why can you not go and see Miss Lois alone?"

"I should be welcome, at any rate; *she* adores me."

"Does she, indeed!"

"Yes, Miss Douglas, she does. She pretends otherwise, but that is always the way with women. Oh! I know the world."

"You are only one year older than I am."

"In actual time, perhaps; but twenty years older in knowledge."

"What will you be, then, when you come back from college? An old man?"

"By no means; for *I* shall stay where I am. But in the mean time you will catch up with me."

Handsome Rast had passed through his novitiate, so he thought. His knowledge of the world was derived partly from Lieutenant Walters, who, although fresh from West Point, was still several years older than young Pronando, and patronized him accordingly, and partly from a slender, low-voiced Miss Carew, who was thirty, but appeared twenty, after the manner of slender yellow-white blondes who have never possessed any rose-tints, having always been willowy and amber-colored. Miss Carew sailed, for a summer's amusement through the Great Lakes of the West; and then returned Eastward with the opinion that they were but so many raw, blank, inland oceans, without sensations or local coloring enough to rouse her. The week on the island, which was an epoch in Rast's life, had held for her but languid interest; yet even the languid work of a master-hand has finish and power, and Rast was melancholy and silent for fifteen days after the enchantress had departed. Then he wrote to her one or two wild letters, and received no answer; then he grew bitter. Then Walters came, with his cadet's deep experience in life, and the youth learned from him, and re-appeared on the surface again with a tinge of cynicism which filled Anne with wonder. For he had never told her the story of the summer; it was almost the only event in his life which she had not shared. But it was not that he feared to tell her, they were as frank with each other as two children; it was because he thought she would not understand it.

"I do not like Mr. Walters," she said, one day.

"He was very much liked at the Point, I assure you," said Rast, with significant emphasis. "By the ladies, I mean, who come there in the summer."

"How could they like him, with that important, egotistical air?"

"But it is to conquer him they like," said Tita, looking up from her corner.

"Hear the child!" said Rast, laughing. "Are *you* going to conquer, Tita?"

"Yes," said Tita, stroking the cat which shared the corner with her—a soft coated yellow pussy that was generally sleepy and quiet, but which had, nevertheless, at times, extraordinary fits of galloping round in a circle, and tearing the bark from the trees as though she was possessed—an eccentricity of character which the boys attributed to the direct influence of Satan.

Miss Lois lived in the church-house. It was an ugly house; but then, as is often said of a plain woman, "so good!" It did not leak or rattle, or fall down or smoke, or lean or sag, as did most of the other houses in the village, in regard to their shingles, their shutters, their chimneys, their side walls, and their roof-trees. It stood straightly and squarely on its stone foundation, and every board, nail and latch was in its proper position. Years before, missionaries had been sent from New England to work among the Indians of this neighborhood, who had obtained their ideas of Christianity, up to that time, solely from the Roman Catholic priests, who had succeeded each other in an unbroken line from that adventurous Jesuit, the first explorer of these inland seas, Father Marquette. The Presbyterians came, established their mission, built a meeting-house, a school-house, and a house for their pastor, the buildings being as solid as their belief. Money was collected for this enterprise from all over New England, that old-time, devout, self-sacrificing community whose sternness and faith were equal; tall spare men came westward to teach the Indians, earnest women with bright steadfast eyes and lath-like forms were their aiders, wives, and companions. Among these came Miss Lois—then young Lois Hinsdale—carried Westward by an aunt whose missionary zeal was burning splendidly up an empty chimney which might have been filled with family loves and cares, but was not: shall we say better filled? The missionaries worked faithfully; but, as the Indians soon moved further westward, the results of their efforts can not be statistically estimated now, or the accounts balanced.

"The only good Indian is a dead Indian," is a remark that crystallizes the floating opinion of the border. But a border population has not a missionary spirit. New England, having long ago chased out, shot down, and exterminated all her own Indians, had become peaceful and pious, and did not agree with these Western carriers of shot-guns. Still, when there were no more Indians to come to this island school, it was of necessity closed, no matter which side was right. There were still numbers of Chippewas living on the other islands and on the mainland; but they belonged to the Roman Catholic faith, and were under the control of Père Michaux.

23

The Protestant church—a square New England meeting-house, with steeple and bell—was kept open during another year; but the congregation grew so small that at last knowledge of the true state of affairs reached the New England purses, and it was decided that the minister in charge should close this mission, and go southward to a more promising field among the prairie settlers of Illinois. All the teachers connected with the Indian school had departed before this—all save Miss Lois and her aunt; for Priscilla Hinsdale, stricken down by her own intense energy, which had consumed her as an inward fire, was now confined to her bed, partially paralyzed. The New England woman had sold her farm, and put almost all her little store of money into island property. "I shall live and die here," she had said; "I have found my life-work." But her work went away from her; her class of promising squaws departed with their pappooses and their braves, and left her scholarless.

"With all the blessed religious privileges they have here, besides other advantages, I can not at all understand it—I can not understand it," she repeated many times, especially to Sandy Forbes, an old Scotchman and fervent singer of psalms.

"Aweel, aweel, Miss Priscilla, I donnot suppose ye can," replied Sandy, with a momentary twinkle in his old eyes.

While still hesitating over her future course, illness struck down the old maid, and her life-work was at last decided for her: it was merely to lie in bed, motionless, winter and summer, with folded hands and whatever resignation she was able to muster. Niece Lois, hitherto a satellite, now assumed the leadership. This would seem a simple enough charge, the household of two women, poor in purse, in a remote village on a Northern frontier. But exotics of any kind require nursing and vigilance, and the Hinsdale household was an exotic. Miss Priscilla required that every collar should be starched in the New England fashion, that every curtain should fall in New England folds, that every dish on the table should be of New England origin, and that every clock should tick with New England accuracy. Lois had known no other training; and remembering as she did also the ways of the old home among the New Hampshire hills with a child's fidelity and affection, she went even beyond her aunt in faithfulness to her ideal; and although the elder woman had long been dead, the niece never varied the habits or altered the rules of the house which was now hers alone.

"A little New England homestead strangely set up here on this far Western island," William Douglas had said.

The church house, as the villagers named it, was built by the Presbyterian missionaries, many of them laboring with their own hands at the good work, seeing, no doubt, files of Indian converts rising up in another world to call them blessed. When it came into the hands of Miss Priscilla, it came, therefore, ready-made as to New England ideas of rooms and closets, and only required a new application of white and green paint to become for her an appropriate and rectangular bower. It stood near the closed meeting-house, whose steeple threw a slow-moving shadow across its garden, like a great sun-dial, all day. Miss Lois had charge of the key of the meeting-house, and often she unlocked its door, went in, and walked up and down the aisle, as if to revive the memories of the past. She remembered the faith and sure hope that used to fill the empty spaces, and shook her head and sighed. Then she upbraided herself for sighing, and sang in her thin husky voice softly a verse or two of one of their old psalms by way of reparation. She sent an annual report of the condition of the building to the Presbyterian Board of Missions, but in it said nothing of the small repairs for which her own purse paid. Was it a silent way of making amends to the old walls for having deserted their tenets?

"Cod-fish balls for breakfast on Sunday morning, of course," said Miss Lois, "and fried hasty-pudding. On Wednesdays a boiled dinner. Pies on Tuesdays and Saturdays."

The pins stood in straight rows on her pincushion; three times each week every room in the house was swept, and the floors as well as the furniture dusted. Beans were baked in an earthen pot on Saturday night, and sweet-cake was made on Thursday. Rast Pronando often dropped in to tea on Thursday. Winter or summer, through scarcity or plenty, Miss Lois never varied her established routine, thereby setting an example, she said, to the idle and shiftless. And certainly she was a faithful guide-post, continually pointing out an industrious and systematic way, which, however, to the end of time, no French-blooded, French-hearted person will ever travel, unless dragged by force. The villagers preferred their lake trout to Miss Lois's salt cod-fish, their savory stews and soups to her corned beef, their tartines to her corn-meal puddings, and their eau-de-vie to her green tea; they loved their disorder and their comfort; her bar soap and scrubbing-brush were a horror to their eyes. They washed the household clothes two or three times a year: was not that enough? Of what use the endless labor of this sharp-nosed woman with glasses over her eyes at the church-house? Were not, perhaps, the glasses the consequences of such toil? And her figure of a long leanness also?

The element of real heroism, however, came into Miss Lois's life in her persistent effort to employ Indian servants. The old mission had been established for their conversion and education; any descendant of that mission, therefore, should continue to the utmost of her ability the beneficent work. The meeting-house was closed, the school-house abandoned, she could reach the native race by no other influence save personal; that personal influence, then, she would use. Through long years had she persisted, through long years would she

24

continue to persist. A succession of Chippewa squaws broke, stole, and skirmished their way through her kitchen with various degrees of success, generally in the end departing suddenly at night with whatever booty they could lay their hands on. It is but justice to add, however, that this was not much, a rigid system of keys and excellent locks prevailing in the well-watched household. Miss Lois's conscience would not allow her to employ half-breeds, who were sometimes endurable servants; duty required, she said, that she should have full-blooded natives. And she had them. She always began to teach them the alphabet within three days after their arrival, and the spectacle of a tearful, freshly caught Indian girl, very wretched in her calico dress and white apron, worn out with the ways of the kettles and brasses, dejected over the fish-balls, and appalled by the pudding, standing confronted by a large alphabet on the well-scoured table, and Miss Lois by her side with a pointer, was frequent and even regular in its occurrence, the only change being in the personality of the learners. No one of them had ever gone through the letters; but Miss Lois was not discouraged. Patiently she began over again—she was always beginning over again. And in the mean time she was often obliged not only to do almost all the household work with her own hands, but to do it twice over in order to instruct the new-comer. By the unwritten law of public opinion, Dr. Gaston was obliged to employ only Protestant servants; by the unwritten law of her own conscience, Miss Lois was obliged to employ only Indians. But in truth she did not employ them so much as they employed her.

Miss Lois received her young friends in the sitting-room. There was a parlor with Brussels carpet and hair-cloth sofa across the hall, but its blinds were closed, and its shades drawn down. The parlor of middle-class households in the cold climate of the Northern States generally is a consecrated apartment, with the chill atmosphere and much of the solemnity of a tomb. It may be called the high altar of the careful housewife; but even here her sense of cleanliness and dustless perfection is such that she keeps it cold. No sacred fire burns, no cheerful ministry is allowed; everything is silent and veiled. The apartment is of no earthly use—nor heavenly, save perhaps for ghosts. But take it away, and the housewife is miserable; leave it, and she lives on contentedly in her sitting-room all the year round, knowing it is *there*.

Miss Lois's sitting-room was cheery; it had a rag-carpet, a bright fire, and double-glass panes instead of the heavy woollen curtains which the villagers hung over their windows in the winter—curtains that kept out the cold, but also the light. Miss Lois's curtains were of white dimity with knotted fringe, and her walls were freshly whitewashed. Her framed sampler, and a memorial picture done with pen and ink, representing two weeping-willows overshadowing a tombstone, ornamented the high mantel-piece, and there were also two gayly colored china jars filled with dried rose-leaves. They were only wild-brier roses; the real roses, as she called them, grew but reluctantly in this Northern air. Miss Lois never loved the wild ones as she had loved the old-fashioned cinnamon-scented pink and damask roses of her youth, but she gathered and dried these leaves of the brier from habit. There was also hanging on the wall a looking-glass tilted forward at such an angle that the looker-in could see only his feet, with a steep ascent of carpet going up hill behind him. This looking-glass possessed a brightly hued picture at the top, divided into two compartments, on one side a lovely lady with a large bonnet modestly concealing her face, very bare shoulders, leg-of-mutton sleeves, and a bag hanging on her arm; on the other old Father Time, scythe in hand, as if he was intended as a warning to the lovely lady that minutes were rapid and his stroke sure.

"Why do you keep your glass tilted forward so far that we can not look in it, Miss Lois?" Rast had once asked.

Miss Lois did it from habit. But she answered: "To keep silly girls from looking at themselves while they are pretending to talk to me. They say something, and then raise their eyes quickly to see how they looked when they said it. I have known them keep a smile or a particular expression half a minute while they studied the effect—ridiculous calves!"

"Calves have lovely eyes sometimes," said Rast.

"Did I say the girls were ugly, Master Pert? But the homely girls look too."

"Perhaps to see how they can improve themselves."

"Perhaps," said the old maid, dryly. "Pity they never learn!"

In the sitting-room was a high chest of drawers, an old clock, a chintz-covered settle, and two deep narrow old rocking-chairs, intended evidently for scant skirts; on an especial table was the family Bible, containing the record of the Hinsdale family from the date of the arrival of the *Mayflower*. Miss Lois's prayer-book was not there; it was up stairs in a bureau drawer. It did not seem to belong to the old-time furniture of the rooms below, nor to the Hinsdale Bible.

The story of Miss Lois's change from the Puritan to the Episcopal ritual might to-day fill a volume if written by one of those brooding, self-searching woman-minds of New England—those unconscious, earnest egotists who bring forth poetry beautiful sometimes to inspiration, but always purely subjective. And if in such a volume the feelings, the arguments, and the change were all represented as sincere, conscientious, and prayerful, they would be represented with entire truth. Nevertheless, so complex are the influences which move our lives, and so deep the under-powers which we ourselves may not always recognize, that it could be safely added by a man of the world as a comment that Lois Hinsdale would never have felt these changes, these doubts, these conflicts, if William Douglas had not been of another creed. For in those days Douglas had a creed—the creed of his young bride.

"Miss Hinsdale, we have come to offer you our New-Year's good wishes," said Rast, taking off his cap and making a ceremonious bow. "Our equipage will wait outside. How charming is your apartment, madam! And yourself—how Minerva-like the gleam of the eye, the motion of the hand, which—"

"Which made the pies now cooling in the pantry, Rast Pronando, to whose fragrance, I presume, I owe the honor of this visit."

"Not for myself, dear madam, but for Anne. She has already confided to me that she feels a certain sinking sensation that absolutely requires the strengthening influence of pie."

Anne laughed. "Are you going to stay long?" she asked, still standing at the doorway.

"Certainly," replied Rast, seating himself in one of the narrow rocking-chairs; "I have a number of subjects to discuss with our dear Miss Lois."

"Then I will leave you here, for Tita is waiting for me. I have promised to take them all over to Père Michaux's house this afternoon."

Miss Lois groaned—two short abrupt groans on different keys.

"Have you? Then I'm going too," said Rast, rising.

"Oh no, Rast; please do not," said the girl, earnestly. "When you go, it is quite a different thing—a frolic always."

"And why not?" said Rast.

"Because the children go for religious instruction, as you well know; it is their faith, and I feel that I ought to give them such opportunities as I can to learn what it means."

"It means mummery!" said Miss Lois, loudly and sternly.

Anne glanced toward her old friend, but stood her ground firmly. "I must take them," she said; "I promised I would do so as long as they were children, and under my care. When they are older they can choose for themselves."

"To whom did you make that promise, Anne Douglas?"

"To Père Michaux."

"And you call yourself a Protestant!"

"Yes; but I hope to keep a promise too, dear Miss Lois."

"Why was it ever made?"

"Père Michaux required it, and—father allowed it."

Miss Lois rubbed her forehead, settled her spectacles with her first and third fingers, shook her head briskly once or twice to see if they were firmly in place, and then went on with her knitting. What William Douglas allowed, how could she disallow?

Rast, standing by Anne's side putting on his fur gloves, showed no disposition to yield.

"Please do not come, Rast," said the girl again, laying her hand on his arm.

"I shall go to take care of you."

"It is not necessary; we have old Antoine and his dogs, and the boys are to have a sled of their own. We shall be at home before dark, I think, and if not, the moon to-night is full."

"But I shall go," said Rast.

"Nonsense!" said Miss Lois. "Of course you will not go; Anne is right. You romp and make mischief with those children always. Behave now, and you shall come back this evening, and Anne shall come too, and we will have apples and nuts and gingerbread, and Anne shall recite."

"Will you, Annet? I will yield if you promise."

"If I must, I must," said Anne, reluctantly.

"Go, then, proud maid; speed upon your errand. And in the mean time, Miss Lois, something fragrant and spicy in the way of a reward *now* would not come amiss, and then some music."

Among the possessions which Miss Lois had inherited from her aunt was a small piano. The elder Miss Hinsdale, sent into the world with an almost Italian love of music, found herself unable to repress it even in cold New England; turning it, therefore, into the channel of the few stunted psalms and hymns and spiritual songs of

26

the day, she indulged it in a cramped fashion, like a full-flowing stream shut off and made to turn a mill. When the missionary spirit seized her in its fiery whirlwind, she bargained with it mentally that her piano should be included; she represented to the doubting elder that it would be an instrument of great power among the savages, and that even David himself accompanied the psalms with a well-stringed harp. The elder still doubted; he liked a tuning-fork; and besides, the money which Miss Priscilla would pay for the transportation of "the instrument" was greatly needed for boots for the young men. But as Miss Priscilla was a free agent, and quite determined, he finally decided, like many another leader, to allow what he could not prevent, and the piano came. It was a small, old-fashioned instrument, which had been kept in tune by Dr. Douglas, and through long years the inner life of Miss Lois, her hopes, aspirations, and disappointments, had found expression through its keys. It was a curious sight to see the old maid sitting at her piano alone on a stormy evening, the doors all closed, the shutters locked, no one stirring in the church-house save herself. Her playing was old-fashioned, her hands stiff; she could not improvise, and the range of the music she knew was small and narrow, yet unconsciously it served to her all the purposes of emotional expression. When she was sad, she played "China"; when she was hopeful, "Coronation." She made the bass heavy in dejection, and played the air in octaves when cheerful. She played only when she was entirely alone. The old piano was the only confidant of the hidden remains of youthful feeling buried in her heart.

Rast played on the piano and the violin in an untrained fashion of his own, and Anne sang; they often had small concerts in Miss Lois's parlor. But a greater entertainment lay in Anne's recitations. These were all from Shakspeare. Not in vain had the chaplain kept her tied to its pages year after year; she had learned, almost unconsciously, as it were, large portions of the immortal text by heart, and had formed her own ideals of the characters, who were to her real persons, although as different from flesh-and-blood people as are the phantoms of a dream. They were like spirits who came at her call, and lent her their personality; she could identify herself with them for the time being so completely, throw herself into the bodies and minds she had constructed for them so entirely, that the effect was startling, and all the more so because her conceptions of the characters were girlish and utterly different from those that have ruled the dramatic stage for generations. Her ideas of Juliet, of Ophelia, of Rosalind, and Cleopatra were her own, and she never varied them; the very earnestness of her personations made the effect all the more extraordinary. Dr. Gaston had never heard these recitations of his pupil; William Douglas had never heard them; either of these men could have corrected her errors and explained to her her mistakes. She herself thought them too trifling for their notice; it was only a way she had of amusing herself. Even Rast, her playmate, found it out by chance, coming upon her among the cedars one day when she was Ophelia, and overhearing her speak several lines before she saw him; he immediately constituted himself an audience of one, with, however, the peremptory manners of a throng, and demanded to hear all she knew. Poor Anne! the great plays of the world had been her fairy tales; she knew no others. She went through her personations timidly, the wild forest her background, the open air and blue Straits her scenery. The audience found fault, but, on the whole, enjoyed the performance, and demanded frequent repetitions. After a while Miss Lois was admitted into the secret, and disapproved, and was curious, and listened, and shook her head, but ended by liking the portraitures, which were in truth as fantastic as phantasmagoria. Miss Lois had never seen a play or read a novel in her life. For some time the forest continued Anne's theatre, and more than once Miss Lois had taken afternoon walks, for which her conscience troubled her: she could not decide whether it was right or wrong. But winter came, and gradually it grew into a habit that Anne should recite at the church-house now and then, the Indian servant who happened to be at that time the occupant of the kitchen being sent carefully away for the evening, in order that her eye should not be guiltily glued to the key-hole during the exciting visits of Ophelia and Juliet. Anne was always reluctant to give these recitations now that she had an audience. "Out in the woods," she said, "I had only the trees and the silence. I never thought of myself at all."

"But Miss Lois and I are as handsome as trees; and as to silence, we never say a word," replied Rast. "Come, Annet, you know you like it."

"Yes; in—in one way I do."

"Then let us take that way," said Rast.

CHAPTER IV.

—"Sounding names as any on the page of history—Lake Winnipeg, Hudson Bay, Ottaway, and portages innumerable; Chipeways, Gens de Terre, Les Pilleurs, the Weepers, and the like. An immense, shaggy, but sincere country, adorned with chains of lakes and rivers, covered with snows, with hemlocks and fir-trees. There is a naturalness in this traveller, and an unpretendingness, as in a Canadian winter, where life is preserved through low temperature and frontier dangers by furs, and within a stout heart. He has truth and moderation worthy of the father of history, which belong only to an intimate experience; and he does not defer much to literature."—Thoreau.

Immediately after the early dinner the little cavalcade set out for the hermitage of Père Michaux, which was on an island of its own at some distance from the village island; to reach it they journeyed over the ice. The boys' sled went first, André riding, the other two drawing: they were to take turns. Then came old Antoine and his dogs, wise-looking, sedate creatures with wide-spread, awkward legs, big paws, and toes turned in. René and Lebeau were the leaders; they were dogs of age and character, and as they guided the sledge they also kept an eye to the younger dogs behind. The team was a local one; it was not employed in carrying the mails, but was used by the villagers when they crossed to the various islands, the fishing grounds, or the Indian villages on the mainland. Old Antoine walked behind with Anne by his side: she preferred to walk. Snugly ensconced in the sledge in a warm nest of furs was Tita, nothing visible of her small self save her dark eyes, which were, however, most of the time closed: here there was nothing to watch. The bells on the dogs sounded out merrily in the clear air: the boys had also adorned themselves with bells, and pranced along like colts. The sunshine was intensely bright, the blue heavens seemed full of its shafts, the ice below glittered in shining lines; on the north and south the dark evergreens of the mainland rose above the white, but toward the east and west the fields of ice extended unbroken over the edge of the horizon. Here they were smooth, covered with snow; there they were heaped in hummocks and ridges, huge blocks piled against each other, and frozen solid in that position where the wind and the current had met and fought. The atmosphere was cold, but so pure and still that breathing was easier than in many localities farther toward the south. There was no dampness, no strong raw wind; only the even cold. A feather thrown from a house-top would have dropped softly to the ground in a straight line, as drop one by one the broad leaves of the sycamore on still Indian summer days. The snow itself was dry; it had fallen at intervals during the winter, and made thicker and thicker the soft mantle that covered the water and land. When the flakes came down, the villagers always knew that it was warmer, for when the clouds were steel-bound, the snow could not fall.

"I think we shall have snow again to-morrow," said old Antoine in his voyageur dialect. "Step forward, then, genteelly, René. Hast thou no conscience, Lebeau?"

The two dogs, whose attention had been a little distracted by the backward vision of André conveying something to his mouth, returned to their duty with a jerk, and the other dogs behind all rang their little bells suddenly as they felt the swerve of the leaders back into the track. For there was a track over the ice toward Père Michaux's island, and another stretching off due eastward—the path of the carrier who brought the mails from below; besides these there were no other ice-roads; the Indians and hunters came and went as the bird flies. Père Michaux's island was not in sight from the village; it was, as the boys said, round the corner. When they had turned this point, and no longer saw the mission church, the little fort, and the ice-covered piers, when there was nothing on the shore side save wild cliffs crowned with evergreens, then before them rose a low island with its bare summer trees, its one weather-beaten house, a straight line of smoke coming from its chimney. It was still a mile distant, but the boys ran along with new vigor. No one wished to ride; André, leaving his place, took hold with the others, and the empty sled went on toward the hermitage at a fine pace.

"You could repose yourself there, mademoiselle," said Antoine, who never thoroughly approved the walking upon her own two feet kept up—nay, even enjoyed—by this vigorous girl at his side. Tita's ideas were more to his mind.

"But I like it," said Anne, smiling. "It makes me feel warm and strong, all awake and joyous, as though I had just heard some delightful news."

"But the delightful news in reality, mademoiselle—one hears not much of it up here, as I say to Jacqueline."

"Look at the sky, the ice-fields; that is news every day, newly beautiful, if we will only look at it."

"Does mademoiselle think, then, that the ice is beautiful?"

"Very beautiful," replied the girl.

The cold air had brought the blood to her cheeks, a gleaming light to her strong, fearless eyes that looked the sun in the face without quailing. Old Antoine caught the idea for the first time that she might, perhaps, be beautiful some day, and that night, before his fire, he repeated the idea to his wife.

"Bah!" said old Jacqueline; "that is one great error of yours, my friend. Have you turned blind?"

"I did not mean beautiful in my eyes, of course; but one kind of beauty pleases me, thank the saints, and that is, without doubt, your own," replied the Frenchman, bowing toward his withered, bright-eyed old spouse with courtly gravity. "But men of another race, now, like those who come here in the summer, might they not think her passable?"

But old Jacqueline, although mollified, would not admit even this. A good young lady, and kind, it was to be hoped she would be content with the graces of piety, since she had not those of the other sort. Religion was all-merciful.

The low island met the lake without any broken ice at its edge; it rose slightly from the beach in a gentle slope, the snow-path leading directly up to the house door. The sound of the bells brought Père Michaux himself to the entrance. "Enter, then, my children," he said; "and you, Antoine, take the dogs round to the kitchen. Pierre is there."

Pierre was a French cook. Neither conscience nor congregation requiring that Père Michaux should nourish his inner man with half-baked or cindered dishes, he enjoyed to the full the skill and affection of this small-sized old Frenchman, who, while learning in his youth the rules, exceptions, and sauces of his profession, became the victim of black melancholy on account of a certain Denise, fair but cold-hearted, who, being employed in a conservatory, should have been warmer. Perhaps Denise had her inner fires, but they emitted no gleam toward poor Pierre; and at last, after spoiling two breakfasts and a dinner, and drawing down upon himself the epithet of "imbécile," the sallow little apprentice abandoned Paris, and in a fit of despair took passage for America, very much as he might have taken passage for Hades *viâ* the charcoal route. Having arrived in New York, instead of seeking a place where his knowledge, small as it was, would have been prized by exiled Frenchmen in a sauceless land, the despairing, obstinate little cook allowed himself to drift into all sorts of incongruous situations, and at last enlisted in the United States army, where, as he could play the flute, he was speedily placed in special service as member of the band. Poor Pierre! his flute sang to him only "Denise! Denise!" But the band-master thought it could sing other tunes as well, and set him to work with the score before him. It was while miserably performing his part in company with six placid Germans that Père Michaux first saw poor Pierre, and recognizing a compatriot, spoke to him. Struck by the pathetic misery of his face, he asked a few questions of the little flute-player, listened to his story, and gave him the comfort and help of sympathy and shillings, together with the sound of the old home accents, sweetest of all to the dulled ears. When the time of enlistment expired, Pierre came westward after his priest: Père Michaux had written to him once or twice, and the ex-cook had preserved the letters as a guide-book. He showed the heading and the postmark whenever he was at a loss, and travelled blindly on, handed from one railway conductor to another like a piece of animated luggage, until at last he was put on board of a steamer, and, with some difficulty, carried westward; for the sight of the water had convinced him that he was to be taken on some unknown and terrible voyage.

The good priest was surprised and touched to see the tears of the little man, stained, weazened, and worn with travel and grief; he took him over to the hermitage in his sharp-pointed boat, which skimmed the crests of the waves, the two sails wing-and-wing, and Pierre sat in the bottom, and held on with a death-grasp. As soon as his foot touched the shore, he declared, with regained fluency, that he would never again enter a boat, large or small, as long as he lived. He never did. In vain Père Michaux represented to him that he could earn more money in a city, in vain he offered to send him Eastward and place him with kind persons speaking his own tongue, who would procure a good situation for him; Pierre was obstinate. He listened, assented to all, but when the time came refused to go.

"Are you or are you not going to send us that cook of yours?" wrote Father George at the end of two years. "This is the fifth time I have made ready for him."

"He will not go," replied Père Michaux at last; "it seems that I must resign myself."

"If your Père Michaux is handsomer than I am," said Dr. Gaston one day to Anne, "it is because he has had something palatable to eat all this time. In a long course of years saleratus tells."

Père Michaux was indeed a man of noble bearing; his face, although benign, wore an expression of authority, which came from the submissive obedience of his flock, who loved him as a father and revered him as a pope. His parish, a diocese in size, extended over the long point of the southern mainland; over the many islands of the Straits, large and small, some of them unnoted on the map, yet inhabited perhaps by a few half-breeds, others dotted with Indian farms; over the village itself, where stood the small weather-beaten old Church of St. Jean; and over the dim blue line of northern coast, as far as eye could reach or priest could go. His roadways were over the water, his carriage a boat; in the winter, a sledge. He was priest, bishop, governor, judge, and physician; his word was absolute. His party-colored flock referred all their disputes to him, and abided by his decisions—questions of fishing-nets as well as questions of conscience, cases of jealousy together with cases of fever. He stood alone. He was not propped. He had the rare leader's mind. Thrown away on that wild Northern border? Not any more than Bishop Chase in Ohio, Captain John Smith in Virginia, or other versatile and autocratic pioneers. Many a man can lead in cities and in camps, among precedents and rules, but only a born leader can lead in a wilderness where he must make his own rules and be his own precedent every hour.

The dogs trotted cheerfully, with all their bells ringing, round to the back door. Old Pierre detested dogs, yet always fed them with a strange sort of conscientiousness, partly from compassion, partly from fear. He could never accustom himself to the trains. To draw, he said, was an undoglike thing. To see the creatures rush by the island on a moonlight night over the white ice, like dogs of a dream, was enough to make the hair elevate itself.

"Whose hair?" Rast had demanded. "Yours, or the dogs'?" For young Pronando was a frequent visitor at the hermitage, not as pupil or member of the flock, but as a candid young friend, admiring impartially both the priest and his cook.

"Hast thou brought me again all those wide-mouthed dogs, brigands of unheard-of and never-to-be-satisfied emptiness, robbers of all things?" demanded Pierre, appearing at the kitchen door, ladle in hand. Antoine's leathery cheeks wrinkled themselves into a grin as he unharnessed his team, all the dogs pawing and howling, and striving to be first at the entrance of this domain of plenty.

"Hold thyself quiet, René. Wilt thou take the very sledge in, Lebeau?" he said, apostrophizing the leaders. But no sooner was the last strap loosened than all the dogs by common consent rushed at and over the little cook and into the kitchen in a manner which would have insured them severe chastisement in any other kitchen in the diocese. Pierre darted about among their gaunt yellow bodies, railing at them for knocking down his pans, and calling upon all the saints to witness their rapacity; but in the mean time he was gathering together quickly fragments of whose choice and savory qualities René and Lebeau had distinct remembrance, and the other dogs anticipation. They leaped and danced round him on their awkward legs and shambling feet, bit and barked at each other, and rolled on the floor in a heap. Anywhere else the long whip would have curled round their lank ribs, but in old Pierre's kitchen they knew they were safe. With a fiercely delivered and eloquent selection from the strong expressions current in the Paris of his youth, the little cook made his way through the snarling throng of yellow backs and legs, and emptied his pan of fragments on the snow outside. Forth rushed the dogs, and cast themselves in a solid mass upon the little heap.

"Hounds of Satan?" said Pierre.

"They are, indeed," replied Antoine. "But leave them now, my friend, and close the door, since warmth is a blessed gift."

But Pierre still stood on the threshold, every now and then darting out to administer a rap to the gluttons, or to pull forward the younger and weaker ones. He presided with exactest justice over the whole repast, and ended by bringing into the kitchen a forlorn and drearily ugly young animal that had not obtained his share on account of the preternaturally quick side snatchings of Lebeau. To this dog he now presented an especial banquet in an earthen dish behind the door.

"If there is anything I abhor, it is the animal called dog," he said, seating himself at last, and wiping his forehead.

"That is plainly evident," replied old Antoine, gravely.

In the mean time, Anne, Tita, and the boys had thrown off their fur cloaks, and entered the sitting-room. Père Michaux took his seat in his large arm-chair near the hearth, Tita curled herself on a cushion at his feet, and the boys sat together on a wooden bench, fidgeting uneasily, and trying to recall a faint outline of their last lesson, while Anne talked to the priest, warming first one of her shapely feet, then the other, as she leaned against the mantel, inquiring after the health of the birds, the squirrels, the fox, and the tame eagle, Père Michaux's companions in his hermitage. The appearance of the room was peculiar, yet picturesque and full of comfort. It was a long, low apartment, the walls made warm in the winter with skins instead of tapestry, and the floor carpeted with blankets; other skins lay before the table and fire as mats. The furniture was rude, but cushioned and decorated, as were likewise the curtains, in a fashion unique, by the hands of half-breed women, who had vied with each other in the work; their primitive embroidery, whose long stitches sprang to the centre of the curtain or cushion, like the rays of a rising sun, and then back again, was as unlike modern needle-work as the vase-pictured Egyptians, with eyes in the sides of their heads, are like a modern photograph; their patterns, too, had come down from the remote ages of the world called the New, which is, however, as old as the continent across the seas. Guns and fishing-tackle hung over the mantel, a lamp swung from the centre of the ceiling, little singing-birds flew into and out of their open cages near the windows, and the tame eagle sat solemnly on his perch at the far end of the long room. The squirrels and the fox were visible in their quarters, peeping out at the new-comers; but their front doors were barred, for they had broken parole, and were at present in disgrace. The ceiling was planked with wood, which had turned to a dark cinnamon hue; the broad windows let in the sunshine on three sides during the day, and at night were covered with heavy curtains, all save one, which had but a single thickness of red cloth over the glass, with a candle behind which burned all night, so that the red gleam shone far across the ice, like a winter light-house for the frozen Straits. More than one despairing man, lost in the cold and darkness, had caught its ray, and sought refuge, with a thankful heart. The broad deep fire-place of this room was its glory: the hearts of giant logs glowed there: it was a fire to dream of on winter nights, a fire to paint on canvas for Christmas pictures to hang on the walls of barren furnace-heated houses, a fire to remember before that noisome thing, a close stove. Round this fire-place were set like tiles rude bits of pottery found in the vicinity, remains of an earlier race, which the half-breeds brought to Père Michaux whenever their ploughs upturned them—arrow-heads, shells from the wilder beaches, little green pebbles from Isle Royale, agates, and fragments of fossils, the whole forming a rough mosaic, strong in its story of the region. From two high shelves the fathers of the Church and the classics of the world looked down upon this scene. But Père Michaux was no bookworm; his books were men. The needs and faults of his flock absorbed all his days, and, when the moon was bright, his evenings also. "There goes Père Michaux," said the half-breeds, as the broad sail of his boat went gleaming by in the summer night, or the sound of his sledge bells came through their closed doors; "he has been to see the dying wife of Jean," or "to carry medicine to François." On the wild nights and the dark nights, when no one could stir abroad, the old priest lighted his lamp, and fed his mind with its old-time nourishment. But he had nothing modern; no newspapers. The nation was to him naught. He was one of a small but distinctly marked class in America that have a distaste for and disbelief in the present, its ideals, thoughts, and actions, and turn for relief to the past; they represent a reaction. This class is made up of foreigners like the priest, of native-born citizens with artistic tastes who have lived much abroad, modern Tories who regret the Revolution, High-Church Episcopalians who would like archbishops and an Establishment, restless politicians who seek an empire—in all, a very small number compared with the mass of the nation at large, and not important enough to be counted at all numerically, yet not without its influence. And not without its use too, its members serving their country, unconsciously perhaps, but powerfully, by acting as a balance to the self-asserting blatant conceit of the young nation—a drag on the wheels of its too-rapidly speeding car. They are a sort of Mordecai at the gate, and are no more disturbed than he was by being in a minority. In any great crisis this element is fused with the rest at once, and disappears; but in times of peace and prosperity up it comes again, and lifts its scornful voice.

Père Michaux occupied himself first with the boys. The religious education of Louis, Gabriel, and André was not complex—a few plain rules that three colts could have learned almost as well, provided they had had speech. But the priest had the rare gift of holding the attention of children while he talked with them, and thus the three boys learned from him gradually and almost unconsciously the tenets of the faith in which their young mother had lived and died. The rare gift of holding the attention of boys—O poor Sunday-school teachers all over the land, ye know how rare that gift is!—ye who must keep restless little heads and hands quiet while some well-meaning but slow, long-winded, four-syllabled man "addresses the children." It is sometimes the superintendent, but more frequently a visitor, who beams through his spectacles benevolently upon the little flock before him, but has no more power over them than a penguin would have over a colony of sparrows.

But if the religion of the boys was simple, that of Tita was of a very different nature; it was as complex, tortuous, unresting, as personal and minute in detail, as some of those religious journals we have all read, diaries of every thought, pen-photographs of every mood, wonderful to read, but not always comfortable when translated into actual life, where something less purely self-engrossed, if even less saintly, is apt to make the household wheels run more smoothly. Tita's religious ideas perplexed Anne, angered Miss Lois, and sometimes wearied even the priest himself. The little creature aspired to be absolutely perfect, and she was perfect in rule and form. Whatever was said to her in the way of correction she turned and adjusted to suit herself; her mental ingenuity was extraordinary. Anne listened to the child with wonder; but Père Michaux understood and treated with kindly carelessness the strong selfism, which he often encountered among older and deeply devout women, but not often in a girl so young. Once the elder sister asked with some anxiety if he thought Tita was tending toward conventual life.

"Oh no," replied the old man, smiling; "anything but that."

"But is she not remarkably devout?"

"As Parisiennes in Lent."

"But it is Lent with her all the year round."

"That is because she has not seen Paris yet."

"But we can not take her to Paris," said Anne, in perplexity.

"What should I do if I had to reply to you always, mademoiselle?" said the priest, smiling, and patting her head.

"You mean that I am dull?" said Anne, a slight flush rising in her cheeks. "I have often noticed that people thought me so."

"I mean nothing of the kind. But by the side of your honesty we all appear like tapers when the sun breaks in," said Père Michaux, gallantly. Still, Anne could not help thinking that he did think her dull.

To-day she sat by the window, looking out over the ice. The boys, dismissed from their bench, had, with the sagacity of the dogs, gone immediately to the kitchen. The soft voice of Tita was repeating something which sounded like a litany to the Virgin, full of mystic phrases, a selection made by the child herself, the priest requiring no such recitation, but listening, as usual, patiently, with his eyes half closed, as the old-time school-teacher listened to Wirt's description of Blennerhasset's Island. Père Michaux had no mystical tendencies. His life was too busy; in the winter it was too cold, and in the summer the sunshine was too brilliant, on his Northern island, for mystical thoughts. At present, through Tita's recitation, his mind was occupied with a poor fisherman's family over on the mainland, to whom on the morrow he was going to send assistance. The three boys came round on the outside, and peered through the windows to see whether the lesson was finished. Anne ordered them back by gesture, for they were bareheaded, and their little faces red with the cold. But they pressed their noses against the panes, glared at Tita, and shook their fists. "It's all ready," they said, in sepulchral tones, putting their mouths to the crack under the sash, "and it's a pudding. Tell her to hurry up, Annet."

But Tita's murmuring voice went steadily on, and the Protestant sister would not interrupt the little Catholic's recitation; she shook her head at the boys, and motioned to them to go back to the kitchen. But they danced up and down to warm themselves, rubbed their little red ears with their hands, and then returned to the crack, and roared in chorus, "Tell her to hurry up; we shall not have time to eat it."

"True," said Père Michaux, overhearing this triple remonstrance. "That will do for to-day, Tita."

"But I have not finished, my father."

"Another time, child."

"I shall recite it, then, at the next lesson, and learn besides as much more; and the interruption was not of my making, but a crime of those sacrilegious boys," said Tita, gathering her books together. The boys, seeing Père Michaux rise from his chair, ran back round the house to announce the tidings to Pierre; the priest came forward to the window.

"That is the mail-train, is it not?" said Anne, looking at a black spot coming up the Strait from the east.

"It is due," said Père Michaux; "but the weather has been so cold that I hardly expected it to-day." He took down a spy-glass, and looked at the moving speck. "Yes, it is the train. I can see the dogs, and Denis himself. I will go over to the village with you, I think. I expect letters."

Père Michaux's correspondence was large. From many a college and mission station came letters to this hermit of the North, on subjects as various as the writers: the flora of the region, its mineralogy, the Indians and their history, the lost grave of Father Marquette (in these later days said to have been found), the legends of the fur-trading times, the existing commerce of the lakes, the fisheries, and kindred subjects were mixed with discussions kept up with fellow Latin and Greek scholars exiled at far-off Southern stations, with games of chess played by letter, with recipes for sauces, and with humorous skirmishing with New York priests on topics of the day, in which the Northern hermit often had the best of it.

A hurrah in the kitchen, an opening of doors, a clattering in the hall, and the boys appeared, followed by old Pierre, bearing aloft a pudding enveloped in steam, exhaling fragrance, and beautiful with raisins, currants, and citron—rarities regarded by Louis, Gabriel, and André with eager eyes.

"But it was for your dinner," said Anne.

"It is still for my dinner. But it would have lasted three days, and now it will end its existence more honorably in one," replied the priest, beginning to cut generous slices.

Tita was the last to come forward. She felt herself obliged to set down all the marks of her various recitations in a small note-book after each lesson; she kept a careful record, and punished or rewarded herself accordingly, the punishments being long readings from some religious book in her corner, murmured generally half aloud, to the exasperation of Miss Lois when she happened to be present, Miss Lois having a vehement dislike for "sing-song." Indeed, the little, soft, persistent murmur sometimes made even Anne think that the whole family bore their part in Tita's religious penances. But what could be said to the child? Was she not engaged in saving her soul?

The marks being at last all set down, she took her share of pudding to the fire, and ate it daintily and dreamily, enjoying it far more than the boys, who swallowed too hastily; far more than Anne, who liked the simplest food. The priest was the only one present who appreciated Pierre's skill as Tita appreciated it. "It is délicieux," she said, softly, replacing the spoon in the saucer, and leaning back against the cushions with half-closed eyes.

"Will you have some more, then?" said Anne.

Tita shook her head, and waved away her sister impatiently.

"She is as thorough an epicure as I am," said the priest, smiling; "it takes away from the poetry of a dish to be asked to eat more."

It was now time to start homeward, and Père Michaux's sledge made its appearance, coming from a little islet near by. Old Pierre would not have dogs upon his shores; yet he went over to the other island himself every morning, at the expense of much time and trouble, to see that the half-breed in charge had not neglected them. The result was that Père Michaux's dogs were known as far as they could be seen by their fat sides, the only rotundities in dog-flesh within a circle of five hundred miles. Père Michaux wished to take Tita with him in his sledge, in order that Anne might ride also; but the young girl declined with a smile, saying that she liked the walk.

"Do not wait for us, sir," she said; "your dogs can go much faster than ours."

But the priest preferred to make the journey in company with them; and they all started together from the house door, where Pierre stood in his red skull-cap, bowing farewell. The sledges glided down the little slope to the beach, and shot out on the white ice, the two drivers keeping by the side of their teams, the boys racing along in advance, and Anne walking with her quick elastic step by the side of Père Michaux's conveyance, talking to him with the animation which always came to her in the open air. The color mounted in her cheeks; with her head held erect she seemed to breathe with delight, and to rejoice in the clear sky, the cold, the crisp sound of her own footsteps, while her eyes followed the cliffs of the shore-line crowned with evergreens— savage cliffs which the short summer could hardly soften. The sun sank toward the west, the air grew colder; Tita drew the furs over her head, and vanished from sight, riding along in her nest half asleep, listening to the bells. The boys still ran and pranced, but more, perhaps, from a sense of honor than from natural hilarity. They were more exact in taking their turns in the sledge now, and more slow in coming out from the furs upon call; still, they kept on. As the track turned little by little, following the line of the shore, they came nearer to the mail-train advancing rapidly from the east in a straight line.

"Denis is determined to have a good supper and sleep to-night," said Père Michaux; "no camp to make in the snow *this* evening." Some minutes later the mail-train passed, the gaunt old dogs which drew the sledge never even turning their heads to gaze at the party, but keeping straight on, having come in a direct line, without a break, from the point, ten miles distant. The young dogs in Antoine's team pricked up their ears, and betrayed a disposition to rush after the mail-train; then René and Lebeau, after looking round once or twice, after turning in their great paws more than usual as they walked, and holding back resolutely, at length sat deliberately down on their haunches, and stopped the sledge.

"And thou art entirely right, René, and thou too, Lebeau," said old Antoine. "To waste breath following a mail-train at a gallop is worthy only of young-dog silliness."

So saying he administered to the recreant members of the team enough chastisement to make them forget the very existence of mail-trains, while René and Lebeau waited composedly to see justice done; they then rose in a dignified manner and started on, the younger dogs following now with abject humility. As they came nearer the village the western pass opened out before them, a long narrow vista of ice, with the dark shore-line on each side, and the glow of the red sunset shining strangely through, as though it came from a tropical country beyond. A sledge was crossing down in the west—a moving speck; the scene was as wild and arctic as if they had been travelling on Baffin's Bay. The busy priest gave little attention to the scene, and the others in all the winters of their lives had seen nothing else: to the Bedouins the great desert is nothing. Anne noted every feature and hue of the picture, but unconsciously. She saw it all, but without a comment. Still, she saw it. She was to see it again many times in after-years—see it in cities, in lighted drawing-rooms, in gladness and in sorrow, and more than once through a mist of tears.

Later in the evening, when the moon was shining brightly, and she was on her way home from the church-house with Rast, she saw a sledge moving toward the northern point. "There is Père Michaux, on his way home," she said. Then, after a moment, "Do you know, Rast, he thinks me dull."

"He would not if he had seen you this evening," replied her companion.

A deep flush, visible even in the moonlight, came into the girl's face. "Do not ask me to recite again," she pleaded; "I can not. You *must* let me do what I feel is right."

"What is there wrong in reciting Shakspeare?"

"I do not know. But something comes over me at times, and I am almost swept away. I can not bear to think of the feeling."

"Then don't," said Rast.

"You do not understand me."

"I don't believe you understand yourself; girls seldom do."

"Why?"

"Let me beg you not to fall into the power of that uncomfortable word, Annet. Walters says women of the world never use it. They never ask a single question."

33

"But how can they learn, then?"

"By observation," replied young Pronando, oracularly.

CHAPTER V.

"It was Peboan, the winter!

From his eyes the tears were flowing

As from melting lakes the streamlets,

And his body shrunk and dwindled

As the shouting sun ascended;

And the young man saw before him,

On the hearth-stone of the wigwam,

Where the fire had smoked and
smouldered,

Saw the earliest flower of spring-time,

Saw the miskodeed in blossom.

Thus it was that in that Northland

Came the spring with all its splendor,

All its birds and all its blossoms,

All its flowers and leaves and grasses."

—Longfellow. *The Song of Hiawatha.*

On this Northern border Spring came late—came late, but in splendor. She sent forward no couriers, no hints in the forest, no premonitions on the winds. All at once she was there herself. Not a shy maid, timid, pallid, hesitating, and turning back, but a full-blooming goddess and woman. One might almost say that she was not Spring at all, but Summer. The weeks called spring farther southward showed here but the shrinking and fading of winter. First the snow crumbled to fine dry grayish powder; then the ice grew porous and became honeycombed, and it was no longer safe to cross the Straits; then the first birds came; then the far-off smoke of a steamer could be seen above the point, and the village wakened. In the same day the winter went and the summer came.

On the highest point of the island were the remains of an old earth-work, crowned by a little surveyor's station, like an arbor on stilts, which was reached by the aid of a ladder. Anne liked to go up there on the first spring day, climb the ice-coated rounds, and, standing on the dry old snow that covered the floor, gaze off toward the south and east, where people and cities were, and the spring; then toward the north, where there was still only fast-bound ice and snow stretching away over thousands of miles of almost unknown country, the great wild northland called British America, traversed by the hunters and trappers of the Hudson Bay Company—vast empire ruled by private hands, a government within a government, its line of forts and posts extending from James Bay to the Little Slave, from the Saskatchewan northward to the Polar Sea. In the early afternoon she stood there now, having made her way up to the height with some difficulty, for the ice-crust was broken, and she was obliged to wade knee-deep through some of the drifts, and go round others that were over her head, leaving a trail behind her as crooked as a child's through a clover field. Reaching the plateau on the summit at last, and avoiding the hidden pits of the old earth-work, she climbed the icy ladder, and stood on the white floor again with delight, brushing from her woollen skirt and leggings the dry snow which still clung to them. The sun was so bright and the air so exhilarating that she pushed back her little fur cap, and drew a long breath of enjoyment. Everything below was still white-covered—the island and village, the Straits and the mainland; but coming round the eastern point four propellers could be seen floundering in the loosened ice, heaving the porous cakes aside, butting with their sharp high bows, and then backing briskly to get headway to start forward again, thus breaking slowly a passageway for themselves, and churning the black water behind until it boiled white as soap-suds as the floating ice closed over it. Now one boat, finding by chance a weakened spot, floundered through it without pause, and came out triumphantly some distance in advance of the rest; then another, wakened to new exertions by this sight, put on all steam, and went pounding along with a crashing sound until her bows were on a line with the first. The two boats left behind now started together with much splashing and sputtering, and veering toward the shore, with the hope of finding a new weak place in the floe, ran against hard ice with a thud, and stopped short; then there was much backing out and floundering round, the engines panting and the little bells ringing wildly, until the old channel was reached, where they rested awhile, and then made another beginning. These manœuvres were repeated over and over again, the passengers and crew of each boat laughing and chaffing each other as they passed and repassed in the slow pounding race. It had happened more than once that these first steamers had been frozen in after reaching the Straits, and had been obliged to spend several days in company fast bound in the ice. Then the passengers and crews visited each other, climbing down the sides of the steamers and walking across. At that early season the passengers were seldom pleasure-travellers, and therefore they endured the delay philosophically. It is only the real pleasure-traveller who has not one hour to spare.

The steamers Anne now watched were the first from below. The lower lakes were clear; it was only this northern Strait that still held the ice together, and kept the fleets at bay on the east and on the west. White-winged vessels, pioneers of the summer squadron, waited without while the propellers turned their knife-bladed bows into the ice, and cut a pathway through. Then word went down that the Straits were open, all the freshwater fleet set sail, the lights were lit again in the light-houses, and the fishing stations and lonely little wood docks came to life.

"How delightful it is!" said Anne, aloud.

There are times when a person, although alone, does utter a sentence or two, that is, thinks aloud; but such times are rare. And such sentences, also, are short—exclamations. The long soliloquies of the stage, so convenient in the elucidation of plot, do not occur in real life, where we are left to guess at our neighbor's motives, untaught by so much as a syllable. How fortunate for Dora's chances of happiness could she but overhear that Alonzo thinks her a sweet, bigoted little fool, but wants that very influence to keep him straight, nothing less than the intense convictions of a limited intelligence and small experience in life being of any use in sweeping him over with a rush by means of his feelings alone, which is what he is hoping for. Having worn out all the pleasure there is to be had in this world, he has now a mind to try for the next.

What an escape for young Conrad to learn from Honoria's own passionate soliloquy that she is marrying him from bitterest rage against Manuel, and that those tones and looks that have made him happy are second-hand wares, which she flings from her voice and eyes with desperate scorn! Still, we must believe that Nature knows what she is about; and she has not as yet taught us to think aloud.

But sometimes, when the air is peculiarly exhilarating, when a distant mountain grows purple and gold tipped as the sun goes down behind it, sometimes when we see the wide ocean suddenly, or come upon a bed of violets, we utter an exclamation as the bird sings: we hardly know we have spoken.

"Yes, it *is* delightful," said some one below, replying to the girl's sentence.

It was Rast, who had come across the plateau unseen, and was now standing on the old bastion of the fort beneath her. Anne smiled, then turned as if to descend.

"Wait; I am coming up," said Rast.

"But it is time to go home."

"Apparently it was not time until I came," said the youth, swinging himself up without the aid of the ladder, and standing by her side. "What are you looking at? Those steamers?"

"Yes, and the spring, and the air."

"You can not see the air."

"But I can feel it; it is delicious. I wonder, if we should go far away, Rast, and see tropical skies, slow rivers, great white lilies, and palms, whether they would seem more beautiful than this?"

"Of course they would; and we are going some day. We are not intending to stay here on this island all our lives, I hope."

"But it is our home, and I love it. I love this water and these woods, I love the flash of the light-houses, and the rushing sound the vessels make sweeping by at night under full sail, close in shore."

"The island is well enough in its way, but there are other places; and I, for one, mean to see the world," said young Pronando, taking off his cap, throwing it up, and catching it like a ball.

"Yes, you will see the world," answered Anne; "but I shall stay here. You must write and tell me all about it."

"Of course," said Rast, sending the cap up twice as high, and catching it with unerring hand. Then he stopped his play, and said, suddenly, "Will you care very much when I am gone away?"

"Yes," said Anne; "I shall be very lonely."

"But shall you care?" said the youth, insistently. "You have so little feeling, Annet; you are always cold."

35

"I shall be colder still if we stay here any longer," said the girl, turning to descend. Rast followed her, and they crossed the plateau together.

"How much shall you care?" he repeated. "You never say things out, Annet. You are like a stone."

"Then throw me away," answered the girl, lightly. But there was a moisture in her eyes and a slight tremor in her voice which Rast understood, or, rather, thought he understood. He took her hand and pressed it warmly; the two fur gloves made the action awkward, but he would not loosen his hold. His spirits rose, and he began to laugh, and to drag his companion along at a rapid pace. They reached the edge of the hill, and the steep descent opened before them; the girl's remonstrances were in vain, and it ended in their racing down together at a break-neck pace, reaching the bottom, laughing and breathless, like two school-children. They were now on the second plateau, the level proper of the island above the cliffs, which, high and precipitous on three sides, sank down gradually to the southwestern shore, so that one might land there, and drag a cannon up to the old earth work on the summit—a feat once performed by British soldiers in the days when the powers of the Old World were still fighting with each other for the New. How quaint they now seem, those ancient proclamations and documents with which a Spanish king grandly meted out this country from Maine to Florida, an English queen divided the same with sweeping patents from East to West, and a French monarch, following after, regranted the whole virgin soil on which the banners of France were to be planted with solemn Christian ceremony! They all took possession; they all planted banners. Some of the brass plates they buried are turned up occasionally at the present day by the farmer's plough, and, wiping his forehead, he stops to spell out their high-sounding words, while his sunburned boys look curiously over his shoulder. A place in the county museum is all they are worth now.

Anne Douglas and Rast went through the fort grounds and down the hill path, instead of going round by the road. The fort ladies, sitting by their low windows, saw them, and commented.

"That girl does not appreciate young Pronando," said Mrs. Cromer. "I doubt if she even sees his beauty."

"Perhaps it is just as well that she does not," replied Mrs. Rankin, "for he must go away and live his life, of course; have his adventures."

"Why not she also?" said Mrs. Bryden, smiling.

"In the first place, she has no choice; she is tied down here. In the second, she is a good sort of girl, without imagination or enthusiasm. Her idea of life is to marry, have meat three times a week, fish three times, lights out at ten o'clock, and, by way of literature, Miss Edgeworth's novels and Macaulay's *History of England*."

"And a very good idea," said Mrs. Bryden.

"Certainly, only one can not call that adventures."

"But even such girls come upon adventures sometimes," said Mrs. Cromer.

"Yes, when they have beauty. Their beauty seems often to have an extraordinary power over the most poetical and imaginative men, too, strange as it may appear. But Anne Douglas has none of it."

"How you all misunderstand her!" said a voice from the little dining-room opening into the parlor, its doorway screened by a curtain.

"Ah, doctor, are you there?" said Mrs. Bryden. "We should not have said a word if we had known it."

"Yes, madam, I am here—with the colonel; but it is only this moment that I have lifted my head to listen to your conversation, and I remain filled with astonishment, as usual, at the obtuseness manifested by your sex regarding each other."

"Hear! hear!" said the colonel.

"Anne Douglas," continued the chaplain, clearing his throat, and beginning in a high chanting voice, which they all knew well, having heard it declaiming on various subjects during long snow-bound winter evenings, "is a most unusual girl."

"Oh, come in here, doctor, and take a seat; it will be hard work to say it all through that doorway," called Mrs. Bryden.

"No, madam, I will not sit down," said the chaplain, appearing under the curtain, his brown wig awry, his finger impressively pointed. "I will simply say this, namely, that as to Anne Douglas, you are all mistaken."

"And who is to be the judge between us?"

"The future, madam."

"Very well; we will leave it to the future, then," said Mrs. Bryden, skillfully evading the expected oration.

"We may safely do that, madam—safely indeed; the only difficulty is that we may not live to see it."

"Oh, a woman's future is always near at hand, doctor. Besides, we are not so very old ourselves."

"True, madam—happily true for all the eyes that rest upon you. Nevertheless, the other side, I opine, is likewise true, namely, that Anne Douglas is very young."

"She is sixteen; and I myself am only twenty," said Mrs. Rankin.

"With due respect, ladies, I must mention that not one of you was ever in her life so young as Anne Douglas at the present moment."

"What in the world do you mean, doctor?"

"What I say. I can see you all as children in my mind's eye," continued the chaplain, unflinchingly; "pretty, bright, precocious little creatures, finely finished, finely dressed, quick-witted, graceful, and bewitching. But at that age Anne Douglas was a—"

"Well, what?"

"A mollusk," said the chaplain, bringing out the word emphatically.

"And what is she now, doctor?"

"A promise."

"To be magnificently fulfilled in the future?"

"That depends upon fate, madam; or rather circumstances."

"For my part, I would rather be fulfilled, although not perhaps magnificently, than remain even the most glorious promise," said Mrs. Rankin, laughing.

The fort ladies liked the old chaplain, and endured his long monologues by adding to them running accompaniments of their own. To bright society women there is nothing so unendurable as long arguments or dissertations on one subject. Whether from want of mental training, or from impatience of delay, they are unwilling to follow any one line of thought for more than a minute or two; they love to skim at random, to light and fly away again, to hover, to poise, and then dart upward into space like so many humming-birds. Listen to a circle of them sitting chatting over their embroidery round the fire or on a piazza; no man with a thoroughly masculine mind can follow them in their mental dartings hither and thither. He has just brought his thoughts to bear upon a subject, and is collecting what he is going to say, when, behold! they are miles away, and he would be considered stupid to attempt to bring them back. His mental processes are slow and lumbering compared with theirs. And when, once in a while, a woman appears who likes to search out a subject, she finds herself out of place and bewildered too, often a target for the quick tongues and light ridicule of her companions. If she likes to generalize, she is lost. Her companions never wish to generalize; they want to know not the general view of a subject, but what Mrs. Blank or Mr. Star thinks of it. Parents, if you have a daughter of this kind, see that she spends in her youth a good portion of every day with the most volatile swift-tongued maidens you can find; otherwise you leave her without the current coin of the realm in which she must live and die, and no matter if she be fairly a gold mine herself, her wealth is unavailable.

Spring burst upon the island with sudden glory; the maples showed all at once a thousand perfect little leaflets, the rings of the juniper brightened, the wild larches beckoned with their long green fingers from the height. The ice was gone, the snow was gone, no one knew whither; the Straits were dotted with white sails. Bluebells appeared, swinging on their hair-like stems where late the icicles hung, and every little Indian farm set to work with vigor, knowing that the time was short. The soldiers from the fort dug in the military garden under the cliff, turning up the mould in long ridges, and pausing to hang up their coats on the old stockade with a finely important air of heat: it was so long since they had been too warm! The little village was broad awake now; there was shipping at the piers again, and a demand for white-fish; all the fishing-boats were out, and their half-breed crews hard at work. The violins hung unused on the walls of the little cabins that faced the west, for the winter was ended, and the husbands and lovers were off on the water: the summer was their time for toil.

And now came the parting. Rast was to leave the island, and enter the Western college which Dr. Gaston had selected for him. The chaplain would have sent the boy over to England at once to his own *alma mater* had it been possible; but it was not possible, and the good man knew little or nothing of the degree of excellence possessed by American colleges, East or West. Harvard and Yale and old Columbia would not have believed this; yet it was true.

Rast was in high spirits; the brilliant world seemed opening before him. Everything in his life was as he wished it to be; and he was not disturbed by any realization that this was a rare condition of affairs which might never occur again. He was young, buoyant, and beautiful; everybody liked him, and he liked everybody. He was going to set sail into his far bright future, and he would find, probably, an island of silver and diamonds, with peacocks walking slowly about spreading their gorgeous feathers, and pleasure-boats at hand with silken sails and golden oars. It was not identically this that he dreamed, but things equally shining and unattainable—that is, to such a nature as his. The silver and diamond islands are there, but by a law of equalization only hard-featured prosaic men attain them and take possession, forming thereafterward a lasting contrast to their own

37

surroundings, which then goes into the other scale, and amuses forever the poverty-stricken poets who, in their poor old boats, with ragged canvas and some small ballast of guitars and lutes, sail by, eating their crusts and laughing at them.

"I shall not go one step, even now, unless you promise to write regularly, Annet," said Rast, the evening before his departure, as they stood together on the old piazza of the Agency watching for the lights of the steamer which was to carry him away.

"Of course I shall write, Rast; once a week always."

"No; I wish no set times fixed. You are simply to promise that you will immediately answer every letter *I* write."

"I will answer; but as to the time—I may not always be able—"

"You may if you choose; and I will not go unless you promise," said Rast, with irritation. "Do you want to spoil everything, my education and all my future? I would not be so selfish, Annet, if I were you. What is it I ask? A trifle. I have no father, no mother, no sister; only you. I am going away for the first time in my life, and you grudge me a letter!"

"Not a letter, Rast, but a promise; lest I might not be able to fulfill it. I only meant that something might happen in the house which would keep me from answering within the hour, and then my promise would be broken. I will always answer as soon as I can."

"You will not fail me, then?"

The girl held out her hand and clasped his with a warm, honest pressure; he turned and looked at her in the starlight. "God bless you for your dear sincere eyes!" he said. "The devil himself would believe you."

"I hope he would," said Anne, smiling.

What with Miss Lois's Calvinism, and the terrific picture of his Satanic Majesty at the death-bed of the wicked in the old Catholic church, the two, as children, had often talked about the devil and his characteristics, Rast being sure that some day he should see him. Miss Lois, overhearing this, agreed with the lad dryly, much to Anne's dismay.

"What is the use of the devil?" she had once demanded.

"To punish the wicked," answered Miss Lois.

"Does he enjoy it?"

"I suppose he does."

"Then he must be very wicked himself?"

"He is."

"Who created him?"

"You know as well as I do, Anne. God created him, of course."

"Well," said the child, after a silence, going as usual to the root of the matter, "I don't think *I* should have made him at all if I couldn't have made him better."

The next morning the sun rose as usual, but Rast was gone. Anne felt a loneliness she had never felt before in all her life. For Rast had been her companion; hardly a day had passed without his step on the piazza, his voice in the hall, a walk with him or a sail; and always, whether at home or abroad, the constant accompaniment of his suggestions, his fault-findings, his teachings, his teasings, his grumblings, his laughter and merry nonsense, the whole made bearable—nay, even pleasant—by the affection that lay underneath. Anne Douglas's nature was faithful to an extraordinary degree, faithful to its promises, its duties, its love; but it was an intuitive faithfulness, which never thought about itself at all. Those persons who are in the habit of explaining voluminously to themselves and everybody else the lines of argument, the struggles, and triumphant conclusions reached by their various virtues, would have considered this girl's mind but a poor dull thing, for Anne never analyzed herself at all. She had never lived for herself or in herself, and it was that which gave the tinge of coldness that was noticed in her. For warm-heartedness generally begins at home, and those who are warm to others are warmer to themselves; it is but the overflow.

Meantime young Pronando, sailing southward, felt his spirits rise with every shining mile. Loneliness is crowded out of the mind of the one who goes by the myriad images of travel; it is the one who stays who suffers. But there was much to be done at the Agency. The boys grew out of their clothes, the old furniture fell to pieces, and the father seemed more lost to the present with every day and hour. He gave less and less attention to the wants of the household, and at last Anne and Miss Lois together managed everything without troubling him even by a question. For strange patience have loving women ever had with dreamers like William Douglas—men who, viewed by the eyes of the world, are useless and incompetent; tears are shed over their graves oftentimes long after the successful are forgotten. For personally there is a sweetness and gentleness in their natures which make them very dear to the women who love them. The successful man, perhaps, would not care for such love, which is half devotion, half protection; the successful man wishes to domineer. But as he grows old he notices that Jane is always quiet when the peach-trees are in bloom, and that gray-haired sister Catherine always bends down her head and weeps silently whenever the choir sings "Rockingham"; and then he remembers who it was that died when the peach-trees showed their blossoms, and who it was who went about humming "Rockingham," and understands. Yet always with a slow surprise, and a wonder at women's ways, since both the men were, to his idea, failures in the world and their generation.

Any other woman of Miss Lois's age and strict prudence, having general charge of the Douglas household, would have required from Anne long ago that she should ask her father plainly what were his resources and his income. To a cent were all the affairs of the church-house regulated and balanced; Miss Lois would have been unhappy at the end of the week if a penny remained unaccounted for. Yet she said nothing to the daughter, nothing to the father, although noticing all the time that the small provision was no larger, while the boys grew like reeds, and the time was at hand when more must be done for them. William Douglas's way was to give Anne at the beginning of each week a certain sum. This he had done as far back as his daughter could remember, and she had spent it under the direction of Miss Lois. Now, being older, she laid it out without much advice from her mentor, but began to feel troubled because it did not go as far. "It goes as far," said Miss Lois, "but the boys have gone farther."

"Poor little fellows! they must eat."

"And they must work."

"But what can they do at their age, Miss Lois?"

"Form habits," replied the New England woman, sternly. "In my opinion the crying evil of the country to-day is that the boys are not trained; educated, I grant you, but not trained—trained as they were when times were simpler, and the rod in use. Parents are too ambitious; the mechanic wishes to make his sons merchants, the merchant wishes to make his gentlemen; but, while educating them and pushing them forward, the parents forget the homely habits of patient labor, strict veracity in thought and action, and stern self-denials which have given *them* their measure of success, and so between the two stools the poor boys fall to the ground. It is my opinion," added Miss Lois, decisively, "that, whether you want to build the Capitol at Washington or a red barn, you must first have a firm foundation."

"Yes, I know," replied Anne. "And I *do* try to control them."

"Oh, General Putnam! *you* try!" said Miss Lois. "Why, you spoil them like babies."

Anne always gave up the point when Miss Lois reverted to Putnam. This Revolutionary hero, now principally known, like Romulus, by a wolf story, was the old maid's glory and remote ancestor, and helped her over occasional necessities for strong expressions with ancestral kindness. She felt like reverting to him more than once that summer, because, Rast having gone, there was less of a whirlwind of out-door life, of pleasure in the woods and on the water, and the plain bare state of things stood clearly revealed. Anne fell behind every month with the household expenses in spite of all her efforts, and every month Miss Lois herself made up the deficiency. The boys were larger, and careless. The old house yawned itself apart. Of necessity the gap between the income and the expenditure must grow wider and wider. Anne did not realize this, but Miss Lois did. The young girl thought each month that she must have been unusually extravagant; she counted in some item as an extra expense which would not occur again, gave up something for herself, and began anew with fresh hope. On almost all subjects Miss Lois had the smallest amount of patience for what she called blindness, but on this she was silent. Now and then her eyes would follow Anne's father with a troubled gaze; but if he looked toward her or spoke, she at once assumed her usual brisk manner, and was even more cheerful than usual. Thus, the mentor being silent, the family drifted on.

The short Northern summer, with its intense sunshine and its cool nights, was now upon them. Fire crackled upon the hearth of the Agency sitting-room in the early morning, but it died out about ten o'clock, and from that time until five in the afternoon the heat and the brightness were peculiarly brilliant and intense. It seemed as though the white cliffs must take fire and smoulder in places where they were without trees to cover them; to climb up and sit there was to feel the earth burning under you, and to be penetrated with a sun-bath of rays beating straight down through the clear air like white shafts. And yet there was nothing resembling the lowland heats in this atmosphere, for all the time a breeze blew, ruffling the Straits, and bearing the vessels swiftly on to the east and the west on long tacks, making the leaves in the woods flutter on their branchlets, and keeping the wild-brier bushes, growing on angles and points of the cliff, stretched out like long whip-cords wreathed in pink and green. There was nothing, too, of the stillness of the lowlands, for always one could hear the rustling and laughing of the forest, and the wash of the water on the pebbly beach. There were seldom any clouds in the summer sky, and those that were there were never of that soft, high-piled white downiness that belongs to summer clouds farther south. They came up in the west at evening in time for the sunset, or they lay along the east in the early morning, but they did not drift over the zenith in white laziness at noontide, or come together violently in sudden thunder-storms. They were sober clouds of quiet hue, and they seemed to know that they were not to have a prominent place in the summer procession of night, noon, and morning in that Northern sky, as though there was a law that the sun should have uninterrupted sway during the short season allotted to him. Anne walked in the woods as usual, but not far. Rast was gone. Rast always hurried everybody; left alone, she wandered slowly through the aisles of the arbor vitæ on the southern heights. The close ranks of these trees hardly made what is called a grove, for the flat green plats of foliage rose straight into the air, and did not arch or mingle with each other; a person walking there could always see the open sky above. But so dense was the thickness on each side that though the little paths with which the wood was intersected often ran close to each other, sometimes side by side, persons following them had no suspicion of each other's presence unless their voices betrayed them. In the hot sun the trees exhaled a strong aromatic fragrance, and as the currents of air did not penetrate their low green-walled aisles, it rested there, although up above everything was dancing along— butterflies, petals of the brier, waifs and strays from the forest, borne lakeward on the strong breeze. The atmosphere in these paths was so hot, still, and aromatic that now and then Anne loved to go there and steep herself in it. She used to tell Miss Lois that it made her feel as though she was an Egyptian princess who had been swathed in precious gums and spices for a thousand years.

Over on the other side of the island grew the great pines. These had two deeply worn Indian trails leading through them from north to south, not aimless, wandering little paths like those through the arbor vitæ, but one straight track from the village to the western shore, and another leading down to the spring on the beach. The cliffs on whose summit these pines grew were high and precipitous, overlooking deep water; a vessel could have sailed by so near the shore that a pebble thrown from above would have dropped upon her deck. With one arm round an old trunk, Anne often sat on the edge of these cliffs, looking down through the western pass. She had never felt any desire to leave the island, save that sometimes she had vague dreams of the tropics—visions of palm-trees and white lilies, the Pyramids and minarets, as fantastic as her dreams of Shakspeare. But she loved the island and the island trees; she loved the wild larches, the tall spires of the spruces bossed with lighter green, the gray pines, and the rings of the juniper. She had a peculiar feeling about trees. When she was a little girl she used to whisper to them how much she loved them, and even now she felt that they noticed her. Several times since these recent beginnings of care she had turned back and gone over part of the path a second time, because she felt that she had not been as observant as usual of her old friends, and that they would be grieved by the inattention. But this she never told.

There was, however, less and less time for walking in the woods; there was much to do at home, and she was faithful in doing it: every spring of the little household machinery felt her hand upon it, keeping it in order. The clothes she made for Tita and the boys, the dinners she provided from scanty materials, the locks and latches she improvised, the paint she mixed and applied, the cheerfulness and spirit with which she labored on day after day, were evidences of a great courage and unselfishness; and if the garments were not always successful as regards shape, nor the dinners always good, she was not disheartened, but bore the fault-findings cheerfully, promising to do better another time. For they all found fault with her, the boys loudly, Tita quietly, but with a calm pertinacity that always gained its little point. Even Miss Lois thought sometimes that Anne was careless, and told her so. For Miss Lois never concealed her light under a bushel. The New England woman believed that household labor held the first place among a woman's duties and privileges; and if the housekeeper spent fourteen hours out of the twenty-four in her task, she was but fulfilling her destiny as her Creator had intended. Anne was careless in the matter of piece-bags, having only two, whereas four, for linen and cotton, colors and black materials, were, as every one knew, absolutely necessary. There was also the systematic halving of sheets and resewing them at the first signs of wear somewhat neglected, and also a particularity as to the saving of string. Even the vaguely lost, thought-wandering father, too, finding that his comforts diminished, spoke of it, not with complaint so much as surprise; and then the daughter restored what he had missed at any sacrifice. All this was done without the recognition by anybody that it was much to do. Anne did not think of it in that way, and no one thought for her. For they were all so accustomed to her strong, cheerful spirit that they took what she did as a matter of course. Dr. Gaston understood something of the life led at the Agency; but he too had fallen into a way of resting upon the girl. She took a rapid survey of his small housekeeping whenever she came up to his cottage for a lesson, which was not as often now as formerly, owing to her manifold home duties. But Père Michaux shook his head. He believed that all should live their lives, and that one should not be a slave to others; that the young should be young, and that some natural simple pleasure should be put into each twenty-four hours. To all his flock he preached this doctrine. They might be poor, but children should be made happy; they might be poor, but youth should not be overwhelmed with the elders' cares; they might be poor, but they could have family love round the poorest hearthstone; and there was always time for a little pleasure, if they would seek it simply and moderately. The fine robust old man lived in an atmosphere above the subtleties of his leaner brethren in cities farther southward, and he was left untrammelled in his water diocese. Privileges are allowed to scouts preceding the army in an Indian country, because it is not every man who can be a scout. Not but that the old priest understood the mysteries, the introverted gaze, and indwelling thoughts that belong to one side of his religion; they were a part of his experience, and he knew their beauty and their dangers. They were good for some minds, he said; but it was a strange fact, which he had proved more than once during the long course of his ministry, that the minds which needed them the least loved them the most dearly, revelled in them, and clung to them with pertinacity, in spite of his efforts to turn them into more practical channels.

In all his broad parish he had no penitent so long-winded, exhaustive, and self-centred as little Tita. He took excellent care of the child, was very patient with her small ceremonies and solemnities, tried gently to lead her aright, and, with rare wisdom, in her own way, not his. But through it all, in his frequent visits to the Agency, and in the visits of the Douglas family to the hermitage, his real interest was centred in the Protestant sister, the tall unconscious young girl who had not yet, as he said to himself, begun to live. He shook his head often as he thought of her. "In France, even in England, she would be guarded," he said to himself; "but here! It is an excellent country, this America of theirs, for the pioneer, the New-Englander, the adventurer, and the farmer; but for a girl like Anne? No." And then, if Anne was present, and happened to meet his eye, she smiled back so frankly that he forgot his fears. "After all, I suppose there are hundreds of such girls in this country of theirs," he admitted, in a grumbling way, to his French mind, "coming up like flowers everywhere, without any guardianship at all. But it is all wrong, all wrong."

The priest generally placed America as a nation in the hands of possessive pronouns of the third person plural; it was a safe way of avoiding responsibility, and of being as scornful, without offending any one, as he pleased. One must have some outlet.

The summer wore on. Rast wrote frequently, and Anne, writing the first letters of her life in reply, found that she liked to write. She saved in her memory all kinds of things to tell him: about their favorite trees, about the birds that had nests in the garden that season, about the fishermen and their luck, about the unusual quantity of raspberries on the mainland, about the boys, about Tita. Something, too, about Bacon and Sir Thomas Browne, selections from whose volumes she was now reading under the direction of the chaplain. But she never put down any of her own thoughts, opinions, or feelings: her letters were curious examples of purely impersonal objective writing. Egotism, the under-current of most long letters as of most long conversations also, the telling of how this or that was due to us, affected us, was regarded by us, was prophesied, was commended, was objected to, was feared, was thoroughly understood, was held in restraint, was despised or scorned by us, and all our opinions on the subject, which, however important in itself, we present always surrounded by a large indefinite aureola of our own personality—this was entirely wanting in Anne Douglas's letters and conversation. Perhaps if she had had a girl friend of her own age she might have exchanged with her those little confidences, speculations, and fancies which are the first steps toward independent thought, those mazy whispered discussions in which girls delight, the beginnings of poetry and romance, the beginnings, in fact, of their own personal individual consciousness and life. But she had only Rast, and that was not the same thing. Rast always took the lead; and he had so many opinions of his own that there was no time to discuss, or even inquire about, hers.

In the mean time young Pronando was growing into manhood at the rate of a year in a month. His handsome face, fine bearing, generous ways, and incessant activity both of limb and brain gave him a leader's place among the Western students, who studied well, were careless in dress and manner, spent their money, according to the Western fashion, like princes, and had a peculiar dry humor of their own, delivered with lantern-jawed solemnity.

Young Pronando's preparation for college had been far better than that of most of his companions, owing to Dr. Gaston's care. The boy apprehended with great rapidity—apprehended perhaps more than he comprehended: he did not take the time to comprehend. He floated lightly down the stream of college life. His comrades liked him; the young Western professors, quick, unceremonious, practical men, were constantly running against little rocks which showed a better training than their own, and were therefore shy about finding fault with him; and the old president, an Eastern man, listened furtively to his Oxford pronunciation of Greek, and sighed in spite of himself and his large salary, hating the new bare white-painted flourishing institution over which he presided with a fresher hatred—the hatred of an exile. For there was not a tree on the college grounds: Young America always cuts down all his trees as a first step toward civilization; then, after an interregnum, when all the kings of the forest have been laid low, he sets out small saplings in whitewashed tree-boxes, and watches and tends them with fervor.

Rast learned rapidly—more things than one. The school for girls, which, singularly enough, in American towns, is always found flourishing close under the walls of a college, on the excellent and heroic principle, perhaps, of resisting temptation rather than fleeing from it, was situated here at convenient distance for a variety of strict rules on both sides, which gave interest and excitement to the day. Every morning Miss Corinna Haws and her sister girded themselves for the contest with fresh-rubbed spectacles and vigilance, and every morning the girls eluded them; that is, some of the girls, namely, Louise Ray and Kate and Fanny Meadows, cousins, rivals, and beauties of the Western river-country type, where the full life and languor of the South have fused somewhat the old inherited New England delicacy and fragile contours. These three young girls were all interested in handsome Rast in their fanciful, innocent, sentimental way. They glanced at him furtively in church on Sunday; they took walks of miles to catch a distant glimpse of him; but they would have run away like frightened fawns if he had approached nearer. They wrote notes which they never sent, but carried in their pockets for days; they had deep secrets to tell each other about how they had heard that somebody had told somebody else that the Juniors were going to play ball that afternoon in Payne's meadow, and that if they could only persuade Miss Miriam to go round by the hill, they could see them, and not so very far off either, only two wheat fields and the river between. Miss Miriam was the second Miss Haws, good-tempered and—near-sighted.

That the three girls were interested in one and the same person was part of the pleasure of the affair; each would have considered it a very dreary amusement to be interested all alone. The event of the summer, the comet of that season's sky, was an invitation to a small party in the town, where it was understood that young Pronando, with five or six of his companions, would be present. Miss Haws accepted occasional invitations for her pupils, marshalling them in a bevy, herself robed in pea-green silk, like an ancient mermaid: she said that it gave them dignity. It did. The stern dignity and silence almost solemn displayed by Rast's three worshippers when they found themselves actually in the same room with him were something preternatural. They moved stiffly, as if their elbows and ankles were out of joint; they spoke to each other cautiously in the lowest whispers, with their under jaws rigid, and a difficulty with their labials; they moved their eyes carefully everywhere save toward the point where he was standing, yet knew exactly where he was every moment of the time. When he approached the quadrille which was formed in one corner by Miss Haws's young ladies, dancing virginally by themselves, they squeezed each others' hands convulsively when they passed in "ladies' chain," in token of the great fact that he was looking on. When, after the dance, they walked up and down in the hall, arm in arm, they trod upon each other's slippers as sympathetic perception of the intensity of his presence on the stairs. What an evening! How crowded full of emotions! Yet the outward appearance was simply that of three shy, awkward girls in white muslin, keeping close together, and as far as possible from a handsome, gay-hearted, fast-talking youth who never once noticed them. O the imaginative, happy, shy fancies of foolish school-girls! It is a question whether the real love which comes later ever yields that wild, fairy-like romance which these early attachments exhale; the very element of reality weights it down, and makes it less heavenly fair.

At the end of the summer Rast had acquired a deep experience in life (so he thought), a downy little golden mustache, and a better opinion of himself than ever. The world is very kind to a handsome boy of frank and spirited bearing, one who looks as though he intended to mount and ride to victory. The proud vigor of such a youth is pleasant to tired eyes; he is so sure he will succeed! And most persons older, although knowing the world better and not so sure, give him as he passes a smile and friendly word, and wish him godspeed. It is not quite fair, perhaps, to other youths of equal merit but another bearing, yet Nature orders it so. The handsome, strong, confident boy who looks her in the face with daring courage wins from her always a fine starting-place in the race of life, which seems to advance him far beyond his companions. Seems; but the end is far away.

Rast did not return to the island during the summer vacation; Dr. Gaston wished him to continue his studies with a tutor, and as the little college town was now radiant with a mild summer gayety, the young man was willing to remain. He wrote to Anne frequently, giving abstracts of his life, lists of little events like statistics in a report. He did this regularly, and omitted nothing, for the letters were his conscience. When they were once written and sent, however, off he went to new pleasures. It must be added as well that he always sought the post-office eagerly for Anne's replies, and placed them in his pocket with satisfaction. They were sometimes unread, or half read, for days, awaiting a convenient season, but they were there.

Anne's letters were long, they were pleasant, they were never exciting—the very kind to keep; like friends who last a lifetime, but who never give us one quickened pulse. Alone in his room, or stretched on the grass under a tree, reading them, Rast felt himself strongly carried back to his old life on the island, and he did not resist the feeling. His plans for the future were as yet vague, but Anne was always a part of his dream.

But this youth lived so vigorously and fully and happily in the present that there was not much time for the future and for dreams. He seldom thought. What other people thought, he felt.

CHAPTER VI.

"Into the Silent Land!

Ah! who shall lead us thither?

Clouds in the evening sky more darkly
gather,

And shattered wrecks lie thicker on the
strand.

Who leads us with a gentle hand

Thither, O thither,

Into the Silent Land?

"O Land, O Land,

For all the broken-hearted,

The mildest herald by our fate allotted

Beckons, and with inverted torch doth stand

To lead us with a gentle hand

To the land of the great Departed—

Into the Silent Land!"

—Longfellow. *From the German.*

Early in September William Douglas failed suddenly. From taciturnity he sank into silence, from quiet into lethargy. He rose in the morning, but after that effort he became like a breathing statue, and sat all day in his arm-chair without stirring or noticing anything. If they brought him food he ate it, but he did not speak or answer their questions by motion or gesture. The fort surgeon was puzzled; it was evidently not paralysis. He was a new-comer on the island, and he asked many questions as to the past. Anne sincerely, Miss Lois resolutely, denied that there had ever been any trouble with the brain; Dr. Gaston drummed on the table, and answered sharply that all men of intellect were more or less mad. But the towns-people smiled, and tapped their foreheads significantly; and the new surgeon had noticed in the course of his experience that, with time for observation, the towns-people are generally right. So he gave a few medicines, ordered a generous diet, and looking about him for some friend of the family who could be trusted, selected at last Père Michaux. For Miss Lois would not treat him even civilly, bristling when he approached like a hedge-hog; and with her frank eyes meeting his, he found it impossible to speak to Anne. But he told Père Michaux the true state of his patient, and asked him to break the tidings to the family.

"He can not live long," he said.

"Is it so?" said Père Michaux. "God's will be done. Poor Anne!"

"An odd lot of children he has in that ramshackle old house of his," continued the surgeon. "Two sets, I should say."

"Yes; the second wife was a French girl."

"With Indian blood?"

"Yes."

"I thought so. Who is to have charge of them? The boys will take to the woods, I suppose, but that little Tita is an odd specimen. She would make quite a sensation in New York a few years later."

"May she never reach there!" said the old priest, fervently.

"Well, perhaps you are right. But who is to have the child?"

"Her sister will take charge of her."

"Miss Anne? Yes, she will do her best, of course; she is a fine, frank young Saxon. But I doubt if she understands that elfish little creature."

"She understands her better than we do," said the priest, with some heat.

"Ah? You know best, of course; I speak merely as an outsider," answered the new surgeon, going off about his business.

Père Michaux decided that he would tell Anne herself. He went to the house for the purpose, and called her out on the old piazza. But when she stood before him, her violet eyes meeting his without a suspicion of the tidings he brought, his heart failed him suddenly. He comprehended for the first time what it would be to her, and, making some chance inquiry, he asked to see Miss Lois, and turned away. Anne went in, and Miss Lois came out. The contrast between the priest and the New England woman was more marked than usual as they stood there facing each other on the old piazza, he less composed than he ordinarily was on account of what he had to tell. But it never occurred to him for a moment that Miss Lois would falter. Why should she? He told her. She sank down at his feet as though she had fallen there and died.

Alarmed, he bent over her, and in the twilight saw that she was not dead; her features were working strangely; her hands were clinched over her breast; her faded eyes stared at him behind the spectacles as though he were miles away. He tried to raise her. She struck at him almost fiercely. "Let me alone," she said, in a muffled voice. Then, still lying where she fell, she threw up her arms and wailed once or twice, not loudly, but with a struggling, inarticulate sound, as a person cries out in sleep. Poor old Lois! it was the last wail of her love. But even then she did not recognize it. Nor did the priest. Pale, with uncertain steps and shaking hands, yet tearless, the stricken woman raised herself by the aid of the bench, crossed the piazza, went down the path and into the street, Père Michaux's eyes following her in bewilderment. She was evidently going home, and her prim, angular shape looked strangely bare and uncovered in the lack of bonnet and shawl, for through all the years she had lived on the island she had never once been seen in the open air without them. The precision of her bonnet strings was a matter of conscience. The priest went away also. And thus it happened that Anne was not told at all.

When, late in the evening, Miss Lois returned, grayly pale, but quiet, as she entered the hall a cry met her ears and rang through the house. It had come sooner than any one expected. The sword of sorrow, which sooner or later must pierce all loving hearts, had entered Anne Douglas's breast. Her father was dead.

He had died suddenly, peacefully and without pain, passing away in sleep. Anne was with him, and Tita, jealously watchful to the last. No one else was in the room at the moment. Père Michaux, coming in, had been the first to perceive the change.

Tita drew away quickly to a distant corner, and kneeling down where she could still see everything that went on, began repeating prayers; but Anne, with a wild cry, threw herself down beside her dead, sobbing, holding his hand, and calling his name again and again. She would not believe that he was gone.

Ah, well, many of us know the sorrow. A daughter's love for a kind father is a peculiarly dependent, clinging affection; it is mixed with the careless happiness of childhood, which can never come again. Into the father's grave the daughter, sometimes a gray-haired woman, lays away forever the little pet names and memories which to all the rest of the world are but foolishness. Even though happy in her woman's lot, she weeps convulsively here for a while with a sorrow that nothing can comfort; no other love so protecting and unselfish will ever be hers again.

Anne was crushed by her grief; it seemed to those who watched her that she revealed a new nature in her sorrow. Dr. Gaston and Père Michaux spoke of it to each other, but could find little to say to the girl herself; she had, as it were, drifted beyond their reach, far out on an unknown sea. They prayed for her, and went silently away, only to come back within the hour and meet again on the threshold, recognizing each other's errand. They were troubled by the change in this young creature, upon whom they had all, in a certain way, depended. Singularly enough, Miss Lois did not seem to appreciate Anne's condition: she was suffering too deeply herself. The whole of her repressed nature was in revolt. But faithful to the unconscious secret of her life, she still thought the wild pain of her heart was "sorrow for a friend."

She went about as usual, attending to household tasks for both homes. She was unchanged, yet totally changed. There was a new tension about her mouth, and an unwonted silence, but her hands were as busy as ever. Days had passed after the funeral before she began to perceive, even slightly, the broken condition of Anne. The girl herself was the first to come back to the present, in the necessity for asking one of those sad questions which often raise their heads as soon as the coffin is borne away. "Miss Lois, there are bills to be paid, and I have no money. Do you know anything of our real income?"

The old habits of the elder woman stirred a little; but she answered, vaguely, "No."

"We must look through dear papa's papers," said Anne, her voice breaking as she spoke the name. "He received few letters, none at all lately; whatever he had, then, must be here."

Miss Lois assented, still silently, and the two began their task. Anne, with a quivering lip, unlocked her father's desk. William Douglas had not been a relic-loving man. He had lived, he had loved; but memory was sufficient for him; he needed no tokens. So, amid a hundred mementos of nature, they found nothing personal, not even a likeness of Anne's mother, or lock of her curling brown hair. And amid a mass of miscellaneous papers, writings on every philosophic and imaginative subject, they found but one relating to money—some figures jotted down, with a date affixed, the sum far from large, the date three years before. Below, a later line was added, as if (for the whole was vague) so much had gone, and this was the remainder; the date of this last line was eight months back.

"Perhaps this is it," said Anne; "perhaps this is what he had."

"I'm sure I don't know," said Miss Lois, mechanically.

They went on with the search, and at last came to a package tied in brown paper, which contained money; opening it, they counted the contents.

"Three hundred and ten dollars and eighty-five cents," said Anne.

Miss Lois took a pen and made a calculation, still with the manner of a machine. "That is about what would be left by this time, at the rate of the sums you have had, supposing the memorandum is what you think it is," she said, rubbing her forehead with a shadowy imitation of her old habit.

"It is a large sum," said Anne.

Nothing more was found. It appeared, therefore, that the five children of William Douglas were left alone in the world with exactly three hundred and ten dollars and eighty-five cents.

Dr. Gaston and Père Michaux learned the result that day; the story spread through the village and up to the fort. "I never heard anything so extraordinary in my life," said Mrs. Cromer. "That a man like Dr. Douglas should have gone on for the last four or five years deliberately living on his capital, seeing it go dollar by dollar, without making one effort to save it, or to earn an income—a father with children! I shall always believe, after this, that the villagers were right, and that his mind was affected."

The chaplain stopped these comments gruffly, and the fort ladies forgave him on account of the tremor in his voice. He left them, and went across to his little book-clogged cottage with the first indications of age showing in his gait.

"It is a blow to him; he is very fond of Anne, and hoped everything for her," said Mrs. Bryden. "I presume he would adopt her if he could; but there are the other children."

"They might go to their mother's relatives, I should think," said Mrs. Rankin.

"They could, but Anne will not allow it. You will see."

"I suppose our good chaplain has nothing to bequeath, even if he should adopt Anne?"

"No, he has no property, and has saved nothing from his little salary; it has all gone into books," answered the colonel's wife.

Another week passed. By that time Dr. Gaston and Père Michaux together had brought the reality clearly before Anne's eyes; for the girl had heretofore held such small sums of money in her hands at any one time that the amount found in the desk had seemed to her large. Père Michaux began the small list of resources by proposing that the four children should go at once to their uncle, their mother's brother, who was willing to receive them and give them a home, such as it was, among his own brood of black-eyed little ones. Anne decidedly refused. Dr. Gaston then asked her to come to him, and be his dear daughter as long as he lived.

"I must not come with them, and I can not come without them," was Anne's reply.

There remained Miss Lois. But she seemed entirely unconscious of any pressing necessity for haste in regard to the affairs of the little household, coming and going as usual, but without words; while people round her, with that virtuous readiness as to the duties of their neighbors which is so helpful in a wicked world, said loudly and frequently that she was the nearest friend, and ought to do— Here followed a variety of suggestions, which amounted in the aggregate to everything. At last, as often happens, it was an outside voice that brought the truth before her.

"And what are you thinking of doing, dear Miss Lois, for the five poor orphans?" asked the second Miss Macdougall while paying a visit of general condolence at the church-house.

"Why, what should I do?" said Miss Lois, with a faint remembrance of her old vigilant pride. "They want nothing."

"They want nothing! And not one hundred dollars apiece for them in the wide world!" exclaimed Miss Jean.

"Surely you're joking, my dear. Here's Dr. Gaston wishing to take Anne, as is most kind and natural; but she will not leave those children. Although why they should not go back to the stratum from which they came is a mystery to me. She can never make anything of them: mark my words."

Miss Jean paused; but whether Miss Lois marked her words or not, she made no response, but sat gazing straight at the wall. Miss Jean, however, knew her duty, and did it like a heroine of old. "We thought, perhaps, dear Miss Lois, that *you* would like to take them for a time," she said, "seeing that Anne has proved herself so obstinate as to the other arrangements proposed. The village has thought so generally, and I am not the one to hide it from you, having been taught by my lamented parent to honor and abide by veracity the most precise. We could all help you a little in clothing them for the present, and we will contribute to their support a fish now and then, a bag of meal, a barrel of potatoes, which we would do gladly—right gladly, I do assure you. For no one likes to think of Dr. Douglas's children being on the town."

The homely phrase roused Miss Lois at last. "What in the world are you talking about, Jean Macdougall?" she exclaimed, in wrath. "On the town! Are you clean daft? On the town, indeed! Clear out of my house this moment, you lying, evil-speaking woman!"

The second Miss Macdougall rose in majesty, and drew her black silk visite round her. "Of whom ye are speaking, Miss Hinsdale, I knaw not," she said, growing Scotch in her anger; "but I believe ye hae lost your wits. I tak' my departure freely, and not as sent by one who has strangely forgotten the demeanor of a leddy."

With hands folded, she swept toward the door, all the flowers on her dignified bonnet swaying perceptibly. Pausing on the threshold, she added, "As a gude Christian, and a keeper of my word, I still say, Miss Hinsdale, in spite of insults, that in the matter of a fish or two, or a barrel of potatoes now and then, ye can count upon the Macdougalls."

Left alone, Miss Lois put on her shawl and bonnet with feverish haste, and went over to the Agency. Anne was in the sitting-room, and the children were with her.

"Anne, of course you and the children are coming to live with me whenever you think it best to leave this house," said Miss Lois, appearing on the threshold like an excited ghost in spectacles. "You never thought or planned anything else, I hope?"

"No," said Anne, frankly, "I did not—at least for the present. I knew you would help us, Miss Lois, although you did not speak."

"Speak! was there any need of speaking?" said the elder woman, bursting into a few dry, harsh sobs. "You are all I have in the world, Anne. How could you mistrust me?"

"I did not," said Anne.

And then the two women kissed each other, and it was all understood without further words. And thus, through the intervention of the second Miss Macdougall (who found herself ill rewarded for her pains), Lois Hinsdale came out from the watch-chamber of her dead to real life again, took up her burden, and went on.

Anne now unfolded her plans, for she had been obliged to invent plans: necessity forced her forward. "We must all come to you for a time, dear Miss Lois; but I am young and strong, and I can work. I wish to educate the boys as father would have wished them educated. Do you ask what I can do? I think—that is, I hope—that I can teach." Then, in a lower voice, she added, "I promised father that I would do all I could for the children, and I shall keep my promise."

Miss Lois's eyes filled with tears. But the effect of the loving emotion was only to redden the lids, and make the orbs beneath look smaller and more unbeautiful than before.

For to be born into life with small, inexpressive eyes is like being born dumb. One may have a heart full of feeling, but the world will not believe it. Pass on, then, Martha, with your pale little orbs; leave the feeling to Beatrice with her deep brown glance, to Agnes with her pure blue gaze, to Isabel with hers of passionate splendor. The world does not believe you have any especial feelings, poor Martha. Then do not have them, if you can help it—and pass on.

"I have been thinking deeply," continued Anne, "and I have consulted Dr. Gaston. He says that I have a good education, but probably an old-fashioned one; at least the fort ladies told him that it would be so considered. It seems that what I need is a 'polish of modern accomplishments.' That is what he called it. Now, to obtain a teacher's place, I must have this, and I can not obtain it here." She paused; and then, like one who rides forward on a solitary charge, added, "I am going to write to Miss Vanhorn."

"A dragon!" said Miss Lois, knitting fiercely. Then added, after a moment, "A positive demon of pride." Then, after another silence, she said, sternly, "She broke your mother's heart, Anne Douglas, and she will break yours."

"I hope not," said the girl, her voice trembling a little; for her sorrow was still very near the surface. "She is old now, and perhaps more gentle. At any rate, she is my only living relative, and to her I must appeal."

"How do you know she is alive? The world would be well rid of such a wicked fiend," pursued Miss Lois, quoting unconsciously from Anne's forest Juliet.

"She was living last year, for father spoke of her."

"I did not know he ever spoke of her."

"Only in answer to my questions; for I had found her address, written in mother's handwriting, in an old note-book. She brought up my mother, you know, and was once very fond of her."

"So fond of her that she killed her. If poor Alida had not had that strain upon her, she might have been alive at this day," said Miss Lois.

Anne's self-control left her now, and she began to sob like a child. "Do not make it harder for me than it is," she said, amid her tears. "I *must* ask her; and if she should consent to help me, it will be grief enough to leave you all, without these cruel memories added. She is old: who knows but that she may be longing to repair the harm she did?"

"Can the leopard change his spots?" said Miss Lois, sternly. "But what do you mean by leaving us all? What do you intend to do?"

"I intend to ask her either to use her influence in obtaining a teacher's place for me immediately, or if I am not, in her opinion, qualified, to give me the proper masters for one year. I would study very hard; she would not be burdened with me long."

"And the proper masters are not here, of course?"

"No; at the East."

Miss Lois stopped in the middle of a round, took off her spectacles, rolled up her knitting-work slowly and tightly as though it was never to be unrolled again, and pinned it together with decision; she was pinning in also a vast resolution. Then she looked at Anne in silence for several minutes, saw the tear-dimmed eyes and tired, anxious face, the appealing glance of William Douglas's child.

"I have not one word to say against it," she remarked at last, breaking the silence; and then she walked out of the house and went homeward.

It was a hard battle for her. She was to be left with the four brown-skinned children, for whom she had always felt unconquerable aversion, while the one child whom she loved—Anne—was to go far away. It was a revival of the bitter old feeling against Angélique Lafontaine, the artful minx who had entrapped William Douglas to his ruin. In truth, however, there had been very little art about Angélique; nor was Douglas by any means a rich prey. But women always attribute wonderful powers of strategy to a successful rival, even although by the same ratio they reduce the bridegroom to a condition approaching idiocy; for anything is better than the supposition that he was a free agent, and sought his fate from the love of it.

The thought of Anne's going was dreadful to Miss Lois; yet her long-headed New England thrift and calculation saw chances in that future which Anne did not see. "The old wretch has money, and no near heirs," she said to herself, "why should she not take a fancy to this grandniece? Anne has no such idea, but her friends should, therefore, have it for her." Still, the tears would rise and dim her spectacles as she thought of the parting. She took off the gold-rimmed glasses and rubbed them vigorously. "One thing is certain," she added, to herself, as a sort of comfort, "Tita will have to do her mummeries in the garden after this."

Poor old Lois! in these petty annoyances and heavy cures her great grief was to be pressed down into a subdued under-current, no longer to be indulged or made much of even by herself.

Anne knew but little of her grandaunt. William Douglas would not speak of what was the most bitter memory of his life. The address in the old note-book, in her mother's unformed girlish handwriting, was her only guide. She knew that Miss Vanhorn was obstinate and ill-tempered; she knew that she had discarded her mother on account of her disobedient marriage, and had remained harsh and unforgiving to the last. And this was all she knew. But she had no choice. Hoping, praying for the best, she wrote her letter, and sent it on its way. Then they all waited. For Père Michaux had been taken into the conference also, and had given hearty approval to Anne's idea—so hearty, indeed, that both the chaplain and Miss Lois looked upon him with disfavor. What did he mean? He did not say what he meant, but returned to his hermitage cheerfully. Dr. Gaston, not so cheerfully, brought out his hardest chess problems, and tried to pass away the time in mathematical combinations of the deepest kind. Miss Lois, however, had combinations at hand of another sort. No sooner was the letter gone than she advanced a series of conjectures which did honor even to her New England origin.

The first was that Miss Vanhorn had gone abroad: those old New-Yorkers were "capable of wishing to ride on camels, even"; she added, from habit, "through the eye of a needle." The next day she decided that paralysis would be the trouble: those old New-Yorkers were "often stricken down in that way, owing to their high living and desperate wine-bibbing." Anne need give no more thought to her letter; Miss Vanhorn would not be able even to read it. The third day, Miss Vanhorn would read the letter, but would immediately throw it on the floor and stamp on it: those old New-Yorkers "had terrible tempers," and were "known to swear like troopers even on the slightest provocation." The fourth day, Miss Vanhorn was mad; the fifth day, she was married; the sixth, she was dead: those old New-Yorkers having tendencies toward insanity, matrimony, and death which, Miss Lois averred, were known to all the world, and indisputable. That she herself had never been in New York in her life made no difference in her certainties: women like Miss Lois are always sure they know all about New York.

Anne, weary and anxious, and forced to hear all these probabilities, began at last to picture her grandaunt as a sort of human kaleidoscope, falling into new and more fantastic combinations at a moment's notice.

They had allowed two weeks for the letter to reach the island, always supposing that Miss Vanhorn was not on a camel, paralyzed, obstinate, mad, married, or dead. But on the tenth day the letter came. Anne took it with a hand that trembled. Dr. Gaston was present, and Miss Lois, but neither of them comprehended her feelings. She felt that she was now to be confronted by an assent which would strain her heart-strings almost to snapping, yet be ultimately for the best, or by a refusal which would fill her poor heart with joy, although at the same time pressing down upon her shoulders a heavy, almost hopeless, weight of care. The two could not enter into her feelings, because in the depths of their hearts they both resented her willingness to leave them. They never said this to each other, they never said it to themselves; yet they both felt it with the unconscious selfishness of those who are growing old, especially when their world is narrowed down to one or two loving young hearts. They did not realize that it was as hard for her to go as it was for them to let her go; they did not realize what a supreme effort of courage it required to make this young girl go out alone into the wide world, and face its vastness and its strangeness; they did not realize how she loved them, and how every tree, every rock of the island, also, was dear to her strongly loving, concentrated heart.

After her father's death Anne had been for a time passive, swept away by grief as a dead leaf on the wind. But cold necessity came and stood by her bedside silently and stonily, and looked at her until, recalling her promise, she rose, choked back her sorrow, and returned to common life and duty with an aching but resolute heart. In the effort she made to speak at all it was no wonder that she spoke quietly, almost coldly; having, after sleepless nights of sorrow, nerved herself to bear the great change in her lot, should it come to her, could she trust herself to say that she was sorry to go? Sorry!—when her whole heart was one pain!

The letter was as follows:

"Grandniece Anne,—I did not know that you were in existence. I have read your letter, and have now to say the following. Your mother willfully disobeyed me, and died. I, meanwhile, an old woman, remain as strong as ever.

"While I recognize no legal claim upon me (I having long since attended to the future disposal of all my property according to my own wishes), I am willing to help you to a certain extent, as I would help any industrious young girl asking for assistance. If what you say of your education is true, you need only what are called modern accomplishments (of which I personally have small opinion, a grimacing in French and a squalling in Italian being not to my taste) to make you a fairly well qualified teacher in an average country boarding-school, which is all you can expect. You may, therefore, come to New York at my expense, and enter Madame Moreau's establishment, where, as I understand, the extreme of everything called 'accomplishment' is taught, and much nonsense learned in the latest style. You may remain one year; not longer. And I advise you to improve the time, as nothing more will be done for you by me. You will bring your own clothes, but I will pay for your books. I send no money now, but will refund your travelling expenses (of which you will keep strict account, without extras) upon your arrival in the city, which must not be later than the last of October. Go directly to Madame Moreau's (the address is inclosed), and remember that you are simply Anne Douglas, and not a relative of your obedient servant,

Katharine Vanhorn."

Anne, who had read the letter aloud in a low voice, now laid it down, and looked palely at her two old friends.

"A hard letter," said the chaplain, indignantly. "My child, remain with us. We will think of some other plan for you. Let the proud, cold-hearted old woman go."

"I told you how it would be," said Miss Lois, a bright spot of red on each cheek-bone. "She was cruel to your mother before you, and she will be cruel to you. You must give it up."

"No," said Anne, slowly, raising the letter and replacing it in its envelope; "it is a matter in which I have no choice. She gives me the year at school, as you see, and—there are the children. I promised father, and I must keep the promise. Do not make me falter, dear friends, for—I *must* go." And unable longer to keep back the tears, she hurriedly left the room.

Dr. Gaston, without a word, took his old felt hat and went home. Miss Lois sat staring vaguely at the window-pane, until she became conscious that some one was coming up the path, and that "some one" Père Michaux. She too then went hurriedly homeward, by the back way, in order to avoid him. The old priest, coming in, found the house deserted. Anne was on her knees in her own room, sobbing as if her heart would break; but the walls were thick, and he could not hear her.

Then Tita came in. "Annet is going away," she said, softly; "she is going to school. The letter came to-day."

"So Miss Vanhorn consents, does she? Excellent! excellent!" said Père Michaux, rubbing his hands, his eyes expressing a hearty satisfaction.

"When will you say 'Excellent! excellent!' about me?" said Tita, jealously.

"Before long, I hope," said the priest, patting her small head.

"But are you sure, mon père?"

"Well, yes," said Père Michaux, "on the whole, I am."

He smiled, and the child smiled also; but with a deep quiet triumph remarkable in one so young.

CHAPTER VII.

"To all appearance it was chiefly by Accident, and the grace of Nature."—Carlyle.

It was still September; for great sorrows come, graves are made and turfed over, and yet the month is not out. Anne had written her letter immediately, accepting her grandaunt's offer, and Père Michaux gave her his approval and praise; but the others did not, could not, and she suffered from their silence. It made, however, no change in her purpose; she went about her tasks steadily, toiling all day over the children's clothes, for she had used part of the money in her hands to make them comfortable, and part was to be given to Miss Lois. Her own garments troubled her little; two strong, plain black gowns she considered amply sufficient. Into the midst of all this swift sewing suddenly one day came Rast.

"Why did I do it?" he said, in answer to everybody. "Do you suppose I was going to let Annet go away for a whole long year without saying even good-by? Of course not."

"It is very kind," said Anne, her tired eyes resting on his handsome face gratefully, her sewing for the moment cast aside. Her friends had not been overkind to her lately, and she was deeply touched by this proof of attachment from her old playmate and companion. Rast expressed his affection, as usual, in his own way. He did not say that he had come back to the island because he wished to see her, but because he knew that she wished to see him. And Anne willingly agreed. Dr. Gaston, as guardian of this runaway collegian, gave him a long lecture on his escapade and its consequences, his interrupted studies, a long train of disasters to follow being pictured with stern distinctness. Rast listened to the sermon, or rather sat through it, without impatience: he had a fine sunny temper, and few things troubled him. He seldom gave any attention to subtleties of meaning, or under-currents, but took the surface impression, and answered it promptly, often putting to rout by his directness trains of reasoning much deeper than his own. So now all he said was, "I could not help coming, sir, because Annet is going away; I wanted to see her." And the old man was silenced in spite of himself.

As he was there, and it could not be helped, Rast, by common consent of the island, was allowed to spend several days unmolested among his old haunts. Then they all began to grow restive, to ask questions, and to speak of the different boats. For the public of small villages has always a singular impatience as to anything like uncertainty in the date of departure of its guests. Many a miniature community has been stirred into heat because it could not find out the day and hour when Mrs. Blank would terminate her visit at her friend's mansion, and with her trunk and bag depart on her way to the railway station; and this not because the community has any objection to Mrs. Blank, or any wish to have her depart, but simply because if she is going, they wish to know *when*, and have it settled. The few days over, Rast himself was not unwilling to go. He had seen Anne, and Anne was pressed with work, and so constantly threatened by grief that she had to hold it down with an iron effort at almost every moment. If she kept her eyes free from tears and her voice steady, she did all she could; she had no idea that Rast expected more. Rast meanwhile had learned clearly that he was a remarkably handsome, brilliant young fellow, and that the whole world was before him where to choose. He was fond of Anne; the best feelings of his nature and the associations of his whole boyhood's life were twined round her; and yet he was conscious that he had always been very kind to her, and this coming back to the island on purpose to see her—that was remarkably kind. He was glad to do it, of course; but she must appreciate it. He began now to feel that as he had seen her, and as he could not in any case stay until she went, he might as well go. He yielded, therefore, to the first suggestion of the higher powers, saying, however, frankly, and with real feeling, that it was hard to bid farewell for so long a time to his old playmate, and that he did not know how he could endure the separation. As the last words were spoken it was Rast who had tear-dimmed eyes; it was Rast's voice that faltered. Anne was calm, and her calmness annoyed him. He would have liked a more demonstrative sorrow. But as he went down the long path on his way to the pier where the steamboat was waiting, the first whistle having already sounded, he forgot everything save his affection for her and the loneliness in store for him after her departure. While she was on their island she seemed near, but New York was another world.

49

Down in the shadow of the great gate there was an ancient little cherry-tree, low and gnarled, which thrust one crooked arm across the path above the heads of the passers-by. As Rast approached he saw in the dusky twilight a small figure perched upon this bough, and recognized Tita.

"Is that you, child?" he said, pausing and looking up. She answered by dropping into his arms like a kitten, and clinging to him mutely, with her face hidden on his shoulder.

"What an affectionate little creature she is, after all!" he thought, stroking her dark hair. Then, after saying good-by, and giving her a kiss, he disengaged himself without much ceremony, and telling her to be a good girl and mind Miss Lois during the winter, he hurried down to the pier, the second whistle summoning all loiterers on board with shrill harshness. Tita, left alone, looked at her arms, reddened by the force with which she had resisted his efforts to unclasp them. They had been pressed so closely against the rough woollen cloth of his coat that the brown flesh showed the mark of the diagonal pattern.

"It is a hurt," she said, passionately—"it is a hurt." Her eyes flashed, and she shook her small fist at the retreating figure. Then, as the whistle sounded a third time, she climbed quickly to the top of the great gates, and sat there high in the air while the steamer backed out from the piers, turned round, and started westward through the Straits, nothing now save a moving line of lights, the short Northern twilight having faded into night.

When the long sad day of parting was at last over, and everything done that her hands could find to do in that amount of time, Anne, in her own room alone, let her feelings come forth; she was the only watcher in the old house, every other eye was closed in sleep. These moments alone at night, when she allowed herself to weep and think, were like breathing times; then her sorrows came forth. According to her nature, she did not fear or brood upon her own future so much as upon the future of the children; the love in her heart made it seem to her a bitter fate to be forced to leave them and the island. The prospect of the long journey, the city school, the harsh aunt, did not dishearten her; they were but parts of her duty, the duty of her life. It was after midnight; still she sat there. The old shutters, which had been rattling for some time, broke their fastenings, and came violently against the panes with a sound like the report of a pistol.

"The wind is rising," she thought, vaguely, as she rose to fasten them, opening one of the windows for the purpose. In rushed the blast, blowing out the candle, driving books and papers across the floor, and whirling the girl's long loosened hair over her face and round her arms like the coils of a boa-constrictor. Blinded, breathless, she hastily let down the sash again, and peered through the small wrinkled panes. A few stars were visible between the light clouds which drove rapidly from north to south in long regular lines like bars, giving a singular appearance to the sky, which the girl recognized at once, and in the recognition came back to present life. "The equinoctial," she said to herself; "and one of the worst. Where can the *Huron* be? Has she had time to reach the shelter of the islands?"

The *Huron* was the steamer which had carried Rast away at twilight. She was a good boat and stanch. But Anne knew that craft as stanch had been wrecked and driven ashore during these fierce autumn gales which sweep over the chain of lakes suddenly, and strew their coasts with fragments of vessels, and steamers also, from the head of Superior to the foot of Ontario. If there was more sea-room, vessels might escape; if there were better harbors, steamers might seek port; in a gale, an ocean captain has twenty chances for his vessel where the lake captain has one. Anne stood with her face pressed against the window for a long time; the force of the wind increased. She took her candle and went across to a side room whose windows commanded the western pass: she hoped that she might see the lights of the steamer coming back, seeking the shelter of the island before the worst came. But all was dark. She returned to her room, and tried to sleep, but could not. Dawn found her at the window, wakeful and anxious. There was to be no sun that day, only a yellow white light. She knelt down and prayed; then she rose, and braided anew her thick brown hair. When she entered the sitting-room the vivid rose freshness which always came to her in the early morning was only slightly paled by her vigil, and her face seemed as usual to the boys, who were waiting for her. Before breakfast was ready, Miss Lois arrived, tightly swathed in a shawl and veils, and carrying a large basket.

"There is fresh gingerbread in there," she said; "I thought the boys might like some; and—it will be an excellent day to finish those jackets, Anne. No danger of interruption."

She did not mention the gale or Rast; neither did Anne. They sat down to breakfast with the boys, and talked about thread and buttons. But, while they were eating, Louis exclaimed, "Why, there's Dr. Gaston!" and looking up, they saw the chaplain struggling to keep his hat in place as he came up the path sideways, fighting the wind.

"He should just have wrapped himself up, and scudded before it as I did," said Miss Lois.

Anne ran to open the door, and the old clergyman came panting in.

"It is such a miserable day that I thought you would like to have that dictionary, dear; so I brought it down to you," he said, laying the heavy volume on the table.

"Thanks. Have you had breakfast?" said Anne.

"Well, no. I thought I would come without waiting for it this morning, in order that you might have the book, you know. What! *you* here, Miss Lois?"

"Yes, sir. I came to help Anne. We are going to have a good long day at these jackets," replied Miss Lois, briskly.

They all sat down at the table again, and Gabriel was going to the kitchen for hot potatoes, when he spied another figure struggling through the gate and driving up the long path. "Père Michaux!" he cried, running to open the door.

In another moment the priest had entered, and was greeting them cheerfully. "As I staid in town overnight, I thought, Anne, that I would come up and look over those books. It is a good day for it; there will be no interruption. I think I shall find a number of volumes which I may wish to purchase."

"It is very kind; I shall like to think of my dear father's books in your hands. But have you breakfasted?"

No, the priest acknowledged that he had not. In truth, he was not hungry when he rose; but now that he saw the table spread, he thought he might eat something after all.

So they sat down again, and Louis went out to help Gabriel bring in more coffee, potatoes, and eggs. There was a good deal of noise with the plates, a good deal of passing to and fro the milk, cream, butter, and salt; a good deal of talking on rather a high key; a great many questions and answers whose irrelevancy nobody noticed. Dr. Gaston told a long story, and forgot the point; but Miss Lois laughed as heartily as though it had been acutely present. Père Michaux then brought up the venerable subject of the lost grave of Father Marquette; and the others entered into it with the enthusiasm of resurrectionists, and as though they had never heard of it before, Miss Lois and Dr. Gaston even seeming to be pitted against each other in the amount of interest they showed concerning the dead Jesuit. Anne said little; in truth, there was no space left for her, the others keeping up so brisk a fire of phrases. It was not until Tita, coming into the room, remarked, as she warmed her hands, that breakfast was unusually early, that any stop was made, and then all the talkers fell upon her directly, in lieu of Father Marquette. Miss Lois could not imagine what she meant. It was sad, indeed, to see such laziness in so young a child. Before long she would be asking for breakfast in bed! Dr. Gaston scouted the idea that it was early; he had often been down in the village an hour earlier. It was a fine bracing morning for a walk.

All this time the high ceaseless whistle of the wind, the roar of the water on the beach, the banging to and fro of the shutters here and there on the wide rambling old mansion, the creaking of the near trees that brushed its sides, and the hundred other noises of the gale, made the room seem strange and uncomfortable; every now and then the solid old frame-work vibrated as a new blast struck it, and through the floor and patched carpet puffs of cold air came up into the room and swept over their feet. All their voices were pitched high to overcome these sounds.

Tita listened to the remarks addressed to her, noted the pretense of bustle and hearty appetite, and then, turning to the window, she said, during a momentary lull in the storm, "I do not wonder that you can not eat, when poor Rast is somewhere on that black water."

Dr. Gaston pushed away his plate, Miss Lois sat staring at the wall with her lips tightly compressed, while Anne covered her face with her hands to keep back the tears. Père Michaux rose and began to walk up and down the room; for a moment, besides his step, there was no sound save the roar of the storm. Tita's words had ended all pretense, clothed their fear in language, and set it up in their midst. From that moment, through the long day, there was no more disguise; every cloud, every great wave, was watched, every fresh fierce blast swept through four anxious hearts. They were very silent now, and as the storm grew wilder, even the boys became awed, and curled themselves together on the broad window-seat, speaking in whispers. At noon a vessel drove by under bare poles; she seemed to be unmanageable, and they could see the signals of the sailors as they passed the island. But there was no life-boat, and nothing else could live in that sea. At two o'clock a large bark came into view, and ran ashore on the reef opposite; there she lay, pounding to pieces for two hours. They saw the crew try to launch the boats; one was broken into fragments in a moment, then another. The third and last floated, filled with humanity, and in two minutes she also was swamped, and dark objects that they knew were men were sucked under. Then the hull of a schooner, with one mast standing, drove aimlessly by, so near the shore that with the glass they could see the features of the sailors lashed to the pole.

"Oh! if we could but save them!" said Anne. "How near they are!" But even as she spoke the mast fell, and they saw the poor fellows drown before their eyes.

At four the *Huron* came into sight from the western pass, laboring heavily, fighting her way along inch by inch, but advancing. "Thanks be to the Lord for this!" said the chaplain, fervently. Père Michaux took off his velvet cap, and reverently made the sign of the cross.

"'Twouldn't be any harm to sing a hymn, I guess," said Miss Lois, wiping her eyes. Then Anne sang the "De Profundis." Amid the storm all the voices rose together, the children and Miss Lois and the two priests joining in the old psalm of King David, which belongs to all alike, Romanist and Protestant, Jew and Christian, bond and free.

"I do feel better," said Miss Lois. "But the steamer is still far off."

"The danger will be when she attempts to turn," said Père Michaux.

They all stood at the windows watching the boat as she rolled and pitched in the heavy sea, seeming half the time to make no headway at all, but on the contrary to be beaten back, yet doggedly persisting. At five o'clock she had reached the point where she must turn and run the gauntlet in order to enter port, with the gale striking full upon her side. Every front window in the village now held gazing faces, and along the piers men were clustered under the lee of the warehouses with ropes and hooks, waiting to see what they could do. The steamer seemed to hesitate a moment, and was driven back. Then she turned sharply and started in toward the piers with all steam on. The watchers at the Agency held their breath. For a moment or two she advanced rapidly, then the wind struck her, and she careened until her smoke-stacks seemed almost to touch the water. The boys cried out; Miss Lois clasped her hands. But the boat had righted herself again by changing her course, and was now drifting back to her old station. Again and again she made the attempt, now coming slowly, now with all the sudden speed she could muster; but she never advanced far before the lurch came, throwing her on her side, with one paddle-wheel in the air, and straining every timber in her frame. After half an hour of this work she drew off, and began to ply slowly up and down under the partial shelter of the little island opposite, as if resting. But there was not a place where she could cast anchor, nor any safety in flight; the gale would outlast the night, and the village harbor was her best hope. The wind was increasing, the afternoon sinking into night; every one on the island and on board also knew that when darkness fell, the danger, already great, would be trebled. Menacing and near on every side were long low shore-lines, which looked harmless enough, yet held in their sands the bones of many a drowned man, the ribs of many a vessel.

"Why doesn't she make another trial?" said Dr. Gaston, feverishly wiping his eyeglasses. "There is no use in running up and down under that island any longer."

"The captain is probably making everything ready for a final attempt," answered Père Michaux.

And so it seemed, for, after a few more minutes had passed, the steamer left her shelter, and proceeded cautiously down to the end of the little island, keeping as closely in shore as she could, climbing each wave with her bows, and then pitching down into the depth on the other side, until it seemed as if her hind-quarters must be broken off, being too long to fit into the watery hollows under her. Having reached the end of the islet, she paused, and slowly turned.

"Now for it," said Père Michaux.

It was sunset-time in pleasant parts of the land; here the raw, cold, yellow light, which had not varied since early morning, giving a peculiar distinctness to all objects near or far, grew more clear for a few moments—the effect, perhaps, of the after-glow behind the clouds which had covered the sky all day unmoved, fitting as closely as the cover upon a dish. As the steamer started out into the channel, those on shore could see that the passengers were gathered on the deck as if prepared for the worst. They were all there, even the children. But now no one thought any more, only watched; no one spoke, only breathed. The steamer was full in the gale, and on her side. Yet she kept along, righting herself a little now and then, and then careening anew. It seemed as though she would not be able to make headway with her one wheel, but she did. Then the islanders began to fear that she would be driven by too far out; but the captain had allowed for that. In a few seconds more it became evident that she would just brush the end of the longest pier, with nothing to spare. Then the men on shore ran down, the wind almost taking them off their feet, with ropes, chains, grappling-irons, and whatever they could lay their hands on. The steamer, now unmanageable, was drifting rapidly toward them on her side, the passengers clinging to her hurricane-deck and to the railings. A great wave washed over her when not twenty feet from the pier, bearing off several persons, who struggled in the water a moment, and then disappeared. Anne covered her eyes with her hands, and prayed that Rast might not be among these. When she looked again, the boat was fastened by two, by ten, by twenty, ropes and chains to the end of the pier, bows on, and pulling at her halters like an unmanageable steed, while women were throwing their children into the arms of those below, and men were jumping madly over, at the risk of breaking their ankle-bones. Anything to be on the blessed shore! In three minutes a hundred persons were on the pier, and Rast among them. Anne, Dr. Gaston, Père Michaux, Miss Lois, and the children all recognized his figure instantly, and the two old men started down through the storm to meet him, in their excitement running along like school-boys, hand in hand.

Rast was safe. They brought him home to the Agency in triumph, and placed him in a chair before the fire. They all wanted to touch him, in order to feel that he was really there, to be glad over him, to make much of him; they all talked together. Anne came to his side with tender affection. He was pale and moved. Instinctively and naturally as a child turns to its mother he turned to her, and, before them all, laid his head down upon her shoulder, and clung to her without speaking. The elders drew away a little; the boys stopped their clamor. Only Tita kept her place by the youth's side, and frowned darkly on the others.

Then they broke into a group again. Rast recovered himself, Dr. Gaston began to make puns, and Père Michaux and Miss Lois revived the subject of Father Marquette as a safe ladder by which they could all come down to common life again. A visit to the kitchen was made, and a grand repast, dinner and supper combined, was proposed and carried into effect by Miss Lois, Père Michaux, and the Irish soldier's wife, the three boys acting as volunteers. Even Dr. Gaston found his way to the distant sanctuary through the series of empty rooms that preceded it, and proffering his services, was set to toasting bread—a duty he accomplished by attentively burning one side of every slice, and forgetting the other, so that there was a wide latitude of choice, and all tastes were suited. With his wig pushed back, and his cheery face scarlet from the heat, he presented a fine contrast to Père Michaux, who, quietly and deliberately as usual, was seasoning a stew with scientific care, while Miss Lois, beating eggs, harried the Irish soldier's wife until she ran to and fro, at her wits' end.

Tita kept guard in the sitting-room, where Anne had been decisively ordered to remain and entertain Rast; the child sat in her corner, watching them, her eyes narrowed under their partly closed lids. Rast had now recovered his usual spirits, and talked gayly; Anne did not say much, but leaned back in her chair listening, thankfully quiet and happy. The evening was radiant with contentment; it was midnight when they separated. The gale was then as wild as ever; but who cared now whether the old house shook?

Rast was safe.

At the end of the following day at last the wind ceased: twenty-two wrecks were counted in the Straits alone, with many lives lost. The dead sailors were washed ashore on the island beaches and down the coast, and buried in the sands where they were found. The friends of those who had been washed overboard from the steamer came up and searched for their bodies up and down the shores for miles; some found their lost, others, after days of watching in vain, went away sorrowing, thinking, with a new idea of its significance, of that time "when the sea shall give up her dead."

After the storm came halcyon days. The trees now showed those brilliant hues of the American autumn which as yet no native poet has so strongly described, no native artist so vividly painted, that the older nations across the ocean have fit idea of their splendor. Here, in the North, the scarlet, orange, and crimson trees were mingled with pines, which made the green of the background; indeed, the islets all round were like gorgeous bouquets set in the deep blue of the water, and floating quietly there.

Rast was to return to college in a few days. He was in such gay spirits that Miss Lois was vexed, although she could hardly have told why. Père Michaux, however, aided and encouraged all the pranks of the young student. He was with him almost constantly, not returning to the hermitage at all during the time of his stay; Miss Lois was surprised to see how fond he was of the youth.

"No one can see Rast a moment alone now," she said, complainingly; "Père Michaux is always with him."

"Why do you want to see him alone?" said Tita, from her corner, looking up for a moment from her book.

"Don't you know that it is rude to ask questions?" said Miss Lois, sharply. But although she gave no reasons, it was plain that for some reason she was disappointed and angry.

The last day came, the last afternoon; the smoke of the coming steamer could be seen beyond the blue line of the point. No danger now of storm; the weather would be fair for many days. Père Michaux had proposed that Anne, Rast, and himself should go up to the heights behind the house and watch the sunset hues for the last time that year; they were to come back to the Agency in time to meet Dr. Gaston and Miss Lois, and take tea there all together, before the steamer's departure. Tita announced that she wished to go to the heights also.

"Come along then, Puss," said Rast, giving her his hand.

They set out through the garden, and up the narrow winding path; but the ascent was steep, and the priest climbed slowly, pausing now and then to take breath. Rast staid with him, while Anne strolled forward; Tita waited with Rast. They had been sitting on a crag for several minutes, when suddenly Rast exclaimed: "Hallo! there's Spotty's dog! he has been lost for three days, the scamp. I'll go up and catch him, and be back in a moment." While still speaking he was already scaling the rocks above them, not following the path by which Anne had ascended, but swinging himself up, hand over hand, with the dexterity and strength of a mountaineer; in a minute or two he was out of sight. Spotty's dog was a favorite in the garrison, Spotty, a dilapidated old Irish soldier, being his owner in name. Spotty said that the dog had "followed" him, when he was passing through Detroit; if he did, he had never repeated the act, but had persistently gone in the opposite direction ever since. But the men always went out and hunted for him all over the island, sooner or later finding him and bringing him back; for they liked to see him dance on his mournful hind legs, go through the drill, and pretend to be dead—feats which once formed parts of his répertoire as member of the travelling canine troupe which he had deserted at Detroit. It was considered quite an achievement to bring back this accomplished animal, and Rast was not above the glory. But it was not to be so easy as he had imagined: several minutes passed and he did not return, Spotty's dog having shown his thin nose and one eye but an instant at the top of the height, and then withdrawn them, leaving no trace behind.

"We will go up the path, and join Anne," said Père Michaux; "we will not wait longer for Rast. He can find us there as well as here."

They started; but after a few steps the priest's foot slipped on a rolling stone; he lost his balance, and half fell, half sank to the ground, fortunately directly along the narrow path, and not beyond its edge. When he attempted to rise, he found that his ankle was strained: he was a large man, and he had fallen heavily. Tita bound up the place as well as she could with his handkerchief and her own formed into a bandage; but at best he could only hobble. He might manage to go down the path to the house, but evidently he could not clamber further. Again they waited for Rast, but he did not come. They called, but no one answered. They were perched half way up the white cliff, where no one could hear them. Tita's whole face had grown darkly red, as though the blood would burst through; she looked copper-colored, and her expression was full of repressed impatience. Père Michaux, himself more perturbed and angry than so slight a hurt would seem to justify, happening to look at her, was seized with an idea. "Run up, child," he said, "and join Anne; do not leave her again. Tell her what has happened, and—mind what I say exactly, Tita—do not leave her."

Tita was off up the path and out of sight in an instant. The old priest, left to himself, hobbled slowly down the hill and across the garden to the Agency, not without some difficulty and pain.

Anne had gone up to the heights, and seated herself in good faith to wait for the others; Rast had gone after the dog in good faith, and not to seek Anne. Yet they met, and the others did not find them.

The dog ran away, and Rast after him, down the north path for a mile, and then straight into the fir wood, where nothing can be caught, man or dog. So Rast came back, not by the path, but through the forest, and found Anne sitting in a little nook among the arbor vitæ, where there was an opening, like a green window, overlooking the harbor. He sat down by her side, and fanned himself with his hat for a few moments, and then he went down to find Père Michaux and bring him up thither. But by that time the priest had reached the house, and he returned, saying that he saw by the foot-marks that the old man had for some reason gone down the hill again, leaving them to watch their last sunset alone. He threw himself down by Anne's side, and together they looked through their green casement.

"The steamer has turned the point," said Anne.

They both watched it in silence. They heard the evening gun from the fort.

"I shall never forgive myself, Rast, for having let you go before so carelessly. When the gale began that night, every blast seemed to go through my heart."

"I thought you did not appear to care much," said Rast, in an aggrieved tone.

"Did you notice it, then? It was only because I have to repress myself every moment, dear, lest I should give way entirely. You know I too must go far away—far away from all I love. I feel it very deeply."

She turned toward him as she spoke, with her eyes full of tears. Her hat was off, and her face, softened by emotion, looked for the first time to his eyes womanly. For generally that frank brow, direct gaze, and impersonal expression gave her the air of a child. Rast had never thought that Anne was beautiful; he had never thought of himself as her lover. He was very fond of her, of course; and she was very fond of him; and he meant to be good to her always. But that was all. Now, however, suddenly a new feeling came over him; he realized that her eyes were very lovely, and that her lips trembled with emotion. True, even then she did not turn from him, rather toward him; but he was too young himself to understand these indications, and, carried away by her sweetness, his own affection, and the impulse of the moment, he put his arm round her, and drew her toward him, sure that he loved her, and especially sure that she loved him. Poor Anne, who would soon have to part with him—dear Anne, his old playmate and friend!

Half an hour later he came into the Agency sitting-room, where the others were waiting, with a quick step and sparkling eyes, and, with the tone and manner of a young conqueror, announced, "Dr. Gaston, and all of you, I am going to marry Annet. We are engaged."

CHAPTER VIII.

"Shades of evening, close not o'er us,

Leave our lonely bark awhile;

Morn, alas! will not restore us

Yonder dear and fading isle.

Though 'neath distant skies we wander,

Still with thee our thoughts must dwell:

Absence makes the heart grow fonder—

Isle of beauty, fare thee well!"

—Thomas Haynes Bayly.

"We are engaged."

Dr. Gaston, who was standing, sat down as though struck down. Miss Lois jumped up, and began to laugh and cry in a breath. Père Michaux, who was sitting with his injured foot resting on a stool, ground his hands down suddenly on the arms of his chair with a sharp displeasure visible for an instant on his face. But only for an instant; it was gone before any one saw it.

"Oh, my darling boy!" said Miss Lois, with her arms round Rast's neck. "I always knew you would. You are made for each other, and always were. *Now* we shall have you both with us always, thank the Lord!" Then she sobbed again, and took a fresh and tighter hold of him. "I'll take the boys, dear; you need not be troubled with them. And I'll come over here and live, so that you and Annet can have the church-house; it's in much better repair; only there should be a new chimney. The dearest wish of my heart is now fulfilled, and I am quite ready to die."

Rast was kind always; it was simply impossible for him to say or do anything which could hurt the feelings of any one present. Such a course is sometimes contradictory, since those who are absent likewise have their feelings; but it is always at the moment agreeable. He kissed Miss Lois affectionately, thanked her, and led her to her chair; nor did he stop there, but stood beside her with her hand in his until she began to recover her composure, wipe her eyes, and smile. Then he went across to Dr. Gaston, his faithful and early friend.

"I hope I have your approval, sir?" he said, looking very tall and handsome as he stood by the old man's chair.

"Yes, yes," said the chaplain, extending his hand. "I was—I was startled at first, of course; you have both seemed like children to me. But if it must be, it must be. Only—make her happy, Rast; make her happy."

"I shall try, sir."

"Come, doctor, acknowledge that you have always expected it," said Miss Lois, breaking into permanent sunshine, and beginning to wipe her spectacles in a business-like way, which showed that the moisture was ended for the present.

"No—yes; I hardly know what I have expected," answered the chaplain, still a little suffocated, and speaking thickly. "I do not think I have expected anything."

"Is there any one else you would prefer to have Rast marry? Answer me that."

"No, no; certainly not."

"Is there any one you would prefer to have Anne marry?"

"Why need she marry at all?" said the chaplain, boldly, breaking through the chain of questions closing round him. "I am sure you yourself are a bright example, Miss Hinsdale, of the merits of single life."

But, to his surprise, Miss Lois turned upon him.

"What! have Anne live through my loneliness, my always-being-misunderstood-ness, my general sense of a useless ocean within me, its breaking waves dashed high on a stern and rock-bound coast?" she said, quoting vehemently from the only poem she knew. "Never!"

While Dr. Gaston was still gazing at her, Rast turned to Père Michaux. "I am sure of your approval," he said, smiling confidently. "I have had no doubt of that."

"Haven't you?" said the priest, dryly.

"No, sir: you have always been my friend."

"And I shall continue to be," said Père Michaux. But he rose as he spoke, and hobbled into the hall, closing the door behind him.

Tita was hurrying through the garden on her way from the heights; he waited for her.

"Where have you been?" he asked, sternly.

The child seemed exhausted, her breath came in panting gasps; her skirt was torn, her hair streaming, and the dark red hue of her face was changed to a yellow pallor.

"I have run and run, I have followed and followed, I have listened with my ear on the ground; I have climbed trees to look, I have torn a path through bushes, and I have not found them," she said, huskily, a slight froth on her dry lips as she spoke, her eyes bright and feverish.

"They are here," said Père Michaux; "they have been at home some time. What can you have been about, Angélique?"

"I have told you," said the child, rolling her apron tightly in her small brown hands. "I followed his track. He went down the north path. I traced him for a mile; then I lost him. In the fir wood. Then I crept, and looked, and listened."

"You followed Rast, then, when I told you to go to Anne! Enough. I thought, at least, you were quick, Tita; but it seems you are dull—dull as an owl," said the priest, turning away. He hobbled to the front door and sat down on the threshold. "After all my care," he said to himself, "to be foiled by a rolling stone!"

Through the open window he heard Miss Lois ask where Anne was. "Did she not come back with you, Rast?"

"Yes, but she was obliged to go directly to the kitchen. Something about the tea, I believe."

"Oh no; it was because she did not want to face us," said Miss Lois, archly. "I will go and bring her, the dear child!"

Père Michaux smiled contemptuously in the twilight outside; but he seemed to have recovered his equanimity also. "Something about the tea!" he said to himself. "Something about the tea!" He rose and hobbled into the sitting-room again with regained cheerfulness. Miss Lois was leading in Anne. "Here she is," said the old maid. "I found her; hiding, of course, and trembling."

Anne, smiling, turned down her cuffs, and began to light the lamp as usual. "I had to watch the broiling of the birds," she said. "You would not like to have them burned, would you?"

Père Michaux now looked thoroughly happy. "By no means," he replied, hobbling over and patting her on the head—"by no means, my dear." Then he laughed contentedly, and sat down. The others might talk now; he was satisfied.

When the lamp was lighted, everybody kissed Anne formally, and wished her happiness, Père Michaux going through the little rite with his finest Parisian courtesy. The boys added their caresses, and Gabriel said, "Of course *now* you won't go away, Annet?"

"Yes, dear, I must go just the same," said the sister.

"Certainly," said Père Michaux. "Erastus can not marry yet; he must go through college, and afterward establish himself in life."

"They could be married next spring," suggested Miss Lois: "we could help them at the beginning."

"Young Pronando is less of a man than I suppose, if he allows any one save himself to take care of his wife," said Père Michaux, sententiously.

"Of course I shall not," said Rast, throwing back his handsome head with an air of pride.

"That is right; stand by your decision," said the priest. "And now let us have tea. Enough has happened for one day, I think, and Rast must go at dawn. He can write as many letters as he pleases, but in real life he has now to show us what metal he is made of; I do not doubt but that it will prove pure ore."

Dr. Gaston sat silent; he drank his tea, and every now and then looked at Anne. She was cheerful and contented; her eyes rested upon Rast with confidence; she smiled when he spoke as if she liked to hear his voice; but of consciousness, embarrassment, hesitation, there was not a trace. The chaplain rubbed his forehead again and again, and pushed his wig so far back that it looked like a brown aureole. But if he was perplexed, Miss Lois was not; the happy old maid supplied all the consciousness, archness, and sentimental necessities of the occasion. She had kept them suppressed for years, and had a large store on hand. She radiated romance.

While they were taking tea, Tita entered, languid and indifferent as a city lady. No, she did not care for any tea, she said; and when the boys, all together, told her the great news, she merely smiled, fanned herself, and said she had long expected it.

Miss Lois looked up sharply, with the intention of contradicting this statement, but Tita gazed back at her so calmly that she gave it up.

After Père Michaux had left her in the hall, she had stolen to the back door of the sitting-room, laid her ear on the floor close to the crack under it, and overheard all. Then, trembling and silent, she crept up to her own room, bolted the door, and, throwing herself down upon the floor, rolled to and fro in a sort of frenzy. But she was a supple, light little creature, and made no sound. When her anger had spent itself, and she had risen to her feet, those below had no consciousness that the ceiling above them had been ironed all over on its upper side by the contact of a fierce little body, hot and palpitating wildly.

Père Michaux threw himself into that evening with all the powers he possessed fully alert; there were given so many hours to fill, and he filled them. The young lover Rast, the sentimental Miss Lois, the perplexed old chaplain, even the boys, all gave way to his influence, and listened or laughed at his will. Only Tita sat apart, silent and cold. Ten o'clock, eleven o'clock—it was certainly time to separate. But the boys, although sleepy and irritable, refused to go to bed, and fought with each other on the hearth-rug. Midnight; the old priest's flow of fancy and wit was still in full play, and the circle unbroken.

At last Dr. Gaston found himself yawning. "The world will not stop, even if we do go to bed, my friends," he said, rising. "We certainly ought not to talk or listen longer to-night."

Père Michaux rose also, and linked his arm in Rast's. "I will walk home with you, young sir," he said, cordially. "Miss Lois, we will take you as far as your gate."

Miss Lois was willing, but a little uncertain in her movements; inclined toward delay. Would Anne lend her a shawl? And, when the young girl had gone up stairs after it, would Rast take the candle into the hall, lest she should stumble on her way down?

"She will not stumble," said Père Michaux. "She never stumbled in her life, Miss Lois. Of what are you thinking?"

Miss Lois put on the shawl; and then, when they had reached the gate, "Run back, Rast," she said; "I have left my knitting."

"Here it is," said the priest, promptly producing it. "I saw it on the table, and took charge of it."

Miss Lois was very much obliged; but she was sure she heard some one calling. Perhaps it was Anne. If Rast—

"Only a night-bird," said Père Michaux, walking on. He left Miss Lois at the church-house; and then, linking his arm again in Rast's, accompanied him to his lodgings. "I am going to give you a parting present," he said—"a watch, the one I am wearing now. I have another, which will do very well for this region."

The priest's watch was a handsome one, and Rast was still young enough to feel an immense satisfaction in such a possession. He took it with many thanks, and frankly expressed delight. The old priest accompanied his gift with fatherly good wishes and advice. It was now so late that he would take a bed in the house, he thought. In this way, too, he would be with Rast, and see the last of him.

But love laughs at parsons.

Père Michaux saw his charge to bed, and went to bed himself in an adjoining room. He slept soundly; but at the first peep of dawn his charge was gone—gone to meet Anne on the heights, as agreed between them the night before.

O wise Père Michaux!

The sun was not yet above the horizon, but Anne was there. The youth took her hands in his, and looked at her earnestly. He was half surprised himself at what he had done, and he looked at her again to see how it had happened. All his life from earliest childhood she had been his dearest companion and friend; but now she was his betrothed wife, would she be in any way different? The sun came up, and showed that she was just the same—calm, clear-eyed, and sweet-voiced. What more could he ask?

"*Do* you love me, Annet?" he said more than once, looking at her as though she ought to be some new and only half-comprehended person.

"You know I do," she answered. Then, as he asked again, "Why do you ask me?" she said. "Has not my whole life shown it?"

"Yes," he answered, growing more calm. "I believe you *have* loved me all your life, Annet."

"I have," replied the girl.

He kissed her gently. "I shall always be kind to you," he said. Then, with a half-sigh, "You will like to live here?"

"It is my home, Rast. However, other places will not seem strange after I have seen the great city. For of course I must go to New York, just the same, to learn to be a teacher, and help the children: we may be separated for years."

"Oh no; I shall be able to take care of you all before long," said Rast, grandly. "As soon as I have been through college I shall look about and decide upon something. Would you like me to be a lawyer? Or a surgeon? Then there is always the army. Or we might have a farm."

57

"There is only Frobisher's."

"Oh, you mean here on the island? Well, Frobisher's would do. We could repair the old house, and have a pony-cart, and drive in to town." Here the steamer sounded its first whistle. That meant that it would start in half an hour. Rast left the future and his plans in mid-air, and took Anne in his arms with real emotion. "Good-by, dear, good-by," he said. "Do not grieve, or allow yourself to be lonely. I shall see you soon in some way, even if I have to go to New York for the purpose. Remember that you are my betrothed wife now. That thought will comfort you."

"Yes," said Anne, her sincere eyes meeting his. Then she clung to him for a few moments, sobbing. "You must go away, and I must go away," she said, amid her tears: "nothing is the same any more. Father is dead, and the whole world will be between us. Nothing is the same any more. Nothing is the same."

"Distance is nothing nowadays," said the youth, soothing her; "I can reach you in almost no time, Annet."

"Yes, but nothing is the same any more; nothing ever will be the same ever again," she sobbed, oppressed for the first time in her life by the vague uncertainties of the future.

"Oh yes, it will," said her companion, decidedly. "I will come back here if you wish it so much, and you shall come back, and we will live here on this same old island all our lives. A man has but to choose his home, you know."

Anne looked somewhat comforted. Yet only part of her responded to his words; she still felt that nothing would ever be quite the same again. She could not bring back her father; she could not bring back their long happy childhood. The door was closed behind them, and they must now go out into the wide world.

The second whistle sounded—another fifteen minutes gone. They ran down the steep path together, meeting Miss Lois on her way up, a green woollen hood on her head as a protection against the morning air.

"You will want a ring, my dears," she said, breathlessly, as she kissed them—"an engagement ring; it is the custom, and fortunately I have one for you."

With a mixture of smiles and tears of delight and excitement, she took from a little box an old-fashioned ring, and handed it to Rast.

"It was your mother's, dear," she said to Anne; "your father gave it to me as a memento of her when you were a baby. It is most fit that you should wear it."

Rast examined the slender little circlet without much admiration. It was a hoop of very small rubies placed close together, with as little gold visible as was possible. "I meant to give Annet a diamond," he said, with the tone of a young duke.

"Oh no, Rast," exclaimed the girl.

"But take this for the present," urged the old maid. "You must not let her go from you without one; it would be a bad sign. Put it on yourself, Rast; I want to see you do it."

Rast slipped the circlet into its place on Anne's finger, and then, with a little flourish which became him well, he uncovered his head, bent his knee, and raised the hand to his lips.

"But you have put it on the right hand," said Miss Lois, in dismay.

"It does not make any difference," said Rast. "And besides, I like the right hand; it means more."

Rast did not admire the old-fashioned ring, but to Anne it was both beautiful and sacred. She gazed at it with a lovely light in her eyes, and an earnest thoughtfulness. Any one could see how gravely she regarded the little ceremony.

When they came back to the house, Dr. Gaston was already there, and Père Michaux was limping up the path from the gate. He caught sight of Rast and Anne together. "Check!" he said to himself. "So much for being a stupid old man. Outwitted yesterday by a rolling stone, and to-day by your own inconceivable dullness. And you gave away your watch—did you?—to prevent what has happened! The girl has probably bound herself formally, and now you will have her conscience against you as well as all the rest. Bah!"

But while thinking this, he came forward and greeted them all happily and cheerfully, whereas the old chaplain, who really had no especial objection to the engagement, was cross and silent, and hardly greeted anybody. He knew that he was ill-tempered, and wondered why he should be. "Anything unexpected is apt to disturb the mind," he remarked, apologetically, to the priest, taking out his handkerchief and rubbing his forehead violently, as if to restore equanimity by counter-circulation. But however cross or quiet the others might be, Miss Lois beamed for all; she shed forth radiance like Roman candles even at that early hour, when the air was still chill and the sky gray with mist. The boys came down stairs with their clothes half on, and then Rast said good-by, and hurried down to the pier, and they all stood together on the old piazza, and watched the steamer back out into the stream, turn round, and start westward, the point of the island soon hiding it from

58

view. Then Dr. Gaston took his unaccountable ill temper homeward, Père Michaux set sail for the hermitage, Anne sat down to sew, and only Miss Lois let every-day life take care of itself, and cried on.

"I know there will be no more storms," she said; "it isn't that. But it is everything that has happened, Anne dear: the engagement, and the romance of it all!"

Tita now entered: she had not appeared before. She required that fresh coffee should be prepared for her, and she obtained it. For the Irish soldier's wife was almost as much afraid of her as the boys were. She glanced at Miss Lois's happy tears, at Anne's ruby ring, at the general disorder.

"And all this for a mere boy!" she said, superbly.

Miss Lois stopped crying from sheer astonishment. "And pray, may I ask, what are you?" she demanded.

"A girl; and about on a line with the boy referred to," replied Miss Tita, composedly. "Anne is much too old."

The boys gave a laugh of scorn. Tita turned and looked at them, and they took to the woods for the day. Miss Lois cried no more, but began to sew; there was a vague dread in her heart as to what the winter would be with Tita in the church-house. "If I could only cut off her hair!" she thought, with a remembrance of Samson. "Never was such hair seen on any child before."

As Tita sat on her low bench, the two long thick braids of her black hair certainly did touch the floor; and most New England women, who, whether from the nipping climate or their Roundhead origin, have, as a class, rather scanty locks, would have agreed with Miss Lois that "such a mane" was unnatural on a girl of that age—indeed, intolerable.

Amid much sewing, planning, and busy labor, time flew on. Dr. Gaston did not pretend to do anything else now save come down early in the morning to the Agency, and remain nearly all day, sitting in an arm-chair, sometimes with a book before him, but hardly turning a page. His dear young pupil, his almost child, was going away. He tried not to think how lonely he should be without her. Père Michaux came frequently; he spoke to Tita with a new severity, and often with a slight shade of sarcasm in his voice. "Are you not a little too severe with her?" asked Miss Lois one day, really fearing lest Tita, in revenge, might go out on some dark night and set fire to the house.

"He is my priest, isn't he, and not yours? He shall order me to do what he pleases, and I shall do it," answered the small person whom she had intended to defend.

And now every day more and more beautiful grew the hues on the trees; it was a last intensity of color before the long, cold, dead-white winter. All the maple and oak leaves were now scarlet, orange, or crimson, each hue vivid; they died in a glory to which no tropical leaf ever attains. The air was warm, hazy, and still—the true air of Indian summer; and as if to justify the term, the Indians on the mainland and islands were busy bringing potatoes and game to the village to sell, fishing, cutting wood, and begging, full of a tardy activity before the approach of winter. Anne watched them crossing in their canoes, and landing on the beach, and when occasionally the submissive, gentle-eyed squaws, carrying their little pappooses, came to the kitchen door to beg, she herself went out to see them, and bade the servant give them something. They were Chippewas, dark-skinned and silent, wearing short calico skirts, and a blanket drawn over their heads. Patient and uncomplaining by nature, they performed almost all the labor on their small farms, cooked for their lords and masters, and took care of the children, as their share of the duties of life, the husbands being warriors, and above common toil. Anne knew some of these Chippewa women personally, and could talk to them in their own tongue; but it was not old acquaintance which made her go out and see them now. It was the feeling that they belonged to the island, to the life which she must soon leave behind. She felt herself clinging to everything—to the trees, to the white cliffs, to the very sunshine—like a person dragged along against his will, who catches at every straw.

The day came at last; the eastern-bound steamer was at the pier; Anne must go. Dr. Gaston's eyes were wet; with choked utterance he gave her his benediction. Miss Lois was depressed; but her depression had little opportunity to make itself felt, on account of the clamor and wild behavior of the boys, which demanded her constant attention. The clamor, however, was not so alarming as the velvety goodness of Tita. What could the child be planning? The poor old maid sighed, as she asked herself this question, over the life that lay before her. But twenty such lives would not wear out Lois Hinsdale. Père Michaux was in excellent spirits, and kept them all in order. He calmed the boys, encouraged Anne, cheered the old chaplain and Miss Lois, led them all down the street and on board the boat, then back on the pier again, where they could see Anne standing on the high deck above them. He shook the boys when they howled in their grief too loudly, and as the steamer moved out into the stream he gave his arm to Miss Lois, who, for the moment forgetting everything save that the dear little baby whom she had loved so long was going away, burst into convulsive tears. Tita sat on the edge of the pier, and watched the boat silently. She did not speak or wave her handkerchief; she shed no tears. But long after the others had gone home, when the steamer was a mere speck low down on the eastern horizon, she sat there still.

Yes, Anne was gone.

And now that she was gone, it was astonishing to see what a void was left. No one had especially valued or praised her while she was there; she was a matter of course. But now that she was absent, the whole life of the village seemed changed. There was no one to lead the music on Sundays, standing by the organ and singing clearly, and Miss Lois's playing seemed now doubly dull and mechanical. There was no one going up to the fort at a certain hour every morning, passing the windows where the fort ladies sat, with books under her arm. There was no one working in the Agency garden; no one coming with a quick step into the butcher's little shop to see what he had, and consult him, not without hidden anxiety, as to the possibility of a rise in prices. There was no one sewing on the piazza, or going out to find the boys, or sailing over to the hermitage with the four black-eyed children, who plainly enough needed even more holy instruction than they obtained. They all knew everything she did, and all her ways. And as it was a small community, they missed her sadly. The old Agency, too, seemed to become suddenly dilapidated, almost ruinous; the boys were undeniably rascals, and Tita "a little minx." Miss Lois was without doubt a dogmatic old maid, and the chaplain not what he used to be, poor old man—fast breaking up. Only Père Michaux bore the test unaltered. But then he had not leaned upon this young girl as the others had leaned—the house and garden, the chaplain as well as the children: the strong young nature had in one way supported them all.

Meanwhile the girl herself was journeying down the lake. She stood at the stern, watching the island grow distant, grow purple, grow lower and lower on the surface of the water, until at last it disappeared; then she covered her face and wept. After this, like one who leaves the vanished past behind him, and resolutely faces the future, she went forward to the bow and took her seat there. Night came on; she remained on deck through the evening: it seemed less lonely there than among the passengers in the cabin. She knew the captain; and she had been especially placed in his charge, also, by Père Michaux, as far as one of the lower-lake ports, where she was to be met by a priest and taken to the eastern-bound train. The captain, a weather-beaten man, past middle age, came after a while and sat down near her.

"What is that red light over the shore-line?" said Anne to her taciturn companion, who sat and smoked near by, protecting her paternally by his presence, but having apparently few words, and those husky, at his command.

"Fire in the woods."

"Is it not rather late in the season for a forest fire?"

"Well, there it is," answered the captain, declining discussion of the point in face of obvious fact.

Anne had already questioned him on the subject of light-houses. Would he like to live in a light-house?

No, he would not.

But they might be pleasant places in summer, with the blue water all round them: she had often thought she would like to live in one.

Well, *he* wouldn't.

But why?

Resky places sometimes when the wind blew: give him a good stiddy boat, now.

After a time they came nearer to the burning forest. Anne could see the great columns of flame shoot up into the sky; the woods were on fire for miles. She knew that the birds were flying, dizzy and blinded, before the terrible conqueror, that the wild-cats were crying like children, that the small wolves were howling, and that the more timid wood creatures were cowering behind fallen trunks, their eyes dilated and ears laid flat in terror. She knew all this because she had often heard it described, fires miles long in the pine forests being frequent occurrences in the late summer and early autumn; but she had never before seen with her own eyes the lurid splendor, as there was no unbroken stretch of pineries on the Straits. She sat silently watching the great clouds of red light roll up into the dark sky, and the shower of sparks higher still. The advance-guard was of lapping tongues that caught at and curled through the green wood far in front; then came a wall of clear orange-colored roaring fire, then the steady incandescence that was consuming the hearts of the great trees, and behind, the long range of dying fires like coals, only each coal was a tree. It grew late; she went to her state-room in order that the captain might be relieved from his duty of guard. But for several hours longer she sat by her small window, watching the flames, which turned to a long red line as the steamer's course carried her farther from the shore. She was thinking of those she had left behind, and of the island; of Rast, and her own betrothal. The betrothal seemed to her quite natural; they had always been together in the past, and now they would always be together in the future; she was content that it was so. She knew so little of the outside world that few forebodings as to her own immediate present troubled her. She was on her way to a school where she would study hard, so as soon to be able to teach, and help the children; the boys were to be educated one by one, and after the first year, perhaps, she could send for Tita, since Miss Lois never understood the child aright, failing to comprehend her peculiar nature, and making her, poor little thing, uncomfortable. It would be a double relief—to Miss Lois as well as Tita. It was a pity that her grand-aunt was so hard and ill-tempered; but probably she was old and infirm. Perhaps if she could see Tita, she might take a fancy to the child; Tita was so small and so soft-voiced, whereas she, Anne, was so overgrown and awkward. She gave a thought of regret to her own deficiencies, but hardly a sigh. They were matters of fact which she had long ago accepted. The coast fire had now faded into a line of red dots and a dull light above them; she knelt down and prayed, not without the sadness which a lonely young traveller might naturally feel on the broad dark lake.

At the lower-lake port she was met by an old French priest, one of Père Michaux's friends, who took her to the railway station in a carriage, bought her ticket, checked her trunk, gave her a few careful words of instruction as to the journey, and then, business matters over, sat down by her side and talked to her with enchanting politeness and ease until the moment of departure. Père Michaux had arranged this: although not of their faith, Anne was to travel all the way to New York in the care of the Roman Catholic Church, represented by its priests, handed from one to the next, and met at the entrance of the great city by another, who would cross the river for the purpose, in order that her young island eyes might not be confused by the crowd and turmoil. At first Dr. Gaston had talked of escorting Anne in person; but it was so long since he had travelled anywhere, and he was so absent-minded, that it was evident even to himself that Anne would in reality escort him. Miss Lois had the children, and of course could not leave them.

"I would go myself if there was any necessity for it," said Père Michaux, "but there is not. Let me arrange it, and I promise you that Anne shall reach her school in safety; I will have competent persons to meet her all along the route—unless, indeed, you have friends of your own upon whom you prefer to rely?"

This was one of the little winds which Père Michaux occasionally sent over the self-esteem of his two Protestant companions: he could not help it. Dr. Gaston frowned: he had not an acquaintance between New York and the island, and Père Michaux knew it. But Miss Lois, undaunted, rushed into the fray.

"Oh, certainly, it would be quite easy for us to have her met by friends on the way," she began, making for the moment common and Protestant cause with Dr. Gaston; "it would require only a few letters. In New England I should have my own family connections to call upon—persons of the highest respectability, descendants, most of them, of the celebrated patriot Israel Putnam."

"Certainly," replied Père Michaux. "I understand. Then I will leave Anne to you."

"But unfortunately, as Anne is going to New York, not Boston, my connections do not live along the route, exactly," continued Miss Lois, the adverb standing for a small matter of a thousand miles or so; "nor," she added, again admitting Dr. Gaston to a partnership, "can we make them."

"There remain, then, the pastors of your church," said the priest.

"Certainly—the pastors. It will be the simplest thing in the world for Dr. Gaston to write to them; they will be delighted to take charge of any friend of ours."

The chaplain pushed his wig back a little, and murmured, "Church Almanac."

Miss Lois glanced at him angrily. "I am sure I do not know what Dr. Gaston means by mentioning 'Church Almanac' in that way," she said, sharply. "We know most of the prominent pastors, of course. Dr. Shepherd, for instance, and Dr. Dell."

Dr. Shepherd and Dr. Dell, who occasionally came up to the island during the summer for a few days of rest, lived in the lower-lake town where Anne's long railway journey began. They were not pastors, but rectors, and the misuse of the terms grated on the chaplain's Anglican ear. But he was a patient man, and accustomed now to the heterogeneous phrasing of the Western border.

"And besides," added Miss Lois, triumphantly, "there is the bishop!"

Now the bishop lived five miles farther. It was not evident, therefore, to the ordinary mind what aid these reverend gentlemen could give to Anne, all living, as they did, at the western beginning of her railway journey; but Miss Lois, who, like others of her sex, possessed the power (unattainable by man) of rising above mere logical sequence, felt that she had conquered.

"I have no bishops to offer," said Père Michaux, with mock humility; "only ordinary priests. I will therefore leave Anne to your care, Miss Lois—yours and Dr. Gaston's."

So the discussion ended, and Miss Lois came off with Protestant colors flying. None the less Père Michaux wrote his letters; and Dr. Gaston did not write his. For the two men understood each other. There was no need for the old chaplain to say, plainly, "I have lived out of the world so long that I have not a single clerical friend this side of New York upon whom I can call"; the priest comprehended it without words. And there was no need for Père Michaux to parade the close ties and net-work of communication which prevailed in the ancient Church to which he belonged; the chaplain knew them without the telling. Each understood the other; and being men, they could do without the small teasing comments, like the buzzing of flies, with which women enliven their days. Thus it happened that Anne Douglas travelled from the northern island across to the great city on the ocean border in the charge of the Roman Catholic Church.

She arrived in New York worn out and bewildered, and having lost her sense of comparison by the strangeness and fatigue of the long journey, she did not appreciate the city's size, the crowded streets, and roar of traffic, but regarded everything vaguely, like a tired child who has neither surprise nor attention to give.

At length the carriage stopped; she went up a broad flight of stone steps; she was entering an open door. Some one was speaking to her; she was in a room where there were chairs, and she sank down. The priest who had brought her from the other side of the river was exchanging a few words with a lady; he was going; he was gone. The lady was coming toward her.

"You are very tired, my child;" she said. "Let me take you a moment to Tante, and then you can go to your room."

"To Tante?" said Anne.

"Yes, to Tante, or Madame Moreau, the principal of the school. She expects you."

CHAPTER IX.

"Manners—not what, but *how*. Manners are happy ways of doing things; each once a stroke of genius or of love—now repeated and hardened into usage. Manners require time; nothing is more vulgar than haste."—Emerson.

Madame Moreau was a Frenchwoman, small and old, with a thin shrewd face and large features. She wore a plain black satin gown, the narrow skirt gathered in the old-fashioned style, and falling straight to the floor; the waist of the gown, fastened behind, was in front plaited into a long rounded point. Broad ruffles of fine lace shielded her throat and hands, and her cap, garnished with violet velvet, was trimmed with the same delicate fabric. She was never a handsome woman even in youth, and she was now seventy-five years of age; yet she was charming.

She rose, kissed the young girl lightly on each cheek, and said a few words of welcome. Her manner was affectionate, but impersonal. She never took fancies; but neither did she take dislikes. That her young ladies were all charming young persons was an axiom never allowed to be brought into question; that they were simply and gracefully feminine was with equal firmness established. Other schools of modern and American origin might make a feature of public examinations, with questions by bearded professors from boys' colleges; but the establishment of Madame Moreau knew nothing of such innovations. The Frenchwoman's idea was not a bad one; good or bad, it was inflexible. She was a woman of marked character, and may be said to have accomplished much good in a mannerless generation and land. Thoroughly French, she was respected and loved by all her American scholars; and it will be long ere her name and memory fade away.

Miss Vanhorn did not come to see her niece until a week had passed. Anne had been assigned to the lowest French class among the children, had taken her first singing lesson from one Italian, fat, rosy, and smiling, and her first Italian lesson from another, lean, old, and soiled, had learned to answer questions in the Moreau French, and to talk a little, as well as to comprehend the fact that her clothes were remarkable, and that she herself was considered an oddity, when one morning Tante sent word that she was to come down to the drawing-room to see a visitor.

The visitor was an old woman with black eyes, a black wig, shining false teeth, a Roman nose, and a high color (which was, however, natural), and she was talking to Tante, who, with her own soft gray hair, and teeth which if false did not appear so, looked charmingly real beside her. Miss Vanhorn was short and stout; she was muffled in an India shawl, and upon her hands were a pair of cream-colored kid gloves much too large for her, so that when she fumbled, as she did every few moments, in an embroidered bag for aromatic seeds coated with sugar, she had much difficulty in finding them, owing to the empty wrinkled ends of the glove fingers. She lifted a gold-rimmed eye-glass to her eyes as Anne entered, and coolly inspected her.

"Dear me! dear me!" she said. Then, in execrable French, "What can be done with such a young savage as this?"

"How do you do, aunt?" said Anne, using the conventional words with a slight tremor in her voice. This was the woman who had brought up her mother—her dear, unremembered mother.

"Grandaunt," said Miss Vanhorn, tartly. "Sit down; I can not bear to have people standing in front of me. How old are you?"

"I am seventeen, grandaunt."

Miss Vanhorn let her eyeglass drop, and groaned. "*Can* anything be done with her?" she asked, closing her eyes tightly, and turning toward Tante, while Anne flushed crimson, not so much from the criticism as the unkindness.

"Oh yes," said Tante, taking the opportunity given by the closed eyes to pat the young girl's hand encouragingly. "Miss Douglas is very intelligent; and she has a fine mezzo-soprano voice. Signor Belzini is much pleased with it. It would be well, also, I think, if you would allow her to take a few dancing lessons."

"She will have no occasion for dancing," answered Miss Vanhorn, still with her eyes closed.

"It was not so much for the dancing itself as for grace of carriage," replied Tante. "Miss Douglas has a type of figure rare among American girls."

"I should say so, indeed!" groaned the other, shaking her head gloomily, still voluntarily blinded.

"But none the less beautiful in its way," continued Tante, unmoved. "It is the Greek type."

"I am not acquainted with any Greeks," replied Miss Vanhorn.

"You are still as devoted as ever to the beautiful and refined study of plant life, dear madame," pursued Tante, changing the current of conversation. "How delightful to have a young relative to assist you, with the fresh and ardent interest belonging to her age, when the flowers bloom again upon the rural slopes of Haarderwyck!" As Tante said this, she looked off dreamily into space, as if she saw aunt and niece wandering together through groves of allegorical flowers.

"She is not likely to see Haarderwyck," answered Miss Vanhorn. Then, after a moment's pause—a pause which Tante did not break—she peered at Anne with half-open eyes, and asked, abruptly, "Do you, then, know anything of botany?"

Tante made a slight motion with her delicate withered old hand. But Anne did not comprehend her, and answered, honestly, "No, grandaunt, I do not."

"Bah!" said Miss Vanhorn; "I might have known without the asking. Make what you can of her, madame. I will pay your bill for one year: no longer. But no nonsense, no extras, mind that." Again she sought a caraway seed, pursuing it vindictively along the bottom of her bag, and losing it at the last, after all.

"As regards wardrobe, I would advise some few changes," said Tante, smoothly. "It is one of my axioms that pupils study to greater advantage when their thoughts are not disturbed by deficiencies in dress. Conformity to our simple standard is therefore desirable."

"It may be desirable; it is not always, on that account, attainable," answered Miss Vanhorn, conveying a finally caught seed to her mouth, dropping it at the last moment, and carefully and firmly biting the seam of the glove finger in its place.

"Purchases are made for the pupils with discretion by one of our most experienced teachers," continued Tante.

"Glad to hear it," said her visitor, releasing the glove finger, and pretending to chew the seed which was not there.

"But I do not need anything, Tante," interposed Anne, the deep color deepening in her cheeks.

"So much the better," said her grandaunt, dryly, "since you will have nothing."

She went away soon afterward somewhat placated, owing to skillful reminiscences of a favorite cousin, who, it seemed, had been one of Tante's "dearest pupils" in times past; "a true Vanhorn, worthy of her Knickerbocker blood." The word "Neeker-bo-ker," delicately comprehended, applied, and, what was more important still, limited, was one of Tante's most telling achievements—a shibboleth. She knew all the old Dutch names, and remembered their intermarriages; she was acquainted with the peculiar flavor of Huguenot descent; she comprehended the especial aristocracy of Tory families, whose original property had been confiscated by a raw republic under George Washington. Ah! skillful old Tante, what a general you would have made!

Anne Douglas, the new pupil, was now left to face the school with her island-made gowns, and what courage she could muster. Fortunately the gowns were black and severely plain. Tante, not at all disturbed by Miss Vanhorn's refusal, ordered a simple cloak and bonnet for her through an inexpensive French channel, so that in the street she passed unremarked; but, in the house, every-day life required more courage than scaling a wall. Girls are not brutal, like boys, but their light wit is pitiless. The Southern pupils, provided generously with money in the lavish old-time Southern way, the day scholars, dressed with the exquisite simplicity of Northern school-girls of good family, glanced with amusement at the attire of this girl from the Northwest. This girl, being young, felt their glances; as a refuge, she threw herself into her studies with double energy, and gaining confidence respecting what she had been afraid was her island patois, she advanced so rapidly in the French classes that she passed from the lowest to the highest, and was publicly congratulated by Tante herself. In Italian her progress was more slow. Her companion, in the class of two, was a beautiful dark-eyed Southern girl, who read musically, but seldom deigned to open her grammar. The forlorn, soiled old exile to whom, with unconscious irony, the bath-room had been assigned for recitations in the crowded house, regarded this pupil with mixed admiration and despair. Her remarks on Mary Stuart, represented by Alfieri, were nicely calculated to rouse him to patriotic fury, and then, when the old man burst forth in a torrent of excited words, she would raise her soft eyes in surprise, and inquire if he was ill. The two girls sat on the bath-tub, which was decorously covered over and cushioned; the exile had a chair for dignity's sake. Above, in a corresponding room, a screen was drawn round the tub, and a piano placed against it. Here, all day long, another exile, a German music-master, with little gold rings in his ears, gave piano lessons, and Anne was one of his pupils. To Signor Belzini, the teacher of vocal music, the drawing-room itself was assigned. He was a prosperous and smiling Italian, who had a habit of bringing pieces of pink cream candy with him, and arranging them in a row on the piano for his own refreshment after each song. There was an atmosphere of perfume and mystery about Belzini. It was whispered that he knew the leading opera-singers, even taking supper with them sometimes after the opera. The pupils exhausted their imaginations in picturing to each other the probable poetry and romance of these occasions.

Belzini was a musical trick-master; but he was not ignorant. When Anne came to take her first lesson, he smiled effusively, as usual, took a piece of candy, and, while enjoying it, asked if she could read notes, and gave her the "Drinking Song" from *Lucrezia Borgia* as a trial. Anne sang it correctly without accompaniment, but slowly and solemnly as a dead march. It is probable that "Il Segreto" never heard itself so sung before or since. Belzini was walking up and down with his plump hands behind him.

"You have never heard it sung?" he said.

"No," replied Anne.

"Sing something else, then. Something you like yourself."

After a moment's hesitation, Anne sang an island ballad in the voyageur patois.

"May I ask who has taught you, mademoiselle?"

"My father," said the pupil, with a slight tremor in her voice.

"He must be a cultivated musician, although of the German school," said Belzini, seating himself at the piano and running his white fingers over the keys. "Try these scales."

It was soon understood that "the islander" could sing as well as study. Tolerance was therefore accorded to her. But not much more. It is only in "books for the young" that poorly clad girls are found leading whole schools by the mere power of intellectual or moral supremacy. The emotional type of boarding-school, also, is seldom seen in cities; its home is amid the dead lethargy of a winter-bound country village.

The great event in the opening of Anne's school life was her first opera. Tante, not at all blinded by the country garb and silence of the new pupil, had written her name with her own hand upon the opera list for the winter, without consulting Miss Vanhorn, who would, however, pay for it in the end, as she would also pay for the drawing and dancing lessons ordered by the same autocratic command. For it was one of Tante's rules to cultivate every talent of the agreeable and decorative order which her pupils possessed; she bathed them as the photographer bathes his shadowy plate, bringing out and "setting," as it were, as deeply as possible, their colors, whatever they happened to be. Tante always attended the opera in person. Preceded by the usher, the old Frenchwoman glided down the awkward central aisle of the Academy of Music, with her inimitable step, clad in her narrow satin gown and all her laces, well aware that tongues in every direction were saying: "There is Madame Moreau at the head of her school, as usual. What a wonderful old lady she is!" While the pupils were filing into their places, Tante remained in the aisle fanning herself majestically, and surveying them with a benignant smile. When all were seated, with a graceful little bend she glided into her place at the end, the motion of sitting down and the bend fused into one in a manner known only to herself.

Anne's strong idealism, shown in her vivid although mistaken conceptions of Shakspeare's women, was now turned into the channel of opera music. After hearing several operas, she threw herself into her Italian songs with so much fervor that Belzini sat aghast; this was not the manner in which demoiselles of private life should sing. Tante, passing one day (by the merest chance, of course) through the drawing-room while Anne was singing, paused a moment to listen. "Ma fille," she said, when the song was ended, tapping Anne's shoulder affably, "give no more expression to the Italian words you sing than to the syllables of your scales. Interpretations are not required." The old Frenchwoman always put down with iron hand what she called the predominant tendency toward too great freedom—sensationalism—in young girls. She spent her life in a constant struggle with the American "jeune fille."

During this time Rast wrote regularly; but his letters, not being authorized by Miss Vanhorn, Anne's guardian, passed first through the hands of one of the teachers, and the knowledge of this inspection naturally dulled the youth's pen. But Anne's letters to him passed the same ordeal without change in word or in spirit. Miss Lois and Dr. Gaston wrote once a week; Père Michaux contented himself with postscripts added to the long, badly spelled, but elaborately worded epistles with which Mademoiselle Tita favored her elder sister. It was evident to Anne that Miss Lois was having a severe winter.

The second event in Anne's school life was the gaining of a friend.

At first it was but a musical companion. Helen Lorrington lived not far from the school; she was one of Tante's old scholars, and this Napoleon of teachers especially liked this pupil, who was modelled after her own heart. Helen held what may be called a woman's most untrammelled position in life, namely, that of a young widow, protected but not controlled, rich, beautiful, and without children. She was also heir to the estate of an eccentric grandfather, who detested her, yet would not allow his money to go to any collateral branch. He detested her because her father was a Spaniard, whose dark eyes had so reprehensibly fascinated his little Dutch daughter that she had unexpectedly plucked up courage to marry in spite of the paternal prohibition, and not only that, but to be very happy also during the short portion of life allotted to her afterward. The young Spanish husband, with an unaccountable indifference to the wealth for which he was supposed to have plotted so perseveringly, was pusillanimous enough to die soon afterward, leaving only one little pale-faced child, a puny girl, to inherit the money. The baby Helen had never possessed the dimples and rose tints that make the beauty of childhood; the girl Helen had not the rounded curves and peach-like bloom that make the beauty of youth. At seventeen she was what she was now; therefore at seventeen she was old. At twenty-seven she was what she was then; therefore at twenty-seven she was young.

She was tall, and extremely, marvellously slender; yet her bones were so small that there were no angles visible in all her graceful length. She was a long woman; her arms were long, her throat was long, her eyes and face were long. Her form, slight enough for a spirit, was as natural as the swaying grasses on a hill-side. She was as flexible as a ribbon. Her beauties were a regally poised little head, a delicately cut profile, and a remarkable length of hair; her peculiarities, the color of this hair, the color of her skin, and the narrowness of her eyes. The hue of her hair was called flaxen; but it was more than that—it was the color of bleached straw. There was not a trace of gold in it, nor did it ever shine, but hung, when unbound, a soft even mass straight down below the knee. It was very thick, but so fine that it was manageable; it was never rough, because there were no short locks. The complexion which accompanied this hair was white, with an under-tint of ivory. There are skins with under-tints of pink, of blue, and of brown; but this was different in that it shaded off into cream, without any indication of these hues. This soft ivory-color gave a shade of fuller richness to the slender straw-haired woman—an effect increased by the hue of the eyes, when visible under the long light lashes. For Helen's eyes were of a bright dark unexpected brown. The eyes were so long and narrow, however, that generally only a line of bright brown looked at you when you met their gaze. Small features, narrow cheeks, delicate lips, and little milk-white teeth, like a child's, completed this face which never had a red tint, even the lips being but faintly colored. There were many men who, seeing Helen Lorrington for the first time, thought her exquisitely beautiful; there were others who, seeing her for the first time, thought her singularly ugly. The *second* time, there was never a question. Her grandfather called her an albino; but he was nearly blind, and could only see the color of her hair. He could not see the strong brown light of her eyes, or the soft ivory complexion, which never changed in the wind, the heat, or the cold.

Mrs. Lorrington was always dressed richly, but after a fashion of her own. Instead of disguising the slenderness of her form, she intensified it; instead of contrasting hues, she often wore amber tints like her hair. Amid all her silks, jewels, and laces, there was always supreme her own personality, which reduced her costumes to what, after all, costumes should be, merely the subordinate coverings of a beautiful woman.

Helen had a clear, flute-like voice, with few low notes, and a remarkably high range. She continued her lessons with Belzini whenever she was in the city, more in order that he might transpose her songs for her than for any instruction he could now bestow. She was an old pupil of his, and the sentimental Italian adored her; this adoration, however, did not prevent him from being very comfortable at home with his portly wife. One morning Helen, coming in for a moment to leave a new song, found Anne at the piano taking her lesson. Belzini, always anxious to please his fair-haired divinity, motioned to her to stay and listen. Anne's rich voice pleased her ears; but she had heard rich voices before. What held her attention now was the girl herself. For although Helen was a marvel of self-belief, although she made her own peculiar beauty an object of worship, and was so saturated with knowledge of herself that she could not take an attitude which did not become her, she yet possessed a comprehension of other types of beauty, and had, if not an admiration for, at least a curiosity about, them. In Anne she recognized at once what Tante had also recognized—unfolding beauty of an unfamiliar type, the curves of a nobly shaped form hidden under an ugly gown, above the round white throat a beautiful head, and a singularly young face shadowed by a thoughtfulness which was very grave and impersonal when compared with the usual light, self-centred expressions of young girls' faces. At once Helen's artistic eye had Anne before her, robed in fit attire; in imagination she dressed her slowly from head to foot as the song went on, and was considering the question of jewels when the music ceased, and Belzini was turning toward her.

"I hope I may become better acquainted with this rich voice," she said, coming back gracefully to the present. "May I introduce myself? I should like to try a duet with you, if you will allow me, Miss—"

"Douglas," said Belzini; "and this, mademoiselle, is Mrs. Lorrington."

Such was the beginning.

In addition to Helen's fancy for Anne's fair grave face, the young girl's voice proved a firmer support for her high soprano than it had ever obtained. Her own circle in society and the music classes had been searched in vain more than once. For she needed a soprano, not a contralto. And as soprani are particularly human, there had never been any lasting co-operation. Anne, however, cheerfully sang whatever Belzini put before her, remained admiringly silent while Helen executed the rapid runs and trills with which she always decorated her part, and then, when the mezzo was needed again, gave her full voice willingly, supporting the other as the notes of an organ meet and support a flute after its solo.

Belzini was in ecstasies; he sat up all night to copy music for them. He said, anxiously, to Helen: "And the young girl? You like her, do you not? Such a voice for you!"

"But I can not exactly buy young girls, can I?" said Mrs. Lorrington, smiling.

More and more, however, each day she liked "the young girl" for herself alone. She was an original, of course; almost an aboriginal; for she told the truth exactly upon all occasions, appropriate or inappropriate, and she had convictions. She was not aware, apparently, of the old-fashioned and cumbrous appearance of these last-named articles of mental furniture. But the real secret of Helen's liking lay in the fact that Anne admired her, and was at the same time neither envious nor jealous, and from her youth she had been troubled by the sure development of these two feelings, sooner or later, in all her girl companions. In truth, Helen's lot *was* enviable; and also, whether consciously or unconsciously, she had a skill in provoking jealousy. She was the spoiled child of fortune. It was no wonder, therefore, that those of her own sex and age seldom enjoyed being with her: the contrast was too great. Helen was, besides, the very queen of Whim.

The queen of Whim! By nature; which means that she had a highly developed imagination. By the life she had led, having never, save for the six short months of her husband's adoring rule, been under the control, or even advice, of any man. For whim can be thoroughly developed only in feminine households: it is essentially feminine. And Helen had been brought up by a maiden aunt, who lived alone. A man, however mild, demands in a home at least a pretense of fixed hours and regularity; only a household of women is capable of no regularity at all, of changing the serious dinner hour capriciously, and even giving up dinner altogether. Only a household of women has sudden inspirations as to journeys and departures within the hour; brings forth sudden ideas as to changes of route while actually on the way, and a going southward instead of westward, with a total indifference to supper. Helen's present whim was Anne.

"I want you to spend part of the holidays with me," she said, a few days before Christmas. "Come on Monday, and stay over New-Year's Day."

"Oh, I can not," said Anne, startled.

"Why not? Tante will consent if I ask her; she always does. Do you love this crowded house so much that you can not leave it?"

"It is not that. But—"

"But you are shy. But Miss Vanhorn might not like it. You do not know Aunt Margaretta. You have no silk gown. Now let *me* talk. I will write to Miss Vanhorn. Aunt Margaretta is as gentle as a dove. I am bold enough for two. And the silk dress shall come from me."

"I could not take that, Mrs. Lorrington."

"Because you are proud?"

"No; but because I would rather not. It would be too great an obligation."

"You repay me by your voice a thousandfold, Anne. I have never had the right voice for mine until now; and therefore the obligation is on my side. I do not speak of the pleasure your visit will give me, because I hope to make that mutual. But say no more. I intend to have my way."

And she had her way. "I have always detested Miss Vanhorn, with her caraway seeds, and her malice," she explained to Tante. "Much as I like Anne for herself alone, it will be delicious also to annoy the old dragon by bringing into notice this unknown niece whom she is hiding here so carefully. Now confess, Tante, that it will be delicious."

Tante shook her head reprovingly. But she herself was in her heart by no means fond of Miss Vanhorn; she had had more than one battle royal with that venerable Knickerbocker, which had tested even her celebrated suavity.

Helen's note was as follows:

"Dear Miss Vanhorn,—I very much wish to persuade your charming niece, Miss Douglas, to spend a portion of the holidays with me. Her voice is marvellously sweet, and Aunt Margaretta is most anxious to hear it; while *I* am desirous to have her in my own home, even if but for a few days, in order that I may learn more of her truly admirable qualities, which she inherits, no doubt, from your family.

"I trust you will add your consent to Tante's, already willingly bestowed, and make me thereby still more your obliged friend,

"Helen Roosbroeck Lorrington."

The obliged friend had the following answer:

"Miss Vanhorn presents her compliments to Mrs. Lorrington, with thanks for her note, which, however, was an unnecessary attention, Miss Vanhorn claiming no authority over the movements of Anne Douglas (whose relationship to her is remote), beyond a due respect for the rules of the institution where she has been placed. Miss Vanhorn is gratified to learn that Miss Douglas's voice is already of practical use to her, and has the honor of remaining Mrs. Lorrington's obliged and humble servant.

"Madison Square, *Tuesday*."

Tears sprang to Anne's eyes when Helen showed her this note.

"Why do you care? She was always a dragon; forget her. Now, Anne, remember that it is all understood, and the carriage will come for you on Monday." Then, seeing the face before her still irresolute, she added: "If you are to have pupils, some of them may be like me. You ought, therefore, to learn how to manage *me*, you know."

"You are right," said Anne, seriously. "It is strange how little confidence I feel."

Helen, looking at her as she stood there in her island gown, coarse shoes, and old-fashioned collar, did not think it strange at all, but wondered, as she had wondered a hundred times before, why it was that this girl did not think of herself and her own appearance. "And you must let me have my way, too, about something for you to wear," she added.

"It shall be as you wish, Helen. It can not be otherwise, I suppose, if I go to you. But—I hope the time will come when I can do something for you."

"Never fear; it will. I feel it instinctively. You will either save my life or take it—one or the other; but I am not sure which."

Monday came; and after her lonely Christmas, Anne was glad to step into Miss Teller's carriage, and be taken to the home on the Avenue. The cordial welcome she received there was delightful to her, the luxury novel. She enjoyed everything simply and sincerely, from the late breakfast in the small warm breakfast-room, from which the raw light of the winter morning was carefully excluded, to the chat with Helen over the dressing-room fire late at night, when all the house was still. Helen's aunt, Miss Teller, was a thin, light-eyed person of fifty-five years of age. Richly dressed, very tall, with a back as immovable and erect as though made of steel, and a tower of blonde lace on her head, she was a personage of imposing aspect, but in reality as mild as a sheep.

"Yes, my dear," she said, when Anne noticed the tinted light in the breakfast-room; "I take great care about light, which I consider an influence in our households too much neglected. The hideous white glare in most American breakfast-rooms on snowy winter mornings has often made me shudder when I have been visiting my friends; only the extremely vigorous can enjoy this sharp contact with the new day. Then the æsthetic effect: children are always homely when the teeth are changing and the shoulder-blades prominent; and who wishes to see, besides, each freckle and imperfection upon the countenances of those he loves? I have observed, too, that even morning prayer, as a family observance, fails to counter-act the influence of this painful light. For if as you kneel you cover your face with your hands, the glare will be doubly unbearable when you remove them; and if you do *not* cover your brow, you will inevitably blink. Those who do not close their eyes at all are the most comfortable, but I trust we would all prefer to suffer rather than be guilty of such irreverence."

"Now that is Aunt Gretta exactly," said Helen, as Miss Teller left the room. "When you are once accustomed to her height and blonde caps, you will find her soft as a down coverlet."

Here Miss Teller returned. "My dear," she said, anxiously, addressing Anne, "as to soap for the hands—what kind do you prefer?"

"Anne's hands are beautiful, and she will have the white soap in the second box on the first shelf of the store-room—the rose; *not* the heliotrope, which is mine," said Helen, taking one of the young girl's hands, and spreading out the firm taper fingers. "See her wrists! Now my wrists are small too, but then there is nothing but wrist all the way up."

"My dear, your arms have been much admired," said Miss Margaretta, with a shade of bewilderment in her voice.

"Yes, because I choose they shall be. But when I spoke of Anne's hands, I spoke artistically, aunt."

"Do you expect Mr. Blum to-day?" said Miss Teller.

"Oh no," said Helen, smiling. "Mr. Blum, Anne, is a poor artist whom Aunt Gretta is cruel enough to dislike."

"Not on account of his poverty," said Miss Margaretta, "but on account of my having half-brothers, with large families, all with weak lungs, taking cold, I may say, at a breath—a mere breath; and Mr. Blum insists upon coming here without overshoes when there has been a thaw, and sitting all the evening in wet boots, which naturally makes me think of my brothers' weak families, to say nothing of the danger to himself."

"Well, Mr. Blum is not coming. But Mr. Heathcote is."

"Ah."

"And Mr. Dexter may."

"I am always glad to see Mr. Dexter," said Aunt Margaretta.

Mr. Heathcote did not come; Mr. Dexter did. But Anne was driving with Miss Teller, and missed the visit.

"A remarkable man," said the elder lady, as they sat at the dinner table in the soft radiance of wax lights.

"You mean Mr. Blum?" said Helen. "This straw-colored jelly exactly matches me, Anne."

"I mean Mr. Dexter," said Miss Teller, nodding her head impressively. "Sent through college by the bounty of a relative (who died immediately afterward, in the most reprehensible way, leaving him absolutely nothing), Gregory Dexter, at thirty-eight, is to-day a man of modern and distinct importance. Handsome—you do not contradict me there, Helen?"

"No, aunt."

"Handsome," repeated Miss Teller, triumphantly, "successful, moral, kind-hearted, and rich—what would you have more? I ask you, Miss Douglas, what would you have more?"

"Nothing," said Helen. "Anne has confided to me—nothing. Long live Gregory Dexter! And I feel sure, too, that he will outlive us all. I shall go first. You will see. I always wanted to be first in everything—even the grave."

"My dear!" said Miss Margaretta.

"Well, aunt, now would you like to be last? Think how lonely you would be. Besides, all the best places would be taken," said Helen, in business-like tones, taking a spray of heliotrope from the vase before her.

New-Year's Day was, in the eyes of Margaretta Teller, a solemn festival; thought was given to it in June, preparation for it began in September. Many a call was made at the house on that day which neither Miss Margaretta, nor her niece, Mrs. Lorrington, attracted, but rather the old-time dishes and the old-time punch on their dining-room table. Old men with gouty feet, amateur antiquarians of mild but obstinate aspect, to whom Helen was "a slip of a girl," and Miss Margaretta still too youthful a person to be of much interest, called regularly on the old Dutch holiday, and tasted this New-Year's punch. They cherished the idea that they were thus maintaining the "solid old customs," and they spoke to each other in moist, husky under-tones when they met in the hall, as much as to say, "Ah, ah! you here? That's right—that's right. A barrier, sir—a barrier against modern innovation!"

Helen had several friends besides Anne to assist her in receiving, and the young island girl remained, therefore, more or less unnoticed, owing to her lack of the ready, graceful smiles and phrases which are the current coin of New-Year's Day. She passed rapidly through the different phases of timidity, bewilderment, and fatigue; and then, when more accustomed to the scene, she regained her composure, and even began to feel amused. She ceased hiding behind the others; she learned to repeat the same answers to the same questions without caring for their inanity; she gave up trying to distinguish names, and (like the others) massed all callers into a constantly arriving repetition of the same person, who was to be treated with a cordiality as impersonal as it was glittering. She tried to select Mr. Dexter, and at length decided that he was a certain person standing near Helen—a man with brown hair and eyes; but she was not sure, and Helen's manner betrayed nothing.

The fatiguing day was over at last, and then followed an hour or two of comparative quiet; the few familiar guests who remained were glad to sink down in easy-chairs, and enjoy connected sentences again. The faces of the ladies showed fine lines extending from the nostril to the chin; the muscles that had smiled so much were weary.

And now Anne discovered Gregory Dexter; and he was not the person she had selected. Mr. Dexter was a tall, broad-shouldered man, with an appearance of persistent vigor in his bearing, and a look of determination in his strong, squarely cut jaw and chin. His face was rather short, with good features and clear gray eyes, which met the gazer calmly; and there was about him that air of self-reliance which does not irritate in a large strong man, any more than imperiousness in a beautiful woman.

The person with brown eyes proved to be Mr. Heathcote. He seemed indolent, and contributed but few words to the general treasury of conversation.

Mr. Blum was present also; but on this occasion he wore the peculiarly new, shining, patent-leather boots dear to the hearts of his countrymen on festal occasions, and Miss Teller's anxieties were quiescent. Helen liked artists; she said that their ways were a "proud assertion that a ray of beauty outvalued all the mere utilities of the world."

"Are bad boots rays of beauty?" inquired Miss Margaretta.

"Yes. That is, a man whose soul is uplifted by art may not always remember his boots; to himself, no doubt, his feet seem winged."

"Very far from winged are Blum's feet," responded Miss Margaretta, shaking her head gravely. "Very, very far."

Late in the evening, when almost all the guests had departed, Helen seemed seized with a sudden determination to bring Anne into prominence. Mr. Dexter still lingered, and the artist. Also Ward Heathcote.

"Anne, will you sing now? First with me, then alone?" she said, going to the piano.

A bright flush rose in Anne's face; the prominent blue eyes of the German artist were fixed upon her; Gregory Dexter had turned toward her with his usual prompt attention. Even the indolent Heathcote looked up as Helen spoke. But having once decided to do a thing, Anne knew no way save to do it; having accepted Helen's generous kindness, she must now do what Helen asked in return. She rose in silence, and crossed the brightly lighted room on her way to the piano. Few women walk well; by well, is meant naturally. Helen was graceful; she had the lithe shape and long step which give a peculiar swaying grace, like that of elm branches. Yet Helen's walk belonged to the drawing-room, or at best the city pavement; one could not imagine her on a country road. Anne's gait was different. As she crossed the room alone, it drew upon her for the first time the full attention of the three gentlemen who were present. Blum stared gravely. Dexter's eyes moved up to her face, as if he saw it now with new interest. Heathcote leaned back on the sofa with an amused expression, glancing from Anne to Helen, as if saying, "I understand."

Anne wore one of Helen's gifts, a soft silk of pale gray, in deference to her mourning garb; the dress was high over the shoulders, but cut down squarely in front and behind, according to a fashion of the day. The sleeves came to the elbow only; the long skirt was severely plain. They had taken off their gloves, and the girl's beautiful arms were conspicuous, as well as her round, full, white throat.

The American Venus is thin.

American girls are slight; they have visible collar-bones and elbows. When they pass into the fullness of womanhood (if they pass at all), it is suddenly, leaving no time for the beautiful pure virginal outlines which made Anne Douglas an exception to her kind. Anne's walk was entirely natural, her poise natural; yet so perfect were her proportions that even Tante, artificial and French as she was, refrained from the suggestions and directions as to step and bearing which encircled the other pupils like an atmosphere.

The young girl's hair had been arranged by Helen's maid, under Helen's own direction, in a plain Greek knot, leaving the shape of the head, and the small ear, exposed; and as she stood by the piano, waiting, she looked (as Helen had intended her to look) like some young creature from an earlier world, startled and shy, yet too proud to run away.

They sang together; and in singing Anne recovered her self-possession. Then Helen asked her to sing without accompaniment a little island ballad which was one of her favorites, and leading her to the centre of the room, left her there alone. Poor Anne! But, moved by the one desire of pleasing Helen, she clasped her hands in simple child-like fashion, and began to sing, her eyes raised slightly so as to look above the faces of her audience. It was an old-fashioned ballad or chanson, in the patois of the voyageurs, with a refrain in a minor key, and it told of the vanishing of a certain petite Marie, and the sorrowing of her mother—a common-place theme long drawn out, the constantly recurring refrain, at first monotonous, becoming after a while sweet to the ear, like the wash of small waves on a smooth beach. But it was the ending upon which Helen relied for her effect. Suddenly the lament of the long-winded mother ended, the time changed, and a verse followed picturing the rapture of the lovers as they fled away in their sharp-bowed boat, wing and wing, over the blue lake. Anne sang this as though inspired; she forgot her audience, and sang as she had always sung it on the island for Rast and the children. Her voice floated through the house, she shaded her eyes with her hand, and leaned forward, gazing, as though she saw the boat across the water, and then she smiled, as, with a long soft note, the song ended.

But the instant it was over, her timidity came back with double force, and she hastily sought refuge beside Helen, her voice gone, in her eyes a dangerous nearness to tears.

There was now an outburst of compliments from Blum; but Helen kindly met and parried them. Mr. Dexter began a few well-chosen sentences of praise; but in the midst of his fluent adjectives, Anne glanced up so beseechingly that he caught the mist in her eyes, and instantly ceased. Nor was this all; he opened a discussion with Miss Teller, dragging in Heathcote also (against the latter's will), and thus secured for Anne the time to recover herself. She felt this quick kindness, and was grateful. She decided that she liked him; and she wondered whether Helen liked him also.

The next morning the fairy-time was over; she went back to school.

CHAPTER X.

"There are three sorts of egoists: those who live themselves and let others live; those who live themselves and don't let others live; and those who neither live themselves nor let others live."

"With thoughts and feelings very simple but very strong."—Tourguénieff.

The winter passed. The new pupil studied with diligence, and insisted upon learning the beginnings of piano-playing so thoroughly that the resigned little German master with ear-rings woke up and began to ask her whether she could not go through a course of ten years or so, and become "a real blayer, not like American blayers, who vant all to learn de same biece, and blay him mit de loud pedal down." Sometimes Helen bore her away to spend a Sunday; but there were no more New-Year's Days, or occasions for the gray silk. When together at Miss Teller's, the two sat over the dressing-room fire at night, talking with that delightful mixture of confidence and sudden little bits of hypocrisy in which women delight, and which undress seems to beget. The bits of hypocrisy, however, were all Helen's.

She had long ago gathered from Anne her whole simple history; she was familiar with the Agency, the fort, Miss Lois, Père Michaux, Dr. Gaston, Rast, Tita, and the boys, even old Antoine and his dogs, René and Lebeau. Anne, glad to have a listener, had poured out a flood of details from her lonely homesick heart, going back as far as her own lost mother, and her young step-mother Angélique. But it was not until one of these later midnight talks that the girl had spoken of her own betrothal. Helen was much surprised—the only surprise she had shown. "I should never have dreamed it, Crystal!" she exclaimed. "Never!" (Crystal was her name for Anne.)

"Why not?"

"Because you are so—young."

"But it often happens at my age. The fort ladies were married at eighteen and nineteen, and my own dear mother was only twenty."

"You adore this Rast, I suppose?"

"Yes, I like him."

"Nonsense! You mean that you adore him."

"Perhaps I do," said Anne, smiling. "I have noticed that our use of words is different."

"And how long have you adored him?"

"All my life."

The little sentence came forth gravely and sincerely. Helen surveyed the speaker with a quizzical expression in her narrow brown eyes. "No one 'adores' all one's life," she answered. Then, as Anne did not take up the challenge, she paused, and, after surveying her companion in silence for a moment, added, "There is no time fixed as yet for this marriage?"

"No; Rast has his position to make first. And I myself should be better pleased to have four or five years to give to the children before we are married. I am anxious to educate the boys."

"Bon!" said Helen. "All will yet end well, Virginie. My compliments to Paul. It is a pretty island pastoral, this little romance of yours; you have my good wishes."

The island pastoral was simple indeed compared with the net-work of fancies and manœuvres disclosed by Helen. Her life seemed to be a drama. Her personages were masked under fictitious names; the Poet, the Haunted Man, the Knight-errant, the Chanting Tenor, and the Bishop, all figured in her recitals, to which Anne listened with intense interest. Helen was a brilliant story-teller. She could give the salient points of a conversation, and these only. She colored everything, of course, according to her own fancy; but one could forgive her that for her skillful avoidance of dull details, whose stupid repetition, simply because they are true, is a habit with which many good people are afflicted.

The narrations, of course, were of love and lovers: it is always so in the midnight talks of women over the dying fire. Even the most secluded country girl will on such occasions unroll a list as long as Leporello's. The listener may know it is fictitious, and the narrator may know that she knows it. But there seems to be a fascination in the telling and the hearing all the same.

Helen amused herself greatly over the deep interest Anne took in her stories; to do her justice, they were generally true, the conversations only being more dramatic than the reality had been. This was not Helen's fault; she performed her own part brilliantly, and even went over, on occasion, and helped on the other side. But the American man is not distinguished for conversational skill. This comes, not from dullness or lack of appreciation, but rather from overappreciation. Without the rock-like slow self-confidence of the Englishman, the Frenchman's never-failing wish to please, or the idealizing powers of the German, the American, with a quicker apprehension, does not appear so well in conversation as any one of these compeers. He takes in an idea so quickly that elaborate comment seems to him hardly worth while; and thus he only has a word or two where an Englishman has several well-intentioned sentences, a Frenchman an epigram, and a German a whole cloud of philosophical quotations and comments. But it is, more than all else, the enormous strength which ridicule as an influence possesses in America that makes him what he is; he shrinks from the slightest appearance of "fine talking," lest the ever-present harpies of mirth should swoop down and feed upon his vitals.

Helen's friends, therefore, might not always have recognized themselves in her sparkling narratives, as far as their words were concerned; but it is only justice to them to add that she was never obliged to embellish their actions. She related to Anne apart, during their music lessons, the latest events in a whisper, while Belzini gave two minutes to cream candy and rest; the stories became the fairy tales of the school-girl's quiet life. Through all, she found her interest more and more attracted by "the Bishop," who seemed, however, to be anything but an ecclesiastical personage.

Miss Vanhorn had been filled with profound astonishment and annoyance by Helen's note. She knew Helen, and she knew Miss Teller: what could they want of Anne? After due delay, she came in her carriage to find out.

Tante, comprehending her motive, sent Anne up stairs to attire herself in the second dress given by Helen—a plain black costume, simply but becomingly made, and employed the delay in talking to her visitor mellifluously on every conceivable subject save the desired one. She treated her to a dissertation on intaglii, to an argument or two on architecture, and was fervently asking her opinion of certain recently exhibited relics said to be by Benvenuto Cellini, when the door opened and Anne appeared.

The young girl greeted her grandaunt with the same mixture of timidity and hope which she had shown at their first interview. But Miss Vanhorn's face stiffened into rigidity as she surveyed her.

"She is impressed at last," thought the old Frenchwoman, folding her hands contentedly and leaning back in her chair, at rest (temporarily) from her labors.

But if impressed, Miss Vanhorn had no intention of betraying her impression for the amusement of her ancient enemy; she told Anne curtly to put on her bonnet, that she had come to take her for a drive. Once safely in the carriage, she extracted from her niece, who willingly answered, every detail of her acquaintance with Helen, and the holiday visit, bestowing with her own eyes, meanwhile, a close scrutiny upon the black dress, with whose texture and simplicity even her angry annoyance could find no fault.

"She wants to get something out of you, of course," she said, abruptly, when the story was told; "Helen Lorrington is a thoroughly selfish woman. I know her well. She introduced you, I suppose, as Miss Vanhorn's niece?"

"Oh no, grandaunt. She has no such thought."

"What do you know of her thoughts! You continue to go there?"

"Sometimes, on Sundays—when she asks me."

"Very well. But you are not to go again when company is expected; I positively forbid it. You were not brought down from your island to attend evening parties. You hear me?"

"Yes."

"Perhaps you are planning for a situation here at Moreau's next winter?" said the old woman, after a pause, peering at Anne suspiciously.

"I could not fill it, grandaunt; I could only teach in a country school."

"At Newport, or some such place, then?"

"I could not get a position of that kind."

"Mrs. Lorrington could help you."

"I have not asked her to help me."

"I thought perhaps she had some such idea of her own," continued Miss Vanhorn. "You can probably prop up that fife-like voice of hers in a way she likes; and besides, you are a good foil for her, with your big shoulders and bread-and-milk face. You little simpleton, don't you know that to even the most skillful flirt a woman friend of some kind or other is necessary as background and support?"

"No, I did not know it," said Anne, in a disheartened voice.

"What a friend for Helen Lorrington! No wonder she has pounced upon you! You would never see one of her manœuvres, although done within an inch of you. With your believing eyes, and your sincerity, you are worth your weight in silver to that straw-faced mermaid. But, after all, I do not interfere. Let her only obtain a good situation for you next year, and pay you back in more useful coin than fine dresses, and I make no objection."

She settled herself anew in the corner of the carriage, and began the process of extracting a seed, while Anne, silent and dejected, gazed into the snow-covered street, asking herself whether Helen and all this world were really as selfish and hypocritical as her grandaunt represented. But these thoughts soon gave way to the predominant one, the one that always came to her when with Miss Vanhorn—the thought of her mother.

"During the summer, do you still live in the old country house on the Hudson, grandaunt?"

Miss Vanhorn, who had just secured a seed, dropped it. "I am not aware that my old country house is anything to you," she answered, tartly, fitting on her flapping glove-fingers, and beginning a second search.

A sob rose in Anne's throat; but she quelled it. Her mother had spent all her life, up to the time of her marriage, at that old river homestead.

Soon after this, Madame Moreau sent out cards of invitation for one of her musical evenings. Miss Vanhorn's card was accompanied by a little note in Tante's own handwriting.

"The invitation is merely a compliment which I give myself the pleasure of paying to a distinguished patron of my school" (wrote the old French lady). "There will be nothing worthy of her ear—a simple school-girls' concert, in which Miss Douglas (who will have the kind assistance of Mrs. Lorrington) will take part. I can not urge, for so unimportant an affair, the personal presence of Miss Vanhorn; but I beg her to accept the inclosed card as a respectful remembrance from

"Hortense-Pauline Moreau."

"That will bring her," thought Tante, sealing the missive, in her old-fashioned way, with wax.

She was right; Miss Vanhorn came.

Anne sang first alone. Then with Helen.

"Isn't that Mrs. Lorrington?" said a voice behind Miss Vanhorn.

"Yes. My Louise tells me that she has taken up this Miss Douglas enthusiastically—comes here to sing with her almost every day."

"Who is the girl?"

Miss Vanhorn prepared an especially rigid expression of countenance for the item of relationship which she supposed would follow. But nothing came; Helen was evidently waiting for a more dramatic occasion. She felt herself respited; yet doubly angry and apprehensive.

When the song was ended, there was much applause of the subdued drawing-room kind—applause, however, plainly intended for Helen alone. Singularly enough, Miss Vanhorn resented this. "If I should take Anne, dress her properly, and introduce her as my niece, the Lorrington would be nowhere," she thought, angrily. It was the first germ of the idea.

It was not allowed to disappear. It grew and gathered strength slowly, as Tante and Helen intended it should; the two friendly conspirators never relaxed for a day their efforts concerning it. Anne remained unconscious of these manœuvres; but the old grandaunt was annoyed, and urged, and flattered, and menaced forward with so much skill that it ended in her proposing to Anne, one day in the early spring, that she should come and spend the summer with her, the children on the island to be provided for meanwhile by an allowance, and Anne herself to have a second winter at the Moreau school, if she wished it, so that she might be fitted for a higher position than otherwise she could have hoped to attain.

"Oh, grandaunt!" cried the girl, taking the old loosely gloved hand in hers.

"There is no occasion for shaking hands and grandaunting in that way," said Miss Vanhorn. "If you wish to do what I propose, do it; I am not actuated by any new affection for you. You will take four days to consider; at the end of that period, you may send me your answer. But, with your acceptance, I shall require the strictest obedience. And—no allusion whatever to your mother."

"What are to be my duties?" asked Anne, in a low voice.

"Whatever I require," answered the old woman, grimly.

At first Anne thought of consulting Tante. But she had a strong under-current of loyalty in her nature, and the tie of blood bound her to her grandaunt, after all: she decided to consult no one but herself. The third day was

Sunday. In the twilight she sat alone on her narrow bed, by the window of the dormitory, thinking. It was a boisterous March evening; the wildest month of the twelve was on his mad errands as usual. Her thoughts were on the island with the children; would it not be best for them that she should accept the offered allowance, and go with this strange grandaunt of hers, enduring as best she might her cold severity? Miss Lois's income was small; the allowance would make the little household comfortable. A second winter in New York would enable her to take a higher place as teacher, and also give the self-confidence she lacked. Yes; it was best.

But a great and overwhelming loneliness rose in her heart at the thought of another long year's delay before she could be with those she loved. Rast's last letter was in her pocket; she took it out, and held it in her hand for comfort. In it he had written of the sure success of his future; and Anne believed it as fully as he did. Her hand grew warmer as she held the sheet, and as she recalled his sanguine words. She began to feel courageous again. Then another thought came to her: must she tell Miss Vanhorn of her engagement? In their new conditions, would it not be dishonest to keep the truth back? "I do not see that it can be of any interest to her," she said to herself. "Still, I prefer to tell her." And then, having made her decision, she went to Tante.

Tante was charmed with the news (and with the success of her plan). She discoursed upon family affection in very beautiful language. "You will find a true well-spring of love in the heart of your venerable relative," she remarked, raising her delicate handkerchief, like the suggestion of a happiness that reached even to tears. "Long, long have I held your cherished grandaunt in a warm corner of my memory and heart."

This was true as regarded the time and warmth; only the latter was of a somewhat peppery nature.

The next morning Helen was told the news. She threw back her head in comic despair. "The old dragon has taken the game out of my hands at last," she said, "and ended all the sport. Excuse the title, Anne. But I am morally certain she has all sorts of vinegarish names for me. And now—am I to congratulate you upon your new home?"

"It is more a matter of duty, I think, than congratulation," said Anne, thoughtfully. "And next, I must tell her of my engagement."

"I wouldn't, if I were you, Crystal."

"Why?"

"She would rather have you free."

"I shall be free, as far as she is concerned."

"Do not be too sure of that. And take my advice—do not tell her."

Anne, however, paid no heed to this admonition; some things she did simply because she could not help doing them. She had intended to make her little confession immediately; but Miss Vanhorn gave her no opportunity. "That is enough talking," she said. "I have neuralgia in my eyebrow."

"But, grandaunt, I feel that I ought to tell you."

"Tell me nothing. Don't you know how to be silent? Set about learning, then. When I have neuralgia in my eyebrow, you are to speak only from necessity; when I have it in the eye itself, you are not to speak at all. Find me a caraway, and don't bungle."

She handed her velvet bag to Anne, and refitted the fingers of her yellow glove: evidently the young girl's duties were beginning.

Several days passed, but the neuralgia always prevented the story. At last the eyebrow was released, and then Anne spoke. "I wish to tell you, grandaunt, before I come to you, that I am engaged—engaged to be married."

"Who cares?" said Miss Vanhorn. "To the man in the moon, I suppose; most school-girls are."

"No, to—"

"Draw up my shawl," interrupted the old woman. "*I* do not care who it is. Why do you keep on telling me?"

"Because I did not wish to deceive you."

"Wait till I ask you not to deceive me. Who is the boy?"

"His name is Erastus Pronando," began Anne; "and—"

"Pronando?" cried Katharine Vanhorn, in a loud, bewildered voice—"Pronando? And his father's name?"

"John, I believe," said Anne, startled by the change in the old face. "But he has been dead many years."

Old Katharine rose; her hands trembled, her eyes flashed. "You will give up this boy at once and forever," she said, violently, "or my compact with you is at an end."

"How can I, grandaunt? I have promised—"

"I believe I am mistress of my own actions; and in this affair I will have no sort of hesitation," continued the old woman, taking the words from Anne, and tapping a chair back angrily with her hand. "Decide now—this moment. Break this engagement, and my agreement remains. Refuse to break it, and it falls. That is all."

"You are unjust and cruel," said the girl, roused by these arbitrary words.

Miss Vanhorn waved her hand for silence.

"If you will let me tell you, aunt—"

The old woman bounded forward suddenly, as if on springs, seized her niece by both shoulders, and shook her with all her strength. "There!" she said, breathless. "*Will* you stop talking! All I want is your answer—yes, or no."

The drawing-room of Madame Moreau had certainly never witnessed such a sight as this. One of its young ladies shaken—yes, absolutely shaken like a refractory child! The very chairs and tables seemed to tremble, and visibly hope that there was no one in the *salon des élèves*, behind.

Anne was more startled than hurt by her grandaunt's violence. "I am sorry to displease you," she said, slowly and very gravely; "but I can not break my engagement."

Without a word, Miss Vanhorn drew her shawl round her shoulders, pinned it, crossed the room, opened the door, and was gone. A moment later her carriage rolled away, and Anne, alone in the drawing-room, listened to the sound of the wheels growing fainter and fainter, with a chilly mixture of blank surprise, disappointment, and grief filling her heart. "But it *was* right that I should tell her," she said to herself as she went up stairs—"it *was* right."

Right and wrong always presented themselves to her as black and white. She knew no shading. She was wrong; there are grays. But, so far in her life, she had not been taught by sad experience to see them. "It *was* right," she repeated to Helen, a little miserably, but still steadfastly.

"I am not so sure of that," replied Mrs. Lorrington. "You have lost a year's fixed income for those children, and a second winter here for yourself; and for what? For the sake of telling the dragon something which does not concern her, and which she did not wish to know."

"But it was true."

"Are we to go out with trumpets and tell everything we know, just because it is true? Is there not such a thing as egotistical truthfulness?"

"It makes no difference," said Anne, despairingly. "I had to tell her."

"You are stubborn, Crystal, and you see but one side of a question. But never fear; we will circumvent the dragon yet. I wonder, though, why she was so wrought up by the name Pronando? Perhaps Aunt Gretta will know."

Miss Teller did not know; but one of the husky-voiced old gentlemen who kept up the "barrier, sir, against modern innovation," remembered the particulars (musty and dusty now) of Kate Vanhorn's engagement to one of the Pronandos—the wild one who ran away. He was younger than she was, a handsome fellow (yes, yes, he remembered it all now), and "she was terribly cut up about it, and went abroad immediately." Abroad—great panacea for American woes! To what continent can those who live "abroad" depart when trouble seizes *them* in its pitiless claws?

Time is not so all-erasing as we think. Old Katharine Vanhorn, at seventy, heard from the young lips of her grandniece the name which had not been mentioned in her presence for nearly half a century—the name which still had power to rouse in her heart the old bitter feeling. For John Pronando had turned from her to an uneducated common girl—a market-gardener's daughter. The proud Kate Vanhorn resented the defection instantly; she broke the bond of her betrothal, and sailed for England before Pronando realized that she was offended. This idyl of the gardener's daughter was but one of his passing amusements; and so he wrote to his black-browed goddess. But she replied that if he sought amusement of that kind during the short period of betrothal, he would seek it doubly after marriage, and *then* it would not be so easy to sail for Europe. She considered that she had had an escape. Pronando, handsome, light-hearted, and careless, gave up his offended Juno without much heartache, and the episode of Phyllis being by this time finished, he strayed back to his Philadelphia home, to embroil himself as usual with his family, and, later, to follow out the course ordained for him by fate. Kate Vanhorn had other suitors; but the old wound never healed.

"Come and spend the summer with me," said Helen. "I trust I am as agreeable as the dragon."

"No; I must stay here. Even as it is, she is doing a great deal for me; I have no real claim upon her," replied Anne, trying not to give way to the loneliness that oppressed her.

"Only that of being her nearest living relative, and natural heir."

"I have not considered the question of inheritance," replied the island girl, proudly.

"I know you have not; yet it is there. Old ladies, however, instead of natural heirs, are apt to prefer unnatural ones—cold-blooded Societies, Organizations, and the endless Heathen. But I am in earnest about the summer, Crystal: spend it with me."

"You are always generous to me," said Anne, gratefully.

"No; I never was generous in my life. I do not know how to be generous. But this is the way it is: I am rich; I want a companion; and I like *you*. Your voice supports mine perfectly, and is not in the least too loud—a thing I detest. Besides, we look well together. You are an excellent background for me; you make me look poetic; whereas most women make me look like a caricature of myself—of what I really am. As though a straw-bug should go out walking with a very attenuated grasshopper. Now if the straw-bug went out always with a plump young toad or wood-turtle, people might be found to admire even *his* hair-like fineness of limb and yellow transparency, by force, you know, of contrast."

Anne laughed; but there was also a slight change of expression in her face.

"I can read you, Crystal," said Helen, laughing in her turn. "Old Katharine has already told you all those things—sweet old lady! She understands me so well! Come; call it selfishness or generosity, as you please; but accept."

"It is generosity, Helen; which, however, I must decline."

"It must be very inconvenient to be so conscientious," said Mrs. Lorrington. "But mind, I do not give it up. What! lose so good a listener as you are? To whom, then, can I confide the latest particulars respecting the Poet, the Bishop, the Knight-errant, and the Haunted Man?"

"I like the Bishop," said Anne, smiling back at her friend. She had acquired the idea, without words, that Helen liked him also.

The story of Miss Vanhorn's change was, of course, related to Tante: Anne had great confidence both in the old Frenchwoman's kindness of heart and excellent judgment.

Tante listened, asked a question or two, and then said: "Yes, yes, I see. For the present, nothing more can be done. She will allow you to finish your year here, and as the time is of value to you, you shall continue your studies through the vacation. But not at my New Jersey farm, as she supposes; at a better place than that. You shall go to Pitre."

"A place, Tante?"

"No; a friend of mine, and a woman."

Mademoiselle Jeanne-Armande Pitre was not so old as Tante (Tante had friends of all ages); she was about fifty, but conveyed the impression of never having been young. "She is an excellent teacher," continued the other Frenchwoman, "and so closely avaricious that she will be glad to take you even for the small sum you will pay. She is employed in a Western seminary somewhere, but always returns to this little house of hers for the summer vacation. Your opportunity for study with her will be excellent; she has a rage for study. Write and tell your grandaunt, ma fille, what I have decided."

"Ma fille" wrote; but Miss Vanhorn made no reply.

Early in June, accompanied by "monsieur," Anne started on her little journey. The German music master said farewell with hearty regret. He was leaving also; he should not be with Madame Moreau another winter, he said. The Italian atmosphere stifled him, and the very sight of Belzini made him "dremble vit a er-righteous er-rage." He gave Anne his address, and begged that she would send to him when she wanted new music; "music *vort* someding." Monsieur Laurent, Anne's escort, was a nephew of Tante's, a fine-looking middle-aged Frenchman, who taught the verbs with a military air. But it was not so much his air as his dining-room which gave him importance in the eyes of the school. The "salle à manger de monsieur" was a small half-dark apartment, where he took his meals by himself. It was a mysterious place; monsieur was never seen there; it was not known even at what hour he dined. But there were stories in whispered circulation of soups, sauces, salads, and wines served there in secret, which made the listeners hungry even in the mere recital. They peered into the dim little room as they passed, but never saw anything save a brown linen table-cloth, an old caster, and one chair. It was stated, however, that this caster was not a common caster, but that it held, instead of the ordinary pepper and mustard, various liquids and spices of mysterious nature, delightfully and wickedly French.

In less than an hour the travellers reached Lancaster. Here monsieur placed Anne in a red wagon which was in waiting, said good-by hastily (being, perhaps, in a hurry to return to his dining-room), and caught the down train back to the city. He had lived in America so long that he could hurry like a native.

The old horse attached to the red wagon walked slowly over a level winding road, switching his tail to and fro, and stopping now and then to cough, with the profundity which only a horse's cough possesses. At last, turning into a field, he stopped before what appeared to be a fragment of a house.

"Is this the place?" said Anne, surprised.

"It's Miss Peter's," replied the boy driver.

The appearance of Mademoiselle Pitre in person at the door now removed all doubt as to her abode. "I am glad to see you," she said, extending a long yellow hand. "Enter."

The house, which had never been finished, was old; the sides and back were of brick, and the front of wood, temporarily boarded across. The kitchen and one room made all the depth; above, there were three small chambers. After a while, apparently, windows and a front door had been set in the temporary boarding, and a flight of steps added. Mademoiselle had bought the house in its unfinished condition, and had gradually become an object of great unpopularity in the neighborhood because, as season after season rolled by, she did nothing more to her purchase. What did she mean, then? Simple comment swelled into suspicion; the penny-saving old maid was now considered a dark and mysterious person at Lancaster. Opinions varied as to whether she had committed a crime in her youth, or intended to commit one in her age. At any rate, she was not like other people—in the country a heinous crime.

The interior of this half-house was not uncomfortable, although arranged with the strictest economy. The chief room had been painted a brilliant blue by the skillful hands of mademoiselle herself; there was no carpet, but in summer one can spare a carpet; and Anne thought the bright color, the growing plants and flowers, the gayly colored crockery, the four white cats, the sunshine, and the cool open space unfilled by furniture, quaintly foreign and attractive.

The mistress of the house was tall and yellow. She was attired in a black velvet bodice, and a muslin skirt whereon a waving design, like an endless procession of spindling beet roots, or fat leeches going round and round, was depicted in dark crimson. This muslin was secretly admired in the neighborhood; but as mademoiselle never went to church, and, what was worse, made no change in her dress on the Sabbath-day, it was considered a step toward rationalism to express the liking.

Anne slept peacefully on her narrow bed, and went down to a savory breakfast the next morning. The old Irish servant, Nora, who came out from the city every summer to live with mademoiselle, prepared with skill the few dishes the careful mistress ordered. But when the meal was over, Anne soon discovered that the careful mistress was also an expert in teaching. Her French, Italian, music, and drawing were all reviewed and criticised, and then Jeanne-Armande put on her bonnet, and told her pupil to make ready for her first lesson in botany.

"Am I to study botany?" said Anne, surprised.

"All study botany who come to me," replied Jeanne-Armande, much in the tone of "Lasciate ogni speranza voi ch' entrate." "Is that all the bonnet you have? It is far too fine. I will buy you a Shaker at the shop." And with her tin flower case slung from her shoulder, she started down the road toward the country store at the corners; here she bought a Shaker bonnet for her pupil, selecting one that was bent, and demanding a reduction in price in consequence of the "irreparable injury to the fibre of the fabric." The shop-keeper, an anxious little man with a large family, did his best to keep on good terms with "the foreigner" privately, and to preserve on other occasions that appearance of virtuous disapproval which the neighborhood required of him. He lived haunted by a fear lest the Frenchwoman and her chief detractors should meet face to face in the narrow confines of his domain; and he had long determined that in case of such event he would be down in the cellar drawing molasses—an operation universally known to consume time. But the sword of Damocles does not fall; in this instance, as in others, mademoiselle departed in safety, bearing Anne away to the woods, her face hidden in the depths of the Shaker.

Wild flowers, that seem so fresh and young, are, singularly enough, the especial prey of old maids. Young girls love the garden flowers; beautiful women surround themselves with hot-house hues and perfumes. But who goes into the woods, explores the rocky glens, braves the swamps? Always the ardent-hearted old maid, who, in her plain garb and thick shoes, is searching for the delicate little wild blossoms, the world over.

Jeanne-Armande had an absorbing love for flowers, a glowing enthusiasm for botany. She now taught Anne the flower study with what Tante would have called "a rage." More than once the pupil thought how strange it was that fate should have forced into her hands at this late hour the talisman that might once have been the key to her grandaunt's favor. It did not occur to her that Tante was the Fate.

Letters had come from all on the island, and from Rast. Regarding her course in telling Miss Vanhorn of her engagement, Miss Lois wrote that it was "quite unnecessary," and Dr. Gaston that it was "imprudent." Even Rast (this was hardest to bear) had written, "While I am proud, dearest, to have your name linked with mine, still, I like better to think of the time when I can come and claim you in person, in the face of all the grandaunts in the world, who, if they *knew* nothing, could not in the mean time harass and annoy you."

Père Michaux made no comment. Anne looked through Tita's letters for some time expectantly, but no message in his small, clear handwriting appeared.

The weeks passed. The pupil learned the real kindness of the teacher, and never thought of laughing at her oddities, until—Helen came.

For Helen came: on her way home from her grandfather's bedside, whither she had been summoned (as usual two or three times each year) "to see him die."

"Grandpapa always recovers as soon as I enter the door," she said. "I should think he would insist upon my living there as a safeguard! This time I did not even see him—he did not wish me in the room; and so, having half a day to spare, I decided to send my maid on, and stop over and see *you*, Crystal."

Anne, delighted and excited, sat looking at her friend with happy eyes. "I am so glad, glad, to see you!" she said.

"Then present me to your hostess and jailer. For I intend to remain overnight, and corrupt the household."

Jeanne-Armande was charmed with their visitor; she said she was "a lady decidedly as it should be." Helen accompanied them on their botany walk, observed the velvet bodice and beet-root muslin, complimented the ceremonious courses of the meagre little dinner, and did not laugh until they were safely ensconced in Anne's cell for the night.

"But, Crystal," she said, when she had imitated Jeanne-Armande, and Anne herself as pupil, with such quick and ridiculous fidelity that Anne was obliged to bury her face in the pillow to stifle her laughter, "I have a purpose in coming here. The old dragon has appeared at Caryl's, where Aunt Gretta and I spent last summer, and where we intend to spend the remainder of this; she is even there to-night, caraway seeds, malice, and all. Now I want you to go back with me, as my guest for a week or two, and together we will annihilate her."

"Do not call her by that name, Helen."

"Not respectful enough? Grand Llama, then; the double l scintillates with respect. The Grand Llama being present, I want to bring you on the scene as a charming, botanizing, singing niece whom she has strangely neglected. Will you go?"

"Of course I can not."

"You have too many principles; and, mind you, principles are often shockingly egotistical and selfish. I would rather have a mountain of sins piled up against me on the judgment-day, and a crowd of friends whom I had helped and made happy, than the most snowy empty pious record in the world, and no such following."

"One does not necessitate the other," said Anne, after her usual pause when with Helen: she was always a little behind Helen's fluent phrases. "One can have friends without sins."

"Wait and see," said Helen.

In the morning the brilliant visitor took her departure, and the half-house fell back into its usual quietude. Anne did not go with Helen; but Helen avowed her purpose of bringing her to Caryl's yet, in spite of fate. "I am not easily defeated," she said. "When I wish a thing, it always happens. But, like the magicians, nobody notices how hard I have worked to have it happen."

She departed. And within a week she filled Caryl's with descriptions of Jeanne-Armande, the velvet bodice, the beet-root skirt, the blue room, the white cats, and the dinner, together with the solitary pupil, whose knowledge of *botany* was something unparalleled in the history of the science. Caryl's was amused with the descriptions, and cared nothing for the reality. But when Miss Vanhorn heard the tale, it was the reality that menaced her. No one knew as yet the name of the solitary pupil, nor the relationship to herself; but of course Mrs. Lorrington was merely biding her time. What was her purpose? In her heart she pondered over this new knowledge of botany, expressly paraded by Helen; her own eyes and hands were not as sure and deft as formerly. Sometimes now when she stooped to gather a flower, it was only a leaf with the sun shining on it, or a growth of fungus, yellowly white. "Of course it is all a plan of old Moreau's," she said to herself. "Anne would never have thought of studying botany to gain my favor; she hasn't wit enough. It is old Moreau and the Lorrington together. Let us see what will be their next step."

But Helen merely decorated her stories, and told nothing new. One day some one asked: "But who is this girl? All this while you have not told us; nor the place where this remarkable half-house is."

"I am not at liberty to tell," replied Helen's clear even voice. "That is not permitted—at present."

Miss Vanhorn fidgeted in her corner, and put up her glass to catch any wandering expressions that might be turning in her direction; but there were none. "She is giving me a chance of having Anne here peaceably," she thought. "If, after a reasonable time, I do not accept it, she will declare war, and the house will ring with my hard-heartedness. Fortunately I do not care for hard-heartedness."

She went off on her solitary drive; mistook two flowers; stumbled and hurt her ankle; lost her magnifying-glass. On her way home she sat and meditated. It would be comfortable to have young eyes and hands to assist her. Also, if Anne was really there in person, then, when all the duets were sung, and the novelty (as well as difficulty) over, Mrs. Lorrington would be the first to weary of her protégée, and would let her fall like a faded leaf. And that would be the end of that. Here a sudden and new idea came to her: might not this very life at

Caryl's break up, of itself, the engagement which was so obnoxious? If she should bring Anne here and introduce her as her niece, might not her very ignorance of the world and crude simplicity attract the attention of some of the loungers at Caryl's, who, if they exerted themselves, would have little difficulty in effacing the memory of that boy on the island? They would not, of course, be in earnest, but the result would be accomplished all the same. Anne was impressionable, and truthfulness itself. Yes, it could be done.

Accompanied by her elderly maid, she went back to New York; and then out to the half-house.

"I have changed my mind," she announced, abruptly, taking her seat upon Jeanne-Armande's hard sofa. "You are to come with me. This is the blue room, I suppose; and there are the four cats. Where is the bodiced woman? Send her to me; and go pack your clothes immediately."

"Am I to go to Caryl's—where Helen is?" said Anne, in excited surprise.

"Yes; you will see your Helen. You understand, I presume, that she is at the bottom of all this."

"But—do you like Helen, grandaunt?"

"I am extremely fond of her," replied Miss Vanhorn, dryly. "Run and make ready; and send the bodiced woman to me. I give you half an hour; no longer."

Jeanne-Armande came in with her gliding step. In her youth a lady's footfall was never heard. She wore long narrow cloth gaiters without heels, met at the ankles by two modest ruffles, whose edges were visible when the wind blew. The exposure of even a hair's-breadth rim of ankle would have seemed to her an unpardonable impropriety. However, there was no danger; the ruffles swept the ground.

The Frenchwoman was grieved to part with her pupil; she had conceived a real affection for her in the busy spot which served her as a heart. She said good-by in the privacy of the kitchen, that Miss Vanhorn might not see the tears in her eyes; then she returned to the blue room and went through a second farewell, with a dignity appropriate to the occasion.

"Good-by," said Anne, coming back from the doorway to kiss her thin cheek a second time. Then she whispered: "I may return to you after all, mademoiselle. Do not forget me."

"The dear child!" said Jeanne-Armande, waving her handkerchief as the carriage drove away. And there was a lump in her yellow old throat which did not disappear all day.

CHAPTER XI.

"Those who honestly make their own way without the aid of fortunate circumstances and by the force of their own intelligence. This includes the great multitude of Americans."

—George William Curtis.

"He is a good fellow, spoiled. Whether he can be unspoiled, is doubtful. It might be accomplished by the Blessing we call Sorrow."

When the two travellers arrived at Caryl's, Helen was gone. Another telegraphic dispatch had again summoned her to her frequently dying grandfather.

"You are disappointed," said Miss Vanhorn.

"Yes, grandaunt."

"You will have all the more time to devote to me," said the old woman, with her dry little laugh.

Caryl's was a summer resort of an especial kind. Persons who dislike crowds, persons who seek novelty, and, above all, persons who spend their lives in carefully avoiding every thing and place which can even remotely be called popular, combine to make such nooks, and give them a brief fame—a fame which by its very nature must die as suddenly as it is born. Caryl's was originally a stage inn, or "tarvern," in the dialect of the district. But the stage ran no longer, and as the railway was several miles distant, the house had become as isolated as the old road before its door, which went literally nowhere, the bridge which had once spanned the river having fallen into ruin. Some young men belonging to those New York families designated by Tante as "Neeker-bokers" discovered Caryl's by chance, and established themselves there as a place free from new people, with some shooting, and a few trout. The next summer they brought their friends, and from this beginning had swiftly grown the present state of things, namely, two hundred persons occupying the old building and hastily erected cottages, in rooms which their city servants would have refused with scorn.

The crowd of summer travellers could not find Caryl's; Caryl's was not advertised. It was not on the road to anywhere. It was a mysterious spot. The vogue of such places changes as fantastically as it is created; the people who make it take flight suddenly, and never return. If it exist at all, it falls into the hands of another class; and there is a great deal of wondering (deservedly) over what was ever found attractive in it. The nobler ocean beaches, grand mountains, and bounteous springs will always be, must always be, popular; it is Nature's ironical method, perhaps, of forcing the would-be exclusives to content themselves with her second best, after all.

Caryl's, now at the height of its transient fame, was merely a quiet nook in the green country, with no more attractions than a hundred others; but the old piazza was paced by the little high-heeled shoes of fashionable women, the uneven floors swept by their trailing skirts. French maids and little bare-legged children sported in the old-fashioned garden, and young men made up their shooting parties in the bare office, and danced in the evening—yes, really danced, not leaving it superciliously to the boys—in the rackety bowling-alley, which, refloored, did duty as a ball-room. There was a certain woody, uncloying flavor about Caryl's (so it was asserted), which could not exist amid the gilding of Saratoga. All this Miss Vanhorn related to her niece on the day of their arrival. "I do not expect you to understand it," she said; "but pray make no comment; ask no question. Accept everything, and then you will pass."

Aunt and niece had spent a few days in New York, *en route*. The old lady was eccentric about her own attire; she knew that she could afford to be eccentric. But for her niece she purchased a sufficient although simple supply of summer costumes, so that the young girl made her appearance among the others without attracting especial attention. Helen was not there; no one identified Miss Douglas as the *rara avis* of her fantastic narrations. And there was no surface sparkle about Anne, none of the usual girlish wish to attract attention, which makes the eyes brighten, the color rise, and the breath quicken when entering a new circle.

That old woman of the world, Katharine Vanhorn, took no step to attract notice to her niece. She knew that Anne's beauty was of the kind that could afford to wait; people would discover it for themselves. Anne remained, therefore, quietly by her side through several days, while she, not unwilling at heart to have so fresh a listener, talked on and instructed her. Miss Vanhorn was not naturally brilliant, but she was one of those society women who, in the course of years of fashionable life, have selected and retained for their own use excellent bits of phrasing not original with themselves, idiomatic epithets, a way of neatly describing a person in a word or two as though you had ticketed him, until the listener really takes for brilliancy what is no more than a thread-and-needle shop of other people's wares.

"Any man," she said, as they sat in the transformed bowling-alley—"any man, no matter how insignificant and unattractive, can be made to believe that any woman, no matter how beautiful or brilliant, is in love with him, at the expense of two looks and one sigh."

"But who cares to make him believe?" said Anne, with the unaffected, cheerful indifference which belonged to her, and which had already quieted Miss Vanhorn's fears as to any awkward self-consciousness.

"Most women."

"Why?"

"To swell their trains," replied the old woman. "Isabel Varce, over there in blue, and Rachel Bannert, the one in black, care for nothing else."

"Mrs. Bannert is very ugly," said Anne, with the calm certainty of girlhood.

"Oh, is she?" said Miss Vanhorn, laughing shortly. "You will change your mind, my Phyllis; you will learn that a dark skin and half-open eyes are superb."

"If *Helen* was here, people would see real beauty," answered Anne, with some scorn.

"They are a contrast, I admit; opposite types. But we must not be narrow, Phyllis; you will find that people continue to look at Mrs. Bannert, no matter who is by. Here is some one who seems to know you."

"Mr. Dexter," said Anne, as the tall form drew near. "He is a friend of Helen's."

"Helen has a great many friends. However, I happen to have heard of this Mr. Dexter. You may present him to me—I hope you know how."

All Madame Moreau's pupils knew how. Anne performed her task properly, and Dexter, bringing forward one of the old broken-backed chairs (which formed part of the "woody and uncloying flavor" of Caryl's), sat down beside them.

"I am surprised that you remembered me, Mr. Dexter," said the girl. "You saw me but once, and on New-Year's Day too, among so many."

"But you remembered me, Miss Douglas."

"That is different. You were kind to me—about the singing. It is natural that I should remember."

"And why not as natural that I should remember the singing?"

"Because it was not good enough to have made any especial impression," replied Anne, looking at him calmly with her clear violet eyes.

"It was at least new—I mean the simplicity of the little ballad," said Dexter, ceasing to compliment, and speaking only the truth.

"Simplicity!" said Miss Vanhorn: "I am tired of it. I hope, Anne, you will not sing any simplicity songs here; those ridiculous things about bringing an ivy leaf, only an ivy leaf, and that it was but a little faded flower. They show an extremely miserly spirit, I think. If you can not give your friends a whole blossom or a fresh one, you had better not give them any at all."

"Who was it who said that he was sated with poetry about flowers, and that if the Muses must come in everywhere, he wished they would not always come as green-grocers?" said Dexter, who knew perfectly the home of this as of every other quotation, but always placed it in that way to give people an opportunity of saying, "Charles Lamb, wasn't it?" or "Sheridan?" It made conversation flowing.

"The flowers do not need the Muses," said Miss Vanhorn—"slatternly creatures, with no fit to their gowns. And that reminds me of what Anne was saying as you came up, Mr. Dexter; she was calmly and decisively observing that Mrs. Bannert was very ugly."

A smile crossed Dexter's face in answer to the old woman's short dry laugh.

"I added that if Mrs. Lorrington was here, people would see real beauty," said Anne, distressed by this betrayal, but standing by her guns.

Miss Vanhorn laughed again. "Mr. Dexter particularly admires Mrs. Bannert, child," she said, cheerfully, having had the unexpected amusement of two good laughs in an evening.

But Anne, instead of showing embarrassment, turned her eyes toward Dexter, as if in honest inquiry.

"Mrs. Bannert represents the Oriental type of beauty," he answered, smiling, as he perceived her frank want of agreement.

"Say creole," said Miss Vanhorn. "It is a novelty, child, which has made its appearance lately; a reaction after the narrow-chested type which has so long in America held undisputed sway. We absolutely take a quadroon to get away from the consumptive, blue-eyed saint, of whom we are all desperately tired."

"New York city is now developing a type of its own, I think," said Dexter. "You can tell a New York girl at a glance when you meet her in the West or the South. Women walk more in the city than they do elsewhere, and that has given them a firm step and bearing, which are noticeable."

"To think of comparisons between different parts of this raw land of ours, as though they had especial characteristics of their own!" said Miss Vanhorn, looking for a seed.

"You have not traveled much in this country, I presume," said Dexter.

"No, man, no. When I travel, I go abroad."

"I have never been abroad," answered Dexter, quietly. "But I can see a difference between the people of Massachusetts and the people of South Carolina, the people of Philadelphia and the people of San Francisco, which is marked and of the soil. I even think that I can tell a Baltimore, Buffalo, Chicago, Louisville, or St. Louis family at sight."

"You go to all those places?" said Miss Vanhorn, half closing her eyes, and speaking in a languid voice, as if the subject was too remote for close attention.

"Yes. You are not aware that I am a business man."

"Ah? What is it you do?" said the old woman, who knew perfectly Dexter's entire history, but wanted to hear his own account of himself.

"I am interested in iron; that is, I have iron mills, and—other things."

"Exactly; as you say—other things. Does that mean politics?"

"Partly," said Dexter, smiling.

"And oil?"

"No. I have never had any opportunity to coin gold with the Aladdin's lamp found in Pennsylvania. There is no magic in any of my occupations; they are all regular and commonplace."

"Are you in Congress now?"

"No; I was only there one term."

"A bore, isn't it?"

"Not to me."

"Congress is always a riot," said Miss Vanhorn, still with her eyes closed.

"I can not agree with you," said Dexter, his face taking on one of its resolute expressions. "I have small patience with those Americans who affect to be above any interest in the government of the country in which

80

they live. It *is* their country, and they can no more alter that fact than they can change their plain grandfathers into foreign noblemen."

"Dear me! dear me!" said Miss Vanborn, carelessly. "You talk to me as if I were a mass-meeting."

"I beg your pardon," said Dexter, his former manner returning. "I forgot for the moment that no one is in earnest at Caryl's."

"By-the-way, how did *you* ever get in here?" said Miss Vanhorn, with frank impertinence.

"I came because I like to see all sides of society," he replied, smiling down upon her with amused eyes.

"Give me your arm. You amount to something," said the old woman, rising. "We will walk up and down for a few moments; and, Anne, you can come too."

"I am almost sure that he is Helen's Knight-errant," thought Anne. "And I like him *very* much."

A niece of Miss Vanhorn's could not of course be slighted. The next day Isabel Varce came up and talked a while; later, Mrs. Bannert and the others followed. Gregory Dexter was with aunt and niece frequently; and Miss Vanhorn was pleased to be very gracious. She talked to him herself most of the time, while Anne watched the current of the new life round her. Other men had been presented to her; and among them she thought she recognized the Chanting Tenor and the Poet of Helen's narratives. She could not write to Helen; the eccentric grandfather objected to letters. "Fools and women clog the mails," was one of his favorite assertions. But although Anne could not write, Helen could smuggle letters occasionally into the outgoing mail-bags, and when she learned that Anne was at Caryl's, she wrote immediately. "Have you seen Isabel Varce yet?" ran the letter. "And Rachel Bannert? The former is my dearest rival, the latter my deadliest friend. Use your eyes, I beg. What amusement I shall have hearing your descriptions when I come! For of course you will make the blindest mistakes. However, a blind man has been known to see sometimes what other people have never discovered. How is the Grand Llama? I conquered her at last, as I told you I should. With a high pressure of magnanimity. But it was all for my own sake; and now, behold, I am here! But you can study the Bishop, the Poet, the Tenor, and the Knight-errant in the flesh; how do you like the Knight?"

"This place is a prison," wrote Helen, again; "and I am in the mean time consumed with curiosity to know *what* is going on at Caryl's. Please answer my letters, and put the answers away until I come; it is the only method I can think of by which I can get the aroma of each day. Or, rather, not the aroma, but the facts; you do not know much of aromas. If facts were 'a divine thing' to Frederick the Great (Mr. Dexter told me that, of course), they are certainly extremely solemn to you. Tell me, then, what everybody is doing. And particularly the Bishop and the Knight-errant."

And Anne answered the letters faithfully, telling everything she noticed, especially as to Dexter. Who the Bishop was she had not been able to decide.

In addition to the others, Ward Heathcote had now arrived at Caryl's, also Mr. Blum.

In the mean time Miss Vanhorn had tested without delay her niece's new knowledge of botany. Her face was flushed and her hand fairly trembled with eagerness as she gave Anne her first wild flower, and ordered her to analyze it. Would she blunder, or show herself dull and incompetent? One thing was certain: no pretended zeal could deceive old Katharine—she knew the reality too well.

But there was no pretense. Anne, honest as usual, analyzed the flower with some mistakes, but with real interest; and the keen black eyes recognized the genuine hue of the feeling, as far as it went. After that initiation, every morning they drove to the woods, and Anne searched in all directions, coming back loaded down with spoil. Every afternoon there followed analyzing, pressing, drying, and labelling, for hours.

"Pray leave the foundations of our bridge intact," called Isabel Varce, passing on horseback, accompanied by Ward Heathcote, and looking down at Anne digging up something on the bank below, while at a little distance Miss Vanhorn's coupé was waiting, with the old lady's hard face looking out through the closed window.

Anne laughed, and turned her face, glowing with rose-color, upward to look at them.

"Do you like that sort of thing?" said Isabel, pausing, having noted at a glance that the young girl was attired in old clothes, and appeared in every way at a disadvantage. She had no especial malice toward Anne in this; she merely acted on general principles as applied to all of her own sex. But even the most acute feminine minds make mistakes on one subject, namely, they forget that to a man dress is not the woman. Anne, in her faded gown, down on the muddy bank, with her hat off, her boots begrimed, and her zeal for the root she was digging up, seemed to Ward Heathcote a new and striking creature. The wind ruffled her thick brown hair and blew it into little rings and curls about her face, her eyes, unflinching in the brilliant sunshine, laughed back at them as they looked over the railing; the lines of her shoulder and extended arms were of noble beauty. To a woman's eyes a perfect sleeve is of the highest importance; it did not occur to Isabel that through the ugly, baggy, out-of-date sleeve down there on the bank, the wind, sturdily blowing, was revealing an arm whose outline silk and lace could never rival. Satisfied with her manœuvre, she rode on: Anne certainly looked what all women would have called "a fright."

Yet that very evening Heathcote approached, recalled himself to Miss Vanhorn's short memory, and, after a few moments of conversation, sat down beside Anne, who received him with the same frank predisposition to be pleased which she gave to all alike. Heathcote was not a talker like Dexter; he seemed to have little to say at any time. He was one of a small and unimportant class in the United States, which would be very offensive to citizens at large if it came in contact with them; but it seldom does. To this class there is no city in America save New York, and New York itself is only partially endurable. National reputations are nothing, politics nothing. Money is necessary, and ought to be provided in some way; and generally it is, since without it this class could not exist in a purely democratic land. But it is inherited, not made. It may be said that simply the large landed estates acquired at an early date in the vicinity of the city, and immensely increased in value by the growth of the metropolis, have produced this class, which, however, having no barriers, can never be permanent, or make to itself laws. Heathcote's great-grandfather was a landed proprietor in Westchester County; he had lived well, and died at a good old age, to be succeeded by his son, who also lived well, and died not so well, and poorer than his father. The grandson increased the ratio in both cases, leaving to his little boy, Ward, but a small portion of the original fortune, and departing from the custom of the house in that he died early. The boy, without father, mother, brother, or sister, grew up under the care of guardians, and, upon coming of age, took possession of the remnant left to him. A good portion of this he himself had lost, not so much from extravagance, however, as carelessness. He had been abroad, of course, and had adopted English ways, but not with any violence. He left that to others. He passed for good-natured in the main; he was not restless. He was quite willing that other men should have more luxuries than he had—a yacht, for instance, or fine horses; he felt no irritation on the subject. On the other hand, he would have been much surprised to learn that any one longed to take him out and knock him down, simply as an insufferable object. Yet Gregory Dexter had that longing at times so strongly that his hand fairly quivered.

Heathcote was slightly above middle height, and well built, but his gait was indolent and careless. Good features unlighted by animation, a brown skin, brown eyes ordinarily rather lethargic, thick brown hair and mustache, and heavy eyebrows standing out prominently from the face in profile view, were the items ordinarily given in a general description. He had a low-toned voice and slow manner, in which, however, there was no affectation. What was the use of doing anything with any particular effort? He had no antipathy for persons of other habits; the world was large. It was noticed, however (or rather it was *not* noticed), that he generally got away from them as soon as he quietly could. He had lived to be thirty-two years old, and had on the whole enjoyed life so far, although he was neither especially important, handsome, nor rich. The secret of this lay in one fact: women liked him.

What was it that they found to like in him? This was the question asked often in irritation by his brother man. And naturally. For the women themselves could not give a reasonable reason. The corresponding side of life is not the same, since men admire with a reason; the woman is plainly beautiful, or brilliant, or fascinating round whom they gather. At Caryl's seven or eight men were handsomer than Heathcote; a number were more brilliant; many were richer. Yet almost all of these had discovered, at one time or another, that the eyes they were talking to were following Heathcote furtively; and they had seen attempts that made them tingle with anger—all the more so because they were so infinitesimally delicate and fine, as became the actions of well-bred women. One or two, who had married, had had explained to them elaborately by their wives what it was they (in their free days, of course) had liked in Heathcote—elaborately, if not clearly. The husbands gathered generally that it was only a way he had, a manner; the liking was half imaginative, after all. Now Heathcote was not in the least imaginative. But the women were.

Manly qualities, good hearts, handsome faces, and greater wealth held their own in fact against him. Marriages took place in his circle, wedding chimes pealed, and brides were happy under their veils in spite of him. Yet, as histories of lives go, there was a decided balance in his favor of feminine regard, and no one could deny it.

He had now but a small income, and had been obliged to come down to a very simple manner of life. Those who disliked him said that of course he would marry money. As yet, however, he had shown no signs of fulfilling his destiny in this respect. He seldom took the trouble to express his opinions, and therefore passed as having none; but those who were clear-sighted knew better. Dexter was one of these, and this entire absence of self-assertion in Ward Heathcote stung him. For Dexter always asserted himself; he could not help it. He came in at this moment, and noted Heathcote's position near Anne. Obeying an impulse, he crossed the room immediately, and began a counter-conversation with Miss Vanhorn, the chaperon.

"Trying to interest that child," he thought, as he listened to the grandaunt with the air of deferential attention she liked so well. With eyes that apparently never once glanced in their direction, he kept close watch of the

82

two beyond. "She is no match for him," he thought, with indignation; "she has had no experience. It ought not to be allowed."

But Dexter always mistook Heathcote; he gave him credit for plans and theories of which Heathcote never dreamed. In fact, he judged him by himself. Heathcote was merely talking to Anne now in the absence of other entertainment, having felt some slight curiosity about her because she had looked so bright and contented on the mud-bank under the bridge. He tried to recall his impression of her on New-Year's Day, and determined to refresh his memory by Blum; but, in the mean time, outwardly, his manner was as though, silently of course, but none the less deeply, he had dwelt upon her image ever since. It was this impalpable manner which made Dexter indignant. He knew it so well! He said to himself that it was a lie. And, generally speaking, it was. But possibly in this case (as in others) it was not so much the falsity of the manner as its success which annoyed the other man.

He could not hear what was said; and the words, in truth, were not many or brilliant. But he knew the sort of quiet glance with which they were being accompanied. Yet Dexter, quick and suspicious as he was, would never have discovered that glance unaided. He had learned it from another, and that other, of course, a woman. For once in a while it happens that a woman, when roused to fury, will pour out the whole story of her wrongs to some man who happens to be near. No man does this. He has not the same need of expression; and, besides, he will never show himself at such a disadvantage voluntarily, even for the sake of comfort. He would rather remain uncomforted. But women of strong feelings often, when excited, cast wisdom to the winds, and even seem to find a desperate satisfaction in the most hazardous imprudences, which can injure only themselves. In a mood of this kind, some one had poured out to Gregory Dexter bitter testimony against Heathcote, one-sided, perhaps, but photographically accurate in all the details, which are so much to women. Dexter had listened with inward anger and contempt; but he had listened. And he had recognized, besides, the accent of truth in every word. The narrator was now in Austria with a new and foreign husband, apparently as happy as the day is long. But the listener had never forgotten or forgiven her account of Heathcote's method and manner. He said to himself that he despised it, and he did despise it. Still, in some occult way, one may be jealous of results attained even by ways and means for which one feels a righteous contempt; and the more so when one has a firm confidence in his own abilities, which have not yet, however, been openly recognized in that field. In all other fields Gregory Dexter was a marked type of American success.

As the days moved slowly on, he kept watch of Heathcote. It was more a determination to foil him than interest in Anne which made him add himself as a third whenever he could unobtrusively; which was not often, since Miss Vanhorn liked to talk to him herself, and Anne knew no more how to aid him than a nun. After a while Heathcote became conscious of this watchfulness, and it amused him. His idea of Dexter was "a clever sort of fellow, who has made money, and is ambitious. Goes in for politics, and that sort of thing. Talks well, but too much. Tiresome." He began to devote himself to Anne now in a different way; hitherto he had been only entertaining himself (and rather languidly) by a study of her fresh naïve truthfulness. He had drawn out her history; he, too, knew of the island, the fort, and the dog trains. Poor Anne was always eloquent on these subjects. Her color rose, her words came quickly.

"You are fond of the island," he said, one evening, as they sat on the piazza in the moonlight, Dexter within three feet of them, but unable to hear their murmured words. For Heathcote had a way of interposing his shoulder between listeners and the person to whom he was talking, which made the breadth of woollen cloth as much a barrier as a stone wall; he did this more frequently now that he had discovered Dexter's watchfulness.

"Yes," said Anne, in as low a voice as his own. Then suddenly, plainly visible to him in the moonlight, tears welled up and dropped upon her cheeks.

She had been homesick all day. Sometimes Miss Vanhorn was hard and cold as a bronze statue in winter; sometimes she was as quick and fiery as if charged with electricity. Sometimes she veered between the two. To-day had been one of the veering days, and Anne had worked over the dried plants five hours in a close room, now a mark for sarcastic darts of ridicule, now enduring an icy silence, until her lot seemed too heavy to bear. She had learned to understand the old woman's moods, but understanding pain does not make it lighter. Released at last, a great wave of homesickness had swept over her, which did not, however, break bounds until Heathcote's words touched the spring; then the gates opened and the tears came.

They had no sooner dropped upon her cheeks, one, two, three, than she was overwhelmed with hot shame at having allowed them to fall, and with fear lest any one should notice them. Mr. Heathcote had seen them, that was hopelessly certain; but if only she could keep them from her grandaunt! Yet she did not dare to lift her handkerchief lest its white should attract attention.

But Heathcote knew what to do.

As soon as he saw the tears (to him, of course, totally unexpected; but girls are so), he raised his straw hat, which lay on his knee, and, holding it by the crown, began elaborately to explain some peculiarity in the lining (he called it South American) invented for the occasion, at the same time, by the motion, screening her face completely from observation on the other side. But Anne could not check herself; the very shelter brought thicker drops. He could not hold his hat in that position forever, even to look at Brazilian linings. He rose suddenly, and standing in front so as to screen her, he cried, "A bat! a bat!" at the same time making a pass with his hat as though he saw it in the air.

Every one on the piazza rose, darted aside hither and thither, the ladies covering their heads with their fans and handkerchiefs, the men making passes with their hats, as usual on bat occasions; every one was sure the noxious creature flew by. For a number of minutes confusion reigned. When it was over, Anne's cheeks were dry, and a little cobweb tie had been formed between herself and Heathcote. It was too slight to be noticed, but it was there.

CHAPTER XII.

"Le hasard sait ce qu'il fait!"—*French Proverb.*

The next day there was a picnic. No one wished to go especially save Isabel Varce, but no one opposed her wish. At Caryl's they generally followed whatever was suggested, with indolent acquiescence. Miss Vanhorn, however, being a contrary planet revolving in an orbit of her own, at first declined to go; there were important plants to finish. But Mr. Dexter persuaded her to change her mind, and, with Anne, to accompany him in a certain light carriage which he had ordered from the next town, more comfortable than the Caryl red wagons, and not so heavy as her own coupé. Miss Vanhorn liked to be comfortable, and she was playing the part also of liking Gregory Dexter; she therefore accepted. She knew perfectly well that Dexter's "light carriage" had not come from the next town, but from New York; and she smiled at what she considered the effort of this new man to conceal his lavishness. But she was quite willing that he should spend his money to gain her favor (she having already decided to give it to him), and therefore it was with contentment that she stepped into the carriage—a model of its kind—on the morning of the appointed day, and put up her glass to watch the others ascending, by a little flight of steps, to the high table-land of the red wagons. Mr. Heathcote was on horseback; he dismounted, however, to assist Mrs. Bannert to her place. He raised his hat to Anne with his usual quiet manner, but she returned his salutation with a bright smile. She was grateful to him. Had he not been kind to her?

The picnic was like most picnics of the sort—heavy work for the servants, languid amusement, not unmixed with only partially concealed ennui, on the part of the guests. There was but little wandering away, the participants being too few for much severance. They strolled through the woods in long-drawn links; they went to see a view from a knoll; they sang a few songs gently, faint pipings from the ladies, and nothing from the men (Blum being absent) save the correct bass of Dexter, which seemed very far down indeed in the cellars of melody, while the ladies were on the high battlements. The conversation was never exactly allowed to die out, yet it languished. Almost all would rather have been at home. The men especially found small pleasure in sitting on the ground; besides, a distinct consciousness that the attitude was not becoming. For the American does not possess a taste for throwing himself heartily down upon Mother Earth. He can camp; he can hunt, swim, ride, walk, use Indian clubs, play base-ball, drive, row, sail a yacht, or even guide a balloon; but when it comes to grass, give him a bench.

Isabel Varce, in a wonderful costume of woodland green, her somewhat sharp features shaded by a shepherdess hat, carried out her purpose—the subjugation of a certain Peter Dane, a widower of distinction, a late arrival at Caryl's. Mrs. Bannert had Ward Heathcote by her side, apparently to the satisfaction of both. Other men and women were contented or discontented as it happened; and two or three school-girls of twelve or thirteen really enjoyed themselves, being at the happy age when blue sky and golden sunshine, green woods and lunch on the grass, are all that is necessary for supreme happiness.

There was one comic element present, and by mistake. A reverend gentleman of the kind that calls everybody "brother" had arrived unexpectedly at Caryl's; he was journeying for the purpose of distributing certain thin pamphlets of powerfully persuasive influence as to general virtue, and as he had not been over that ground for some years, he had no suspicion that Caryl's had changed, or that it was any more important than Barr's, Murphy's, Allen's, and other hamlets in the neighborhood and possessive case, with whose attributes he was familiar. Old John Caryl had taken him in for a night or two, and had ordered the unused school-house at the cross-roads to be swept out for a hamlet evening service; but the hamlet could not confine the Reverend Ezra Sloane. His heart waxed warm within him at the sight of so many persons, all well-to-do, pleasant to the eye, and apparently not pressed for time. He had spent his life in ministering to the poor in this world's goods, and to the workers who had no leisure; it was a new pleasure to him simply to be among the agreeable, well-dressed, and unanxious. He took his best coat from his lean valise, and wore it steadily. He was so happy in his child-like satisfaction that no one rebuffed him, and when he presented himself, blandly smiling, to join the picnic party, no one had the heart to tell him of his mistake. As he climbed complacently into one of the wagons, however, stiff old Mrs. Bannert, on the back seat, gave John Caryl, standing at the horses' heads, a look which he understood. The Reverend Ezra must depart the next morning, or be merged—conclusively merged—in the hamlet. His fate was sealed. But to-day he disported himself to his heart's content; his smiling face was everywhere. He went eagerly through the woods, joining now one group, now another; he laughed when they laughed, understanding, however, but few of their allusions. He was restlessly anxious to join in the singing, but could not, as he did not know their songs, and he proposed, in entire good faith, one or two psalms, giving them up, however, immediately, when old Mrs. Bannert, who had taken upon herself the task of keeping him down, remarked sternly that no one knew the tunes. He went to see the view, and extending his hand, said, in his best manner, "Behold! brethren, is there not hill, and dale, and mountain, and valley, and—river?" As he said "river" he closed his eyes impressively, and stood there among them the image of self-complacence. The wind blew out his black coat, and showed how thin it was, and the wearer as well.

"Why is it always a thin, weakly man like that who insists upon calling people 'brethren'?" said Heathcote, as they stood a little apart.

"Because, being weakly, we can not knock him down for it, as we certainly should do if he was stronger," said Dexter.

But it was especially at lunch that the Reverend Ezra shone forth; rising to the occasion, he brought forth all the gallant speeches of his youth, which had much the air of his grandfather's Green Mountain musket. Some of his phrases Anne recognized: Miss Lois used them. The young girl was pained to see how out of place he was, how absurd in his well-intentioned efforts; and she therefore drew him a little apart, and strove to entertain him herself. She had known plain people on the island, and had experienced much of their faithful goodness and generosity in times of trouble; it hurt her to have him ridiculed. It came out, during this conversation, that he knew something of botany, and on the strength of this passport she took him to Miss Vanhorn. The Reverend Ezra really did understand the flora of the district, through which he had journeyed many times in former years on his old mare; Miss Vanhorn's sharp questions brought out what he knew, and gave him also the grateful sensation of imparting valuable information. He now appeared quite collected and sensible. He mentioned, after a while, that an orchid grew in these very woods at some distance up the mountain—an orchid which was rare. Miss Vanhorn had never seen that particular orchid in its wild state; a flush rose in her cheek.

"We can drive out to-morrow and look for it, grandaunt," said Anne.

"No," replied Miss Vanhorn, firmly; "that orchid must be found to-day, while Mr.—Mr.—"

"Sloane," said the minister, affably.

"—while Mr. Stone is with you to point out the exact locality. I desire you to go with him immediately, Anne; *this* is a matter of importance."

"It is about two miles up the mountain," objected the missionary, loath to leave the festival.

"Anne is not afraid of two short miles," replied the old woman, inflexibly. "And as for yourself, Mr. Doane, no doubt you will be glad to abandon this scene of idle frivolity." And then the Reverend Ezra, a little startled by this view of the case, yielded, and sought his hat and cane.

This conversation had taken place at one side. Mr. Dexter, however, talking ceremoniously with old Mrs. Bannert, overheard it, and immediately thought of a plan by which it might be made available for his own purposes. The picnic had not given him much satisfaction so far; it had been too languid. With all his effort, he could not quite enter into the continuous indolence of Caryl's. True, he had taken Anne from Heathcote, thus checking for the moment that gentleman's lazy supremacy, at least in one quarter; but there were other quarters, and Heathcote was now occupying the one which Dexter himself coveted most of all, namely, the seat next to Rachel Bannert. Rachel was a widow, and uncomfortably dependent upon her mother-in-law. The elder Mrs. Bannert was sharp-eyed as a hawk, wise as a serpent, and obstinate as a hedge-hog; Rachel as soft-voiced and soft-breasted as a dove; yet the latter intended to have, and did in the end have, the Bannert estate, and in the mean time she "shared her mother-in-law's home." There were varying opinions as to the delights of that home.

Dexter, fretted by Heathcote's unbroken conversation with Rachel, and weary of the long inaction of the morning, now proposed that they should all go in search of the orchid; his idea was that at least it would break up existing proximities, and give them all something to do. Lunch had been prolonged to the utmost extent of its vitality, and the participants were in the state of nerveless leaves in Indian summer, ready to float away on the first breeze. They strolled off, therefore, all save the elder ladies, through the wood, led by the delighted Ezra, who had that "God-bless-you-all-my-friends" air with which many worthy people are afflicted. The apparent self-effacement effected by good-breeding, even in the wicked, is certainly more agreeable to an ordinary world than the unconscious egotism of a large class of the good.

After a quarter of an hour the woodman's trail they were following turned and went up the mountain-side. No one save Anne and the missionary had the slightest intention of walking two miles to look for a flower, but they were willing to stroll on for a while. They came to the main road, and crossed it, making many objections to its being there, with its commonplace daylight, after the shade, flickering sunbeams, and vague green vistas of the forest. But on this road, in the dust, a travelling harp-player was trudging along, accompanied by a wizened little boy and a still more wizened monkey.

"Let us carry them off into the deepest woods, and have a dance," said Isabel. "We will be nymphs and dryades, and all sorts of woodland things."

It is difficult to dance on uneven ground, in the middle of the day, to the sound of an untuned old harp, and a violin held upside down, and scraped by a melancholy boy. But Isabel had her way, or rather took it, and they all set off somewhat vaguely for "the deepest woods," leaving the woodman's path, and following another track, which Isabel pronounced "such a dear little trail it must lead somewhere." The Reverend Ezra was disturbed. He thought he held them all under his own guidance, when, lo! they were not only leaving him and his orchid without a word of excuse, but were actually departing with a wandering harpist to find a level spot on which to dance!

"I—I think that path leads only to an old quarry," he said, with a hesitating smile.

But no one paid any attention to him, save Anne, who had paused also, uncertain what to do.

"We will get the orchid afterward, Miss Douglas," said Dexter. "I promise that you shall have it."

"But Mr. Sloane," said Anne, glancing toward the deserted missionary.

"Come with us, dominie," said Dexter, with the ready good-nature that was one of his outward characteristics. It was a quick, tolerant good-nature, and seemed to belong to his broad, strong frame.

But the dominie had a dignity of his own, after all. When he realized that he was forsaken, he came forward and said quietly that he would go up the mountain alone and get the orchid, joining them at the main-road crossing on the way back.

"As you please," said Dexter. "And I, for one, shall feel much indebted to you, sir, if you bring back the flower, because I have promised Miss Douglas that she should have it, and should be obliged to go for it myself, ignorant as I am, were it not for your kindness."

He raised his hat courteously, and went off with Anne to join the others, already out of sight.

"I suppose he does not approve of the dancing," said the girl, looking back.

But Dexter did not care whether he approved or disapproved; he had already dismissed the dominie from his mind.

The path took them to a deserted stone-quarry in the side of the hill. There was the usual yawning pit, floored with broken jagged masses, and chips of stone, the straight bare wall of rock above, and the forest greenery coming to the edge of the desolation on all sides, and leaning over to peep down. The quarrymen had camped below, and the little open space where once their lodge of boughs had stood was selected by Isabel for the dancing floor. The harpist, a small old man clad in a grimy velveteen coat, played a waltz, to which the little Italian boy added a lagging accompaniment; the monkey, who seemed to have belonged to some defunct hand-organ, sat on a stump and surveyed the scene. They did not all dance, but Isabel succeeded in persuading a few to move through a quadrille whose figures she improvised for the occasion. But the scene was more picturesque when, after a time, the dull partners in coats were discarded, and the floating draperies danced by themselves, joining hands in a ring, and circling round and round with merry little motions which were charmingly pretty, like kittens at play. Then they made the boy sing, and he chanted a tune which had (musically) neither beginning nor end, but a useful quality of going on forever. But whatever he did, and whatever they gave him, made no difference in his settled melancholy, which the monkey's small face seemed to caricature. Then they danced again, and this time Dexter took part, while the other coated ones remained on the grass, smoking. It ended in his waltzing with them all in turn, and being overwhelmed with their praises, which, however, being levelled at the heads of the others by strongly implied comparison, were not as valuable as they seemed. Dexter knew that he gained nothing by joining in that dance; but where there was something to do, he could not resist doing it. When the waltz was over, and the wandering musicians sent on their way with a lavish reward of silver, which the monkey had received cynically as it was placed piece by piece in his little paw, Isabel led off all the ladies "to explore the quarry," expressly forbidding the others to follow. With an air of great enjoyment in their freedom and solitude the floating draperies departed, and the smokers were left under the trees, content, on their side also, to have half an hour of quiet. Mr. Peter Dane immediately and heartily yawned at full width, and was no longer particular as to the position of his legs. In truth, it was the incipient fatigue on the face of this distinguished widower which had induced Isabel to lead off her exploring party; for when a man is over fifty, nothing is more dangerous than to tire him. He never forgives it.

Isabel led her band round to an ascent, steep but not long; her plan was to go up the hill through the wood, and appear on the top of the quarry, so many graceful figures high in the air against the blue sky, for the indolent smokers below to envy and admire. Isabel was a slender creature with a pale complexion; the slight color produced by the exercise would be becoming. Rachel, who was dimpled, "never could climb"; her "ankles" were "not strong." (And certainly they were very small ankles for such a weight of dimples.) The party now divided itself under these two leaders; those who were indolent staid with Rachel; those who were not afraid of exercise went with Isabel. A few went for amusement, without motive; among these was Anne. One went for wrath; and this was Valeria Morle.

It is hard for a neutral-faced girl with a fixed opinion of her own importance to learn the lesson of her real insignificance, when removed from the background of home, at a place like Caryl's. Valeria was there, mistakenly visiting an aunt for two weeks, and with the calm security of the country mind, she had mentally selected Ward Heathcote as her knight for the time being, and had bestowed upon him in consequence several little speeches and smiles carefully calculated to produce an impression, to mean a great deal to any one who was watching. But Heathcote was not watching; the small well-regulated country smiles had about as much effect as the twitterings of a wren would have in a wood full of nightingales. Miss Morle could not understand it; had they not slain their thousands, nay, ten thousands (young lady's computation), in Morleville? She now went up the hill in silent wrath, glad to do something and to be away from Heathcote. Still, she could not help believing that he would miss her; men had been known to be very much interested in girls, and yet make no sign for a long time. They watched them from a distance. In this case Valeria was to have her hopes realized. She was to be watched, and from a distance.

The eight who reached the summit sported gayly to and fro for a while, now near the edge, now back, gathering flowers and throwing them over, calling down to the smokers, who lay and watched them, without, however, any burning desire especially visible on their countenances to climb up and join them. Valeria, with a stubborn determination to make herself in some way conspicuous, went to the edge of the cliff, and even leaned over; she had one arm round a young tree, but half of her shoes (by no means small ones) were over the verge, and the breeze showed that they were. Anne saw it, and spoke to Isabel.

"If she will do it, she will," answered Isabel; "and the more we notice her, the more she will persist. She is one of those dull girls intended by Nature to be always what is called sensible. And when one of *those* girls takes to making a fool of herself, her idiocy is colossal."

But Isabel's philosophy did not relieve Anne's fear. She called to Valeria, warningly, "You are very near the edge, Miss Morle; wouldn't it be safer to step back a little?"

But Valeria would not. They were all noticing her at last. They should see how strong her nerves were, how firm her poise. The smokers below, too, were now observing her. She threw back her head, and hummed a little tune. If the edge did not crumble, she was, in truth, safe enough. To a person who is not dizzy, five inches of foot-hold is as safe as five yards.

But—the edge did crumble. And suddenly. The group of women behind had the horror, of seeing her sway, stagger, slip down, frantically writhe on the verge half an instant, and then, with an awful scream, slide over out of sight, as her arm was wrenched from the little tree. Those below had seen it too. They sprang to their feet, and ran first forward, then round and up the hill behind.

For she had not slipped far. The cliff jutted out slightly a short distance below the verge, and, by what seemed a miracle, the girl was held by this second edge. Eight inches beyond, the sheer precipice began, with the pile of broken stones sixty feet below. Anne was the first to discover this, reaching the verge as the girl sank out of sight; the others, shuddering, put their hands over their eyes and clung together.

"She has not fallen far," cried Anne, with a quick and burning excitement. "Lie still, Valeria," she called down. "Close your eyes, and make yourself perfectly motionless; hardly breathe. We will save you yet."

She took hold of the young tree to test its strength, at the same time speaking rapidly to the others. "By lying down, and clasping that tree trunk with one arm, and then stretching over, I can just reach her hand, I think, and seize it. Do you see? That is what I am going to try to do. I can not tell how strong this tree is; but—there is not a moment to lose. After I am down, and have her hand, do anything you think best to secure us. Either hold me yourselves or make ropes of your sacques and shawls. If help comes soon, we can save her." While still speaking, she threw herself down upon the edge, clasped one arm strongly round the tree trunk, and stretching down sideways, her head and shoulder over the verge, she succeeded in first touching, then clasping, the wrist of the girl below, who could not see her rescuer as she lay facing the precipice with closed eyes, helpless and inert. It was done, but only two girls' wrists as a link.

The others had caught hold of Anne as strongly as they could.

"No," said Isabel, taking command excitedly; "one of you hold her firmly, and the rest clasp arms and form a chain, all sitting down, to that large tree in the rear. If the strain comes, throw yourselves toward the large tree."

So they formed a chain. Isabel, looking over, saw that the girl below had clasped Anne's wrist with her own fingers also—a strong grasp, a death-grasp. If she slipped farther, Anne must slip too.

All this had not taken two minutes—scarcely a minute and a half. They were now all motionless; they could hear the footsteps of the men hurrying up the hill behind, coming nearer and nearer. But how slow they were! How long! The men were exactly three minutes, and it is safe to say that never in their lives had they rushed up a hill with such desperate haste and energy. But—women expect wings.

Heathcote and Dexter reached the summit first. There they beheld five white-cheeked women, dressed in various dainty floating fabrics, and adorned with ferns and wild flowers, sitting on the ground, clasping each others' hands and arms. They formed a line, of which the woman at one end had her arm round a large tree, and the woman at the other round the body of a sixth, who was half over the cliff. A seventh and free person, Isabel, stood at the edge, her eyes fixed on the heavy form poised along the second verge below. No one spoke but Isabel. "She has caught on something, and Anne is holding her," she explained, in quick although low tones, as if afraid to disturb even the air. But while she was speaking the two men had gone swiftly to the edge, at a little distance below the group, and noted the position themselves.

"Let me—" began Dexter.

"No, you are too heavy," answered Heathcote. "*You* must hold *me*."

"Yes," said Isabel. "Quick! quick!" A woman in a hurry would say "Quick!" to the very lightning.

But if men are slow, they are sure. Heathcote stretched himself down carefully on the other side of the little tree, but without touching it, that being Anne's chief support, and bearing his full weight upon Dexter, who in turn was held by the other men, who had now come up, he seized Valeria's arm firmly above Anne's hand, and told Anne to let go her hold. They were face to face; Anne's forehead was suffused with red, owing to her cramped position.

"I can not; she has grasped my wrist," she answered.

"Let go, Miss Morle," called Heathcote. "I have you firmly; do you not feel my hand?"

But Valeria would not; perhaps could not.

"Some of you take hold of Miss Douglas, then," called Heathcote to the men above. "The girl below will not loosen her hold, and you will have to draw us all up together."

"Ready?" called the voices above, after an instant.

"Ready," answered Heathcote.

Then he felt himself drawn upward slowly, an inch, two inches; so did Anne. The two downward-stretched arms tightened; the one upward-lifted arm began to rise from the body to which it belonged. But what a weight for that one arm! Valeria was a large, heavy girl, with a ponderous weight of bone. In the position in which she lay, it seemed probable that her body might swing over the edge, and almost wrench the arm from its socket by its weight.

"Stop," said Heathcote, perceiving this. The men above paused. "Are you afraid to support her for one instant alone, Anne?" he asked.

"No," murmured Anne. Her eyes were blood-shot; she saw him through a crimson cloud.

"Keep me firmly," he called out, warningly, to Dexter. Then, letting go his first hold, he stretched down still farther, made a slight spring forward, and succeeded in grasping Valeria's waist. "*Now* pull up, and quickly," he said, panting.

And thus, together, Valeria firmly held by Heathcote, the two rescuers and the rescued were drawn safely up from danger to safe level again. Only a few feet, but all the difference between life and death.

When the others looked down upon the now uncovered space, they saw that it was only the stump of a slender cedar sapling, a few inches in height, and two little edges of rock standing up unevenly here and there, which had formed the parapet. A person might have tried all day, with an acrobat's net spread below for safety, to cling there, without success; Valeria had fallen at the one angle and in the one position which made it possible. Two arms were strained, and that was all.

Isabel was white with nervous fear; the others showed traces of tears. But the cause of all this anxiety and trouble, although entirely uninjured and not nervous (she had not seen herself), sat smiling upon them all in a sweet suffering-martyr way, and finally went down the hill with masculine escort on each side—apotheosis not before attained. Will it be believed that this girl, fairly well educated and in her sober senses, was simpleton enough to say to Heathcote that evening, in a sentimental whisper, "How I wish that Miss Douglas had not touched me!" There was faint moonlight, and the simpering expression of the neutral face filled him with astonishment. Dexter would have understood: Dexter was accustomed to all varieties of women, even the Valeria variety: but Heathcote was not. All he said, therefore, was, "Why?"

"Because then *you* alone would have saved me," murmured Valeria, sweetly.

"If Miss Douglas had not grasped you as she did, we might all have been too late," replied Heathcote, looking at her in wonder.

"Ah, no; I did not slip farther. You would have been in time," said the belle of Morleville, with what she considered a telling glance. And she actually convinced herself that she had made an impression.

"I ought not to have done it, of course, Louisa," she said to her bosom-friend, in the privacy of her own room, after her return to Morleville; "but I really felt that he deserved at least *that* reward for his great devotion to me, poor fellow!"

"And why couldn't you like him, after all, Valeria dear?" urged Louisa, deeply interested, and not a little envious.

"I could not—I could not," replied Valeria, slowly and virtuously, shaking her head. "He had not the principles I require in a man. But—I felt sorry for him."

Oh, ineffable Valerias! what would life be without you?

Dexter had been the one to offer his arm to Anne when she felt able to go down the hill. At the main-road crossing they found the Reverend Mr. Sloane faithfully sitting on a dusty bank, with the orchid in his hand, waiting for them. It seemed to Anne that a long and vague period of time had passed since they parted from him. But she was glad to get the orchid; she knew that no slight extraneous affair, such as the saving of a life, would excuse the absence of that flower. Rachel Bannert had chafed Heathcote's strained arm with her soft hands, and arranged a sling for it made of her sash. She accompanied him back to the picnic ground. It was worth while to have a strained arm.

Miss Vanhorn considered that it was all nonsense, and was inclined to reprove her niece. But she had the orchid; and when Dexter came up, and in a few strong words expressed his admiration for the young girl's courage, she changed her mind, and agreed with him, although regretting "the display."

"Girls like that Morle should be manacled," she said.

"And I, for one, congratulate myself that there was, as you call it, a display—a display of the finest resolution I have ever seen in a young girl," said Dexter, warmly. "Miss Douglas was not even sure that the little tree was firm; and of course she could not tell how long it would take us to come."

"They all assisted, I understand," said Miss Vanhorn, impassively.

"They all assisted *afterward*. But not one of them would have taken her place. Miss Morle seized her wrist immediately, and with the grasp of a vise. They must inevitably have gone over together."

"Well, well; that is enough, I think," said Miss Vanhorn. "We will drive home now," she added, giving her orders as though both the carriage and its owner were her own property.

When she had been assisted into her place, and Anne had taken her seat beside her, Heathcote, who had not spoken to his fellow-rescuer since they reached level ground, came forward to the carriage door, with his arm in its ribbon sling, and offered his hand. He said only a word or two; but, as his eyes met hers, Anne blushed—blushed suddenly and vividly. She was realizing for the first time how she must have looked to him, hanging in her cramped position, with crimson face and wild falling hair.

CHAPTER XIII.

"So on the tip of his subduing tongue

All kinds of arguments and questions

deep."

—Shakspeare.

"What is the use of so much talking? Is not this wild rose sweet without a comment?"—Hazlitt.

Early the next morning Miss Vanhorn, accompanied by her niece, drove off on an all-day botanizing expedition. Miss Vanhorn understood the worth of being missed. At sunset she returned; and the girl she brought back with her was on the verge of despair. For the old woman had spent the hours in making her doubt herself in every possible way, besides covering her with ridicule concerning the occurrences of the day before. It was late when they entered the old ball-room, Anne looking newly youthful and painfully shy; as they crossed the floor she did not raise her eyes. Dexter was dancing with Rachel, whose soft arms were visible under her black gauze, encircled with bands of old gold. Anne was dressed in a thick white linen fabric (Miss Vanhorn having herself selected the dress and ordered her to wear it), and appeared more like a school-girl than ever. Miss Vanhorn, raising her eye-glass, had selected her position on entering, like a general on the field: Anne was placed next to Isabel on the wooden bench that ran round the room. And immediately Miss Varce seemed to have grown suddenly old. In addition, her blonde beauty was now seen to be heightened by art. Isabel herself did not dream of this. Hardly any woman, whose toilet is a study, can comprehend beauty in unattractive unfashionable attire. So she kept her seat unconsciously, sure of her Paris draperies, while the superb youth of Anne, heightened by the simplicity of the garb she wore, reduced the other woman, at least in the eyes of all the men present, to the temporary rank of a faded wax doll.

Dexter soon came up and asked Anne to dance. She replied, in a low voice and without looking up, that she would rather not; her arm was still painful.

"Go," said Miss Vanhorn, overhearing, "and do not be absurd about your arm. I dare say Miss Morle's aches quite as badly." She was almost always severe with her niece in Dexter's presence: could it have been that she wished to excite his sympathy?

Anne rose in silence; they did not dance, but, after walking up and down the room once or twice, went out on the piazza. The windows were open: it was the custom to sit here and look through at the dancers within. They sat down near a window.

"I have not had an opportunity until now, Miss Douglas, to tell you how deeply I have admired your wonderful courage," began Dexter.

"Oh, pray do not speak of it," said Anne, with intense embarrassment. For Miss Vanhorn had harried her niece so successfully during the long day, that the girl really believed that she had overstepped not only the edge of the cliff, but the limits of modesty as well.

"But I must," said Dexter. "In the life I have lived, Miss Douglas, I have seen women of all classes, and several times have been with women in moments of peril—on the plains during an Indian attack, at the mines after an explosion, and once on a sinking steamer. Only one showed anything like your quick courage of yesterday, and she was a mother who showed it for her child. You did your brave deed for a stranger; and you seem, to my eyes at least, hardly more than a child yourself. It is but another proof of the innate nobility of our human nature, and I, an enthusiast in such matters, beg you to let me personally thank you for the privilege of seeing your noble act." He put out his hand, took hers, and pressed it cordially.

It was a set speech, perhaps—Dexter made set speeches; but it was cordial and sincere. Anne, much comforted by this view of her impulsive action, looked at him with thankfulness. This was different from Miss Vanhorn's idea of it; different and better.

"I once helped one of my little brothers, who had fallen over a cliff, in much the same way," she said, with a little sigh of relief. "I am glad you think it was excusable."

"Excusable? It was superb," said Dexter. "And permit me to add, too, that I am a better judge of heroism than the people here, who belong, most of them, to a small, prejudiced, and I might say ignorant, class. They have no more idea of heroism, of anything broad and liberal, or of the country at large, than so many canary-birds born and bred in a cage. They ridicule the mere idea of being in earnest about anything in this ridiculous world. Yet the world is not so ridiculous as they think, and earnestness carries with it a tremendous weight sometimes. All the great deeds of which we have record have been done by earnest beliefs and earnest enthusiasms, even though mistaken ones. It is easy enough, by carefully abstaining from doing anything one's self, to maintain the position of ridiculing the attempts of others; but it is more than probable—in fact it is almost certain—that those very persons who ridicule and criticise could not themselves do the very least of those deeds, attain the very lowest of those successes, which afford them so much entertainment in others."

So spoke Dexter; and not without a tinge of bitterness, which he disguised as scorn. A little of the indifference to outside opinion which characterized the very class of whom he spoke would have made him a contented, as he already was a successful, man. But there was a surface of personal vanity over his better qualities which led him to desire a tribute of universal liking; and this is the tribute the class referred to always refuses—to the person who appears to seek it.

"But, in spite of ridicule, self-sacrifice is still heroic, faith in our humanity still beautiful, and courage still dear, to all hearts that have true nobility," he continued. Then it struck him that he was generalizing too much, feminine minds always preferring a personal application. "I would rather have a girl who was brave and truthful for my wife than the most beautiful woman on earth," he said, with the quick, sudden utterance he used when he wished to appear impulsive.

"But beautiful women can be truthful too," said Anne, viewing the subject impartially, with no realization of any application to herself.

"Can, but rarely are. I have, however, known—that is, I think I now know—*one*," he added, with quiet emphasis, coming round on another tack.

"I hope you do," said Anne; "and more than one. Else your acquaintance must be limited." As she spoke, the music sounded forth within, and forgetting the subject altogether, she turned with girlish interest to watch the dancers.

Dexter almost laughed aloud to himself in his shadowed corner, she was so unconscious. He had not thought her beautiful, save for the perfection of her youthful bloom; but now he suddenly began to discover the purity of her profile, and the graceful shape of her head, outlined against the lighted window. His taste, however, was not for youthful simplicity; he preferred beauty more ripened, and heightened by art. Having lived among the Indians in reality, the true children of nature, he had none of those dreams of ideal perfection in a brown skin and in the wilderness which haunt the eyes of dwellers in cities, and mislead even the artist. To him Rachel in her black floating laces, and Helen Lorrington in her shimmering silks, were far more beautiful than an Indian girl in her calico skirt could possibly be. But—Anne was certainly very fair and sweet.

"Of what were you thinking, Miss Douglas, during the minutes you hung suspended over that abyss?" he asked, moving so that he could rest his head on his hand, and thus look at her more steadily.

Anne turned. For she always looked directly at the person who spoke to her, having none of those side glances, tableaux of sweeping eyelashes, and willful little motions which belong to most pretty girls. She turned. And now Dexter was surprised to see how she was blushing, so deeply and slowly that it must have been physically painful.

"She is beginning to be conscious of my manner at last," he said to himself, with self-gratulation. Then he added, in a lower voice, "*I* was thinking only of you; and what a brutal sacrifice it would be if your life should be given for that other!"

"Valeria is a good girl, I think," said Anne, recovering herself, and answering as impersonally as though he had neither lowered his voice nor thrown any intensity into his eyes. "However, none of the ladies here approach Helen—Mrs. Lorrington; and I am sure *you* agree with me in thinking so, Mr. Dexter."

"You are loyal to your friend."

"No one has been so kind to me; I both love her and warmly admire her. How I hope she may come soon! And when she does, as I can not help loving to be with her, I suppose I shall see a great deal more of *you*," said the girl, smiling, and in her own mind addressing the long-devoted Knight-errant.

"Shall you?" thought Dexter, not a little piqued by her readiness to yield him even to her friend. "I will see that you do not long continue quite so indifferent," he added to himself, with determination. Then, in pursuance of this, he decided to go in and dance with some one else; that should be a first step.

"I believe I am engaged to Mrs. Bannert for the next dance," he said, regretfully. "Shall I take you in?"

"No; please let me stay here a while. My arm really aches dully all the time, and the fresh air is pleasant."

"And if Miss Vanhorn should ask?"

"Tell her where I am."

"I will," answered Dexter. And he fully intended to do it in any case. He liked, when she was not with him, to have Anne safely under her grandaunt's watchful vigilance, not exactly with the spirit of the dog in the manger, but something like it. He was conscious, also, that he possessed the chaperon's especial favor, and he did not intend to forfeit it; he wished to use it for his own purposes.

But Rachel marred his intention by crossing it with one of her own.

Dexter admired Mrs. Bannert. He could not help it. When she took his arm, he was for the time being hers. She knew this, and being piqued by some neglect of Heathcote's, she met the other man at the door, and made him think, without saying it, that she wished to be with him awhile on the moon-lit piazza; for Heathcote was there. Dexter obeyed. And thus it happened that Miss Vanhorn was not told at all; but supposing that her niece was still with the escort she had herself selected, the fine-looking owner of mines and mills, the future Senator, the "type of American success," she rested mistakenly content, and spent the time agreeably in making old Mrs. Bannert's life a temporary fever by relating to her in detail some old buried scandals respecting the departed Bannert, pretending to have forgotten entirely the chief actor's name.

In the mean while Heathcote, sauntering along the piazza in his turn, came upon Anne sitting alone by the window, and dropped into the vacant place beside her. He said a few words, playing with the fringe of Rachel's sash, which he still wore, "her colors," some one remarked, but made no allusion to the occurrences of the previous day. What he said was unimportant, but he looked at her rather steadily, and she was conscious of his glance. In truth, he was merely noting the effect of her head and throat against the lighted window, as Dexter had done, the outline being very distinct and lovely, a profile framed in light; but she thought it was something different. A painful timidity again seized her; instead of blushing, she turned pale, and with difficulty answered clearly. "*He* does not praise me," she thought. "*He* does not say that what I did yesterday was greater than anything among Indians and mines and on sinking steamers. *He* is laughing at me. Grandaunt was right, and no doubt he thinks me a bold, forward girl who tried to make a sensation."

Heathcote made another unimportant remark, but Anne, being now nervously sensitive, took it as having a second meaning. She turned her head away to hide the burning tears that were rising; but although unshed, Heathcote saw them. His observation was instantaneous where women were concerned; not so much active as intuitive. He had no idea what was the matter with her: this was the second inexplicable appearance of tears. But it would take more than such little damp occasions to disconcert him; and rather at random, but with sympathy and even tenderness in his voice, he said, soothingly, "Do not mind it," "it" of course representing whatever she pleased. Then, as the drops fell, "Why, you poor child, you are really in trouble," he said, taking her hand and holding it in his. Then, after a moment: "I do not know, of course, what it is that distresses you, but I too, although ignorant, am distressed by it also. For since yesterday, Anne, you have occupied a place in my memory which will never give you up. You will be an image there forever."

It was not much, after all; most improbable was it that any of those who saw her risk her life that day would soon forget her. Yet there was something in the glance of his eye and in the clasp of his hand that soothed Anne inexpressibly. She never again cared what people thought of her "boyish freak" (so Miss Vanhorn termed it), but laid the whole memory away, embalmed shyly in sweet odors forever.

Other persons now came in sight. "Shall we walk?" said Heathcote. They rose; she took his arm. He did not lead her out to the shadowed path below the piazza; they remained all the time among the lights and passing strollers. Their conversation was inconclusive and unmomentous, without a tinge of novel interest or brilliancy; not one sentence would have been worth repeating. Yet such as it was, with its few words and many silences which the man of the world did not exert himself to break, it seemed to establish a closer acquaintance between them than eloquence could have done. At least it was so with Anne, although she did not define it. Heathcote had no need to define; it was an old story with him.

As the second dance ended, he took her round, as though by chance, to the other side of the piazza, where he knew Rachel was sitting with Mr. Dexter. Here he skillfully changed companions, simply by one or two of his glances. For Rachel understood from them that he was bored, repentant, and lonely; and once convinced of this, she immediately executed the manœuvre herself, with the woman's usual means of natural little phrases and changes of position, Heathcote meanwhile standing passive until it was all done. Heathcote generally stood passive. But Dexter often had the appearance of exerting himself and arranging things.

Thus it happened that Miss Vanhorn saw Anne re-enter with the same escort who had taken her forth.

Another week passed, and another. Various scenes in the little dramas played by the different persons present followed each other with more or less notice, more or less success. One side of Dexter's nature was completely fascinated with Rachel Bannert—with her beauty, which a saint-worshipper would have denied, although why saintliness should be a matter of blonde hair remains undiscovered; with her dress and grace of manner; with her undoubted position in that narrow circle which he wished to enter even while condemning—perhaps merely to conquer it and turn away again. His rival with Rachel was Heathcote; he had discovered that. He was conscious that he detested Heathcote. While thus secretly interested in Rachel, he yet found time, however, to give a portion of each day to Anne; he did this partly from policy and partly from jealous annoyance. For here too he found the other man. Heathcote, in truth, seemed to be amusing himself in much the same way. If Dexter waltzed with Rachel, Heathcote offered his arm to Anne and took her out on the piazza; if Dexter walked with Anne there, Heathcote took Rachel into the rose-scented dusky garden. But Dexter had Miss Vanhorn's favor, if that was anything. She went to drive with him and took Anne; she allowed him to accompany them on their botanizing expeditions; she talked to him, and even listened to his descriptions of his life and adventures. In reality she cared no more for him than for a Choctaw; no more for his life than for that of Robinson Crusoe. But he was a rich man, and he would do for Anne, who was not a Vanhorn, but merely a Douglas. He had showed some liking for the girl; the affair should be encouraged and clinched. She, Katharine Vanhorn, would clinch it. He must be a very different man from the diagnosis she had made up of him if he did not yield to her clinching.

During these weeks, therefore, there had been many long conversations between Anne and Mr. Dexter; they had talked on many subjects appropriate to the occasion—Dexter was always appropriate. He had quoted pages of poetry, and he quoted well. He had, like Othello, related his adventures, and they were thrilling and true. Then, when more sure of her, he had turned the conversation upon herself. It is a fascinating subject—one's self! Anne touched it timidly here and there, but, never having had the habit or even the knowledge of self-analysis, she was more uncomfortable than pleased, after all, and inclined mentally to run away. She did not know herself whether she had more imagination than timidity, whether conscientiousness was more developed in her than ideality, or whether, if obliged to choose between saving the life of a brother or a husband, she would choose the former or the latter. Dexter had to drag her opinions of her own character from her almost by main strength. But he persisted. He had never known an imaginative young girl at the age when all things are problems to her who was not secretly, often openly, fascinated by a sympathetic research into her own timid little characteristics, opening like buds within her one by one. Dexter's theory was correct, his rule a good one probably in ninety-nine cases out of a hundred; only—Anne was the hundredth. She began to be afraid of him as he came toward her, kind, smiling, with his invisible air of success about him, ready for one of their long conversations. Yet certainly he was as pleasant a companion as a somewhat lonely young girl, isolated at a place like Caryl's, could wish for; at least that is what every one would have said.

During these weeks there had been no long talks with Heathcote. Miss Vanhorn did not ask him to accompany them to the woods; she did not utter to him the initiative word in passing which gives the opportunity. Still, there had been chance meetings and chance words, of course—five-minute strolls on the piazza, five-minute looks at the sunset or at the stars, in the pauses between the dances. But where Heathcote took a minute, Dexter had, if he chose, an hour.

Although in one way now so idle, Anne seemed to herself never to have been so busy before. Miss Vanhorn kept her at work upon plants through a large portion of each day, and required her to be promptly ready upon all other occasions. She barely found time to write to Miss Lois, who was spending the summer in a state betwixt anger and joy, veering one way by reason, the other by wrath, yet unable to refrain entirely from satisfaction over the new clothes for the children which Miss Vanhorn's money had enabled her to buy. The allowance was paid in advance; and it made Anne light-hearted whenever she thought, as she did daily, of the comforts it gave to those she loved. To Rast, Anne wrote in the early morning, her only free time. Rast was now on the island, but he was to go in a few days. This statement, continually repeated, like lawyers' notices of sales postponed from date to date, had lasted all summer, and still lasted. He had written to Anne as usual, until Miss Vanhorn, although without naming him, had tartly forbidden "so many letters." Then Anne asked him to write less frequently, and he obeyed. She, however, continued to write herself as before, describing her life at Caryl's, while he answered (as often as he was allowed), telling of his plans, and complaining that they were to be separated so long. But he was going to the far West, and there he should soon win a home for her. He counted the days till that happy time.

And then Anne would sit and dream of the island: she saw the old house, Rast, and the children, Miss Lois's thin, energetic face, the blue Straits, the white fort, and the little inclosure on the heights where were the two graves. She closed her eyes and heard their voices; she told them all she hoped. Only this one more winter, and then she could see them again, send them help, and perhaps have one of the children with her. And then, the year after— But here Miss Vanhorn's voice calling her name broke the vision, and with a sigh she returned to Caryl's again.

Helen's letters had ceased; but Anne jotted down a faithful record of the events of the days for her inspection when she came. Rumors varied at Caryl's respecting Mrs. Lorrington. Now her grandfather had died, and left her everything; and now he had miraculously recovered, and deeded his fortune to charitable institutions. Now he had existed without nourishment for weeks, and now he had the appetite of ten, and exhibited the capabilities of a second Methuselah. But in the mean time Helen was still absent. Under these circumstances, Anne, if she had been older, and desirous, might have collected voluminous expressions of opinion as to the qualities, beauty, and history, past and present, of the absent one from her dearest friends on earth. But the dearest friends on earth had not the habit of talking to this young girl as a companion and equal; to them she was simply that "sweet child," that "dear fresh-faced school-girl," to whom they confided only amiable platitudes. So Anne continued to hold fast undisturbed her belief in her beautiful Helen—that strong, grateful, reverent feeling which a young girl often cherishes for an older woman who is kind to her.

One still, hazy morning Miss Vanhorn announced her programme for the day. She intended to drive over to the county town, and Anne was to go with her six miles of the distance, and be left at a certain glen, where there was a country saw-mill. They had been there together several times, and had made acquaintance with the saw-miller, his wife, and his brood of white-headed children. The object of the present visit was a certain fern—the Camptosorus, or walking-leaf—which Miss Vanhorn had recently learned grew there, or at least had grown there within the memory of living botanists. That was enough. Anne was to search for the plant unflinchingly (the presence of the mill family being a sufficient protection) throughout the entire day, and be in waiting at the main-road crossing at sunset, when her grandaunt's carriage would stop on its return home. In order that there might be no mistake as to the time, she was allowed to wear one of Miss Vanhorn's watches. There were fourteen of them, all heirlooms, all either wildly too fast in their motions or hopelessly too slow, so that the gift was an embarrassing one. Anne knew that if she relied upon the one intrusted to her care, she would be obliged to spend about three hours at the crossing to allow for the variations in one direction or the other which might erratically attack it during the day. But her hope lay in the saw-miller's bright-faced little Yankee clock. At their early breakfast she prepared a lunch for herself in a small basket, and before Caryl's had fairly awakened, the old coupé rolled away from the door, bearing aunt and niece into the green country. When they reached the wooded hills at the end of the six miles, Anne descended with her basket, her digging trowel, and her tin plant case. She was to go over every inch of the saw-miller's ravine, and find that fern, living or dead. Miss Vanhorn said this, and she meant the plant; but it sounded as if she meant Anne. With renewed warnings as to care and diligence, she drove on, and Anne was left alone. It was ten o'clock, and a breathless August day. She hastened up the little path toward the saw-mill, glad to enter the wood and escape the heat of the sun. She now walked more slowly, and looked right and left for the fern; it was not there, probably, so near the light, but she had conscientiously determined to lose no inch of the allotted ground. Owing to this slow search, half an hour had passed when she reached the mill. She had perceived for some time that it was not in motion; there was no hum of the saw, no harsh cry of the rent boards: she said to herself that the miller was getting a great log in place on the little cart to be drawn up the tramway. But when she reached the spot, the miller was not there; the mill was closed, and only the peculiar fresh odor of the logs recently sawn asunder told that but a short time before the saw had been in motion. She went on to the door of the little house, and knocked; no one answered. Standing on tiptoe, she peeped in through the low window, and saw that the rooms were empty, and in that shining order that betokens the housewife's absence. Returning to the mill, she walked up the tramway; a bit of paper, for the information of chance customers, was pinned to the latch: "All hands gone to the sirkus. Home at sunset." She sat down, took off her straw hat, and considered what to do.

Three hundred and sixty-four days of that year Saw-miller Pike, his wife, his four children, and his hired man, one or all of them, were on that spot; their one absence chance decreed should be on this particular August Thursday when Anne Douglas came there to spend the day. She was not afraid; it was a quiet rural neighborhood without beggars or tramps. Her grandaunt would not return until sunset. She decided to look for the fern, and if she found it within an hour or two, to walk home, and send a boy back on horseback to wait for Miss Vanhorn. If she did not find it before afternoon, she would wait for the carriage, according to agreement. Hanging her basket and shawl on a tree branch near the mill, she entered the ravine, and was soon hidden in its green recesses. Up and down, up and down the steep rocky sides she climbed, her tin case swinging from her shoulder, her trowel in her belt; she neglected no spot, and her track, if it had been visible, would have shown itself almost as regular as the web of the geometric spider. Up and down, up and down, from the head of the ravine to its foot on one side: nothing. It seemed to her that she had seen the fronds and curled crosiers of a thousand ferns. Her eyes were tired, and she threw herself down on a mossy bank not far from the mill to rest a moment. There was no use in looking at the watch; still, she did it, and decided that it was either half past eleven or half past three. The remaining side of the ravine gazed at her steadily; she knew that she must clamber over every inch of those rocks also. She sighed, bathed her flushed cheeks in the brook, took down her hair, and braided it in two long school-girl braids, which hung down below her waist; then she tied her straw hat to a branch, pinned her neck-tie on the brim, took off her linen cuffs, and laid them within together with her gloves, and leaving the tin plant case and the trowel on the bank, started on her search. Up and down, up and down, peering into every cranny, standing on next to nothing, swinging herself from rock to rock; making acquaintance with several very unpleasant rock spiders, and hastily constructing bridges for them of small twigs, so that they could cross from her skirt to their home ledge in safety; finding a trickling spring, and drinking from it; now half way down the ravine, now three-quarters; and still no walking-leaf. She sat down on a jutting crag to take breath an instant, and watched a bird on a tree branch near by. He was one of those little brown songsters that sing as follows:

Seeing her watching him, he now chanted his little anthem in his best style.

"Very well," said Anne, aloud.

"Oh no; only so-so," said a voice below. She looked down, startled, It was Ward Heathcote.

CHAPTER XIV.

"From beginning to end it was all undeniable nonsense; but not necessarily the worse for that."—Nathaniel Hawthorne.

Heathcote was sitting under a tree by the brook-side, as though he had never been anywhere else.

"When did you come?" said Anne, looking down from her perch.

"Fifteen minutes or so ago," he answered, looking up from his couch.

"*Why* did you come?"

"To see you, of course."

"No; I can not believe that. The day is too warm."

"You, at any rate, look cool enough."

"It is cool up here among the rocks; but it must be intense out on the high-road."

"I did not come by the high-road."

"How, then, did you come?"

"Across the fields."

"Why?"

"Miss Douglas, were you born in New Hampshire? As I can not call all this information you require up hill, I shall be obliged to come up myself."

As he rose, Anne saw that he was laden with her dinner basket and shawl, her plant case and trowel, and her straw hat and its contents, which he balanced with exaggerated care. "Oh, leave them all there," she called down, laughingly.

But no, Heathcote would not; he preferred to bring them all with him. When he reached her rock, he gravely delivered them into her hands, and took a seat beside her, fanning himself with his hat.

"And now, how does it happen that you are here?" repeated Anne, placing her possessions in different niches.

"You insist? Why not let it pass for chance? No? Well, then, by horseback to Powell's: horse loses shoe; blacksmith's shop. Blacksmith talkative; second customer that morning; old coupé, fat old coachman, and fat brown horse, who also loses shoe. Coachman talkative; tells all about it; blacksmith tells *me*; young lady left at saw-mill to be taken up on return. I, being acquainted with said saw-mill and young lady, come across by lane through the fields. Find a dinner basket; look in; conclude to bring it on. Find a small tin coffin, and bring that too. Find a hat, ditto. Hat contains—"

"Never mind," said Anne, laughing. "But where is your horse?"

"Tied to a tree."

"And what are you going to do?"

"At present, nothing. By-and-by, if you will permit it, I *may*—smoke a cigar."

"I have no idea what time it is," said Anne, after a pause, while Heathcote, finding a comfortable place with his back against the rocks, seemed disposed to enjoy one of his seasons of silence.

He drew out his watch, and without looking at it held it toward her. "You need not tell; *I* do not want to know," he said.

"In spite of that, I feel it to be my duty to announce that it is nearly half past twelve; you may still reach home in time for lunch."

"Thanks. I know what I shall have for lunch."

"What?"

"One small biscuit, three slices of cake, one long corpulent pickle, and an apple."

"You have left nothing for me," said Anne, laughing over this disclosure of the contents of her basket.

"On the contrary, I have brought you something," said Heathcote, gravely producing two potatoes uncooked, a pinch of salt in paper, and a quarter of a loaf of bread, from the pockets of his blue flannel coat.

Anne burst into a peal of laughter, and the last shadow of timidity vanished. Heathcote seemed for the moment as young as Rast himself.

"Where have you been foraging?" she said.

"Foraging? I beg your pardon; nothing of the kind. I bought these supplies regularly from a farmer's wife, and paid for them in the coin of the land. I remarked to her that I should be out all day, and hated hunger; it was so sanguinary."

"But you will not be out all day."

"Until eight minutes of six, precisely; that is the time I have selected for my return." Then, seeing that she looked grave, he dropped into his usual manner, and added, "Of course, Miss Douglas, I shall only remain a little while—until the noon heat is over. You are looking for a rare flower, I believe?"

"A fern."

"What is the color of its flower?"

Anne laughed again. "A fern has no flower," she explained. "See, it is like this." And plucking a slender leaf, she described the wished-for plant minutely. "It stretches out its long tip—so; touches the earth—so; puts down a new little root from the leaf's end—so; and then starts on again—so."

"In a series of little green leaps?"

"Yes."

Heathcote knew as much of ferns as he did of saurians; but no subject was too remote for him when he chose to appear interested. He now chose to appear so, and they talked of ferns for some time. Then Anne said that she must finish the remaining quarter of the ravine. Heathcote decided to smoke a cigar where he was first; then he would join her.

But when, half an hour later, she came into view again beside the brook below him, apparently he had not stirred. "Found it?" he said.

"No."

"There is a sort of thin, consumptive, beggarly little leaf up here which looks something like your description. Shall I bring him down?"

"No, no; do not touch it," she answered, springing up the rocks toward him. "If it should be! But—I don't believe you know."

But he did know; for it was there. Very small and slender, creeping close to the rocks in the shyest way, half lost in the deep moss; but there! Heathcote had not moved; but the shrinking little plant happened to have placed itself exactly on a line with his idle eyes.

"It is unfair that you should find it without stirring, while I have had such a hard climb all in vain," said Anne, carefully taking up the little plant, with sufficient earth and moss to keep it comfortable.

"It is ever so," replied her companion, lazily, watching the spirals of cigar smoke above his head: "wait, and in time everything will come to you. If not in this world, then certainly in the next, which is the world I have selected for my own best efforts."

When the fern was properly bedded in the tin case, and the cover closed, Anne sat down for a moment to rest.

"When shall we have lunch?" asked the smoker.

"*You?*"

"Yes; I am bitterly hungry."

"But you said you were only going to stay a short time."

"Half an hour longer."

"What time is it now?"

"I have no idea."

"You can look."

"I refuse to look. Amiability has its limit."

"I had intended to walk home, if I found the fern in time," said Anne.

"Ah? But I think we are going to have a storm. Probably a thunder-storm," said Heathcote, languidly.

"How do you know? And—what shall we do?"

"I know, because I have been watching that little patch of sky up there. As to what we shall do—we can try the mill."

They rose as he spoke. Anne took the plant case. "I will carry this," she said; "the walking-leaf must be humored."

"So long as I have the dinner basket I remain sweet-tempered," answered Heathcote.

She put on her hat, but her neck-tie and cuffs were gone.

"I have them safe," he said. "They are with the potatoes."

Reaching the mill, they tried the door, but found it securely fastened. They tried the house door and windows, with the same result. Unless they broke several panes of glass they could not gain entrance, and even then it was a question whether Heathcote would be able to thrust inward the strong oaken stick above, which held the sash down.

"Do mount your horse and ride home," urged Anne. "I shall be safe here, and in danger of nothing worse than a summer shower. I will go back in the ravine and find a beech-tree. Its close, strong little leaves will keep off the rain almost entirely. Why should both of us be drenched?"

"Neither of us shall be. Come with me, and quickly, for the storm is close upon us. There is a little cave, or rather hollow in the rock, not far above the road; I think it will shelter us. I, for one, have no desire to be out in your 'summer shower,' and ride home to Caryl's afterward in a limp, blue-stained condition."

"How long will it take us to reach this cave?" said Anne, hesitating.

"Three minutes, perhaps."

"I suppose we had better go, then," she said, slowly. "But pray do not take those things. They will all have to be brought down again."

"They shall be," said Heathcote, leading the way toward the road.

It was not a long climb, but in some places the ascent was steep. A little path was their guide to the "cave"—a hollow in the ledge, which the boys of the neighborhood considered quite a fortress, a bandit's retreat. A rude ladder formed the front steps of their rock nest, and Anne was soon ensconced within, her gray shawl making a carpet for them both. The cave was about seven feet in depth, and four or five in breadth; the rock roof was high above their heads. Behind there was a dark, deep little recess, blackened with smoke, which the boys had evidently used as an oven. The side of the hill jutted out slightly above them, and this, rather than the seven feet of depth possessed by the niche, made it possible that they would escape the rain.

The cave was in an angle of the hill. From Heathcote's side part of the main road could be seen, and the saw-mill; but Anne, facing the other way, saw only the fields and forest, the sparkle of the little mill-stream, and the calmer gleam of the river. One half of the sky was of the deepest blue, one half of the expanse of field and forest golden in the sunshine. Over the other half hung a cloud and a shadow of deep purple-black, which were advancing rapidly, although there was not, where the two gazers sat, so much as a breath of stirred air.

"It will soon be here," said Heathcote. "See that white line across the forest? That is the wind turning over the leaves. In the fields it makes the grain look suddenly gray as it is bent forward."

"I should not have known it was the wind," said Anne. "I have only seen storms on the water."

"That yellow line is the Mellport plank-road; all the dust is whirling. Are you afraid of lightning?"

"Shall we have it?"

"Yes; here it is." And, with a flash, the wind was upon them. A cloud of dust rose from the road below; they bent their heads until the whirlwind had passed by on its wild career down the valley. When, laughing and breathless, Anne opened her eyes again, her hair, swept out of its loose braids, was in a wild mass round her shoulders, and she barely saved her straw hat, which was starting out to follow the whirlwind. And now the lightning was vivid and beautiful, cutting the blue-black clouds with fierce golden darts, while the thunder followed, peal after peal, until the hill itself seemed to tremble. A moment later came the rain, hiding both the valley and sky with its thick gray veil: they were shut in.

As Heathcote had thought, the drops only grazed their doorway. They moved slightly back from the entrance; he took off his hat, hung it on a rock knob, and inquired meekly if they might not *now* have lunch. Anne, who, between the peals, had been endeavoring to recapture her hair, and had now one long thick braid in comparative order, smiled, and advised him to stay his hunger with the provisions in his own pockets. He took them out and looked at them.

"If the boys who use this hole for an oven have left us some wood, we will roast and toast these, and have a hot lunch yet," he said, stretching back to search. Lighting a match, he examined the hole; the draught that blew the flame proved that it had an outlet above. "Boys know something, after all. And here is their wood-pile," he said, showing Anne, by the light of a second match, a cranny in the rock at one side neatly filled with small sticks and twigs. The rain fell in a thick dark sheet outside straight down from the sky to the ground with a low rushing sound. In a minute or two a tiny blue flame flickered on their miniature hearth, went out, started again, turned golden, caught at the twigs, and grew at last into a brisk little fire. Heathcote, leaning on his elbow, his hands and cuffs grimed, watched and tended it carefully. He next cut his quarter loaf into slices, and toasted—or rather heated—them on the point of his knife-blade; he put his two potatoes under hot ashes, like two Indian mounds, arranged his pinch of salt ceremoniously upon a stone, and then announced that he had prepared a meal to which all persons present were generously invited, with a polite unconsciousness as to any covered

97

baskets they might have in their possession, or the supposed contents of said receptacles. Anne, having finished the other long braid and thrown it behind her, was now endeavoring to wash her hands in the rain. In this attempt Heathcote joined her, but only succeeded in broadening the grimy spots. The girl's neck-tie and cuffs were still confiscated. She was aware that a linen collar, fastened only with a white pin, is not what custom requires at the base of a chin, and that wrists bare for three inches above the hand are considered indecorous. At least in the morning, certain qualities in evening air making the same exposure, even to a much greater extent, quite different. But she was not much troubled; island life had made her indifferent even to these enormities.

The rain did not swerve from its work; it came down steadily; they could not see through the swift lead-colored drops. But, within, the little cave was cheery in the fire-light, and the toasted bread had an appetizing fragrance. At least Heathcote said so; Anne thought it was burned. She opened her basket, and they divided the contents impartially—half a biscuit, half a pickle, half an apple, and a slice and a half of cake for each. The potatoes were hardly warmed through, but Heathcote insisted that they should be tasted, "in order not to wickedly waste the salt." Being really hungry, they finished everything, he stoutly refusing to give up even a crumb of his last half-slice of cake, which Anne begged for on the plea of being still in school. By this time they were full of merriment, laughing and paying no attention to what they said, talking nonsense and enjoying it. Anne's cheeks glowed, her eyes were bright as stars, her brown hair, more loosely fastened than usual, lay in little waves round her face; her beautiful arched lips were half the time parted in laughter, and her rounded arms and hands seemed to fall into charming poses of their own, whichever way she turned.

About three o'clock the veil of rain grew less dense; they could see the fields again; from where he sat, Heathcote could see the road and the mill.

"Can we not go now?" said Anne.

"By no means, unless you covet the drenching we have taken so much care to escape. But by four I think it will be over." He lit a cigar, and leaning back against the rock, said, "Tell me some more about that island; about the dogs and the ice."

"No," said Anne, coloring a little; "you are laughing at me. I shall tell you no more."

Then he demanded autocratically that she should sing. "I choose the song you sang on New-Year's night; the ballad."

And Anne sang the little chanson, sang it softly and clearly, the low sound of the rain forming an accompaniment.

"Do you know any Italian songs?"

"Yes."

"Please sing me one."

She sang one of Belzini's selections, and remembered to sing it as Tante had directed.

"You do not sing that as well as the other; there is no expression. However, that could hardly be expected, I suppose."

"Yes, it could, and I know how. Only Tante told me not to do it," said the girl, with a touch of annoyance.

"Tante not being here, I propose that you disobey."

And Anne, not unwillingly, began; it had always been hard for her to follow Tante's little rule. She had heard the song more than once in the opera to which it belonged, and she knew the Italian words. She put her whole heart into it, and when she ended, her eyes were dimmed with emotion.

Heathcote looked at her now, and guardedly. This was not the school-girl of the hour before. But it was, and he soon discovered that it was. Anne's emotion had been impersonal; she had identified herself for the time being with the song, but once ended, its love and grief were no more to her—her own personality as Anne Douglas—than the opera itself.

"Curious!" thought the man beside her.

And then his attention was diverted by a moving object advancing along the main road below. Through the rain he distinguished the light buggy of Gregory Dexter and his pair of fine black horses. They had evidently been under shelter during the heaviest rain-fall, and had now ventured forth again. Heathcote made no sign, but watched. Anne could not see the road. Dexter stopped at the mill, tied his horses to a post, and then tried the doors, and also the door of the miller's little cottage, peering through the windows as they had done. Then he went up the ravine out of sight, as if searching for some one. After five minutes he returned, and waited, hesitating, under a tree, which partially protected him from the still falling drops. Heathcote was now roused to amusement. Dexter was evidently searching for Anne. He lit another cigar, leaned back against the rock in a comfortable position, and began a desultory conversation, at the same time watching the movements of his rival below. A sudden after-shower had now come up—one of those short but heavy bursts of rain on the departing edge of a thunder-storm, by which the unwary are often overtaken. Dexter, leaving his tree, and seizing the cushions of the buggy, hurried up the tramway to the mill door again, intending to force an entrance. But the solid oak stood firm in spite of his efforts, and the rain poured fiercely down. Heathcote could see him look upward to the sky, still holding the heavy cushions, and his sense of enjoyment was so great that he leaned forward and warmly shook hands with Anne.

"Why do you do that?" she asked, in surprise.

"I remembered that I had not shaken hands with you all day. If we neglect our privileges, the gods take them from us," he answered. And then, he had the exquisite pleasure of seeing the man below attempt to climb up to one of the small mill windows, slip down twice, and at last succeed so far as to find footing on a projecting edge, and endeavor to open the stubborn sash, which plainly would not yield. He was exerting all his strength. But without avail. It was a true dog-day afternoon, the rain having made the air more close and lifeless than before. The strong draught up the chimney of their cave had taken the heat of the small fire away from them; yet even there among the cool rocks they had found it necessary to put out the little blaze, as making their niche too warm. Down below in the open valley the heat was unbroken; and to be wet and warm, and obliged to exert all one's strength at the same time, is hard for a large man like Gregory Dexter. The rain dripped from the roof directly down upon his hat, and probably, the looker-on thought with glee, was stealing down his back also. At any rate he was becoming impatient, for he broke a pane of glass and put his hand through to try and reach the sash-spring. But the spring was broken; it would not move. And now he must be growing angry, for he shivered all the panes, broke the frame, and then tried to clamber in; the cushions were already sacrificed down on the wet boards below. But it is difficult for a broad-shouldered heavy man to climb through a small window, especially if he have no firm foot-hold as a beginning. Heathcote laughed out aloud now, and Anne leaned forward to look also.

"Who is it?" she said, as she caught sight of the struggling figure. At this moment Dexter had one knee on the sill and his head inside, but he was too broad for the space.

"He is caught! He can neither get in nor out," said Heathcote, in an ecstasy of mirth.

"Who is it?" said Anne again.

"Dexter, of course; he is here looking for you. There! he has slipped—he is in real danger! No; he has firm hold with his hands. See him try to find the edge with his feet. Oh, this is too good!" And throwing back his head, Heathcote laughed until his brown eyes shone.

But Anne, really alarmed, held her breath; then, when the struggling figure at last found its former foot-hold, she gave a sigh of relief. "We must go down," she said.

"And why, Miss Douglas?"

"Did you not say he had come for me?"

"That was a supposition merely. And did not I come for you too?"

"But as he is there, would it not be better for us to go down?"

"Have we not done well enough by ourselves so far? And besides, at this late hour, I see no object in getting a wetting merely for his sake."

"It is not raining hard now."

"But it is still raining."

She leaned forward and looked down at Dexter again; he was standing under a tree wiping his hat with his handkerchief.

"Please let me go down," she said, entreatingly, like a child.

"No," said Heathcote, smiling back, and taking her hand as if to make sure. "Do you remember the evening after the quarry affair, Anne? and that I took your hand, and held it as I am doing now? Did you think me impertinent?"

"I thought you very kind. After that I did not mind what grandaunt had said."

"And what had she said? But no matter; something disagreeable, without doubt. Even the boys who frequent this retreat could not well have grimier hands than we have now: look at them. No, you can not be released, unless you promise."

"What?"

"Not to go down until I give you leave: I will give it soon."

"I promise."

With a quiet pressure, and one rather long look, he relinquished her hand, and leaned back against the rock again.

"I wonder how Dexter knew that you were here?"

"Perhaps he met grandaunt. I heard him say that he was going to Mellport to-day."

"That is it. The roads cross, and he must have met her. Probably, then, he has her permission to take you home. Miss Douglas, will you accept advice?"

"I will at least listen to it," said Anne, smiling.

"When the rain stops, as it will in a few minutes, go down alone. And say nothing to Mr. Dexter about me. Now do not begin to batter me with that aggressive truthfulness of yours. You can, of course, tell Miss Vanhorn the whole; but certainly you are not accountable to Gregory Dexter."

"But why should I not tell him?"

"Because it is as well that he should not know I have been here with you all day," said Heathcote, quietly, but curious to hear what she would answer.

"Was it wrong?"

"It was a chance. But he would think I planned it. Of course I supposed the miller and his family were here."

"But if it was wrong for you to be here when you found them absent, why did you stay?" said Anne, looking at him gravely.

"The storm came up, you know; of course I could not leave you. Do not look so serious; all is well if we keep it to ourselves. And Miss Vanhorn's first command to you will be the same. She will look blackly at me for a day or two, but I shall be able to bear that. Take my advice; to Dexter, at least, say nothing." Then, seeing her still unconvinced, he added, "On my own account, too, I wish you would not tell him."

"You mean it?"

"Yes."

"Then I will not," she answered, raising her sincere eyes to his.

Heathcote laughed, lightly lifted her hand, and touched the blue-veined wrist with his lips. "You true-hearted little girl!" he said. "I was only joking. As far as I am concerned, you may tell Dexter and the whole world. But seriously, on your own account, I beg you to refrain. Promise me not to tell him until you have seen Miss Vanhorn."

"Very well; I promise that," said Anne.

"Good-by, then. The rain is over, and he will be going. I will not show myself until I see you drive away. What good fortune that my horse was tied out of sight! Must you carry all those things, basket, tin case, and all? Why not let me try to smuggle some of them home on horseback? You would rather not? I submit. There, your hat has fallen off; I will tie it on."

"But the strings do not belong there," said Anne, laughing merrily as he knotted the two blue ribbons with great strength (as a man always ties a ribbon) under her chin.

"Never mind; they look charming."

"And my cuffs?"

"You can not have them; I shall keep them as souvenirs. And now—have you had a pleasant day, Anne?"

"Very," replied the girl, frankly.

They shook hands in farewell, and then she went down the ladder, her shawl, plant case, and basket on her arm. Heathcote remained in the cave. When she had reached the ground, and was turning to descend the hill, a low voice above said, "Anne."

She glanced up; Heathcote was lying on the floor of the cave with his eyes looking over the edge. "Shake hands," he said, cautiously stretching down an arm.

"But I did."

"Once more."

She put down her shawl, plant case, and basket, and, climbing one round of the ladder, extended her hand; their finger-tips touched.

"Thanks," said the voice above, and the head was withdrawn.

Dexter, after doing what he could to make the buggy dry, was on the point of driving away, when he saw a figure coming toward him, and recognized Anne. He jumped lightly out over the wheel (he could be light on occasion), and came to meet her. It was as they had thought; he had met Miss Vanhorn, and learning where Anne was, had received permission to take her home.

"I shall not be disappointed after all," he said, his white teeth gleaming as he smiled, and his gray eyes resting upon her with cordial pleasure. He certainly was a fine-looking man. But—too large for a mill window. Fortunately mill windows are not standards of comparison.

"It has been raining a long time; where did you find shelter?" he asked, as the spirited horses, fretted by standing, started down the moist brown road at a swift pace.

"In a little cave in the hill-side above us," answered Anne, conscious that at that very moment Heathcote was probably watching them. She hesitated, and then, in spite of a distinct determination not to do it, could not help turning her head and glancing backward and upward for a second behind her companion's broad shoulders. In answer, a handkerchief fluttered from above; he was watching, then. A bright flush rose in her cheeks, and she talked gayly to Dexter during the six-mile drive between the glistening fields, over the wet dark bridge, and up to the piazza of Caryl's, where almost every one was sitting enjoying the coolness after the rain, and the fresh fragrance of the grateful earth. Rachel Bannert came forward as they alighted, and resting her hand caressingly on Anne's shoulder, hoped that she was not tired—and were they caught in the rain?—and did they observe the peculiar color of the clouds?—and so forth, and so forth. Rachel was dressed for the evening in black lace over black velvet, with a crimson rose in her hair; the rich drapery trailed round her in royal length, yet in some way failed to conceal entirely the little foot in its black slipper. Anne did not hurry away; she stood contentedly where she was while Rachel asked all her little questions. Dexter had stepped back into the buggy with the intention of driving round himself to the stables; he had no desire to expose the wrinkled condition of his attire to the groups on the piazza. But in that short interval he noted (as Rachel had intended he should note) every detail of her appearance. Her only failure was that he failed to note also, by comparison, the deficiencies of Anne.

When he was gone, being released, Anne ran up to her room, placed the fern in water, and then, happening to think of it, looked at herself in the glass. The result was not cheering. Like most women, she judged herself by the order of her hair and dress; they were both frightful.

Miss Vanhorn, also caught in the storm, did not return until late twilight. Anne, not knowing what she would decree when she heard the story of the day, had attired herself in the thick white school-girl dress which had been selected on another occasion of penance—the evening after the adventure at the quarry. It was an inconvenient time to tell the story. Miss Vanhorn was tired and cross, tea had been sent up to the room, and Bessmer was waiting to arrange her hair. "What have you been doing now?" she said. "Climbing trees? Or breaking in colts?"

Anne told her tale briefly. The old woman listened, without comment, but watching her closely all the time.

"And he said to tell you," said Anne, in conclusion, "but not to tell Mr. Dexter, unless you gave me permission."

"Mr. Dexter alone?"

"Mr. Dexter or—any one, I suppose."

"Very well; that will do. And Mr. Heathcote is right; you are not to breathe a word of this adventure to any one. But what fascination it is, Anne Douglas, which induces you to hang yourself over rocks, and climb up into caves, I can not imagine! Luckily this time you had not a crowd of spectators. Bring me the fern, and—But what, in the name of wonder, are you wearing? Go to your room immediately and put on the lavender silk."

"Oh, grandaunt, *that*?"

"Do as I bid you. Bessmer, you can come in now. I suppose it is ordered for the best that young girls should be such hopeless simpletons!"

CHAPTER XV.

"No summer ever came back, and no two summers ever were alike. Times change, and people change; and if our hearts do not change as readily, so much the worse for us."—Nathaniel Hawthorne.

"But, ah! who ever shunn'd by precedent

The destined ills she must herself assay?"

—Shakspeare.

When Miss Vanhorn and her niece entered the ball-room, late in the evening, heads were turned to look at them; for the old woman wore all her diamonds, fine stones in old-fashioned settings, and shone like a little squat-figured East Indian god. Anne was beside her, clad in pale lavender—an evening costume simply made, but more like full dress than anything she had yet worn. Dexter came forward instantly, and asked her to dance. He thought he had never seen her look so well—so much like the other ladies; for heretofore there had been a marked difference—a difference which he had neither comprehended nor admired. Anne danced. New invitations came, and she accepted them. She was enjoying it all frankly, when through a window she caught sight of Heathcote on the piazza looking in. She happened to be dancing with Mr. Dexter, and at once she felt nervous in the thought that he might at any moment ask her some question about the day which she would find difficulty in answering. But she had not thought of this until her eyes fell on Heathcote.

Dexter had seen Heathcote too, and he had also seen her sudden nervousness. He was intensely vexed. Could Ward Heathcote, simply by looking through a window, make a girl grow nervous in that way, and a girl with whom he, Dexter, was dancing? With inward angry determination, he immediately asked her to dance again. But he need not have feared interference; Heathcote did not enter the room during the evening.

From the moment Miss Vanhorn heard the story of that day her method regarding her niece changed entirely; for Mr. Heathcote would never have remained with her, storm or no storm, through four or five hours, unless he either admired her, had been entertained by her, or liked her for herself alone, as men will like occasionally a frank, natural young girl.

According to old Katharine, Anne was not beautiful enough to excite his admiration, not amusing enough to entertain him; it must be, therefore, that he liked her to a certain degree for herself alone. Mr. Heathcote was not a favorite of old Katharine's, yet none the less was his approval worth having, and none the less, also, was he an excellent subject to rouse the jealousy of Gregory Dexter. For Dexter was not coming forward as rapidly as old Katharine had decreed he should come. Old Katharine had decided that Anne was to marry Dexter; but if in the mean time her girlish fancy was attracted toward Heathcote, so much the better. It would all the more surely eliminate the memory of that fatal name, Pronando. Of course Heathcote was only amusing himself, but he must now be encouraged to continue to amuse himself. She ceased taking Anne to the woods every day; she made her sit among the groups of ladies on the piazza in the morning, with worsted, canvas, and a pattern, which puzzled poor Anne deeply, since she had not the gift of fancy-work, nor a talent for tidies. She asked Heathcote to teach her niece to play billiards, and she sent her to stroll on the river-bank at sunset with him under a white silk parasol. At the same time, however, she continued to summon Mr. Dexter to her side with the same dictatorial manner she had assumed toward him from the first, and to talk to him, and encourage him to talk to her through long half-hours of afternoon and evening. The old woman, with her airs of patronage, her half-closed eyes, and frank impertinence, amused him more than any one at Caryl's. With his own wide, far-reaching plans and cares and enterprises all the time pushing each other forward in his mind, it was like coming from a world of giants to one of Lilliputians to sit down and talk with limited, prejudiced, narrow old Katharine. She knew that he was amused; she was even capable of understanding it, viewed from his own stand-point. That made no difference with her own.

After three or four days of the chaperon's open arrangement, it grew into a custom for Heathcote to meet Anne at sunset in the garden, and stroll up and down with her for half an hour. She was always there, because she was sent there. Heathcote never said he would come again; it was supposed to be by chance. But one evening Anne remarked frankly that she was very glad he came; her grandaunt sent her out whether she wished to come or not, and the resources of the small garden were soon exhausted. They were sitting in an arbor at the end of the serpentine walk. Heathcote, his straw hat on the ground, was braiding three spears of grass with elaborate care.

"You pay rather doubtful compliments," he said.

"I only mean that it is very kind to come so regularly."

"You will not let even that remain a chance?"

"But it is not, is it?"

"Well, no," he answered, after a short silence, "I can not say that it is." He dropped the grass blades, leaned back against the rustic seat, and looked at her. It was a great temptation; he was a finished adept in the art of flirtation at its highest grade, and enjoyed the pastime. But he had not really opened that game with this young girl, and he said to himself that he would not now. He leaned over, found his three spears of grass, and went on braiding. But although he thus restrained himself, he still continued to meet her, as Miss Vanhorn, with equal pertinacity, continued to send her niece to meet him. They were not alone in the garden, but their conversation was unheard.

One evening tableaux were given: Isabel, Rachel, and others had been admired in many varieties of costume and attitude, and Dexter had been everything from Richard the Lion-hearted to Aladdin. Heathcote had refused

102

to take part. And now came a tableau in which Anne, as the Goddess of Liberty, was poised on a barrel mounted on three tables, one above the other. This airy elevation was considered necessary for the goddess, and the three tables were occupied by symbolical groups of the Seasons, the Virtues, and the Nations, all gathered together under the protection of Liberty on her barrel. Liberty, being in this case a finely poised young person, kept her position easily, flag in hand, while the merry groups were arranged on the tables below. When all was ready, the curtain was raised, lowered, then raised again for a second view, Anne looking like a goddess indeed (although a very young one), her white-robed form outlined against a dark background, one arm extended, her head thrown back, and her eyes fixed upon the outspread flag. But at the instant the curtain began to rise for this second view, she had felt the barrel broaden slightly under her, and knew that a hoop had parted. At the same second came the feeling that her best course was to stand perfectly motionless, in the hope that the staves would still support her until she could be assisted down from her isolated height. For she was fifteen feet above the stage, and there was nothing within reach which she could grasp. A chill ran over her; she tried not to breathe. At the same moment, however, when the sensation of falling was coming upon her, two firm hands were placed upon each side of her waist from behind, very slightly lifting her, as if to show her that she was safe even if the support did give way beneath her. It was Heathcote, standing on the table below. He had been detailed as scene-shifter (Rachel, being behind the scenes herself, had arranged this), had noticed the barrel as it moved, and had sprung up unseen behind the draperied pyramid to assist the goddess. No one saw him. When the curtain reached the foot-lights again he was assisting all the allegorical personages to descend from their heights, and first of all Liberty, who was trembling. No one knew this, however, save himself. Rachel, gorgeous as Autumn, drew him away almost immediately, and Anne had no opportunity to thank him until the next afternoon.

"You do not know how frightful it was for the moment," she said. "I had never felt dizzy in my life before. I had nothing with which I could save myself, and I could not jump down on the tables below, because there was no footing: I should only have thrown down the others. How quick you were, and how kind! But you are always kind."

"Few would agree with you there, Miss Douglas. Mr. Dexter has far more of what is called kindness than I have," said Heathcote, carelessly.

They were sitting in the same arbor. Anne was silent a moment, as if pondering. "Yes," she said, thoughtfully, "I believe you are right. You are kind to a few; he is kind to all. It would be better if you were more like him."

"Thanks. But it is too late, I fear, to make a Dexter of me. I have always been, if not exactly a grief to my friends, still by no means their pride. Fortunately I have no father or mother to be disturbed by my lacks; one does not mind being a grief to second cousins." He paused; then added, in another tone, "But life is lonely enough sometimes."

Two violet eyes met his as he spoke, gazing at him so earnestly, sincerely, and almost wistfully that for an instant he lost himself. He began to speculate as to the best way of retaining that wistful interest; and then, suddenly, as a dam gives way in the night and lets out the flood, all his good resolutions crumbled, and his vagrant fancy, long indulged, asserted its command, and took its own way again. He knew that he could not approach her to the ordinary degree and in the ordinary way of flirtation; she would not understand or allow it. With the intuition which was his most dangerous gift he also knew that there was a way of another kind. And he used it.

His sudden change of purpose had taken but a moment. "Lonely enough," he repeated, "and bad enough. Do you think there is any use in trying to be better?" He spoke as if half in earnest.

"We must all try," said the girl, gravely.

"But one needs help."

"It will be given."

He rose, walked to the door of the arbor, as if hesitating, then came back abruptly. "*You* could help me," he said, standing in front of her, with his eyes fixed upon her face.

She started slightly, and turned her eyes away, but did not speak. Nor did he. At last, as the silence grew oppressive, she said, in a low voice: "You are mistaken, I think. I can not."

He sat down again, and began slowly to excavate a hole in the sand with the end of his cane, to the consternation of a colony of ants who lived in a thriving village under the opposite bench, but still in dangerous proximity to the approaching tunnel.

"I have never pretended to be anything but an idle, useless fellow," he said, his eyes intent upon his work. "But my life does not satisfy me always, and at times I am seized by a horrible loneliness. I am not all bad, I hope. If any one cared enough—but no one has ever cared."

"You have many friends," said Anne, her eyes fixed upon the hues of the western sky.

"As you see them. The people here are examples of my friends."

103

"You must have others who are nearer."

"No, no one. I have never had a home." He looked up as he said this, and met her eyes, withdrawn for a moment from the sunset; they expressed so much pity that he felt ashamed of himself. For his entire freedom from home ties was almost the only thing for which he had felt profoundly grateful in his idle life. Other boys had been obliged to bend to the paternal will; other fellows had not been able to wander over the world and enjoy themselves as he had wandered and enjoyed. But—he could not help going on now.

"I pretend to be indifferent, and all that. No doubt I succeed in appearing so—that is, to the outside world. But there come moments when I would give anything for some firm belief to anchor myself to, something higher and better than I am." (The tunnel was very near the ants now.) "I believe, Miss Douglas, I can not help believing, that *you* could tell me what that is."

"Oh no; I am very ignorant," said Anne, hurriedly, returning to the sunset with heightened color.

"But you believe. I will never make a spectacle of myself; I will never ask the conventional questions of conventional good people, whom I hate. *You* might influence me—But what right have I to ask you, Anne? Why should I think that you would care?"

"I do care," said the low voice, after a moment, as if forced to answer.

"Then help me."

"How can I help you?"

"Tell me what you believe. And make me believe it also."

"Surely, Mr. Heathcote, you believe in God?"

"I am not sure that I do."

She clasped her hands in distress. "How *can* you live!" she cried, almost in tears.

Again Heathcote felt a touch of compunction. But he could not make himself stop now; he was too sincerely interested.

"There is no use; I can not argue," Anne was saying. "If you do not *feel* God, I can not make you believe in him."

"Tell me how *you* feel; perhaps I can learn from you."

Poor Anne! she did not know how she felt, and had no words ready. Undeveloped, unused to analysis, she was asked to unfold her inmost soul in the broad garish light of day.

"I—I can not," she murmured, in deep trouble.

"Never mind, then," said Heathcote, with an excellent little assumption of disappointment masked by affected carelessness. "Forget what I have said; it is of small consequence at best. Shall we go back to the house, Miss Douglas?"

But Anne was struggling with herself, making a desperate effort to conquer what seemed to her a selfish and unworthy timidity. "I will do anything I can," she said, hurriedly, in a low voice.

They had both risen. "Let me see you to-morrow, then."

"Yes."

"It is a beginning," he said. He offered his arm gravely, almost reverently, and in silence they returned to the house. It seemed to Anne that many long minutes passed as they walked through the garden, brushed by the roses on each side: in reality the minutes were three.

For that evening meteors had been appointed by the astronomers and the newspapers. They were, when they came, few and faint; but they afforded a pretext for being out on the hill. Anne was there with Mr. Dexter, and other star-gazers were near. Heathcote and Rachel, however, were not visible, and this disturbed Dexter. In spite of himself, he could never be quite content unless he knew where that dark-eyed woman was. But his inward annoyance did not affect either his memory or the fine tones of his voice. No one on the hill that night quoted so well or so aptly grand star-like sentences, or verses appropriate to the occasion.

"When standing alone on a hill-top during a clear night such as this, Miss Douglas," he said, "the roll of the earth eastward is almost a palpable movement. The sensation may be caused by the panoramic glide of the stars past earthly objects, or by the wind, or by the solitude; but whatever be its origin, the impression of riding along is vivid and abiding. We are now watching our own stately progress through the stars."

"Hear Dexter quote," said Heathcote, in his lowest under-tone, to Rachel. They were near the others, but, instead of standing, were sitting on the grass, with a large bush for background; in its shadow their figures were concealed, and the rustle of its leaves drowned their whispers.

"Hush! I like Mr. Dexter," said Rachel.

"I know you do. You will marry that man some day."

104

"Do *you* say that, Ward?"

An hour later, Anne, in her own room, was timidly adding the same name to her own petitions before she slept.

The next day, and the next, they met in the garden at sunset as before, and each time when they parted she was flushed and excited by the effort she was making, and he was calm and content. On the third afternoon they did not meet, for there was another picnic. But as the sun sank below the horizon, and the rich colors rose in the sky, Heathcote turned, and, across all the merry throng, looked at her as if in remembrance. After that he did not see her alone for several days: chance obstacles stood in the way, and he never forced anything. Then there was another unmolested hour in the arbor; then another. Anne was now deeply interested. How could she help being so, when the education of a soul was placed in her hands? And Heathcote began to be fascinated too.

By his own conversion?

August was nearly over. The nights were cool, and the early mornings veiled in mist. The city idlers awakened reluctantly to the realization that summer was drawing to its close; and there was the same old surprise over the dampness of the yellow moonlight, the dull look of the forest; the same old discovery that the golden-rods and asters were becoming prominent in the departure of the more delicate blossoms. The last four days of that August Anne remembered all her life.

On the 28th there occurred, by unexpected self-arrangement of small events, a long conversation of three hours with Heathcote.

On the 29th he quarrelled with her, and hotly, leaving her overwhelmed with grief and surprise.

On the 30th he came back to her. They had but three minutes together on the piazza, and then Mr. Dexter joined them. But in those minutes he had asked forgiveness, and seemed also to yield all at once the points over which heretofore he had been immovable.

On the 31st Helen came.

It was late. Anne had gone to her room. She had not seen Heathcote that day. She had extinguished the candle, and was looking at the brassy moon slowly rising above the trees, when a light tap sounded on her door.

"Who is it?" she said.

"Helen, of course," answered a sweet voice she knew. She drew back the bolt swiftly, and Mrs. Lorrington came in, dressed in travelling attire. She had just arrived. She kissed Anne, saying, gayly: "Are you not glad to see me? Grandfather has again recovered, and dismissed me. I spend my life on the road. Are you well, Crystal? And how do you like Caryl's? No, do not light the candle; I can see you in the moonlight, all draped in white. I shall stay half an hour—no longer. My maid is waiting, and I must not lose my beauty-sleep. But I wanted to see you first of all. Tell me about yourself, and everything. Did you put down what happened in a note-book, as I asked you?"

"Yes; here it is. But the record is brief—only names and dates. How glad I am to see you, Helen! How very, very glad! It seemed as if you would never come." She took Helen's hands, and held them as she spoke. She was very deeply attached to her brilliant friend.

Helen laughed, kissed her again, and began asking questions. She was full of plans. "Heretofore they have not staid at Caryl's in the autumn," she said, "but this year I shall make them. September and part of October would be pleasant here, I know. Has any one spoken of going?"

"Mrs. Bannert has, I think."

"You mean my dearest friend Rachel. But she will stay now that *I* have come; that is, if I succeed in keeping—somebody else. The Bishop has been devoted to her, of course, and likewise the Tenor; the Haunted Man and others skirmish on her borders. Even the Knight-errant is not, I am sorry to say, above suspicion. Who has it especially been?"

"I do not know; every one seems to admire her. I think she has not favored one more than another."

"Oh, has she not?" said Mrs. Lorrington, laughing. "It is well I have come, Crystal. You are too innocent to live." She tapped her cheek as she spoke, and then turned her face to the moonlight. "And whom do you like best?" she said. "Mr. Dexter?"

"Yes," said Anne; "I like him sincerely. And you will find his name very often there," she added, looking at the note-book by Helen's side.

"Yes, but the others too, I hope. What *I* want to know, of course, is the wicked career of the Knight-errant."

"But is not Mr. Dexter the Knight-errant?"

"By no means. Mr. Dexter is the Bishop; have you not discovered that? The Knight-errant is very decidedly some one else. And, by-the-way, how do you like Some One Else—that is, Mr. Heathcote?"

"Mr. Heathcote!"

"It is not polite to repeat one's words, Crystal. But—I suppose you do *not* like him; and half the time, I confess, he is detestable. However, now that I have come, he shall behave better, and I shall make you like each other, for my sake. There is just one question I wish to ask here: has he been much with Rachel?"

"No—yes—yes, I suppose he has," murmured Anne, sitting still as a statue in the shadow. The brassy moon had gone slowly and coldly behind a cloud, and the room was dim.

"You suppose? Do you not know?"

"Yes, I know he has." She stopped abruptly. She had never before thought whether Heathcote was or was not with Rachel more than with others; but now she began to recall. "Yes, he *has* been with her," she said again, struck by a sudden pang.

"Very well; I shall see to it, now that I am here," said Helen, with a sharp tone in her voice. "He will perhaps be sorry that I have arrived just at the end of the season—the time for grand climaxes, you know; but he will have to yield. My half-hour is over; I must go. How is the Grand Llama? Endurable?"

"She is helping the children; I am grateful to her," replied Anne's voice, mechanically.

"Which means that she is worse than ever. What a dead-alive voice you said it in! Now that I am here, I will do battle for you, Crystal, never fear. I must go. You shall see my triumphal entrance to-morrow at breakfast. Our rooms are not far from yours. Good-night."

She was gone. The door was closed. Anne was alone.

CHAPTER XVI.

"You who keep account

Of crisis and transition in this life,

Set down the first time Nature says plain 'no'

To some 'yes' in you, and walks over you

In gorgeous sweeps of scorn. We all begin

By singing with the birds, and running fast

With June days hand in hand; but, once for all,

The birds must sing against us, and the sun

Strike down upon us like a friend's sword, caught

By an enemy to slay us, while we read

The dear name on the blade which bites at us."

—Elizabeth Barrett Browning.

It is easy for the young to be happy before the deep feelings of the heart have been stirred. It is easy to be good when there has been no strong temptation to be evil; easy to be unselfish when nothing is ardently craved; easy to be faithful when faithfulness does not tear the soul out of its abiding-place. Some persons pass through all of life without strong temptations; not having deep feelings, they are likewise exempt from deep sins. These pass for saints. But when one thinks of the cause of their faultlessness, one understands perhaps better the meaning of those words, otherwise mysterious, that "joy shall be in heaven over one sinner that repenteth, more than over ninety and nine just persons, which need no repentance."

Anne went through that night her first real torture; heretofore she had felt only grief—a very different pain.

Being a woman, her first feeling, even before the consciousness of what it meant, was jealousy. What did Helen mean by speaking of him as though he belonged to her? She had never spoken in that way before. Although she—Anne—had mistaken the fictitious titles, still, even under the title, there had been no such open appropriation of the Knight-errant. What did she mean? And then into this burning jealous anger came the low-voiced question, asked somewhere down in the depths of her being, as though a judge was speaking, "What—

106

is—it—to—you?" And again, "What is it to you?" She buried her face tremblingly in her hands, for all at once she realized what it was, what it had been, unconsciously perhaps, but for a long time really, to her.

She made no attempt at self-deception. Her strongest trait from childhood had been her sincerity, and now it would not let her go. She had begun to love Ward Heathcote unconsciously, but now she loved him consciously. That was the bare fact. It confronted her, it loomed above her, a dark menacing shape, from whose presence she could not flee. She shivered, and her breath seemed to stop during the slow moment while the truth made itself known to her. "O God!" she murmured, bursting into tears; and there was no irreverence in the cry. She recognized the faithlessness which had taken possession of her—unawares, it is true, yet loyal hearts are not conquered so. She had been living in a dream, and had suddenly found the dream reality, and the actors flesh and blood—one of them at least, a poor wildly loving girl, with the mark of Judas upon her brow. She tried to pray, but could think of no words. For she was false to Rast, she loved Heathcote, and hated Helen, yet could not bring herself to ask that any of these feelings should be otherwise. This was so new to her that she sank down upon the floor in utter despair and self-abasement. She was bound to Rast; she was bound to Helen. Yet she had, in her heart at least, betrayed them both.

Still, so complex is human nature that even here in the midst of her abasement the question stole in, whispering its way along as it came, "*Does* he care for me?" And "he" was not Rast. She forgot all else to weigh every word and look of the weeks and days that had passed. Slowly she lived over in memory all their conversations, not forgetting the most trivial, and even raised her arm to get a pillow in order that she might lie more easily; but the little action brought reality again, and her arm fell, while part of her consciousness drew off, and sat in judgment upon the other part. The sentence was scathing.

Then jealousy seized her again. She had admired Helen so warmly as a woman, that even now she could not escape the feeling. She went over in quick, hot review all that the sweet voice and delicate lips had ever said concerning the person veiled under the name of Knight-errant, and the result was a miserable conviction that she had been mistaken; that there was a tie of some kind—slight, perhaps, yet still a tie. And then, as she crushed her hands together in impotent anger, she again realized what she was thinking, and began to sob in her grief like a child. Poor Anne! she would never be a child again. Never again would be hers that proud dauntless confidence of the untried, which makes all life seem easy and secure. And here suddenly into her grief darted this new and withering thought: Had Heathcote perceived her feeling for him? and had he been playing upon it to amuse himself?

Anne knew vaguely that people treated her as though she was hardly more than a child. She was conscious of it, but did not dispute it, accepting it humbly as something—some fault in herself—which she could not change. But now the sleeping woman was aroused at last, and she blushed deeply in the darkness at the thought that while she had remained unconscious, this man of the world had perhaps detected the truth immediately, and had acted as he had in consequence of it. This was the deepest sting of all, and again hurriedly she went over all their conversations a second time; and imagined that she found indications of what she feared. She rose to her feet with the nervous idea of fleeing somewhere, she did not know where.

The night had passed. The sun had not yet risen, but the eastern sky was waiting for his coming with all its banners aflame. Standing by the window, she watched the first gold rim appear. The small birds were twittering in the near trees, the earth was awaking to another day, and for the first time Anne realized the joy of that part of creation which knows not sorrow or care; for the first time wished herself a flower of the field, or a sweet-voiced bird singing his happy morning anthem on a spray. There were three hours yet before breakfast, two before any one would be stirring. She dressed herself, stole through the hall and down the stairs, unbolted the side door, and went into the garden; she longed for the freshness of the morning air. Her steps led her toward the arbor; she stopped, and turned in another direction—toward the bank of the little river. Here she began to walk to and fro from a pile of drift-wood to a bush covered with dew-drops, from the bush back to the drift-wood again. Her feet were wet, her head ached dully, but she kept her mind down to the purpose before her. The nightmare of the darkness was gone; she now faced her grief, and knew what it was, and had decided upon her course. This course was to leave Caryl's. She hoped to return to Mademoiselle at the half-house, and remain there until the school opened—if her grandaunt was willing. If her grandaunt was willing—there came the difficulty. Yet why should she not be willing? The season was over; the summer flowers were gone; it was but anticipating departure by a week or two. Thus she reasoned with herself, yet felt all the time by intuition that Miss Vanhorn would refuse her consent. And if she should so refuse, what then? It could make no difference in the necessity for going, but it would make the going hard. She was considering this point when she heard a footstep. She looked up, and saw—Ward Heathcote. She had been there some time; it was now seven o'clock. They both heard the old clock in the office strike as they stood there looking at each other. In half an hour the early risers would be coming into the garden.

107

Anne did not move or speak; the great effort she had made to retain her composure, when she saw him, kept her motionless and dumb. Her first darting thought had been to show him that she was at ease and indifferent. But this required words, and she had not one ready; she was afraid to speak, too, lest her voice should tremble. She saw, standing there before her, the man who had made her forget Rast, who had made her jealous of Helen, who had played with her holiest feelings, who had deceived and laughed at her, the man whom she—hated? No, no—whom she loved, loved, loved: this was the desperate ending. She turned very white, standing motionless beside the dew-spangled bush.

And Heathcote saw, standing there before him, a young girl with her fair face strangely pale and worn, her eyes fixed, her lips compressed; she was trembling slightly and constantly, in spite of the rigidity of her attitude.

He looked at her in silence for a moment; then, knocking down at one blow all the barriers she had erected, he came to her and took her cold hands in his. "What is it she has said to you?" he asked.

She drew herself away without speaking.

"What has Helen said to you? Has she told you that I have deceived you? That I have played a part?"

But Anne did not answer; she turned, as if to pass him.

"You shall not leave me," he said, barring the way. "Stay a moment, Anne; I promise not to keep you long. You will not? But you shall. Am *I* nothing in all this? My feelings nothing? Let me tell you one thing: whatever Helen may have said, remember that it was all before I knew—*you*."

Anne's hands shook in his as he said this. "Let me go," she cried, with low, quick utterance; she dared not say more, lest her voice should break into sobs.

"I will not," said Heathcote, "until you hear me while I tell you that I have *not* played a false part with you, Anne. I did begin it as an experiment, I confess that I did; but I have ended by being in earnest—at least to a certain degree. Helen does not know me entirely; one side of me she has never even suspected."

"Mrs. Lorrington has not spoken on the subject," murmured Anne, feeling compelled to set him right, but not looking up.

"Then what *has* she said about me, that you should look as you do, my poor child?"

"You take too much upon yourself," replied the girl, with an effort to speak scornfully. "Why should you suppose we have talked of you?"

"I do not suppose it; I know it. I have not the heart to laugh at you, Anne: your white face hurts me like a sharp pain. Will you at least tell me that you do not believe I have been amusing myself at your expense—that you do not believe I have been insincere?"

"I am glad to think that you were not wholly insincere."

"And you will believe also that I like you—like you very, very much, with more than the ordinary liking?"

"That is nothing to me."

"Nothing to you? Look at me, Anne; you shall look once. Ah, my dear child, do you not see that I can not help loving you? And that you—love me also?" As he spoke he drew her close and looked down into her eyes, those startled violet eyes, that met his at last—for one half-moment.

Then she sprang from him, and burst into tears. "Leave me," she said, brokenly. "You are cruel."

"No; only human," answered Heathcote, not quite master of his words now. "I have had your confession in that look, Anne, and you shall never regret it."

"I regret it already," she cried, passionately; "I shall regret it all my life. Do you not comprehend? can you not understand? I am engaged—engaged to be married. I was engaged before we ever met."

"*You* engaged, when I thought you hardly more than a child!" He had been dwelling only upon himself and his own course; possibilities on the other side had not occurred to him. They seldom do to much-admired men.

"I can not help what you thought me," replied Anne. At this moment they heard a step on the piazza; some one had come forth to try the morning air. Where they stood they were concealed, but from the garden walk they would be plainly visible.

"Leave me," she said, hurriedly.

"I will; I will cross the field, and approach the house by the road, so that you will be quite safe. But I shall see you again, Anne." He bent his head, and touched her hand with his lips, then sprang over the stone wall, and was gone, crossing the fields toward the distant turnpike.

Anne returned to the house, exchanging greetings as she passed with the well-preserved jaunty old gentleman who was walking up and down the piazza twenty-five times before breakfast. She sought her own room, dressed herself anew, and then tapped at her grandaunt's door; the routine of the day had her in its iron grasp, and she was obliged to follow its law.

Mrs. Lorrington came in to breakfast like a queen: it was a royal progress. Miss Teller walked behind in amiable majesty, and gathered up the overflow; that is, she shook hands cordially with those who could not reach Helen, and smiled especially upon those whom Helen disliked. Helen was robed in a soft white woollen material that clung closely about her; she had never seemed more slender. Her pale hair, wound round her small head, conveyed the idea that, unbound, it would fall to the hem of her dress. She wore no ornaments, not even a ring on her small fair hands. Her place was at some distance from Miss Vanhorn's table, but as soon as she was seated she bowed to Anne, and smiled with marked friendliness. Anne returned the salutation, and wondered that people did not cry out and ask her if she was dying. But life does not go out so easily as miserable young girls imagine.

"Eggs?" said the waiter.

She took one.

"I thought you did not like eggs," said Miss Vanhorn. She was in an ill-humor that morning because Bessmer had upset the plant-drying apparatus, composed of bricks and boards.

"Yes, thanks," said Anne, vaguely. Mr. Dexter was bowing good-morning to her at that moment, and she returned the salutation. Miss Vanhorn, observing this, withheld her intended rebuke for inattention. Dexter had bowed on his way across to Helen; he had finished his own breakfast, and now took a seat beside Miss Teller and Mrs. Lorrington. At this instant a servant entered bearing a basket of flowers, not the old-fashioned country flowers of Caryl's, but the superb cream-colored roses of the city, each on its long stalk, reposing on a bed of unmixed heliotrope, Helen's favorite flower. All eyes coveted the roses as they passed, and watched to see their destination. They were presented to Mrs. Lorrington.

Every one supposed that Dexter was the giver. The rich gift was like him, and perhaps also the time of its presentation. But the time was a mistake of the servant's; and was not Mrs. Lorrington bowing her thanks?— yes, she was bowing her thanks, with a little air of consciousness, yet with openness also, to Mr. Heathcote, who sat by himself at the end of the long room. He bowed gravely in return, thus acknowledging himself the sender.

"Well," said Miss Vanhorn, crossly, yet with a little shade of relief too in her voice, "of all systematic coquettes, Helen Lorrington is our worst. I suppose that we shall have no peace, now that she has come. However, it will not last long."

"You will go away soon, then, grandaunt?" said Anne, eagerly.

Miss Vanhorn put up her eyeglass; the tone had betrayed something. "No," she said, inspecting her niece coolly; "nothing of the sort. I shall remain through September, perhaps later."

Anne's heart sank. She would be obliged, then, to go through the ordeal. She could eat nothing; a choking sensation had risen in her throat when Heathcote bowed to Helen, acknowledging the flowers. "May I go, grandaunt?" she said. "I do not feel well this morning."

"No; finish your breakfast like a Christian. I hate sensations. However, on second thoughts, you *may* go," added the old woman, glancing at Dexter and Helen. "You may as well be re-arranging those specimens that Bessmer stupidly knocked down. But do not let me find the Lorrington in my parlor when I come up; do you hear?"

"Yes," said Anne, escaping. She ran up stairs to her own room, locked the door, and then stood pressing her hands upon her heart, crying out in a whisper: "Oh, what shall I do! What shall I do! How can I bear it!" But she could not have even that moment unmolested: the day had begun, and its burdens she must bear. Bessmer knocked, and began at once tremulously about the injured plants through the closed door.

"Yes," said Anne, opening it, "I know about them. I came up to re-arrange them."

"It wouldenter been so bad, miss, if it hadenter been asters. But I never could make out asters; they all seem of a piece to me," said Bessmer, while Anne sorted the specimens, and replaced them within the drying-sheets. "Every fall there's the same time with 'em. I just dread asters, I do; not but what golden-rods is almost worse."

"Anne," said a voice in the hall.

Anne opened the door; it was Helen, with her roses.

"These are the Grand Llama's apartments, I suppose," she said, peeping in. "I will not enter; merely gaze over the sacred threshold. Come to my room, Crystal, for half an hour; I am going to drive at eleven."

"I must finish arranging these plants."

"Then come when you have finished. Do not fail; I shall wait for you." And the white robe floated off down the dark sidling hall, as Miss Vanhorn's heavy foot made itself heard ascending the stairs. When Bessmer had gone to her breakfast, to collect what strength she could for another aster-day, Anne summoned her courage.

"Grandaunt, I would like to speak to you," she said.

"And I do not want to be spoken to; I have neuralgia in my cheek-bones."

"But I would like to tell you—"

"And I do not want to be told. You are always getting up sensations of one kind or another, which amount to nothing in the end. Be ready to drive to Updegraff's glen at eleven; that is all I have to say to you now." She went into the inner room, and closed the door.

"It does not make any difference," thought Anne, drearily; "I shall tell her at eleven."

Then, nerving herself for another kind of ordeal, she went slowly toward Helen's apartments.

But conventionality is a strong power: she passed the first fifteen minutes of conversation without faltering. Then Helen said: "You look pale, Crystal. What is the matter?"

"I did not sleep well."

"And there is some trouble besides! I see by the note-book that you have been with the Bishop almost constantly; confess that you like him!"

"Yes, I like him."

"Very much?"

"Yes."

"*Very* much?"

"You know, Helen, that I am engaged."

"That! for your engagement," said Mrs. Lorrington, taking a rose and tossing it toward her. "I know you are engaged. But I thought that if the Bishop would only get into one of his dead-earnest moods—he is capable of it—you would have to yield. For you are capable of it too."

"Capable of what? Breaking a promise?"

"Do not be disagreeable; I am complimenting you. No; I mean capable of loving—really loving."

"All women can love, can they not?"

"Themselves! Yes. But rarely any one else. And now let me tell you something delightful—one of those irrelevant little inconsistencies which make society amusing: *I* am going to drive with the Bishop this morning, and not you at all."

"I hope you will enjoy the drive."

"You take it well," said Mrs. Lorrington, laughing merrily. "But I will not tease you, Crystal. Only tell me one thing—you are always truthful. Has anything been said to you—anything that really *means* anything—since you have been here?"

"By whom?" said Anne, almost in a whisper.

"The Bishop, of course. Who else should it be?"

"Oh, no, no," answered the girl, rising hurriedly, as if uncertain what to do. "Why do you speak to me so constantly of Mr. Dexter? I have been with—with others too."

"You have been with him more than with the 'others' you mention," said Helen, mimicking her tone. "The note-book tells that. However, I will say no more; merely observe. You are looking at my driving costume; jealous already? But I tell you frankly, Crystal, that regarding dress you must yield to me. With millions you could not rival me; on that ground I am alone. Rachel looked positively black with envy when she saw me this morning; she is ugly in a second, you know, if she loses that soft Oriental expression which makes you think of the Nile. Imagine Rachel in a Greek robe like this, loosely made, with a girdle! I shall certainly look well this morning; but never fear, it shall be for your sake. I shall talk of you, and make you doubly interesting by what I do and do not say; I shall give thrilling glimpses only."

The maid entered, and Anne sat through the change of dress and the rebraiding of the pale soft hair.

"I do not forbid your peeping through the hall window to see us start," said Mrs. Lorrington, gayly, as she drew on her gloves. "Good-by."

Anne went to her own room. "Are they all mad?" she thought. "Or am I? Why do they all speak of Mr. Dexter so constantly, and not of—"

"You are late," said Miss Vanhorn's voice. "I told you not to keep me waiting. Get your hat and gloves, and come immediately; the carriage is there."

But it was not as strange in reality as it seemed to Anne that Helen, Miss Vanhorn, and others spoke of Mr. Dexter in connection with herself. Absorbed in a deeper current, she had forgotten that others judge by the surface, and that Mr. Dexter had been with her openly, and even conspicuously, during a portion of every day for several weeks. To her the two hours or three with him had been but so many portions of time before she

110

could see, or after she had seen, Heathcote. But time is not divided as young people suppose; she forgot that ordinary eyes can not see the invisible weights which make ten minutes—nay, five—with one person outbalance a whole day with another. In the brief diary which she had kept for Helen, Dexter's name occurred far more frequently than Heathcote's, and Helen had judged from that. Others did the same, with their eyes. If old Katharine had so far honored her niece as to question her, she might have learned something more; but she did not question, she relied upon her own sagacity. It is a dispensation of Providence that the old, no matter how crowded their own youth may have been, always forget. What old Katharine now forgot was this: if a man like Gregory Dexter is conspicuously devoted to one woman, but always in the presence of others, making no attempt to secure her attention for a few moments alone here and there, it is probable that there is another woman for whom he keeps those moments, and a hidden feeling stronger than the one openly displayed. Rachel never allowed observable devotion. This, however, did not forbid the unobserved.

"Grandaunt," began Anne, as the carriage rolled along the country road. Her voice faltered a little, and she paused to steady it.

"Wait a day," said Miss Vanhorn, with grim sarcasm; "then there will be nothing to tell. It is always so with girls."

It was her nearest approach to good-humor: Anne took courage. "The summer is nearly over, grandaunt—"

"I have an almanac."

"—and, as school will soon begin—"

"In about three weeks."

"—I should like to go back to Mademoiselle until then, if you do not object."

Miss Vanhorn put up her eyeglass, and looked at her niece; then she laughed, sought for a caraway-seed, and by good luck found one, and deposited it safely in the tight grasp of her glittering teeth. She thought Anne was jealous of Mr. Dexter's attentions to Helen.

"You need not be afraid, child," she said, still laughing. "If you have a rival, it is the Egyptian, and not that long white creature you call your friend."

"I am unhappy here, grandaunt. Please let me go."

"Girls are always unhappy, or thinking themselves so. It is one of their habits. Of course you can not go; it would be too ridiculous giving way to any such childish feeling. You will stay as long as I stay."

"But I can not. I *must* go."

"And who holds the authority, pray?"

"Dear grandaunt, do not compel me," said Anne, seizing the old woman's hands in hers. But Miss Vanhorn drew them away angrily.

"What nonsense!" she said. "Do not let me hear another word. You will stay according to my pleasure (which should be yours also), or you forfeit your second winter at Moreau's and the children's allowance." She tapped on the glass, and signaled to the coachman to drive homeward. "You have spoiled the drive with your obstinacy; I do not care to go now. Spend the day in your own room. At five o'clock come to me."

And at five Anne came.

"Have you found your senses?" asked the elder woman, and more gently.

"I have not changed my mind."

Miss Vanhorn rose and locked the door. "You will now give me your reasons," she said.

"I can not."

"You mean that you will not."

Anne was silent, and Miss Vanhorn surveyed her for a moment before letting loose the dogs of war. In her trouble the girl looked much older; it was a grave, sad, but determined woman who was standing there to receive her sentence, and suddenly the inquisitor changed her course.

"There, there," she said; "never mind about it now. Go back to your room; Bessmer shall bring you some tea, and then you will let her dress you precisely as I shall order. You will not, I trust, disobey me in so small a matter as that?"

"And may I go to-morrow?"

"We will see. You can not go to-night, at any rate; so do as I bid you."

Anne obeyed; but she was disappointed that all was not ended and the contest over. For the young, to wait seems harder than to suffer.

Miss Vanhorn thought that her niece was jealous of Helen in regard to Dexter, and that this jealousy had opened her eyes for the first time to her own faithlessness; being conscientious, of course she was, between the two feelings, made very wretched. And the old woman's solution of the difficulty was to give Dexter one more and perfect opportunity, if she, Katharine Vanhorn, could arrange it. And there was, in truth, very little that old Katharine could not arrange if she chose, since she was a woman not afraid to use on occasion that which in society is the equivalent of force, namely, directness. She was capable of saying, openly, "Mr. Dexter, will you take Anne out on the piazza for a while? The air is close here," and then of smiling back upon Rachel, Isabel, or whoever was left behind, with the malice of a Mazarin. Chance favored old Katharine that night once and again.

CHAPTER XVII.

"That which is not allotted, the hand can not reach, and what is allotted will find you wherever you may be. You have heard with what toil Secunder penetrated to the land of darkness, and that, after all, he did not taste the water of immortality."—Saadi.

"When a woman hath ceased to be quite the same to us, it matters little how different she becomes."—Walter Savage Landor.

The last dance of the season had been appointed for the evening, and Mrs. Lorrington's arrival had stimulated the others to ordain "full dress"; they all had one costume in reserve, and it was an occasion to bring all the banners upon the field, and the lance also, in a last tournament. Other contests, other rivalries, had existed, other stories besides this story of Anne; it never happens in real life that one woman usurps everything. That this dance should occur on this particular evening was one of the chances vouchsafed to old Katharine and her strategy.

For the fairest costume ordered for Anne had not been worn, and at ten o'clock Bessmer with delight was asking a white-robed figure to look at itself in the glass, while on her knees she spread out the cloud of fleecy drapery that trailed softly over the floor behind. The robe was of white lace, and simple. But nothing could have brought out so strongly the rich, noble beauty of this young face and form. There was not an ornament to break the outline of the round white throat, or the beautiful arms, bared from the shoulder. For the first time the thick brown hair was released from its school-girl simplicity, and Anne's face wore a new aspect, as young faces will under such changes. For one may be sorrowful, and even despairing, yet at eighteen a few waving locks will make a fair face fairer than ever, even in spite of one's own determined opposition.

When they entered the ball-room, the second chance vouchsafed to old Katharine came to meet them, and no strategy was necessary. For Mr. Dexter, with an unwonted color on his face, offered his arm to Anne immediately, asking for that dance, and "as many dances besides as you can give me, Miss Douglas."

All who were near heard his words; among them Rachel. She looked at him with soft deprecation in her eyes. But he returned her gaze directly and haughtily, and bore Anne away. They danced once, and then went out on the piazza. It was a cool evening, and presently Miss Vanhorn came to the window. "It is too damp for you here, child," she said. "If you do not care to dance, take Mr. Dexter up to see the flowers in our parlor; and when you come down, bring my shawl."

"Mr. Dexter does not care about flowers, I think," answered Anne, too absorbed in her own troubles to be concerned about her grandaunt's open manœuvre. She spoke mechanically.

"On the contrary, I am very fond of flowers," said Dexter, rising immediately. "And I particularly thank you, Miss Vanhorn, for giving me this opportunity to—admire them." He spoke with emphasis, and bowed as he spoke. The old lady gave him a stately inclination in return. They understood each other; the higher powers were agreed.

When Anne, still self-absorbed and unconscious, entered the little parlor, she was surprised to find it brightly lighted and prepared, as if for their reception. The red curtains were closed, a small fire crackled on the hearth, the rich perfume of the flowers filled the warm air; in the damp September evening the room was a picture of comfort, and in the ruddy light her own figure, in its white lace dress, was clearly outlined and radiant. "Here are the flowers," she said, going toward the table. Dexter had closed the door; he now came forward, and looked at the blossoms a moment absently. Then he turned toward the sofa, which was covered with the same red chintz which hung over the windows to the floor.

"Shall we sit here awhile? The room is pleasant, if you are in no hurry to return."

"No, I am in no hurry," replied Anne. She was glad to be quiet and away from the dancers; she feared to meet Heathcote. Mr. Dexter always talked; she would not be obliged to think of new subjects, or to make long replies.

But to-night Mr. Dexter was unusually silent. She leaned back against the red cushions, and looked at the point of her slipper; she was asking herself how long this evening would last.

"Miss Douglas," began Dexter at length, and somewhat abruptly, "I do not know in what light you regard me, or what degree of estimation you have conferred upon me; but—" Here he paused.

"It is of no consequence," said Anne.

"What?"

"I mean," she said, rousing herself from her abstraction, "that it does not matter one way or the other. I am going away to-morrow, Mr. Dexter. I see now that I ought never to have come. But—how could I know?"

"Why do you go?" said her companion, pausing a moment also, in his own train of thought.

"I have duties elsewhere," she began; then stopped. "But that is not the real reason," she added.

"You are unhappy, Miss Douglas; I can always read your face. I will not obtrude questions now, although most desirous to lift the burdens which are resting upon you. For I have something to ask you. Will you listen to me for a few moments?"

"Oh yes," said Anne, falling back into apathy, her eyes still on the point of her slipper.

"It is considered egotistical to talk of one's self," began Dexter, after a short silence; "but, under the circumstances, I trust I may be pardoned." He took an easier attitude, and folded his arms. "I was born in New Hampshire." (Here Anne tried to pay attention; from this beginning, she felt that she must attend. But she only succeeded in repeating, vaguely, the word "New Hampshire?" as though she had reasons for thinking it might be Maine.)

"Yes, New Hampshire. My father was a farmer there; but when I was five years old he died, and my mother died during the following year. A rich relative, a cousin, living in Illinois, befriended me, homeless as I was, and gave me that best gift in America, a good education. I went through college, and then—found myself penniless. My cousin had died without a will, and others had inherited his estate. Since then, Miss Douglas, I have led a life of effort, hard, hard work, and bitter fluctuations. I have taught school; I have dug in the mines; I have driven a stage; I have been lost in the desert, and have lived for days upon moss and berries. Once I had a hundred thousand dollars—the result of intensest labor and vigilance through ten long years—and I lost it in an hour. Then for three days, shovel in hand, I worked on an embankment. I tell you all this plainly, so that if it, or any part of it, ever comes up, you will not feel that you have been deceived. The leading power of my whole life has been action; whether for good or for ill—action. I am now thirty-eight years old, and I think I may say that I—am no worse than other men. The struggle is now over; I am rich. I will even tell you the amount of my fortune—"

"Oh no," said Anne, hurriedly.

"I prefer to do so," replied Dexter, with a formal gesture. "I wish you to understand clearly the whole position, both as regards myself and all my affairs."

"Myself and all my affairs," repeated itself buzzingly in Anne's brain.

"My property is now estimated at a little more than a million, and without doubt it will increase in value, as it consists largely of land, and especially mines."

He paused. He was conscious that he had not succeeded in controlling a certain pride in the tone of his voice, and he stopped to remedy it. In truth, he *was* proud. No one but the man who has struggled and labored for that sum, unaided and alone, knows how hard it is to win it, and how rare and splendid has been his own success. He has seen others go down on all sides of him like grain before the scythe, while he stood upright. He knows of disappointed hopes, of bitter effort ended in the grave; of men, strong and fearless as himself, who have striven desperately, and as desperately failed. He was silent for a moment, thinking of these things.

"It must be pleasant to have so much money," said Anne, sighing a little, and turning her slipper point slightly, as though to survey it in profile.

Dexter went on with his tale. He was as much for the moment absorbed in himself as she was in herself; they were like two persons shut up in closely walled towers side by side.

"For some years I have lived at the East, and have been much in what is called society in New York and Washington," he continued, "and I have had no cause to be dissatisfied with the reception accorded to me. I have seen many beautiful faces, and they have not entirely withheld their kindness from me. But—Miss Douglas, young girls like romance, and I have, unfortunately, little that I can express, although I believe that I have at heart more true chivalry toward women than twenty of the idle *blasé* men about here. But that had been better left unsaid. What I wish to say to you is this: will you be my wife? Anne, dear child, will you marry me?" He had ended abruptly, and even to himself unexpectedly, as though his usually fluent speech had failed him. He took her hand, and waited for her answer, his face showing signs of emotion, which seemed to be more his own than roused by anything in her.

Anne had started back in surprise; she drew her hand from his. They were both gloved; only the kid-skins had touched each other. "You are making a mistake," she said, rising. "You think I am Mrs. Lorrington."

Dexter had risen also; an involuntary smile passed over his face at her words. He took her hand again, and held it firmly.

"Do you not suppose I know to whom I am talking?" he said, "I am talking to you, Anne, and thinking only of you. I ask you again, will you be my wife?"

"Of course not. You do not love me in the least, and I do not love you. Of what are you dreaming, Mr. Dexter?" She walked across the little room, and stood between the windows, the red light full upon her. A brightness had risen in her eyes; she looked very beautiful in her youthful scorn.

Dexter gazed at her, but without moving. "You are mistaken," he said, gravely. "I do love you."

"Since when?" asked the sweet voice, with a touch of sarcasm. Anne was now using the powers of concealment which nature gives to all women, even the youngest, as a defense. Mr. Dexter should know nothing, should not be vouchsafed even a glimpse, of her inner feelings; she would simply refuse him, as girls did in books. And she tried to think what they said.

But the man opposite her was not like a man in a book. "Since six o'clock this evening," he answered, quietly.

Anne looked at him in wonder.

"Do you wish to hear the whole?" he asked.

"No; it is nothing to me. Since you only began at six, probably you can stop at twelve," she answered, still with her girlish scorn perceptible in her voice.

But Dexter paid no attention to her sarcasm. "I will tell you the whole when you are my wife," he said. "Let it suffice now that at the hour named I became aware of the worthlessness and faithlessness of women; and—I speak God's truth, Anne—even at that bitter moment I fell back upon the thought of *you* as a safeguard—a safeguard against total disbelief in the possibility of woman's fidelity. I knew then that I had revered you with my better self all the while—that, young as you are, I had believed in you. I believe in you now. Be my wife; and from this instant I will devote all the love in me—and I have more than you think—to you alone." He had crossed the room, and was standing beside her.

Anne felt at once the touch of real feeling. "I am very sorry," she said, gently, looking up into his face. "I should have said it at first, but that I did not think you were in earnest until now. I am engaged, Mr. Dexter; I was engaged before I came here."

"But," said Dexter, "Miss Vanhorn—"

"Yes, I know. Grandaunt does not approve of it, and will not countenance it. But that, of course, makes no difference."

He looked at her, puzzled by her manner. In truth, poor Anne, while immovably determined to keep her promise to Rast, even cherishing the purpose, also, of hastening the marriage if he wished it, was yet so inefficient an actress that she trembled as she spoke, and returned his gaze through a mist of tears.

"You *wish* to marry this man, I suppose—I am ignorant of his name?" he asked, watching her with attention.

"His name is Erastus Pronando; we were children together on the island," she answered, in a low voice, with downcast eyes.

"And you wish to marry him?"

"I do."

Gregory Dexter put another disappointment down upon the tablets of his memory—a disappointment and a surprise; he had not once doubted his success.

In this certainty he had been deceived partly by Miss Vanhorn, and partly by Anne herself; by her unstudied frankness. He knew that she liked him, but he had mistaken the nature of her regard. He could always control himself, however, and he now turned to her kindly. He thought she was afraid of her aunt. "Sit down for a few minutes more," he said, "and tell me about it. Why does Miss Vanhorn disapprove?"

"I do not know," replied Anne; "or, rather, I do know, but can not tell you. Never mind about me, Mr. Dexter. I am unhappy; but no one can help me. I must help myself."

"Mr. Pronando should esteem it his dearest privilege to do so," said Dexter, who felt himself growing old and cynical under this revelation of fresh young love.

114

"Yes," murmured Anne, then stopped. "If you will leave me now," she said, after a moment, "it would be very kind."

"I will go, of course, if you desire it; but first let me say one word. Your aunt objects to this engagement, and you have neither father nor mother to take your part. I have a true regard for you, which is not altered by the personal disappointment I am at present feeling; it is founded upon a belief in you which can not change. Can I not help you, then, as a friend? For instance, could I not help Mr. Pronando—merely as a friend? I know what it is to have to make one's own way in the world unaided. I feel for such boys—I mean young men. What does he intend to do? Give me his address."

"No," said Anne, touched by this prompt kindness. "But I feel your generosity, Mr. Dexter; I shall never forget it." Her eyes filled with tears, but she brushed them away. "Will you leave me now?" she said.

"Would it not be better if we returned together? I mean, would not Miss Vanhorn notice it less? You could excuse yourself soon afterward."

"You are right. I will go down with you. But first, do I not show—" she went toward the mirror.

"Show what?" said Dexter, following her, and standing by her side. "That you are one of the loveliest young girls in the world—as you look to-night, the loveliest?" He smiled at her reflection in the mirror as he spoke, and then turned toward the reality. "You show nothing," he said, kindly; "and my eyes are very observant."

They went toward the door; as they reached it, he bent over her. "If this engagement should by any chance be broken, then could you not love me a little, Anne—only a little?" he murmured, looking into her eyes questioningly.

"I wish I could," she answered, gravely. "You are a generous man. I would like to love you."

"But you could not?"

"I can not."

He pressed her hand in silence, opened the door, and led the way down to the hall-room. They had been absent one hour.

Blum, who was standing disconsolately near the entrance, watching Helen, came up and asked Anne to dance. Reluctant to go to her grandaunt before it was necessary, she consented. She glanced nervously up and down the long room as they took their places, but Heathcote was not present. Her gaze then rested upon another figure moving through the dance at some distance down the hall. Mrs. Lorrington in her costume that evening challenged criticism. She did this occasionally—it was one of her amusements. Her dress was of almost the same shade of color as her hair, the hue unbroken from head to foot, the few ornaments being little stars of topaz. Her shoulders and arms were uncovered; and here also she challenged criticism, since she was so slight that in profile view she looked like a swaying reed. But as there was not an angle visible anywhere, her fair slenderness seemed a new kind of beauty, which all, in spite of sculptor's rules, must now admire. Rachel called her, smilingly, "the amber witch." But Isabel said, "No; witch-hazel; because it is so beautiful, and yellow, and sweet." Rachel, Isabel, and Helen always said charming things about each other in public: they had done this unflinchingly for years.

Miss Vanhorn was watching her niece from her comfortable seat on the other side of the room, and watching with some impatience. But the Haunted Man was now asking Anne to dance, and Anne was accepting. After that dance she went out on the piazza for a few moments; when she returned, Heathcote was in the room, and waltzing with Helen.

All her courage left her before she could grasp it, and hardly knowing what she was doing, she went directly across the floor to Miss Vanhorn, and asked if she might go to her room.

Miss Vanhorn formed one of a majestic phalanx of old ladies. "Are you tired?" she asked.

"Very tired," said Anne, not raising her eyes higher than the stout waist before her, clad in shining black satin.

"She does look pale," remarked old Mrs. Bannert, sympathizingly.

"Anne is always sleepy at eight or nine, like a baby," replied Miss Vanhorn, well aware that the dark-eyed Rachel was decidedly a night-bird, and seldom appeared at breakfast at all; "and she has also a barbarous way of getting up at dawn. Go to bed, child, if you wish; your bowl of bread and milk will be ready in the morning." Then, as Anne turned, she added: "You will be asleep when I come up; I will not disturb you. Take a good rest." Which Anne interpreted, "I give you that amount of time: think well before you act." The last respite was accorded.

But even a minute is precious to the man doomed to death. Anne left the ball-room almost with a light heart: she had the night. She shut herself in her room, took off the lace dress, loosened her hair, and sat down by the window to think. The late moon was rising; a white fog filled the valley and lay thickly over the river; but she left the sash open—the cool damp air seemed to soothe her troubled thoughts. For she knew—and despised herself in the knowledge—that the strongest feeling in her heart now was jealousy, jealousy of Helen dancing with Heathcote below. Time passed unheeded; she had not stirred hand or foot when, two hours later, there was a tap on her door. It was Helen.

"Do not speak," she whispered, entering swiftly and softly, and closing the door; "the Grand Llama is coming up the stairs. I wanted to see you, and I knew that if I did not slip in before she passed, I could not get in without disturbing her. Do not stir; she will stop at your door and listen."

They stood motionless; Miss Vanhorn's step came along the hall, and, as Helen had predicted, paused at Anne's door. There was no light within, and no sound; after a moment it passed on, entered the parlor, and then the bedroom beyond.

"If Bessmer would only close the bedroom door," whispered Helen, "we should be quite safe." At this moment the maid did close the door; Helen gave a sigh of relief. "I never could whisper well," she said. "Only cat-women whisper nicely. Isabel is a cat-woman. Now when it comes to a murmur—a faint, clear, sweet murmur, I am an adept. I wonder if Isabel will subdue her widower? You have been here long enough to have an opinion. Will she?"

"I do not know," said Anne, wondering at her own ability to speak the words.

"And I—do not care! I am tired, Crystal: may I lie on your bed? Do close that deathly window, and come over here, so that we can talk comfortably," said Helen, throwing herself down on the white coverlet—a long slender shape, with its white arms clasped under its head. The small room was in shadow. Anne drew a chair to the bedside and sat down, with her back to the moonlight.

"This is a miserable world," began Mrs. Lorrington. Her companion, sitting with folded arms and downcast eyes, mentally agreed with her.

"Of course *you* do not think so," continued Helen, "and perhaps, being such a crystal-innocent, you will never find it out. There are such souls. There are also others; and it is quite decided that I hate—Rachel Bannert, who is one of them."

Anne had moved nervously, but at that name she fell back into stillness again.

"Rachel is the kind of woman I dread more than any other," continued Helen. "Her strength is feeling. Feeling! I tell you, Crystal, that you and I are capable of loving, and suffering for the one we love, through long years of pain, where Rachel would not wet the sole of her slipper. Yet men believe in her! The truth is, men are fools: one sigh deceives them."

"Then sigh," said the figure in the chair.

"No; that is not my talent: I must continue to be myself. But *I* saw her on the piazza with Ward to-night; and I detest her."

"With—Mr. Heathcote?"

"Yes. Of course nothing would be so much to her disadvantage as to marry Ward, and she knows it; he has no fortune, and she has none. But she loves to make me wretched. I made the greatest mistake of my life when I let her see once, more than a year ago, how things were."

"How things were?" repeated Anne—that commonplace phrase which carries deep meanings safely because unexpressed.

"Of course there is no necessity to tell *you*, Crystal, what you must already know—that Ward and I are in a certain way betrothed. It is an old affair: we have known each other always."

"Yes," said the other voice, affirmatively and steadily.

"Some day we shall be married, I suppose: we like each other. But there is no haste at present: I think we both like to be free. Heigh-ho! Do you admire this dress, Crystal?"

"It is very beautiful."

"And yet he only came in and danced with me once!"

"Perhaps he does not care for dancing," said Anne. She was accomplishing each one of her sentences slowly and carefully, like answers in a lesson.

"Yes, he does. Do not be deceived by his indolent manner, Crystal; he is full of all sorts of unexpected strong likings and feelings, in spite of his lazy look. Do you think I should be likely to fall in love with a stick?"

Anne made no reply.

"*Do* you?" said Helen, insistently, stretching out her arms, and adjusting the chains of topaz stars that decked their slenderness.

Anne leaned forward and drew down her friend's hands, holding them closely in her own. "Helen," she said, "tell me: do you love Mr. Heathcote?"

116

"What is love?" said Mrs. Lorrington, lightly.

"Tell me, Helen."

"Why do you wish to know?"

"I *do* wish to know."

"Ward Heathcote is not worth my love."

"Is he worth Rachel Bannert's, then?" said Anne, touching the spring by which she had seen the other stirred.

"Rachel Bannert!" repeated Helen, with a tone of bitter scorn. Then she paused. "Anne, you are a true-hearted child, and I *will* tell you. I love Ward Heathcote with my whole heart and soul."

She spoke in clear tones, and did not turn away or hide her face; she lay looking up at the moonlight on the rough white wall. It was Anne who turned, shivering, and shading her eyes with her hand.

"I love him so much," Helen continued, "that if he should leave me, I believe I should die. Not suddenly, or with any sensation, of course. I only mean that I should not be able to live."

Again there was silence. Then the clear soft voice went on.

"I have always loved him. Ever since I can remember. Do not be shocked, but I loved him even when I married Richard. I was very young, and did it in a sort of desperate revenge because he did not, would not, care for me. I was not punished for my madness, for Richard loved me dearly, and died so soon, poor fellow, that he never discovered the truth. And then it all began over again. Only *this* time Ward was—different."

Another silence followed. Anne did not move or speak.

"Do not be unhappy about me, child," said Helen at last, turning on her arm to look at her companion; "all will come right in time. It was only that I was vexed about this evening. For he has not seemed quite himself lately, and of course I attribute it to Rachel: her deadly sweetness is like that of nightshade and tube-roses combined. Now tell me about yourself: how comes on the quarrel with the Llama?"

"I hardly know."

"I saw you stealing away in your white lace with Gregory Dexter this evening," pursued Helen. "He was as agreeable as ever this morning. However, there it is again; just before six, Nightshade strolled off toward the ravine 'to see the sunset' (one sees the sunset so well from there, you know, facing the east), and Dexter seemed also to have forgotten the points of the compass, for—he followed her."

"Then it was Mrs. Bannert," said Anne, half unconsciously.

"It is always Mrs. Bannert. I do not in the least know what you mean, but—it is always Mrs. Bannert. What did he say about her?"

"Of course I can not tell you, Helen. But—I really thought it was you."

"What should *I* have to do with it? How you play at cross-purposes, Crystal! Is it possible that during all this time you have not discovered how infatuated our Gregory is with Rachel? Ward is only amusing himself; but Gregory is, in one sense, carried away. However, I doubt if it lasts, and I really think he has a warm regard for you, a serious one. It is a pity you could not—"

Anne stopped the sentence with a gesture.

"Yes, I see that little ring," said Helen. "But the world is a puzzle, and we often follow several paths before we find the right one. How cold your hands are! The nights are no longer like summer, and the moon is Medusa. The autumn moon is a cruel moon always, reminding us of the broken hopes and promises of the lost summer. I must go, Crystal. You are pale and weary; the summer with the Llama has been too hard. I believe you will be glad to be safely back at Moreau's again. But I can not come over now and tell you romances, can I? You know the personages, and the charm will be gone. To-morrow I am going to ride. You have not seen me in my habit? I assure you even a mermaid can not compare with me. Do you know, I should be happy for life if I could but induce Rachel to show herself once on horseback by my side: on horseback Rachel looks—excuse the word, but it expresses it—sploshy. The trouble is that she knows it, and will not go; she prefers moonlight, a piazza, and sylphide roses in her hair, with the background of fluffy white shawl."

Then, with a little more light nonsense, Helen went away—went at last. Anne bolted the door, threw herself down upon her knees beside the bed, with her arms stretched out and her face hidden. There had been but this wanting to her misery, and now it was added: Helen loved him.

For she was not deceived by the flippant phrases which had surrounded the avowal: Helen would talk flippantly on her death-bed. None the less was she in earnest when she spoke those few words. In such matters a woman can read a woman: there is a tone of voice which can not be counterfeited. It tells all.

CHAPTER XVIII.

"What is this that thou hast been fretting and fuming and lamenting and self-tormenting on account of? Say it in a word: is it not because thou art not *happy*? Foolish soul! what act of Legislature was there that *thou* shouldst be happy? There is in Man a higher than Happiness; he can do without Happiness, and instead thereof find Blessedness. This is the everlasting Yea, wherein all contradiction is solved."—Carlyle.

After an hour of mute suffering, Anne sought the blessed oblivion of sleep. She had conquered herself; she was exhausted. She would try to gain strength for the effort of the coming day. But nothing avails against that fever, strong as life and sad as death, which we call Love, and which, in spite of the crowd of shallower feelings that masquerade under and mock its name, still remains the master-power of our human existence. Anne had no sooner laid her head upon the pillow than there rose within her, and ten times stronger than before, her love and her jealousy. She would stay and contest the matter with Helen. Had he not said, had he not looked—And then she caught herself back in an agony of self-reproach. For it is always hard for the young to learn the lesson of human weakness. It is strange and humiliating to them to discover that there are powers within them stronger than their own wills. The old know this so well that they excuse each other silently; but, loath to shake the ignorant faith of innocence, they leave the young to find it out for themselves. The whole night with Anne was but a repetition of efforts and lapses, followed toward morning, however, by a struggling return to self-control. For years of faithfulness even as a child are not thrown away, but yield, thank Heaven! a strength at last in times of trial; else might we all go drown ourselves. At dawn, with tear-stained cheeks, she fell asleep, waking with a start when Bessmer knocked and inquired if she was ill. Miss Vanhorn had gone down to breakfast.

"Please send me some coffee," said Anne, without opening the door. "I do not care for anything else. I will be ready soon."

She dressed herself slowly, swallowing the coffee. But youth is strong; the cold bath and the fresh white morning dress made her look as fair as ever. Miss Vanhorn was waiting for her in the little parlor. Bessmer was sent away, and the door closed. The girl remained standing, and took hold of the back of a chair to nerve herself for the first step along the hard, lonely road stretching out before her like a desert.

"Anne," began Miss Vanhorn, in a magisterial voice, "what did Mr. Dexter say to you last evening?"

"He asked me to be his wife."

"I hardly expected it so soon, although I knew it would come in time," said the old woman, with a swallow of satisfaction. "Sit down. And don't be an idiot. You will now listen to *me*. Mr. Dexter is a rich man; he is what is called a rising man (if any one wants to rise); he is a good enough man also, as men go. He has no claim as regards family; neither have you. He is a thorough and undiluted American; so are you. He will be a kind husband, and one far higher in the world than you had any right to expect. On the other hand, you will do very well as his wife, for you have fair ability and a pretty face (it is of course your pink and white beauty that has won him), and principles enough for both. Like all people who have made money rapidly, he is lavish, and will deny you nothing; he will even allow you, I presume, to help one and all of that colony of children, priests, old maids, and dogs, up on that island. See what power will be put into your hands! You might labor all your life, and not accomplish one-hundredth part of that which, as Gregory Dexter's wife, you could do in one day.

"As to your probable objection—the boy-and-girl engagement in which you were foolish enough to entangle yourself—I will simply say, leave it to time; it will break itself. How do you know that it is not, in fact, broken already? The Pronando blood is faithless in its very essence," added the old woman, bitterly. "Mr. Dexter is a man of the world. I will explain it to him myself; he will understand, and will not urge you at present. He will wait, as I shall, for the natural solution of time. But in the mean while you must not offend him; he is not at all a man whom a woman can offend with impunity. He is vain, and has a singularly mistaken idea of his own importance. Agree to what I propose—which is simple quiescence for the present—and you shall go back to Moreau's, and the allowance for the children shall be continued. I have never before in my life made so many concessions; it is because you have had at times lately a look that brings back—Alida."

Anne's lips trembled; a sudden weakness came over her at this allusion to her mother.

"Well?" said Miss Vanhorn, expectantly.

There was a pause. Then a girl's voice answered: "I can not, grandaunt. I must go."

"You *may* go, I tell you, back to Moreau's on the 1st of October."

"I mean that I can not marry Mr. Dexter."

"No one asks you to marry him now."

"I can never marry him."

"Why?" said Miss Vanhorn, with rising color. "Be careful what you say. No lies."

"I—I am engaged to Rast."

"Lie number one. Look at me. If your engagement was ended, *then* would you marry Mr. Dexter?"

Anne half rose, as if to escape, but sank back again. "I could not marry him, because I do not love him," she answered.

"And whom do you love, that you know so much about it, and have your 'do not' and 'can not' so promptly ready? Never tell me that it is that boy upon the island who has taught you all these new ways, this faltering and fear of looking in my face, of which you knew nothing when you came. Do you wish me to tell you what I think of you?"

"No," cried the girl, rushing forward, and falling on her knees beside the arm-chair; "tell me nothing. Only let me go away. I can not, can not stay here; I am too wretched, too weak. You can not have a lower opinion of me than I have of myself at this moment. If you have any compassion for me—for the memory of my mother—say no more, and let me go." She bowed her head upon the arm of the chair and sobbed aloud.

But Miss Vanhorn rose and walked away. "I know what this means," she said, standing in the centre of the room. "Like mother, like daughter. Only Alida ran after a man who loved her, although her inferior, while you have thrown yourself at the feet of a man who is simply laughing at you. Don't you know, you fool, that Ward Heathcote will marry Helen Lorrington—the woman you pretend to be grateful to, and call your dearest friend? Helen Lorrington will be in every way a suitable wife for him. It has long been generally understood. The idea of *your* trying to thrust yourself between them is preposterous—I may say a maniac's folly."

"I am not trying: only let me go," sobbed Anne, still kneeling by the chair.

"You think I have not seen," continued Miss Vanhorn, her wrath rising with every bitter word; "but I have. Only I never dreamed that it was as bad as this. I never dreamed that Alida's daughter could be bold and immodest—worse than her mother, who was only love-mad."

Anne started to her feet. "Miss Vanhorn," she said, "I will not hear this, either of myself or my mother. It is not true."

"As to not hearing it, you are right; you will not hear my voice often in the future. I wash my hands of you. You are an ungrateful girl, and will come to an evil end. When I think of the enormous selfishness you now show in thus throwing away, for a mere matter of personal obstinacy, the bread of your sister and brothers, and leaving them to starve, I stand appalled. What do you expect?"

"Nothing—save to go."

"And you *shall* go."

"To-day?"

"This afternoon, at three." As she said this, Miss Vanhorn seated herself with her back toward Anne, and took up a book, as though there was no one in the room.

"Do you want me any longer, grandaunt?"

"Never call me by that name again. Go to your room; Bessmer will attend to you. At two o'clock I will see you for a moment before you go."

Without a reply, Anne obeyed. Her tears were dried as if by fever; words had been spoken which could not be forgiven. Inaction was impossible; she began to pack. Then, remembering who had given her all these clothes, she paused, uncertain what to do. After reflection, she decided to take with her only those she had brought from the half-house; and in this she was not actuated by any spirit of retaliation, her idea was that her grandaunt would demand the gifts in any case. Miss Vanhorn was not generous. She worked steadily; she did not wish to think; yet still the crowding feelings pursued her, caught up with her, and then went along with her, thrusting their faces close to hers, and forcing recognition. Was she, as Miss Vanhorn had said, enormously selfish in thus sacrificing the new comfort of the pinched household on the island to her own obstinacy? But, as she folded the plain garments brought from that home, she knew that it was not selfishness; as she replaced the filmy ball dress in its box, she said to herself that she could not deceive Mr. Dexter by so much even as a silence. Then, as she wrapped the white parasol in its coverings, the old burning, throbbing misery rolled over her, followed by the hot jealousy which she thought she had conquered; she seized the two dresses given by Helen, and added them to those left behind. But the action brought shame, and she replaced them. And now all the clothes faced her from the open trunks; those from the island, those which Rast had seen, murmured, "Faithless!" Helen's gifts whispered, "Ingratitude!" and those of her grandaunt called more loudly, "Fool!" She closed the lids, and turned toward the window; she tried to busy her mind with the future: surely thought and plans were needed. She was no longer confident, as she had been when she first left her Northern island; she knew now how wide the world was, and how cold. She could not apply at the doors of schools without letters or recommendations; she could not live alone. Her one hope began and ended in Jeanne-Armande. She dressed herself in travelling garb and sat down to wait. It was nearly noon, probably she would not see Helen, as she always slept through the morning after a ball, preserving by this changeless care the smooth fairness of her delicate complexion. She decided to write a note of farewell, and leave it with Bessmer; but again and again she tore up her beginnings, until the floor was strewn with fragments. She had so very much not to say. At last she succeeded in putting together a few sentences, which told nothing, save that she was going away; she bade her good-by, and thanked her for all her kindness, signing, without any preliminary phrases (for was she "affectionately" or "sincerely" Helen's "friend"?), merely her name, Anne Douglas.

At one o'clock Bessmer entered with luncheon. Evidently she had received orders to enter into no conversation with the prisoner; but she took the note, and promised to deliver it with her own hands. At two the door opened, and Miss Vanhorn came in.

The old woman's eye took in at a glance the closed trunks and the travelling dress. She had meant to try her niece, to punish her; but even then she could not believe that the girl would really throw away forever all the advantages she had placed within her grasp. She sat down, and after waiting a moment, closed her eyes. "Anne Douglas," she began, "daughter of my misguided niece Alida Clanssen, I have come for a final decision. Answer my questions. First, have you, or have you not, one hundred dollars in the world?"

"I have not."

"Have you, or have you not, three brothers and one sister wholly dependent upon you?"

"I have."

"Is it just or honorable to leave them longer to the charity of a woman who is poor herself, and not even a relative?"

"It is neither."

"Have I, or have I not, assisted you, offered also to continue the pension which makes them comfortable?"

"You have."

"Then," said the old woman, still with her eyes closed, "why persist in this idiotic stubbornness? In offending me, are you not aware that you are offending the only person on earth who can assist you? I make no promises as to the future; but I am an old woman now, one to whom you could at least be dutiful. There—I want no fine words. Show your fineness by obeying my wishes."

"I will stay with *you*, grandaunt, willingly, gladly, gratefully, if you will take me away from this place."

"No conditions," said Miss Vanhorn. "Come here; kneel down in front of me, so that I can look at you. Will you stay with me *here*, if I yield everything concerning Mr. Dexter?" She held her firmly, with her small keen eyes searching her face.

Anne was silent. Like the panorama which is said to pass before the eyes of the drowning man, the days and hours at Caryl's as they would be, must be, unrolled themselves before her. But there only followed the same desperate realization of the impossibility of remaining; the misery, the jealousy; worse than all, the self-doubt. The misery, the jealousy, she could perhaps bear, deep as they were. But what appalled her was this new doubt of herself, this new knowledge, that, in spite of all her determination, she might, if tried, yield to this love which had taken possession of her unawares, yield to certain words which he might speak, to certain tones of his voice, and thus become even more faithless to Rast, to Helen, and to herself, than she already was. If he would go away—but she knew that he would not. No, *she* must go. Consciousness came slowly back to her eyes, which had been meeting Miss Vanhorn's blankly.

"I can not stay," she said.

Miss Vanhorn thrust her away violently. "I am well paid for having had anything to do with Douglas blood," she cried, her voice trembling with anger. "Get back into the wilderness from whence you came! I will never hear your name on earth again." She left the room.

In a few moments Bessmer appeared, her eyes reddened by tears, and announced that the wagon was waiting. It was at a side door. At this hour there was no one on the piazzas, and Anne's trunk was carried down, and she herself followed with Bessmer, without being seen by any one save the servants and old John Caryl.

"I am not to say anything to you, Miss Douglas, if you please, but just the ordinary things, if you please," said Bessmer, as the wagon bore them away. "You are to take the three o'clock train, and go—wherever you please, she said. I was to tell you."

"Yes, Bessmer; do not be troubled. I know what to do. Will you tell grandaunt, when you return, that I beg her to forgive what has seemed obstinacy, but was only sad necessity. Can you remember it?"

"Yes, miss; only sad necessity," repeated Bessmer, with dropping tears. She was a meek woman, with a comfortable convexity of person, which, however, did not seem to give her confidence.

"I was not to know, miss, if you please, where you bought tickets to," she said, as the wagon stopped at the little station. "I was to give you this, and then go right back."

She handed Anne an envelope containing a fifty-dollar note. Anne looked at it a moment. "I will not take this, I think; you can tell grandaunt that I have money enough for the present," she said, returning it. She gave her hand kindly to the weeping maid, who was then driven away in the wagon, her sun-umbrella held askew over her respectable brown bonnet, her broad shoulders shaken with her sincere grief. A turn in the road soon hid even this poor friend of hers from view. Anne was alone.

The station-keeper was not there; his house was near by, but hidden by a grove of maples, and Anne, standing on the platform, seemed all alone, the two shining rails stretching north and south having the peculiarly solitary aspect which a one-track railway always has among green fields, with no sign of life in sight. No train has passed, or ever will pass. It is all a dream. She walked to and fro. She could see into the waiting-room, which was adorned with three framed texts, and another placard not religiously intended, but referring, on the contrary, to steamboats, which might yet be so interpreted, namely, "Take the Providence Line." She noted the drearily ugly round stove, faded below to white, planted in a sand-filled box; she saw the bench, railed off into single seats by iron elbows, and remembered that during her journey eastward, two, if not three, of these places were generally filled with the packages of some solitary female of middle age, clad in half-mourning, who remained stonily unobservant of the longing glances cast upon the space she occupied. These thoughts came to her mechanically. When a decision has finally been made, and for the present nothing more can be done, the mind goes wandering off on trivial errands; the flight of a bird, the passage of the fairy car of thistle-down, are sufficient to set it in motion. It seemed to her that she had been there a long time, when a step came through the grove: Hosea Plympton—or, as he was called in the neighborhood, Hosy Plim—was unlocking the station door. Anne bought her ticket, and had her trunk checked; she hoped to reach the half-house before midnight.

Hosy having attended to his official business with dignity, now came out to converse unofficially with his one passenger. "From Caryl's, ain't you?"

"Yes," replied Anne.

"Goin' to New York?"

"Yes."

"I haven't yet ben to that me-tropo-lis," said Hosy. "On some accounts I should admire to go, on others not. Ben long at Caryl's?"

"Yes, some time."

"My wife's cousin helps over there; Mirandy's her name. And she tells me, Mirandy does, that the heap of washing over to that house is a sight to see. She tells me, Mirandy does, that they don't especial dress up for the Sabbath over there, not so much even as on other days."

"That is true, I believe."

"Sing'lar," said the little man, "what folks 'll do as has the money! They don't seem to be capable of enj'ying themselves exactly; and p'r'aps that's what Providence intends. We haven't had city folks at Caryl's until lately, miss, you see; and I confess they've ben a continooal study to me ever since. 'Tis amazin' the ways the Lord'll take to make us contented with our lot. Till I *see* 'em, I thought 'em most downright and all everlastin' to be envied. But *now* I feel the ba'm of comfort and innard strengthenin' when I see how little they know *how* to enj'y themselves, after all. Here's the train, miss."

In another moment Anne felt herself borne away—away from the solitary station, with its shining lines of rails; from the green hills which encircled Caryl's; from the mountain-peaks beyond. She had started on her journey into the wide world.

In darkness, but in safety, she arrived at the half-house, in the station-keeper's wagon, a few minutes before midnight. A light was still burning, and in response to her knock Jeanne-Armande herself opened the door, clad in a wrapper, with a wonderful flannel cap on her head. She was much astonished to see her pupil, but received her cordially, ordered the trunk brought in, and herself attended to the beating down of the station-keeper's boy to a proper price for his services. She remarked upon his audacity and plainly criminal tendencies; she thoroughly sifted the physical qualities of the horse; she objected to the shape of the wagon; and finally, she had noted his manner of bringing in the trunk, and shaving its edges as well as her doorway, and she felt that she must go over to the station herself early in the morning, and lodge a complaint against him. What did he mean by— But here the boy succumbed, and departed with half-price, and Jeanne-Armande took breath, and closed the door in triumph.

"You see that I have come back to you, mademoiselle," said Anne, with a faint smile. "Shall I tell you why?"

"Yes; but no, not now. You are very weary, my child; you look pale and worn. Would you like some coffee?"

"Yes," said Anne, who felt a faint exhaustion stealing over her. "But the fast-day coffee will do." For there was one package of coffee in the store-room which went by that name, and which old Nora was instructed to use on Fridays. Not that Jeanne-Armande followed strict rules and discipline; but she had bought that coffee at an auction sale in the city for a very low price, and it proved indeed so low in quality that they could not drink it more than once a week. Certainly, therefore, Friday was the appropriate day.

"No," said the hostess, "you shall have a little of the other, child. Come to the kitchen. Nora has gone to bed, but I will arrange a little supper for you with my own hands."

They went to the bare little room, where a mouse would have starved. But mademoiselle was not without resources, and keys. Soon she "arranged" a brisk little fire and a cheery little stew, while the pint coffee-pot sent forth a delicious fragrance. Sitting there in a wooden chair beside the little stove, Anne felt more of home comfort than she had ever known at Caryl's, and the thin miserly teacher was kinder than her grandaunt had ever been. She ate and drank, and was warmed; then, sitting by the dying coals, she told her story, or rather as much of it as it was necessary mademoiselle should know.

"It is a pity," said Jeanne-Armande, "and especially since she has no relative, this grandaunt, nearer than yourself. Could nothing be done in the way of renewal, as to heart-strings?"

"Not at present. I must rely upon you, mademoiselle; in this, even Tante can not help me."

"That is true; she can not. She even disapproved of my own going forth into the provinces," said Jeanne-Armande, with the air of an explorer. "We have different views of life, Hortense Moreau and I; but there!—we respect each other. Of how much money can you dispose at present, my child?"

Anne told the sum.

"If it is so little as that," said Jeanne-Armande, "it will be better for you to go westward with me immediately. I start earlier than usual this year; you can take the journey with me, and share expenses; in this way we shall both be able to save. Now as to chances: there is sometimes a subordinate employed under me, when there is a press of new scholars. This is the autumn term: there *may* be a press. I must prepare you, however, for the lowest of low salaries," said the teacher, her voice changing suddenly to a dry sharpness. "I shall present you as a novice, to whom the privilege of entering the institution is an equivalent of money."

"I expect but little," said Anne. "A beginner must take the lowest place."

On the second day they started. Jeanne-Armande was journeying to Weston this time by a roundabout way. By means of excursion tickets to Valley City, offered for low rates for three days, she had found that she could (in time) reach Weston *viâ* the former city, and effect a saving of one dollar and ten cents. With the aid of her basket, no additional meals would be required, and the money saved, therefore, would be pure gain. There was only one point undecided, namely, should she go through to Valley City, or change at a junction twenty miles this side for the northern road? What would be the saving, if any, by going on? What by changing? No one could tell her; the complication of excursion rates to Valley City for the person who was not going there, and the method of night travel for a person who would neither take a sleeping-car, nor travel in a day car, combined themselves to render more impassive still the ticket-sellers, safely protected in their official round towers from the rabble of buyers outside. Regarding the main lines between New York and Weston, and all their connections, it would be safe to say that mademoiselle knew more than the officials themselves. The remainder of the continent was an unknown wilderness in her mind, but these lines of rails, over which she was obliged to purchase her way year after year, she understood thoroughly. She had tried all the routes, and once she had gone through Canada; she had looked at canal-boats meditatively. She was haunted by a vision that some day she might find a clean captain and captain's wife who would receive her as passenger, and allow her to cook her own little meals along shore. Once, she explained to Anne, a Sunday-school camp-meeting had reduced the rates, she being apparently on her way thither. She had always regretted that the season of State fairs was a month later: she felt herself capable of being on her way to all of them.

"But now, whether to go on to Valley City, or to leave the train at Stringhampton Junction, is the question I can not decide," she said, with irritation, having returned discomfited from another encounter with a ticket-seller.

"We reach Weston by both routes, do we not?" said Anne.

"Of course; that follows without saying. Evidently you do not comprehend the considerations which are weighing upon me. However, I will get it out of the ticket agent at New Macedonia," said mademoiselle, rising. "Come, the train is ready."

They were going only as far as New Macedonia that night; mademoiselle had slept there twice, and intended to sleep there again. Once, in her decorous maiden life, she had passed a night in a sleeping-car, and never again would her foot "cross the threshold of one of those outrageous inventions." She remembered even now with a shudder the processions of persons in muffled drapery going to the wash-rooms in the early morning. New

Macedonia existed only to give suppers and breakfasts; it had but two narrow sleeping apartments over its abnormal development of dining-room below. But the military genius of Jeanne-Armande selected it on this very account; for sleeping-rooms where no one ever slept, half-price could in conscience alone be charged. All night Anne was wakened at intervals by the rushing sound of passing trains. Once she stole softly to the uncurtained window and looked out; clouds covered the sky, no star was visible, but down the valley shone a spark which grew and grew, and then turned white and intense, as, with a glare and a thundering sound, a locomotive rushed by, with its long line of dimly lighted sleeping-cars swiftly and softly following with their unconscious human freight, the line ending in two red eyes looking back as the train vanished round a curve.

"Ten hours' sleep," said mademoiselle, awaking with satisfaction in the morning. "I now think we can sit up to-night in the Valley City waiting-room, and save the price of lodgings. Until twelve they would think we were waiting for the midnight train; after that, the night porter, who comes on duty then, would suppose it was the early morning express."

"Then you have decided to go through to Valley City?" asked Anne.

"Yes, since by this arrangement we can do it without expense."

Two trains stopped at New Macedonia for breakfast, one eastward bound from over the Alleghanies, the other westward bound from New York. Jeanne-Armande's strategy was to enter the latter while its passengers were at breakfast, and take bodily possession of a good seat, removing, if necessary, a masculine bag or two left there as tokens of ownership; for the American man never makes war where the gentler sex is concerned, but retreats to another seat, or even to the smoking-car, with silent generosity.

Breakfast was now over; the train-boy was exchanging a few witticisms with the pea-nut vender of the station, a brakeman sparred playfully with the baggage porter, and a pallid telegraph operator looked on from his window with interest. Meanwhile the conductor, in his stiff official cap, pared a small apple with the same air of fixed melancholy and inward sarcasm which he gave to all his duties, large and small; when it was eaten, he threw the core with careful precision at a passing pig, looked at his watch, and called out, suddenly and sternly, "All aboard!" The train moved on.

It was nine o'clock. At ten there came into the car a figure Anne knew—Ward Heathcote.

CHAPTER XIX.

"Man is a bundle of contradictions, tied together with fancies."—Persian Proverb.

"The might of one fair face sublimes my love,

For it hath weaned my heart from low desires.

Nor death I heed, nor purgatorial fires.

Forgive me if I can not turn away

From those sweet eyes that are my earthly

heaven,

For they are guiding stars, benignly given

To tempt my footsteps to the upward way."

—Michael Angelo.

Dire was the wrath of Helen Lorrington when, having carefully filled the measure of her lost sleep, she sent a little note across to Anne, and answer was returned that Miss Douglas was gone.

Mrs. Lorrington, with compliments to Miss Vanhorn, then begged (on a card) to be informed *where* Miss Douglas was gone. Miss Vanhorn, with compliments to Mrs. Lorrington (also on a card), returned answer that she did not know. Mrs. Lorrington, deeply grieved to disturb Miss Vanhorn a second time, then requested to be favored with Miss Douglas's address. Miss Vanhorn, with assurances that it was no disturbance, but always a pleasure to oblige Mrs. Lorrington, replied that she did not possess it. Then Helen waited until the old coupé rolled away for an afternoon drive, its solitary occupant inside, her profile visible between the two closed glass windows like an object mounted for a microscope, and going across, beguiled the mild Bessmer to tell all she knew. This was not much; but the result was great anger in Helen's mind, and a determination to avenge the harsh deed. Bessmer did not know causes, but she knew actions. Anne had been sent away in disgrace, the maid being forbidden to know even the direction the lonely traveller had taken. Helen, quick to solve riddles, solved this, at least as far as one side of it was concerned, and the quick, partially correct guesses of a quick-witted woman are often, by their very nearness, more misleading than any others. Mr. Dexter had been with Anne during the evening of the ball; probably he had asked her to be his wife. Anne, faithful to her engagement, had refused him; and Miss Vanhorn, faithful to her cruel nature, had sent her away in disgrace. And when Helen learned that Mr. Dexter had gone also—gone early in the morning before any one was stirring—she took it as confirmation of her theory, and was now quite sure. She would tell all the house, she said to herself. She began by telling Heathcote.

They were strolling in the garden. She turned toward the little arbor at the end of the path.

"Not there," said Heathcote.

"Why not? Have you been there so much with Rachel?" said his companion, in a sweet voice.

"Never, I think. But arbors are damp holes."

"Nevertheless, I am going there, and you are going with me."

"As you please."

"Ward, how much have you been with Rachel?" she asked, when they were seated in the little bower, which was overgrown with the old-fashioned vine called matrimony.

"Oh!" said Heathcote, with a sound of fatigue in his voice. "Are we never to have an end to that subject?"

"Yes; when you *make* an end."

"One likes to amuse one's self. You do."

"Whom do you mean now?" said Helen, diverted from her questions for the moment, as he intended she should be.

To tell the truth, Heathcote did not mean any one; but he never hesitated. So now he answered, promptly, "Dexter." He had long ago discovered that he could make any woman believe he was jealous of any man, no matter whom, even one to whom she had never spoken; it presupposed that the other man had been all the time a silent admirer, and on this point the grasp of the feminine imagination is wide and hopeful.

"How like you that is! Mr. Dexter is nothing to me."

"You have been out driving with him already," said Heathcote, pursuing his advantage; "and you have not been out with me."

"He has gone; so we need not quarrel about him."

"When did he go?"

"Early this morning. And to show you how unjust you are, he went because last evening Anne Douglas refused him."

"Then he was refused twice in one day," said Heathcote. "Mrs. Bannert refused him at six."

"How do you know?"

"She told me."

"Traitorous creature!"

"Oh no; she is an especial—I may say confidential—friend of mine."

"Then what am I?"

"Not a friend at all, I hope," said the man beside her. "Something more." He was pulling a spray of vine to pieces, and did not look up; but Helen was satisfied, and smiled to herself brightly. She now went back to Anne. "Did you know poor Anne was gone too, Ward?"

"Gone!" said Heathcote, starting. Then he controlled himself. "What do you mean?" he asked.

"I mean that Miss Vanhorn cruelly sent her away this afternoon without warning, and with only a little money; Bessmer was not even allowed to inquire what she intended to do, or where she was going. I have been haunted ever since I heard it by visions of the poor child arriving in New York all alone, and perhaps losing her way: she only knew that one up-town locality near Moreau's."

"Do you mean to say that no one knows where she has gone?"

"No one. Bessmer tells me that the old dragon was in one of her black rages. Mr. Dexter was with Anne for some time in the little parlor during the ball last evening, and Miss Vanhorn had the room made ready, as though she expected him. Here are the few lines the poor child left for me: they are constrained, and very unlike her; but I suppose she was too troubled to choose her words. She told me herself only the day before that she was very unhappy."

Heathcote took the little note, and slipped it into an inner pocket. He said nothing, and went on stripping the vine.

"There is one thing that puzzles me," continued Helen. "Bessmer heard the old woman say, violently, 'You have thrown yourself at the feet of a man who is simply laughing at you.' Now Anne never threw herself at any man's feet—unless, indeed, it might be the feet of that boy on the island to whom she is engaged. I do not know how she acts when with him."

"It is a pity, since Bessmer overheard so much, that while she was about it she did not overhear more," said Heathcote, dryly.

"You need not suspect her: she is as honest as a cow, and as unimaginative. She happened to catch that sentence because she had entered the next room for something; but she went out again immediately, and heard no more. What I fear is that Miss Vanhorn has dismissed her entirely, and that I shall not see her again, even at Moreau's. In the note she says that she will send me her address when she can, which is oddly expressed, is it not? I suppose she means that she will send it when she knows where she is to be. Poor child! think of her to-night out in the hard world all alone!"

"I *do* think of her."

"It is good of you to care so much. But you know how much attached to her I am."

"Yes."

"She is an odd girl. Undeveloped, yet very strong. She would refuse a prince, a king, without a thought, and work all her life like a slave for the man she loved, whoever he might be. In truth, she has done what amounts to nearly the same thing, if my surmises are correct. Those children on the island were pensioned, and I presume the old dragon has stopped the pension."

"Have you no idea where she has gone?"

"Probably to Mademoiselle Pitre at Lancaster, on the Inside Road; I stopped there once to see her. It would be her first resource. I shall hear from her, of course, in a few days, and then I shall help her in every way in my power. We will not let her suffer, Ward."

"No."

Then there was a pause.

"Are you not chilly here, Helen?"

"It *is* damp," said Mrs. Lorrington, rising. She always followed the moods of this lethargic suitor of hers as closely as she could divine them; she took the advance in every oblique and even retrograde movement he made so swiftly that it generally seemed to have originated with herself. In five minutes they were in the house, and she had left him.

In what was called the office, a group of young men were discussing, over their cigars, a camping party; the mountains, whose blue sides lay along the western sky, afforded good hunting ground still, and were not as yet farmed out to clubs. The men now at Caryl's generally camped out for a few weeks every year; it was one of their habits. Heathcote, with his hands in the pockets of his sack-coat, walked up and down, listening. After a while, "I think I'll go with you," he said.

"Come along, then, old fellow; I wish you would."

"When are you going?"

"To-morrow morning—early."

"By wagon?"

"Train to the junction; then wagons."

"How long shall you stay?"

"A week or two."

"I'll go," said Heathcote. He threw away his cigar, and started toward his room. Helen was singing in the parlor as he passed; he paused outside for a moment to listen. Every one was present save Anne and Gregory Dexter; yet the long room wore to him already the desolate and empty aspect of summer resorts in September. He could see the singer plainly; he leaned against the wall and looked at her. He liked her; she fitted into all the grooves of his habits and tastes. And he thought she would marry him if he pushed the matter. While he was thus meditating, a soft little hand touched his arm in the darkness. "I saw you," said Rachel, in a whisper, "and came round to join you. You are looking at Helen; what a flute-like voice she has! Let us go out and listen to her on the piazza."

Mr. Heathcote would be delighted to go. He hated that parlor, with all those people sitting round in a row. How could Rachel stand it?

Rachel, with a pathetic sigh, answered, How could she do as she wished? She had no talent for deception.

Heathcote regretted this; he wished with all his heart that she had.

His heart was not all his to wish with, Rachel suggested, in a cooing murmur.

He answered that it was. And then they went out on the piazza.

Helen missed Rachel, and suspected, but sang on as sweetly as ever. At last, however, even Rachel could not keep the recreant admirer longer. He went off to his room, filled a travelling bag, lit a cigar, and then sat down to write a note:

"Dear Helen,—I have decided suddenly to go with the camping party to the mountains for a week or two; we leave early in the morning. I shall hope to find you still here when I return.

W. H."

He sealed this missive, threw it aside, and then began to study a railway guide. To a person going across to the mountains in a wagon, a knowledge of the latest time-tables was, of course, important.

The next morning, while her maid was coiling her fair hair, Mrs. Lorrington received the note, and bit her lips with vexation.

The hunting party drove over to the station soon after six, and waited there for the early train. Hosy sold them their tickets, and then came out to gain a little information in affable conversation. All the men save Heathcote were attired in the most extraordinary old clothes, and they wore among them an assortment of hats which might have won a prize in a collection. Hosy regarded them with wonder, but his sharp freckled face betrayed no sign. They were men, and he was above curiosity. He ate an apple reflectively, and took an inward inventory: "Hez clothes that I wouldn't be seen in, and sports 'em proud as you please. Hats like a pirate. The strangest set of fellers!"

As the branch road train, with a vast amount of self-important whistling, drew near the junction with the main line, Heathcote said carelessly that he thought he would run down to the city for a day or two, and join them later. There was hue and cry over this delinquency, but he paid his way to peace by promising to bring with him on his return a certain straw-packed basket, which, more than anything else, is a welcome sight to poor hard-worked hunters in a thirsty land. The wagons rolled away with their loads, and he was left to take the southern-bound express. He reached the city late in the evening, slept there, and early the next morning went out to Lancaster Station. When he stepped off the train, a boy and a red wagon were in waiting; nothing else save the green country.

"Does a French lady named Pitre live in this neighborhood?" he inquired of the boy, who was holding the old mare's head watchfully, as though, if not restrained, she would impetuously follow the receding train. This was the boy with whom Jeanne-Armande had had her memorable contest over Anne's fare. Here was his chance to make up from the pockets of this stranger—fair prey, since he was a friend of hers—the money lost on that field.

"Miss Peters lives not fur off. I can drive you there if you want ter go."

Heathcote took his seat in the wagon, and slowly as possible the boy drove onward, choosing the most roundabout course, and bringing the neighborhood matrons to their windows to see that wagon pass a second time with the same stranger in it, going no one knew where. At last, all the cross-roads being exhausted, the boy stopped before the closed half-house.

"Is this the place? It looks uninhabited," said Heathcote.

"'T always looks so; she's such a screw, she is," replied Eli, addressed as "Li" by his friends.

Heathcote knocked; no answer. He went round to the back door, but found no sign of life.

"There is no one here. Would any one in the neighborhood know where she has gone?"

"Mr. Green might, over to the store," said Li.

"Drive there."

"I've got to meet the next train, but I'll take you as fur as the door; 'tain't but a step from there to the station. And you might as well pay me now," he added, carelessly, "because the mare she's very fiery, and won't stand." Pocketing his money—double price—he drove off, exultant. It was a mile and a half to the station, and a hot, cloudless morning.

Heathcote made acquaintance with Mr. Green, and asked his question. There was no one in the shop at the moment, and Mr. Green responded freely that he knew Miss Peters very well; in fact, they were old friends. She had gone to Valley City—had, in fact, left that very morning in the same red wagon which had brought the inquirer to his door; he, Green, looking out by chance, had seen her pass. What did she do in Valley City? Why, she taught—in fact, kept school. She had kept school there for ten years, and he, Green, was the only one in the neighborhood who knew it, since she—Miss Peters—wasn't much liked about there, perhaps on account of her being a Papist. But in such matters, he, Green, was liberal. Did she have any one with her? Yes, she had; in fact,

Miss Douglas—same young lady as was there the fore part of the summer. No, they warn't going to stop at all in New York; going right through to the West. Hoped there was no bad news?

"No," replied Heathcote.

But his monosyllable without details convinced the hearer that there was, and before night the whole neighborhood was humming with conjecture. The darkest of the old suspicions about mademoiselle's past were now held to have been verified.

Heathcote walked back to the station over the red clay road, and looked for that boy. But Li had taken care to make good his retreat. By the delay two trains were missed, and he was obliged to wait; when he reached the city it was two o'clock, and it seemed to him that the pavements had never exhaled such withering heat. His rooms were closed; he went to the hotel, took a bath, took two, but could not recover either his coolness or his temper. Even after dinner he was still undecided. Should he go westward to Valley City by the ten o'clock train? or wait till morning? or throw it all up and join the other men at the mountains? It was a close evening. Anne was at that moment on the ferry-boat.

Mademoiselle had carefully misled her friend Mr. Green; so great was her caution, so intricate her manœuvres, that she not only never once told him the truth, but also had taken the trouble to invent elaborate fictions concerning herself and her school at Valley City every time she closed the half-house and bade him good-by. The only person who knew where she really was was the Roman Catholic priest who had charge of the mission church at the railway-car shops three miles distant; to this secret agent was intrusted the duty of walking over once a week, without exciting the notice of the neighborhood, to see if the half-house remained safe and undisturbed. For this service mademoiselle paid a small sum each week to the mission; and it was money well earned. The priest, a lank, lonely, sad-eyed young Irishman, with big feet in low shoes, came down the track once in seven days to Lancaster, as if for a walk, taking the half-house within his varying circuit, and, with the tact of his nation and profession, never once betraying his real object. On this occasion Jeanne-Armande had even showed Mr. Green her tickets to Valley City: what could be surer?

At sunset, in the city, the air grew cooler, a salt breeze came up the harbor from the ocean, tossing bluely outside. Heathcote decided to take another glass of wine, and the morning train. To the mountains?

The next day he was somewhat disgustedly eating breakfast at New Macedonia; and going through the cars an hour later, came upon Anne. He had not expected to see her. He was as much surprised as she was.

Why had he followed her? He could hardly have given a clear answer, save perhaps that he was accustomed to follow his inclinations wherever they led him, without hinderance or question. For there existed no one in the world who had the right to question him; and therefore he was without the habit of accounting for what he did, even to himself. It may, perhaps, be considered remarkable that, with such a position and training, he was, as a man, no worse than he was; that is, that he should be so good a fellow, after all, when he had possessed such unlimited opportunities to be a bad one. But natural refinement and fine physical health had kept the balance from swaying far; and the last-named influence is more powerful than is realized. Many a man of fine mind—even genius—is with the dolts and the brutes in the great army of the fallen, owing to a miserable, weak, and disappointing body. Of course he should have learned, early in life, its deficiencies, should have guarded it, withheld it and himself from exertions which to his neighbor are naught; but he does not always learn this lesson. The human creature who goes through his allotted course with vigorous health and a physical presence fine enough to command the unconscious respect of all with whom he comes in contact has no conception of the humiliations and discouragements, the struggles and failures, which beset the path of his weak-bodied and physically insignificant brother. Heathcote, indolent as he was, had a superb constitution, for which and of which, ungratefully, he had never thought long enough to be thankful.

But why was he following Anne?

She had told him of her engagement. Even if he could have broken that engagement, did he wish to break it? He said to himself that it was because his chivalry, as a man, had been stirred by the maid's story of Miss Vanhorn's harsh words—words which he had at once construed as an allusion to himself. Was he not partially, perhaps wholly, responsible for her banishment? But, even if this were true, could he not have acted through Helen, who was by far the most fitting agent? Instead of this, here he was following her himself!

Why?

Simply because of one look he had had deep down into violet eyes.

He had not expected to find her so soon. In truth, he was following in rather a purposeless fashion, leaving much to chance, and making no plans. They had gone to Valley City; he would go to Valley City. Perhaps he should meet her in the street there; or perhaps he should leave a letter; perhaps he should do neither, but merely turn round, his impulse satisfied, and go home again. There was no need to decide now. He was on the way; that was enough. And more than enough.

Then, suddenly, he saw her.

She was sitting next the aisle. He put out his hand; she gave hers, and mechanically mentioned his name to mademoiselle, who, helmeted in her travelling bonnet surmounted by a green veil, presented a martial front to all beholders. There was no vacant place near; he remained standing.

"How fortunate that I have met you!" he said, with conventional cordiality. "The day promised to be intolerably long and dull."

Mademoiselle, who at a glance had taken in his appearance from head to foot as only a Frenchwoman can, inquired if he was going far, in a voice so harmonious, compared with the bonnet, that it was an agreeable surprise.

"To Valley City," replied Heathcote.

"We also are going to Valley City," said Jeanne-Armande, graciously. "It is a pity there happens to be no vacant place near for monsieur. If some of these good people—" Here she turned the helmet toward her neighbors behind.

"Pray do not give yourself any trouble," said Heathcote. "I was on my way to the last car, hoping to find more air and space. If I am so fortunate as to find there two vacant seats, may I not return for you? It will be a charity to my loneliness."

"And a pleasure, monsieur, to ourselves," said mademoiselle.

He bowed his thanks, and glanced again at Anne. She had not spoken, and had not looked at him since her first startled glance. But Jeanne-Armande was gracious for two; she was charmed to have a monsieur of such distinguished appearance standing in the aisle by their side, and she inwardly wished that she had worn her second instead of her third best gloves and veil.

"Mrs. Lorrington misses you sadly," said Heathcote to the silent averted face, more for the sake of saying something than with any special meaning.

A slight quiver in the downcast eyelids, but no answer.

"She hopes that you will soon send her your address."

"It is uncertain as yet where I shall be," murmured Anne.

"I thought you were to be at Valley City?"

She made no reply, but through her mind passed the thought that he could not know, then, their real destination. He had been speaking in a low voice; mademoiselle had not heard. But he could not carry on a conversation long with a person who would not answer. "I will go to the last car, and see if I can find those seats," he said, speaking to mademoiselle, and smiling as he spoke. She thought him charming.

As soon as he turned away, Anne said: "Please do not tell him that ours are excursion tickets, mademoiselle. Let him think that our destination is really Valley City."

"Certainly, if you wish it," replied Jeanne-Armande, who had a sympathy with all mysteries; this little speech of Anne's gave a new spice to the day. "He is one of the circle round your grandaunt, probably?"

"Yes; I met him at Caryl's."

"A most distinguished personage; entirely as it should be. And did I not overhear the name of the charming Mrs. Lorrington also?"

"He is a friend of Helen's. I think, I am not sure, but still I think that they are engaged," said Anne, bravely.

"And most appropriate. I do not know when I have been more comforted than by the culture and manner of that elegant friend of yours who sought you out at my little residence; I hope it may be my fortunate privilege to entertain her there again. From these two examples, I am naturally led to think that the circle round your grandaunt is one adjusted to that amiable poise so agreeable to the feelings of a lady."

Anne made no reply; the circle round her grandaunt seemed to her a world of dark and menacing terrors, from which she was fleeing with all the speed she could summon. But, one of these terrors had followed her.

Presently Heathcote returned. He had found two vacant seats, and the car was much better ventilated than this one; there was no dust, and no one was eating either pea-nuts or apples; the floor was clean; the covering of the seats seemed to have been recently renewed. Upon hearing the enumeration of all these advantages, mademoiselle arose immediately, and "monsieur" was extremely attentive in the matter of carrying shawls, packages, and baskets. But when they reached the car, they found that the two seats were not together; one was at the end, the other separated from it by the aisle and four intervening places.

"I hoped that you would be kind enough to give me the pleasure of being with you by turns," said Heathcote, gallantly, to mademoiselle, "since it was impossible to find seats together." As he spoke, he placed Jeanne-Armande in one of the seats, and Anne in the other; and then gravely, but with just the scintillation of a smile in his brown eyes, he took his own place, not beside Anne, but beside the delighted Frenchwoman, who could scarcely believe her good fortune to be real until she found him actually assisting her in the disposal of basket, shawl, bag, India-rubber shoes, and precious although baggy umbrella.

CHAPTER XX.

"*Philip.* Madam, a day may sink or save a realm.

Mary. A day may save a heart from breaking, too."—
Tennyson.

Mr. Heathcote retained his place beside mademoiselle through a whole long hour. She had time to get over her fear that he would go away soon, time to adjust her powers, time to enlarge, and to do justice to herself and several subjects adapted elegantly and with easy grace to the occasion. In her hard-working life she had seldom enjoyed a greater pleasure. For Jeanne-Armande had good blood in her veins; the ends of her poor old fingers were finely moulded, and there had been a title in the family long ago in Berri. And when at last monsieur did go, it was not hastily. The proper preliminaries were spoken, the first little movement made, and then, later, the slow rising, as if with reluctance, to the feet. Jeanne-Armande was satisfied, and smiled with honeyed graciousness, as, after another moment's delay, he bowed and went back to the place behind, where Anne was sitting.

In truth, Heathcote had not been unwilling to take the hour himself; it was not necessary to talk—Jeanne-Armande would talk for two. The sight of Anne had been unexpected; he had not decided what he should say to her even at Valley City, much less here. After an hour's thought, he took his place beside her. And remarked upon—the beauty of the day.

Dexter would have said something faultless, and all the more so if he had wished to disguise his thoughts. But all Heathcote said was, "What a lovely day!"

"Yes," replied Anne. In her mind surged to and fro one constant repetition: "Ah, my dear child, do you not see that I can not help loving you? and that you—love me also?" "Do you not see that I can not help loving you? and that you—love me also?"

"They improve things, after all," said Heathcote. "The last time I went over this road the train-boy was a poor little cripple, and therefore one couldn't quite throw his books on the floor." This was in allusion to the progress of a brisk youth through the car for the purpose of depositing upon the patient knees of each passenger a paper-covered novel, a magazine or two, and a song-book.

—"And that you—love me also," ran Anne's thoughts, as she looked out on the gliding fields.

There was a silence. Then Heathcote moved nearer.

"Anne," he said, in a low tone, "I was very much disturbed when I found that you had gone. From the little I was able to learn, I fear you were harshly treated by that hard old woman who calls herself your aunt."

"Not according to her view of it," said Anne, her face still turned to the window.

"I wish you would look at me, instead of at those stupid fields," said Heathcote, after a moment, in an aggrieved tone. "Here I have escaped from Caryl's under false pretenses, told dozens of lies, spent a broiling morning at a hole of a place called Lancaster, melted myself in the hot city, and bought tickets for all across the continent, just for the chance of seeing you a moment, and you will not even look at me."

But she had turned now. "Did you go out to the half-house?" she said, with a little movement of surprise.

"Yes," he answered, immediately meeting her eyes, and holding them with his own. (They had not precisely the kind of expression which is appropriate to the man who has decided to perform the part of "merely a kind friend." But then Heathcote always looked more than he said.)

"I am very sorry," she murmured—"I mean, sorry that you have followed me."

"Why are you sorry? You do not know how distressed I was when Mrs. Lorrington told me."

"Helen!" said Anne, her eyes falling at the sound of the name.

"She does not know where I am; no one knows. They think I have gone to the mountains. But—I could not be at peace with myself, Anne, until I had seen you once more. Do you remember the last time we met, that morning in the garden?" She made a mute gesture which begged for silence; but he went on: "I can never forget that look of yours. In truth, I fear I have done all this, have come all this distance, and in spite of myself, for—another."

There was no one behind them; they had the last seat. Anne was thinking, wildly, "Oh, if he would but speak in any other tone—say anything else than that!" Then she turned, at bay. "Mrs. Lorrington told me that you were engaged to her," she said, announcing it quietly, although her face was very pale.

"Did she? It is partly true. But—I love *you*, Anne."

The last words that Ward Heathcote had intended to speak, when he took that seat beside her, he had now spoken; the last step he had intended to take he had now taken. What did he mean? He did not know himself. He only knew that her face was exquisitely sweet to him, and that he was irresistibly drawn toward her, whether he would or no. "I love you," he repeated.

What could be said to such a plain, direct wooer as this? Anne, holding on desperately to her self-possession, and throwing up barriers mentally, made of all her resolutions and duties, her pride and her prayers, drew away, coldly answering: "However you may have forgotten your own engagement, Mr. Heathcote, I have not forgotten mine. It is not right for you to speak and for me to hear such words."

"Right is nothing," said Heathcote, "if we love each other."

"We do not," replied Anne, falling into the trap.

"We do; at least *I* do."

This avowal, again repeated, was so precious to the poor humiliated pride of the woman's heart within her that she had to pause an instant. "I was afraid you would think," she said, blushing brightly—"I was afraid you would think that I—I mean, that I can not help being glad that you—"

"That I love you? I do. But just as truly as I love you, Anne, you love me. You can not deny it."

"I will not discuss the subject. I shall soon be married, Mr. Heathcote, and you—"

"Never mind me; I can take care of myself. And so you are going to marry a man you do not love?"

"I do love him. I loved him long before I knew you; I shall love him long after you are forgotten. Leave me; I will not listen to you. Why do you speak so to me? Why did you follow me?"

"Because, dear, I love you. I did not fully know it myself until now. Believe me, Anne, I had no more intention of speaking in this way when I sat down here than I had of following you when I first heard you had gone; but the next morning I did it. Come, let everything go to the winds, as I do, and say you love me; for I know you do."

The tears were in Anne's eyes now; she could not see. "Let me go to mademoiselle," she said, half rising as if to pass him. "It is cruel to insult me."

"Do not attract attention; sit down for one moment. I will not keep you long; but you shall listen to me. Insult you? Did I ever dream of insulting you? Is it an insult to ask you to be my wife? That is what I ask now. I acknowledge that I did not follow you with any such intention. But now that I sit here beside you, I realize what you are to me. My darling, I love you, child as you have seemed. Look up, and tell me that you will be my wife."

"Never."

"Why?" said Heathcote, not in the least believing her, but watching the intense color flush her face and throat, and then die away.

"I shall marry Rast. And you—will marry Helen."

"As I said before, *I* can take care of myself. The question is *you*." As he spoke he looked at her so insistently that, struggling and unwilling, she yet felt herself compelled to meet his eyes in return.

"Helen loves you dearly," she said, desperately.

They were looking full at each other now. In the close proximity required by the noise of the train, they could see the varying lights and shadows in the depths of each other's eyes. The passengers' faces were all turned forward; there was no one on a line with them; virtually they were alone.

"I do not know what your object is in bringing in Mrs. Lorrington's name so often," said Heathcote. "She does not need your championship, I assure you."

"How base to desert her so!"

"Not any more base than to marry a man you do not love," replied Heathcote. "I hardly know anything more base than that. But marry *me*, my darling," he added, his voice softening as he bent toward her, "and you shall see how I will love you."

"You said I could go," said the girl, turning from him, and putting her hand over her eyes.

"You may go, if you are afraid. But I hardly think you a coward. No; let us have it out now. Here you are, engaged. Here I am, half engaged. We meet. Do you suppose I wish to love you? Not at all. You are by no means the wife I have intended to have. Do you wish to love me? No. You wish to be faithful to your engagement. In a worldly point of view we could not do a more foolish deed than to marry each other. You have nothing, and a burden of responsibilities; I have very little, and a much heavier burden of bad habits and idleness. What is the result? By some unknown enchantment I begin to love you, you begin to love me. The very fact that I am sitting here to-day conclusively proves the former. I am as fond of you as a school-boy, Anne. In truth, you have made me act like a school-boy. This is a poor place to woo you in; but, dear, just look at me once, only once more."

But Anne would not look. In all her struggles and all her resolutions, all her jealousy and her humiliation, she had made no provision against this form of trial, namely, that he should love her like this.

"Oh, go, go; leave me," she murmured, hardly able to speak. He gathered the words more from the movement of her lips than from any sound.

"I will go if you wish it. But I shall come back," he said. And then, quietly, he left her alone, and returned to Jeanne-Armande.

The Frenchwoman was charmed; she had not expected him so soon. She said to herself, with a breath of satisfaction, that her conversation had fallen in fit places.

Alone, looking at the hills as they passed in procession, Anne collected her scattered resolves, and fought her battle. In one way it was a sweet moment to her. She had felt dyed with eternal shame at having given her love unsought, uncared for; but he loved her—even if only a little, he loved her. This was balm to her wounded heart, and diffused itself like a glow; her cold hands grew warm, her life seemed to flow more freely. But soon the realization followed that now she must arm herself in new guise to resist the new temptation. She must keep her promise. She would marry Rast, if he wished it, though the earth were moved, and the hills carried into the midst of the sea. And Heathcote would be far happier with Helen; his feeling for herself was but a fancy, and would pass, as no doubt many other fancies had passed. In addition, Helen loved him; her life was bound up in him, whether he knew it or no. Helen had been her kindest friend; if all else were free, this alone would hold her. "But I *am* glad, glad to the bottom of my heart, that he did care for me, even if only a little," she thought, as she watched the hills. "My task is now to protect him from himself, and—and what is harder, myself from myself. I will do it. But I *am* glad—I am glad." Quieted, she waited for his return.

When he came she would speak so calmly and firmly that his words would be quelled. He would recognize the uselessness of further speech. When he came. But he did not come. The hills changed to cliffs, the cliffs to mountains, the long miles grew into thirty and forty, yet he did not return. He had risen, but did not come to her; he had gone forward to the smoking-car. He had, in truth, caught the reflection of her face in a mirror, and decided not to come. It is not difficult to make resolutions; there is a fervidness in the work that elevates and strengthens the heart. But once made, one needs to exercise them, otherwise they grow cold and torpid on one's hands.

Jeanne-Armande, finding herself alone, barricaded her seat with basket and umbrella, so as to be able to return thither (and perhaps have other conversations), and came across to Anne.

"A most accomplished gentleman!" she said, with effusion. "Mrs. Lorrington, charming as she is, is yet to be herself congratulated. He has even been in Berri," she added, as though that was a chief accomplishment, "and may have beheld with his own eyes the château of my ancestors." Rarely indeed did Jeanne-Armande allude to this château: persons with château ancestors might be required to sustain expenses not in accordance with her well-arranged rules.

"Where does this train stop?" asked Anne, with some irrelevance as to the château.

"At Centerville, for what they call dinner; and at Stringhampton Junction in the evening. It is the fast express."

"Do we meet an eastward-bound train at Centerville?"

"I presume we do; but we shall not get out, so the crowd in the dining-room will not incommode us. The contents of my basket will be sufficient. But if you wish a cup of coffee, it will be eight cents. There is a species of German cake at Centerville, remarkably filling for the price. They bring them through the cars."

"What time is it now?"

"About half past twelve; we reach Centerville at two. What age has Monsieur Heathcote, my dear?"

"Thirty-two or thirty-three, I believe."

"A gentleman of independent fortune, I presume?"

"He is independent, but, I was told, not rich."

"The position I should have supposed," said mademoiselle. "What penetrating eyes he possesses; penetrating, yet soft. There is something in his glance, coming from under those heavy brows, which is particularly moving—one might almost say tender. Have you observed it?"

131

Yes, Anne had observed it.

Jeanne-Armande, protected as she supposed from indiscretion by the engagement to the charming Mrs. Lorrington, rambled on, enjoying the real pleasure of being sentimental and romantic, without risk, cost, or loss of time, on this eventful day.

"I wish you could have seen Mr. Dexter, mademoiselle," said Anne, making an effort to turn the tide. "He is considered handsome, and he has a large fortune—"

"But not inherited, I presume," interposed mademoiselle, grandly. "Mr. Heathcote, as I understand, lives upon his paternal revenues."

If Heathcote had been there, he might have answered that he tried to, but never succeeded. He was not there, however; and Anne could only reply that she did not know.

"He has undoubtedly that air," said Jeanne-Armande, faithful to her distinguished escort, and waving away all diversions in favor of unknown Dexters. "Do you know when they are to be married?"

"No," said Anne, drearily, looking now at the cliffs which bounded the narrow valley through which the train was rushing.

"Let us hope that it will be soon; for life is short at best. Though not romantic by nature, I own I should be pleased to possess a small portion of the wedding cake of that amiable pair," pursued Jeanne-Armande, fixing her eyes upon the suspended lamp of the car, lost in sentimental reverie.

"I think I will buy a newspaper," said Anne, as the train-boy came toward them.

"Buy a paper? By no means," said mademoiselle, descending hastily to earth again. "I have yesterday's paper, which I found on the ferry-boat. It is in good order; I smoothed it out carefully; you can read that." She produced it from some remote pocket, and Anne took refuge in its pages, while Jeanne-Armande closed her eyes under the helmet, no doubt to meditate further on the picture of felicity she had called up.

Anne felt all the weariness of long suspense. It was one o'clock; it was half past one; it was nearly two; still he did not appear. Even mademoiselle now roused herself, looked at her watch, and in her turn began to ask where he could be; but she had the comfort of asking it aloud.

The speed was now perceptibly slackened, and the brakeman announced at the door: "Cen—ter—ville. Twen—timinets for dinner," in a bar of music not unlike a hoarse Gregorian chant. At this instant Heathcote entered from the next car.

"Ah! there he is," said mademoiselle, with satisfaction. "Do you think he will partake of a little taste with us?" He joined them, and she repeated her question in the shape of a modest allusion to the contents of her basket.

"No, thanks; I shall go out and walk up and down to breathe the air. But first, will you not go with me, and see what they have? Perhaps we might find something not altogether uneatable."

Mademoiselle declined, with her most gracious smile. She would content herself with the contents of her basket; but perhaps Anne—

The eastward-bound train was in, drawn up beside them.

"Yes," said Anne, "I should like to go." Then, as soon as they were in the open air, "I only wish to speak to you for a moment," she began. "I shall not go to the dining-room."

"Take my arm, then, and we will walk up and down."

"Yes, let us walk," she said, moving onward.

"We can not walk well unless you take my arm."

"I do not wish to walk well," she answered angrily.

He never would act according to her plan or theory. Here was all this persistence about a trifle, while she was wrought up to matters of deep moment.

"I do not care whether you wish to take it or not; you must. There! *Now* what do you want to say to me?" He was not wrought up at all; he was even smiling, and looking at her in the same old way. It was hard to begin under such circumstances; but she did begin. "Mr. Heathcote, while I thank you for all your kindness—"

"I have not been kind; I only said that I loved you. That is either above or below kindness, certainly not on a level with that tepid feeling."

But Anne would not listen, "While I thank you, I wish at the same time to say that I understand quite well that it is but an impulse which—"

"It *was* but an impulse, I grant," said Heathcote, again interrupting her, "but with roots too strong for me to break—as I have found to my dismay," he added, smiling, as he met her eyes.

"I wish you, I beg you, to return to New York on this train now waiting," said the girl, abandoning all her carefully composed sentences, and bringing forward her one desire with an earnestness which could not be doubted.

"I shall do nothing of the kind."

"But what is the use of going on?"

"I never cared much about use, Miss Douglas."

"And then there is the pain."

"Not for me."

"For me, then," she said, looking away from him across the net-work of tracks, and up the little village street ending in the blue side of the mountain. "Putting everything else aside, do you care nothing for my pain?"

"I can not help caring more for the things you put aside, since *I* happen to be one of them."

"You are selfish," she said, hotly. "I ask you to leave me; I tell you your presence pains me; and you will not go." She drew her arm from his, and turned toward the car. He lifted his hat, and went across to the dining-hall.

Mademoiselle was eating cold toast. She considered that toast retained its freshness longer than plain bread. Anne sat down beside her. She felt a hope that Heathcote would perhaps take the city-bound train after all. She heard the bell ring, and watched the passengers hasten forth from the dining-hall. The eastward-bound train was going—was gone; a golden space of sunshine and the empty rails were now where had been its noise and bell and steam.

"Our own passengers will soon be returning," said Jeanne-Armande, brushing away the crumbs, and looking at herself in the glass to see if the helmet was straight.

"May I sit here with you?" said Anne.

"Certainly, my dear. But Mr. Heathcote—will he not be disappointed?"

"No," replied the girl, dully. "I do not think he will care to talk to me this afternoon."

Jeanne-Armande said to herself that perhaps he would care to talk to some one else. But she made no comment.

The train moved on. An hour passed, and he did not appear. The Frenchwoman could not conceal her disappointment. "If he intended to leave the train at Centerville, I am surprised that he should not have returned to make us his farewells," she said, acidly.

"He is not always attentive to such things," said Anne.

"On the contrary. *I* have found him extremely attentive," retorted mademoiselle, veering again.

But at this stage Heathcote entered, and Anne's hope that he had left them was dashed to the ground. He noted the situation; and then he asked mademoiselle if she would not join him in the other seat for a while. The flattered Frenchwoman consented, and as he followed her he gave Anne a glance which said, "Check." And Anne felt that it was "check" indeed.

He had no intention of troubling her; he would give her time to grow tired.

But she was tired already.

At last, however, he did come. They were in plain sight now, people were sitting behind them; she could not childishly refuse to let him take the vacant place beside her. But at least, she thought, his words must be guarded, or people behind would make out what he said, even from the motion of his lips.

But Heathcote never cared for people.

"Dear," he said, bending toward her, "I am so glad to be with you again!" After all, he had managed to place himself so that by supporting his cheek with his hand, the people behind could not see his face at all, much less make out what he said.

Anne did not reply.

"Won't you even look at me? I must content myself, then, with your profile."

"You are ungenerous," she answered, in a tone as low as his own. "It will end in my feeling a contempt for you."

"And I—never felt so proud of myself in all my life before. For what am I doing? Throwing away all my fixed ideas of what life should be, for your sake, and glad to do it."

"Mr. Heathcote, will you never believe that I am in earnest?"

"I know very well that you are in earnest. But I shall be equally in earnest in breaking down the barriers between us. When that Western lover of yours is married to some one else, and Mrs. Lorrington likewise, *then* shall we not be free?"

"Helen will never marry any one else."

"Why do you not say that Mr. Pronando never will?"

"Because I am not sure," she answered, with sad humility.

"Are you going to tell him all that has happened?"

"Yes."

"And leave the decision to him?"

"Yes."

"You will put yourself in a false position, then. If you really intend to marry him, it would be safer to tell him nothing," said Heathcote, in an impartial tone. "No man likes to hear that sort of thing, even if his wife tells it herself. Though he may know she has loved some one else, he does not care to have it stated in words; he would rather leave it disembodied." Anne was looking at him; a sudden pain, which she did not have time to conceal, showed itself in her face as he spoke. "You darling child!" said Heathcote, laughing. "See how you look when I even *speak* of your marrying any one save me!"

She shrank back, feeling the justice of his inference. Her resolution remained unchanged; but she could not withstand entirely the personal power of his presence. She gazed at the afternoon sunshine striking the mountain-peaks, and asked herself how she could bear the long hours that still lay between her and the time of release—release from this narrow space where she must sit beside him, and feel the dangerous subtle influence of his voice and eyes. Then suddenly an idea came to her, like a door opening silently before a prisoner in a cell. She kept her face turned toward the window, while rapidly and with a beating heart she went over its possibilities. Yes, it could be done. It should be done. With inward excitement she tried to arrange the details.

Heathcote had fallen into silence; but he seemed quite content to sit there beside her without speaking. At last, having decided upon her course, and feeling nervously unable to endure his wordless presence longer, she began to talk of Caryl's, Miss Vanhorn, mademoiselle, the half-house—anything and everything which possessed no real importance, and did not bear upon the subject between them. He answered her in his brief fashion. If she wished to pad the dangerous edges of the day with a few safe conventionalities, he had no objection; women would be conventional on a raft in mid-ocean. The afternoon moved on toward sunset. He thought the contest was over, that although she might still make objection, at heart she had yielded; and he was not unwilling to rest. Why should they hurry? The whole of life was before them.

As night fell, they reached Stringhampton Junction, and the great engine stopped again. The passengers hastened hungrily into the little supper-room, and Heathcote urged mademoiselle to accompany him thither, and taste a cup of that compound found at railway stations called Japan tea. Jeanne-Armande looked half inclined to accept this invitation, but Anne, answering for both, said: "No; we have all we need in our basket. You can, however, if you will be so kind, send us some tea." This decision being in accordance with Jeanne-Armande's own rules, she did not like to contravene it, in spite of the satisfaction it would have given her to enter the supper-room with her decorous brown glove reposing upon such a coat sleeve. Heathcote bowed, and went out. Anne watched his figure entering the doorway of the brightly lighted supper-room, which was separated by a wide space from the waiting train. Then she turned.

"Mademoiselle," she said, her burning haste contrasting with her clear calm utterance of the moment before, "I beg you to leave this train with me without one instant's delay. The peace of my whole life depends upon it."

"What *can* you mean?" said the bewildered teacher.

"I can not explain now; I will, later. But if you have any regard for me, any compassion, come at once."

"But our bags, our—"

"I will take them all."

"And our trunks—they are checked through to Valley City. Will there be time to take them off?" said Jeanne-Armande, confusedly. Then, with more clearness, "But why should we go at all? I have no money to spend on freaks."

"This is Stringhampton Junction; we can cross here to the northern road, as you originally intended," explained Anne, rapidly. "All the additional expense I will pay. Dear mademoiselle, have pity on me, and come. Else I shall go alone."

The voice was eloquent; Jeanne-Armande rose. Anne hurried her through the almost empty car toward the rear door.

"But where *are* we going?"

"Out of the light," answered Anne.

They climbed down in the darkness on the other side of the train, and Anne led the way across the tracks at random, until they reached a safe country road-side beyond, and felt the soft grass under their feet.

"Where *are* we going?" said the Frenchwoman again, almost in tears. "Monsieur Heathcote—what will he think of us?"

"It is from him I am fleeing," replied Anne. "And now we must find the cross-road train. Do you know where it is?"

"It is, or should be, over there," said Jeanne-Armande, waving her umbrella tragically.

But she followed: the young girl had turned leader now.

They found the cross-road train, entered, and took their seats. And then Anne feverishly counted the seconds, expecting with each one to see Heathcote's face at the door. But the little branch train did not wait for supper; the few passengers were already in their places, and at last the bell rang, and the engine started northward, but so slowly that Anne found herself leaning forward, as though to hasten its speed. Then the wheels began to turn more rapidly—clank, clank, past the switches; rumble, rumble, over the bridge; by the dark line of the wood-pile; and then onward into the dark defiles of the mountains. They were away.

CHAPTER XXI.

"How heavy do I journey on the way

When what I seek, my weary travel's end,

Doth teach that ease and that repose to say,

'Thus far the miles are measured from my friend.'"

—*Shakspeare's Sonnets.*

In the mean time Ward Heathcote was in the supper-room. After selecting the best that the little country station afforded, and feeing a servant to take it across to the train, he sat down to eat a nondescript meal with some hunger.

The intelligent mulatto boy who carried the waiter consumed as many minutes as possible in his search for "the two ladies in that car, on the right-hand side opposite the fourth window," who, plainly, were not there. He had the fee in his pocket, there would not be another, and the two "suppers" were paid for. It was decidedly a case for delay. He waited, therefore, until the warning bell rang, and he was then encountered in hot haste hurrying to meet his patron, the waiter still balanced on his shoulder.

"No ladies there, sah. Looked everywhere fur 'em, sah."

There was no time for further parley. Heathcote hurried forward, and the train started. They must be there, of course; probably the cars had been changed or moved forward while the train was waiting. But although he went from end to end of the long file of carriages, he found no one. They were under full headway now; the great engine did not need gradual beginnings. He could not bring himself to ask questions of the passengers whose faces he remembered in the same car; they would open upon him a battery of curiosity in return. He went to the rear door, opened it, and looked out; the two grime-encircled eyes of a brakeman met his gravely. He stepped outside, closed the door, and entered into conversation with the eyes.

Yes, he seed two ladies get off; they come out this here end door, and climbed down on the wrong side. Seemed to be in a hurry. Didn't know where they went. Called after 'em that that warn't the way to the dining-room, and the young one said, "Thanks," but didn't say no more. Was they left behind? No, train didn't stop this side of Valley City; but the gentleman could telegraph back, and they could come on safe and sound in the morning express. 'Twarn't likely they'd gone north by the little branch road, was it? Branch connects at Stringhampton for the Northern Line.

But this suggestion made no impression upon Heathcote. Mademoiselle lived in Valley City; he had seen her tickets for Valley City. No, it was some unlooked-for mistake or accident. He gave the brakeman a dollar, and went back into the car. But everything was gone—bags, shawls, basket, cloak, bundle, and umbrella, all the miscellaneous possessions with which mademoiselle was accustomed to travel; there had been, then, deliberation enough to collect them all. He sat down perplexed, and gradually the certainty stole coldly over him that Anne had fled. It must be this.

For it was no freak of the Frenchwoman's; she had been too much pleased with his escort to forego it willingly. He was deeply hurt. And deeply surprised. Had he not followed her to ask her to be his wife? (This was not true, but for the moment he thought it was.) Was this a proper response?

Never before had he received such a rebuff, and after brooding over it an hour in the dismal car, it grew into an insult. His deeper feelings were aroused. Under his indolence he had a dominant pride, even arrogance of nature, which would have astonished many who thought they knew him. Whether his words had or had not been the result of impulse, now that they were spoken, they were worthy of at least respect. He grew more angry as the minutes passed, for he was so deeply hurt that he took refuge in anger. To be so thwarted and played upon— he, a man of the world—by a young girl; a young girl regarding whom, too, there had sprung up in his heart almost the only real faith of his life! He had believed in that face, had trusted those violet eyes, he did not know how unquestioningly until now. And then, feeling something very like moisture coming into his own eyes, he rose, angry over his weakness, went forward to the smoking car, lit a cigar, and savagely tried to think of other things. A pretty fool he was to be on a night train in the heart of Pennsylvania, going no one knew whither.

But, in spite of himself, his mind stole back to Anne. She was so different from the society women with whom he had always associated; she had so plainly loved him. Poor, remorseful, conscientious, struggling, faithful heart! Why had she fled from him? It did not occur to him that she was fleeing from herself.

He arrived at Valley City at eleven o'clock, and had the very room with gaudy carpet he had pictured to himself. The next morning, disgusted with everything and out of temper as he was, he yet so far postponed his return journey as to make inquiries concerning schools for girls—one in particular, in which a certain Mademoiselle Pitre had been teaching French and music for several years. The clerk thought it must be the "Young Ladies' Seminary." Heathcote took down the address of this establishment, ordered a carriage, and drove thither, inquiring at the door if Mademoiselle Pitre had arrived.

There was no such person there, the maid answered. No; he knew that she had not yet arrived. But when was she expected?

The maid (who admired the stranger) did not take it upon herself to deny his statement, but went away, and returned with the principal, Professor Adolphus Bittinger. Professor Bittinger was not acquainted with Mademoiselle Pitre. Their instructress in the French language was named Blanchard, and was already there. Heathcote then asked if there were any other young ladies' seminaries in Valley City, and was told (loftily) that there were not. No schools where French was taught? There might be, the professor thought, one or two small establishments for day scholars. The visitor wrote down the new addresses, and drove away to visit four day schools in succession, sending a ripple of curiosity down the benches, and exciting a flutter in the breasts of four French teachers, who came in person to answer the inquiries of monsieur. One of them, a veteran in the profession, who had spent her life in asking about the loaf made by the distant one-eyed relative of the baker, answered decidedly that there was no such person in Valley City. "Monsieur" was beginning to think so himself; but having now the fancy to exhaust all the possibilities, he visited the infant schools, and a private class, and at two o'clock returned to the hotel, having seen altogether about five hundred young Americans in frocks, from five years old to seventeen.

According to the statement of the little shop-keeper at Lancaster, mademoiselle had been teaching in Valley City for a number of years: there remained, then, the chance that she was in a private family as governess. Heathcote lingered in Valley City three days longer on this governess chance. He ate three more dinners in the comfortless dining-room, slept three more nights in the gaudy bedroom, and was at the railway station five times each day, to wit, at the hours when the trains arrived from the east. If they had waited at Stringhampton until he had had time to return to New York, they would be coming on now. But no one came. The fourth day opened with dull gray rain; the smoke of the manufactories hung over the valley like a pall. In the dining-room there was a sour odor of fresh paint, and from the window he could see only a line of hacks, the horses standing in the rain with drooping heads, while the drivers, in a row against an opposite wall, looked, in their long oil-skin coats, as though they were drawn up there in their black shrouds to be shot. In a fit of utter disgust he rang for his bill, ordered a carriage, and drove to the station: he would take the morning train for New York.

Yet when the carriage was dismissed, he let the express roll away without him, while he walked to and fro, waiting for an incoming train. The train was behind time; when it did come, there was no one among its passengers whom he had ever seen before. With an anathema upon his own folly, he took the day accommodation eastward. He would return to New York without any more senseless delays. And then at Stringhampton Junction he was the only person who alighted. His idea was to make inquiries there. He spent two hours of that afternoon in the rain, under a borrowed umbrella, and three alone in the waiting-room. No such persons as he described had been seen at Stringhampton, and as the settlement was small, and possessed of active curiosity, there remained no room for doubt. There was the chance that they had followed him to Valley City an hour later on a freight train with car attached, in which case he had missed them. And there was the other chance that they had gone northward by the branch road. But why should they go northward? They lived in Valley City, or near there; their tickets were marked "Valley City." The branch led to the Northern Line, by which one could reach Chicago, St. Louis, Omaha, the wilderness, but not Valley City. The gentleman might go up as far as the Northern Line, and inquire of the station agent there, suggested the Stringhampton ticket-seller, who balanced a wooden tooth-pick in his mouth lightly, like a cigarette. But the gentleman, who had already been looking up the narrow line of wet rails under his umbrella for an hour, regarded the speaker menacingly, and turned away with the ironical comment in his own mind that the Northern Line and its station agent might be—what amounted to Calvinized—before *he* sought them.

The night express came thundering along at midnight. It bore away the visitor. Stringhampton saw him no more.

In the mean time Anne and her companion had ridden on during the night, and the younger woman had explained to the elder as well as she could the cause of her sudden action. "It was not right that I should hear or that he should speak such words."

"He had but little time in which to speak them," said Jeanne-Armande, stiffly. "He spent most of the day with me. But, in any case, why run away? Why could you not have repelled him quietly, and with the proper dignity of a lady, and yet remained where you were, comfortably, and allowed me to remain as well?"

"I *could* not," said Anne. Then, after a moment, "Dear mademoiselle," she added, "do not ask me any more questions. I have done wrong, and I have been very, very unhappy. It is over now, and with your help I hope to have a long winter of quiet and patient labor. I am grateful to you; you do not know how grateful. Save those far away on the island, you seem to me now the only friend I have on earth." Her voice broke.

Jeanne-Armande's better feelings were touched. "My poor child!" she said, pityingly.

And then Anne laid her head down upon the Frenchwoman's shoulder, and sobbed as if her heart would break.

They reached Weston the next day. The journey was ended.

Mademoiselle selected new lodgings, in a quarter which overlooked the lake. She never occupied the same rooms two seasons in succession, lest she should be regarded as "an old friend," and expected to make concessions accordingly. On the second day she called ceremoniously upon the principal of the school, sending in her old-fashioned glazed card, with her name engraved upon it, together with a minute "Paris" in one corner. To this important personage she formally presented her candidate, endowing her with so large a variety of brilliant qualities and accomplishments that the candidate was filled with astonishment, and came near denying them, had she not been prevented by the silent meaning pressure of a gaiter that divined her intention, and forbade the revelation. Fortunately an under-teacher was needed, and half an hour later Anne went away, definitely, although at a very small salary, engaged.

She went directly home, locked her door, took paper and pen, and began to write. "Dear Rast," she wrote. Then, with a flood of remorseful affection, "Dear, dear Rast." Her letter was a long one, without break or hesitation. She told him all save names, and asked him to forgive her. If he still loved her and wished her to be his wife, she was ready; in truth, she seemed almost to urge the marriage, that is, if he still loved her. When the letter was completed she went out and placed it in a letter-box with her own hands, coming home with a conscience more free. She had done what she could. The letter was sent to the island, where Rast still was when she had heard from him the last time before leaving Caryl's; for only seven days had passed since then. They seemed seven years.

A day later she wrote to Miss Lois, telling of Miss Vanhorn's action, her new home and change of position. She said nothing of her letter to Rast or the story it told; she left that to him to relate or not as he pleased. In all things he should be now her master.

When this second letter was sent, she asked herself whether she could write to Helen. But instantly the feeling came surging over her that she could not. In addition there was the necessity of keeping her new abode hidden. No one knew were mademoiselle was, and the younger woman had now the benefit of that carefully woven mystery. She was safe. She must not disturb that safety.

To one other person she felt that she must write, namely, Miss Vanhorn. Harsh as had been the treatment she had received, it came from her mother's aunt. She wrote, therefore, briefly, stating that she had obtained a teacher's place, but without saying where it was. This letter, inclosed in another envelope, was sent to a friend of Jeanne-Armande in Boston, and mailed from that city. Anne had written that a letter sent to the Boston address, which she inclosed, would be immediately forwarded to her. But no reply came. Old Katharine never forgave.

The school opened; the young teacher had a class of new scholars. To her also were given the little brothers who were allowed to mingle with the flock until they reached the age of eleven, when they were banished to rougher trials elsewhere; to these little boys she taught Latin grammar, and the various pursuits in the imperfect tense of those two well-known grammar worthies, Caius and Balbus. Jeanne-Armande had not failed to proclaim far and wide her candidate's qualifications as to vocal music. "A pupil of Belzini," she remarked, with a stately air, "was not often to be obtained so far inland." The principal, a clear-headed Western woman, with a keen sense of humor, perceived at once (although smiling at it) the value of the phrase. It was soon in circulation. And it was understood that at Christmas-time the pupil of Belzini, who was not often to be obtained so far inland, would assume charge of the music class, and lift it to a plane of Italian perfection hitherto unattained.

The autumn opened. Anne, walking on the lake shore at sunset, saw the vessels steal out from port one by one, and opening white sails, glide away in the breeze of evening silently as spirits. Then came the colored leaves. The town, even in its meanest streets, was now so beautiful that the wonder was that the people did not leave their houses, and live out-of-doors altogether, merely to gaze; every leaf was a flower, and brighter than the brightest blossom. Then came a wild storm, tearing the splendor from the branches in a single night; in the morning, November rain was falling, and all was desolate and bare. But after this, the last respite, came Indian summer.

If there is a time when the American of to-day recalls the red-skinned men who preceded him in this land he now calls his own, it is during these few days of stillness and beauty which bear the name of the vanished race. Work is over in the fields, they are ready for their winter rest; the leaves are gone, the trees are ready too. The last red apple is gathered; men and the squirrels together have gleaned the last nut. There is nothing more to be done; and he who with a delicate imagination walks abroad, or drives slowly along country roads, finds himself thinking, in the stillness, of those who roved over this same ground not many years ago, and tardily gathering in at this season their small crops of corn beside the rivers, gave to the beautiful golden-purple-hued days the name they bear. Through the naked woods he sees them stealing, bow in hand; on the stream he sees their birch-bark canoes; the smoke in the atmosphere must surely rise from their hidden camp fires. They have come back to their old haunts from the happy hunting grounds for these few golden days. Is it not the Indian summer? The winter came early, with whirling snow followed by bitter cold. Ice formed; navigation was over until spring. Anne had heard from Dr. Gaston and Miss Lois, but not from Rast. For Rast had gone; he had started on his preliminary journey through the western country, where he proposed to engage in business enterprises, although their nature remained as yet vague. The chaplain wrote that a letter addressed to Erastus in her handwriting had been brought to him the day after the youth's departure, and that he had sent it to the frontier town which was to be his first stopping-place. Erastus had written to her the day before his departure, but the letter had of course gone to Caryl's. Miss Vanhorn, without doubt, would forward it to her niece. The old man wrote with an effort to appear cheerful, but he confessed that he missed his two children sadly. The boys were well, and Angélique was growing pretty. In another year it would be better that she should be with her sister; it was somewhat doubtful whether Miss Lois understood the child.

Miss Lois's letter was emphatic, beginning and ending with her opinion of Miss Vanhorn in the threefold character of grandaunt, Christian, and woman. She was able to let out her feelings at last, unhindered by the now-withdrawn allowance. The old bitter resentment against the woman who had slighted William Douglas found vent, and the characterization was withering and picturesque. When she had finished the arraignment, trial, and execution, at least in words, she turned at last to the children; and here it was evident that her pen paused and went more slowly. The boys, she hoped (rather as a last resort), were "good-hearted." She had but little trouble, comparatively, with Tita now; the child was very attentive to her lessons, and had been over to Père Michaux at his hermitage almost every other day. The boys went sometimes; and Erastus had been kind enough to accompany the children, to see that they were not drowned. And then, dropping the irksome theme, Miss Lois dipped her pen in romance, and filled the remainder of her letter with praise of golden-haired Rast, not so much because she herself loved him, as because Anne did. For the old maid believed with her whole heart in this young affection which had sprung into being under her fostering care, and looked forward to the day when the two should kneel together before Dr. Gaston in the little fort chapel, to receive the solemn benediction of the marriage service, as the happiest remaining in her life on earth. Anne read the fervid words with troubled heart. If Rast felt all that Miss Lois said he felt, if he had borne as impatiently as Miss Lois described their present partial separation, even when he was sure of her love, how would he suffer when he read her letter! She looked forward feverishly to the arrival of his answer; but none came. The delay was hard to bear.

Dr. Gaston wrote a second time. Rast had remained but a day at the first town, and not liking it, had gone forward. Not having heard from Anne, he sent, inclosed to the chaplain's care, a letter for her. With nervous haste she opened it; but it contained nothing save an account of his journey, with a description of the frontier village—"shanties, drinking saloons, tin cans, and a grave-yard already. This will never do for a home for us. I shall push on farther." The tone of the letter was affectionate, as sure as ever of her love. Rast had always been

138

sure of that. She read the pages sadly; it seemed as if she was willfully deceiving him. Where was her letter, the letter that told all? She wrote to the postmaster of the first town, requesting him to return it. After some delay, she received answer that it had been sent westward to another town, which the person addressed, namely, Erastus Pronando, had said should be his next stopping-place. But a second letter from Rast, sent also to the chaplain's care, had mentioned passing through that very town without stopping—"it was such an infernal den"; and again Anne wrote, addressing the second postmaster, and asking for the letter. This postmaster replied, after some tardiness, owing to his conflicting engagements as politician, hunter, and occasionally miner, that the letter described had been forwarded to the Dead-letter Office. This correspondence occupied October and November; and during this time Rast was still roaming through the West, writing frequently, but sending no permanent address. Now rumors of a silver mine attracted him; now it was a scheme for cattle-raising; now speculation in lands along the line of the coming railway It was impossible to follow him—and in truth he did not wish to be followed. He was tasting his first liberty. He meant to look around the world awhile before choosing his home: not long, only awhile. Still, awhile.

The chaplain added a few lines of his own when he sent these letters to Anne. Winter had seized them; they were now fast fettered; the mail came over the ice. Miss Lois was kind, and sometimes came up to regulate his housekeeping; but nothing went as formerly. His coffee was seldom good; and he found himself growing peevish—at least his present domestic, a worthy widow named McGlathery, had remarked upon it. But Anne must not think the domestic was in fault; he had reason to believe that she meant well even when she addressed him on the subject of his own short-comings. And here the chaplain's old humor peeped through, as he added, quaintly, that poor Mistress McGlathery's health was far from strong, she being subject to "inward tremblings," which tremblings she had several times described to him with tears in her eyes, while he had as often recommended peppermint and ginger, but without success; on the contrary, she always went away with a motion of the skirts and a manner as to closing the door which, the chaplain thought, betokened offense. Anne smiled over these letters, and then sighed. If she could only be with him again—with them all! She dreamed at night of the old man in his arm-chair, of Miss Lois, of the boys, of Tita curled in her furry corner, which she had transferred, in spite of Miss Lois's remonstrances, to the sitting-room of the church-house. Neither Tita nor Père Michaux had written; she wondered over their new silence.

Anne's pupils had, of course, exhaustively weighed and sifted the new teacher, and had decided to like her. Some of them decided to adore her, and expressed their adoration in bouquets, autograph albums, and various articles in card-board supposed to be of an ornamental nature. They watched her guardedly, and were jealous of every one to whom she spoke; she little knew what a net-work of plots, observation, mines and countermines, surrounded her as patiently she toiled through each long monotonous day. These adorations of school-girls, although but unconscious rehearsals of the future, are yet real while they last; Anne's adorers went sleepless if by chance she gave especial attention to any other pupil. The adored one meanwhile did not notice these little intensities; her mind was absorbed by other thoughts.

Four days before Christmas two letters came; one was her own to Rast, returned at last from the Dead-letter Office; the other was from Miss Lois, telling of the serious illness of Dr. Gaston. The old chaplain had had a stroke of paralysis, and Rast had been summoned; fortunately his last letter had been from St. Louis, to which place he had unexpectedly returned, and therefore they had been able to reach him by message to Chicago and a telegraphic dispatch. Dr. Gaston wished to see him; the youth had been his ward as well as almost child, and there were business matters to be arranged between them. Anne's tears fell as she read of her dear old teacher's danger, and the impulse came to her to go to him at once. Was she not his child as well as Rast? But the impulse was checked by the remainder of the letter. Miss Lois wrote, sadly, that she had tried to keep it from Anne, but had not succeeded: since August her small income had been much reduced, owing to the failure of a New Hampshire bank, and she now found that with all her effort they could not quite live on what was left. "Very nearly, dear child. I think, with *thirty* dollars, I can manage until spring. Then everything will be *cheaper*. I should not have kept it from you if it had not happened at the *very time* of your trouble with that *wicked old woman*, and I did not wish to add to your care. But the boys have what is called *fine* appetites (I wish they were not quite so 'fine'), and of course *this* winter, and never before, my provisions were spoiled in my own cellar."

Anne had intended to send to Miss Lois all her small savings on Christmas-day. She now went to the principal of the school, asked that the payment of her salary might be advanced, and forwarded all she was able to send to the poverty-stricken little household in the church-house. That night she wept bitter tears; the old chaplain was dying, and she could not go to him; the children were perhaps suffering. For the first time in a life of poverty she felt its iron hand crushing her down. Her letter to Rast lay before her; she could not send it now and disturb the last hours on earth of their dear old friend. She laid it aside and waited—waited through those long hours of dreary suspense which those must bear who are distant from the dying beds of their loved ones.

In the mean time Rast had arrived. Miss Lois wrote of the chaplain's joy at seeing him. The next letter contained the tidings that death had come; early in the morning, peacefully, with scarcely a sigh, the old man's soul had passed from earth. Colonel Bryden, coming in soon afterward, and looking upon the calm face, had said, gently,

"Then steal away, give little warning,

Choose thine own time;

Say not good-night, but, in some brighter
clime,

Bid me good-morning."

When Anne knew that the funeral was over, that another grave had been made under the snow in the little military cemetery, and that, with the strange swiftness which is so hard for mourning hearts to realize, daily life was moving on again in the small island circle where the kind old face would be seen no more, she sent her letter, the same old letter, unaltered and travel-worn. Then she waited. She could not receive her answer before the eighth or ninth day. But on the fifth came two letters; on the seventh, three. The first were from Miss Lois and Mrs. Bryden; the others from Tita, Père Michaux, and—Rast. And the extraordinary tidings they brought were these: Rast had married Tita. The little sister was now his wife.

CHAPTER XXII.

"A slave had long worn a chain upon his ankle. By the order of his master it was removed. 'Why dost thou spring aloft and sing, O slave? Surely the sun is as fierce and thy burden as heavy as before.' The slave replied: 'Ten times the sun and the burden would seem light, now that the chain is removed.'"—*From the Arabic.*

Miss Lois's letter was a wail:

"My poor dear outraged Child,—What *can* I say to you? There is no use in trying to *prepare* you for it, since you would never *conceive* such *double-dyed* blackness of heart! Tita has *run away*. She slipped off clandestinely, and they think she has followed *Rast*, who left yesterday on his way back to St. Louis and the West. Père Michaux has followed *her*, saying that if he found them together he should, acting as Tita's guardian, insist upon a *marriage* before he returned! He feels himself responsible for *Tita*, he says, and paid no attention when I asked him if no one was to be responsible for *you*! My poor child, it seems that I have been blind all along; I never *dreamed* of what was going on. The little minx deceived me completely. I thought her so much improved, so studious, while all the time she was meeting Erastus, or planning to meet him, with a skill far beyond *my* comprehension. All last summer, they tell me, she was with him constantly; those daily journeys to Père Michaux's island were for that purpose, while I supposed they were for prayers. What *Erastus* thought or meant, no one seems to know; but they all combined in declaring that the child (child no longer!) was deeply in love with him, and that everybody saw it save *me*. My New England blood could not, I am proud to say, grasp it! You know, my poor darling, the opinion I have *always* had concerning Tita's mother, who slyly and artfully inveigled your honored father into a *trap*. Tita has therefore but followed in her mother's footsteps.

"That Erastus has ever *cared*, or cares now in the least, for her, save as a plaything, I will *never* believe. But Père Michaux is like a *mule* for stubbornness, as you know, and I fear he will marry them in *any* case. He did not seem to think of *you* at all, and when I said, 'Anne will *die* of grief!' he only smiled—yes, *smiled*—and Frenchly shrugged his shoulders! My poor child, I have but little hope, because if he appeals to Erastus's *honor*, what can the boy do? He is the soul of honor.

"I can hardly write, my brain has been so overturned. To think that *Tita* should have outwitted us all at her age, and gained her point over everything, over you and over Rast—poor, poor Rast, who will be so *miserably* sacrificed! I will write again to-morrow; but if Père Michaux carries out his strange *Jesuitical* design, you will hear from him probably before you can hear again from me. Bear up, my dearest Anne. I acknowledge that, so far, I have found it difficult to see the Divine purpose in this, unless indeed it be to inform us that we are all but cinders and ashes; which, however, I for one have long known."

Mrs. Bryden's letter:

"Dear Anne,—I feel drawn toward you more closely since the illness and death of our dear Dr. Gaston, who loved you so tenderly, and talked so much of you during his last days with us. It is but a short time since I wrote to you, giving some of the messages he left, and telling of his peaceful departure; but now I feel that I must write again upon a subject which is painful, yet one upon which you should have, I think, all the correct details immediately. Miss Hinsdale is no doubt writing to you also; but she does not know all. She has not perceived, as we have, the gradual approaches to this catastrophe—I can call it by no other name.

"When you went away, your half-sister was a child. With what has seemed lightning rapidity she has grown to womanhood, and for months it has been plainly evident that she was striving in every way to gain and hold the attention of Erastus Pronando. He lingered here almost all summer, as you will remember; Tita followed him everywhere. Miss Hinsdale, absorbed in the cares of housekeeping, knew nothing of it; but daily, on one pretext or another, they were together. Whether Erastus was interested I have no means of knowing; but that Tita is now extremely pretty in a certain style, and that she was absorbed in him, we could all see. It was not our affair; yet we might have felt called upon to make it ours if it had not been for Père Michaux. He was her constant guardian.

"Erastus went away yesterday in advance of the mail-train. He bade us all good-by, and I am positive that he had no plan, not even a suspicion of what was to follow. We have a new mail-carrier this winter, Denis being confined to his cabin with rheumatism. Tita must have slipped away unperceived, and joined this man at dusk on the ice a mile or two below the island; her track was found this morning. Erastus expected to join the mail-train to-day, and she knew it, of course; the probability is, therefore, that they are now together. It seems hardly credible that so young a head could have arranged its plans so deftly; yet it is certainly true that, even if Rast wished to bring her back, he could not do so immediately, not until the up-train passed them. Père Michaux started after them this morning, travelling in his own sledge. He thinks (it is better that you should know it, Anne) that Erastus *is* fond of Tita, and that only his engagement to you has held him back. Now that the step has been taken, he has no real doubt but that Rast himself will wish to marry her, and without delay.

"All this will seem very strange to you, my dear child; but I trust it will not be so hard a blow as Miss Hinsdale apprehends. Père Michaux told me this morning in so many words: 'Anne has never loved the boy with anything more than the affection of childhood. It will be for her a release.' He was convinced of this, and went off on his journey with what looked very much like gladness. I hope, with all my heart, that he is right." Then, with a few more words of kindly friendship, the letter ended.

The other envelope bore the rude pen-and-ink postmark of a Northwestern lumber settlement, where travellers coming down, from the North in the winter over the ice and snow met the pioneer railway, which had pushed its track to that point before the blockade of the cold began.

Tita's letter:

"Deerest Sister,—You will not I am sure blaime your little Tita for following the impulse of her *hart*. Since you were hear I have grown up and it is the truth that Rast has loved me for *yeers* of his own accord and because he could not help it—deerest sister who can. But he never ment to break his word to you and he tryed not to but was devowered by his love for me and you will forgive him deerest sister will you not since there is no more hope for you as we were married by Père Michaux an hour ago who approved of all and has hartily given us his bennydiction. Since my spiritual directeur has no reproche you will not have enny I am sure and remain your loving sister,

Angélique Pronando."

"P. S. We go to Chicago to-day. Enny money for *close* for me could be sent to the Illinois Hotel, where my deerest husband says we are to stay.

A. P."

Père Michaux's letter:

"Dear Anne,—It is not often that I speak so bluntly as I shall speak now. In marrying, this morning, your half-sister Angélique to Erastus Pronando I feel that I have done you a great service. You did not love him with the real love of a nature like yours—the love that will certainly come to you some day; perhaps has already come. I have always known this, and, in accordance with it, did all I could to prevent the engagement originally. I failed; but this day's work has made up for the failure.

"Angélique has grown into a woman. She is also very beautiful, after a peculiar fashion of her own. All the strength of her nature, such as it is, is concentrated upon the young man who is now her husband. From childhood she has loved him; she was bitterly jealous of you even before you went away. I have been aware of this, but until lately I was not sure of Rast. Her increasing beauty, however, added to her intense absorbed interest in him, has conquered. Seeing this, I have watched with satisfaction the events of the past summer, and have even assisted somewhat (and with a clear conscience) in their development.

"Erastus, even if you had loved him, Anne, could not have made you happy. And neither would you have made him happy; for he is quick-witted, and he would have inevitably, and in spite of all your tender humility, my child, discovered your intellectual superiority, and in time would have angrily resented it. For he is vain; his nature is light; he needs adulation in order to feel contented. On the other hand, he is kind-hearted and affectionate, and to Tita will be a demi-god always. The faults that would have been death to you, she will never see. She is therefore the fit wife for him.

"You will ask, Does he love her? I answer, Yes. When he came back to the island, and found her so different, the same elfish little creature, but now strangely pretty, openly fond of him, following him everywhere, with the words of a child but the eyes of a woman, he was at first surprised, then annoyed, then amused, interested, and finally fascinated. He struggled against it. I give him the due of justice—he did struggle. But Tita was always *there*. He went away hurriedly at the last, and if it had not been for Dr. Gaston's illness and his own recall to the island, it might not have gone farther. Tita understood this as well as I did; she made the most of her time. Still, I am quite sure that he had no suspicion she intended to follow him; the plan was all her own. She did follow him. And I followed her. I caught up with them that very day at sunset, and an hour ago I married them. If you have not already forgiven me, Anne, you will do so some day. I have no fear. I can wait. I shall go on with them as far as Chicago, and then, after a day or two, I shall return to the island. Do not be disturbed by anything Miss Lois may write. She has been blindly mistaken from the beginning. In truth, there is a vein of obstinate weakness on some subjects in that otherwise estimable woman, for which I have always been at a loss to account."

Ah, wise old priest, there are some things too deep for even you to know!

Rast's letter was short. It touched Anne more than any of the others:

"What must you think of me, Annet? Forgive me, and forget me. I *did* try. But would you have cared for a man who had to try? When I think of you I scorn myself. But she is the sweetest, dearest, most winning little creature the world ever saw; and my only excuse is that—I love her.

E. P."

These few lines, in which the young husband made out no case for himself, sought no shield in the little bride's own rashness, but simply avowed his love, and took all the responsibility upon himself, pleased the elder sister. It was manly. She was glad that Tita had a defender.

She had read these last letters standing in the centre of her room, Jeanne-Armande anxiously watching her from the open door. The Frenchwoman had poured out a glass of water, and had it in readiness: she thought that perhaps Anne was going to faint. With no distinct idea of what had happened, she had lived in a riot of conjecture for two days.

But instead of fainting, Anne, holding the letters in her hand, turned and looked at her.

"Well, dear, will you go to bed?" she said, solicitously.

"Why should I go to bed?"

"I thought perhaps you had heard—had heard bad news."

"On the contrary," replied Anne, slowly and gravely, "I am afraid, mademoiselle, that the news is good—even very good."

For her heart had flown out of its cage and upward as a freed bird darts up in the sky. The bond, on her side at least, was gone; she was free. *Now* she would live a life of self-abnegation and labor, but without inward thralldom. Women had lived such lives before she was born, women would live such lives after she was dead. She would be one of the sisterhood, and coveting nothing of the actual joy of love, she would cherish only the ideal, an altar-light within, burning forever. The cares of each day were as nothing now: she was free, free!

In her exaltation she did not recognize as wrong the opposite course she had intended to follow before the lightning fell, namely, uniting herself to one man while so deeply loving another. She was of so humble and unconscious a spirit regarding herself that it had not seemed to her that the inner feelings of her heart would be of consequence to Rast, so long as she was the obedient, devoted, faithful wife she was determined with all her soul to be. For she had not that imaginative egotism which so many women possess, which makes them spend their lives in illusion, weaving round their every thought and word an importance which no one else can discern. According to these women, there are a thousand innocent acts which "he" (lover or husband) "would not for an instant allow," although to the world at large "he" appears indifferent enough. They go through long turmoil, from which they emerge triumphantly, founded upon some hidden jealousy which "he" is supposed to feel, so well hidden generally, and so entirely supposed, that persons with less imagination never observe it. But after all, smile as we may, it is only those who are in most respects happy and fortunate wives who can so entertain themselves. For cold unkindness, or a harsh and brutal word, will rend this filmy fabric of imagination immediately, never to be rewoven again.

Anne wrote to Rast, repeating the contents of the old letter, which had been doomed never to reach him. She asked him to return the wanderer unopened when it was forwarded to him from the island; there was a depth of feeling in it which it was not necessary now that he should see. She told him that her own avowal should lift from him all the weight of wrong-doing; she had first gone astray. "We were always like brother and sister, Rast; I see it now. It is far better as it is."

A few days later Père Michaux wrote again, and inclosed a picture of Tita. The elder sister gazed at it curiously. This was not Tita; and yet those were her eyes, and that the old well-remembered mutinous expression still lurking about the little mouth. Puzzled, she took it to mademoiselle. "It is my little sister," she said. "Do you think it pretty?"

Jeanne-Armande put on her spectacles, and held it frowningly at different distances from her eyes.

"It is odd," she said at last. "Ye—es, it is pretty too. But, for a child's face, remarkable."

"She is not a child."

"Not a child?"

"No; she is married," replied Anne, smiling.

Mademoiselle pursed up her lips, and examined the picture with one eye closed. "After all," she said, "I can believe it. The *eyes* are mature."

The little bride was represented standing; she leaned against a pillar nonchalantly, and outlined on a light background, the extreme smallness of her figure was clearly shown. Her eyes were half veiled by their large drooping lids and long lashes; her little oval face looked small, like that of a child. Her dress was long, and swept over the floor with the richness of silk: evidently Père Michaux had not stinted the lavish little hands when they made their first purchase of a full-grown woman's attire. For the priest had taken upon himself this outlay; the "money for close," of which Tita had written, was provided from his purse. He wrote to Anne that as he was partly responsible for the wedding, he was also responsible for the trousseau; and he returned the money which with great difficulty the elder sister had sent.

"She must be very small," said mademoiselle, musingly, as they still studied the picture.

"She is; she has the most slender little face I ever saw."

Tita's head was thrown back as she leaned against the pillar; there was a half-smile on her delicate lips; her thick hair was still braided childishly in two long braids which hung over her shoulders and down on the silken skirt behind; in her small ears were odd long hoops of gold, which Père Michaux had given her, selecting them himself on account of their adaptation to her half-Oriental, half-elfin beauty. Her cheeks showed no color; there were brown shadows under her eyes. On her slender brown hand shone the wedding ring. The picture was well executed, and had been carefully tinted under Père Michaux's eye: the old priest knew that it was Rast's best excuse.

Now that Anne was freed, he felt no animosity toward the young husband; on the contrary, he wished to advance his interests in every way that he could. Tita was a selfish little creature, yet she adored her husband. She would have killed herself for him at any moment. But first she would have killed him.

He saw them start for the far West, and then he returned northward to his island home. Miss Lois, disheartened by all that had happened, busied herself in taking care of the boys dumbly, and often shook her head at the fire when sitting alone with her knitting. She never opened the old piano now, and she was less stringent with her Indian servants; she would even have given up quietly her perennial alphabet teaching if Père Michaux had not discovered the intention, and quizzically approved it, whereat, of course, she was obliged to go on. In truth, the old man did this purposely, having noticed the change in his old antagonist. He fell into the habit of coming to the church-house more frequently—to teach the boys, he said. He did teach the little rascals, and taught them well, but he also talked to Miss Lois. The original founders of the church-house would have been well astonished could they have risen from their graves and beheld the old priest and the New England woman sitting on opposite sides of the fire in the neat shining room, which still retained its Puritan air in spite of years, the boys, and Episcopal apostasy.

Regarding Rast's conduct, Miss Lois maintained a grim silence. The foundations of her faith in life had been shaken; but how could she, supposed to be a sternly practical person, confess it to the world—confess that she had dreamed like a girl over this broken betrothal?

"Do you not see how much happier, freer, she is?" the priest would say, after reading one of Anne's letters. "The very tone betrays it."

Miss Lois sighed deeply, and poked the fire.

"Pooh! pooh! Do you want her to be *un*happy?" said the old man. "Suppose that it had been the other way? Why not rejoice as I do over her cheerfulness?"

"Why not indeed?" thought Miss Lois. But that stubborn old heart of hers would not let her.

The priest had sent to her also one of the pictures of Tita. One day, after his return, he asked for it. She answered that it was gone.

"Where?"

"Into the fire."

"She cannot forgive," he thought, glancing cautiously at the set face opposite.

But it was not Tita whom she could not forgive; it was the young mother, dead long years before.

The winter moved on. Anne had taken off her engagement ring, and now wore in its place a ring given by her school-girl adorers, who had requested permission in a formal note to present one to their goddess. As she had refused gems, they had selected the most costly plain gold circlet they could find in Weston, spending a long and happy Saturday in the quest. "But it is a wedding ring," said the jeweller.

But why should brides have all the heavy gold? the school-girls wished to know. Other persons could wear plain gold rings also if they pleased.

So they bought the circlet and presented it to Anne with beating hearts and cheeks flushed with pleasure, humbly requesting in return, for each a lock of her hair. Then ensued a second purchase of lockets for this hair: it was well that their extravagant little purses were well filled.

To the school-girls the ring meant one thing, to Anne another; she mentally made it a token of the life she intended to lead. Free herself, he was not free; Helen loved him. Probably, also, he had already forgotten his fancy for the lonely girl whom he had seen during those few weeks at Caryl's. She would live her life out as faithfully as she could, thankful above all things for her freedom. Surely strength would be given her to do this. The ring was like the marriage ring of a nun, the token of a vow of patience and humility. During all these long months she had known no more, heard no more, of her companions of that summer than as though they had never existed. The newspapers of Weston and the country at large were not concerned about the opinions and movements of the unimportant little circle left behind at Caryl's. Their columns had contained burning words; but they were words relating to the great questions which were agitating the land from the Penobscot to the Rio Grande. Once, in a stray number of the *Home Journal*, she found the following paragraph: "Miss Katharine Vanhorn is in Italy at present. It is understood that Miss Vanhorn contemplates an extended tour, and will not return to this country for several years. Her Hudson River residence and her house in the city are both closed." Anne no longer hoped for any softening of that hard nature; yet the chance lines hurt her, and gave her a forsaken feeling all day.

CHAPTER XXIII.

"War! war! war!

A thunder-cloud in the south in the early

spring—

The launch of a thunder-bolt; and then,

With one red flare, the lightning stretched its

wing,

And a rolling echo roused a million men."

—Edmund Clarence Stedman.

April. The sound of military music; the sound of feet keeping step exactly, and overcoming by its regularity the noise of thousands of other feet hurrying on irregularly in front of them, abreast of them, and behind them. A crowd in the square so dense that no one could pass through; the tree branches above black with boys; the windows all round the four sides filled with heads. And everywhere women pressing forward, waving handkerchiefs, some pallid, some flushed, but all deeply excited, forgetful of self, with eyes fixed on the small compact lines of military caps close together, moving steadily onward in the midst of the accompanying throng. And happy the one who had a place in the front rank: how she gazed! If a girl, no matter how light of heart and frivolous, a silence and soberness came over her for a moment, and her eyes grew wistful. If a woman, one who had loved, no matter how hard and cold she had grown, a warmer heart came back to her then, and tears rose. What was it? Only a few men dressed in the holiday uniform these towns-people had often seen; men many of whom they knew well, together with their shortcomings and weaknesses, whose military airs they had laughed at; men who, taken singly, had neither importance nor interest. What was it, then, that made the women's eyes tearful, and sent the great crowd thronging round and after them as though each one had been crowned king? What made the groups on the steps and piazzas of each house keep silence after they had passed, and watch them as long as they could distinguish the moving lines? It was that these men had made the first reply of this town to the President's call. It was because these holiday soldiers were on their way to real battle-fields, where balls would plough through human flesh, and leave agony and death behind. The poorest, dullest, soldier who was in these ranks from a sense of loyalty, however dim and inarticulate it might be, gave all he had: martyr or saint never gave more. Not many of the gazing people thought of this; but they did think of death by bayonet and ball as the holiday ranks marched by.

Down through the main street went the little troop, and the crowd made a solid wall on the sidewalk, and a moving guard before and behind. From the high windows above, the handkerchiefs of the work-girls fluttered, while underneath from the law offices, and below from the door-ways, men looked out soberly, realizing that this meant War indeed—real and near War.

By another way, down the hill toward the railway-station, rattled the wheels of an artillery company; also a little holiday troop, with holiday guns shining brightly. The men sat in their places with folded arms; the crowd, seeing them, knew them all. They were only Miller, and Sieberling, and Wagner, and others as familiar; six months ago—a month ago—they would have laughed inexhaustibly at the idea of calling Tom Miller a hero, or elevating Fritz Wagner to any other pedestal than the top of a beer barrel. But now, as they saw them, they gave a mighty cheer, which rang through the air splendidly, and raised a hue of pride upon the faces of the artillerymen, and perhaps the first feeling in some of their hearts higher than the determination not to "back out," which had been until then their actuating motive. The two shining little guns rattled down the hill; the infantry company marched down behind them. The line of cars, with locomotive attached, was in waiting, and, breaking ranks, helter-skelter, in any way and every way, hindered by hand-shaking, by all sorts of incongruous parting gifts thrust upon them at the last moment by people they never saw before, blessed by excited, tearful women, made heart-sick themselves by the sight of the grief of their mothers and wives, the soldiers took their places in the cars, and the train moved out from the station, followed by a long cheer, taken up and repeated again and again, until nothing but a dark speck on the straight track remained for the shouters to look at, when they stopped suddenly, hoarse and tired, and went silently homeward, pondering upon this new thing which had come into their lives. The petty cares of the day were forgotten. "War is hideous; but it banishes littleness from daily life."

Anne, brought up as she had been in a remote little community, isolated and half foreign, was in a measure ignorant of the causes and questions of the great struggle which began in America in April, 1861. Not hers the prayerful ardor of the New England girl who that day willingly gave her lover, saw him brought home later dead, buried him, and lived on, because she believed that he had died to free his brother man, as Christ had died for her. Not hers the proud loyalty of the Southern girl to her blood and to her State, when that day she bade her lover go forth and sweep their fanatical assailants back, as the old Cavaliers, from whom they were descended, swept back the crop-eared Puritans into the sea.

Jeanne-Armande was not especially stirred; save by impatience—impatience over this interference with the prosperity of the country. It might injure property (the half-house), and break up music classes and schools! What sympathy she felt, too, was with the South; but she was wise enough to conceal this from all save Anne, since the school was burning with zeal, and the principal already engaged in teaching the pupils to make lint. But if Jeanne-Armande was lukewarm, Miss Lois was at fever heat; the old New England spirit rose within her like a giant when she read the tidings. Far away as she was from all the influences of the time, she yet wrote long letters to Anne which sounded like the clash of spears, the call of the trumpet, and the roll of drums, so fervid were the sentences which fell of themselves into the warlike phraseology of the Old Testament, learned by heart in her youth. But duty, as well as charity, begins at home, and even the most burning zeal must give way before the daily needs of children. Little André was not strong; his spine was becoming curved, they feared. In his languor he had fallen into the habit of asking Miss Lois to hold him in her arms, rock with him in the old rocking-chair, and sing. Miss Lois had not thought that she could ever love "those children"; but there was a soft spot in her heart now for little André.

In June two unexpected changes came. Little André grew suddenly worse; and Jeanne-Armande went to Europe. A rich merchant of Weston, wishing to take his family abroad, engaged mademoiselle as governess for his two daughters, and French speaker for the party, at what she herself termed "the salary of a princess." The two announcements came on the same day. Jeanne-Armande, excited and tremulous, covered a sheet of paper with figures to show to herself and Anne the amount of the expected gain. As she could not retain her place in the school without the magic power of being in two places at once, the next best course was to obtain it for Anne, with the understanding that the successor was to relinquish it immediately whenever called upon to do so. As they were in the middle of a term, the principal accepted Miss Douglas, who, although young, had proved herself competent and faithful. And thus Anne found herself unexpectedly possessed of a higher salary, heavier duties, and alone. For Jeanne-Armande, in the helmet bonnet, sailed on the twentieth of the month for England, in company with her charges, who, with all their beauty and bird-like activity, would find it impossible to elude mademoiselle, who would guard them with unflinching vigilance, and, it is but fair to add, would earn every cent of even that "salary of a princess" (whatever that may be) which had attracted her.

Before mademoiselle departed it had been decided that in consequence of little André's illness Miss Lois should close the church-house, and take the child to the hot springs not far distant, in Michigan, and that Louis and Gabriel should come to their elder sister for a time. The boys were to travel to Weston alone, Père Michaux putting them in charge of the captain of the steamer, while Anne was to meet them upon their arrival. Miss Lois wrote that they were wild with excitement, and had begged all sorts of farewell presents from everybody, and packed them in the two chests which Père Michaux had given them—knives, cord, hammers, nails, the last being "a box-stove, old and rusty, which they had actually taken to pieces and hidden among their clothes." Jeanne-Armande went away on Monday; the boys were to arrive on Saturday. Anne spent all her leisure time in preparing for them. Two of the little black-eyed fellows were coming at last, the children who had clung to her skirts, called her "Annet," and now and then, when they felt like it, swarmed up all together to kiss her, like so many affectionate young bears. They were very dear to her—part of her childhood and of the island. The day arrived; full of expectation, she went down to meet the steamer. Slowly the long narrow craft threaded its way up the crooked river; the great ropes were made fast, the plank laid in place; out poured the passengers, men, women, and children, but no Louis, no Gabriel. Anne watched until the last man had passed, and the deck hands were beginning to roll out the freight; then a voice spoke above, "Is that Miss Douglas?"

She looked up, and saw the captain, who asked her to come on board for a moment. "I am very much troubled, Miss Douglas," he began, wiping his red but friendly face. "The two boys—your half-brothers, I believe—placed in my care by Père Michaux, have run away."

Anne gazed at him in silence.

"They must have slipped off the boat at Hennepin, which is the first point where we strike a railroad. It seems to have been a plan, too, for they managed to have their chests put off also."

"You have no idea where they have gone?"

"No; I sent letters back to Hennepin and to Père Michaux immediately, making inquiries. The only clew I have is that they asked a number of questions about the plains of one of our hands, who has been out that way."

"The plains!"

"Yes; they said they had a sister living out there."

A pain darted through Anne's heart. Could they have deserted her for Tita? She went home desolate and disheartened; the empty rooms, where all her loving preparations were useless now, seemed to watch her satirically. Even the boys did not care enough for her to think of her pain and disappointment.

Père Michaux had had no suspicion of the plan: but he knew of one dark fact which might have, he wrote to Anne, a bearing upon it. Miss Lois had mysteriously lost, in spite of all her care, a sum of money, upon which she had depended for a part of the summer's expenses, and concerning which she had made great lamentation; it had been made up by the renting of the church-house; but the mystery remained. If the boys had taken it, bad as the action was, it insured for a time at least their safety. The priest thought they had started westward to join Rast and Tita, having been fascinated by what they had overheard of Rast's letters.

The surmise was correct. After what seemed to Anne very long delay, a letter came; it was from Rast. The night before, two dirty little tramps, tired and hungry, with clothes soiled and torn, had opened the door and walked in, announcing that they were Louis and Gabriel, and that they meant to stay. They had asked for food, but had fallen asleep almost before they could eat it. With their first breath that morning they had again declared that nothing should induce them to return eastward, either to the island or to Anne. And Rast added that he thought they might as well remain; he and Tita would take charge of them. After a few days came a letter from the boys themselves, printed by Louis. In this document, brief but explicit, they sent their love, but declined to return. If Père Michaux came after them, they would run away again, and *this* time no one should ever know where they were, "exsep, purhaps, the *Mormons*." With this dark threat the letter ended.

Père Michaux, as in the case of Tita, took the matter into his own hands. He wrote to Rast to keep the boys, and find some regular occupation for them as soon as possible. Anne's ideas about them had always been rather Quixotic; he doubted whether they could ever have been induced to attend school regularly. But now they would grow to manhood in a region where such natural gifts as they possessed would be an advantage to them, and where, also, their deficiencies would not be especially apparent. The old priest rather enjoyed this escapade. He considered that three of the Douglas children were now, on the whole, well placed, and that Anne was freed from the hampering responsibility which her father's ill-advised course had imposed upon her. He sailed round his water parish with brisker zeal than ever, although in truth he was very lonely. The little white fort was empty; even Miss Lois was gone; but he kept himself busy, and read his old classics on stormy evenings when the rain poured down on his low roof.

But Anne grieved.

As several of her pupils wished to continue their music lessons during the vacation, it was decided by Miss Lois and herself that she should remain where she was for the present; the only cheer she had was in the hope that in autumn Miss Lois and the little boy would come to her. But in spite of all her efforts, the long weeks of summer stretched before her like a desert; in her lonely rooms without the boys, without mademoiselle, she was pursued by a silent depression unlike anything she had felt before. She fell into the habit of allowing herself to sit alone in the darkness through the evening brooding upon the past. The kind-hearted woman who kept the house, in whose charge she had been left by mademoiselle, said that she was "homesick."

"How can one be homesick who has no home?" answered the girl, smiling sadly.

One day the principal of the school asked her if she would go on Saturdays for a while, and assist those who were at work in the Aid Rooms for the soldiers' hospitals. Anne consented languidly; but once within the dingy walls, languor vanished. There personal sorrow seemed small in the presence of ghastly lists of articles required for the wounded and dying. At least those she loved were not confronting cannon. Those in charge of the rooms soon learned to expect her, this young teacher, a stranger in Weston, who with a settled look of sadness on her fair face had become the most diligent worker there. She came more regularly after a time, for the school had closed, the long vacation begun.

On Sunday, the 21st of July, Anne was in church; it was a warm day; fans waved, soft air came in and played around the heads of the people, who, indolent with summer ease, leaned back comfortably, and listened with drowsy peacefulness to the peaceful sermon. At that very moment, on a little mill-stream near Washington, men were desperately fighting the first great battle of the war, the Sunday battle of Bull Run. The remnant of the Northern army poured over Long Bridge into the capital during all that night, a routed, panic-stricken mob.

The North had suffered a great defeat; the South had gained a great victory. And both sides paused.

The news flashed over the wires and into Weston, and the town was appalled. Never in the four long years that followed was there again a day so filled with stern astonishment to the entire North as that Monday after Bull Run. The Aid Rooms, where Anne worked during her leisure hours, were filled with helpers now; all hearts were excited and in earnest. West Virginia was the field to which their aid was sent, a mountain region whose streams were raised in an hour into torrents, and whose roads were often long sloughs of despond, through which the soldiers of each side gloomily pursued each other by turns, the slowness of the advancing force only equalled by that of the pursued, which was encountering in front the same disheartening difficulties. The men in hospital on the edges of this region, worn out with wearying marches, wounded in skirmishes, stricken down by the insidious fever which haunts the river valleys, suffered as much as those who had the names of great battles wherewith to identify themselves; but they lacked the glory.

One sultry evening, when the day's various labor was ended, Anne, having made a pretense of eating in her lonely room, went across to the bank of the lake to watch the sun set in the hazy blue water, and look northward toward the island. She was weary and sad: where were now the resolution and the patience with which she had meant to crown her life? You did not know, poor Anne, when you framed those lofty purposes, that suffering is just as hard to bear whether one is noble or ignoble, good or bad. In the face of danger the heart is roused, and in the exaltation of determination forgets its pain; it is the long monotony of dangerless days that tries the spirit hardest.

A letter had come to her that morning, bearing a Boston postmark; the address was in the neat, small handwriting of Jeanne-Armande's friend. Anne, remembering that it was this Boston address which she had sent to her grandaunt, opened the envelope eagerly. But it was only the formal letter of a lawyer. Miss Vanhorn had died, on the nineteenth of June, in Switzerland, and the lawyer wrote to inform "Miss Anne Douglas" that a certain portrait, said in the will to be that of "Alida Clanssen," had been bequeathed to her by his late client, and would be forwarded to her address, whenever she requested it. Anne had expected nothing, not even this. But an increased solitariness came upon her as she thought of that cold rigid face lying under the turf far away in Switzerland—the face of the only relative left to her.

The sun had disappeared; it was twilight. The few loiterers on the bank were departing. The sound of carriage wheels roused her, and turning she saw that a carriage had approached, and that three persons had alighted and were coming toward her. They proved to be the principal of the school and the president of the Aid Society, accompanied by one of her associates. They had been to Anne's home, and learning where she was, had followed her. It seemed that one of the city physicians had gone southward a few days before to assist in the regimental hospitals on the border; a telegraphic dispatch had just been received from him, urging the Aid Society to send without delay three or four nurses to that fever-cursed district, where men were dying in delirium for want of proper care. It was the first personal appeal which had come to Weston; the young Aid Society felt that it must be answered. But who could go? Among the many workers at the Aid Rooms, few were free; wives, mothers, and daughters, they could give an hour or two daily to the work of love, but they could not leave their homes. One useful woman, a nurse by profession, was already engaged; another, a lady educated and

147

refined, whose hair had been silvered as much by affliction as by age, had offered to go. There were two, then; but they ought to send four. Many had been asked during that afternoon, but without success. The society was at its wits' end. Then some one thought of Miss Douglas.

She was young, but she was also self-controlled and physically strong. Her inexperience would not be awkwardness; she would obey with intelligence and firmness the directions given her. Under the charge of the two older women, she could go—if she would!

It would be but for a short time—two weeks only; at the end of that period the society expected to relieve these first volunteers with regularly engaged and paid nurses. The long vacation had begun; as teacher, she would lose nothing; her expenses would be paid by the society. She had seemed so interested; it would not be much more to go for a few days in person; perhaps she would even be glad to go. All this they told her eagerly, while she stood before them in silence. Then, when at last their voices ceased, and they waited for answer, she said, slowly, looking from one to the other: "I could go, if it were not for one obstacle. I have music scholars, and I can not afford to lose them. I am very poor."

"They will gladly wait until you return, Miss Douglas," said the principal. "When it is known where you have gone, you will not only retain all your old scholars, but gain many new ones. They will be proud of their teacher."

"Yes, proud!" echoed the associate. Again Anne remained silent; she was thinking. In her loneliness she was almost glad to go. Perhaps, by the side of the suffering and the dying, she could learn to be ashamed of being so down-hearted and miserable. It was but a short absence. "Yes, I will go," she said, quietly. And then the three ladies kissed her, and the associate, who was of a tearful habit, took out her handkerchief. "It is so sweet, and so—so martial!" she sobbed.

The next morning they started. Early as it was, a little company had gathered to see them off. The school-girls were there, half in grief, half in pride, over what they were pleased to call the "heroism" of their dear Miss Douglas. Mrs. Green, Anne's landlady, was there in her Sunday bonnet, which was, however, but a poor one. These, with the principal of the school and the other teachers, and the ladies belonging to the Aid Society, made quite a snowy shower of white handkerchiefs as the train moved out from the station, Anne's young face contrasting with the strong features and coarse complexion of Mary Crane, the professional nurse, on one side, and with the thin cheeks and silver hair of Mrs. Barstow on the other, as they stood together at the rear door of the last car. "Good-by! good-by!" called the school-girls in tears, and the ladies of the Aid Society gave a shrill little feminine cheer. They were away.

CHAPTER XXIV.

"When we remember how they died—

In dark ravine and on the mountain-
side,...

How their dear lives were spent

By lone lagoons and streams,

In the weary hospital tent,...

....it seems

Ignoble to be alive!"

—Thomas Bailey Aldrich.

The three nurses travelled southward by railway, steamboat, and wagon. On the evening of the third day they came to the first hospital, having been met at the river by an escort, and safely guided across a country fair with summer and peaceful to the eye, but harassed by constant skirmishing—the guerrilla warfare that desolated that border during the entire war. The houses they passed looked home-like and quiet; if the horses had been stolen and the barns pillaged, at least nothing of it appeared in the warm sunshine of the still August day. At the door of the hospital they were welcomed cordially, and within the hour they were at work, Anne timidly, the others energetically. Mary Crane had the worst cases; then followed Mrs. Barstow. To Anne was given what was called the light work; none of her patients were in danger. The men here had all been stricken down by fever; there were no wounded. During the next day and evening, however, stories began to come to the little post, brought by the country people, that a battle had been fought farther up the valley toward the mountains, and that

Hospital Number Two was filled with wounded men, many of them lying on the hard floor because there were not beds enough, unattended and suffering because there were no nurses. Anne, who had worked ardently all day, chafing and rebelling in spirit at the sight of suffering which could have been soothed by a few of the common luxuries abundant in almost every house in Weston, felt herself first awed, then chilled, by this picture of far worse agony beyond, whose details were pitilessly painted in the plain rough words of the country people. She went to the door and looked up the valley. The river wound slowly along, broad, yellow, and shining; it came from the mountains, but from where she stood she could see only round-topped hills. While she was still wistfully gazing, a soldier on horseback rode up to the door and dismounted; it was a messenger from Number Two, urgently asking for help.

"Under the circumstances, I do not see how I can refuse," said the surgeon of Number One, with some annoyance in his tone, "because none of my men are wounded. People never stop to think that fever is equally dangerous. I was just congratulating myself upon a little satisfactory work. However, I shall have to yield, I suppose. I can not send you all; but I ought to spare two, at least for some days. Mary Crane of course can do the most good; and as Miss Douglas can not be left here alone, perhaps it would be best that she should go with Mary."

"You retain Mrs. Barstow here?" asked Anne.

"Yes; I have, indeed, no choice. *You* are too young to be retained alone. I suppose you are willing? (Women always are wild for a change!) Make ready, then; I shall send you forward to-night." The surgeon of Number One was a cynic.

At nine o'clock they started. The crescent of a young moon showed itself through the light clouds, which, low as mist, hung over the valley. Nothing stirred; each leaf hung motionless from its branchlet as they passed. Even the penetrating sing-song chant of the summer insects was hushed, and the smooth river as they followed its windings made no murmur. They were in a light wagon, with an escort of two mounted men.

"If you go beyond Number Two, you'll have to take to horseback, I reckon," said their driver, a countryman, who, without partisan feeling as to the two sides of the contest, held on with a tight grip to his horses, and impartially "did teaming" for both.

"Is there still another hospital beyond?" inquired Anne.

"Yes, there's Peterson's, a sorter hospital; it's up in the mountains. And heaps of sick fellers there too, the last time I was up."

"It does not belong to this department," said Mary Crane.

"I reckon they suffer pooty much the same, no matter where they belong," replied the driver, flicking the wheel reflectively with his whip-lash. "There was a feller up at Number Two the other day as hadn't any face left to speak of; yet he was alive, and quite peart."

Anne shuddered.

"There now, hold up, won't you?" said Mary Crane. "This young lady ain't a real nurse, as I am, and such stories make her feel faint."

"If she ain't a real nurse, what made her come?" said the man, glancing at Anne with dull curiosity.

"'Twas just goodness, and the real downright article of patriotism, I guess," said the hearty nurse, smiling.

"Oh no," said Anne; "I was lonely and sad, and glad to come."

"It *doos* kinder rouse one up to see a lot of men hit in all sorts of ways, legs and arms and everything flying round," remarked the driver, as if approving Anne's selection of remedies for loneliness.

They reached Number Two at dawn, and found the wounded in rows upon the floor of the barn dignified by the name of hospital. There had been no attempt to classify them after the few beds were filled. One poor torn fragment of humanity breathed his last as the nurses entered, another an hour later. Mary Crane set herself to work with ready skill; Anne, after going outside two or three times to let her tears flow unseen over the sorrowful sights, was able to assist in taking care of two kinds of cases—those who were the least hurt and those who were beyond hope, the slightly wounded and the dying. One man, upon whose face was the gray shadow of death, asked her in a whisper to write a letter for him. She found paper and pen, and sat down beside the bed to receive his farewell message to his wife and children. "And tell little Jim he must grow up and be a comfort to his mother," he murmured; and then turning his quiet gaze slowly upon the nurse: "His mother is only twenty-two years old now, miss. I expect she'll feel bad, Mary will, when she hears." Poor young wife! The simple country phraseology covered as much sorrow as the finest language of the schools. During the night the man died.

The new nurses remained at Number Two six days. Anne's work consisted principally in relieving Mary Crane at dawn, and keeping the watch through the early morning hours while she slept; for the head surgeon and Mary would not allow her to watch at night. The surgeon had two assistants; with one of these silent old men (they were both gray-haired) she kept watch while the sun rose slowly over the hill-tops, while the birds twittered, and the yellow butterflies came dancing through the open doors and windows, over the heads of the poor human sleepers. But Number Two had greater ease now. The hopelessly wounded were all at rest, their sufferings in this life over. Those who were left, in time would see health again.

On the seventh day a note came to the surgeon in charge from the temporary hospital at Peterson's Mill, asking for medicines. "If you can possibly spare us one or two nurses for a few days, pray do so. In all my experience I have never been so hard pushed as now," wrote the other surgeon. "The men here are all down with the fever, and I and my assistant are almost crazed with incessant night-work. If we could be relieved for one night even, it would be God's charity."

The surgeon of Number Two read this note aloud to Anne as they stood by a table eating their hasty breakfast. "It is like the note you sent to us at Number One," she said.

"Oh no; that was different, *I* never send and take away other people's nurses," said Dr. Janes, laughingly.

"I should like to go," she said, after a moment.

"You should like to go? I thought you were so much interested here."

"So I am; but after what I have seen, I am haunted by the thought that there may be worse suffering beyond. That is the reason I came here. But the men here are more comfortable now, and those who were suffering hopelessly have been relieved forever from earthly pain. If we are not needed, some of us ought to go."

"But if we pass you on in this way from post to post, we shall get you entirely over the mountains, and into the Department of the Potomac, Miss Douglas. What you say is true enough, but at present I refuse. I simply can not spare you two. If they should send us a nurse from Rivertown as they promised, we might get along without you for a while; but not now. Charity, you know, begins at home."

Anne sighed, but acquiesced. The surgeon knew best. But during that day, not only did the promised nurse from the Rivertown Aid Society arrive, but with her a volunteer assistant, a young girl, her face flushed with exaltation and excitement over the opportunity afforded her to help and comfort "our poor dear wounded heroes." The wounded heroes were not poetical in appearance; they were simply a row of ordinary sick men, bandaged in various ways, often irritable, sometimes profane; their grammar was defective, and they cared more for tobacco than for texts, or even poetical quotations. The young nurse would soon have her romance rudely dispelled. But as there was good stuff in her, she would do useful work yet, although shorn of many illusions. The other woman was a professional nurse, whose services were paid for like those of Mary Crane.

"*Now* may we go?" said Anne, when the new nurse had been installed.

Dr. Janes, loath to consent, yet ashamed, as he said himself, of his own greediness, made no long opposition, and the countryman with the non-partisan horses was engaged to take them to Peterson's Mill. For this part of the road no escort was required. They travelled in the wagon for ten miles. Here the man stopped, took the harness from the horses, replaced it with two side-saddles which he had brought with him, drew the wagon into a ravine safely out of sight, effaced the trace of the wheels, and then wiping his forehead after his exertions, announced that he was ready. Anne had never been on horseback in her life. Mary Crane, who would have mounted a camel imperturbably if it came into the line of her business, climbed up sturdily by the aid of a stump, and announced that she felt herself "quite solid." The horse seemed to agree with her. Anne followed her example, and being without physical nervousness, she soon became accustomed to the motion, and even began to imagine how exhilarating it would be to ride rapidly over a broad plain, feeling the wind on her face as she flew along. But the two old brown horses had no idea of flying. They toiled patiently every day, and sometimes at night as well, now for one army, now for the other; but nothing could make them quicken their pace. In the present case they were not asked to do it, since the road was but a bridle-path through the ravines and over the hills which formed the flank of the mountains they were approaching, and the driver was following them on foot. The ascents grew steeper, the ravines deeper and wilder.

"I no longer see the mountains," said Anne.

"That's because you're in 'em," answered the driver.

At night-fall they reached their destination. It was a small mountain mill, in a little green valley which nestled confidingly among the wild peaks as though it was not afraid of their roughness. Within were the fever patients, and the tired surgeon and his still more tired assistant could hardly believe their good fortune when the two nurses appeared. The assistant, a tall young medical student who had not yet finished growing, made his own bed of hay and a coverlet so hungrily in a dusky corner that Anne could not help smiling; the poor fellow was fairly gaunt from loss of sleep, and had been obliged to walk up and down during the whole of the previous night to keep himself awake. The surgeon, who was older and more hardened, explained to Mary Crane the condition of the men, and gave her careful directions for the night; then he too disappeared. Anne and Mary moved about softly, and when everything was ready, sat down on opposite sides of the room to keep the vigil. If the men were restless, Mary was to attend to them; Anne was the subordinate, merely obeying Mary's orders. The place was dimly lighted by two candles set in bottles; the timbers above were festooned with cobwebs whitened with meal, and the floor was covered with its fine yellow dust. A large spider came slowly out from behind a beam near by, and looked at Anne; at least she thought he did. He was mealy too, and she fell to wondering whether he missed the noise of the wheel, and whether he asked himself what all these men meant by coming in and lying down in rows upon his floor to disturb his peacefulness. At sunrise the surgeon came in, but he was obliged to shake the student roughly before he could awaken him from his heavy slumber. It was not until the third day that the poor youth lost the half-mad expression which had shone in his haggard face when they arrived, and began to look as though he was composed of something besides big jaws, gaunt cheeks, and sunken eyes, which had seemed to be all there was of him besides bones when they first came.

The fever patients at Peterson's Mill were not Western men, like the inmates of Number One and Number Two; they belonged to two New York regiments. Mary Crane did excellent work among them, her best; her systematic watchfulness, untiring vigilance, and strict rules shook the hold of the fever, and in many cases routed the dismal spectre, and brought the victims triumphantly back to hope of health again.

One morning Anne, having written a letter for one of the men, was fanning him as he lay in his corner; the doors were open, but the air was sultry. The man was middle-aged and gaunt, his skin was yellow and lifeless, his eyes sunken. Yet the surgeon pronounced him out of danger; it was now merely a question of care, patience, and nourishment. The poor mill-hospital had so little for its sick! But boxes from the North were at last beginning to penetrate even these defiles; one had arrived during the previous night, having been dragged on a rude sledge over places where wheels could not go, by the non-partisan horses, which were now on their patient way with a load of provisions to a detachment of Confederates camped, or rather mired, in the southern part of the county. The contents of that box had made the mill-hospital glad; the yellow-faced skeleton whom Anne was fanning had tasted lemons at last, and almost thought he was in heaven. Revived and more hopeful, he had been talking to his nurse. "I should feel easier, miss, if I knew just where our captain was. You see, there was a sort of a scrimmage, and some of us got hurt. He wasn't hurt, but he was took down with the fever, and so bad that we had to leave him behind at a farm-house. And I've heard nothing since."

"Where was he left—far from here?"

"No; sing'lerly enough, 'twas the very next valley to this one. *We* went in half a dozen directions after that, and tramped miles in the mud, but he was left there. We put him in charge of a woman, who *said* she'd take care of him, but I misdoubt her. She was a meaching-looking creature."

"Probably, then, as you have heard nothing, he has recovered, and is with his regiment again," said Anne, with the cheerful optimism which is part of a nurse's duty.

"Yes, miss. And yet perhaps he ain't, you know. I thought mebbe you'd ask the surgeon for me. I'm only a straggler here, anyway; the others don't belong to my regiment. Heathcote was the name; Captain Ward Heathcote. A city feller he was, but wuth a heap, for all that."

What was the matter with the nurse that she turned so pale? And now she was gone! And without leaving the fan too. However, he could hardly have held it. He found his little shred of lemon, lifted it to his dry lips, and closed his eyes patiently, hardly remembering even what he had said.

Meanwhile Anne, still very pale, had drawn the surgeon outside the door, and was questioning him. Yes, he knew that an officer had been left at a farm-house over in the next valley; he had been asked to ride over and see him. But how could he! As nothing had been heard from him since, however, he was probably well by this time, and back with his regiment again.

"Probably"—the very word she had herself used when answering the soldier. How inactive and cowardly it seemed now! "I must go across to this next valley," she said.

"My dear Miss Douglas!" said Dr. Flower, a grave, portly man, whose ideas moved as slowly as his small fat-encircled eyes.

"I know a Mr. Heathcote; this may be the same person. The Mr. Heathcote I know is engaged to a friend of mine, a lady to whom I am much indebted. I must learn whether this officer in the next valley is he."

"But even if it is the same man, no doubt he is doing well over there. Otherwise we should have heard from them before this time," said the surgeon, sensibly.

But Anne did not stop at sense. "It is probable, but not certain. There must be no room for doubt. If *you* will ride over, I will stay. Otherwise I must go."

"I can not leave; it is impossible."

"Where can I procure a horse, then?"

"I do not think I ought to allow it, Miss Douglas. It is nearly fifteen miles to the next valley; of course you can not go alone, and I can not spare Mary Crane to go with you." The surgeon spoke decidedly; he had daughters of his own at home, and felt himself responsible for this young nurse.

Anne looked at him. "Oh, do help me!" she cried, with an outburst of sudden emotion. "I must go; even if I go alone, and walk every step of the way, I must, must go!"

Dr. Caleb Flower was a slow man; but anything he had once learned he remembered. He now recognized the presence of what he called "one of those intense impulses which make even timid women for the time being inflexible as adamant."

"You will have to pay largely for horses and a guide," he said, in order to gain time, inwardly regretting meanwhile that he had not the power to tie this nurse to her chair.

"I have a little money with me."

"But even if horses are found, you can not go alone; and, as I said before, I can not spare Mary."

"Why would not Diana do?" said Anne.

"Diana!" exclaimed Dr. Flower, his lips puckering as if to form a long whistle.

Diana was a middle-aged negro woman, who, with her husband, July, lived in a cabin near the mill, acting as laundress for the hospital. She was a silent, austere woman; in her there was little of the light-heartedness and plenitude of person which generally belong to her race. A devout Baptist, quoting more texts to the sick soldiers than they liked when she was employed in the hospital, chanting hymns in a low voice while hanging out the clothes, Diana had need of her austerity, industry, and leanness to balance July, who was the most light-hearted, lazy, and rotund negro in the mountains.

"But you know that Mary Crane has orders not to leave you?" said Dr. Flower.

"I did not know it."

"Yes; so she tells me. The ladies of the Aid Society who sent her arranged it. And I wish with all my heart that our other young nurses were as well taken care of!" added the surgeon, a comical expression coming into his small eyes.

"On ordinary occasions I would not, of course, interfere with these orders," said Anne, "but on this I must. You must trust me with Diana, doctor—Diana and July. They will take good care of me."

"I suppose I shall *have* to yield, Miss Douglas. But I regret, regret exceedingly, that I have not full authority over you. I feel it necessary to say formally that your going is against my wishes and my advice. And now, since you *will* have your own way in any case, I must do what I can for you."

An hour later, two mules were ascending the mountain-side, following an old trail; Anne was on one, the tall grave Diana on the other. July walked in front, with his gun over his shoulder.

"No danjah hyah," he assured them volubly; "soldiers doan' come up dis yer way at all. Dey go draggin' 'long in de mud below always; seem to like 'em."

But Anne was not thinking of danger. "Could we not go faster by the road?" she asked.

"'Spec's we could, miss. But wudn't darst to, ef I was you."

"No, no, miss," said Diana. "Best keep along in dese yere woods; dey's safe."

The hours were endless. At last it seemed to Anne as if they were not moving at all, but merely sitting still in their saddles, while a continuous procession of low trees and high bushes filed slowly past them, now pointing upward, now slanting downward, according to the nature of the ground. In reality they were moving forward, crossing a spur of the mountain, but so dense was the foliage of the thicket, and so winding the path, that they could not see three feet in any direction, and all sense of advance was therefore lost. Anne fell into a mental lethargy, which was troubled every now and then by that strange sense of having seen particular objects before which occasionally haunts the brain. Now it was a tree, now a bird; or was it that she had known July in some far-off anterior existence, and that he had kicked a stone from his path in precisely that same way?

It was late twilight when, after a long descent still shrouded in the interminable thicket, the path came out suddenly upon a road, and Anne's eyes seemed to herself to expand as the view expanded. She saw a valley, the gray smoothness of water, and here and there roofs. July had stopped the mules in the shadow.

"Can you tell me which house it mought be, miss?" he asked, in a low, cautious tone.

"No," replied Anne. "But the person I am trying to find is named Heathcote—Captain Heathcote. We must make inquiries."

"Now do be keerful, miss," urged July, keeping Anne's mule back. "I'll jes' go and peer roun' a bit. But you stay hyar with Di."

"Yes, miss," said Diana. "We'll go back in de woods a piece, and wait. July'll fin' out all about 'em."

Whether willingly or unwillingly, Anne was obliged to yield; the two women rode back into the woods, and July stole away cautiously upon his errand.

It was ten o'clock before he returned; Anne had dismounted, and was walking impatiently to and fro in the warm darkness.

"Found 'em, miss," said July. "But it's cl'ar 'cross de valley. Howsomever, valley's safe, dey say, and you can ride right along ober."

"Was it Mr. Heathcote?" said Anne, as the mules trotted down a cross-road and over a bridge, July keeping up with a long loping run.

"Yes, miss; Heathcote's de name. I saw him, and moughty sick he looked."

"What did he say?"

"Fever's in him head, miss, and didn't say nothing. Senses clean done gone."

Anne had not thought of this, it changed her task at once. He would not know her; she could do all that was necessary in safety, and then go unrecognized away. "What will he say?" she had asked herself a thousand times. Now, he would say nothing, and all would be simple and easy.

"Dis yere's de place," said July, pausing.

It was a low farm-house with a slanting roof; there was a light in the window, and the door stood open. Anne, springing from her saddle, and followed by Diana, hastened up the little garden path. At first there seemed to be no one in the room into which the house door opened; then a slight sound behind a curtain in one corner attracted her attention, and going across, she drew aside the drapery. The head moving restlessly to and fro on the pillow, with closed eyes and drawn mouth, was that of Ward Heathcote.

She spoke his name; the eyes opened and rested upon her, but there was no recognition in the glance.

"Bless you! his senses has been gone for days," said the farmer's wife, coming up behind her and looking at her patient impartially. "He don't know nobody no more'n a day-old baby!"

CHAPTER XXV.

"Love is not love

Which alters when it alteration finds,

Or tends with the remover to remove:

Love's not Time's fool, though rosy lips and

cheeks

Within his bending sickle's compass come:

Love alters not with his brief hours and weeks,

But bears it out even to the edge of doom."

—Shakspeare.

"Why did you not send across to the hospital at the mill?" said Anne. "Dr. Flower, receiving no second message, supposed that Captain Heathcote had recovered."

"Well, you see, I reckon I know as much about this yer fever as the doctors do as never had it," replied Mrs. Redd. "The captain couldn't be moved; that was plain as day. And we hadn't a horse, nuther. Our horse and mules have all been run off and stole."

Mrs. Redd was a clay-colored woman, with a figure which, cavernous in front, was yet so rounded out behind that if she could have turned her head round she would have been very well shaped. Her knowledge of the fever was plainly derived from personal experience; she explained that she had it "by spells," and that "Redd he has it too," and their daughter Nancy as well. "Redd he isn't to home now, nor Nancy nuther. But Redd he'll be back by to-morrow night, I reckon. If you want to stay, I can accommodate you. You can have the loft, and the niggers can sleep in the barn. But they'll have to cook for themselves. I shall be mighty glad to have some help in tending on the captain; I'm about wore out."

Mrs. Redd did not mention that she had confiscated the sick man's money, and hidden it safely away in an old tea-pot, and that all her knowledge of arithmetic was at work keeping a daily account of expenses which should in the end exactly balance the sum. She had no intention of stealing the money—certainly not. But of course her

153

"just account" must be paid. She could still work at this problem, she thought, and earn something as well from the new-comers, who would also relieve her from all care of the sick man: it was clearly a providence. In the glow of this expected gain she even prepared supper. Fortunately in summer her kitchen was in the open air, and the room where Heathcote lay was left undisturbed.

Anne had brought the hospital medicines with her, and careful instructions from Mary Crane. If she had come upon Heathcote before her late experiences, she would have felt little hope, but men whose strength had been far more reduced than his had recovered under her eyes. Diana was a careful nurse; July filled the place of valet, sleeping on straw on the floor. She ordered down the bed-curtains and opened all the windows; martial law regarding air, quiet, and medicines was proclaimed. The sick man lay quietly, save for the continued restless motion of his head.

"If we could only stop his slipping his head across and back in that everlasting way, I believe he'd be better right off," said Mrs. Redd.

"It done him good, 'pears to me," said July, who already felt a strong affection in his capacious vagabondizing heart for the stranger committed to his care. "Yo' see, it kinder rests his mind like."

"Much mind *he's* got to rest with!" said Mrs. Redd, contemptuously.

With her two assistants, it was not necessary that Anne should remain in the room at night, and she did not, at least in personal presence; but every half-hour she was at the top of the stairway, silently watching to see if Diana fulfilled her duties. On the third day the new medicines and the vigilance conquered. On the fifth day the sick man fell into his first natural slumber. The house was very still. Bees droned serenely. There was no breeze. Anne was sitting on the door-steps. "Ought I to go now before he wakens?" she was thinking. "But I *can* not until the danger is surely over. He may not recognize me even now." She said to herself that she would stay a short time longer, but without entering the room where he was; Diana could come to her for orders, and the others must not allude to her presence. Then, as soon as she was satisfied that his recovery was certain, she could slip away unseen. She went round to the back of the house to warn the others; it was all to go on as though she was not there.

Heathcote wakened at last, weak but conscious. He had accepted without speech the presence of Diana and July, and had soon fallen asleep again, "like a chile." He ate some breakfast the next morning, and the day passed without fever. Mrs. Redd pronounced him convalescent, and declared decisively that all he needed was to "eat hearty." The best medicine now would be "a plenty of vittals." In accordance with this opinion she prepared a meal of might, carried it in with her own hands, and in two minutes, forgetting all about the instructions she had received, betrayed Anne's secret. Diana, who was present, looked at her reproachfully: the black skin covered more faithfulness than the white.

"Well, I do declare to Jerusalem I forgot!" said the hostess, laughing. "However, now you know it, Miss Douglas might as well come in, and make you eat if she can. For eat you must, captain. Why, man alive, if you could see yourself! You're just skin and rattling bones."

And thus it all happened. Anne, afraid to lay so much as a finger's weight of excitement of any kind upon him in his weak state, hearing his voice faintly calling her name, and understanding at once that her presence had been disclosed, came quietly in with a calm face, as though her being there was quite commonplace and natural, and taking the plate from Diana, sat down by the bedside and began to feed him with the bits of chicken, which was all of the meal of might that he would touch. She paid no attention to the expression which grew gradually in his feeble eyes as they rested upon her and followed her motions, at first vaguely, then with more and more of insistence and recollection.

"Anne?" he murmured, after a while, as if questioning with himself. "It is Anne?"

She lifted her hand authoritatively. "Yes," she said; "but you must not talk. Eat."

He obeyed; but he still gazed at her, and then slowly he smiled. "You will not run away again?" he whispered.

"Not immediately."

"Promise that you will not go to-night or to-morrow."

"I promise."

And then, as if satisfied, he fell asleep.

He slept all night peacefully. But Anne did not once lose consciousness. At dawn she left her sleepless couch, and dressed herself, moving about the room cautiously, so as not to awaken the sleeper below. When she was ready to go down, she paused a moment, thinking. Raising her eyes, she found herself standing by chance opposite the small mirror, and her gaze rested half unconsciously upon her own reflected image. She drew nearer, and leaning with folded arms upon the chest of drawers, looked at herself, as if striving to see something hitherto hidden.

We think we know our own faces, yet they are in reality less known to us than the countenances of our acquaintances, of our servants, even of our dogs. If any one will stand alone close to a mirror, and look intently at his own reflection for several minutes or longer, the impression produced on his mind will be extraordinary. At first it is nothing but his own well-known, perhaps well-worn, face that confronts him. Whatever there may be of novelty in the faces of others, there is certainly nothing of it here. So at least he believes. But after a while it grows strange. What do those eyes mean, meeting his so mysteriously and silently? Whose mouth is that? Whose brow? What vague suggestions of something stronger than he is, some dormant force which laughs him to scorn, are lurking behind that mask? In the outline of the features, the curve of the jaw and chin, perhaps he notes a suggested likeness to this or that animal of the lower class—a sign of some trait which he was not conscious he possessed. And then—those strange eyes! They are his own; nothing new; yet in their depths all sorts of mocking meanings seem to rise. The world, with all its associations, even his own history also, drops from him like a garment, and he is left alone, facing the problem of his own existence. It is the old riddle of the Sphinx.

Something of this passed through Anne's mind at that moment. She was too young to accept misery, to generalize on sorrow, to place herself among the large percentage of women to whom, in the great balance of population, a happy love is denied. She felt her own wretchedness acutely, unceasingly, while the man she loved was so near. She knew that she would leave him, that he would go back to Helen; that she would return to her hospital work and to Weston, and that that would be the end. There was not in her mind a thought of anything else. Yet this certainty did not prevent the two large slow tears that rose and welled over as she watched the eyes in the glass, watched them as though they were the eyes of some one else.

Diana's head now appeared, giving the morning bulletin: the captain had slept "like a cherrb," and was already "'mos' well." Anne went down by the outside stairway, and ate her breakfast under the trees not far from Mrs. Redd's out-door hearth. She told July that she should return to the hospital during the coming night, or, if the mountain path could not be traversed in the darkness, they must start at dawn.

"I don't think it's quite fair of you to quit so soon," objected Mrs. Redd, loath to lose her profit.

"If you can find any one to escort me, I will leave you Diana and July," answered Anne. "For myself, I can not stay longer."

July went in with the sick man's breakfast, but came forth again immediately. "He wants *yo'* to come, miss."

"I can not come now. If he eats his breakfast obediently, I will come in and see him later," said the nurse.

"Isn't much trouble 'bout *eating*," said July, grinning. "Cap'n he eats like he 'mos' starved."

Anne remained sitting under the trees, while the two black servants attended to her patient. At ten o'clock he was reported as "sittin' up in bed, and powerful smart." This bulletin was soon followed by another, "Him all tired out now, and gone to sleep."

Leaving directions for the next hour, she strolled into the woods behind the house. She had intended to go but a short distance, but, led on by her own restlessness and the dull pain in her heart, she wandered farther than she knew.

Jacob Redd's little farm was on the northern edge of the valley; its fields and wood-lot ascended the side of the mountain. Anne, reaching the end of the wood-lot, opened the gate, and went on up the hill. She followed a little trail. The trees were larger than those through which she had travelled on the opposite side of the valley; it was a wood, not a thicket; the sunshine was hot, the green silent shade pleasant. She went on, although now the trail was climbing upward steeply, and rocks appeared. She had been ascending for half an hour, when she came suddenly upon a narrow, deep ravine, crossing from left to right; the trail turned and followed its edge; but as its depths looked cool and inviting, and as she thought she heard the sound of a brook below, she left the little path, and went downward into the glen. When she reached the bottom she found herself beside a brook, flowing along over white pebbles; it was not more than a foot wide, but full of life and merriment, going no one knew whither, and in a great hurry about it. A little brook is a fascinating object to persons unaccustomed to its coaxing, vagrant witcheries. There were no brooks on the island, only springs that trickled down from the cliffs into the lake in tiny silver water-falls. Anne followed the brook. Absorbed in her own thoughts, and naturally fearless, it did not occur to her that there might be danger even in this quiet forest. She went round a curve, then round another, when—what was that? She paused. Could he have seen her? Was he asleep? Or—dead?

It was a common sight enough, a dead soldier in the uniform of the United States infantry. He was young, and his face, turned toward her, was as peaceful as if he was sleeping; there was almost a smile on his cold lips. With beating heart she looked around. There were twisted broken branches above on the steep side of the ravine; he had either fallen over, or else had dragged himself down to be out of danger, or perhaps to get water from the brook. The death-wound was in his breast; she could see traces of blood. But he could not have been long dead. It had been said that there was no danger in that neighborhood at present; then what was this? Only one of the chances of war, and a common one in that region: an isolated soldier taken off by a bullet from behind a tree. She stood looking sorrowfully down upon the prostrate form; then a thought came to her. She stooped to see if she could discover the identity of the slain man from anything his pockets contained. There was no money, but various little possessions, a soldier's wealth—a puzzle carved in wood and neatly fitted together, a pocket-knife, a ball of twine, a pipe, and a ragged song-book. At last she came upon what she had hoped to find—a letter. It was from the soldier's mother, full of love and little items of neighborhood news, and ending, "May God bless you, my dear and only son!" The postmark was that of a small village in Michigan, and the mother's name was signed in full.

One page of the letter was blank; with the poor soldier's own pencil Anne drew upon this half sheet a sketch of his figure, lying there peacefully beside the little brook. Then she severed a lock of his hair, and went sadly away. July should come up and bury him; but the mother, far away in Michigan, should have something more than the silence and heart-breaking suspense of that terrible word "missing." The lock of hair, the picture, and the poor little articles taken from his pockets would be her greatest earthly treasures. For the girl forgets her lover, and the wife forgets her husband; but the mother never forgets her dear and only son.

When Anne reached the farm-house it was nearly four o'clock. July's black anxious face met hers as she glanced through the open door of the main room; he was sitting near the bed waving a long plume of feathers backward and forward to keep the flies from the sleeping face below. The negro came out on tiptoe, his enormous patched old shoes looking like caricatures, yet making no more sound, as he stole along, than the small slippers of a woman. "Cap'en he orful disappointed 'cause you worn't yere at dinner-time," he whispered. "An' Mars' Redd, Mis' Redd's husband, you know, him jess come home, and they's bote gone 'cross de valley to see some pusson they know that's sick; but they'll back 'fore long. And Di she's gone to look fer *you*, 'cause she was moughty oneasy 'bout yer. An' she's been gone so long that *I'm* moughty oneasy 'bout Di. P'r'aps you seen her, miss?"

No, Anne had not seen her. July looked toward the mountain-side anxiously. "Cap'en he's had 'em broth, and taken 'em medicine, and has jess settled down to a good long sleep; reckon he won't wake up till sunset. If you'll allow, miss, I'll run up and look for Di."

Anne saw that he intended to go, whether she wished it or not: the lazy fellow was fond of his wife. She gave her consent, therefore, on the condition that he would return speedily, and telling him of the dead soldier, suggested that when Farmer Redd returned the two men should go up the mountain together and bury him. Was there a burial-ground or church-yard in the neighborhood?

No; July knew of none; each family buried its dead on its own ground, "in a corner of a meddar." He went away, and Anne sat down to keep the watch.

She moved the long plume to and fro, refraining from even looking at the sleeper, lest by some occult influence he might feel the gaze and waken. Mrs. Redd's clock in another room struck five. The atmosphere grew breathless; the flies became tenacious, almost adhesive; the heat was intense. She knew that a thunder-storm must be near, but from where she sat she could not see the sky, and she was afraid to stop the motion of the waving fan. Each moment she hoped to hear the sound of July's returning footsteps, or those of the Redds, but none came. Then at last with a gust and a whirl of hot sand the stillness was broken, and the storm was upon them. She ran to close the doors, but happily the sleeper was not awakened. The flies retreated to the ceiling, and she stood looking at the black rushing rain. The thunder was not loud, but the lightning was almost incessant. She now hoped that in the cooler air his sleep would be even deeper than before.

But when the storm had sobered down into steady soft gray rain, so that she could open the doors again, she heard a voice speaking her name:

"Anne."

She turned. Heathcote was awake, and gazing at her, almost as he had gazed in health.

Summoning all her self-possession, yet feeling drearily, unshakenly sure, even during the short instant of crossing the floor, that no matter what he might say (and perhaps he would say nothing), she should not swerve, and that this little moment, with all its pain and all its sweetness, would, for all its pain and all its sweetness, soon be gone, she sat down by the bedside, and taking up the fan, said, quietly:

"I am glad you are so much better. As the fever has not returned, in a week or two you may hope to be quite strong again. Do not try to talk, please. I will fan you to sleep."

"Very well," replied Heathcote, but reaching out as he spoke, and taking hold of the edge of her sleeve, which was near him.

"Why do you do that?" said his nurse, smiling, like one who humors the fancies of a child.

"To keep you from going away. You said you would be here at dinner, and you were not."

"I was detained. I intended to be here, but—"

She stopped, for Heathcote had closed his eyes, and she thought he was falling asleep. But no.

156

"It is raining," he said presently, still with closed eyes.

"Yes; a summer shower."

"Do you remember that thunder-storm when we were in the little cave? You are changed since then."

She made no answer.

"Your face has grown grave. No one would take you for a child now, but that day in the cave you were hardly more than one."

"You too are changed," she answered, turning the conversation from herself; "you are thin and pale. You must sleep and eat. Surrender yourself to that duty for the time being." She spoke with matter-of-fact cheerfulness, but her ears were strained to catch the sound of footsteps. None came, and the rain fell steadily. She began to dread rain.

Heathcote in his turn did not reply, but she was conscious that his eyes were open, and that he was looking at her. At last he said, gently,

"*I* should have placed it there, Anne."

She turned; his gaze was fixed upon her left hand, and the gold ring given by the school-girls.

"He is kind to you? And you—are happy?" he continued, still gazing at the circlet.

She did not speak; she was startled and confused. He supposed, then, that she was married. Would it not be best to leave the error uncorrected? But—could she succeed in this?

"You do not answer," said Heathcote, lifting his eyes to her face. "Are you not happy, then?"

"Yes, I am happy," she answered, trying to smile. "But please do not talk; you are not strong enough for talking."

"I hope he is not here, or expected. Do not let him come in *here*, Anne: promise me."

"He is not coming."

"He is in the army, I suppose, somewhere in the neighborhood; and you are here to be near him?"

"No."

"Then how is it that you are here?"

"I have been in the hospitals for a short time as nurse. But if you persist in talking, I shall certainly leave you. Why not try to sleep?"

"He must be a pretty sort of fellow to let you go into the hospitals," said Heathcote, paying no heed to her threat. "I have your fatal marriage notice, Anne; I have always kept it."

"You have my marriage notice?" she repeated, startled out of her caution.

"Yes. Put your hand under my pillow and you will find my wallet; the woman of the house has skillfully abstracted the money, but fortunately she has not considered a newspaper slip as of any value." He took the case from her hand, opened it, and gave her a folded square paper, cut from the columns of a New York journal. Anne opened it, and read the notice of the marriage of "Erastus Pronando, son of the late John Pronando, Esquire, of Philadelphia, and Angélique, daughter of the late William Douglas, surgeon, United States Army."

The slip dropped from her hand. "Père Michaux must have sent it," she thought.

"It was in all the New York and Philadelphia papers for several days," said Heathcote. "There seemed to be a kind of insistence about it."

And there was. Père Michaux had hoped that the Eastern Pronandos would see the name, and, moved by some awakening of memory or affection, would make inquiry for this son of the lost brother, and assist him on his journey through the crowded world.

"I did not know that 'Anne' was a shortening of 'Angélique'; I thought yours was the plain old English name. But Helen knew; I showed the notice to her."

Anne's face altered; she could not control the tremor that seized her, and he noticed it.

"Are you *not* married then, after all? Tell me, Anne, tell me. You can not deceive; you never could, poor child; I remember that well."

She tried to rise, but he held her arm with both hands, and she could not bring herself to use force against that feeble hold.

"Why should you not tell me what all the world is free to know?" he continued. "What difference does it make?"

"You are right; it makes no difference," she answered, seating herself, and taking up the fan again. "It is of no especial consequence. No, I am not married, Mr. Heathcote. Angélique is the name of my little sister Tita, of whom you have heard me speak; we first called her Petite, then Tita. Mr. Pronando and Tita are married."

"The same Pronando to whom you were engaged?"

"Yes. He is—"

"Oh, I do not care to hear anything about *him*. Give me your hand, Anne. Take off that ring."

"No; it was a present from my pupils," she said, drawing back with a smile, but at the same time an inward sigh of relief that the disclosure was over. "They—"

"If you knew what I suffered when I read that notice!" pursued Heathcote, without heeding her. "The world seemed all wrong then forever. For there was something about you, Anne, which brought out what small good there was in my worthless self, and young as you were, you yet in one way ruled me. I might have borne the separation itself, but the thought that any other man should call you wife was intolerable to me. I had—I still have it—a peculiar feeling about you. In some mysterious way you had come to be the one real faith of my life. I was bitterly hurt and angry when you ran away from me; but angry as I was, I still searched for you, and would have searched again if Helen had not—But never mind that now. If I have loved you, Anne, you have loved me just as dearly. And now you are here, and I am here, let us ask no more questions, but just—be happy."

"But," said the girl, breathlessly, "Helen—?" Then she stopped.

Heathcote was watching her. She tried to be calm, but her lips trembled. A little skill in deception now, poor Anne, would have been of saving help. Heathcote still watched her in silence—watched her until at last she turned toward him.

"Did you not know," he said, slowly meeting her eyes—"did you not know that Helen was—married?"

"Married? And not to you?"

There was a perceptible pause. Then he answered. "Not to me."

A silence followed. A whirl of conflicting feelings filled Anne's heart; she turned her face away, blushing deeply, and conscious of it. "I hope she is happy," she murmured at last, striving to speak naturally.

"I think she is." Then he stretched out his hands and took hers. "Turn this way, so that I can see you," he said, beseechingly.

She turned, and it seemed to him that eyes never beheld so exquisite a face.

"My darling, do you love me? Tell me so. If I was not a poor sick fellow, I should take you in my arms and draw your sweet face down upon my shoulder. But, as it is—" He moved nearer, and tried to lift himself upon his elbow.

There was a feebleness in the effort which went to Anne's heart. She loved him so deeply! They were both free now, and he was weak and ill. With a sudden impulse she drew nearer, so that his head could rest on her shoulder. He silently put out his hand; she took it in hers; then he closed his eyes as if content.

As for Anne, she felt an outburst of happiness almost too great to bear; her breath came and went so quickly that Heathcote perceived it, and raising her hand he pressed it to his lips. Still he did not open his eyes, or speak one word further to the blushing, beautiful woman whose arm was supporting him, and whose eyes, timid yet loving, were resting upon his face. If he had been strong, she would never have yielded so far. But nothing appeals so powerfully to a woman's heart as the sudden feebleness of a strong man—the man she loves. It is so new and perilously sweet that he should be dependent upon her, that her arm should be needed to support him, that his weak voice should call her name with childish loneliness and impatience if she is not there. And so Anne at last no longer turned her eyes away, but looked down upon the face lying upon her shoulder—a face worn by illness and bronzed by exposure, but the same face still, the face of the summer idler at Caryl's, the face she had seen during those long hours in the sunset arbor in the garden that morning, the face of the man who had followed her westward, and who now, after long hopeless loneliness and pain, was with her again, and her own forever. A rush of tenderest pity came over her as she noted the hollows at the temples, and the dark shadows under the closed eyes. She bent her head, and touched his closely cut hair with her lips.

"Do not," said Heathcote.

She had not thought that he would perceive the girlish little caress; she drew back quickly. Then he opened his eyes. It seemed almost as if he had been trying to keep them shut.

"It is of no use," he murmured, looking at her. "Kiss me, Anne. Kiss me once. Oh, my darling! my darling!" And with more strength than she supposed him to possess, he threw his arms round her, drew her lovely face down to his and kissed her fondly, not once, but many times.

And she, at first resisting love's sweet violence, at last yielded to it; for, she loved him.

The rain still fell; it was growing toward twilight. Footsteps were approaching.

"It is Diana," said Anne.

158

But Heathcote still held her.

"Please let me go," she said, smiling happily.

"Then tell me you love me."

"You know I do, Ward," she answered, blushing deeply, yet with all the old honesty in her sincere eyes.

"Will you come and say good-night to me if I let you go now?"

"Yes."

Her beautiful lips were near his; he could not help kissing her once more. Then he released her.

The room was dim. Opening the door, she saw Diana and July coming through the shed toward her, their clothes wet and streaked with red clay. Diana explained their long absence gravely. July had not been able to restrain his curiosity about the dead soldier, and when he finally found his wife, where she was searching for "miss," they were both so far up the mountain that he announced his intention of going to "find the pore fellow anyway," and that she might go with him or return homeward as she pleased.

"Sence he would go, it was better fo' me to go too, miss," said the black wife, glancing at her husband with some severity. "An' while we was about it, we jess buried him."

The sternly honest principles of Diana countenanced no rifling of pockets, no thefts of clothing; she would not trust July alone with the dead man. Who knew what temptation there might be in the shape of a pocket-knife? Without putting her fears into words, however—for she always carefully guarded her husband's dignity—she accompanied him, stood by while he made his examination, and then waited alone in the ravine while he went to a farm-house a mile or two distant and returned with two other blacks, who assisted in digging the grave. The rain pattered down upon the leaves overhead, and at last reached her and the dead, whose face she had reverently covered with her clean white apron. When all was ready, they carefully lowered the body to its last resting-place, first lining the hollow with fresh green leaves, according to the rude unconscious poetry which the negroes, left to themselves, often display. Diana had then kneeled down and "offered a powerfu' prayer," so July said. Then, having made a "firs'-rate moun' ober him," they had come away, leaving him to his long repose.

Half an hour later the Redds returned also. By contrast with the preceding stillness, the little house seemed full to overflowing. Anne busied herself in household tasks, and let the others wait upon the patient. But she did not deny herself the pleasure of looking at him from the other side of the room now and then, and she smiled brightly whenever his eyes met hers and gave back her mute salutation.

Heathcote was so much better that only July was to watch that night; Diana was to enjoy an unbroken night's rest, with a pillow and a blanket upon the hay in the barn. July went out to arrange this bed for his wife, and then, as the patient was for the moment left alone, Anne stole down from her loft to keep her promise.

"Good-night," she murmured, bending over him. "Do not keep me, good-night."

He drew her toward him, but, laughing lightly and happily, she slipped from his grasp and was gone.

When July returned, there was no one there but his patient, who did not have so quiet a night as they had anticipated, being restless, tormented apparently by troubled dreams.

CHAPTER XXVI.

"My only wickedness is that I love you; my only goodness, the same."—Anonymous.

"A Durwaish in his prayer said: 'O God, show kindness toward the wicked; for on the good Thou hast already bestowed kindness enough by having created them virtuous.'"—Saadi.

Anne passed the next day in the same state of vivid happiness. The mere joy of the present was enough for her; she thought not as yet of the future, of next month, next week, or even to-morrow. It sufficed that they were there together, and free without wrong to love each other. During the morning there came no second chance for their being alone, and Heathcote grew irritated as the slow hours passed. Farmer Redd esteemed it his duty, now that he was at home again, to entertain his guest whenever, from his open eyes, he judged him ready for conversation; and Mrs. Redd, July, and Diana seemed to have grown into six persons at least, from their continuous appearances at the door. At last, about five o'clock, Anne was left alone in the room, and his impatient eyes immediately summoned her. Smiling at his irritation, she sat down by the bedside and took up the fan.

"You need not do that," he said; "or rather, yes, do. It will keep you here, at any rate. Where *have* you been all day?"

They could talk in low tones unheard; but through the open door Mrs. Redd and Diana were visible, taking down clothes from the line. Heathcote watched them for a moment, and then looked at his nurse with silent wistfulness.

"But it is a great happiness merely to be together," said Anne, answering the look in words.

"Yes, I know it; but yet— Tell me, Anne, do you love me?"

"You know I do; in truth, you have told me you knew it more times than was generous," she answered, almost gayly. She was fairly light-hearted now with happiness.

"That is not what I want. Look at me and tell me; do, dear." He spoke urgently, almost feverishly; a sombre restless light burned in his eyes.

And then she bent forward and looked at him with so much love that his inmost heart was stirred. "I love you with all my heart, all my being," she murmured, even the fair young beauty of her face eclipsed by the light from the soul within. He saw then what he had seen before—how deep was her love for him. But this time there was in it no fear; only perfect trust.

He turned his head away as if struggling with some hidden emotion. But Anne, recovering herself, fell back into her former content, and began to talk with the child-like ease of happiness. She told him of her life, all that had happened since their parting. Once or twice, when her story approached their past, and she made some chance inquiry, he stopped her. "Do not ask questions," he said; "let us rest content with what we have;" and she, willing to follow his fancy, smiled and refrained. He lay silently watching her as she talked. Her faith in him was absolute; it was part of her nature, and he knew her nature. It was because she was what she was that he had loved her, when all the habits and purposes of his life were directly opposed to it.

"Anne," he said, "when will you marry me?"

"Whenever you wish," she answered, with what was to him the sweetest expression of obedience that a girl's pure eyes ever held.

"Will you go with me, as soon as I am able, and let some clergyman in the nearest village marry us?"

"I would rather have Miss Lois come, and little André; still, Ward, it shall be as you wish."

He took her hand, and laid his hot cheek upon it; a moisture gathered in his eyes. "You trust me entirely. You would put your hand in mine to-night and go out into the world with me unquestioning?"

"Yes."

"Kiss me once, love—just once more." His face was altering; its faint color had faded, and a brown pallor was taking its place.

"You are tired," said Anne, regretfully; "I have talked to you too long." What he had said made no especial impression upon her; of course she trusted him.

"Kiss me," he said again; "only once more, love." There was a strange dulled look in his eyes; she missed the expression which had lain there since the avowal of the day before. She turned; there was no one in sight—the women had gone to the end of the garden. She bent over and kissed him with timid tenderness, and as her lips touched his cheek, tears stole from his eyes under the closed lashes. Then, as steps were approaching, he turned his face toward the wall, and covered his eyes with his hand. She thought that he was tired, that he had been overtaxed by all that had happened, and going out softly she cautioned the others. "Do not go in at present; I think he is falling asleep."

"Well, then, I'll jest take this time to run across to Miss Pendleton's and git some of that yere fine meal; I reckon the captain will like a cake of it for supper," said Mrs. Redd. "And, Di, you go down to Dawson's and git a young chicken for briling. No one need say as how the captain don't have enough to eat yere."

July was left in charge. Anne took her straw hat, passed through the garden, and into the wood-lot behind, where she strolled to and fro, looking at the hues of the sunset through the trees, although not in reality conscious of the colors at all, save as part of the great boundless joy of the day.

She had been there some time, when a sound roused her; she lifted her eyes. Was it a ghost approaching?

Weak, holding on by the trees, a shadow of his former self, it was Ward Heathcote who was coming toward her as well as he could, swerving a little now and then, and moving unsteadily, yet walking. July had deserted his post, and the patient, left alone, had risen, dressed himself unaided, and was coming to find her.

With a cry she went to meet him, and drew him down upon a fallen tree trunk. "What *can* you mean?" she said, kneeling down to support him.

"Do not," he answered (and the voice was unlike Heathcote's). "I will move along so that I can lean against this tree. Come where I can see you, Anne; I have something to say."

"Let us first go back to the house. Then you can say it."

160

But he only made a motion of refusal, and, startled by his manner, she came and stood before him as he desired. He began to speak at once, and rapidly.

"Anne, I have deceived you. Helen is married; but *I*—am her husband."

She gazed at him. Not a muscle or feature had stirred, yet her whole face was altered.

"I did not mean to deceive you; there was no plan. It was a wild temptation that swept over me suddenly when I found that you were free—not married as I had thought; that you still loved me, and that you—did not know. I said to myself, let me have the sweetness of her love for one short day, one short day only, and then I will tell her all. Yet I might have let it go on for a while longer, Anne, if it had not been for your own words this afternoon: you would go with me anywhere, at any time, trusting me utterly, loving me as you only can love. Your faith has humiliated me; your unquestioning trust has made me ashamed. And so I have come to tell you the deception, and to tell you also that I love you so that I will no longer trust myself. I do not say that I can not, but that I will not. And I feel the strongest self-reproach of my life that I took advantage of your innocent faith to draw out, even for that short time, the proof which I did not need; for ever since that morning in the garden, Anne, I have known that you loved me. It was that which hurt me in your marriage. But you are so sweet, so dangerously sweet to me, and I—have not been accustomed to deny myself. This is no excuse; I do not offer it as such. But remember what kind of a man I have been; remember that I love you, and—forgive me."

For the first time he now looked at her. Still and white as a snow statue, she met his gaze mutely.

"I can say no more, Anne, unless you tell me you forgive me."

She did not answer. He moved as if to rise and come to her, but she stretched out her hand to keep him back.

"You are too weak," she murmured, hurriedly. "Yes, yes, I forgive you."

"You will wish to know how it all happened," he began again, and his voice showed his increasing exhaustion.

"No; I do not care to hear."

"I will write it, then."

There was a momentary pause; he closed his eyes. The girl, noting, amid her own suffering, the deathly look upon his face, came to his side. "You must go back to the house," she said. "Will my arm be enough? Or shall I call July?"

He looked at her; a light came back into his eyes. "Anne," he whispered, "would not the whole world be well lost to us if we could have but love and each other?"

She returned his gaze. "Yes," she said, "it would—if happiness were all."

"Then you *would* be happy with me, darling?"

"Yes."

"Alone with me, and—in banishment?"

"In banishment, in disgrace, in poverty, pain, and death," she answered, steadily.

"Then you will go with me, trusting to me only?" He was holding her hands now, and she did not withdraw them.

"No," she answered; "never. If happiness were all, I said. But it is not all. There is something nearer, higher than happiness." She paused. Then rapidly and passionately these words broke from her: "Ward, Ward, you are far more than my life to me. Do not kill me, kill my love for you, my faith in you, by trying to tempt me more. You could not succeed; I tell you plainly you could never succeed; but it is not on that account I speak. It is because it would kill me to lose my belief in you, my love, my only, only love!"

"But I am not so good as you think," murmured Heathcote, leaning his head against her. His hands, still holding hers, were growing cold.

"But you are brave. And you *shall* be true. Go back to Helen, and try to do what is right, as *I* also shall try."

"But you—that is different. *You* do not care."

"Not care!" she repeated, and her voice quivered and broke. "You *know* that is false."

"It is. Forgive me."

"Promise me that you will go back; promise for my sake, Ward. Light words are often spoken about a broken heart; but I think, if you fail me now, my heart will break indeed."

"What must I do?"

"Go back to Helen—to your life, whatever it is."

"And shall I see you again?"

"No."

161

"It is too hard, too hard," he whispered, putting his arms round her.

But she unclasped them. "I have your promise?" she said.

"No."

"Then I *take* it." And lightly touching his forehead with her lips, she turned and was gone.

When July and Diana came to bring back their foolhardy patient, they found him lying on the earth so still and cold that it seemed as if he were dead. That night the fever appeared again. But there was only Diana to nurse him now; Anne was gone.

Farmer Redd acted as guide and escort back to Peterson's Mill; but the pale young nurse would not stop, begging Dr. Flower to send her onward immediately to Number Two. She was so worn and changed that the surgeon feared that fever had already attacked her, and he sent a private note to the surgeon of Number Two, recommending that Miss Douglas should at once be returned to Number One, and, if possible, sent northward to her home. But when Anne arrived at Number One, and saw again the sweet face of Mrs. Barstow, when she felt herself safely surrounded by the old work, she said that she would stay for a few days longer. While her hands were busy, she could think; as she could not sleep, she would watch. She felt that she had now to learn life entirely anew; not only herself, but the very sky, sunshine, and air. The world was altered.

On the seventh morning a letter came; it was from Heathcote, and had been forwarded from Peterson's Mill. She kept it until she had a half-hour to herself, and then, going to the bank of the river, she sat down under the trees and opened it. Slowly; for it might be for good, or it might be for evil; but, in any case, it was her last. She would not allow herself to receive or read another.

It was a long letter, written with pencil upon coarse blue-lined paper. After saying that the fever had disappeared, and that before long he should try to rejoin his regiment, the words went on as follows:

"I said that I would write and tell you all. When you ran away from me last year, I was deeply hurt; I searched for you, but could find no clew. Then I went back eastward, joined the camping party, and after a day or two returned with them to Caryl's. No one suspected where I had been. From Caryl's we all went down to the city together, and the winter began.

"I was, in a certain way, engaged to Helen; yet I was not bound. Nor was she. I liked her: she had known how to adapt herself to me always. But I had never been in any haste; and I wondered sometimes why she held to me, when there were other men, worth more in every way than Ward Heathcote, who admired her as much as I did. But I did not then know that she loved me. I know it now.

"After our return to the city, I never spoke of you; but now and then she mentioned your name of her own accord, and I—listened. She was much surprised that you did not write to her; she knew no more where you were than I did, and hoped every day for a letter; so did I. But you did not write.

"All this time—I do not like to say it, yet it is part of the story—she made herself my slave. There was nothing I could say or do, no matter how arbitrary, to which she did not yield, in which she did not acquiesce. No word concerning marriage was spoken, even our former vague lovers' talk had ceased; for, after you hurt me so deeply, Anne, I had not the heart for it. My temper was anything but pleasant. The winter moved on; I had no plan; I let things take their course. But I always expected to find you in some way, to see you again, until—that marriage notice appeared. I took it to Helen. 'It is Anne, I suppose?' I said. She read it, and answered, 'Yes.' She was deceived, just as I was."

Here Anne put down the letter, and looked off over the river. Helen knew that Tita's name was Angélique, and that the sister's was plain Anne. It was a lie direct. But Heathcote did not know it. "He shall never know through me," she thought, with stern sadness.

The letter went on: "I think she had not suspected me before, Anne—I mean in connection with you: she was always thinking of Rachel. But she did then, and I saw it. I was so cut up about it that I concealed nothing. About a week after that she was thrown from her carriage. They thought she was dying, and sent for me. Miss Teller was in the hall waiting; she took me into the library, and said that the doctors thought Helen might live if they could only rouse her, but that she seemed to be sinking into a stupor. With tears rolling down her cheeks, she said, 'Ward, I know you love her, and she has long loved you. But you have said nothing, and it has worn upon her. Go to her and save her life. *You* can.'

"She took me into the room, and went out, closing the door. Helen was lying on a couch; I thought she was already dead. But when I bent over her and spoke her name, she opened her eyes, and knew me immediately. I was shocked by her death-like face. It was all so sudden. I had left her the night before, dressed for a ball. She whispered to me to lift her in my arms, so that she might die there; but I was afraid to move her, lest her suffering should increase. She begged with so much earnestness, however, that at last, gently as I could, I lifted and held her. 'I am going to die,' she whispered, 'so I need not care any more, or try. I have always loved you, Ward. I loved you even when I married Richard.' I thought her mind was wandering; and she must have seen that I did, because she spoke again, and this time aloud. 'I am perfectly myself. I tell you that I have always loved you; you *shall* know it before I die.' Miss Teller said, 'And he loves you also, my darling child; he has told me so. Now, for *his* sake you will try to recover and be his wife.'

"We were married two days later. The doctors advised it, because when I was not there Helen sank rapidly. I took care of the poor girl for weeks; she ate only from my hand. As she grew stronger, I taught her to walk again, and carried her in my arms up and down stairs. When at last she began to improve, she gained strength rapidly; she is now well, save that she will never be able to walk far or dance. I think she is happy. It seems a feeble thing to say, and yet it is something—I am always kind to Helen.

"As for you—it was all a wild, sudden temptation.

"I will go back to my regiment (as to my being in the army, after that attack on Sumter it seemed to me the only thing to do). I will make no attempt to follow you. In short, I will do—as well as I can. It may not be very well.

W. H."

That was all. Anne, miserable, lonely, broken-hearted, as she was, felt that she had in one way conquered. She leaned her head against the tree trunk, and sat for some time with her eyes closed. Then she tore the letter into fragments, threw them into the river, and watched the slow current bear them away. When the last one had disappeared, she rose and went back to the hospital.

"The clean clothes have been brought in, Miss Douglas," said the surgeon's assistant. "Can you sort them?"

"Yes," she replied. And dull life moved on again.

CHAPTER XXVII.

"O Toil, O Loneliness, O Poverty, doing the right makes ye no easier."

The next morning the new nurses, long delayed, sent by the Weston Aid Society, arrived at Number One, and Mary Crane, Mrs. Barstow, and Anne were relieved from duty, and returned to their Northern home. During the journey Anne decided that she must not remain in Weston. It was a hard decision, but it seemed to her inevitable. This man whom she loved knew that her home was there. He had said that he would not follow her; but could she depend upon his promise? Even in saying that he would try to do as well as he could, he had distinctly added that it might "not be very well." She must leave no temptation in his path, or her own. She must put it out of his power to find her, out of hers to meet him. She must go away, leaving no trace behind.

She felt deeply thankful that at the present moment her movements were not cramped by the wants of the children; for if they had been in pressing need, she must have staid—have staid and faced the fear and the danger. Now she could go. But whither? It would be hard to go out into the broad world again, this time more solitary than before. After much thought, she decided to go eastward to the half-house, Jeanne-Armande having given her permission to use it. It would be at least a shelter over her head, and probably old Nora would be glad to come and stay with her. With this little home as background, she hoped to be able to obtain pupils in the city, little girls to whom she could be day governess, giving lessons in music and French. But the pupils: how could she obtain them? Whose influence could she hope for? She could not go to Tante, lest Helen should hear of her presence. At first it seemed as if there were no one; she went over and over in vain her meagre list of friends. Suddenly a remembrance of the little German music-master, who had taught classical music, and hated Belzini, came to her; he was no longer at the Moreau school, and she had his address. He had been especially kind. She summoned her courage and wrote to him. Herr Scheffel's reply came promptly and cordially. "I have your letter received, and I remember you entirely. I know not now all I can promise, as my season of lessons is not yet begun, but two little girls you can have at once for scales, though much they will not pay. But with your voice, honored Fräulein, a place in a church choir is the best, and for that I will do my very best endeavor. But while you make a beginning, honored Fräulein, take my wife and I for friends. Our loaf and our cup, and our hearts too, are all yours."

The little German had liked Anne: this pupil, and this one only, had cheered the dull hours he had spent in the little third-story room, where he, the piano, and the screen had their cramped abode. Anne smiled as she gratefully read his warm-hearted letter, his offer of his cup and his loaf; she could hear him saying it—his "gup" and his "loave," and "two liddle girls for sgales, though moche they will not bay." She had written to old Nora also, and the answer (a niece acting as scribe) declared, with Hibernian effusiveness, and a curious assemblage of negatives, that she would be glad to return to the half-house on Jeanne-Armande's old terms, namely, her living, but no wages. She did not add that, owing to rheumatism, she was unable to obtain work where she was;

she left Anne to find that out for herself. But even old Nora, bandaged in red flannel, her gait reduced to a limp, was a companion worth having when one is companionless. During the interval, Anne had received several letters from Miss Lois. Little André was better, but the doctors advised that he should remain where he was through the winter. Miss Lois wrote that she was willing to remain, in the hope of benefit to the suffering boy, and how great a concession this was from the careful housekeeper and home-lover only Anne could know. (But she did not know how close the child had grown to Miss Lois's heart.) This new plan would prevent their coming to Weston at present. Thankful now for what would have been, under other circumstances, a great disappointment, Anne resigned her position in the Weston school, and went away, at the last suddenly, and evading all inquiries. Mrs. Green was absent, the woman in temporary charge of the lodgings was not curious, and the lonely young teacher was able to carry out her design. She left Weston alone in the cold dawn of a dark morning, her face turned eastward.

It was a courageous journey; only Herr Scheffel to rely upon, and the great stony-hearted city to encounter in the hard struggle for daily bread. Yet she felt that she must not linger in Weston; and she felt, too, that she must not add herself to Miss Lois's cares, but rather make a strong effort to secure a new position as soon as possible, in order to send money to André. She thought that she would be safely hidden at the half-house. Heathcote knew that Jeanne-Armande was in Europe, and therefore he would not think of her in connection with Lancaster, but would suppose that she was still in Weston, or, if not there, then at home on her Northern island. In addition, one is never so well hidden as in the crowds of a large city. But when she saw the spires, as the train swept over the salt marshes, her heart began to beat: the blur of roofs seemed so vast, and herself so small and alone! But she made the transit safely, and drove up to the door of the half-house in the red wagon, with Li as driver, at sunset. A figure was sitting on the steps outside, with a large bundle at its feet; it was Nora. Anne opened the door with Jeanne-Armande's key, and they entered together.

"Oh, wirra, wirra! Miss Douglas dear, and did ye know she'd taken out all the furrrniture? Sure the ould shell is empty." It was true, and drearily unexpected.

Jeanne-Armande, finding time to make a flying visit to her country residence the day before she sailed, had been seized with the sudden suspicion that certain articles were missing, notably a green wooden pail and a window-curtain. The young priest, who had met her there by appointment, and opened the door for her with his key (what mazes of roundabout ways homeward, in order to divert suspicion, Jeanne-Armande required of him that day!), was of the opinion that she was mistaken. But no; Jeanne-Armande was never mistaken. She knew just where she had left that pail, and as for the pattern of the flowers upon that curtain, she knew every petal. Haunted by a vision of the abstraction of all her household furniture, piece by piece, during her long absence— tables, chairs, pans, and candle-sticks following each other through back windows, moved by invisible hands— she was seized with an inspiration on the spot: she would sell off all her furniture by public sale that very hour, and leave only an empty house behind her. She knew that she was considered a mystery in the neighborhood; probably, then, people would come to a Mystery's sale, and pay good prices for a Mystery's furniture. Of one thing she was certain—no buyer in that region knew how to buy for prices as low as she herself had paid. Her method of buying was genius. In five minutes a boy and a bell were secured, in half an hour the whole neighborhood had heard the announcement, and, as mademoiselle had anticipated, flocked to the sale. She attended to all negotiations in person, still in her rôle of a Mystery, and sailed for Europe the next day in triumph, having in her pocket nearly twice the sum she had originally expended. She did not once think of Anne in connection with this. Although she had given her authority to use the half-house, and had intrusted to her care her own key, it seemed almost impossible that the young girl would wish to use it. For was she not admirably established at Weston, with all the advantages of mademoiselle's own name and position behind her?

And thus it was that only bare walls met Anne's eyes as, followed by Nora, she went from room to room, asking herself silently what she should do in this new emergency that confronted her. One door they found locked; it was the door of the store-room: there must, then, be something within. Li was summoned to break the lock, and nothing loath, he broke it so well that it was useless from that hour. Yes, here was something—the unsold articles, carefully placed in order. A chair, a kitchen table, an iron tea-kettle with a hole in it, and two straw beds—the covers hanging on nails, and the straw tied in bundles beneath; there was also a collection of wooden boxes, which mademoiselle had endeavored, but without success, to dispose of as "old, superior, and well-seasoned kindling-wood." It was a meagre supply of furniture with which to begin housekeeping, a collection conspicuous for what it lacked. But Anne, summoning courage, directed Li to carry down stairs all the articles, such as they were, while she cheered old Nora with the promise to buy whatever was necessary, and asked her to unpack the few supplies she had herself purchased on her way through the city. The kitchen stove was gone; but there was a fire-place, and Li made a bright fire with some of the superior kindling-wood, mended the kettle, filled it, and hung it over the crackling flame. The boy enjoyed it all greatly. He stuffed the cases with straw, and dragged them down stairs, he brought down the chair and table, and piled up boxes for a second seat, he pinned up Anne's shawl for a curtain, and then volunteered to go to the store for whatever was necessary, insisting, however, upon the strict allowance of two spoons, two plates, and two cups only. It was all like *Robinson Crusoe* and *The Swiss Family Robinson*, and more than two would infringe upon the severe paucity required by those admirable narratives. When he returned with his burden, he affably offered to remain and take supper with them; in truth, it was difficult to leave such a fascinating scene as two straw beds on the floor, and a kettle swinging over a hearth fire, like a gypsy camp—at least as Li imagined it, for that essence of vagrant romanticism is absent from American life, the so-called gypsies always turning out impostors, with neither donkeys, tents, nor camp fires, and instead of the ancient and mysterious language described by Borrow, using generally the well-known and unpoetical dialect that belongs to modern and Americanized Erin. At last, however, Li departed; Anne fastened the door. Old Nora was soon asleep on the straw, but not her young mistress, in whose mind figures, added together and set opposite each other, were inscribing themselves like letters of fire on a black wall. She had not expected any such outlay as would now be required, and the money she had brought with her would not admit it. At last, troubled and despairing, she rose from her hard couch, went to the window, and looked out. Overhead the stars were serenely shining; her mind went back to the little window of her room in the old Agency. These were the same stars; God was the same God; would He not show her a way? Quieted, she returned to her straw, and soon fell asleep.

In the morning they had a gypsy breakfast. The sun shone brightly, and even in the empty rooms the young day looked hopeful. The mistress of the house went in to the city on the morning train, and in spite of all lacks, in spite of all her trouble and care, it was a beautiful girl who entered the train at Lancaster station, and caused for a moment the chronically tired business men to forget their damp-smelling morning papers as they looked at her. For Anne was constantly growing more beautiful; nothing had had power as yet to arrest the strong course of nature. Sorrow had but added a more ripened charm, since now the old child-like openness was gone, and in its place was a knowledge of the depth and the richness and the pain of life, and a reticence. The open page had been written upon, and turned down. Riding on toward the city, she was, however, as unconscious of any observation she attracted as if she had been a girl of marble. Hers was not one of those natures which can follow at a time but one idea; yet something of the intensity which such natures have—the nature of all enthusiasts and partisans—was hers, owing to the strength of the few feelings which absorbed her. For the thousand-and-one changing interests, fancies, and impulses which actuate most young girls there was in her heart no room. It was not that she thought and imagined less, but that she loved more.

Herr Scheffel received her in his small parlor. It was over the shop of a musical instrument maker, a German also. Anne looked into his small show-window while she was waiting for the street door to be opened, noted the great brass tubes disposed diagonally, the accordions in a rampart, the pavement of little music-boxes with views of Switzerland on their lids, and the violins in apotheosis above. Behind the inner glass she saw the instrument maker himself dusting a tambourine. She imagined him playing on it all alone on rainy evenings for company, with the other instruments looking on in a friendly way. Here Herr Scheffel's cheery wife opened the door, and upon learning the name, welcomed her visitor heartily, and ushered her up the narrow stairway.

"How you haf zhanged!" said Herr Scheffel, lifting his hands in astonishment as he met her at the entrance. "But not for the vorse, Fräulein. On the gontrary!" He bowed gallantly, and brought forward his best arm-chair, then bowed again, sat down opposite, folded his hands, and was ready for business or pleasure, as she saw fit to select. Anne had come to him hoping, but not expecting. Fortune favored her, however; or rather, as usual, some one had taken hold of Fortune, and forced her to extend her favor, the some one in this instance being the little music-master himself, who had not only bestowed two of his own scholars as a beginning, but had also obtained for her a trial place in a church choir. He now went with her without delay to the residence of the little pupils, and arranged for the first lesson; then he took her to visit the contralto of the choir, whose good-will he had already besought for the young stranger. The contralto was a thin, disappointed little woman, with rather a bad temper; but as she liked Anne's voice, and hated the organist and tenor, she mentally organized an alliance offensive and defensive on the spot, contralto, soprano, and basso against the other two, with possibilities as to the rector thrown in. For, as the rector regularly attended the rehearsals (under the mild delusion that he was directing the choir), the contralto hoped that the new soprano's face, as well as voice, would draw him out of his guarded neutrality, and give to their side the balance of power. So, being in a friendly mood, she went over the anthems with Anne, and when the little rehearsal was ended, Herr Scheffel took her thin hand, and bowed over it profoundly. Miss Pratt was a native of Maine, and despised romance, yet she was not altogether displeased with that bow. Sunday morning came; the new voice conquered. Anne was engaged to fill the vacant place in the choir. Furniture was now purchased for the empty little home, but very sparingly. It looked as though it would be cold there in the winter. But—winter was not yet come.

Slowly she gained other pupils; but still only little girls "for the sgales," as Herr Scheffel said. The older scholars for whom she had hoped did not as yet seek her. But the little household lived.

In the mean while Père Michaux on the island and Miss Lois at the springs had both been taken by surprise by Anne's sudden departure from Weston. They knew nothing of it until she was safely in the half-house. But poor

Miss Lois, ever since the affair of Tita and Rast, had cynically held that there was no accounting for anybody or anything in this world, and she therefore remained silent. Père Michaux divined that there was something behind; but as Anne offered no explanation, he asked no question. In truth, the old priest had a faith in her not unlike that which had taken possession of Heathcote. What was it that gave these two men of the world this faith? It was not her innocence alone, for many are innocent. It was her sincerity, combined with the peculiar intensity of feeling which lay beneath the surface—an intensity of which she was herself unconscious, but which their eyes could plainly perceive, and, for its great rarity, admire, as the one perfect pearl is admired among the thousands of its compeers by those who have knowledge and experience enough to appreciate its flawlessness. But the majority have not this knowledge; they admire mere size, or a pear-like shape, or perhaps some eccentricity of color. Thus the perfect one is guarded, and the world is not reduced to despair.

During these days in the city Anne had thought often of Helen. Her engagements were all in another quarter, distant from Miss Teller's residence; she would not have accepted pupils in that neighborhood. But it was not probable that any would be offered to her in so fashionable a locality. She did not allow herself even to approach that part of the city, or to enter the streets leading to it, yet many times she found herself longing to see the house in spite of her determination, and thinking that if she wore a thick veil, so that no one would recognize her, there would be no danger, and she might catch a glimpse of Miss Teller, or even of Helen. But she never yielded to these longings. October passed into November, and November into December, and she did not once transgress her rules.

Early in December she obtained a new pupil, her first in vocal music. She gave two lessons without any unusual occurrence, and then—Of all the powers that make or mar us, the most autocratic is Chance. Let not the name of Fate be mentioned in its presence; let Luck hide its head. For Luck is but the man himself, and Fate deals only with great questions; but Chance attacks all irrelevantly and at random. Though man avoids, arranges, labors, and plans, one stroke from its wand destroys all. Anne had avoided, arranged, labored, and planned, yet on her way to give the third lesson to this new pupil she came suddenly upon—Helen.

On the opposite side a carriage had stopped; the footman opened the door, and a servant came from the house to assist its occupant. Anne's eyes by chance were resting upon the group. She saw a lady lifted to the pavement; then saw her slowly ascend the house steps, while a maid followed with shawls and wraps. It was Helen. Anne's eyes recognized her instantly. She was unchanged—proud, graceful, and exquisitely attired as ever, in spite of her slow step and need of assistance. Involuntarily the girl opposite had paused; then, recovering herself, she drew down her veil and walked on, her heart beating rapidly, her breath coming in throbs. But no one had noticed her. Helen was already within the house, and the servant was closing the door; then the footman came down the steps, sprang up to his place, and the carriage rolled away.

She went on to her pupil's residence, and, quietly as she could, asked, upon the first opportunity, her question.

"A lady who was assisted up the steps? Oh yes, I know whom you mean; it is Mrs. Ward Heathcote," replied the girl-pupil. "Isn't she too lovely! Did you see her face?"

"Yes. Does she live in that house?"

"I am delighted to say that she *does*. She used to live with her aunt, Miss Teller, but it seems that she inherited this old house over here from her grandfather, who died not long ago, and she has taken a fancy to live in it. Of course *I* think all her fancies are seraphic, and principally this one, since it has brought her near *us*. I look at her half the time; just gaze and gaze!" Cora was sixteen, and very pretty; she talked in the dialect of her age and set. Launched now on a favorite topic, she rushed on, while the teacher, with downcast eyes, listened, and rolled and unrolled the sheet of music in her hands. Mrs. Heathcote's beauty; Mrs. Heathcote's wealth; Mrs. Heathcote's wonderful costumes; Mrs. Heathcote's romantic marriage, after a fall from her carriage; Mrs. Heathcote's husband, "*chivalrously* in the army, with a pair of *eyes*, Miss Douglas, which, I do assure you, are—well, *murderously* beautiful is not a word to express it! Not that he *cares*. The most *indifferent* person! Still, if you could *see* them, you would *know* what I mean." Cora told all that she knew, and more than she knew. The two households had no acquaintance, Anne learned; the school-girl had obtained her information from other sources. There would, then, be no danger of discovery in that way. The silent listener could not help listening while Cora said that Captain Heathcote had not returned home since his first departure; that he had been seriously ill somewhere in the West, but having recovered, had immediately returned to his regiment without coming home on furlough, as others always did, after an illness, or even the pretense of one, which conduct Cora considered so "perfectly grand" that she wondered "the papers" did not "blazon it aloft." At last even the school-girl's volubility and adjectives were exhausted, and the monologue came to an end. Then the teacher gave her lesson, and the words she had heard sounded in her ears like the roar of the sea in a storm—it seemed as though she must be speaking loudly in order to drown it. But her pupil noticed nothing, save that Miss Douglas was more quiet than usual, and perhaps more pale. When she went away, she turned eastward, in order not to pass the house a second time—the house that held Helen. But she need not have taken the precaution;

hers was not a figure upon which the eyes of Mrs. Heathcote would be likely to dwell. In the city, unfashionable attire is like the ring of Gyges, it renders the wearer, if not invisible, at least unseen.

That night she could not sleep; she could do nothing but think of Helen, Helen, her once dearly loved friend—Helen, his wife. She knew that she must give up this new danger, and she knew also that she loved the danger—these chances of a glimpse of Helen, Helen's home, and—yes, it might be, at some future time, Helen's husband. But she conquered herself again. In the morning she wrote a note to Cora's mother, saying that she found herself unable to continue the lessons; as Cora had the manuscript music-books which Dr. Douglas had himself prepared for his daughter when she was a little girl on the island, she added that she would come for them on Monday, and at the same time take leave of her pupil, from whom she parted with regret.

Saturday and Sunday now intervened. At the choir rehearsal on Saturday a foreboding came over her; occult malign influences seemed hovering in the air. The tenor and organist, the opposition party, were ominously affable. In this church there was, as in many another, an anomalous "music committee," composed apparently of vestrymen, but in reality of vestrymen's wives. These wives, spurred on secretly by the tenor and organist, had decided that Miss Douglas was not the kind of soprano they wished to have. She came into the city by train on the Sabbath day; she was dressed so plainly and unfashionably that it betokened a want of proper respect for the congregation; in addition, and in spite of this plain attire, there was something about her which made "the gentlemen turn and look at her." This last was the fatal accusation. Poor Anne could not have disproved these charges, even if she had known what they were; but she did not. Her foreboding of trouble had not been at fault however, for on Monday morning came a formal note of dismissal, worded with careful politeness; her services would not be required after the following Sunday. It was a hard blow. But the vestrymen's wives preferred the other candidate (friend of the organist and tenor), who lived with her mother in the city, and patronized no Sunday trains; whose garments were nicely adjusted to the requirements of the position, following the fashions carefully indeed, but at a distance, and with chastened salaried humility as well; who sang correctly, but with none of that fervor which the vestrymen's wives considered so "out of place in a church"; and whose face certainly had none of those outlines and hues which so reprehensibly attracted "the attention of the gentlemen." And thus Anne was dismissed.

It was a bitterly cold morning. The scantily furnished rooms of the half-house looked dreary and blank; old Nora, groaning with rheumatism, sat drawn up beside the kitchen stove. Anne, who had one French lesson to give, and the farewell visit to make at the residence of Mrs. Iverson, Cora's mother, went in to the city. She gave the lesson, and then walked down to the Scheffels' lodging to bear the dark tidings of her dismissal. The musical instrument maker's window was frosted nearly to the top; but he had made a round hole inside with a hot penny, and he was looking through it when Anne rang the street bell. It was startling to see a human eye so near, isolated by the frost-work—an eye and nothing more; but she was glad he could amuse himself even after that solitary fashion. Herr Scheffel had not returned from his round of lessons. Anne waited some time in the small warm crowded room, where growing plants, canary-birds, little plaster busts of the great musicians, the piano, and the stove crowded each other cheerfully, but he did not come. Mrs. Scheffel urged her to remain all night. "It ees zo beetter cold." But Anne took leave, promising to come again on the morrow. It was after four o'clock, and darkness was not far distant; the piercing wind swept through the streets, blowing the flinty dust before it; the ground was frozen hard as steel. She made her farewell visit at Mrs. Iverson's, took her music-books, and said good-by, facing the effusive regrets of Cora as well as she could, and trying not to think how the money thus relinquished would be doubly needed now. Then she went forth into the darkening street, the door of the warm, brightly lighted home closing behind her like a knell. She had chosen twilight purposely for this last visit, in order that she might neither see nor be seen. She shivered now as the wind struck her, clasped the heavy books with one arm, and turned westward on her way to the railway station. It seemed to her that the city held that night no girl so desolate as herself.

As she was passing the street lamp at the first corner, some one stopped suddenly. "Good heavens! Miss Douglas—Anne—is that you?" said a voice. She looked up. It was Gregory Dexter.

CHAPTER XXVIII.

"Loke who that ... most intendeth ay

To do the generous deedes that he can,

And take *him* for the greatest

gentleman."

—Chaucer.

"Anne! Is it you?" repeated Dexter.

"Yes," she replied, having seen that it was impossible to escape, since he was standing directly in her path. Then she tried to smile. "I should not have thought you would have known me in this twilight."

"I believe I should know you anywhere, even in total darkness. But where are you going? I will accompany you."

"I am on my way to X station, to take a train."

"Let me carry those books for you. X station? That is at some distance; would it not be better to have a carriage? Here, boy, run and call a carriage. There will be a half-dollar for you if you make haste."

He was the same as ever, prompt, kind, and disposed to have his own way. But Anne, who on another occasion might have objected, now stood beside him unopposing. She *was* weary, cold, and disheartened, and she was glad he was there. He had made her take his arm immediately, and even that small support was comforting. The carriage came, they rolled away, Anne leaning back against the cushions, and breathing in the grateful sense of being cared for and protected, taken from the desolate and darkening streets which otherwise she must have traversed alone.

"I only arrived in town to-day," Dexter was saying; "and, on my way to a friend's house where I am to dine, I intended calling upon Mrs. Heathcote. I was going there when I met you. I should have inquired about you immediately, for I have but just seen the account of the disposal of Miss Vanhorn's estate, and was thinking of you. I supposed, Miss Douglas, that you were to be her heir."

"No."

"She certainly allowed me to suppose so."

"I do not think she ever had any such intention," replied Anne.

"You are living near the city?"

"Yes; at Lancaster. I give lessons in town."

"And you come in and out on these freezing days, and walk to and from the station?"

"It is not always so cold."

"Very well; I am going as far as Lancaster with you," said Dexter. "I hope I shall be welcome."

"Mr. Dexter, please do not."

But he simply smiled and threw back his head in his old dictatorial way, helped her from the carriage, bought tickets, secured for her the best seat in the car, and took his place beside her; it seemed to Anne that but a few minutes had passed when they heard "Lancaster," and stepping out on the little platform, found the faithful Li in waiting, his comforter tied over his ears, and jumping up and down to keep himself warm. Anne had not ordered the red wagon, and he was not therefore allowed to bring it out; but the little freckled knight-errant had brought himself instead as faithful escort homeward.

"Is there no carriage here, or any sort of a vehicle?" said Dexter, in his quick, authoritative way. "Boy, bring a carriage."

"There ain't none; but you can have the red wagon. Horse good, and wagon first-rate. It'll be a dollar," answered Li.

"Go and get it, then."

The boy was gone like a dart, and in less time than any one else would have taken, he was back with the wagon, and Mr. Dexter (in spite of her remonstrance) was accompanying Anne homeward in the icy darkness. "But you will lose the return train," she said.

"I intend to lose it."

When they stopped at the gate, no light was visible; Anne knocked, but crippled old Nora was long in coming. When she did open the door, it was a room nearly as cold as the air outside into which the guest was ushered. As Li was obliged to return with the horse, his willing hands were absent, and the young mistress of the house went out herself, brought in candles and kindling-wood, and was stooping to light the fire, when Dexter took the wood from her, led her to a chair, seated her despotically, and made the fire himself. Then, standing before it, he looked all round the room, slowly and markedly and in silence; afterward his eyes came back to her. "So this is where you live—all the home you have!"

"It is but a temporary home. Some day I hope to go back to the island," replied Anne.

"When you have, by teaching, made money enough to live upon, I suppose. It looks like it *here*," he said, with sarcastic emphasis.

168

"It has not been so cold before," answered Anne. "The house has an empty look, I acknowledge; that is because I supposed it was furnished; but finding it bare, I decided to purchase only necessary articles. What is the use of buying much for a temporary home?"

"Of course. So much better to do without, especially in this weather!"

"I assure you we have not been uncomfortable until, perhaps, to-night."

"May I ask the amount, Miss Douglas, of your present income?"

"I do not think you ought to ask," said the poverty-stricken young mistress, bravely.

"But I do ask. And you—will answer."

"It has been, although not large, sufficient for our needs," replied Anne, who, in spite of her desire to hide the truth from him, was yet unable to put the statement into the present tense; but she hoped that he would not notice it.

On the contrary, however, Dexter answered instantly: "Has been? Then it is not now?"

"I have recently lost my place in a church choir; but I hope soon to obtain another position."

"And in the mean time you live on—hope? Forgive me if I seem inquisitive and even harsh, Miss Douglas; but you do not realize how all this impresses me. The last time I saw you you were richly dressed, a favorite in a luxurious circle, the reputed heiress of a large fortune. Little more than a year passes, and I meet you in the street at twilight, alone and desolate; I come to your home, and find it cold and empty; I look at you, and note your dress. You can offer me nothing, hardly a fire. It hurts me, Anne—hurts me deeply—to think that all this time I have had every luxury, while *you* have suffered."

"No, not suffered," she replied. But her voice trembled. This strong assertive kindness touched her lonely heart keenly.

"Then if you have not suffered as yet—and I am thankful to hear you say it—you will suffer; or rather you might have suffered if I had not met you in time. But never again, Anne—never again. Why, my child, do you not remember that I begged you to be my wife? Shall she who, if she had willed it, would now have been so near and dear to me, be left to encounter toil and privation, while *I* have abundance? Never, Anne—never!"

He left his place, took her hand, and held it in his warm grasp. There was nothing save friendly earnestness in his eyes as they met her upward look, and seeing this, she felt herself leaning as it were in spirit upon him: she had indeed need of aid. He smiled, and comprehended all without another word.

"I must go on the ten-o'clock train," he said, cheerfully, coming back to daily life again. "And before I go, in some way or another, that good Irish goblin of yours must manufacture a supper for me; from appearances, I should say she had only to wave her broom-stick. When I met you I was on my way to dine with some friends. What their estimation of me is at this moment I am afraid to think; but that does not make me any the less hungry. With your permission, therefore, I will take off this heavy overcoat, and dine here." As he spoke he removed his large shaggy overcoat—a handsome fur-lined Canadian garment, suited to his strong figure and the bitter weather, appearing in evening dress, with a little spray of fern in his button-hole. "Now," he said, "I am going out to plead with the goblin in person."

"I will go," said Anne, laughing, won from her depression by his buoyant manner.

"On the contrary, you will stay; and not only that, but seated precisely where I placed you. I will encounter the goblin alone." He opened the door, went through, and closed it behind him. Soon Anne heard the sound of laughter in the kitchen, not only old Nora's hearty Irish mirth, but Li's shriller voice added to it. For the faithful Li had hastened back, after the old horse was housed, in order to be in readiness if Miss Douglas, owing to her unexpected visitor, required anything. What Dexter said and did in that bare, dimly lighted kitchen that night was never known, save from results. But certainly he inspired both Nora, Li, and the stove. He returned to the parlor, made up the fire with so much skill that it shone out brightly, and then sat down, allowing Anne to do nothing save lean back in the low chair, which he had cushioned for her with his shaggy coat. Before long Li came in, first with four lighted candles in new candlesticks, which he disposed about the room according to his taste, and then, later, with table-cloth and plates for the dining-table. The boy's face glowed with glee and exercise; he had already been to the store twice on a run, and returned loaded and breathless, but triumphant. After a while pleasant odors began to steal in from the kitchen, underneath all the inspiring fragrance of coffee. At last the door opened, and Nora herself hobbled in, bringing a covered dish, and then a second, and then a third, Li excitedly handing them to her from the kitchen entrance. When her ambition was aroused, the old Irishwoman was a good cook. It had been aroused to-night by Dexter's largess, and the result was an appetizing although nondescript repast, half dinner, half high-tea. The room was now brightly illuminated; the fire-light danced on the bare floor. Dexter, standing by the table, tall and commanding, his face full of friendliness, seemed to Anne a personification of kindly aid and strength. She no longer made any objection, but obeyed him smilingly, even as to where she should sit, and what she should eat. His sudden appearance, at the moment of all others when everything seemed to have failed, was comfort too penetrating to be resisted. And why should it be resisted? There was no suggestion in his manner of a return to the old subject; on the contrary, he had himself spoken of it as a thing of the past. He would not repeat his old request—would not wish to repeat it.

After the repast was over, and Nora and Li were joyously feasting in the kitchen, he drew his chair nearer to hers, and said, "Now tell me about yourself, and what your life has been since we parted." For up to this time, after those few strong words in the beginning, he had spoken only on general topics, or at least upon those not closely connected with herself.

Anne, however, merely outlined her present life and position, clearly, but without explanation.

"And Mrs. Heathcote does not know you are here?"

"She does not know, and she must not know. I have your promise, Mr. Dexter, to reveal nothing."

"You have my promise, and I will keep it. Still, I do not comprehend—"

"It is not possible that you should comprehend. And in addition to keeping my secret, Mr. Dexter, you must tell *me* nothing of her, or of any of the people who were at Caryl's."

"It is a great gulf fixed?"

"Yes."

He looked at her in silence; she was quiet and thoughtful, her gaze resting on the fire. After a while she said again, "You will remember?"

"Yes. I never had the talent of forgetting."

Soon afterward he went away, with Li as guide. As he took her hand at parting, he said, "Are you coming in to the city to-morrow?"

"Yes; I must see Herr Scheffel."

"Will you let me meet you somewhere?"

After a moment's hesitation, she answered, "I would rather not."

"As you please. But I shall come and see you on Wednesday, then. Good-night." He went out in the intense country darkness, preceded by Li, who had disposed his comforter about him in such a manner as to look as much as possible like the shaggy overcoat, which, in his eyes, was fit for the Czar of all the Russias in his diamond crown.

The next day was even colder. Anne went in to the city, gave one lesson, and then faced the bitter wind on her way down to Herr Scheffel's lodgings. Her heart was not so heavy, in spite of the cold, as it had been the day before, since between that time and this she had heard the cordial voice of a friend.

The musical instrument maker's window was entirely frozen over, the frost was like a white curtain shutting him out from the world; it was to be hoped that he found comfort in playing on his tambourine within. This time Herr Scheffel was at home, and he had a hope concerning a place in another choir. Anne returned to Lancaster cheered. As she walked homeward from the railway station down the hard country road, darkness was falling, and she wondered why the faithful Li was not there as usual to meet her. When she came within sight of the half-house, it was blazing with light; from every window radiance streamed, smoke ascended from the chimneys, and she could see figures within moving about as if at work. What could it mean? She went up the steps, opened the door, and entered. Was this her barren home?

Workmen were putting the finishing touches to what seemed to have been an afternoon's labor; Li, in a fever of excitement, was directing everybody. Through the open door Nora could be seen moving to and fro amid barrels, boxes, and bags. The men had evidently received their orders, for as soon as the young mistress of the house appeared they hastily concluded their labors, and, taking their tools, vanished like so many genii of the ring. Anne called them back, but they were already far down the road. Li and Nora explained together that the men and two wagon-loads of furniture had arrived at the door of the half-house at two o'clock, and that the head workman, showing Mr. Dexter's card, had claimed entrance and liberty to carry out his orders; he had a rough plan of the rooms, sketched by Dexter, and was to follow his directions. Li and Nora, already warm adherents, entered into the scheme with all their hearts, and the result was that mademoiselle's little house was now carpeted, and warmed, and filled from top to bottom. The bare store-room was crowded, the cupboards garnished; there were easy-chairs, curtains, pictures, and even flowers—tea-roses in a vase. The furniture was perhaps too massive, the carpets and curtains too costly for the plain abode; Dexter always erred on the side of magnificence. His lavishness had been brought up at Caryl's as a testimony against him, for it was a decided evidence of newness. But on this gloomy freezing winter night no one could have the heart to say that the rich fabrics were not full of comfort both to the eye and touch, and Anne, sinking into one of the easy-chairs, uncertain what to do, was at least not at all uncertain as to the comfort of the cushioned back; it was luxurious.

Later, in her own room, she sat looking at the unexpected gifts which faced her from all sides. What should she do? It was not right to force them upon her; and yet how like him was the lavish quick generosity! In her poverty the gift seemed enormous; yet it was not. The little home possessed few rooms, had seemed hardly more than a toy house to the city workmen who had hastily filled it. But to Anne it seemed magical. Books had been bought for her also, the well-proved standard works which Dexter always selected for his own reading. In his busy life this American had not had time to study the new writers; he was the one person left who still quoted Addison. After looking at the books, Anne, opening the closet door by chance, saw a long cedar case upon the floor; it was locked, but the key was in an envelope bearing her name. She opened the case; a faint fragrance floated out, as, from its wrappings, she drew forth an India shawl, dark, rich, and costly enough for a duchess. There was a note inside the case from Dexter—a note hastily written in pencil:

"Dear Miss Douglas,—I do not know whether this is anything you can wear, but at least it is warm. On the night I first met you you were shivering, and I have thought of it ever since. Please accept the shawl, therefore, and the other trifles, from your friend, G. D."

The trifles were furs—sable. Here, as usual, Dexter had selected the costly; he knew no other way. And thus surrounded by all the new luxury of the room, with the shawl and the furs in her hands, Anne stood, an image of perplexity.

The next day the giver came out. She received him gravely. There was a look in her eyes which told him that he had not won her approval.

"Of course I do not intend to trouble you often with visits," he said, as he gave his furred overcoat to Li. "But one or two may be allowed, I think, from such an old friend."

"And to such a desolate girl."

"Desolate no longer," he answered, choosing to ignore the reproach of the phrase.

He installed himself in one of the new arm-chairs (looking, it must be confessed, much more comfortable than before), and began to talk in a fluent general way, approaching no topics that were personal. Meanwhile old Nora, hearing from Li that the benefactor of the household was present, appeared, strong in the new richness of her store-room, at the door, and dropping a courtesy, wished to know at what hour it would please him to dine. She said "your honor"; she had almost said "your highness." Her homage was so sincere that Anne smiled, and Dexter laughed outright.

"You see I am expected to stay, whether you wish it or not," he said. "Do let me; it shall be for the last time." Then turning to Nora, he said, "At four." And with another reverence, the old woman withdrew.

"It is a viciously disagreeable afternoon. You would not, I think, have the heart to turn out even a dog," he continued, leaning back at ease, and looking at his hostess, his eyes shining with amusement: he was reading her objections, and triumphing over them. Then, as he saw her soberness deepen, he grew grave immediately. "I am staying to-day because I wish to talk with you, Anne," he said. "I shall not come again. I know as well as you do, of course, that you can not receive me while you have no better chaperon than Nora." He paused, looking at her downcast face. "You do not like what I have done?"

"No."

"Why?"

"You have loaded me with too heavy an obligation."

"Any other reason?"

"I can never repay you."

"In addition?"

"It is not right that you should treat me as though I were a child."

"I knew you would object, and strongly; yet I hope to bring you over yet to my view of the case," said Dexter. "You say that I have placed you under too heavy an obligation. But pray consider what a slight affair the little gift seems to me. The house is very small; I have spent but a few hundreds; in all, with the exception of the shawl and furs, not much over five. What is that to an income like mine? You say you can never repay me. You repay me by accepting. It seems to me a noble quality to accept, simply and generously accept; and I have believed that yours was a noble nature. Accept, then, generously what it is such a pleasure to me to give. On my own side, I say this: the woman Gregory Dexter once asked to be his wife shall not suffer from want while Gregory Dexter lives, and knows where to find her. This has nothing to do with you; it is my side of the subject."

He spoke with much feeling. Anne looked at him. Then she rose, and with quiet dignity gave him, as he rose also, her hand. He understood the silent little action. "You have answered my expectation," he said, and the subject was at an end forever.

171

After dinner, in the twilight, he spoke again. "You said, an hour or two ago, that I had treated you as though you were a child. It is true; for you were a child at Caryl's, and I remembered you as you were then. But you are much changed; looking at you now, it is impossible that I should ever think of you in the same way again."

She made no reply.

"Can you tell me nothing of yourself, of your personal life since we parted? Your engagement, for instance?"

"It is ended. Mr. Pronando is married; he married my sister. You did not see the notice?" (Anne's thoughts were back in the West Virginia farm-house now with the folded slip of newspaper.)

"No; I was in the far West until April. I did not come eastward until the war broke out. Then you are free, Anne? Do not be afraid to tell me; I remember every word you said in Miss Vanhorn's little red parlor, and I shall not repeat my mistake. You are, then, free?"

"I can not answer you."

"Then I will not ask; it all belongs to the one subject, I suppose. The only part intrusted to me—the secret of your being here—I will religiously guard. As to your present life—you would rather let this Herr Scheffel continue looking for a place for you?"

"Yes."

"I will not interfere. But I shall write to you now and then, and you must answer. If at the end of a month you have not obtained this position you are hoping for—in a church choir, is it not?—you must let me know. Will you promise?"

"I promise."

"And bear in mind this: you shall never be left friendless again while I am on earth to protect you."

"But I have no right to—"

"Yes, you have; you have been more to me than you know." Here he paused, and looked away as if debating with himself. "I have always intended that you should know it some time," he continued; "perhaps this is as good a time as any. Will you listen?"

"Yes."

He settled himself anew in his chair, meditated a moment, and then, with all his natural fluency, which nothing could abate, with the self-absorption which men of his temperament always show when speaking of themselves, and yet with a certain guarded look at Anne too all the while, as if curious to see how she would take his words, he began:

"You know what my life has been—that is, generally. What I wish to tell you now is an inner phase. When, at the beginning of middle age, at last I had gained the wealth I always intended to have, I decided that I would marry. I wished to have a home. Of course, during all those toiling years, I had not been without what are called love affairs, but I was far too intensely absorbed in my own purposes to spend much time upon them. Besides, I had preserved an ideal.

"I do not intend to conceal or deny that I am ambitious: I made a deliberate effort to gain admittance into what is called the best society in the Eastern cities, and in a measure I succeeded. I enjoyed the life; it was another world; but still, wherever I went it seemed to me that the women were artificial. Beautiful, attractive, women I could not help admiring, but—not like my ideal of what my wife must be. They would never make for me that home I coveted; for while I stood ready to surround that home with luxury, in its centre I wanted, for myself alone, a true and loving heart, a heart absorbed in me. And then, while I knew that I wanted this, while I still cherished my old ideal closely, what did I do? I began to love Rachel Bannert!

"You look at me; you do not understand why I speak in that tone. It is as well that you should not. I can only say that I worshipped her. It was not her fault that I began to love her, but it was her fault that I was borne on so far; for she made me believe that she loved me; she gave me the privileges of a lover. I never doubted (how could I?) that she would be my wife in the end, although, for reasons of her own, she wished to keep the engagement, for the time being, a secret. I submitted, because I loved her. And then, when I was helpless, because I was so sure of her, she turned upon me and cast me off. Like a worn-out glove!

"Anne, I could not believe it. We were in the ravine; she had strolled off in that direction, as though by chance, and I had followed her. I asked her what she meant: no doubt I looked like a dolt. She laughed in my face. It seemed that she had only been amusing herself; that she had never had any intention of marrying me; a 'comedy of the summer.' But no one laughs in my face twice—not even a woman. When, at last, I understood her, my infatuation vanished; and I said some words to her that night which I think she will not soon forget. Then I turned and left.

"Remember that this was no boy whose feelings she had played with, whose respect she had forfeited; it was a man, and one who had expected to find in this Eastern society a perfection of delicacy and refinement not elsewhere seen. I scorned myself for having loved her, and for the moment I scorned all women too. Then it was, Anne, that the thought of *you* saved me. I said to myself that if you would be my wife, I could be happy with your fresh sincerity, and not sink into that unbelieving, disagreeable cynicism which I had always despised in other men. Acting on the impulse, I asked you.

"I did not love you, save as all right-minded men love and admire a sweet young girl; but I believed in you; there was something about you that aroused trust and confidence. Besides—I tell you this frankly—I thought I should succeed. I certainly did not want to be repulsed twice in one day. I see now that I was misled by Miss Vanhorn. But I did not see it then, and when I spoke to you, I fully expected that you would answer yes.

"You answered no, Anne, but you still saved me. I still believed in you. And more than ever after that last interview. I went away from Caryl's early the next morning, and two days later started for the West. I was hurt through and through, angry with myself, disgusted with life. I wanted to breathe again the freedom of the border. Yet through it all your memory was with me as that of one true, pure, steadfast woman-heart which compelled me to believe in goodness and steadfastness as possibilities in women, although I myself had been so blindly befooled. This is what you, although unconsciously, have done for me: it is an inestimable service.

"I was not much moved from my disgust until something occurred which swept me out of myself—I mean the breaking out of the war. I had not believed in its possibility; but when the first gun was fired, I started eastward at an hour's notice." Here Dexter rose, and with folded arms walked to and fro across the floor. "The class of people you met at Caryl's used to smile and shrug their shoulders over what is called patriotism—I think they are smiling no longer."—(Here Anne remembered "After that attack on Fort Sumter, it seemed to me the only thing to do") "but the tidings of that first gun stirred something in *my* breast which is, I suppose, what that word means. As soon as I reached Pennsylvania, I went up to the district where my mines are, gathered together and equipped all the volunteers who would go. I have been doing similar work on a larger scale ever since. I should long ago have been at the front in person were it not that the Governor requires my presence at home, and I am well aware also that I am worth twenty times more in matters of organization than I should be simply as one more man in the field."

This was true. Gregory Dexter's remarkable business powers and energy, together with his wealth, force, and lavish liberality, made him the strong arm of his State throughout the entire war.

He asked for no comment upon his story; he had told it briefly as a series of facts. But from it he hoped that the listener would draw a feeling which would make her rest content under his friendly aid. And he succeeded.

But before he went away she told him that while accepting all the house contained, she would rather return those of his gifts which had been personal to herself.

"Why?"

"I would rather do it, but I do not know how to explain the feeling," she answered, frankly, although her face was one bright blush.

"If you do not, I do," said Dexter, smiling, and looking at her with the beginnings of a new interest in his eyes. "As you please, of course, although I *did* try to buy a good shawl for you, Anne. Are you not very poorly dressed?"

"Plainly and inexpensively. Quite warmly, however."

"But what am I to do with the things? I will tell you what I shall do: I shall keep them just as they are, in the cedar box. Perhaps some day you will accept them."

She shook her head. But he only smiled back in answer, and soon afterward he went away.

The next day she sent the cedar case to his city address. She wrote a note to accompany it, and then destroyed it. Why should she write? All had been said.

Before the month was quite ended, Herr Scheffel succeeded in obtaining for her a place in another church choir. It was a small church, and the salary was not large, but she was glad to accept it, and more than glad to be able to write to Mr. Dexter that she had accepted it. New pupils came with the new year; she was again able to send money to Miss Lois, for the household supplies, so lavishly provided, were sufficient for the little family throughout the winter.

In February, being again in New York, Dexter came out to see her. It was a wild evening; the wind whistled round the house, and blew the hail and sleet against the panes. Most persons would have remained in the city; but after one look at Dexter's face and figure, no one ever spoke to him about the weather. Anne had received a long letter from Jeanne-Armande; she showed it to him. Also one from Père Michaux. "I feel now," she said, "almost as though you were my—"

"Please do not say father."

"Oh no."

"Brother, then?"

"Hardly that."

"Uncle?"

"Perhaps; I never had an uncle. But, after all, it is more like—" Here she stopped again.

"Guardian?" suggested Dexter; "they are always remarkable persons, at least in books. Never mind the name, Anne; I am content to be simply your friend."

During the evening he made one allusion to the forbidden subject. "You asked me to tell you nothing regarding the people who were at Caryl's, but perhaps the prohibition was not eternal. I spent an hour with Mrs. Heathcote this afternoon (never fear; I kept your secret). Would you not like to hear something of her?"

Anne's face changed, but she did not swerve. "No; tell me nothing," she answered. And he obeyed her wish. In a short time he took leave, and returned to the city. During the remainder of the winter she did not see him again.

CHAPTER XXIX.

"The fierce old fires of primitive ages are not dead yet, although we pretend they are. Every now and then each man of us is confronted by a gleam of the old wild light deep down in his own startled heart."

In the middle of wild, snowy March there came a strange week of beautiful days. On the Sunday of this week Anne was in her place in the choir, as usual, some time before the service began.

It was a compromise choir. The dispute between the ideas of the rector and those of the congregation had been ended by bringing the organ forward to the corner near the chancel, and placing in front of it the singers' seats, ornamented with the proper devices: so much was done for the rector. To balance this, and in deference to the congregation, the old quartette of voices was retained, and placed in these seats, which, plainly intended for ten or twelve surpliced choristers, were all too long and broad for the four persons who alone occupied them. The singers sat in one, and kept their music-books in the other, and objecting to the open publicity of their position facing the congregation, they had demanded, and at last succeeded in obtaining (to the despair of the rector), red curtains, which, hanging from the high railing above, modestly concealed them when they were seated, and converted that corner of the church into something between a booth in a fair and a circus tent.

Before the service began, while the people were coming in, the contralto pushed aside a corner of the curtain as usual, and peeped out. She then reported to Anne in a whisper the course of events, as follows, Anne not caring to hear, but quiescent:

"Loads of people to-day. Wonder why? Oh yes, I remember now; the apostolic bishop's going to be here, and preach about the Indians. Don't you love that man? I do; and I wish I was an Indian myself. We'll have *all* the curtains put back for the sermon. More people coming. I declare it's quite exciting. And I forgot gum-drops on this day of all others, and shall probably be hoarse as a crow, and spoil the duet! I hope you won't be raging. Oh, *do* look! Here's such a swell! A lady; Paris clothes from head to foot. And she's going to sit up here near us too. Take a look?" But Anne declined, and the reporter went on. "She has the lightest hair I ever saw. I wonder if it's bleached? And she's as slender as a paper-cutter." (The contralto was stout.) "But I can't deny that she's handsome, and her clothes are stunning. They're right close to us now, and the man's awfully handsome too, come to look at him—her husband, I suppose. A pair of brown eyes and *such* heavy eyebrows! They—"

But the soprano was curious at last, apparently, and the contralto good-naturedly gave up her look-out corner. Yes, there they were, Helen and Ward Heathcote, Mrs. Heathcote and her husband, Captain Heathcote and his wife. Very near her, and unconscious of her presence. Hungrily, and for one long moment, she could not help looking at them. As the light-tongued girl had said, Helen looked very beautiful, more beautiful than ever, Anne thought. She was clad in black velvet from head to foot, and as the day was unexpectedly warm, she had thrown aside her heavy mantle edged with fur, and her slender form was visible, outlined in the clinging fabric. Under the small black velvet bonnet with its single plume her hair, in all its fine abundance, shone resplendent, contrasting with the velvet's richness. One little delicately gloved hand held a prayer-book, and with the other, as Anne looked, she motioned to her husband. He drew nearer, and she spoke. In answer he sought in his pockets, and drew forth a fan. She extended her hand as if to take it, but he opened it himself, and began to fan her quietly. The heat in the church was oppressive; his wife was delicate; what more natural than that he should do this? Yet the gazer felt herself acutely miserable. She knew Helen so well also that although to the rest of the congregation the fair face preserved unchanged its proud immobility, Anne's eyes could read at once the wife's happiness in her husband's attention.

174

She drew back. "I can not sing to-day," she said, hurriedly; "I am not well. Will you please make my excuses to the others?" As she spoke she drew on her gloves. (She had a fancy that she could not sing with her hands gloved.)

"Why, what in the world—" began the contralto. "But you *do* look frightfully pale. Are you going to faint? Let me go with you."

"I shall not faint, but I must get to the open air as soon as possible. Please stay and tell the others, perhaps Miss Freeborn will sing in my place."

Having succeeded in saying this, her white cheeks and trembling hands witnesses for her, she went out through the little choir door, which was concealed by the curtain, and in another moment was in the street. The organist, hidden in his oaken cell, looked after her in surprise. When the basso came in, with a flower in his mouth, he took the flower out, and grew severely thoughtful over the exigencies of the situation. After a few minutes of hurried discussion, the basso, who was also the leader, came forth from the circus tent and made a majestic progress to the rector's pew, where sat the lily-like Miss Freeborn, the rector's daughter; and then, after another consultation, she rose, and the two made a second majestic progress back to the circus tent, the congregation meanwhile looking on with much interest. When the tenor came, a rather dissipated youth who had been up late the night before, he was appalled by the presence of the lily-like Miss Freeborn, and did not sing as well as usual, Miss Freeborn, although lily-like, keeping him sternly to his notes, and not allowing him any of those lingering little descents after the other singers have finished, upon which he, like many tenors, relied for his principal effects.

Meanwhile Anne was walking rapidly down the street; a mile soon lay between her and the church, yet still she hastened onward. She was in a fever, yet a chill as well. Now she was warm with joy, now cold with grief. She had seen him. Her eyes had rested upon his face at last, and he was safe, he was well and strong again. Was not this joy enough?

And yet he was with Helen. And Helen loved him.

She had asked him to go back to Helen. He had gone back. She had asked him to do his part in life bravely. And he was doing it. Was not this what she wished?

And yet—was it so hard to go back—to go back to beautiful Helen who loved him so deeply? Did his part in life require bravery? Did he look as though it was a sacrifice, a hardship? And here she tried to recall how in truth he had looked—how, to the eyes of a stranger. He was strong again and vigorous; but beyond that she could think only of how he looked to her—the face she knew so well, the profile, the short crisp hair, the heavy eyebrows and brown eyes. He was in citizen's dress; only the bronzed skin and erect bearing betrayed the soldier. How he would have looked to a stranger she could not tell; she only knew, she only felt, how he looked to her. "He is at home on furlough," she thought, with gladness, realizing the great joy it was that he should be safe when so many had been taken. And then, in her memory, blotting out all gladness, rose again the picture of the two figures, side by side, and she hurried onward, she knew not whither. It was jealousy, plain, simple, unconquerable jealousy, which was consuming her; jealousy, terrible passion which the most refined and intellectual share with the poor Hottentots, from which the Christian can not escape any more than the pagan; jealousy, horrible companion of love, its guardian and tormentor. God help the jealous! for they suffer the acutest tortures the human mind can feel. And Anne was jealous.

If she had not admired Helen so deeply, and loved her (save for this one barrier) so sincerely, she would not have suffered as she was suffering. But to her Helen had always been the fairest woman on earth, and even now this feeling could not be changed. All Helen's words came back to her, every syllable of her clear, quietly but intensely uttered avowal; and this man, whom she had loved so deeply, was now her husband.

It was nothing new. Why should she feel it, think of it, in this way? But she was no longer capable of thinking or feeling reasonably. Of course he loved her. In his mind she, Anne, was probably but a far-off remembrance, even if a remembrance at all. Their meeting in West Virginia had been a chance encounter; its impulses, therefore, had been chance impulses, its words chance words, meaning nothing, already forgotten. She, Anne, had taken them as great, and serious, and sincere; and she, Anne, had been a fool. Her life had been built upon this idea. It was a foundation of sand.

She walked on, seeing nothing, hearing nothing. Where were now the resignation and self-sacrifice, the crowned patience and noble fortitude? Ah, yes, but resignation and fortitude were one thing when she had thought that he required them also, another when they were replaced in his life by happiness and content. It is easy to be self-sacrificing when the one we love suffers in companionship with us, and there is no rival. But when there is a rival, self-sacrifice goes to the winds. "He never loved me," was the burning cry of her heart. "I have been a fool—a poor self-absorbed, blinded fool. If he thinks of me at all, it is with a smile over my simple credulity."

175

Through miles of streets she wandered, and at last found herself again in the quarter where the church stood. A sudden desire seized her to look at him, at them, again. If the service had been long, she would be in time to see their carriage pass. She turned, and hastened toward the church, as anxious now to reach it as she had been before to leave it far behind. Now she could see the corner and the porch. No, service was not ended; carriages were waiting without. She was in time. But as she drew near, figures began to appear, coming from the porch, and she took refuge under the steps of a house opposite, her figure hidden in the shadow.

The congregation slowly made its dignified way into the street. St. Lucien's had seldom held so large a throng of worshippers. The little sexton hardly knew, in his excitement, where he was, or what his duty, on such a momentous occasion. At length they appeared, the last of all; only one carriage was left, and that was their own. Slowly, leaning on her husband's arm, the slender fair-haired woman came forth; and Anne, still as a statue, watched with fixed, burning eyes while he threw the velvet cloak round her as they reached the open air, and fastened the clasp. Chance favored the gazer. Helen had left her prayer-book behind in the pew, and while the sexton went back to look for it, husband and wife stood waiting on the steps in the sunshine. Yes, Heathcote had regained all his old vigor, but his expression was changed. He was graver; in repose his face was stern.

It seemed as if Helen felt the fixed although unseen gaze, for she shivered slightly, said something, and they began to go down the steps, the wife supported by her husband's arm as though she needed the assistance. The footman held open the carriage door, but Helen paused. Anne could see her slender foot, in its little winter boot, put out, and then withdrawn, as though she felt herself unable to take the step. Then her husband lifted her in his arms and placed her in the carriage himself, took his place beside her, and the man closed the door. In another minute the sexton had brought the prayer-book, and the carriage rolled away. Anne came out from her hiding-place. The vision was gone.

Again she walked at random through the streets, unheeding where she was. She knew that she had broken her compact with herself—broken it utterly. Of what avail now the long months during which she had not allowed herself to enter the street or the neighborhood where Helen lived? Of what avail that she had not allowed herself to listen to one word concerning them when Mr. Dexter stood ready to tell all? She had looked at them—looked at them voluntarily and long; had gone back to the church door to look at them, to look again at the face for a sight of which her whole heart hungered.

She had broken her vow. In addition, the mist over her blind eyes was dissolved. He had never loved her; it had been but a passing fancy. It was best so. Yet, oh, how easy all the past now seemed, in spite of its loneliness, toil, and care! For *then* she had believed that she was loved. She began to realize that until this moment she had never really given up her own will at all, but had held on through all to this inward belief, which had made her lonely life warm with its hidden secret light. She had thought herself noble, and she had been but selfish; she had thought herself self-controlled, and she had been following her own will; she had thought herself humble, and here she was, maddened by humiliated jealous pride.

At last, worn out with weariness, she went homeward to the half-house as twilight fell. In the morning the ground was white with snow again, and the tumultuous winds of March were careering through the sky, whipping the sleet and hail before them as they flew along; the strange halcyon sunshine was gone, and a second winter upon them. And Anne felt that a winter such as she had never known before was in her heart also.

CHAPTER XXX.

"O eloquent and mightie Death! thou hast drawn together all the farre-stretched greatnesse, all the pride, crueltie, and ambition of men, and covered it all over with these two narrow words, Hic jacet!"—Sir Walter Raleigh.

A month passed. Anne saw nothing more, heard nothing more, but toiled on in her daily round. She taught and sang. She answered Miss Lois's letters and those of Père Michaux. There was no longer any danger in writing to Weston, and she smiled sadly as she thought of the blind, self-important days when she had believed otherwise. She now wrote to her friends there, and letters came in return. Mrs. Barstow's pages were filled with accounts of hospital work, for Donelson had been followed by the great blood-shedding of Shiloh, and the West was dotted with battle-fields.

She had allowed herself no newspapers, lest she should come upon his name. But now she ordered one, and read it daily. What was it to her even if she should come upon his name? She must learn to bear it, so long as they trod the same earth. And one day she did come upon it; but it was merely the two-line announcement that he had returned to the front.

The great city had grown used to the war. There were few signs in its busy streets that a pall hung over the borders of the South. The music teacher on her rounds saw nothing save now and then the ranks of a regiment passing through on its way to a train. Traffic went on unchanged; pleasure was rampant as ever. The shrill voice of the newsboy calling the details of the last battle was often the only reminder of the dread reality. May moved onward. The Scheffels began to make those little excursions into the country so dear to the German heart; but they could not persuade the honored Fräulein to accompany them. For it was not the real country to which they went, but only that suburban imitation of it which thrives in the neighborhood of New York, and Anne's heart was back on her island in the cool blue Northern straits. Miss Lois was now at home again, and her letters were like a breath of life to the homesick girl. Little André was better, and Père Michaux came often to the church-house, and seemed glad to be with them again. With them again! If she could but be with them too!—stand on the heights among the beckoning larches, walk through the spicy aisles of the arbor vitæ, sit under the gray old pines, listening to the wash of the cool blue water below, at rest, afar, afar from all this weariness and sadness and pain!

During these days Stonewall Jackson was making one of his brilliant campaigns in the Valley, the Valley of Virginia, the beautiful valley of the Shenandoah. On the last morning in May, while reading the war news, Anne found in one corner a little list of dead. And there, in small letters, which grew to great size, and inscribed themselves on the walls of the room, one succeeding the other like a horrible dream, was the name, Ward Heathcote. "Captain Ward Heathcote,—— New York Volunteers." She turned the sheet; it was repeated in the latest news column, and again in a notice on the local page. "Captain Ward Heathcote,—— New York Volunteers, is reported among the slain," followed by those brief items of birth, age, and general history which appall our eyes when we first behold them on the printed page, and realize that they are now public property, since they belong only to the dead.

It was early. She was at home in the half-house. She rose, put on her bonnet and gloves, walked to the station, took the first train to the city, and went to Helen.

She reached the house, and was denied entrance. Mrs. Heathcote could see no one.

Was any one with her? Miss Teller?

Miss Teller, the man answered, was absent from the city; but a telegraphic dispatch had been sent, and she was on her way home. There was no relative at present with Mrs. Heathcote; friends she was not able to see. And he looked with some curiosity at this plainly dressed young person, who stood there quite unconscious, apparently, of the atmosphere of his manner. And yet Mr. Simpson had a very well regulated manner, founded upon the best models—a manner which had never heretofore failed in its effect. With a preliminary cough, he began to close the door.

"Wait," said this young person, almost as though she had some authority. She drew forth a little note-book, tore out a leaf, wrote a line upon it, and handed him the improvised card. "Please take this to Mrs. Heathcote," she said. "I think she will see me."

See her—see *her*—when already members of the highest circles of the city had been refused! With a slight smile of superior scorn, Simpson took the little slip, and leaving the stranger on the steps, went within, partially closing the door behind him. But in a few minutes he hastily returned, and with him was a sedate middle-aged woman, whom he called Mrs. Bagshot, and who, although quiet in manner, seemed decidedly to outrank him.

"Will you come with me, if you please?" she said deferentially, addressing Anne. "Mrs. Heathcote would like to see you without delay." She led the way with a quiet unhurrying step up a broad stairway, and opened a door. In the darkened room, on a couch, a white form was lying. Bagshot withdrew, and Anne, crossing the floor, sank down on her knees beside the couch.

"Helen!" she said, in a broken voice; "oh, Helen! Helen!"

The white figure did not stir, save slowly to disengage one hand and hold it out. But Anne, leaning forward, tenderly lifted the slight form in her arms, and held it close to her breast.

"I could not help coming," she said. "Poor Helen! poor, poor Helen!"

She smoothed the fair hair away from the small face that lay still and white upon her shoulder, and at that moment she pitied the stricken wife so intensely that she forgot the rival, or rather made herself one with her; for in death there is no rivalry, only a common grief. Helen did not speak, but she moved closer to Anne, and Anne, holding her in her arms, bent over her, soothing her with loving words, as though she had been a little child.

The stranger remained with Mrs. Heathcote nearly two hours. Then she went away, and Simpson, opening the door for her, noticed that her veil was closely drawn, so that her face was concealed. She went up the street to the end of the block, turned the corner, and disappeared. He was still standing on the steps, taking a breath of fresh air, his portly person and solemn face expressing, according to his idea, a dignified grief appropriate to the occasion and the distinction of the family he served—a family whose bereavements even were above the level of ordinary sorrows, when his attention was attracted by the appearance of a boy in uniform, bearing in his hand an orange-brown envelope. In the possibilities of that well-known hue of hope and dread he forgot for the moment even his occupation of arranging in his own mind elegant formulas with which to answer the inquiries constantly made at the door of the bereaved mansion. The boy ascended the steps; Bagshot, up stairs, with her hand on the knob of Mrs. Heathcote's door, saw him, and came down. The dispatch was for her mistress; she carried it to her. The next instant a cry rang through the house. Captain Heathcote was safe.

The message was as follows:

"To Mrs. Ward Heathcote:

"My name given in list a mistake. Am here, wounded, but not dangerously. Will write. W. H."

It was sent from Harper's Ferry. And two hours later, Mrs. Heathcote, accompanied by Bagshot, was on her way to Harper's Ferry.

It was a wild journey. If any man had possessed authority over Helen, she would never have been allowed to make it; but no man did possess authority. Mrs. Heathcote, having money, courage, and a will of steel, asked advice from no one, did not even wait for Miss Teller, but departed according to a swift purpose of her own, accompanied only by Bagshot, who was, however, an efficient person, self-possessed, calm, and accustomed to travelling. It was uncertain whether they would be able to reach Harper's Ferry, but this uncertainty did not deter Helen: she would go as far as she could. In her heart she was not without hope that Mrs. Heathcote could relax the rules and military lines of even the strictest general in the service. As to personal fear, she had none.

At Baltimore she was obliged to wait for an answer to the dispatch she had sent on starting, and the answer was long in coming. To pass away the time, she ordered a carriage and drove about the city; many persons noticed her, and remembered her fair, delicate, and impatient face, framed in its pale hair. At last the answer came. Captain Heathcote was no longer at Harper's Ferry; he had been sent a short distance northward to a town where there was a better hospital, and Mrs. Heathcote was advised to go round by the way of Harrisburg, a route easier and safer, if not in the end more direct as well.

She followed this advice, although against her will. She travelled northward to Harrisburg, and then made a broad curve, and came southward again, within sight of the green hills later to be brought into unexpected and long-enduring fame—the hills around Gettysburg. But now the whole region was fair with summer, smiling and peaceful; the farmers were at work, and the grain was growing. After some delays she reached the little town, with its barrack-like, white-washed hospital, where her husband was installed under treatment for a wound in his right arm, which, at first appearing serious, had now begun to improve so rapidly that the surgeon in charge decided that he could soon travel northward, and receive what further care he needed among the comforts of his own home.

At the end of five days, therefore, they started, attended only by Bagshot, that useful woman possessing, in addition to her other qualifications, both skill and experience as a nurse.

They started; but the journey was soon ended. On the 11th of June the world of New York was startled, its upper circles hotly excited, and one obscure young teacher in a little suburban home paralyzed, by the great headings in the morning newspapers. Mrs. Heathcote, wife of Captain Ward Heathcote,—— New York Volunteers, while on her way homeward with her husband, who was wounded in the Shenandoah Valley, had been found murdered in her room in the country inn at Timloesville, where they were passing the night. And the evidence pointed so strongly toward Captain Heathcote that he had been arrested upon suspicion.

The city journals appended to this brief dispatch whatever details they knew regarding the personal history of the suspected man and his victim. Helen's beauty, the high position of both in society, and their large circle of friends were spoken of; and in one account the wife's wealth, left by will unconditionally to her husband, was significantly mentioned. One of the larger journals, with the terrible and pitiless impartiality of the great city dailies, added that if there had been a plan, some part of it had signally failed. "A man of the ability of Captain Heathcote would never have been caught otherwise in a web of circumstantial evidence so close that it convinced even the pastoral minds of the Timloesville officials. We do not wish, of course, to prejudge this case; but from the half-accounts which have reached us, it looks as though this blunder, whatever it may have been, was but another proof of the eternal verity of the old saying, Murder will out."

It was the journal containing this sentence which Anne read. She had heard the news of Heathcote's safety a few hours after her visit to Helen. Only a few days had passed, and now her eyes were staring at the horrible words that Helen was dead, and that her murderer was her own husband.

CHAPTER XXXI.

"All her bright hair streaming down,

And all the coverlid was cloth of gold

Drawn to her waist, and she herself in white

All but her face, and that clear-featured
face

Was lovely, for she did not seem as dead,

But fast asleep, and lay as though she
smiled."

—Tennyson.

EXTRACT FROM THE NEW YORK "MARS."

"The following details in relation to the terrible crime with whose main facts our readers are familiar will be of interest at the moment. They were collected by our special reporter, sent in person to the scene of the tragedy, for the purpose of gathering reliable information concerning this case, which promises to be one of the *causes célèbres* of the country, not only on account of the high position and wealth of the parties concerned, but also on account of the close net of purely circumstantial evidence which surrounds the accused man.

"TIMLOESVILLE

is a small village on the border-line between Pennsylvania and Maryland. Legally in Pennsylvania, it possesses personally the characteristics of a Maryland village, some of its outlying fields being fairly over the border. It is credited with about two thousand inhabitants; but the present observer did not see, during his stay, more than about one thousand, including women and children. Timloesville is on a branch railway, which connects with the main line at a junction about thirty miles distant. It possesses two churches and a saw-mill, and was named from a highly esteemed early settler (who may perhaps have marched with our great Washington), Judge Jeremiah Timloe. The agricultural products of the surrounding country are principally hay and maize—wrongly called corn. The intelligence and morality of the community are generally understood to be of a high order. A low fever prevails here in the spring.

"TIMLOE HOTEL.

"At the southern edge of the town, on the line of the railway, stands the Timloe Hotel, presenting an imposing façade to the passengers on the trains as they roll by. It is presided over in a highly liberal and gentlemanly manner by Mr. Casper Graub; it is, in fact, to the genial courtesy of 'mine host' that much of this information is due, and we take this occasion also to state that during all the confusion and excitement necessarily accruing to his house during the present week, the high standard of Mr. Graub's table has never once been relaxed.

"MR. GRAUB'S STORY.

"An army officer, with his right arm in a sling, arrived at the Timloe Hotel, accompanied by his wife, and a maid or nurse named Bagshot, on the evening of June 10, at six o'clock precisely. The officer registered the names as follows: 'Ward Heathcote, Mrs. Heathcote and maid, New York.' He wrote the names with his left hand. A room was assigned to them in the front part of the house, but upon the lady's objecting to the proximity of the trains (generally considered, however, by the majority of Mr. Graub's guests, an enjoyable variety), another apartment in a wing was given to them, with windows opening upon the garden. The wing is shaped like an L. The maid, Bagshot, had a room in the bend of the L, she too having objected, although later, to the room first assigned to her. At half past six o'clock they had supper; the lady then retired to her room, but the husband went out, as he said, to stroll about the town. At half past eight he returned. At nine, Bagshot, having been dismissed for the night, went to her own room; when she left, Captain Heathcote was reading a newspaper, and his wife was writing. It has since been ascertained that this newspaper was the Baltimore *Chronos* of the 9th inst. At ten o'clock exactly Captain Heathcote came down stairs a second time, passed through the office, and stopped to light a cigar. Mr. Graub noticed that he was able to use his left hand quite cleverly, and asked him whether he was naturally left-handed; Captain Heathcote answered that he was not, but had learned the use only since his right arm had been disabled. Mr. Graub, seeing him go toward the door, thought that it was somewhat singular that he should wish to take a second walk, and casually remarked upon the warmth of the evening. Captain Heathcote replied that it was for that very reason he was going out; he could not breathe in the house; and he added something not very complimentary to the air (generally considered unusually salubrious) of Timloesville. Mr. Graub noticed that he walked up and down on the piazza once or twice, *as if he wished to show himself plainly to the persons who were sitting there*. He then strolled away, going toward the main street.

"THE OUTSIDE STAIRWAY.

"As before mentioned, the second room given to Mrs. Heathcote was in a wing. This wing is not much used; in fact, at the time, save this party of three, it had no occupants. It is in the old part of the house. A piazza or gallery runs across a portion of the second story, to which access is had from the garden by a flight of wooden steps, or rather an outside stairway. This stairway is old and sagged; in places the railing is gone. It is probable that Mrs. Heathcote did not even see it. But Captain Heathcote might have noticed it, and probably did notice it, from the next street, through which he passed *when he took his first walk before dark*.

"MRS. BAGSHOT'S TESTIMONY.

"As we have seen, Captain Heathcote left the hotel ostentatiously by the front entrance at ten o'clock. At eleven, Mrs. Bagshot, who happened to be looking from her window in the bend of the L, distinctly saw him (her candle being out) *stealing up by the outside stairway* in the only minute of moonlight there was during the entire evening, the clouds having suddenly and strangely parted, as if for that very purpose. She saw him enter his wife's room through one of the long windows which opened to the floor. In about a quarter of an hour she saw him come forth again, close the blind behind him, and begin to descend the stairway. As there was no longer any moonlight, she could only distinguish him by the light that shone from the room; but in that short space of time, while he was closing the blind, she recognized him *beyond the possibility of a doubt*.

"THE NIGHT PORTER'S TALE.

"A little before midnight, all the hotel entrances being closed save the main door, Captain Heathcote returned. As he passed through the office, the night porter noticed that he looked pale, and that his clothes were disordered; his shirt cuffs especially were wet and creased, as *though they had been dipped in water*. He went up stairs to his room, but soon came down again. He had knocked, but could not awaken his wife. Would the porter be able to open the door by turning back the key? His wife was an invalid; he feared she had fainted.

"THE TRAGEDY.

"The night porter—a most respectable person of Irish extraction, named Dennis Haggerty—came up and opened the door. The lamp was burning within; the blinds of the window were closed. On the bed, stabbed to the heart, apparently while she lay asleep, was the body of the wife.

"DUMB WITNESSES.

"Red marks were found on the shutter, which are pronounced by experts to be the partial print of a *left hand*. On the white cloth which covered the bureau is a slight impression of finger-tips, also belonging to a left hand. These marks are too imperfect to be relied upon in themselves, save that they establish the fact that the hand which touched the cloth and closed the shutter was a *left hand*.

"AN IMPROBABLE STORY.

"Captain Heathcote asserts that he left the hotel at ten, as testified, to smoke a cigar and get a breath of fresh air. That he returned through the garden at eleven, and seeing by the bright light that his wife was still awake, he went up by the outside stairway, which he had previously noted, entered the room through the long window to tell her that he was going to take a bath in the river, and to get towels. He remained a few minutes, put two towels in his pocket, and came out, going down the same stairway, across the garden, and along the main road to the river. (A track, however, has been found to the river through the large meadow behind the house.) At the bend where road and river meet, he undressed himself and took a bath. The disorder in his clothing and his wet cuffs came from his own awkwardness, as he has but partial use of his right arm. He then returned by the road as he had come, but he *forgot the towels*. Probably they would be found on the bank where he left them.

"THE TOWEL.

"No towels were found at the point named. But at the end of the track through the grass meadow, among the reeds on the shore, a towel *was* found, and identified as one belonging to the hotel. This towel is *stained with blood*.

"THE THEORY.

"The theory at Timloesville is that Heathcote had no idea that he would be seen when he stole up that outside stairway. He knew that the entire wing was unoccupied: a servant has testified that she told him it was; and he thought, too, that the maid Bagshot had a room in front, not commanding the garden. Bagshot says that the room was changed without his knowledge, while he was absent on his first walk. He supposed, then, that he would not be seen. He evidently took Mrs. Heathcote's diamond rings, purse, and watch (they are all missing) in order to turn public opinion toward the idea that the murder was for the sake of robbery. He *says* that a man passed him while he was bathing, and spoke to him; proof of this would establish something toward the truth of his story. But, strangely enough, this man can not be found. Yet Timloesville and its neighborhood are by no means so crowded with inhabitants that the search should be a difficult one.

"It may be regarded as a direct misfortune in the cause of justice that the accused heard any of Bagshot's testimony against him before he was called upon to give his own account of the events of the evening. And yet his confused, contradictory story is another proof of the incapacity which the most cunning murderers often display when overtaken by suspicion; they seem to lose all power to protect themselves. If Captain Heathcote had denied Bagshot's testimony in toto, had denied having ascended the outside stairway at all, his chances would have been much brighter, for people might have believed that the maid was mistaken. But he *acknowledges the stairway*, and then denies the rest.

"HIS MOTIVE.

"But how can poor finite man detect so obscure a thing as motive? He must hide his face and acknowledge his feebleness when he stands before this inscrutable, heavy-browed, silent Fate. In this case, two solutions are offered. One, that the wife's large fortune was left by will unconditionally to her husband; the other, that Mrs. Bagshot will testify that there was jealousy and ill feeling between these two, linked together by God's holy ordinance, and that this ill feeling was connected with a third person, and that person—a woman."

EXTRACT FROM THE NEW YORK "ZEUS."

"Mrs. Heathcote was apparently murdered while asleep. When found, her face wore a natural and sweet expression, as though she had passed from slumber into death without even a sigh. The maid testifies that her mistress always removed her rings at night; it is probable, therefore, that they, together with her purse and watch, were on the bureau where the marks of the finger-tips were found.

"We refrain at present from comment upon the close circumstantial evidence which surrounds this case; the strong hand of the law will take hold of it at the proper time, and sift it thoroughly. Meanwhile the attitude of all right-minded persons should be calm and impartial, and the accused man should be held innocent until he is proven guilty. Trial by newspaper is one of the notable evils of our modern American system, and should be systematically discountenanced and discouraged; when a human life is trembling in the balance, the sensation-monger should be silenced, and his evil wares sternly rejected."

This negative impartiality was the nearest approach to friendliness which the accused man received from the combined newspaper columns of New York, Baltimore, and Washington.

The body of poor Helen was brought home, and Miss Teller herself arrayed her darling for her long repose. Friends thronged to see her as she lay in her luxurious drawing-room; flowers were placed everywhere as though for a bridal—the bridal of death. Her figure was visible from head to foot; she seemed asleep. Her still face wore a gentle expression of rest and peace; her small hands were crossed upon her breast; her unbound hair fell in waves behind her shoulders, a few strands lying on the white skirt far below the slender waist, almost to the feet. The long lashes lay upon the oval cheek; no one would ever see those bright brown eyes again, and find fault with them because they were too narrow. The lithe form was motionless; no one would ever again watch it move onward with its peculiar swaying grace, and find fault with it because it was too slender. Those who had not been willing to grant her beauty in life, gazed at her now with tear-dimmed eyes, and willingly gave all the meed of praise they had withheld before. Those who had not loved her while she lived, forgot all, and burst into tears when they saw her now, the delicately featured face once so proud and imperious, quiet forever, grown strangely youthful too, like the face of a young girl.

Miss Teller sat beside her darling; to all she made the same set speech: "Dear Ward, her husband, the one who loved her best, can not be here. I am staying with her, therefore, until she is taken from us; then I shall go to him, as *she* would have wished." For Miss Teller believed no word of the stories with which the newspapers teemed. Indignation and strong affection supplied the place of whatever strength had been lacking in her character, and never before in her life had she appeared as resolute and clear-minded as now.

During the funeral services, Isabel Varce sat beside Miss Teller, sobbing as if her heart would break. Rachel Bannert was next to Isabel. She had looked once at Helen, only once, and her dark face had quivered spasmodically; then she also took her seat beside the fair, still form, and bowed her head. All Helen's companions were clad in mourning garb; the tragedy of this death had invested it with a deeper sadness than belonged to the passing away in the ordinary course of nature of even closer friends. The old-fashioned mansion was full to overflowing; in the halls and doorway, on the front steps, and even on the pavement outside, men were standing, bare-headed and silent, many distinguished faces being among them; society men also, who in general avoided funerals as unpleasant and grewsome ceremonials. These had been Helen's companions and friends; they had all liked and admired her, and as she was borne past them, covered with heliotrope, there was not one whose eyes did not grow stern in thinking of the dastard hand that did the cruel deed.

That night, when darkness fell, many hearts remembered her, lying alone in the far-off cemetery, the cemetery we call Greenwood, although no wood made by Nature's hand alone bears the cold white marble flowers which are found on those fair slopes. And when the next morning dawned, with dull gray clouds and rain, there were many who could not help thinking of the beautiful form which had fared softly and delicately all its life, which had felt only the touch of finest linen and softest silk, which had never suffered from the cold or the storm, now lying there alone in the dark soaked earth, with the rain falling upon its defenseless head, and no one near to replace the wet lilies which the wind had blown from the mound.

But those who were thinking thus were mistaken: some one was near. A girl clad in black and closely veiled stood beside the new-made grave, with tears dropping on her cheeks, and her hand pressed over her heart. There were many mourners yesterday; there was but one to-day. There were many flowers then; now there was only the bunch of violets which this girl had brought. She had knelt beside the mound, her head undefended from the rain, and had prayed silently. Then she had risen, but still she could not go. She paced slowly up and down beside the grave, like a sentinel keeping watch; only when she perceived that one of the men employed in the cemetery was watching her curiously, no doubt wondering why she remained there in the storm, did she turn away at last, and go homeward again by the long route she had traversed in coming.

For Anne had not dared to go to the funeral; had not dared to go to Miss Teller. The hideous sentence in the newspaper had filled her with doubt and vague alarm. It was not possible that she, Anne, was meant; and yet Bagshot, from whom this as yet unrevealed testimony was to come, saw her on the day she visited Helen, after the tidings of her husband's death. Surely this was too slight a foundation upon which to found her vague alarm. She repeated to herself that her dread was unreasonable, yet it would not down. If the danger had been open, she could have faced and defied it; but this mute, unknown something, which was only to be revealed by the power and in the presence of the law, held her back, bound hand and foot, afraid almost to breathe. For her presence or words might, in some way she could not foresee or even comprehend, bring increased danger upon the head of the accused man, already weighted down with a crushing load of suspicion, which grew heavier every hour.

Suspense supplies a calmness of its own. Anne went into the city as usual, gave her lessons, and went through all the forms of her accustomed living, both at home and abroad. Yet all the time she was accompanied by a muffled shape, its ghostly eyes fixed upon her through its dark veil, menacing but silent. It was dread.

When the hour came, and she knew that the old words were being spoken over Helen: "In the midst of life we are in death: of whom may we seek for succor but of Thee?" "Before the mountains were brought forth, or ever the earth and the world were made, Thou art God from everlasting." "A thousand years in Thy sight are but as yesterday, seeing that is past as a watch in the night." "And now, Lord, what is my hope? Truly my hope is even in Thee"—she bowed her head and joined in the sentences mutely, present at least in spirit. The next day, while the rain fell sombrely, she went to the distant cemetery: no one would be there in the storm, and she wished to stand once more by Helen's side—poor Helen, beautiful Helen, taken from this life's errors forever, perhaps already, in another world, understanding all, repentant for all, forgiving all.

There was no one to whom Anne could speak upon the subject which was burning like a constant fire within her heart. And when, a few days later, a letter came from Gregory Dexter, she opened it eagerly: there would be, there must be, comfort here. She read the pages quickly, and her heart stood still. "If I thought that there was the least danger that the secret of this cowardly, cruel deed would not be found out," wrote Dexter, "I should at once leave all this labor in which I am engaged, important as it is, and devote myself to the search for proofs to convict the murderer. Never in my life has my desire for swift, sharp justice been so deeply stirred."

Anne laid down the letter with a trembling hand. If he "thought that there was the least danger"; then he thought there was none. But so far no one had been apprehended, or even suspected, save Ward Heathcote alone. Did he think, then, that Heathcote was guilty? *Could* he think this, knowing him as he did, having been in a certain sense his companion and friend?

Dexter had not liked Heathcote personally, but he was capable of just judgment above his personal likings and dislikings, and Anne knew it. She knew that he had examined the testimony impartially. It must be, then, it must be, that there were grounds for his belief. She took her pen and wrote a burning letter—a letter of entreaty and passionate remonstrance. And then, the next morning, she burned it: she must not write or speak on the subject at all, not even to him.

The slow days moved onward like the processions of a dream. But no one noticed any change in the young teacher, who journeyed wearily through the long hours. Old Nora saw the piles of newspapers in her mistress's room, but as she could not read, they betrayed nothing. She would not, besides, have recognized Helen under the name of Heathcote; the beautiful lady who had visited the half-house in the days of Jeanne-Armande was named Lorrington. The slow days moved on, but not without events. In this case the law had moved speedily. An indictment had been found, and the trial was to take place without delay in the county town of the district to which Timloesville belonged.

Miss Teller had gone to this town; the newspapers said that she had taken a house, and would remain during the trial, or as long as Captain Heathcote was confined there. Anne, reading these items, reading the many descriptions of Heathcote, the suggestions regarding the murder, the theories concerning the blunder (for it was conceded that there had been a blunder), asked herself wonderingly if he had no friends left—no friends on earth, save herself and Miss Teller? The whole world seemed to be against him. But she judged only from the newspapers. There was another side. This was a small, local, but in one way powerful, minority, which stood by the accused man immovably. This minority was composed almost entirely of women—women high in New York society, Helen's own companions and friends. They formed a determined band of champions, who, without condescending to use any arguments, but simply through their own personality, exerted a strong influence, limited, it is true, but despotic. If the case was tried beforehand by the newspapers, it was also tried beforehand by sweet voices and scornful lips in many New York drawing-rooms. Society resolved itself into two parties—those who did and those who did not believe in the guilt of the imprisoned man. Those who did believe were almost all men; those who did not, almost all women; the exceptions being a few men who stood by Heathcote in spite of the evidence, and a few women who, having logical minds, stood by the evidence in spite of themselves.

When the trial began, not only was Miss Teller present, but Mrs. Varce and Isabel, Mrs. Bannert and her daughter-in-law, together with others equally well known as friends of Helen's, and prominent members of New York's fashionable society.

Multomah, the little county town, was excited; its one hotel was crowded. The country people came in to attend the trial from miles around; great lawyers were to be present, there was to be "mighty fine speaking." The gentleman had murdered his wife for the million dollars she constantly carried with her. The gentleman had murdered his wife because she had just discovered that he was already married before he met her, and he was afraid she would reveal the secret. A local preacher improved the occasion by a sermon decked profusely with Apollyons and Abaddons. It was not clearly known what he meant, or where he stood; but the discourse was listened to by a densely packed crowd of farming people, who came out wiping their foreheads, and sat down on convenient tombstones to talk it over, and eat their dinners, brought in baskets, trying the case again beforehand for the five-hundredth time, with texts and Scripture phrases thrown in to give it a Sabbath flavor.

The New York dailies had sent their reporters; every evening Anne read their telegraphic summaries of the day's events; every morning, the account of the same in detail. She was not skillful enough to extract the real evidence from the mass of irrelevant testimony with which it was surrounded, the questions and answers, the confusing pertinacity of the lawyers over some little point which seemed to her as far from the real subject as a blade of grass is from the fixed stars. She turned, therefore, to the printed comments which day by day accompanied the report of the proceedings, gathering from them the progress made, and their ideas of the probabilities which lay in the future. The progress seemed rapid; the probabilities were damning. No journal pretended that they were otherwise. Yet still the able pens of the calmer writers counselled deliberation. "There have been cases with even closer evidence than this," they warningly wrote, "in which the accused, by some unexpected and apparently trivial turn in the testimony, has been proven clearly innocent. In this case, while the evidence is strong, it is difficult to imagine a motive. Mrs. Heathcote was much attached to her husband; she was, besides, a beautiful, accomplished, and fascinating woman. That a man should deliberately plan to murder such a wife, merely in order to obtain possession of wealth which was already practically his, is incredible; and until some more reasonable motive is discovered, many will refuse to believe even the evidence."

Anne, reading this sentence, felt faint. So far the mysterious testimony to which vague allusion had been made in the beginning had not been brought forward; the time had been occupied by the evidence concerning the events at Timloesville, and the questioning and cross-questioning of the Timloesville witnesses. A "more reasonable motive." The veiled shape that accompanied her seemed to assume more definite outline, and to grow from Dread into Fear. And yet she could not tell of what she was afraid.

The days passed, and she wondered how it was that she could still eat, and sleep, and speak as usual, while her whole being was away in that little Pennsylvania town. She did speak and teach as usual, but she did not eat or sleep. Something besides food sustained her. Was it hope? Or fear? Oh, why did not all the world cry out that he was not, could not be guilty! Were people all mad, and deaf, and blind? She lived on in a suspense which was like a continual endurance of suffocation, which yet never quite attains the relief of death.

Miss Teller's lawyers labored with skill and vigilance; all that talent—nay, more, genius—could do, they did. Their theory was that the murder was committed by a third person, who entered Mrs. Heathcote's room by the same outside stairway which her husband had used, after his departure; and they defied the prosecution to prove that they were wrong. In answer to this theory the prosecution presented certain facts, namely: that Heathcote was seen entering by the outside stairway, and that no one else was seen; that the impressions found there were those of a left hand, and that Heathcote was at the time left-handed; that a towel, marked with the name of the hotel and stained with blood, was found on the river-bank at the end of a direct trail from the garden, and that the chamber-maid testified that, whereas she had placed four towels in the room a few hours before, there were in the morning but two remaining, and that no others were missing from the whole number owned by the hotel.

At this stage of the proceedings, Anne, sitting in her own room as usual now in the evening, with one newspaper in her hand and the others scattered on the floor by her side, heard a knock on the door below, but, in her absorption, paid no attention to it. In a few moments, however, Nora came up to say that Mr. Dexter was in the parlor, and wished to see her.

Here was an unexpected trial. She had sent a short, carefully guarded answer to his long letter, and he had not written again. It had been comparatively easy to guard written words. But could she command those that must be spoken? She bathed her face in cold water, and stood waiting until she felt that she had called up a calmer expression; she charged herself to guard every look, every word, even the tones of her voice. Then she went down.

CHAPTER XXXII.

"I can account for nothing you women do, although I have lived among you seventy-five years."—Walter Savage Landor.

As she entered the little parlor, Dexter came forward to meet her. "You are looking very well," he said, almost reproachfully.

"I am very well," she answered. "And you?"

"Not well at all. What with the constant and harassing work I am doing, and this horrible affair concerning poor Helen, I confess that I feel worn and old. It is not often that I acknowledge either. I have been busy in the city all day, and must return to my post on the midnight train; but I had two or three hours to spare, and so I have come out to see you. Before we say anything else, however, tell me about yourself. How is it with you at present?"

Glad of a respite, she described to him, with more details than she had hitherto thought necessary, her position, her pupils, and her daily life. She talked rapidly, giving him no opportunity to speak; she hardly knew herself as she went along. At last, however, he did break through the stream of her words. "I am glad you find interest in these matters," he said, coldly. "With me it is different; I can think of nothing but poor Helen."

It was come: now for self-control. All her words failed suddenly; she could not speak.

"Are you not haunted by it?" he continued. "Do you not constantly see her lying there asleep, that pale hair unbraided, those small helpless hands bare of all their jewels—poor defenseless little hands, decked only with the mockery of that wedding ring?"

He was gazing at the wall, as though it were all pictured there. Anne made no reply, and after a pause he went on. "Helen was a fascinating woman; but she was, or could be if she chose, an intensely exasperating woman as well. I am no coward; I think I may say the reverse; but I would rather be alone with a tigress than with such a woman as she would have been, if roused to jealous fury. She would not have stirred, she would not have raised her voice, but she would have spoken words that would have stung like asps and cut like Damascus blades. No devil would have shown in that kind of torment greater ingenuity. I am a self-controlled man, yet I can imagine Helen Lorrington driving me, if she had tried, into such a state of frenzy that I should hardly know what I was doing. In such a case I should end, I think, by crushing her in my arms, and fairly strangling the low voice that taunted me. But—I could never have stabbed her in her sleep!"

Again he paused, and again Anne kept silence. But he did not notice it; he was absorbed in his own train of thought.

"It is a relief to speak of this to you," he continued, "for you knew Helen, and Heathcote also. Do you know I can imagine just how she worked upon him; how that fair face and those narrow eyes of hers wrought their deadly darts. Her very want of strength was an accessory; for if she could have risen and struck him, if she had been *capable* of any such strong action, the exasperation would have been less. But that a creature so helpless, one whose slight form he had been used to carry about the house in his arms, one who could not walk far unaided—that such a creature should lie there, in all her delicate beauty, and with barbed words deliberately torment him— Anne, I can imagine a rush of madness which might well end in murder and death. But not a plot. If he had killed her in a passion, and then boldly avowed the deed, giving himself up, I should have had some sympathy with him, in spite of the horror of the deed. But to arrange the method of his crime (as he evidently tried to do) so that he would not be discovered, but be enabled quietly to inherit her money—bah! I almost wish I were the hangman myself! Out on the border he would have been lynched long ago."

184

His listener still remained mute, but a little fold of flesh inside her lips was bitten through by her clinched teeth in the effort she made to preserve that muteness.

It seemed to have been a relief to Dexter to let out those strong words. He paused, turned toward Anne, and for the first time noted her dress. "Are you in mourning?" he asked, doubtfully, looking at the unbroken black of her attire.

"It is the same dress I have worn for several months."

He did not know enough of the details of a woman's garb to see that the change came from the absence of white at the throat and wrists. After Helen's death poor Anne had sewed black lace in her plain black gown; it was the only mourning she could allow herself.

The moment was now come when she must say something. Dexter, his outburst over, was leaning back in his chair, looking at her. "Miss Teller has gone to Multomah, I believe," she remarked, neutrally.

"Yes; singularly enough, she believes him innocent. I heard, while in the city to-day, that the Varces and Bannerts and others of that set believe it also, and are all at Multomah 'for the moral effect.' For the moral effect!" He threw back his head and laughed scornfully. "I wish I had time to run up there myself," he added, "to dwell upon the moral effect of all those fine ladies. However, the plain American people have formed their own opinion of this case, and are not likely to be moved by such influences. They understand. This very evening, on the train, I heard a mechanic say, 'If the jurymen were only fine ladies, now, that Heathcote would get off yet.'"

"How can you repeat such words?" said the girl, blazing out suddenly and uncontrollably, as a fire which has been long smothered bursts into sudden and overpowering flame at the last.

"Of course it is bad taste to jest on such a subject. I only— Why, Anne, what is the matter?" For she had risen and was standing before him, her eyes brilliant with an expression which was almost hate.

"You believe that he did it?" she said.

"I do."

"And I do *not*! You say that Helen taunted him, that she drove him into a frenzy; you imagine the scene, and picture its details. Know that Helen loved him with her whole heart. Whatever she may have been to you, to him she was utterly devoted, living upon his words and his smile. She esteemed herself blessed simply to be near him—in his presence; and, on that very night, she said that no wife was ever so happy, and that on her knees she had thanked her Creator for that which made her life one long joy."

Gregory Dexter's face had showed the profoundest wonder while the excited girl was speaking, but by the time she ceased he had, in his quick way, grasped something of the truth, unexpected and astonishing though it was.

"You know this?" he said. "Then she wrote to you."

"Yes."

"On the evening of her death?"

"Yes."

"Bagshot testifies that when she left the room, at nine, Mrs. Heathcote was writing. Was that this letter to you?"

"I presume it was."

"When and how was it mailed? Or rather, what is the date of the postmark?"

"The next morning."

Dexter looked at her searchingly. "This may prove to be very important," he said.

"I know it—now."

"Why have you not spoken before?"

"To whom could I speak? Besides, it has not seemed important to me until now; for no one has suggested that she did not love her husband, that she tormented him and drove him into fury, save yourself alone."

"You will see that others will suggest it also," said Dexter, unmoved by her scorn. "Are you prepared to produce this letter?"

"I have it."

"Can I see it?"

"I would rather not show it."

"There is determined concealment here somewhere, Anne, and I am much troubled; I fear you stand very near great danger. Remember that this is a serious matter, and ordinary rules should be set aside, ordinary feelings sacrificed. You will do well to show me that letter, and, in short, to tell me the whole truth plainly. Do you think you have any friend more steadfast than myself?"

"You are kind. But—you are prejudiced."

"Against Heathcote, do you mean?" said Dexter, a sudden flash coming for an instant into his gray eyes. "Is it possible that *you*, you too, are interested in that man?"

But at this touch upon her heart the girl controlled herself again. She resumed her seat, with her face turned toward the window. "I do not believe that he did it, and you do," she answered, quietly. "That makes a wide separation between us."

But for the moment the man who sat opposite had forgotten the present, to ask himself, with the same old inward wonder and anger, why it was that this other man, who had never done anything or been anything in his life, who had never denied himself, never worked, never accomplished anything—why it was that such a man as this had led captive Helen, Rachel, and now perhaps Anne. If it had been a case of great personal beauty, he could have partially accounted for it, and—scorned it. But it was not. Many a face was more regularly handsome than Heathcote's; he knew that he himself would be pronounced by the majority a handsomer, although of course older, man. But when he realized that he was going over this same old bitter ground, by a strong effort of will he stopped himself and returned to reality. Heathcote's power, whatever it was, and angry as it made him, was nevertheless a fact, and Dexter never contradicted facts. With his accurate memory, he now went back and took up Anne's last answer. "You say I believe it. It is true," he said, turning toward her (he had been sitting with his eyes cast down during this whirl of feeling); "but my belief is not founded upon prejudice, as you seem to think. It rests upon the evidence. Let us go over the evidence together: women are sometimes intuitively right, even against reason."

"I can not go over it."

But he persisted. "It would be better," he said, determined to draw the whole truth from her, if not in one way, then in another. For he realized how important it was that she should have an adviser.

She looked up and met his eyes; they were kind but unyielding. "Very well," she said, making an effort to do even this. She leaned back in her chair and folded her hands: people could endure, then, more than they knew.

Dexter, not giving her a moment's delay, began immediately: his object was to rouse her and draw her out. "We will take at first simply the testimony," he said. "I have the main points here in my note-book. We will even suppose that we do not know the persons concerned, but think of them as strangers." He went over the evidence clearly and briefly. Then the theories. "Note," he said, "the difference. On one side we have a series of facts, testified to by a number of persons. On the other, a series of possibilities, testified to by no one save the prisoner himself. The defense is a theory built to fit the case, without one proof, no matter how small, as a foundation."

Anne had not stirred. Her eyes were turned away, gazing into the darkness of the garden. Dexter closed his note-book, and returned it to his pocket.

"They have advanced no further in the real trial," he said; "but you and I will now drop our rôle of strangers, and go on. We know him; we knew her. Can we think of any cause which would account for such an act? Was there any reason why Ward Heathcote would have been relieved by the death of his wife?"

Anne remained silent.

"The common idea that he wished to have sole control of her wealth will hardly, I think, be received by those who have personally known him," continued Dexter. "He never cared for money. He was, in my opinion, ostentatiously indifferent to it." Here he paused to control the tone of his voice, which was growing bitter. "I repeat—can you imagine any other reason?" he said. Still she did not answer.

"Why do you not answer? I shall begin to suspect that you do."

At this she stirred a little, and he was satisfied. He had moved her from her rigidity. Not wishing to alarm her, he went on, tentatively: "My theory of the motive you are not willing to allow; still, I consider it a possible and even probable one. For they were not happy: *he* was not happy. Beautiful as she was, rich as she was, I was told, when I first came eastward in the spring, soon after their marriage, that had it not been for that accident and the dangerous illness that followed, Helen Lorrington would never have been Ward Heathcote's wife."

"Who told you this?" said Anne, turning toward him.

"I did not hear it from her, but it came from her—Rachel Bannert."

"She is a traitorous woman."

"Yes; but traitors betray—the truth."

He was watching her closely; she felt it, and turned toward the window again, so that he should not see her eyes.

186

"Suppose that he did not love her, but had married her under the influence of pity, when her life hung by a thread; suppose that she loved him—you say she did. Can you not imagine that there might have been moments when she tormented him beyond endurance concerning his past life—who knows but his present also? She was jealous; and she had wonderful ingenuity. But I doubt if you comprehend what I mean: a woman never knows a woman as a man knows her. And Heathcote was not patient. He is a self-indulgent man—a man who has been completely spoiled."

Again he paused. Then he could not resist bringing forward something else, under any circumstances, to show her that she was of no consequence in the case compared with another person. "It is whispered, I hear, that the maid will testify that there was a motive, and a strong one, namely, a rival; that there was another woman whom Heathcote really loved, and that Helen knew this, and used the knowledge."

The formless dread which accompanied Anne began now to assume definite outline and draw nearer. She gazed at her inquisitor with eyes full of dumb distress.

He rose, and took her cold hands in his. "Child," he said, earnestly, "I beseech you tell me all. It will be so much better for you, so much safer. You are suffering intensely. I have seen it all the evening. Can you not trust me?"

She still looked at him in silence, while the tears rose, welled over, and rolled slowly down.

"Can you not trust me?" he repeated.

She shook her head.

"But as you have told me something, why not tell me all?"

"I am afraid to tell all," she whispered.

"For yourself?"

"No."

"For him, then?"

"Yes."

He clinched his hand involuntarily as he heard this answer. Her pale face and agitation were all for him, then—for Ward Heathcote!

"You are really shaken by fear," he said. "I know its signs, or rather those of dread. It is pure dread which has possession of you now. How unlike you, Anne! How unlike yourself you are at this moment!"

But she cared nothing for herself, nothing for the scorn in his voice (the jealous are often loftily scornful), and he saw that she did not.

"Whom do you fear? The maid?"

"Yes."

"What can she say?"

"I do not know; and yet—"

"Is it possible—can it be possible, Anne, that *you* are the person implicated, the so-called rival?"

"I do not know; and it is because I do not know that I am so much afraid," she answered, still in the same low whisper.

"But why should you take this possibility upon yourself? Ward Heathcote is no Sir Galahad, Heaven knows. Probably at this moment twenty women are trembling as you are trembling, fearing lest they be called by name, and forced forward before the world."

He spoke with anger. Anne did not contradict him, but she leaned her head upon her hand wearidly, and closed her eyes.

"How can I leave you?" he said, breaking into his old kindness again. "I ought to go, but it is like leaving a girl in the hands of torturers. If there were only some one to be with you here until all this is over!"

"There is no one. I want no one."

"You puzzle me deeply," he said, walking up and down with troubled anxiety. "I can form no opinion as to whether your dread is purely imaginary or not, because you tell me nothing. If you were an ordinary woman, I should not give much thought to what you say—or rather to what you look, for you say nothing; but you are not ordinary. You are essentially brave, and you have fewer of the fantastic, irrelevant fancies of women than any girl I have ever known. There must be something, then, to fear, since *you* fear so intensely. I like you, Anne; I respect you. I admire you too, more than you know. You are so utterly alone in this trouble that I can not desert you. And I will not."

"Do not stay on my account."

"But I shall. That is, in the city; it is decided. Here is my address. Promise that if you should wish help or advice in any way—mark that I say, in any way—you will send me instantly a dispatch."

"I will."

"There is nothing more that I can do for you?"

"Nothing."

"And nothing that you will tell me? Think well, child."

"Nothing."

Then, as it was late, he made her renew her promise, and went away.

The next morning the package of newspapers was brought to Anne from the station at an early hour as usual. She was in her own room waiting for them. She watched the boy coming along the road, and felt a sudden thrill of anger when he stopped to throw a stone at a bird. To stop with *that* in his hand! Old Nora brought up the package. Anne took it, and closed the door. Then she sat down to read.

Half an hour later, Gregory Dexter received a telegraphic dispatch from Lancaster. "Come immediately. A. D."

CHAPTER XXXIII.

"He was first always. Fortune

Shone bright in his face.

I fought for years; with no effort

He conquered the place.

We ran; my feet were all bleeding,

But he won the race.

"My home was still in the shadow;

His lay in the sun.

I longed in vain; what he asked for,

It straightway was done.

Once I staked all my heart's
treasure;

We played—and he won!"

—Adelaide Procter.

When the dispatch came, Dexter had not yet seen the morning papers. He ate his breakfast hastily, and on the way to the station and on the train he read them with surprise and a tumultuous mixture of other feelings, which he did not stop then to analyze. Mrs. Bagshot had been brought forward a second time by the prosecution, and had testified to an extraordinary conversation which had taken place between Mrs. Heathcote and an unknown young girl on the morning after the news of Captain Heathcote's death in the Shenandoah Valley had been received, parts of which (the conversation) she, in an adjoining room, had overheard. He had barely time to grasp the tenor of the evidence (which was voluminous and interrupted by many questions) when the train reached Lancaster, and he found Li in waiting with the red wagon. All Li could tell was that Miss Douglas was "going on a journey." She was "all ready, with her bonnet on."

In the little parlor he found her, walking up and down, as he had walked during the preceding evening. White as her face was, there was a new expression in her eyes—an expression of energy. In some way she had reached a possibility of action, and consequently a relief. When he had entered, with a rapid motion she closed the doors. "Have you read it?" she said.

"You mean the new testimony? Yes; I read it as I came out."

"And you understood, of course, that it was I?"

"I feared it might be."

"And you see that I must go immediately to Multomah?"

188

"By heavens! no. I see nothing of the kind. Rather should you hasten as far away as possible—to England, Germany—some distant spot where you can safely rest until all danger, danger of discovery, is over."

"So *you* believe it also!" cried the girl, with scathing emphasis. "You believe and condemn! Believe that garbled, distorted story; condemn, when you only know half! Like all the rest of the world, you are in haste to believe, glad to believe, the worst—in haste to join the hue and cry against a hunted man."

She stood in the centre of the room, her form drawn up to its full height, her eyes flashing. She looked inspired—inspired with anger and scorn.

"Then it *is* garbled?" said Dexter, finding time even at that moment to admire her beauty, which had never before been so striking.

"It is. And I must go to Multomah and give the true version. Tell me what train to take."

"First tell *me*, Anne; tell me the whole story. Let me hear it before you give it to the world. Surely there can be no objection to my knowing it now."

"There is no objection; but I can not lose the time. I must start."

A travelling-bag stood on the table beside her shawl and gloves; the red wagon was waiting outside. He comprehended that nothing would stop her, and took his measures accordingly.

"I can arrange everything for you, and I will, and without the least delay. But first you must tell me the whole," he said, sitting down and folding his arms. "I will not work in the dark. As to time, the loss of an hour is nothing compared with the importance of gaining my co-operation, for the moment I am convinced, I will telegraph to the court-room itself, and stop proceedings until you arrive. With my help, my name, my influence, behind you, you can accomplish anything. But what could you do alone? You would he misunderstood, misrepresented, subjected to doubt, suspicion, perhaps insult. Have you thought of this?"

"I mind nothing if I can but save him."

"But if you can save him more effectually with my assistance?"

"How can that be, when you dislike, suspect him?"

"Do you wish to drive me into a rage? Can I not be just to Ward Heathcote whether I like him or not, suspect him or not? Yes, even though I believe him to be guilty? Try me. If I promise to go with you to Multomah to-day, even if I think your presence there will be of no avail, will *that* induce you?"

"Yes."

"Then I promise."

Without pausing, she sat down by the table, taking a newspaper from her pocket. "You have one," she said; "please follow me in the one you have. When I saw the notice of his death, I went immediately to Helen. This woman Bagshot testifies that she was in the next room. I am positive that at first both the doors of Helen's room were closed; Bagshot, therefore, must have slightly opened one of them afterward unobserved by us. There was a curtain hanging partly over this door, but only partly; she could have opened it, therefore, but slightly, or we should have noticed the change. This accounts for the little that she caught—only those sentences that were spoken in an elevated voice, for Helen's room is large. It will shorten the story, I think, if we read the summary on the editorial page." And in a clear voice she read as follows: "'Our readers will remember that at the beginning of the Heathcote trial we expressed the opinion that until some more probable motive for the deed than the desire to obtain control of wealth already practically his own was discovered in connection with the accused, the dispassionate observer would refuse to believe his guilt, despite the threatening nature of the evidence. This motive appears now to have been supplied.' In another column parts of a remarkable conversation are given, overheard by the witness Bagshot—a conversation between Mrs. Heathcote and an unknown and beautiful young girl, who came to the house on the morning after the announcement of Captain Heathcote's death in the Shenandoah Valley, and before the contradiction of the same had been received. This young girl was a stranger to the man Simpson, who opened the front door, and Simpson has been in Mrs. Heathcote's service for some time. He testifies that she was denied entrance, Mrs. Heathcote not being able to see any one. She then tore a leaf from her note-book, wrote a line upon it, and requested him to carry it to his mistress, adding that she thought Mrs. Heathcote would see her. As intimate friends had already been refused, Simpson was incredulous, but performed his duty. To his surprise, Mrs. Heathcote sent Bagshot to say that the stranger was to come to her immediately, and accordingly she was ushered up stairs, and the door closed. Upon being questioned as to what the line of writing was, Simpson replied that he did not read it. Bagshot, however, testifies that, in accordance with her duty, she cast her eye over it, and that it contained the following words: "Do let me come to you. Crystal." The word "Crystal" was a signature, and Mrs. Heathcote seemed to recognize it. Bagshot testifies that the visitor was young and beautiful, although plainly, almost poorly, dressed, and that she remained with Mrs. Heathcote nearly two hours. Very soon after her departure the telegraphic dispatch was received announcing Captain Heathcote's safety, and then the wife started on that fatal journey which was to end in death.

"'This woman, Bagshot, so far the most important witness in the case, testifies that she heard only parts of the conversation—a few detached sentences which were spoken in an elevated tone. But, disconnected as the phrases are, they are brimming with significance. The important parts of her story are as follows: First, she heard Mrs. Heathcote say, "I shall never rest until you tell me all!" Second, that she cried out excitedly: "You have robbed me of his love. I will never forgive you." Third, that she said, rapidly and in a high, strained voice: "Since he saw you he has never loved me; I see it now. He married me from pity, no doubt thinking that I was near death. How many times he must have wished me dead indeed! I wonder *that he has not murdered me.*" Fourth, that later she said: "Yes, he has borne it so far, and now he is dead. But if he were alive, I should have taunted him with it. Do you hear? I say I should have taunted him." Fifth (and most remarkable of all), that this stranger made a strong and open avowal of her own love for the dead man, the extraordinary words of which are given in another column. There are several other sentences, but they are unfinished and comparatively unimportant.

"'The intelligent observer will not fail to note the significance of this testimony, which bears upon the case not only by supplying a motive for the deed, but also, possibly, its immediate cause, in the words of the deeply roused and jealous wife: "I should have taunted him with it. I say I should have taunted him."

"'The witness has been subjected to the closest cross-questioning; it seems impossible to confuse her, or to shake her evidence in the slightest degree. Divest her testimony of all comment and theory, and it still remains as nearly conclusive as any evidence, save ocular, can be. She it is who saw the prisoner enter his wife's room by stealth shortly before the murder; she it is who overheard the avowal of the rival, the rage and bitter jealousy of the wife, and her declaration that if her husband had lived she would have made known to him her discovery, and taunted him with it.

"'He did live; the report of his death was a mistake. It is more than probable that the wife carried out her threat.'"

Here Anne paused and laid the newspaper down; she was composed and grave.

"I will now tell you," she said, lifting her eyes to Dexter's face, "what really occurred and what really was said. As I stated before, upon seeing the announcement of her husband's death, I went to Helen. I wrote upon a slip of paper the line you have heard, and signed the name by which she always called me. As I had hoped, she consented to see me, and this woman, Bagshot, took me up stairs to her room. We were alone. Both doors were closed at first, I know; we supposed that they remained closed all the time. I knelt down by the low couch and took her in my arms. I kissed her, and stroked her hair. I could not cry; neither could she. I sorrowed over her in silence. For some time we did not speak. But after a while, with a long sigh, she said, 'Anne, I deceived him about the name in the marriage notice—Angélique; I let him think that it was you.' I said, 'It is of no consequence,' but she went on. She said that after that summer at Caryl's she had noticed a change in him, but that she did not think of me; she thought only of Rachel Bannert. But when he brought her the marriage notice, and asked if it were I, in an instant an entirely new suspicion leaped into her heart, roused by something in the tone of his voice: she always judged him by his voice. From that moment, she said, she had never been free from the jealous apprehension that he had loved me; and then, looking at me as she lay in my arms, she asked, 'But he never did, did he?'

"If I could have evaded her then, perhaps we should both have been spared all that followed, for we both suffered deeply. But I did not know how; I answered: 'He had fancies, Helen; I may have been one of them. But only for a short time. *You* were his wife.' And then I asked her if her married life had not been happy.

"'Yes, yes,' she answered. 'I worshipped him.' And as she said this she began at last to sob, and the first tears she had shed flowed from her eyes, which had been so dulled and narrowed that they had looked dead. But she had not been satisfied, and later she came back to the subject again. She did it suddenly; seizing my arm, and lifting herself up, she cried out quickly that first sentence overheard by Bagshot—'I shall never rest until you tell me all!' Then, in a beseeching tone, she added: 'Do not keep it from me. I know that he did not love me as I loved him; still, he loved me, and I—was content. What you have to tell, therefore, can not hurt me, for—I was content. Then speak, Anne, speak.'

"I tried to quiet her, but she clung to me entreatingly. 'Tell me—tell me all,' she begged. 'When they bring him home, and I see his still face lying in the coffin, I want to stand beside him with my hand upon his breast, and whisper that I know all, understand all, forgive all, if there were anything to forgive. Anne, he will be glad to hear that—yes, even in death; for I loved him—love him—with all my soul, and he must know it now, there where he has gone. With all my imperfections, my follies, my deceptions, I loved him—loved him—loved him.' She began to weep, and I too burst into tears. It seemed to *me* also that he would be glad to hear that sentence of hers, that forgiveness. And so, judging her by myself, I did tell her all."

190

She paused, and her voice trembled, as though in another moment it would break into sobs.

"What did you tell her?" said Dexter. He was leaning back in his chair, his face divested of all expression save a rigid impartiality.

"Must I repeat it?"

"Of course, if I am to know all."

"I told her that at Caryl's we had been much together," she began, with downcast eyes; "that, after a while, he made himself seem much nearer to me by—by speaking of—by asking me about—sacred things—I mean a religious belief." (Here her listener's face showed a quick gleam of angry contempt, but she did not see it.) "Then, after this, one morning in the garden, when I was in great trouble, he—spoke to me—in another way. And when I went away from Caryl's he followed me, and we were together on a train during one day; mademoiselle was with us. At evening I left the train with mademoiselle: he did not know where we went. At this time I was engaged to Erastus Pronando. In August of the next summer I went to West Virginia to assist in the hospitals for a short time. Here, unexpectedly, I heard of him lying ill at a farm-house in the neighborhood; I did not even know that he was in the army. I went across the mountain to see if he were in good hands, and found him very ill; he did not know me. When the fever subsided, there were a few hours—during which there was a—deception, followed by a confession of the same, and separation. He was to go back to his wife, and he did go back to her. It was because I believed that he had so fully gone back to her—or rather that he had never left her, I having been but a passing fancy—that I told Helen all. She suspected something; it was better that she should know the whole—should know how short-lived had been his interest in me, his forgetfulness of her. But instead of making this impression upon her, it roused in her a passion of excitement. It was then that she exclaimed: 'You have robbed me of his love; I will never forgive you'—the second sentence overheard by that listening spy.

"'Helen,' I answered, 'he did not love me. Do you not see that? *I* am the one humiliated. When I saw you with him at St. Lucien's Church, I knew that he loved you—probably had never loved any one save you.'

"I believed what I said. But this is what she answered: 'It is not true. Since he saw you he has never loved me. I see it now. He married me from pity, no doubt thinking that I was near death. How many times he must have wished me dead indeed! I wonder that he has not murdered me.'

"This, also, Bagshot heard, for Helen had risen to her feet, and spoke in a high, strained voice, unlike her own. I put my arms round her and drew her down again. She struggled, but I would not let her go.

"'Helen,' I said, 'you are beside yourself. You were his wife, and you were happy. That one look I had in church showed me that you were.'

"She relapsed into stillness. After a while she looked up, and said, quietly, 'It is a good thing he is dead.'

"'Hush!' I answered; 'you do not know what you are saying.'

"'Yes, I do. It is a good thing that he is dead,' she repeated; 'for I should have found it out, and made his life a torment. And I should never have died; it would have determined me never to die. I should have lived on forever, an old, old woman, close to him always, so that he could not have *you*.'

"She seemed half mad; I think, at the moment, she was half mad, owing to the shock, and to the dumb grief which was consuming her.

"'It would have been a strange life we should have led,' she went on. 'I would not have left him even for a moment; he should have put on my shawl and carried me to and fro just the same, and I should have kissed him always when he went out and came in, as though we loved each other. I know his nature. It is—O God! I mean it *was*—the kind I could have worked upon. He was generous, very tender to all women; he would have yielded to me always, so far as bearing silently all my torments to the last.'"

Here Dexter interrupted the speaker. "You will acknowledge *now* what I said concerning her?"

"No," replied Anne; "Helen imagined it all. She could never have carried it out. She loved him too deeply."

Her eyes met his defiantly. The old feeling that he was an antagonist rose in her face for a moment, met by a corresponding retort in his. Then they both dropped their glance, and she resumed her narrative.

"It was here that she cried out, 'Yes, he has borne it so far, and now he is dead. But if he were alive, I should have taunted him with it. Do you hear? I say I should have taunted him.' This also Bagshot overheard. And then—" She paused.

"And then?" repeated Dexter, his eyes full upon her face.

"She grew calmer," said the girl, turning her face from him, and speaking for the first time hurriedly; "she even kissed me. 'You were always good and true,' she said. 'But it was easy to be good and true, if you did not love him.' I suppose she felt my heart throb suddenly (she was lying in my arms), for she sprang up, and wound her arms round my neck, bringing her eyes close to mine. *Did* you love him? she asked. 'Tell me—tell me; it will do no harm now.'

"But I drew myself out of her grasp, although she clung to me. I crossed the room. She followed me. 'Tell me,' she whispered; 'I shall not mind it. Indeed, I wish that you *did* love him, that you do love him, for then we would mourn for him together. I can be jealous of his love for you, but not of yours for him, poor child. Tell me, Anne; tell me. I long to know that you are miserable too.' She was leaning on me: in truth, she was too weak to stand alone. She clung to me in the old caressing way. 'Tell me,' she whispered. But I set my lips. Then, still clinging to me, her eyes fixed on mine, she said that I could not love; that I did not know what love meant; that I never would know, because my nature was too calm, too measured. She spoke other deriding words, which I will not repeat; and then—and then—I do not know how it came about, but I pushed her from me, with her whispering voice and shining eyes, and spoke out aloud (we were standing near that door) those words— those words which Bagshot has repeated."

"You said those words?"

"I did."

"Then you loved him?"

"Yes."

"Do you love him now?"

As Dexter asked this question his eyes were fixed upon her with a strange intentness. At first she met his gaze with the same absorbed expression unconscious of self which her face had worn from the beginning. Then a burning blush rose, spread itself over her forehead, and dyed even her throat before it faded. "You have no right to ask that," she said, returning to her narrative with haste, as though it were a refuge.

"After I had said those words, there was no more bitterness between us. I think *then* Helen forgave me. She asked me to come and live with her in her desolation. I answered that perhaps later I could come, but not then; and it was at this time that she said, not what Bagshot has reported, 'You can not conquer hate,' but, 'You can not conquer fate.' And she added: 'We two *must* be together, Anne; we are bound by a tie which can not be severed, even though we may wish it. You must bear with me, and I must suffer you. It is our fate.'

"Later, she grew more feverish; her strength was exhausted. But when at last I rose to go, she went with me to the door. 'If he had lived,' she said, 'one of us must have died.' Then her voice sank to a whisper. 'Changed or died,' she added. 'And as we are not the kind of women who change, it would have ended in the wearing out of the life of one of us—the one who loved the most. And people would have called it by some other name, and that would have been the end. But now it is *he* who has been taken, and—oh! I can not bear it—I can not, can not bear it!'" She paused; her eyes were full of tears.

"Is that all?" said Dexter, coldly.

"That is all."

Then there was a silence.

"Do you not think it important?" she asked at last, with a new timidity in her voice.

"It will make an impression; it will be your word against Bagshot's. The point proved will be that instead of your having separated in anger, with words of bitterness and jealousy, you separated in peace, as friends. Her letter will be important, if it proves this."

"It does. I have also another—a little note telling me of her husband's safety, and dropped into a letter-box on her way to the train. And I have the locket she gave me on the day of our last interview. She took it from her own neck and clasped it round mine a moment before I left her."

"Did Bagshot know of the existence of this locket?"

"She must have known it. For Helen said she always wore it; and Bagshot dressed her daily."

"Will you let me see it? And the two letters also, if they are here?"

"They are up stairs. I will get them."

What he wished to find out was whether she wore the locket. She came back so soon that he said to himself she could not have had it on—there had not been time to remove it; besides, as he held it in his hand it was not warm. He read the two letters carefully. Then he took up the locket again and examined it. It was a costly trinket, set with diamonds; within was a miniature, a life-like picture of Helen's husband.

He looked at his rival silently. The man was in prison, charged with the highest crime in the catalogue of crimes, and Dexter believed him guilty. Yet it was, all the same, above all and through all, the face of his rival still—of his triumphant, successful rival.

He laid down the locket, rose, and went over to Anne.

She was standing by the window, much dejected that he had not been more impressed by the importance of that which she had revealed. She looked up as he came near.

"Anne," he said, "I have promised to take you to Multomah, and I will keep my promise, if you insist. But have you considered that if you correct and restate Bagshot's testimony in all the other points, you will also be required to acknowledge the words of that confession?"

"Yes, I know it," she murmured, turning toward the window again.

"It can not but be horribly repugnant to you. Think how you will be talked about, misunderstood. The newspapers will be black with your name; it will go through the length and breadth of the land accompanied with jests, and possibly with worse than jests. Anne, look up; listen to what I am going to say. Marry me, Anne; marry me to-day; and go on the witness stand—if go you must—as my wife."

She gazed at him, her eyes widened with surprise.

He took her hands, and began to plead. "It is a strange time in which to woo you; but it is a strange ordeal which you have to go through. As my wife, no one will dare to insult you or to misconstrue your evidence; for your marriage will have given the lie beforehand to the worst comment that can be made, namely, that you still love Heathcote, and hope, if he is acquitted, to be his wife. It will be said that you loved him once, but that this tragedy has changed the feeling, and you will be called noble in coming forward of your own accord to acknowledge an avowal which must be now painful to you in the extreme. The 'unknown young girl' will be unknown no longer, when she comes forward as Gregory Dexter's wife, with Gregory Dexter by her side to give her, in the eyes of all men, his proud protection and respect."

Anne's face responded to the warm earnestness of these words: she had never felt herself so powerfully drawn toward him as at that moment.

"As to love, Anne," he continued, his voice softening, "do not fancy that I am feigning anything when I say that I do love you. The feeling has grown up unconsciously. I shall love you very dearly when you are my wife; you could command me, child, to almost any extent. As for your feeling toward me—marry me, and I will *make* you love me." He drew her toward him. "I am not too old, too old for you, am I?" he said, gently.

"It is not that," she answered, in deep distress. "Oh, why, why have you said this?"

"Well, because I am fond of you, I suppose," said Dexter, smiling. He thought she was yielding.

"You do not understand," she said, breaking from him. "You are generous and kind, the best friend I have ever had, and it is for that reason, if for no other, that I would never wrong you by marrying you, because—"

"Because?" repeated Dexter.

"Because I still love him."

"Heathcote?"

"Yes."

His face changed sharply, yet he continued his urging. "Even if you do love him, you would not marry him *now*."

She did not answer.

"You would not marry him with poor Helen's blood between you?"

"It is not between us. He is innocent."

"But if, after escaping conviction, it should yet be made clear to you—perhaps to you alone—that he *was* guilty, then would you marry him?"

"No. But the very greatness of his crime would make him in a certain way sacred to me on account of the terrible remorse and anguish he would have to endure."

"A good way to punish criminals," said Dexter, bitterly. "To give them your love and your life, and make them happy."

"He would not be happy; he would be a wretched man through every moment of his life, and die a wretched death. Whatever forgiveness might come in another world, there would be none in this. Helen herself would wish me to be his friend."

"For the ultra-refinement of self-deception, give me a woman," said Dexter, with even deepened bitterness.

"But why do we waste time and words?" continued Anne. Then seeing him take up his hat and turn toward the door, she ran to him and seized his arm. "You are not going?" she cried, abandoning the subject with a quick, burning anxiety which told more than all the rest. "Will you not take me, as you promised, to Multomah?"

"You still ask me to take you there?"

"Yes, yes."

"What do you think a man is made of?" he said, throwing down his hat, but leaving her, and walking across to the window.

Anne followed him. "Mr. Dexter," she said, standing behind him, shrinkingly, so that he could not see her, "would you wish me to marry you when I love—love *him*, as I said, in those words which you have read, and—even more?" Her face was crimson, her voice broken, her hands were clasped so tightly that the red marks of the pressure were visible.

He turned and looked at her. Her face told even more than her words. All his anger faded; it seemed to him then that he was the most unfortunate man in the whole world. He took her in his arms, and kissed her sadly. "I yield, child," he said. "Think of it no more. But, oh, Anne, Anne, if it could but have been! Why does he have everything, and I nothing?" He bowed his head over hers as it lay on his breast, and stood a moment; then he released her, went to the door, and breathed the outside air in silence.

Closing it, he turned and came toward her again, and in quite another tone said, "Are you ready? If you are, we will go to the city, and start as soon as possible for Multomah."

CHAPTER XXXIV.

"Then she rode forth, clothed on with chastity:

The deep air listen'd round her as she rode,

And all the low wind hardly breathed for fear.

The little wide-mouth'd heads upon the spout

Had cunning eyes to see: the barking cur

Made her cheeks flame: ... the blind walls

Were full of chinks and holes; and overhead

Fantastic gables, crowding, stared: but she

Not less thro' all bore up."—Tennyson.

Gregory Dexter kept his word. He telegraphed to Miss Teller and to Miss Teller's lawyers. He thought of everything, even recalling to Anne's mind that she ought to write to her pupils and to the leader of the choir, telling them that she expected to be absent from the city for several days. "It would be best to resign all the places at once," he said. "After this is over, they can easily come back to you if they wish to do so."

"It may make a difference, then, in my position?" said Anne.

"It will make the difference that you will no longer be an unknown personage," he answered, briefly.

His dispatch had produced a profound sensation of wonder in the mind of Miss Teller, and excitement in the minds of Miss Teller's lawyers. Helen's aunt, so far, had not been able to form a conjecture as to the identity of the mysterious young girl who had visited her niece, and borne part in that remarkable conversation; Bagshot's description brought no image before her mind. The acquaintance with Anne Douglas, the school-girl at Madame Moreau's was such a short, unimportant, and now distant episode in the brilliant, crowded life of her niece that she had forgotten it, or at least never thought of it in this connection. She had never heard Helen call Anne "Crystal." Her imagination was fixed upon a girl of the lower class, beautiful, and perhaps in her way even respectable—"one of those fancies which," she acknowledged, "gentlemen sometimes have," the tears gathering in her pale eyes as she spoke, so repugnant was the idea to her, although she tried to accept it for Heathcote's sake. But how could Helen have known a girl of this sort? Was this, too, one of those concealed trials which wives of "men of the world" were obliged to endure?

Neither did Isabel or Rachel think of Anne. To them she had been but a school-girl, and they had not seen her or heard of her since that summer at Caryl's; she had passed out of their remembrance as entirely as out of their vision. Their idea of Helen's unknown visitor was similar to that which occupied the mind of Miss Teller. And in their hearts they had speculated upon the possibility of using money with such a person, inducing her to come forward, name herself, and deny Bagshot's testimony point-blank, or at least the dangerous portions of it. It could not matter much to a girl of that sort what she had to say, provided she were well paid for it.

194

Miss Teller and the lawyers were waiting to receive Anne, when, late in the evening, she arrived, accompanied by Mr. Dexter. The lawyers had to give way first to Miss Teller.

"Oh, Anne, dear child!" she cried, embracing the young girl warmly; "I never dreamed it was you. And you have come all this way to help us! I do not in the least understand how; but never mind—never mind. God bless you!" She sobbed as she spoke. Then seeing Dexter, who was standing at some distance, she called him to her, and blessed him also. He received her greeting in silence. He had brought Anne, but he was in no mood to appreciate benedictions.

And now the lawyers stepped forward, arranging chairs at the table in a suggestive way, opening papers, and consulting note-books. Anne looked toward Dexter for directions; his eyes told her to seat herself in one of the arm-chairs. He then withdrew to another part of the large room, and Miss Teller, having vainly endeavored to beckon him to her side, so that he might be within reach of her tearful whispers and sympathy-seeking finger, resigned herself to excited listening and silence.

When Anne Douglas appeared on the witness-stand in the Heathcote murder trial, a buzz of curiosity and surprise ran round the crowded court-room.

"A young girl!" was the first whisper. Then, "Pretty, rather," from the women, and "Beautiful!" from the men.

Isabel grasped Rachel's arm. "Is that Anne Douglas?" she said, in a wonder-struck voice. "You remember her—the school-girl, Miss Vanhorn's niece, who was at Caryl's that summer? Helen always liked her; and Ward Heathcote used to talk to her now and then, although Mr. Dexter paid her more real attention."

"I remember her," said Rachel, coldly; "but I do not recollect the other circumstances you mention."

"It *is* Anne," continued Isabel, too much absorbed to notice Rachel's manner. "But older, and a thousand times handsomer. Rachel, that girl is beautiful!"

Anne's eyes were downcast. She feared to see Heathcote, and she did not even know in what part of the room he was placed. She remained thus while she was identified by Bagshot and Simpson, while she gave her name, and went through the preliminary forms; when at last she did raise her eyes, she looked only at the lawyers who addressed her.

And now the ordeal opened. All, or almost all, of that which she had told Gregory Dexter she was now required to repeat here, before this crowded, listening court-room, this sea of faces, these watching lawyers, the judge, and the dreaded jury. She had never been in a court-room before. For one moment, when she first looked up, her courage failed, and those who were watching her saw that it had failed. Then toward whom did her frightened glance turn as if for aid?

"Rachel, it is Gregory Dexter," said Isabel, again grasping her companion's arm excitedly.

"Pray, Isabel, be more quiet," answered Mrs. Bannert. But her own heart throbbed quickly for a moment as she recognized the man who had told her what he thought of her plainly in crude and plebeian Saxon phraseology.

Anne was now speaking. Bagshot's testimony was read to her phrase by phrase. Phrase by phrase she corroborated its truthfulness, but added what had preceded and followed. In this manner all the overheard sentences were repeated amid close attention, the interest increasing with every word.

But still it was evident that all were waiting; the attitude was plainly one of alert expectancy.

For what were they waiting? For the confession of love, to whose "extraordinary words" the New York journals had called attention.

At last it came. An old lawyer read the sentences aloud, slowly, markedly; while the fall of a feather could have been heard in the crowded room, and all eyes were fastened pitilessly upon the defenseless girl; for she seemed at that moment utterly forsaken and defenseless.

"'You say that I can not love,'" slowly read the lawyer, in his clear, dry voice; "'that it is not in my nature. You know nothing about it. You have thought me a child; I am a child no longer. I love Ward Heathcote, your husband, with my whole heart. It was a delight to me simply to be near him, to hear his voice. When he spoke my name, all my being went toward him. I loved him—loved him—so deeply that everything else on the face of the earth is as nothing to me compared with it. I would have been gladly your servant, yes, *yours*, only to be in the same house with him, though I were of no more account in his eyes than the dog on the mat before his door.'"

There was an instant of dead silence after these last passionate words had fallen strangely from the old lawyer's thin lips. Then, "Are these your words?" he asked.

"They are," replied Anne.

In that supreme moment her glance, vaguely turned away from the questioner, met the direct gaze of the prisoner. Until now she had not seen him. It was but an instant that their eyes held each other, but in that instant the thronged court-room faded from her sight, and her face, which, while the lawyer read, had been white and still as marble, was now, though still colorless, so transfigured, so uplifted, so beautiful in its pure sacrifice, that men leaned forward to see her more closely, to print, as it were, that exquisite image upon their memories forever.

Then the crowd took its breath again audibly; the sight was over. Anne had sunk down and covered her face with her hands, and Miss Teller, much agitated, was sending her a glass of water.

Even the law is human sometimes, and there was now a short delay.

So far, while the testimony of the new witness had been dramatic, and in its interest absorbing, it had not proved much, or shaken to any great extent the theory of the prosecution. On the contrary, more than ever now were people inclined to believe that this lovely young girl was in reality the wife's rival. Men whispered to each other, significantly, "Heathcote knew what he was about. That is the most beautiful girl I ever saw in my life; and nothing can alter *that*."

"But now the tide turned. The examination proceeded, and the two unfinished sentences which Bagshot had repeated were read. Anne corrected them.

"'You can not conquer hate,'" read the lawyer.

"Mrs. Heathcote did not say that," began Anne; but her voice was still tremulous, and she paused a moment in order to control it.

"We wish to remark here," said one of Miss Teller's lawyers, "that while the witness named Minerva Bagshot is possessed of an extraordinary memory, and while she has also repeated what she overheard with a correctness and honesty which are indeed remarkable in a person who would deliberately open a door and *listen*, in this instance her careful and conscientious ears will be found to have been mistaken."

He was not allowed to say more. But as he had said all he wished to say, he bore his enforced silence with equanimity.

"Mrs. Heathcote wished me to come and live with her," continued Anne. "She said, not what Mrs. Bagshot has reported, but, 'You can not conquer *fate*.' And then she added, 'We two *must* be together, Anne; we are bound by a tie which can not be severed, even though we may wish it. You must bear with me, and I must suffer you. It is our fate.'"

This produced an effect; it directly contradicted the impression made by Bagshot's phrase, namely, that the two women had parted in anger and hate, the wife especially being in a mood of desperation. True, it was but Anne's word against Bagshot's, and the strange tendency toward believing the worst, which is often seen at criminal trials, inclined most minds toward the elder woman's story. Still, the lawyers for the defense were hopeful.

The last sentence, or portion of a sentence, was now read: "'If he had lived, one of us must have died.'"

It had been decided that Anne should here give all that Helen had said, without omission, as she had given it to Dexter.

"Yes," she answered; "Mrs. Heathcote used those words. But it was in the following connection. When we had said good-by, and I had promised to come again after the funeral, she went with me toward the door. 'If he had lived,' she said, 'one of us must have died.' Then she paused an instant, and her voice sank. 'Changed or died,' she added. 'And as we are not the kind of women who change, it would have ended in the wearing out of the life of one of us—the one who loved the most. And people would have called it by some other name, and that would have been the end. But now it is *he* who has been taken, and—oh! I can not bear it—I can not, can not bear it!'"

She repeated these words of Helen's with such realistic power that tears came to many eyes. Rachel Bannert for the first time veiled her face. All the feeling in her, such as it was, was concentrated upon Heathcote, and Helen's bitter cry of grief, repeated by Anne, had been the secret cry of her own heart every minute since danger first menaced him.

Anne's words had produced a sensation; still, they were but her unsupported words.

But now something else was brought forward; proof which, so far as it went, at least, was tangible. Anne was testifying that, before she went away, Helen had taken from her own neck a locket and given it to her as a token of renewed affection; and the locket was produced. The defense would prove by Bagshot herself that this locket on its chain was round her mistress's neck on the morning of that day, and Mrs. Heathcote must therefore have removed it herself and given it to the present witness, since the latter could hardly have taken it from her by force without being overheard, the door being so very conveniently ajar.

And now the next proof was produced, the hurried note written to Anne by Helen, after the tidings of her husband's safety had been received. After the writing had been identified as Helen's, the note was read.

"Dear Anne,—Ward is safe. It was a mistake. I have just received a dispatch. He is wounded, but not dangerously, and I write this on my way to the train, for I am going to him; that is, if I can get through. All is different now. I trust you. But I love him too much not to try and make him love *me* the most, if I possibly can.

Helen."

This was evidence clear and decided. It was no longer Anne's word, but Helen's own. Whatever else the listeners continued to believe, they must give up the idea that the wife and this young girl had parted in anger and hate; for if the locket as proof could be evaded, the note could not.

But this was not all. An excitement more marked than any save that produced when Anne acknowledged the confession arose in the court-room when the lawyers for the defense announced that they would now bring forward a second letter—a letter written by Mrs. Heathcote to the witness in the inn at Timloesville on the evening of her death—her last letter, what might be called her last utterance on earth. It had been shown that Mrs. Heathcote was seen writing; it would be proved that a letter was given to a colored lad employed in the hotel soon after Captain Heathcote left the room, and that this lad ran across the street to the post-office and dropped it into the mail-box. Not being able to read, he had not made out the address.

When the handwriting of this letter also had been identified, it was, amid eager attention, read aloud. The feeling was as if the dead wife herself were speaking to them from the grave.

"Timloesville, *June 10, half past 8* P.M.

"Dear Anne,—I sent you a few lines from New York, written on my way to the train, but now that I have time, I feel that something more is due to you. I found Ward at a little hospital, his right arm injured, but not seriously. He will not be able to use it readily for some time; it is in a sling. But he is so much better that they have allowed us to start homeward. We are travelling slowly—more, however, on my account than his. I long to have the journey over.

"Dear Anne, I have thought over all our conversation—all that you told me, all that I replied. I am so inexpressibly happy to-night, as I sit here writing, that I can and will do you justice, and tell all the truth—the part that I have hitherto withheld. And that is, Anne, that your influence over him *was* for good, and that your pain and effort have not been thrown away. You asked him to bear his part in life bravely, and he has borne it; you asked him to come back to me, and he did come back. If you were any other woman on earth, I would never confess this—confess that I owe to *you* my happiness of last winter, when he changed, even in his letters, to greater kindness; confess that it was your influence which made him, when he came home later, so much more watchful and gentle in his care of, his manner toward, me. I noticed the change on the first instant, the first letter, and it made my heart bound. If it had been possible, I should have gone to him then, but it was not. He had rejoined his regiment, and I could only watch for his letters like a girl of sixteen. When he did come home, I counted every hour of that short visit as so much happiness greater than I had ever known before. For I had always loved him, and *now* he loved me.

"Do not contradict me; he does love me. At least he is so dear to me, and so kind and tender, that I do not know whether he does or not, but am content. You are a better, nobler woman; yet *I* have the happiness.

"He does not know that I have seen you, and I shall never tell him. He does not know that I know what an effort he has made. But every kind act and tone goes to my heart. For I *did* deceive him, Anne; and if it had not been for that deception, probably he would not now be my husband—he would be free.

"Yet good has come out of evil this time, perhaps on account of my deep love. No wife was ever so thankfully happy as I am to-night, and on my knees I have thanked my Creator for giving me that which makes my life one long joy.

"He has come in, and is sitting opposite, reading. He does not know to whom I am writing—does not dream what I am saying. And he must never know: I can not rise to *that*.

"No, Anne, we must not meet, at least for the present. It is better so, and you yourself will feel that it is. But when I reach home I will write again, and *then* you will answer.

"Always, with warm love, your friend, Helen."

During the reading of this letter, the prisoner for the first time sat with his head bowed, his face shaded by his hand. Miss Teller's sobs could be heard. Anne, too, broke down, and wept silently.

"When I reach home I will write again, and *then* you will answer." Helen *had* reached home, and Anne—had answered.

CHAPTER XXXV.

"The cold neutrality of an impartial judge."—Burke.

The jury were out.

They had been out four hours, but the crowd in the closely packed court-room still kept its ranks unbroken, and even seemed to grow more dense; for if, here and there, one person went away, two from the waiting throng of those in the halls and about the doors immediately pressed their way in to take the vacant place. The long warm summer day was drawing toward its close. The tired people fanned themselves, but would not go, because it was rumored that a decision was near.

Outside, the fair green farming country, which came up almost to the doors, stretched away peacefully in the twilight, shading into the grays of evening down the valley, and at the bases of the hills. The fields were falling asleep; eight o'clock sounding from a distant church bell seemed like a curfew and good-night.

If one had had time to think of it, the picture of the crowded court-room, rising in that peaceful landscape, was a strange one. But no one had time to think of it. Lights had been brought in. The summer beetles, attracted by them, flew in through the open windows, knocked themselves against the wall, fell to the floor, and then slowly took wing again to repeat the process. With the coming of the lights the crowd stirred a little, looked about, and then settled itself anew. The prisoner's chances were canvassed again, and for the hundredth time. The testimony of Anne Douglas had destroyed the theory which had seemed to fill out so well the missing parts of the story; it had proved that the supposed rival was a friend of the wife's, and that the wife loved her; it had proved that Mrs. Heathcote was devoted to her husband, and happy with him, up to the last hour of her life. This was much. But the circumstantial evidence regarding the movements of the prisoner at Timloesville remained unchanged; he was still confronted by the fact of his having been seen on that outside stairway, by the other significant details, and by the print of that left hand.

During this evening waiting, the city papers had come, were brought in, and read. One of them contained some paragraphs upon a point which, in the rapid succession of events that followed each other in the case, had been partially overlooked—a point which the country readers cast aside as unimportant, but which wakened in the minds of the city people present the remembrance that they had needed the admonition.

"But if this conversation (now given in full) was remarkable," wrote the editor far away in New York, "it should not be forgotten that the circumstances were remarkable as well. While reading it one should keep clearly in mind the fact that the subject of it, namely, Captain Heathcote, was, in the belief of both the speakers, dead. Had it not been for this belief of theirs, these words would never have been uttered. He was gone from earth forever—killed suddenly in battle. Such a death brings the deepest feelings of the heart to the surface. Such a death wrings out avowals which otherwise would never be made. Words can be spoken over a coffin— where all is ended—which could never be spoken elsewhere. Death brought together these two women, who seem to have loved each other through and in spite of all. One has gone. And now the menacing shadow of a far worse death has forced the other to come forward, and go through a cruel ordeal, an ordeal which was, however, turned into a triumph by the instant admiration which all rightly minded persons gave to the pure, noble bravery which thus saved a life. For although the verdict has not yet been given, the general opinion is that this new testimony turned the scale, and that the accused man will be acquitted."

But this prophecy was not fulfilled.

Five hours of waiting. Six hours. And now there came a stir. The jury were returning; they had entered; they were in their places. Rachel Bannert bent her face behind her open fan, that people should not see how white it was. Miss Teller involuntarily rose. But as many had also risen in the crowded room, which was not brightly lighted save round the lawyers' tables, they passed unnoticed. The accused looked straight into the faces of the jurors. He was quite calm; this part seemed far less trying to him than that which had gone before.

And then it was told: they had neither convicted nor acquitted him. They had disagreed.

Anne Douglas was not present. She was sitting alone in an unlighted house on the other side of the little country square. Some one walking up and down there, under the maples, had noticed, or rather divined, a figure at the open window behind the muslin curtains of the dark room; he knew that this figure was looking at the lights from the court-room opposite, visible through the trees.

This man under the maples had no more intention of losing the final moment than the most persistent countryman there. But being in the habit of using his money, now that he had it, rather than himself, he had posted two sentinels, sharp-eyed boys whom he had himself selected, one in an upper window of the court-room on the sill, the other outside on the sloping roof of a one-story building which touched it. The boy in the window was to keep watch; the boy on the roof was to drop to the ground at the first signal from the sill, and run. By means of this human telegraph, its designer under the maples intended to reach the window himself, through the little house whose door stood open (its mistress having already been paid for the right of way), in time to hear and see the whole. This intention was carried out—as his intentions generally were. The instant the verdict, or rather the want of verdict, was announced, he left the window, hastened down through the little house, and crossed the square. The people would be slow in leaving the court-room, the stairway was narrow, the crowd dense; the square was empty as he passed through it, went up the steps of the house occupied by Miss Teller, crossed the balcony, and stopped at the open window.

"Anne?" he said.

A figure stirred within.

"They have disagreed. The case will now go over to the November term, when there will be a new trial."

He could see that she covered her face with her hands. But she did not speak.

"It was your testimony that turned the scale," he added.

After a moment, as she still remained silent, "I am going away to-night," he went on; "that is, unless there is something I can do for you. Will you tell me your plans?"

"Yes, always," she answered, speaking low from the darkness. "Everything concerning me you may always know, if you care to know. But so far I have no plan."

"I leave you with Miss Teller; that is safety. Miss Teller claims the privilege now of having you with her always."

"I shall not stay long."

"You will write to me?"

"Yes."

People were now entering the square from the other side. The window-sill was between them; he took her hands, drew her forward from the shadow, and looked at her in the dim light from the street lamp.

"It is my last look, Anne," he said, sadly.

"It need not be."

"Yes; you have chosen. You are sure that there is nothing more that I can do?"

"There is one thing."

"What is it?"

"Believe him innocent. Believe it, not for my sake, but for your own."

"If I try, it will be for yours. Good-by."

He left her, and an hour later was on his way back to his post at the capital of his State. He was needed there; an accumulation of responsibilities awaited him. For that State owed the excellence of its war record, its finely equipped regiments, well-supplied hospitals, and prompt efficiency in all departments of public business throughout those four years, principally to the brain and force of one man—Gregory Dexter.

CHAPTER XXXVI.

"I have no other than a woman's

reason:

I think him so because I think him so."

—Shakspeare.

Summer was at its height. Multomah had returned to its rural quietude; the farmers were busy afield, the court-room was closed, the crowd gone. The interest in the Heathcote case, and the interest in Ward Heathcote, remained as great as ever in the small circle of which he and Helen had formed part; but nothing more could happen until November, and as, in the mean time, the summer was before them, they had found a diversion of thought in discovering an island off the coast of Maine, and betaking themselves thither, leaving to mistaken followers the belief that Caryl's still remained an exclusive and fashionable resort. Beyond this small circle, the attention of the nation at large was absorbed in a far greater story—the story of the Seven Days round Richmond.

Word had come to Anne from the northern island that the little boy, whose failing health had for so many months engrossed all Miss Lois's time and care, had closed his tired eyes upon this world's pain forever. He would no longer need the little crutch, which they had both grieved to think must always be his support; and Miss Lois coming home to the silent church-house after the burial in the little cemetery on the height, and seeing it there in its corner, had burst into bitter tears. For the child, in his helplessness and suffering, had grown into her very heart. But now Anne needed her—that other child whom she had loved so long and so well. And so, after that one fit of weeping, she covered her grief from sight, put a weight of silent remembrance upon it, and with much energy journeyed southward.

For Anne, Miss Lois, and Miss Teller were now linked together by a purpose, a feminine purpose, founded upon faith only, and with outlines vague, yet one none the less to be carried out: to go to Timloesville or its neighborhood, and search for the murderer there.

Miss Teller, who had found occupation in various small schemes for additions to Heathcote's comfort during the summer, rose to excitement when the new idea was presented to her.

"We must have advice about it," she began; "we must consult—" Then seeing in the young face, upon whose expressions she had already come to rely, a non-agreement, she paused.

"The best skill of detectives has already been used," said Anne; "they followed a track, worked from a beginning. We should follow no track, and accept no beginning, save the immovable certainty that he was innocent." She was silent a moment; then with a sigh which was a sad, yet not a hopeless, one, "Dear Miss Teller," she added, "it is said that women divine a truth sometimes by intuition, and against all probability. It is to this instinct—if such there be—that we must trust now."

Miss Teller studied these suggestions with respect; but they seemed large and indistinct. In spite of herself her mind reverted to certain articles of furniture which she had looked at the day before, furniture which was to make his narrow room more comfortable. But she caught herself in these wanderings, brought back her straying thoughts promptly, and fastened them to the main subject with a question—like a pin.

"But how could I go to Timloesville at present, when I have so much planned out to do here? Oh, Anne, I could not leave him here, shut up in that dreary place."

"It seems to me safer that you should not go," replied the girl; "it might be noticed, especially as it is known that you took this house for the summer. But I could go. And there is Miss Lois. She is free now, and the church-house must be very lonely." The tears sprang again as she thought of André, the last of the little black-eyed children who had been so dear.

They talked over the plan. No man being there to weigh it with a cooler masculine judgment, it seemed to them a richly promising one. Anne was imaginative, and Miss Teller reflected Anne. They both felt, however, that its accomplishment depended upon Miss Lois. But Anne's confidence in Miss Lois was great.

"I know of no one for whom I have a deeper respect than for that remarkable woman," said Miss Teller, reverentially. "It will be a great gratification to see her."

"But it would be best, I think, that she should not come here," replied Anne. "I should bid you good-by, and go away; every one would see me go. Then in New York I could meet Miss Lois, and we could go together to Timloesville by another route. At Timloesville nobody would know Miss Lois, and I should keep myself in a measure concealed; there were only a few persons from Timloesville at the trial, and I think I could evade them."

"I should have liked much to meet Miss Hinsdale," said Miss Margaretta, in a tone of regret. "But you know best."

"Oh, no, no," said Anne, letting her arms fall in sudden despondency. "I sometimes think that I know nothing, and worse than nothing! Moments come when I would give years of my life for one hour, only one, of trusting reliance upon some one wiser, stronger, than I—who would tell me what I ought to do."

But this cry of the young heart (brave, but yet so young) distressed Miss Margaretta. If the pilot should lose courage, what would become of the passengers? She felt herself looking into chaos.

Anne saw this. And controlled herself again.

"When should you start?" said the elder lady, relieved, and bringing forward a date. Miss Margaretta always found great support in dates.

"I can not tell yet. We must first hear from Miss Lois."

"I will write to her myself," said Miss Margaretta, putting on her spectacles and setting to work at once. It was a relief to be engaged upon something tangible.

And write she did. The pages she sent to Miss Lois, and the pages with which Miss Lois replied were many, eloquent, and underlined. Before the correspondence was ended they had scientifically discovered, convicted, and hanged the murderer, and religiously buried him.

Miss Lois was the most devoted partisan the accused man had gained. She was pleader, audience, public opinion, detective, judge, and final clergyman, in one. She had never seen Heathcote. That made no difference. She was sure he was a concentration of virtue, and the victim not of circumstances (that was far too mild), but of a "plot" (she wanted to say "popish," but was restrained by her regard for Père Michaux).

Miss Teller saw Heathcote daily. So far, she had not felt it necessary that Anne should accompany her. But shortly before the time fixed for the young girl's departure she was seized with the idea that it was Anne's duty to see him once. For perhaps he could tell her something which would be of use at Timloesville.

"I would rather not; it is not necessary," replied Anne. "You can tell me."

"You should not think of yourself; in such cases ourselves are nothing," said Miss Teller. "The sheriff and the persons in charge under him are possessed of excellent dispositions, as I have had occasion to prove; no one need know of your visit, and I should of course accompany you."

Anne heard her in silence. She was asking herself whether this gentle lady had lost all memory of her own youth, and whether that youth had held no feelings which would make her comprehend the depth of that which she was asking now.

But Miss Teller was not thinking of her youth, or of herself, or of Anne. She had but one thought, one motive—Helen's husband, and how to save him; all the rest seemed to her unimportant. She had in fact forgotten it. "I do not see how you can hesitate," she said, the tears suffusing her light eyes, "when it is for our dear Helen's sake."

"Yes," replied Anne; "but Helen is dead. How can we know—how can we be sure—what she would wish?" She seemed to be speaking to herself. She rose, walked to the window, and stood there looking out.

"She would wish to have him saved, would she not?" answered Miss Teller. "I consider it quite necessary that you should see him before you go. For you could not depend upon my report of what he says. It has, I am sorry to say, been represented to me more than once that I have a tendency to forget what has been variously mentioned as the knob, the point, the gist of a thing."

Anne did not turn.

Miss Teller noted this obstinacy with surprise.

"It is mysterious to me that after the great ordeal of that trial, Anne, you should demur over such a simple thing as this," she said, gently.

But to Anne the sea of faces in the court-room seemed now less difficult than that quiet cell with its one occupant. Then she asked herself whether this were not an unworthy feeling, a weak one? One to be put down at once, and with a strong hand. She yielded. The visit was appointed for the next day.

The county jail with its stone hall; a locked door. They were entering; the jailer retired.

The prisoner rose to receive them; he knew that they were coming, and was prepared. Miss Teller kissed him; he brought forward his two chairs. Then turning to Anne, he said, "It is kind of you to come;" and for a moment they looked at each other.

It was as if they had met in another world, in a far gray land beyond all human error and human dread. Anne felt this suddenly; if not like a chill, it was like the touch of an all-enveloping sadness, which would not pass away. Her fear left her; it seemed to her then that it would never come back.

As she looked at him she saw that he was greatly changed; her one glance in the court-room had not told her how greatly. Part of it was due doubtless to the effects of his wound, to the unaccustomed confinement in the heats of a lowland summer; his face, though still bronzed, was thin, his clothes hung loosely from his broad shoulders. But the marked alteration was in his expression. This was so widely different from that of the brown-eyed lounger of Caryl's, that it seemed another man who was standing there, and not the same. Heathcote's eyes were still brown; but their look was so changed that Gregory Dexter would never have occasion to find fault with it again. His half-indolent carelessness had given place to a stern reticence; his indifference, to a measured self-control. And Anne knew, as though a prophetic vision were passing, that he would carry that changed face always, to his life's end.

Miss Teller had related to him their plan, their womans' plan. He was strongly, unyieldingly, opposed to it. Miss Teller came home every day, won over to his view, and then as regularly changed her mind, in talking with Anne, and went back—to be converted over again. But he knew that Anne had persisted. He knew that he was now expected to search his memory, and see if he could not find there something new. Miss Teller, with a touching eagerness to be of use and business-like, arranged pen, paper, and ink upon the table, and sat down to take notes. She was still a majestic personage, in spite of her grief and anxiety; her height, profile, and flowing draperies were as imposing as ever. But in other ways she had grown suddenly old; her light complexion was now over-spread with a net-work of fine small wrinkles, the last faint blonde of her hair was silvered, and in her cheeks and about her mouth there was a pathetic alteration, the final predominance of old age, and its ineffective helplessness over her own mild personality.

But while they waited, he found that he could not speak. When he saw them sitting there in their mourning garb for Helen, when he felt that Anne too was within the circle of this grief and danger and pain, Anne, in all her pure fair youth and trust and courage, something rose in his throat and stopped utterance. All the past and his own part in it unrolled itself before him like a judgment; all the present, and her brave effort for him; the future, near and dark. For Heathcote, like Dexter, believed that the chances were adverse; and even should he escape conviction, he believed that the cloud upon him would never be cleared away entirely, but that it would rest like a pall over the remainder of his life. At that moment, in his suffering, he felt that uncleared acquittal, conviction, the worst that could come to him, he could bear without a murmur were it only possible to separate Anne—Anne both in the past and present—from his own dark lot. He rose suddenly from the bench where he had seated himself, turned his back to them, went to his little grated window, and stood there looking out.

Miss Teller followed him, and laid her hand on his shoulder. "Dear Ward," she said, "I do not wonder that you are overcome." And she took out her handkerchief.

He mastered himself and came back to the table. Miss Teller, who, having once begun, was unable to stop so quickly, remained where she was. Anne, to break the painful pause, began to ask her written questions from the slip of paper she had brought.

"Can you recall anything concerning the man who came by and spoke to you while you were bathing?" she said, looking at him gravely.

"No. I could not see him; it was very dark."

"What did he say?"

"He asked if the water was cold."

"How did he say it?"

"Simply, 'Is the water cold?'"

"Was there any foreign accent or tone, any peculiarity of pronunciation or trace of dialect, no matter how slight, in his voice or utterance?"

"I do not recall any. Stay, he may have given something of the sound of g to the word—said 'gold,' instead of 'cold.' But the variation was scarcely noticeable. Country people talk in all sorts of ways."

Miss Teller hurriedly returned to her chair, after wiping her eyes, wrote down "gold" and "cold" in large letters on her sheet of paper, and surveyed them critically.

"Is there nothing else you can think of?" pursued Anne.

"No. Why do you dwell upon him?"

"Because he is the man."

"Oh, Anne, is he?—is he?" cried Miss Teller, with as much excitement as though Anne had proved it.

"There is no probability. They have not even been able to find him," said Heathcote.

"Of course it is only my feeling," said the girl.

"But what *Anne* feels is no child's play," commented Miss Teller.

This remark, made in nervousness and without much meaning, seemed to touch Heathcote; he turned to the window again.

"Will you please describe to me exactly what you did from the time you left the inn to take the first walk until you came back after the river-bath?" continued Anne.

He repeated his account of the evening's events as he had first given it, with hardly the variation of a word.

"Are you sure that you took two towels? Might it not be possible that you took only one? For then the second, found at the end of the meadow trail, might have been taken by the murderer."

"No; I took two. I remember it because I put first one in my pocket, and then, with some difficulty, the other, and I spoke to Helen laughingly about my left-handed awkwardness." It was the first time he had spoken his wife's name, and his voice was very grave and sweet as he pronounced it.

Poor Miss Teller broke down again. And Anne began to see her little paper of questions through a blur. But the look of Heathcote's face saved her. Why should he have anything more to bear? She went on quickly with her inquiry.

"Was there much money in the purse?"

"I think not. She gave me almost all she had brought with her as soon as we met."

"Is it a large river?"

"Rather deep; in breadth only a mill-stream."

Then there was a silence. It seemed as if they all felt how little there was to work with, to hope for.

"Will you let Miss Teller draw on a sheet of paper the outline of your left hand?" continued Anne.

He obeyed without comment.

"Now please place your hand in this position, and let her draw the finger-tips." As she spoke, she extended her own left hand, with the finger-tips touching the table, as if she was going to grasp something which lay underneath.

But Heathcote drew back. A flush rose in his cheeks. "I will have nothing to do with it," he said.

"Oh, Ward, when Anne asks you?" said Miss Teller, in distress.

"*I* do not wish her to go to Timloesville," he said, with emphasis; "I have been utterly against it from the first. It is a plan made without reason, and directly against my feelings, my wishes, and my consent. It is unnecessary. It will be useless. And, worse than this, it may bring her into great trouble. Send as many detectives as you please, but do not send her. It is the misfortune of your position and hers that at such a moment you have no one to control you, no man, I mean, to whose better judgment you would defer. My wishes are nothing to you; you override them. You are, in fact, taking advantage of my helplessness."

He spoke to Miss Teller. But Anne, flushing a little at his tone, answered him.

"I can not explain the hope that is in me," she said; "but such a hope I certainly have. I will not be imprudent; Miss Lois shall do everything; I will be very guarded. If we are not suspected (and we shall not be; women are clever in such things), where is the danger? It will be but—but spending a few weeks in the country." She ended hesitatingly, ineffectively. Then, "To sit still and do nothing, to wait—is unendurable!" broke from her in a changed tone. "It is useless to oppose me. I shall go."

Heathcote did not reply.

"No one is to know of it, dear Ward, save ourselves and Miss Hinsdale," said Miss Teller, pleadingly.

"And Mr. Dexter," added Anne.

Heathcote now looked at her. "Dexter has done more for me than I could have expected," he said. "I never knew him well; I fancied, too, that he did not like me."

"Oh, there you are quite mistaken, Ward. He is your most devoted friend," said Miss Teller.

But a change in Anne's face had struck Heathcote. "He thinks me guilty," he said.

"Never! never!" cried Miss Teller. "Tell him no, Anne. Tell him no."

But Anne could not. "He said—" she began; then remembering that Dexter's words, "If I try, it will be for yours," were hardly a promise, she stopped.

"It is of small consequence. Those who could believe me guilty may continue to believe it," said Heathcote. But his face showed that he felt the sting.

He had never cared to be liked by all, or even by many; but when the blow fell it had been an overwhelming surprise to him that any one, even the dullest farm laborer, should suppose it possible that he, Ward Heathcote, could be guilty of such a deed.

It was the lesson which careless men, such as he had been, learn sometimes if brought face to face with the direct homely judgment of the plain people of the land.

"Oh, Anne, how can you have him for your friend? And I, who trusted him so!" said Miss Teller, with indignant grief.

"As Mr. Heathcote has said, it is of small consequence," answered Anne, steadily. "Mr. Dexter brought me here, in spite of his—his feeling, and that should be more to his credit, I think, than as though he had been—one of us. And now, Miss Teller, if there is nothing more to learn, I should like to go."

She rose. Heathcote made a motion as if to detain her, then his hand fell, and he rose also.

"I suppose we can stay until Jason Longworthy knocks?" said Miss Margaretta, hesitatingly.

"I would rather go now, please," said Anne.

For a slow tremor was taking possession of her; the country prison, which had not before had a dangerous look, seemed now to be growing dark and cruel; the iron-barred window was like a menace. It seemed to say that they might talk; but that the prisoner was theirs.

Miss Margaretta rose, disappointed but obedient; she bade Heathcote good-by, and said that she would come again on the morrow.

Then he stepped forward. "I shall not see you again," he said to Anne, holding out his hand. He had not offered to take her hand before.

She gave him hers, and he held it for a moment. No word was spoken; it was a mute farewell. Then she passed out, followed by Miss Teller, and the door was closed behind them.

"Why, you had twenty minutes more," said Jason Longworthy, the deputy, keeping watch in the hall outside.

CHAPTER XXXVII.

"The fisherman, unassisted by destiny, could not catch a fish in the Tigris; and the fish, without fate, could not have died upon dry land."—Saadi.

Anne met Miss Lois in New York. Miss Lois had never been in New York before; but it would take more than New York to confuse Miss Lois. They remained in the city for several days in order to rest and arrange their plans. There was still much to explain which the letters, voluminous as they had been, had not made entirely clear.

But first they spoke of the child. It was Miss Lois at length who turned resolutely from the subject, and took up the tangled coil which awaited her. "Begin at the beginning and tell every word," she said, sitting erect in her chair, her arms folded with tight compactness. If Miss Lois could talk, she could also listen. In the present case she listened comprehensively, sharply, and understandingly. When all was told—"How different it is from the old days when we believed that you and Rast would live always with us on the island, and that that would be the whole," she said, with a long, sad retrospective sigh. Then dismissing the past, "But we must do in this disappointing world what is set before us," she added, sighing again, but this time in a preparatory way. Anew she surveyed Anne. "You are much changed, child," she said. Something of her old spirit returned to her. "I wish those fort ladies could see you *now*!" she remarked, taking off her spectacles and wiping them with a combative air.

Possessed of Anne's narrative, she now began to arrange their plans in accordance with it, and to fit what she considered the necessities of the situation. As a stand-point she prepared a history, which, in its completeness, would have satisfied even herself as third person, forgetting that the mental organizations of the Timloesville people were probably not so well developed in the direction of a conscientious and public-spirited inquiry into the affairs of their neighbors as were those of the meritorious New England community where she had spent her youth. In this history they were to be aunt and niece, of the same name, which, after long cogitation, she decided should be Young, because it had "a plain, respectable sound." She herself was to be a widow (could it have been possible that, for once in her life, she wished to know, even if but reminiscently, how the married state would feel?), and Anne was to be her husband's niece. "Which will account for the lack of resemblance," she said, fitting all the parts of her plan together like those of a puzzle. She had even constructed an elaborate legend concerning said husband, and its items she enumerated with relish. His name, it appeared, had been Asher, and he had been something of a trial to her, although at the last he had experienced religion, and died thoroughly saved. His brother Eleazer, Anne's father, had been a very different person, a sort of New England David. He had taught in an academy, studied for the ministry, and died of "a galloping consumption"—a consolation to all his friends. Miss Lois could describe in detail both of these death-beds, and repeat the inscriptions on the two tombstones. Her own name was Deborah, and Anne's was Ruth. On the second day she evolved the additional item that Ruth was "worn out keeping the accounts of an Asylum for the Aged, in Washington—which is the farthest thing I can think of from teaching children in New York—and I have brought you into the country for your health."

Anne was dismayed. "I shall certainly make some mistake in all this," she said.

"Not if you pay attention. And you can always say your head aches if you don't want to talk. I am not sure but that you had better be threatened with something serious," added Miss Lois, surveying her companion consideringly. "It would have to be connected with the mind, because, unfortunately, you always look the picture of health."

"Oh, please let me be myself," pleaded Anne.

"Never in the world," replied Miss Lois. "Ourselves? No indeed. We've got to *be* conundrums as well as guess them, Ruth Young."

They arrived at their destination, not by the train, but in the little country stage which came from the south. The witnesses from Timloesville present at the trial had been persons connected with the hotel. In order that Anne should not come under their observation, they took lodgings at a farm-house at some distance from the village, and on the opposite side of the valley. Anne was not to enter the village; but of the meadow-paths and woods she would have free range, as the inhabitants of Timloesville, like most country people, had not a high opinion of pedestrian exercise. Anne was not to enter the town at all; but Miss Lois was to examine "its every inch."

The first day passed safely, and the second and third. Anne was now sufficiently accustomed to her new name not to start when she was addressed, and sufficiently instructed in her "headaches" not to repudiate them when inquiries were made; Miss Lois announced, therefore, that the search could begin. She classified the probabilities under five heads.

First. The man must be left-handed.

Second. He must say "gold" for "cold."

Third. As Timloesville was a secluded village to which few strangers came, and as it had been expressly stated at the trial that no strangers were noticed in its vicinity either before or after the murder, the deed had evidently been committed, not as the prosecution mole-blindedly averred, by the one stranger who *was* there, but by no stranger at all—by a resident in the village itself or its neighborhood.

Fourth. As the arrival of Mr. and Mrs. Heathcote was unexpected, the crime must have been one of impulse: there had not been time for a plan.

Fifth. The motive was robbery: the murder was probably a second thought, occasioned, perhaps, by Helen's stirring.

Miss Lois did not waste time. Within a few days she was widely known in Timloesville—"the widow Young, from Washington, staying at Farmer Blackwell's, with her niece, who is out of health, poor thing, and her aunt so anxious about her." The widow was very affable, very talkative; she was considered an almost excitingly agreeable person. But it was strange that she should not have heard of their event, their own particular and now celebrated crime. Mrs. Strain, wife of J. Strain, Esq., felt that this ignorance was lamentable. She therefore proposed to the widow that she should in person go to the Timloe Hotel, and see with her own eyes "the very spot."

"The effect, Mrs. Young, is curdling," she declared.

Mrs. Young was willing to be curdled, if Mrs. Strain would support her in the experience. On the next afternoon, therefore, they went to the Timloe Hotel, and were shown over "the very floor" which had been pressed by the footsteps of the murderer, his beautiful wife, and her highly respectable and observing (one might almost say *providentially* observing) maid. The landlord himself, Mr. Graub, did not disdain to accompany them. Mr. Graub had attended the trial in person, and he had hardly ceased since to admire himself for his own perspicuous cleverness in owning the house where such a very distinguished crime had been committed. There might be localities where a like deed would have injured the patronage of an inn; but the neighborhood of Timloesville was not one of them. The people slowly took in and appreciated their event, as an anaconda is said slowly to take in and appreciate his dinner; they digested it at their leisure. Farmers coming in to town on Saturdays, instead of bringing luncheon in a tin pail, as usual, went to the expense of dining at the hotel, with their wives and daughters, in order to see the room, the blind, and the outside stairway. Mr. Graub, in this position of affairs, was willing to repeat the tale, even to a non-diner. For Mrs. Young was a stranger from Washington, and who knew but that Washington itself might be stirred to a dining interest in the scene of the tragedy, especially as the second trial was still to come?

The impression on the blind was displayed; it was very faint, but clearly that of a left hand.

"And here is the cloth that covered the bureau," continued the landlord, taking it from a paper and spreading it on the old-fashioned chest of drawers. "It is not the identical cloth, for that was required at the trial, together with a fac-simile of the blind; but I can assure you that this one is just like the original, blue-bordered and fringed precisely the same, and we traced the spots on it exactly similar before we let the other go. For we knew that folks would naturally be interested in such a memento."

"It is indeed deeply absorbing," said Mrs. Young. "I wonder, now, what the size of that hand might be? Not yours, Mr. Graub; yours is a very small hand. Let me compare. Suppose I place my fingers so (I will not touch it). Yes, a large hand, without doubt, and a left hand. Do you know of any left-handed persons about here?"

"Why, the man himself was left-handed," answered the landlord and Mrs. Strain together—"Captain Heathcote himself."

"He had been wounded, and carried his right arm in a sling," added Mr. Graub.

"Ah, yes," said the widow; "I remember now. Was this impression measured?"

"Yes; I have the exact figures," replied the landlord, taking out a note-book, and reading the items aloud in a slow, important voice.

"Did you measure it yourself?" asked the widow. "Because if *you* did it, I shall feel sure the figures are correct."

"I did not measure it myself," answered Mr. Graub, not unimpressed by this confidence. "I can, however, re-measure it in a moment if it would be any gratification to you."

"It would be—immense," said the widow. Whereupon he went down stairs for a measure.

"I am subject to dizziness myself, but I *must* hear some one come up that outside stairway," said Mrs. Young to Mrs. Strain during his absence. "*Would* you do it for me? I want to *imagine* the *whole*."

Mrs. J. Strain, though stout, consented; and when her highly decorated bonnet was out of sight, the visitor swiftly drew from her pocket the paper outline of Heathcote's hand which Anne had given her, and compared it with the impression. The outlines seemed different; the hand which had touched the cloth appeared to have been shorter and wider than Heathcote's, the finger-tips broader, as though cushioned with flesh underneath. Mrs. Strain's substantial step was now heard on the outside stairway. But the pattern was already safely returned to the deep pocket of Mrs. Young.

"I have been picturing the entire scene," she said, in an impressive whisper when the bonnet re-appeared, "and I assure you that when I heard your footsteps on those stairs, goose-flesh rose and ran like lightning down my spine." And Mrs. Strain, though out of breath, considered that her services had been well repaid.

Mr. Graub now returned, and measured the prints with the nicest accuracy. Owing to the widow's compliment to his hands, he had stopped to wash them, in order to give a finer effect to the operation. Mrs. Young requested that the figures be written down for her on a slip of paper, "as a memorial"; and then, with one more exhaustive look at the room, the stairway, and the garden, she went away, accompanied by her friend, leaving Mr. Graub more than ever convinced that he was a very unusual man.

Mrs. Strain was easily induced to finish the afternoon's dissipations by going through the grass meadow by the side of the track made by the murderer on his way to the river. They walked "by the side," because the track itself was railed off. So many persons had visited the meadow that Mr. Graub had been obliged to protect his relic in order to preserve its identity, and even existence. The little trail was now conspicuous by the fringing of tall grass which still stood erect on each side of it, the remainder of the meadow having been trodden flat.

"It ends at the river," said Mrs. Young, reflectively.

"Yes, where he came to wash his hands, after the deed was done," responded Mrs. Strain. "And what his visions and inward thoughts must have been at sech a moment I leave you, Mrs. Young, solemnly to consider."

Mrs. Young then returned homeward, after thanking her Timloesville friend for a "most impressive day."

"The outlines are too indistinct to be really of much use, Ruth," she said, as she removed her bonnet. "I believe it was so stated at the trial, wasn't it? But if I have eyes, they do *not* fit."

"Of course not, since it is the hand of another person," replied Anne. "But did you notice, or rather could you see, what the variations were?"

"A broader palm, I should say, and the fingers shorter. The only point, however, which I could make out with certainty was the thick cushion of flesh at the ends of the fingers; that seemed clear enough."

At sunset they went across the fields together to the point on the river-bank where the meadow trail ended.

"The river knows all," said Anne, looking wistfully at the smooth water.

"*They* think so too, for they've dragged it a number of times," responded Miss Lois. "All the boys in the neighborhood have been diving here ever since, I am told; they fancy the purse, watch, and rings are in the mud at the bottom. But they're safe enough in somebody's *pocket*, you may be sure."

"Miss Lois," said the girl, suddenly, "perhaps he went away in a boat!"

"My name is Deborah—Aunt Deborah; and I do wish, Ruth, you would not forget it so constantly. In a boat? Well, perhaps he did. But I don't see how that helps it. To-morrow is market-day, and I must go in to the village and look out for left-handed men; they won't escape me though they fairly dance jigs on their right!"

"He went away in a boat," repeated Anne, as they walked homeward through the dusky fields.

But the man was no nearer or plainer because she had taken him from the main road and placed him on the river; he seemed, indeed, more distant and shadowy than before.

CHAPTER XXXVIII.

"The burnished dragon-fly is thine attendant,

And tilts against the field,

And down the listed sunbeam rides

resplendent,

With steel-blue mail and shield."

—Longfellow.

Miss Lois came home excited. She had seen a left-handed man. True, he was a well-known farmer of the neighborhood, a jovial man, apparently frank and honest as the daylight. But there was no height of impossibility impossible to Miss Lois when she was on a quest. She announced her intention of going to his farm on the morrow under the pretext of looking at his peonies, which, she had been told, were remarkably fine, "for of course I made inquiries immediately, in order to discover the prominent points, if there were any. If it had been onions, I should have been deeply interested in them just the same."

Anne, obliged for the present to let Miss Lois make the tentative efforts, listened apathetically; then she mentioned her wish to row on the river.

"Better stay at home," said Miss Lois. "Then I shall know you are safe."

"But I should like to go, if merely for the air," replied Anne. "My head throbs as I sit here through the long hours. It is not that I expect to accomplish anything, though I confess I *am* haunted by the river, but the motion and fresh air would perhaps keep me from thinking so constantly."

"I am a savage," said Miss Lois, "and you shall go where you please. The truth is, Ruth, that while I am pursuing this matter with my mental faculties, *you* are pursuing it with the inmost fibres of your heart." (The sentence was mixed, but the feeling sincere.) "I will go down this very moment, and begin an arrangement about a boat for you."

She kept her word. Anne, sitting by the window, heard her narrating to Mrs. Blackwell a long chain of reasons to explain the fancy of her niece Ruth for rowing. "She inherits it from her mother, poor child," said the widow, with the sigh which she always gave to the memory of her departed relatives. "Her mother was the daughter of a light-house keeper, and lived, one might say, afloat. Little Ruthie, as a baby, used to play boat; her very baby-talk was full of sailor words. *You* haven't any kind of a row-boat she could use, have you?"

Mrs. Blackwell replied that they had not, but that a neighbor farther down the river owned a skiff which might be borrowed.

"Borrow it, then," said Mrs. Young. "They will lend it to *you*, of course, in a friendly way, and then *we* can pay *you* something for the use of it."

This thrifty arrangement, of which Mrs. Blackwell unaided would never have thought, was carried into effect, and early the next morning the skiff floated at the foot of the meadow, tied to an overhanging branch.

In the afternoon Mrs. Young, in the farm wagon, accompanied by her hostess, and her hostess's little son as driver, set off for John Cole's farm, to see, in Mrs. Blackwell's language, "the pynies." A little later Anne was in the skiff, rowing up the river. She had not had oars in her hands since she left the island.

She rowed on for an hour, through the green fields, then through the woods. Long-legged flies skated on the still surface of the water, insects with gauzy wings floated to and fro. A dragon-fly with steel-blue mail lighted on the edge of the boat. The burnished little creature seemed attracted. He would not leave her, but even when he took flight floated near by on his filmy wings, timing his advance with hers. With one of those vague impulses by which women often select the merest chance to decide their actions, Anne said to herself, "I will row on until I lose sight of him." Turning the skiff, she took one oar for a paddle, and followed the dragon-fly. He flew on now more steadily, selecting the middle of the stream. No doubt he had a dragon-fly's motives; perhaps he was going home; but whether he was or not, he led Anne's boat onward until the river grew suddenly narrower, and entered a ravine. Here, where the long boughs touched leaf-tips over her head, and everything was still and green, she lost him. The sun was sinking toward the western horizon line; it was time to return; but she said to herself that she would come again on the morrow, and explore this cool glen to which her gauzy-winged guide had brought her. When she reached home she found Miss Lois there, and in a state of profound discomfiture. "The man was left-handed enough," she said, "but, come to look at him, he hadn't any little finger at all: chopped off by mistake when a boy. Now the little finger in the impression is the most distinct part of the whole; and so we've lost a day, and the price of the wagon thrown in, not to speak of enough talking about peonies to last a lifetime! There's a fair to-morrow, and of course I must go: more left hands: although now, I confess, they swim round me in a cloud of vexation and peonies, which makes me never want to lay eyes on one of them again;" and she gave a groan, ending in a long yawn. However, the next morning, with patience and energies renewed by sleep, she rose early, like a phœnix from her ashes, and accompanied Mrs. Blackwell to the fair. Anne, again in her skiff, went up the river. She rowed to the glen where she had lost the dragon-fly. Here she rested on her oars a moment. The river still haunted her. "He went away in a boat," had not been out of her mind since it first came to her. "He went away in a boat," she now thought again. "Would he, then, have rowed up or down the stream? If he had wished to escape from the neighborhood, he would have rowed down to the larger river below. He would not have rowed up stream unless he lived somewhere in this region, and was simply going home, because there is no main road in this direction, no railway, nothing but farms which touch each other for miles round. Now, as I believe he was *not* a stranger, but a resident, I will suppose that he went up stream, and I will follow him." She took up her oars and rowed on.

The stream grew still narrower. She had been rowing a long time, and knew that she must be far from home. Nothing broke the green solitude of the shore until at last she came suddenly upon a little board house, hardly more than a shanty, standing near the water, with the forest behind. She started as she saw it, and a chill ran over her. And yet what was it? Only a little board house.

She rowed past; it seemed empty and silent. She turned the skiff, came back, and gathering her courage, landed, and timidly tried the door; it was locked. She went round and looked through the window. There was no one within, but there were signs of habitation—some common furniture, a gun, and on the wall a gaudy picture of the Virgin and the Holy Child. She scrutinized the place with eyes that noted even the mark of muddy boots on the floor and the gray ashes from a pipe on the table. Then suddenly she felt herself seized with fear. If the owner of the cabin should steal up behind her, and ask her what she was doing there! She looked over her shoulder fearfully. But no one was visible, no one was coming up or down the river; her own boat was the only thing that moved, swaying to and fro where she had left it tied to a tree trunk. With the vague terror still haunting her, she hastened to the skiff, pushed off, and paddled swiftly away. But during the long voyage homeward the fear did not entirely die away. "I am growing foolishly nervous," she said to herself, with a weary sigh.

Miss Lois had discovered no left-handed men at the fair; but she had seen a person whom she considered suspicious—a person who sold medicines. "He was middle-sized," she said to Anne, in the low tone they used when within the house, "and he had a down look—a thing I never could abide. He spoke, too, in an odd voice. I suspected him as soon as I laid my eyes upon him, and so just took up a station near him, and watched. He wasn't left-handed *exactly*," she added, as though he might have been so endowed inexactly; "but he is capable of anything—left-handed, web-footed, or whatever you please. After taking a good long look at him, I went round and made (of course by chance, and accidentally) some inquiries. Nobody seemed to know much about him except that his name is Juder (and highly appropriate in my opinion), and he came to the fair the day before with his little hand-cart of medicines, and *went out again*, into the country somewhere, at sunset. Do you mark the significance of that, Ruth Young? He did not stay at the Timloe hotel (prices reduced for the fair, and very reasonable beds on the floor), like the other traders; but though the fair is to be continued over to-morrow, and he is to be there, he took all the trouble to go out of town for the night."

"Perhaps he had no money," said Anne, abstractedly.

"I saw him with my own eyes take in dollars and dollars. Singular that when country people will buy nothing else, they will buy patent medicines. No: the man knows something of that murder, and *could* not stay at that hotel, Ruth Young. And that's *my* theory."

In her turn Anne now related the history of the day, and the discovery of the solitary cabin. Miss Lois was not much impressed by the cabin. "A man is better than a house, any day," she said. "But the thing is to get the man to say 'cold.' I shall ask him to-morrow if he has any pills for a cold in the head or on the lungs; and, as he tells long stories about the remarkable cures his different bottles have effected, I hope, when I once get him started, to hear the word several times. I confess, Ruth, that I have great hopes; I feel the spirit rising within me to run him down."

Miss Lois went again to the fair, her mission bubbling within her. At eight in the morning she started; at nine in the evening she returned. With skirt and shawl bedraggled, and bonnet awry, she came to Anne's room, closed the door, and demanded tragically that the broom-switch should be taken from the shelf and applied to her own thin shoulders. "I deserve it," she said.

"For what?" said Anne, smiling.

Miss Lois returned no answer until she had removed her bonnet and brought forward a chair, seated herself upon it, severely erect, with folded arms, and placed her feet on the round of another. "I went to that fair," she began, in a concentrated tone, "and I followed that medicine man; wherever he stopped his hand-cart and tried to sell, *I* was among his audience. I heard all his stories over and over again; every time he produced his three certificates, *I* read them. I watched his hands, too, and made up my mind that they would do, though I did not catch him in *open* left-handedness. I now tried 'cold.' 'Have you any pills for a cold in the head?' I asked. But all he said was 'yes,' and he brought out a bottle. Then I tried him with a cold on the lungs; but it was just the same. 'What are your testimonials for colds?' I remarked, as though I had not quite made up my mind; and he thereupon told two stories, but they were incoherent, and never once mentioned the word I was waiting to hear. 'Haven't you ever had a cold yourself?' I said, getting mad. 'Can't you speak?' And then, looking frightened, he

208

said he often had colds, and that he took those medicines, and that they always cured him. And then hurriedly, and without waiting for the two bottles which I held in my hand tightly, he began to move on with his cart. But he had said 'gold,' Ruth—he had actually said 'gold!' And, with the stings of a guilty, murderous conscience torturing him, he was going away without the thirty-seven and a half cents each which those two bottles cost! It was enough for me. I tracked him from that moment—at a distance, of course, and in roundabout ways, so that he would not suspect. I think during the day I must have walked, owing to doublings and never stopping, twenty miles. When at last the fair was over, and he started away, I started too. He went by the main road, and I by a lane, and *such* work as I had to keep him in sight, and yet not let him see me! I almost lost him several times, but persevered until he too turned off and went up a hill opposite toward a grove, dragging his little cart behind him. I followed as quickly as I could. He was in the grove as I drew near, stepping as softly as possible, and others were with him; I heard the murmur of voices. 'I have come upon the whole villainous band,' I thought, and I crept softly in among the trees, hardly daring to breathe. Ruth, the voices had a little camp; they had just lighted a fire; and—what do you think they were? Just a parcel of children, the eldest a slip of a girl of ten or eleven! I never was more dumbfounded in my life. Ruth, that medicine man sat down, kissed the children all round, opened his cart, took out bread, cheese, and a little package of tea, while the eldest girl put on a kettle, and they all began to talk. And then the youngest, a little tot, climbed up on his knee, and called him—Mammy! This was too much; and I appeared on the scene. Ruth, he gathered up the children in a frightened sort of way, as if I were going to eat them. 'What do you mean by following me round all day like this?' he began, trying to be brave, though I could see how scared he was. It *was* rather unexpected, you know, my appearing there at that hour so far from town. 'I mean,' said I, 'to know who and what you are. Are you a woman, or are you a man?'

"'Can't you see,' said the poor creature; 'with all these children around? But it's not likely from your looks that *you* ever had any of your own, so you don't know.' She said that," thoughtfully remarked Miss Lois, interrupting her own narrative, "and it has been said before. But how in the world any one can know it at sight is and always will be a mystery to me. Then said I to her, 'Are you the mother, then, of all these children? And if so, how came you to be selling medicines dressed up like a man? It's perfectly disgraceful, and you ought to be arrested.'

"'No one would buy of me if I was a woman,' she answered. 'The cart and medicines belonged to my husband, and he died, poor fellow! four weeks ago, leaving me without a cent. What was I to do? I know all the medicines, and I know all he used to say when he sold them. He was about my size, and I could wear his clothes. I just thought I'd try it for a little while during fair-time for the sake of the children—only for a little while to get started. So I cut my hair and resked it. And it's done tolerably well until *you* come along and nearly scared my life out of me yesterday and to-day. I don't see what on earth you meant by it.'

"Ruth, I took tea with that family on the hill-side, and I gave them all the money I had with me. I have now come home. Any plan you have to propose, I'll follow without a word. I have decided that my mission in this life is *not* to lead. But she *did* say gold for cold," added Miss Lois, with the spirit of "scissors."

"I am afraid a good many persons say it," answered Anne.

The next day Miss Lois gave herself up passively to the boat. They were to take courage in each other's presence, and row to the solitary cabin on the shore. When they reached it, it was again deserted.

"There is no path leading to it or away from it in any direction," said Miss Lois, after peeping through the small window. "The fire is still burning. The owner, therefore, whoever it is, uses a boat, and can not have been long gone either, or the fire would be out."

"If he had gone down the river, we should have met him," suggested Anne, still haunted by the old fear, and watching the forest glades apprehensively.

"How do you know it is a *he*?" said Miss Lois, with grim humor. "Perhaps this, too, is a woman. However, as you say, if he had gone down the river, *probably* we should have met him—a 'probably' is all we have to stand on—and the chances are, therefore, that he has gone up. So we will go up."

They took their places in the skiff again, and the little craft moved forward. After another half-hour they saw, to their surprise, a broad expanse of shining water opening out before them: the river was the outlet of a little lake two miles long.

"This, then, is where they go fishing," said Miss Lois. "The Blackwells spoke of the pond, but I thought it was on the other side of the valley. Push out, Ruth. There are two boats on it, both dug-outs; we'll row by them."

The first boat contained a boy, who said, "Good-day, mums," and showed a string of fish. The second boat, which was farther up the lake, contained a man. He was also fishing, and his face was shaded by an old slouch hat. Anne, who was rowing, could not see him as they approached; but she saw Miss Lois's hands close suddenly upon each other in their lisle-thread gloves, and was prepared for something, she knew not what. No word was spoken; she rowed steadily on, though her heart was throbbing. When she too could look at the man, she saw what it was: he was holding his rod with his left hand.

Their skiff had not paused; it passed him and his dug-out, and moved onward a quarter of a mile—half a mile—before they spoke; they were afraid the very air would betray them. Then Anne beached the boat under the shade of a tree, took off her straw hat, and bathed her pale face in the clear water.

"After all, it is the vaguest kind of a chance," said Miss Lois, rallying, and bringing forward the common-sense view of the case: "no better a one, at this stage, than the peony farmer or my medicine man. You must not be excited, Ruth."

"I am excited only because I have thought so much of the river," said Anne. "The theory that the man who did it went away from the foot of that meadow in a boat, and up this river, has haunted me constantly."

"Theories are like scaffolding: they are not the house, but you can not build the house without them," said Miss Lois. "What we've got to do next is to see whether this man has all his fingers, whether he is a woman, and whether he says, 'gold.' Will you leave it to me, or will you speak to him yourself? On the whole, I think you had better speak to him: your face is in your favor."

When Anne felt herself sufficiently calm, they rowed down the lake again, and passed nearer to the dug-out, and paused.

"Have you taken many fish?" said Anne, in a voice totally unlike her own, owing to the effort she made to control it. The fisherman looked up, took his rod in his right hand, and, with his left, lifted a string of fish.

"Pretty good, eh?" he said, regarding Anne with slow-coming approval. "Have some?"

"Oh no," she answered, almost recoiling.

"But, on the whole, I think I *should* like a few for tea, Ruth," said Miss Lois, hastening to the rescue—"my health," she added, addressing the fisherman, "not being what it was in the lifetime of Mr. Young. How much are your fish? I should like six, if you do not ask too much."

The man named his price, and the widow objected. Then she asked him to hold up the string again, that she might have a better view. He laid his rod aside, held the string in his right hand, and as she selected, still bargaining for the fish she preferred, he detached them with his left hand. Two pairs of eyes, one old, sharp, and aided by spectacles, the other young, soft, intent, yet fearful, watched his every motion. When he held the fish toward them, the widow was long in finding her purse; the palm of his hand was toward them, they could see the underside of the fingers. They were broad, and cushioned with coarse flesh.

Anne had now grown so pale that the elder woman did not dare to linger longer. She paid the money, took the fish, and asked her niece to row on down the lake, not forgetting, even then, to add that she was afraid of the sun's heat, having once had a sun-stroke during the life of the lamented Mr. Young. Anne rowed on, hardly knowing what she was doing. Not until they had reached the little river again, and were out of sight round its curve under the overhanging trees, did they speak.

"Left-handed, and cushions under his finger-tips," said Miss Lois. "But, Ruth, how you acted! You almost betrayed us."

"I could not help it," said Anne, shuddering. "When I saw that hand, and thought— Oh, poor, poor Helen!"

"You must not give way to fancies," said Miss Louis. But she too felt an inward excitement, though she would not acknowledge it.

The fisherman was short in stature, and broad; he was muscular, and his arms seemed too long for his body as he sat in his boat. His head was set on his shoulders without visible throat, his small eyes were very near together, and twinkled when he spoke, while his massive jaw contradicted their ferrety mirthfulness as his muscular frame contradicted the childish, vacant expression of his peculiarly small boyish mouth, whose upper lip protruded over narrow yellow teeth like fangs.

"Faces have little to do with it," said Miss Lois again, half to herself, half to Anne. "It is well known that the portraits of murderers show not a few fine-looking men among them, while the women are almost invariably handsome. What *I* noticed was a certain want in the creature's face, a weakness of some kind, with all his evident craftiness."

When they came to the solitary cabin, Miss Lois proposed that they should wait and see whether it really was the fisherman's home. "It will be another small point settled," she said. "We can conceal our boat, and keep watch in the woods. As he has my money, he will probably come home soon, and very likely go directly down to the village to spend it: that is always the way with such shiftless creatures."

They landed, hid the boat in a little bay among the reeds some distance below the cabin, and then stole back through the woods until they came within sight of its door. There, standing concealed behind two tree trunks, they waited, neither speaking nor stirring. Miss Lois was right in her conjecture: within a quarter of an hour the fisherman came down the river from the lake, stopped at the house, brought out a jug, placed it in his dug-out;

then, relocking the door, he paddled by them down the river. They waited some minutes without stirring. Then Miss Lois stepped from her hiding-place.

"Whiskey!" she said. "And *my* money pays for the damnable stuff!" This reflection kept her silent while they returned to the skiff; but when they were again afloat, she sighed and yielded it as a sacrifice to the emergencies of the quest. Returning to the former subject, she held forth as follows: "It is something, Ruth, but not all. We must not hope too much. What is it? A man lives up the river, and owns a boat; he is left-handed, and has cushions of flesh under his finger-tips: that is the whole. For we can scarcely count as evidence the fact that he is as ugly as a stump fence, such men being not uncommon in the world, and often pious as well. We must do nothing hurriedly, and make no inquiries, lest we scare the game—if it *is* game. To-morrow is market-day; he will probably be in the village with fish to sell, and the best way will be for me to find out quietly who his associates are, by using my eyes and not my tongue. His associates, if he has any, might next be tackled, through their wives, perhaps. Maybe they do sewing, some of them; in that case, we could order something, and so get to speaking terms. There's my old challis, which I have had dyed black—it might be made over, though I *was* going to do it myself. And now do row home, Ruth; I'm dropping for my tea. This exploring work is powerfully wearing on the nerves."

The next day she went to the village.

Anne, finding herself uncontrollably restless, went down and unfastened the skiff, with the intention of rowing awhile to calm her excited fancies. She went up the river for a mile or two. Her mind had fastened itself tenaciously upon the image of the fisherman, and would not loosen its hold. She imagined him stealing up the stairway and leaning over Helen; then escaping with his booty, running through the meadow, and hiding it in his boat, probably the same old black dug-out she had seen. And then, while she was thinking of him, she came suddenly upon him, sitting in his dug-out, not ten feet distant, fishing. Miss Lois had been mistaken in her surmise: he was not in the village, but here.

There had not been a moment of preparation for Anne; yet in the emergency coolness came. Resting on her oars, she spoke: "Have you any fish to-day?"

He shook his head, and held up one. "That's all," he said, drawing his hand over his mouth by way of preparation for conversation.

"I should not think there would be as many fish here as in the lake," she continued, keeping her boat at a distance by a slight motion of her oars.

"When the wind blows hard, there's more in the river," he answered. "Wind blows to-day."

Was she mistaken? Had he given a sound of *d* to *th*?

"But the water of the lake must be colder," she said, hardly able to pronounce the word herself.

"Yes, in places where it's deep. But it's mostly shaller."

"How cold is it? Very cold?" (Was *she* saying "gold" too?)

"No, not very, this time o' year. But cold enough in April."

"What?"

"Cold enough in April," replied the fisherman, his small eyes gazing at her with increasing approbation.

He had given the sound of *g* to the *c*. The pulses in Anne's throat and temples were throbbing so rapidly now that she could not speak.

"I could bring yer some fish to-morrer, I reckon," said the man, making a clicking sound with his teeth as he felt a bite and then lost it.

She nodded, and began to turn the boat.

"Where do you live?" he called, as the space between them widened.

She succeeded in pronouncing the name of her hostess, and then rowed round the curve out of sight, trying not to betray her tremulous haste and fear. All the way home she rowed with the strength of a giantess, not knowing how she was exerting herself until she began to walk through the meadow toward the house, when she found her limbs failing her. She reached her room with an effort, and locking her door, threw herself down on a couch to wait for Miss Lois. It was understood in the house that "poor Miss Young" had one of her "mathematical headaches."

CHAPTER XXXIX.

"God made him; therefore let him pass for a
man."

—Shakspeare.

When Miss Lois returned, and saw Anne's face, she was herself stirred to excitement. "You have seen him!" she said, in a whisper.

"Yes. He is the murderer: I feel it."

"Did he say 'gold'?"

"He did."

They sat down on the couch together, and in whispers Anne told all. Then they looked at each other.

"We must work as lightly as thistle-down," said Miss Lois, "or we shall lose him. He was not in the village to-day, and as he was not, I thought it safer not to inquire about him. I am glad now that I did not. But you are in a high fever, dear child. This suspense must be brought to an end, or it will kill you." She put her arms round Anne and kissed her fondly—an unusual expression of feeling from Miss Lois, who had been brought up in the old-fashioned rigidly undemonstrative New England manner. And the girl put her head down upon her old friend's shoulder and clung to her. But she could not weep; the relief of tears was not yet come.

In the morning they saw the fisherman at the foot of the meadow, and watched him through the blinds, breathlessly. He was so much and so important to them that it seemed as if they must be the same to him. But he was only bringing a string of fish to sell. He drew up his dug-out on the bank, and came toward the house with a rolling step, carrying his fish.

"There's a man here with some fish, that was ordered, he says, by somebody from here," said a voice on the stairs. "Was it you, Mrs. Young?"

"Yes. Come in, Mrs. Blackwell—do. My niece ordered them: you know they're considered very good for an exhausted brain. Perhaps I'd better go down and look at them myself. And, by-the-way, who is this man?"

"It's Sandy Croom; he lives up near the pond."

"Yes, we met him up that way. Is he a German?"

"There's Dutch blood in him, I reckon, as there is in most of the people about here who are not Marylanders," said Mrs. Blackwell, who *was* a Marylander.

"He's a curious-looking creature," pursued Mrs. Young, as they descended the stairs. "Is he quite right in his mind?"

"Some think he isn't; but others say he's sharper than we suppose. He drinks, though."

By this time they were in the kitchen, and Mrs. Young went out to the porch to receive and pay for the fish, her niece Ruth silently following. Croom took off his old hat and made a backward scrape with his foot by way of salutation; his small head was covered with a mat of boyish-looking yellow curls, which contrasted strangely with his red face.

"Here's yer fish," he said, holding them out toward Anne.

But she could not take them: she was gazing, fascinated, at his hand—that broad short left hand which haunted her like a horrible phantom day and night. She raised her handkerchief to her lips in order to conceal, as far as possible, the horror she feared her face must betray.

"You never *could* abide a fishy smell, Ruth," said Mrs. Young, interposing. She paid the fisherman, and asked whether he fished in the winter. He said "no," but gave no reason. He did not, as she had hoped, pronounce the desired word. Then, after another gaze at Anne, he went away, but turned twice to look back before he reached the end of the garden.

"It can not be that he suspects!" murmured Anne.

"No; it's your face, child. Happy or unhappy, you can not help having just the same eyes, hair, and skin, thank the Lord!"

They went upstairs and watched him from the window; he pushed off his dug-out, got in, and paddled toward the village.

"More whiskey!" said Miss Lois, sitting down and rubbing her forehead. "I wish, Ruth Young—I devoutly wish that I knew what it is best to do *now*!"

"Then you think with me?" said Anne, eagerly.

212

"By no means. There isn't a particle of *certainty*. But—I don't deny that there *is* a chance. The trouble is that we can hardly stir in the matter without arousing his suspicion. If he had lived in the village among other people, it would not have been difficult; but, all alone in that far-off cabin—"

Anne clasped her hands suddenly. "Let us send for Père Michaux!" she said. "There was a picture of the Madonna in his cabin—he is a Roman Catholic. Let us send for Père Michaux."

They gazed at each other in excited silence. Miss Lois was the first to speak. "I'm not at all sure but that you have got hold of the difficulty by the right handle at last, Anne," she said, slowly, drawing a long audible breath. It was the first time she had used the name since their departure from New York.

And the letter was written immediately.

"It's a long journey for a small chance," said the elder woman, surveying it as it lay sealed on the table. "Still, I think he will come."

"Yes, for humanity's sake," replied Anne.

"I don't know about humanity," replied her companion, huskily; "but he will come for *yours*. Let us get out in the open air; I'm perfectly tired out by this everlasting whispering. It would be easier to roar."

The letter was sent. Four days for it to go, four days for the answer to return, one day for chance. They agreed not to become impatient before the tenth day.

But on the ninth came, not a letter, but something better—Père Michaux in person.

They were in the fields at sunset, at some distance from the house, when Anne's eyes rested upon him, walking along the country road in his old robust fashion, on his way to the farm-house. She ran across the field to the fence, calling his name. Miss Lois followed, but more slowly; her mind was in a turmoil regarding his unexpected arrival, and the difficulty of making him comprehend or conform to the net-work of fable she had woven round their history.

The old priest gave Anne his blessing; he was much moved at seeing her again. She held his hand in both of her own, and could scarcely realize that it was he, her dear old island friend, standing there in person beside her.

"Dear, dear Père Michaux, how good you are to come!" she said, incoherently, the tears filling her eyes, half in sorrow, half in joy.

Miss Lois now came up and greeted him. "I am glad to see you," she said. Then, in the same breath: "Our names, Father Michaux, are Young; Young—please remember."

"How good you are to come!" said Anne again, the weight on her heart lightened for the moment as she looked into the clear, kind, wise old eyes that met her own.

"Not so very good," said Père Michaux, smiling. "I have been wishing to see you for some time, and I think I should have taken the journey before long in any case. Vacations are due me; it is years since I have had one, and I am an old man now."

"You will never be old," said the girl, affectionately.

"Young is the name," repeated Miss Lois, with unconscious appositeness—"Deborah and Ruth Young."

"I am glad at least that I am not too old to help you, my child," answered Père Michaux, paying little heed to the elder woman's anxious voice.

They were still standing by the road-side. Père Michaux proposed that they should remain in the open air while the beautiful hues of the sunset lasted, and they therefore returned to the field, and sat down under an elm-tree. Under ordinary circumstances, Miss Lois would have strenuously objected to this sylvan indulgence, having peculiarly combative feelings regarding dew; but this evening the maze of doubt in which she was wandering as to whether or not Père Michaux would stay in her web made dew a secondary consideration. Remaining in the fields would at least give time.

Père Michaux was as clear-headed and energetic as ever. After the first few expressions of gladness and satisfaction, it was not long before he turned to Anne, and spoke of the subject which lay before them. "Tell me all," he said. "This is as good a time and place as any we could have, and there should be, I think, no delay."

But though he spoke to Anne, it was Miss Lois who answered: it would have been simply impossible for her not to take that narrative into her own hands.

He listened to the tale with careful attention, not interrupting her many details with so much as a smile or a shrug. This was very unlike his old way with Miss Lois, and showed more than anything else could have done his absorbed interest in the story.

"It is the old truth," he said, after the long stream of words had finally ceased. "Regarding the unravelling of mysteries, women seem sometimes endowed with a sixth sense. A diamond is lost on a turnpike. A man goes along the turnpike searching for it. A woman, searching for it also, turns vaguely off into a field, giving no logical reason for her course, and—finds it."

But while he talked, his mind was in reality dwelling upon the pale girl beside him, the young girl in whom he had felt such strong interest, for whom he had involuntarily cherished such high hope in those early days on the island.

He knew of her testimony at the trial; he had not been surprised. What he had prophesied for her had come indeed. But not so fortunately or so happily as he had hoped. He had saved her from Erastus Pronando for this! Was it well done? He roused himself at last, perceiving that Anne was noticing his abstraction; her eyes were fixed upon him with anxious expectation.

"I must go to work in my own way," he said, stroking her hair. "One point, however, I have already decided: *you* must leave this neighborhood immediately. I wish you had never come."

"But she can not be separated from me," said Miss Lois; "and of course *I* shall be necessary in the search—*I* must be here."

"I do not see that there is any necessity at present," replied Père Michaux. "You have done all you could, and I shall work better, I think, alone." Then, as the old quick anger flashed from her eyes, he turned to Anne. "It is on your account, child," he said. "I must *make* you go. I know it is like taking your life from you to send you away now. But if anything comes of this—if your woman's blind leap into the dark proves to have been guided by intuition, the lime-light of publicity will instantly be turned upon this neighborhood, and you could not escape discovery. Your precautions, or rather those of our good friend Miss Lois, have availed so far: you can still depart in their shadow unobserved. Do so, then, while you can. My first wish is—can not help being—that you should escape. I would rather even have the clew fail than have your name further connected with the matter."

"This is what we get by applying to a *man*," said Miss Lois, in high indignation. "Always thinking of evil!"

"Yes, men do think of it. But Anne will yield to my judgment, will she not?"

"I will do as you think best," she answered. But no color rose in her pale face, as he had expected; the pressing danger and the fear clothed the subject with a shroud.

Miss Lois did not hide her anger and disappointment. Yet she would not leave Anne. And therefore the next morning Mrs. Young and her niece, with health much improved by their sojourn in the country, bade good-by to their hostess, and went southward in the little stage on their way back to "Washington."

Père Michaux was not seen at the farm-house at all; he had returned to the village from the fields, and had taken rooms for a short sojourn at the Timloe hotel.

The "Washington," in this instance, was a small town seventy miles distant; here Mrs. Young and her niece took lodgings, and began, with what patience they could muster, their hard task of waiting.

As for Père Michaux, he went fishing.

EXTRACT FROM THE LETTER OF A SUMMER FISHERMAN.

"I have labored hard, Anne—harder than ever before in my life. I thought I knew what patience was, in my experience with my Indians and half-breeds. I never dreamed of its breadth until now! For my task has been the hard one of winning the trust of a trustless mind—trustless, yet crafty; of subduing its ever-rising reasonless suspicion; of rousing its nearly extinct affections; of touching its undeveloped, almost dead, conscience, and raising it to the point of confession. I said to myself that I would do all this in sincerity; that I would make myself do it in sincerity; that I would teach the poor creature to love me, and having once gained his warped affection, I would assume the task of caring for him as long as life lasted. If I did this in truth and real earnestness I might succeed, as the missionaries of my Church succeed, with the most brutal savages, *because* they are in earnest. Undertaking this, of course I also accepted the chance that all my labor, regarding the hope that *you* have cherished, might be in vain, and that this poor bundle of clay might not be, after all, the criminal we seek. Yet had it been so, my care of him through life must have been the same; having gained his confidence, I could never have deserted him while I lived. Each day I have labored steadily; but often I have advanced so slowly that I seemed to myself not to advance at all.

"I began by going to the pond to fish. We met daily. At first I did not speak; I allowed him to become accustomed to my presence. It was a long time before I even returned his glance of confused respect and acquaintance as our boats passed near each other, for he had at once recognized the priest. I built my foundations with exactest care and patience, often absenting myself in order to remove all suspicion of watchfulness or regularity from his continually suspicious mind; for suspicion, enormously developed, is one of his few mental powers. I had to make my way through its layers as a minute blood-vessel penetrates the cumbrous leathern hide of the rhinoceros.

"I will not tell you all the details now; but at last, one morning, by a little chance event, my long, weary, and apparently unsuccessful labor was crowned with success. He became attached to me. I suppose in all his poor warped life before no one had ever shown confidence in him or tried to win his affection.

"The next step was not so difficult. I soon learned that he had a secret. In his ignorant way, he is a firm believer in the terrors of eternal punishment, and having become attached to me, I could see that he was debating in his own mind whether or not to confide it to me as a priest, and obtain absolution. I did not urge him; I did not even invite his confidence. But I continued faithful to him, and I knew that in time it would come. It did. You are right, Anne; he is the murderer.

"It seems that by night he is tormented by superstitious fear. He is not able to sleep unless he stupefies himself with liquor, because he expects to see his victim appear and look at him with her hollow eyes. To rid himself of this haunting terror, he told all to me under the seal of the confessional. And then began the hardest task of all.

"For as a priest I could not betray him (and I should never have done so, Anne, even for your sake), and yet another life was at stake. I told him with all the power, all the eloquence, I possessed, that his repentance would never be accepted, that he himself would never be forgiven, unless he rescued by a public avowal the innocent man who was suffering in his place. And I gave him an assurance also, which must be kept even if I have to go in person to the Governor, that, in case of public avowal, his life should be spared. His intellect is plainly defective. If Miss Teller, Mr. Heathcote, and the lawyers unite in an appeal for him, I think it will be granted.

"It has been, Anne, very hard, fearfully hard, to bring him to the desired point; more than once I have lost heart. Yet never have I used the lever of real menace, and I wish you to know that I have not. At last, thanks be to the eternal God, patience has conquered. Urged by the superstition which consumes him, he consented to repeat to the local officials, in my presence and under my protection, the confession he had made to me, and to give up the watch and rings, which have lain all this time buried in the earth behind his cabin, he fearing to uncover them until a second crop of grass should be green upon his victim's grave, lest she should appear and take them from him! He did this in order to be delivered in this world and the next, and he will be delivered; for his crime was a brute one, like that of the wolf who slays the lamb.

"I shall see you before long, my dear child; but you will find me worn and old. This has been the hardest toil of my whole life."

Père Michaux did not add that his fatigue of body and mind was heightened by a painful injury received at the hands of the poor wretch he was trying to help. Unexpectedly one morning Croom had attacked him with a billet of wood, striking from behind, and without cause, save that he coveted the priest's fishing-tackle, and, in addition, something in the attitude of the defenseless white-haired old man at that moment tempted him, as a lasso-thrower is tempted by a convenient chance position of cattle. The blow, owing to a fortunate movement of Père Michaux at the same instant, was not mortal, but it disabled the old man's shoulder and arm. And perceiving this, Croom had fled. But what had won his brute heart was the peaceful appearance of the priest at his cabin door early the next morning, where the fisherman had made all ready for flight, and his friendly salutation. "Of course I knew it was all an accident, Croom," he said; "that you did not mean it. And I have come out to ask if you have not something you can recommend to apply to the bruise. You people who live in the woods have better balms than those made in towns; and besides, I would rather ask *your* help than apply to a physician, who might ask questions." He entered the cabin as he spoke, took off his hat, sat down, and offered his bruised arm voluntarily to the hands that had struck the blow. Croom, frightened, brought out a liniment, awkwardly assisted the priest in removing his coat, and then, as the old man sat quietly expectant, began to apply it. As he went on he regained his courage: evidently he was not to be punished. The bruised flesh appealed to him, and before he knew it he was bandaging the arm almost with affection. The priest's trust had won what stood in the place of a heart: it was so new to him to be trusted. This episode of the injured arm, more than anything else, won in the end the confession.

EXTRACT FROM THE NEW YORK "ZEUS."

"Even the story of the last great battle was eclipsed in interest in certain circles of this city yesterday by the tidings which were flashed over the wires from a remote little village in Pennsylvania. Our readers will easily recall the trial of Captain Ward Heathcote on the charge of murder, the murder of his own wife. The evidence against the accused was close, though purely circumstantial. The remarkable incidents of the latter part of the trial have not been forgotten. The jury were unable to agree, and the case went over to the November term.

"The accused, though not convicted, has not had the sympathy of the public. Probably eight out of ten among those who read the evidence have believed him guilty. But yesterday brought the startling intelligence that human judgment has again been proven widely at fault, that the real murderer is in custody, and that he has not only confessed his guilt, but also restored the rings and watch, together with the missing towel. The chain of links is complete.

"The criminal is described as a creature of uncouth appearance, in mental capacity deficient, though extraordinarily cunning. He spent the small amount of money in the purse, but was afraid to touch the rings and watch until a second crop of grass should be growing upon his victim's grave, lest she should appear and take them from him! It is to ignorant superstitious terror of this kind that we owe the final capture of this grotesque murderer.

"His story fills out the missing parts of the evidence, and explains the apparent participation of the accused to have been but an intermingling of personalities. After Captain Heathcote had gone down the outside stairway with the two towels in his pocket, this man, Croom, who was passing the end of the garden at the time, and had seen him come out by the light from the lamp within, stole up the same stairway in order to peer into the apartment, partly from curiosity, partly from the thought that there might be something there to steal. He supposed there was no one in the room, but when he reached the window and peeped through a crack in the old blind, he saw that there was some one—a woman asleep. In his caution he had consumed fifteen or twenty minutes in crossing the garden noiselessly and ascending the stairway, and during this interval Mrs. Heathcote had fallen asleep. The light from the lamp happened to shine full on the diamonds in her rings as they lay, together with her purse and watch, on the bureau, and he coveted the unexpected booty as soon as his eyes fell upon it. Quick as thought he drew open the blind, and crept in on his hands and knees, going straight toward the bureau; but ere he could reach it the sleeper stirred. He had not intended murder, but his brute nature knew no other way, and in a second the deed was done. Then he seized the watch, purse, and rings, went out as he had come, through the window, closing the blind behind him, and stole down the stairway in the darkness. The man is left-handed. It will be remembered that this proved left-handedness of the murderer was regarded as a telling point against Captain Heathcote, his right arm being at the time disabled, and supported by a sling.

"Croom went through the grass meadow to the river-bank, where his boat was tied, and hastily hiding his spoil under the seat, was about to push off, when he was startled by a slight sound, which made him think that another boat was approaching. Stealing out again, he moved cautiously toward the noise, but it was only a man bathing at some distance down the stream, the stillness of the night having made his movements in the water audible. Wishing to find out if the bather were any one he knew, Croom, under cover of the darkness, spoke to him from the bank, asking some chance question. The voice that replied was that of a stranger; still, to make all sure, Croom secreted himself at a short distance, after pretending to depart by the main road, and waited. Presently the bather passed by, going homeward; Croom, very near him, kneeling beside a bush, was convinced by the step and figure that it was no one he knew, that it was not one of the villagers or neighboring farmers. After waiting until all was still, he went to the place where the man had bathed, and searched with his hands on the sand and grass to see if he had not dropped a cigar or stray coin or two: this petty covetousness, when he had the watch and diamonds, betrays the limited nature of his intelligence. He found nothing save the two towels which Captain Heathcote had left behind; he took these and went back to his boat. There, on the shore, the sound of a dog's sudden bark alarmed him; he dropped one of the towels, could not find it among the reeds, and, without waiting longer, pushed off his boat and paddled up the stream toward home. This singular creature, who was bold enough to commit murder, yet afraid to touch his booty for fear of rousing a ghost, has been living on as usual all this time, within a mile or two of the village where his crime was committed, pursuing his daily occupation of fishing, and mixing with the villagers as formerly, without betraying his secret or attracting toward himself the least suspicion. His narrow but remarkable craft is shown in the long account he gives of the intricate and roundabout ways he selected for spending the money he had stolen. The purse itself, together with the watch, rings, and towel, he buried under a tree behind his cabin, where they have lain undisturbed until he himself unearthed them, and delivered them to the priest.

"For this notable confession was obtained by the influence of one of a body of men vowed to good works, a priest of the Roman Catholic Church. Croom was of the same faith, after his debased fashion, and in spite of his weak mind (perhaps on account of it) a superstitious, almost craven, believer.

"The presence of this rarely intelligent and charitable priest in Timloesville at this particular time may be set down as one of these fortunate chances with which a some what unfortunate world is occasionally blessed. Resting after arduous labor elsewhere and engaged in the rural amusement of fishing, this kind-hearted old man noticed the degraded appearance and life of this poor waif of humanity, and in a generous spirit of charity set himself to work to enlighten and instruct him, as much as was possible during the short period of his stay. In this he was successful far beyond his expectation, far beyond his conception, like a laborer ploughing a field who comes upon a vein of gold. He has not only won this poor wretch to repentance, but has also cleared from all suspicion of the darkest crime on the record of crimes the clouded fame of a totally innocent man.

"Never was there a weightier example of the insufficiency of what is called sufficient evidence, and while we, the public, should be deeply glad that an innocent man has been proven innocent, we should also be covered with confusion for the want of perspicacity displayed in the general prejudgment of this case, where minds seem, sheep-like, to have followed each other, without the asking of a question. The people of a rural neighborhood are so convinced of the guilt of the person whom they in their infallibility have arrested that they pay no heed to other possibilities of the case. *Cui bono!* And their wise-acre belief spreads abroad in its brightest hues to the press—to the world. It is the real foundation upon which all the evidence rested.

"A child throws a stone. Its widening ripples stretch across a lake, and break upon far shores. A remote and bucolic community cherishes a surmise, and a continent accepts it. The nineteenth century is hardly to be congratulated upon such indolent inanity, such lambent laxity, as this."

CHAPTER XL.

"Who ordered toil as the condition of life, ordered failure, success; to this person a foremost place, to the other a struggle with the crowd; to each some work upon the ground he stands on until he is laid beneath it.... Lucky he who can bear his failure generously, and give up his broken sword to Fate, the conqueror, with a manly and humble heart."—William Makepeace Thackeray

When set at liberty, Ward Heathcote returned to New York.

The newspapers everywhere had published similar versions of Père Michaux's agency in the discovery of the murderer, and Anne's connection with it was never known. To this day neither Mrs. Blackwell, Mrs. Strain, nor Mr. Graub himself, has any suspicion that their summer visitors were other than the widow Young and her niece Ruth from the metropolis of Washington.

Heathcote returned to New York. And society received him with widely open arms. The women had never believed in his guilt; they now apotheosized him. The men had believed in it; they now pressed forward to atone for their error. But it was a grave and saddened man who received this ovation—an ovation quiet, hardly expressed in words, but marked, nevertheless. A few men did say openly, "Forgive me, Heathcote; you can not be half so severe on me as I am on myself." But generally a silent grip of the hand was the only outward expression.

The most noticeable sign was the deference paid him. It seemed as if a man who had unjustly suffered so much, and been so cruelly suspected, should now be crowned in the sight of all. They could not actually crown him, but they did what they could.

Through this deference and regret, through these manifestations of feeling from persons not easily stirred to feeling or deference, Heathcote passed unmoved and utterly silent, like a man of marble. After a while it was learned that he had transferred Helen's fortune to other hands. At first he had tried to induce Miss Teller to take it, but she had refused. He had then deeded it all to a hospital for children, in which his wife had occasionally evinced some interest. Society divided itself over this action; some admired it, others pronounced it Quixotic. But the man who did it seemed to care nothing for either their praise or their blame.

Rachel asked Isabel if she knew where Anne was.

"The very question I asked dear Miss Teller yesterday," replied Isabel. "She told me that Anne had returned to that island up in the Northwest somewhere, where she used to live. Then I asked, 'Is she going to remain there?' and Miss Teller answered, 'Yes,' but in such a tone that I did not like to question further."

"It has ended, then, as I knew it would," said Rachel. "In spite of all that display on the witness stand, you see he has *not* married her."

"He could not marry her very well at present, I suppose," began Isabel, who had a trace of feeling in her heart for the young girl.

But Rachel interrupted her. "I tell you he will never marry her," she said, her dark eyes flashing out upon the thin blonde face of her companion. For old Mrs. Bannert was dead at last, and her daughter-in-law had inherited the estate. Two weeks later she sailed rather unexpectedly for Europe. But if unexpectedly, not causelessly. She was not a woman to hesitate; before she went she had staked her all, played her game, and—lost it.

Heathcote had never been, and was not now, a saint; but he saw life with different eyes. During the old careless days it had never occurred to him to doubt himself, or his own good (that is, tolerably good—good enough) qualities. Suddenly he had found himself a prisoner behind bars, and half the world, even his own world, believed him guilty. This had greatly changed him. As the long days and nights spent in prison had left traces on his face which would never pass away, so this judgment passed upon him had left traces on his heart which would not be outlived. As regarded both himself and others he was sterner.

Anne had returned with Miss Lois to the island. From New York he wrote to her, "If I can not see you, I shall go back to the army. My old life here is unendurable now."

217

No letters had passed between them: this was the first. They had not seen each other since that interview in the Multomah prison.

She answered simply, Go.

He went.

More than two years passed. Miss Teller journeyed westward to the island, and staid a long time at the church-house, during the first summer, making with reverential respect an acquaintance with Miss Lois. During the second summer Tita came home to make a visit, astonishing her old companions, and even her own sister, by the peculiar beauty of her little face and figure, and her air of indulgent superiority over everything the poor island contained. But she was happy. She smiled sometimes with such real naturalness, her small white teeth gleaming through her delicate little lips, that Anne went across and kissed her out of pure gladness, gladness that she was so content. Rast had prospered—at least he was prospering now (he failed and prospered alternately)—and his little wife pleased herself with silks that trailed behind her over the uncarpeted halls of the church-house, giving majesty (so she thought) to her small figure. If they did not give majesty, they gave an unexpected and bizarre contrast. Strangers who saw Tita that summer went home and talked about her, and never forgot her.

The two boys were tall and strong—almost men; they had no desire to come eastward. Anne must not send them any more money; they did not need it; on the contrary, in a year or two, when they had made their fortunes (merely a question of time), they intended to build for her a grand house on the island, and bestow upon her an income sufficient for all her wants. They requested her to obtain plans for this mansion, according to her taste.

Père Michaux was at work, as usual, in his water parish. He had succeeded in obtaining a commutation of the death sentence, in Croom's case, to imprisonment for a term of years, the criminal's mental weakness being the plea. But he considered the prisoner his especial charge, and never lost sight of him. Such solace and instruction as Croom was capable of receiving were constantly given, if not by the priest himself, then by his influence; and this protection was continued long after the wise, kind old man had passed away.

Jeanne-Armande returned from Europe, and entered into happy possession of the half-house, as it stood, refurnished by the lavish hand of Gregory Dexter.

And Dexter? During the last year of the war he went down to the front, on business connected with a proposed exchange of prisoners. Here, unexpectedly, one day he came upon Ward Heathcote, now in command of a regiment.

Colonel Heathcote was not especially known beyond his own division; in it, he was considered a good officer, cool, determined, and if distinguished at all, distinguished for rigidly obeying his orders, whatever they might be. It was related of him that once having been ordered to take his men up Little Reedy Run, when Big Reedy was plainly meant—Little Reedy, as everybody knew, being within the lines of the enemy, he calmly went up Little Reedy with his regiment. The enemy, startled by the sudden appearance of seven hundred men among their seven thousand, supposed of course that seventy thousand must be behind, and retreated in haste, a mile or two, before they discovered their error. The seven hundred, meanwhile, being wildly recalled by a dozen messengers, came back, with much camp equipage and other booty, together with a few shot in their bodies, sent by the returning and indignant Confederates, one of the balls being in the shoulder of the calm colonel himself.

When Dexter came upon Heathcote, a flush rose in his face. He did not hesitate, however, but walked directly up to the soldier. "Will you step aside with me a moment?" he said. "I want to speak to you."

Heathcote, too, had recognized his former companion at a glance. The two men walked together beyond earshot; then they paused.

But Dexter's fluency had deserted him. "You know?" he said.

"Yes."

"It does not make it any better, I fear, to say that my belief was an honest one."

"You were not alone; there were others who thought as you did. I care little about it now."

"Still, I—I wish to beg your pardon," said Dexter, bringing out the words with an effort. Then, having accomplished his task, he paused. "You are a more fortunate man than I am—than I have ever been," he added, gloomily. "But that does not lighten my mistake."

"Think no more of it," answered Heathcote. "I assure you, it is to me a matter of not the slightest consequence."

The words were double-edged, but Dexter bore them in silence. They shook hands, and separated, nor did they meet again for many years.

CHAPTER XLI.

"Love is strong as death. Many waters can not quench love, neither can floods drown it."—*The Proverbs of Solomon.*

The war was over at last; peace was declared. The last review had been held, and the last volunteer had gone home.

Two persons were standing on the old observatory floor, at the highest point of the island, looking at the little village below, the sparkling Straits, and the blue line of land in the distant north. At least Anne was looking at them. But her lover was looking at her.

"It is enough to repay even the long silence of those long years," he said.

And others might have agreed with him. For it was a woman exquisitely and richly beautiful whom he held in his arms, whose tremulous lips he kissed at his pleasure, until, forgetting the landscape, she turned to him with a clinging movement, and hid her face upon his breast. Her heart, her life, her being, were all his, and he knew it. She loved him intensely.

"Something may be allowed to a starved man," he had said, the first time they were alone together after his arrival, his eyes dwelling fondly on her sweet face. "Do not be careful any more, Anne; show me that you love me. I have suffered, suffered, suffered, since those old days at Caryl's."

On this June afternoon they lingered on the height until the sun sank low in the west.

"We must go, Ward."

"Wait until it is out of sight."

They waited in silence until the gold rim disappeared. Then they turned to each other.

"Your last day alone; to-morrow you will be my wife. Do you remember when I asked you whether the whole world would not be well lost to us if we could but have love and each other? We had love, but the rest was denied. Now we have that also.... Anne, I was, and am still, an idle, selfish fellow. Whatever change there has been or will be is owing to you. For you love me so much, my darling, that you exalt me, and I for very shame try to live up to it."

He looked at her, and she saw the rare tears in his eyes.

Then he brushed them away, smiled, and offered his arm. "Shall we go down now, Mrs. Heathcote?"

They were married the next morning in the little military chapel. Mrs. Rankin was at the fort again, Lieutenant Rankin being major and in command. The other poor wives who had been her companions there were widows now; the battle-fields round Richmond were drawn with lines of fire upon their hearts forever. Mrs. Rankin, though but just arrived, left her household goods unpacked to decorate the chapel with wreaths of the early green. Miss Teller and Miss Lois, both in such excitement that they spoke incoherently, yet seemed to understand each other nevertheless, superintended the preparations at the church-house.

As a wedding gift, Gregory Dexter sent the same package Anne had once returned to him; the only addition was a star for the hair, set with diamonds.

"I said that perhaps you would accept these some time" (he wrote). "Will you accept them now? They were bought for you. It will give me pleasure to think that you are wearing them. I have no right to offer you a ring; but the diamond, in some shape, I must give you, as the one imperishable stone. With unchanging regard,

"Gregory Dexter."

"You have no objection?" said Anne, with a slight hesitation in her voice.

"No," answered Heathcote, carelessly; "it would hurt him too much if we returned them. But what a heavily gorgeous taste he has! Diamonds, sables, and an India shawl!"

He had never been jealous of Dexter. Why should he be jealous now?

The new chaplain read the marriage service, but Père Michaux gave the bride away. Not only the whole village was present, but the whole water parish also, if not within the chapel, then without. People had begun to cross from the mainland and islands at dawn, so as to be in time; the Straits were covered by a small fleet. Miss Teller was the only stranger, save the bridegroom himself.

Anne was dressed simply in soft white; she wore no ornaments. Mr. and Mrs. Heathcote would not be rich; on the contrary, they would begin their married life with a straitened income, that is, in worldly wealth. In youth, beauty, and a love so great that it could not be measured in words, the bridegroom was richer than the proudest king. As for the bride, one look in her eyes was enough.

"I, Anne, take thee, Ward, to my wedded husband, to have and to hold, from this day forward, for better for worse, for richer for poorer, in sickness and in health, to love, cherish, and to obey, till death us do part, according to God's holy ordinance; and thereto I give thee my troth."

"Anne," said Miss Teller, drawing the new-made wife aside, "I want to whisper something. I will not tell Ward—men are different. But I want *you* to know that Helen's grave is covered with heliotrope in Greenwood this morning, and that I am sure she knows all, and is glad."

THE END.

Made in the USA
Monee, IL
29 September 2024

66889391R00122